THE MOST DREADFUL WITNESS

A Tale of Two Guardian Angels

by

Philip Martin Cawlfield

Disclaimer

Ok, this is your typical disclaimer where I say that *all characters in this book are purely fictional and that none of them are real persons living or dead.* I'm *also obligated* to say that *any similarity between characters in this book and actual people is purely coincidental . . . because this is a work of fiction that is not based on any real life events, in part or as a whole.* **In other words, folks, it's just fantasy**. The same is true of places, names of real towns, for instance, aren't used here. Names of restaurants, bars, and other such places are strictly fictional, so you can't find them in any of the towns or places mentioned. Like the people you find here, they are creatures of my imagination.

. . . . And I've got a BIG imagination!

However,

we all know that characters in a book of fiction come from somewhere, and for an author to say that he picked them out of thin air is misleading. In some cases, it might be a blatant lie, and no disclaimer to the contrary will convince level headed people that fictional characters aren't based on real people. As a reader, it's easy to see ourselves in fictional characters. Common sense tells us that there are just so many personality types to pick from, so comparisons between ourselves or people we know well will surely be made.

An author can't be overly concerned about this because he knows that readers aren't looking for themselves in a book.

Entertainment, that's what they're after, but that doesn't mean they will like everything they read. They may not like certain characters, and they take exception to the use of language. This book, for instance, presents readers with quite a few unlikable characters, and the language used here is sometimes explicit. My storyteller doesn't mince words, and he doesn't clean them up either. Bawdy, off-color, explicit language is the order here and will no doubt be offensive to some readers. This is a tough subject, and the story found here involves people who are worldly and often rough and tumble types. But it is also about some sensitive, heart-warming, uplifting things as well. I wrote much of it with a smile on my face, but some of it came about with tears in my eyes.

I taught college for 33 years, and most of that time at a small regional university very similar to the one described in this book. Within that setting, I formed relationships that ranged from casual friends to drinking buddies and real pals. Some of those people are dead and gone now, and some are still around. A few of them, should they read this book, will recognize themselves as the prototype for a character. But they are just prototypes, not the exact character I created for the book. The setting is likewise drawn from places I have lived, but it's not the same either. And I'm there, as are my two children and ex-wife, once again just as a starting point for various characters. Are the events described in this book taken from real occurrences? No. Are the places described here real? No. I'm not an uncaring writer, and I'd never put anything on paper that would purposefully disparage a particular place or person, especially the ones I continue to share this life with. .

Getting this book to market has been a long and exacting process, due mostly to my reluctance to publish it. I've agonized over this book, gone back and forth in trying to decide what to do about it. I had a good time writing it, but that too was difficult from time to time, particularly when the work got close to the bone. I don't like reliving the idiotic things I've done, the pain I've caused other people, and some events and circumstances described here reminded me of a past I'd just as soon forget. But that's the thing, you see, that finally got this book published. It's not about me per se or the people or places I've know . . . but it is about what I used to be, a drunk. I don't like thinking about that, but I know full well that I must remember what life was like back then. I don't ever want to go back to being a drunk, and that keeps me on the straight and narrow now. And maybe, just maybe, what I remember might help someone else. What I've forgotten never will.

And another thing

I'm a lousy proof reader, and I don't have a staff of specialist to do that for me. In other words, I'm my own editor . . . but with some help. My wife helps out by reading through my manuscripts, but she's not a language specialist, just someone who reads a lot. That means you'll likely run across some errors in this book. I hate misspelled words with a passion, and I try to use proper English wherever possible . . . but I'm a long way from being the complete writer. About the best I can do is offer this lame apology for the errors in spelling, punctuation, and grammar. With that said, I'll make a prediction. Betcha don't find many of 'em.

Author's Note: An Introduction

Yeah, I'm a drunk. If the folks at the rehab place I attended back in 1982 got it right, I'd probably been addicted to alcohol since my twenties. That should have been a sobering revelation, but it wasn't. Tell me something I don't know, I thought. And then tell me how to get this monkey off my back. In short, my attitude was pretty much, "I broke it, you fix it." My second revelation, however, was indeed sobering. That's when I was told that there was no cure for what ailed me, that alcoholism couldn't be fixed. No cure, they said, but they could help me learn to live with it and not drink. Day to day maintenance, they said. Treatment and then AA, 12 step program forever, a completely new lifestyle, that was my future.

I vividly remember attending my first AA meeting. The rehab center where I'd checked in made us go, and I sat near the back with some guy I'd just met. A crusty looking cowboy, a handsome old fart with a sweeping handlebar mustache, got up to speak. He stood as straight and erect as a statue and in a monotone voice commenced by saying, "Boys, I walked through that door back there 30 years ago, and they told me to put the plug in the jug, and I did, and ever since life's just been goddamn wonderful."

I looked at the man sitting beside me and said, "If that guy is sober, I might just stay drunk." I said it in jest, but all the while I was thinking there's got to be something more to it than that. There's no doubt that I was miserable because that's what finally drove me to seek help. I'd already learned one of AA's slogans, that I was sick and tired of being sick and tired. I was tired of misery and of feeling helpless and even hopeless. But if my choices were between being sober and miserable and drunk and miserable, I'd opt for the latter.

Fortunately, I started meeting people who had a handle on this alcoholism thing. I voiced my opinion about rather being drunk and miserable than sober and miserable. My main counselor smiled and said, "Well, Phil, the good news is that you can't do it any other way than getting rid of the misery. Sober up, live the new lifestyle we show you, and I promise you the misery will go away." I didn't necessarily believe him at the time, but he didn't lie to me. I've been sober now for a long time, never drank again after treatment. I got free of my whiskey demon, got a new life, and it's been a good one.

My mother was a deeply religious woman, always felt like I made it through all the drunkenness and insanity because I had a guardian angel. She even gave me a book to read about angels, and I read it. I'd been sober less than a few years when things started going poorly for me. My dad died, leaving with mixed emotions and lots of things unresolved. My wife divorced me, took my kids and moved to another state. I was in debt up to my eyebrows. I voiced my doubts about ever having a guardian angel to my mother, saying that if I'd had one back then, he'd apparently forsaken me. "Where is he now that I really need him?" I asked.

"He's probably still resting somewhere. I figure you would've worn one angel completely out," she said.

That started the wheels turning in my head. Guardian angels, huh? What if I had two guardian angels, and what if they didn't see eye to eye on how to look after me. Maybe we're on to something here . . . and we were. It took a while, but I finally started this book. And I worked on it for years, off and on. I went through half dozen computers, moved files here and there, lost parts of the story and had to rewrite them. This project started in 1985, and here we are in 2013, and still no book in print. A former agent read it, said, "I like the story, think it's entertaining, but you tried the impossible. You can't make alcoholism funny."

I didn't try to explain to him that my attempts at humor had little to do with alcoholism itself, just with the circumstances surrounding it. I think back on some of my own drunken forays, escapades . . . and I laugh about them. I don't remember then being all that funny back then, but they got more humorous with each passing year. I'm not about to admit that what's between the covers of this book actually happened to me. I've got a vivid imagination, and even though this is a work of fiction, it has some origins in real life situations I've been privy to . . . either through living them myself or knowing people who did.

A word of caution is in order. This book is straight forward and to the point, a specific point in most cases. My storyteller doesn't mince words, and he doesn't clean them up either. Bawdy, off-color, explicit language is the order here and will no doubt be offensive to some readers. This is a tough subject, and the story found here involves people who are worldly and often rough and tumble types. I've heard rough language described as "explicit language." Explicit, direct and to the point, easily understood . . . that's what I'm after. I offer this caution with no apology. I believe that should I lose you as a reader because of the language used here, I'm actually the better off for it. You probably would've missed the point anyway.

I don't want to overplay the point I've been making about the usefulness of humor in dealing with a serious social problem. Yes, the humor can be useful, but there's more here than funny stories about a drunk . . . much more. Quite a bit of research has gone into this writing project, and there's more to me as a writer than just another college professor who decided he'd take a whack at it. I'm a trained social scientist, one who took his job seriously and worked hard at mastering the subject matter I was required to teach. Mostly, I was a political scientist, but I also studied other social sciences and taught them from time to time. My adventures with alcoholism came twofold: 1) from being one (experience), and 2) from study and research. I wanted this book to be more than just a common sense approach; I wanted what's found here backed with academic outlooks on the problem as well. My plan all along was to make the high brow, academic information about alcoholism more understandable by giving it a whitewashing of everyday language and application. But I didn't quite pull it off, and from that partial failure, I learned something. Without planning it that way, I had developed a discussion of alcoholism featuring both – the more intelligent academic outlook, and the common sense outlook. And low and behold, they often turned out to be the same thing.

"If you have to explain your writing so the reader can understand it, then you need to rewrite it to where he can understand without the explanation," an older and wiser author once told me. And I agree, at least in part. Don't take this introduction as an explanation but rather as simply a preparatory statement that might be useful in understanding the book. I wrote it for you, but I can't follow you through the reading of it. I can't explain every little thing to you. The book is yours now, and I can't be overly concerned about how you interpret it. You can make of this what you can and will, and I have no control passed this point. I hope you enjoy it, and perhaps you'll learn some things in the process.

Prologue

So, you're here at last. I've been waiting for you - waiting and thinking about how I'll tell this story. I'm Doug Anderson. Call me Salty if you want to because that's what most people who've known me well called me. I'm the voice, the storyteller, and I take this duty seriously. This story needs to be told, and there's just the two of us. I can't see you, of course, but I know you're there. You don't have any particular face or form, but I have a good idea who you are and what you look like because . . . well, because I made you up. Actually, I discovered you more than I made you up. I didn't just make up this story either. It really happened, and I discovered it too. I know that you can't see me either and have no idea who I am, but don't let these uneasy dealings booger you to where you cut and run. There's a good story coming your way, and since I'm part of it, you'll get to know what I'm like soon enough. I could be telling it to the whole world and even beyond, but I picked you, so you might as well stick around a while.

Maybe you're wondering why I picked you. Well, it's because you're the best listener, that's why. I like to think of myself as a performer who accepts the challenge of entertaining the most difficult audience of all - one. Large crowds are easy to get lost in, and if you were an audience of thousands, telling this story would be easier. I would see you as a sea of faces, and the relationship would be impersonal, and perhaps distant. But you're not a crowd, you see, and you can sit right there in front of me and look me in the eye as I tell this story. I don't need to know your name, sex, age, race, religion, occupation, education, income, or social status. I don't need to know whether or not you're straight or queer, cute or butt ugly, knee-jerk liberal or knothole conservative, certified genius or post oak stupid, damn Yankee or unreconstructed rebel, camel jock or redneck, happily married or divorced, or stump short or bean pole tall. All I need to know is that you're there, and that you enjoy a good story. I can handle the rest.

Maybe I'm hung on the notion of talking to just one other person because I spent too many years alone. Folks were around me all during that time, and even though they couldn't hear me, I sometimes talked to them. Then I finally got a partner, and that gave me a chance to talk to a real person, and that's when I started understanding how important it is to have someone around who can look you in the eye. That's how most of this story was first told, and since you can't ask questions like he did, I'll tell it in way that satisfies your need for answers.

This story is about an old societal problem - alcoholism. It's about a family and some other people caught up in that problem, but don't fret or get discouraged. You don't need any special knowledge of the subject matter to savvy what I'm going to say. That's why I'm telling it to you - because I know you. You're the person who's a little sick of being preached to about the evils of alcohol, tobacco, fat, cholesterol, caffeine, sugar, salt, and about everything else that tastes or feels good. You're even a little sick of hearing about violence on television and in movies, air and water pollution, radon, ultra-violet rays, teenage pregnancy, abortion, homosexuality, unemployment, anti-feminism, spousal abuse, crime, attention deficit disorder, and a host of other problems. All these things are real problems, and the society we live in needs to do something about them. What we do about them, though, is sometimes misguided.

Some problems like alcoholism shouldn't be left to scholars, health care professionals, psychologist, or scientists. These people certainly shouldn't ignore the problem, should study it and throw their two cents into the pot when it comes to looking for solutions. Some critical thinking is needed, and there's no doubt about that. But what we're talking about here is a horse sense approach to critical thinking. What we need is some good old fashioned practicality, and maybe even some humor. I'm convinced that humor and practicality are intertwined. If we lose our train of practical thought, we lose our humor, and maybe it's the other way around.

I'm not about to contend that all highly educated people can't think in practical terms, but I do think that a lot of scholars in pursuit of solutions to societal problems overlook what's practical because they seems too easy. Too often we go for some modernistic theoretical fix and ignore some of the time honored solutions to age old problems. Just as often, perhaps, we do the reverse and try solving new societal ills with traditional cures. **What this all amounts to is this: Alcoholism is a devastating disease, and there is nothing humorous about the disease itself. Drunks, on the other hand, are often funny, and we can't overlook that. We shouldn't allow the humor to detract from the seriousness of the disease, but if we use it properly, the humor might help us find some new insights into how bad the problem really is and perhaps even how we could better deal with it.**

This story will be told using what I call **sagacious practicality** - a straight forward, common sense, honest, sometimes sad but often humorous narration of what happened. You may not like everything I say, but that's why I narrowed the audience down to you. We all have a sense of humor, but they vary widely from person to person. What I think is wildly funny might strike you as mildly funny, or perhaps as not funny at all. But whether or not you find the humor in this book, you'll still most likely get the point. It's as plain as the nose on your face, funny or not, and that's because it's dished out to you from a practical standpoint. You might even find yourself thinking, "Well, heck, that's just common sense." The humor found in this book is a part of that practicality. It might not seem that way at first, but there's a reason for it . . . and it's a very good reason. If for no other reason, it helps get the point across.

I'm not a wordsmith or anything like that, so don't expect this to be an eloquent narrative. I know the lingo, though, and I've practiced at storytelling enough to have developed a certain style, albeit it somewhat crude. This admission of shortcomings shouldn't be construed as an apology for lack of expertise concerning the subject matter. I know the story, and I know how it should be told. It's just that sometimes the cowboy in me flares up and stomps the crap out of my better judgment about proper grammar. As the reader, it might help if you think of yourself as a clear-minded person with a good sense of humor. If we try hard, maybe we'll both come out of it with a better understanding of what critical thinking really is. Ready?

Part One

The Pundit and the Pupil

CHAPTER 1
Roosevelt Watson

A gal on the second row, sitting in an outside chair on the left side of the isle, crossed her legs and leaned backward, and when she did, I could see all the way to Beaverville. Woody was lecturing a freshman general psychology class and had been talking about the need for a certain amount of excitation and stimulation. Perhaps the gal decided to give him a taste of what he'd been talking about, but if he saw what I'd just seen, he didn't let on. The young woman, apparently disappointed at Woody's lack of interest, shifted her weight in the other direction and re-crossed her legs. Two jocks sitting to her right suddenly started gawking and grinning back and forth at each other, and that got Woody's attention. He snapped his fingers and pointed at them, and the gal, knowing full well she'd caused their censure, straightened up and started looking innocent.

That did it for me. Sitting through a psychology class was bad enough, but having to watch some little tease show off her pink panties was more than I could handle. I needed more excitation and stimuli than that, and I knew just where to find it - the ladies' locker room at the gymnasium. Even though Woody still had another thirty minutes of lecture to go, I got up and walked out. He didn't notice, of course, and neither did anyone else. I knew Woody Pickens for almost fifteen years, and he never saw me. No one around him ever saw me.

The gymnasium was half way across campus from Woody's classroom, and the walk over took only a few minutes. Like most folks who do what I do, I kept to a schedule of sorts. Mornings hardly ever amounted to more than a lot of waiting around, and boredom usually set in early. I'd frequently abandon my official duties and head for the gymnasium, hoping to get there for women's physical education shower time. On this particular morning, however, my mistiming caused me to arrive just as an aerobics class turned out. I crawled to a window ledge just outside the shower room and gave the group a sluggish eyeballing. Mostly faculty wives and women from town, these ladies were nothing to get lathered up about. None of them had a shot at making the centerfold in <u>Playboy</u>, that's for sure, and a few might not have made the centerfold in a swine journal.

Missing a chance to ogle the younger college gals disappointed me some, but love handles and a few stretch marks have never kept me from enjoying a peek at the naked female form. The action slowed as the women finished showering and started dressing, and I had just turned toward the window to lower myself from my perch when I spotted Roosevelt, my supervisor, crawling out of his big Lincoln. When I say he crawled out of his car, I'm not stretching it much. At six feet eight inches tall and three hundred and fifty pounds, Roosevelt didn't fit well in anything, including the big Lincoln he drove. He was much larger than the dozen or so black jocks around campus, and that made mistaking him for anything other than an Angus bull highly unlikely. Besides, I'd never seen a bull drive a Lincoln. After hoisting myself back up to the window ledge for a second look, and I forgot all about shower time.

Roosevelt Watson was an ex-defensive tackle for the Steelers. I'll admit to having some prejudices when it comes to black folks, but prejudice is usually a two way street. It's sort of like my uncle Walt used to say. "I don't feel bad about not liking nobody that don't like me, and niggers don't like me," he'd say and then wink at me. I always got the feeling that Roosevelt didn't like me. I don't know the whole story on him, just what I picked up from occasional conversations between the two of us, but I think his feelings toward me had something to do with how he got here.

He had been a civil rights activist deeply involved in helping the downtrodden and oppressed, particularly other blacks in his native state of Alabama. A bus filled with fifth and sixth graders returning from a pee wee football game plowed into a group of demonstrators protesting racial policies at a segregated elementary school, and Roosevelt was among them. The bus driver, a redneck wearing a T-shirt bearing a rebel flag and inscribed with the words "surrender hell", said the sun had blinded him. The authorities set him free after a brief investigation, and the accident was ruled unavoidable. I don't think Roosevelt ever got over it, at least when it came to shaking his resentment for whites, and my being a Texas cowboy probably didn't made it any easier for him. But Roosevelt, despite his dislike for whites, never treated me badly. He was pretty much a bureaucrat to the core, and sometimes the way he quoted phrases from the rule book reminded me of a fundamentalist bible thumper spouting the scriptures. And he was a hard man to ignore. He wasn't just big; he looked menacing - sort of like a giant-sized Sonny Liston on a bad acid trip. The guy looked like a walking depository for violence, and he could scrunch his face into a scowl that might make Hercules piss his pants.

Perhaps I should have, but I didn't feel particularly intimidated by Roosevelt. Then again, I've always labored under the notion that needless confrontations should be avoided. I jumped down from the ledge, raced from the locker room, and then headed across a parking lot in an attempt to keep from being seen until I was well away from the gymnasium. I didn't make it. He saw me as I tried to sneak behind a line of parked cars near the library, and since I knew he'd seen me, I stopped and gave him a big wave. He waved back and pointed toward a concrete bench beside a sidewalk not far away, and we both started walking toward it.

I kept an eye on him as I walked and noticed a smile on his face, and that spooked me a little. Something's up, I thought. Roosevelt hardly ever smiled and always looked somber and tired. Dark circles under eyes and facial lines aren't usually as noticeable on black folks as on lighter skinned people, and that makes looking weary harder for them. Roosevelt had the hue of a rainy night, but he also had a Deputy Dog face that allowed him to look tired without breaking a sweat. I beat him to the bench and put a foot on it with a forearm resting on the knee. It was a feeble attempt at looking cool and casual.

"What's up, boss man?" I asked as he sauntered up.

"You tell me," he said in return, his feeble smile melting into a frown. "And don't call me boss man."

"How come?"

"I've got a name, so call me that," he said, rolling his eyes skyward in a gesture of weariness. He did that often, and when he did, I sometimes thought I could hear the sound of a bowling ball crashing into pens.

"O.K., Roosevelt it is. What's up?"

"I've got some news for you. The Central Office has sent word that you're getting a partner. He'll be here in a few days," he said, unemotionally and still looking skyward.

"You're yanking my chain, right? They're not really sending some help, are they?"

"Does this look like the face of an insincere messenger?" he asked, looking directly at me for the first time and tapping himself on the cheek. He was right. A face like his was hard to doubt.

"Well, if that don't beat all. I can't believe it. When's he coming? What's his name?"

"He'll be here at 6:30 a.m., the day after tomorrow, and his name is Dewey."

"Dewey? What's his first name?"

"That **is** his first name," Roosevelt said, suddenly looking away.

"Dewey sounds like a redneck name."

"He's a long way from being a redneck," Roosevelt said, working at stifling a smile. His Deputy Dog look suddenly turned wolfish.

"From the way you're acting, I'm thinking this Dewey guy might be somebody I won't like much. I mean, I don't even like the name," I said.

"The name is unimportant, and besides, what difference does it make? You've been hounding me for years for a partner, and now you're getting one. The Central Office picked him, and all I know about him is the name - Dewey Davisson. He's coming by bus, so you'll have to drive over to Cottonwood and pick him up."

"Jesus Christ!" I said, kicking at a pile of grass a grounds keeper had been raking. The fresh mowed grass flew everywhere, and the grounds keeper, a rather dull looking fellow who'd moved some twenty feet away to rake up another mound of grass, turned and gawked. He looked around several times, shrugged, and started raking again.

"He wasn't available. You're getting Dewey instead, and if I were you, I'd try to make the best of the situation," Roosevelt said, trying hard to ignore what I'd just done.

"Make the best of it? What's that supposed to mean?"

"It means you should try hard to get along with him, regardless of what you're first impressions are."

"What kind of guy is this Dewey? Can he handle an assignment like this? What about experience? He's not a greenhorn, is he?" I asked.

"He's just out of training," Roosevelt said.

"I knew it! I knew I'd get a greenhorn," I said, slapping my leg in disgust.

"He'll do a good job. The Central Office knows this assignment is demanding, and I'm sure they've taken that into consideration. I've got to go." He turned to leave, but I wasn't about to let him get off that light.

"That's it? That's all you're going to tell me?" I asked, waving my arms in disgust.

"If I knew more, I'd tell you. Believe me, that's all I know about him."

"Yeah, you said that before, but then you admitted that he was just out of training. You're holding out on me."

"I'm not holding out," Roosevelt said, folding his arms stubbornly.

"What if I don't like him?" I asked.

"Get used to him. There's nothing you can do about it. It's policy, and speaking of policy, why weren't you at your post this morning?" he asked, turning and frowning.

"I took a walk."

"Well, next time, don't walk through the women's locker room. It's time you gave up some of your worldly ways, and the Central Office wouldn't appreciate you're messing around in the women's locker room. Knock off the peeping," he said and pointed a banana-sized finger at me. He had the biggest hands I've ever seen on a man, and his finger looked exceptionally large since it was pointed at the end of my nose. He held the finger in place until I gave him a wary nod.

I held my ground and watched Roosevelt disappear across the parking lot, but as soon as he was out of ear shot, I let out a loud whoop. No need for him to know how delighted I was at having a partner, regardless of how stupid a name he had or how inexperienced he might be. Being at odds about everything was a game we played - with him always being the somewhat self-righteous, paternalistic overlord, and with me being the irresponsible, suspicious underling. I spent the rest of the day entertaining myself with thoughts about how much easier my job would be with a partner.

CHAPTER 2
Transformation

Meeting Dewey Davisson turned out to be the worst disappointment of my life. Sorry, for proper lingo's sake I ought to say that it was the worst disappointment of my afterlife. I've been dead now for about fifteen years, even though it seems a lot longer, and that's only a drop in the bucket considering how long dead is supposed to last. What we're talking about here is one helluva big bucket. Ever think about eternity - I mean, really think about it? Don't burn up any brain cells on it because you'll never figure it out. I try not to think about it because I'm just now starting to figure out what afterlife is all about, and everyone knows without belaboring the point that eternity lasts a long time.

Knowing I'd be dead for eternity upset me for a while, but even that sobering revelation didn't disappoint me as much as meeting Dewey for the first time. Simply saying I was disappointed comes up short of expressing how I really felt because along with it came acute feelings of exacerbation, high dudgeon, and acerbity. In short, I was pissed. I'm pointing this out primarily as a projection of mood from which this story can begin, mostly because being pissed off was the state of mind I found myself in at the time. We'll get back to that later, but right now I need to lay down some background.

I'll start with my name - Salty Anderson. Maybe you've heard of me. I used to be a professional bareback bronc rider before my number came up. My real name's Douglas, but folks on the rodeo circuit called me Salty, mostly because of the way I rode bucking horses, but partly because of my up-front and sometimes abrupt manners. I've always believed in calling a spade a spade, but things are different here. Being dead hasn't changed me much, but I have no idea what my mane is now. My official papers refer to me as T-342,986,864. I figure the T stands for transfer, or transformed, but the number is a mystery. Three hundred and forty two million, nine hundred and eighty six thousand, eight hundred and sixty four – and that certainly doesn't mean that many people died before me. I hate to speculate about it, but that could be the number who came here instead of going to Hell. If I'd gone there, I figure my number would've been lots higher.

We're supposed to refer to ourselves as transformed instead of dead. Dead, they told us, has such a negative sound - so final and too definite to be used gracefully. Dead, transformed, or whatever, take your pick. I won't quibble over terms, and when it gets right down to it, it's not important. It is what it is. I used to be alive and running around here on earth, and now I'm something else and still running around down here. When it comes to names, though, I like being called Salty. Roosevelt and Dewey always called me Doug, but I never cared much for it.

I had a good life before my number came up at the ripe old age of thirty-four. I'm a native Texan who grew up in a small town about a hundred miles south of Dallas. My folks were good country people, ranchers by trade, and they taught me to believe in and hold dear values common to most rural Texans. I'm talking about things like love of country, belief in God, respect for your elders, duty and obligation to family, and, of course, reverence for hard work. That central Texas rearing gave me a chance to grow up as a pretty good kid, but I was all boy - you know, a little ornery behavior now and then. But I was a fairly decent kid who did well in school, all the way through Texas A&M University. I went into the military after graduation for a couple of years, then to the reserves and the rodeo circuit. Things went well for me until my reserve unit got called up. I'd been riding a hot streak that had taken me all the way to number two in the bareback standings, and was about to make a run at my first national championship when they called up my unit and sent me directly to Vietnam. My company caught some heavy action, but I made it to the last month of my tour before I got it.

The way I got it was almost embarrassing. I walked off a ways from my group looking for a place to take a dump, and had just squatted down when I got hit. I took it directly in the chest and went reeling backwards. The next thing I knew, a couple of my men were standing over me. One said something about how I probably didn't suffer much, and I was lying there thinking about telling the dumb bastard that it hurt like hell. I probably would've been embarrassed about getting shot while taking a dump, but it hurt too much at first. Then the pain suddenly went away, and a feeling of euphoria came over me. Pardon the analogy, but when you're dying, you don't care about anything else. Later, I got pissed off, and even to this day the thought of getting shot that way still rankles the hell out of me. Only the worst kind of jerk shoots a man trying to take a dump.

Nothing I'd ever heard about dying turned out to be true. Most accounts had the dying seeing brilliant burst of light, hearing beautiful music, and smelling wonderful smells, and the like, and that's not at all what happened to me. I was lying there looking up, and everything suddenly went black. Worse than that, everything suddenly went nothing. I had no awareness of anything, no fading away of sights or sounds or anything like that. It was like a switch got flicked, and everything disappeared. Then almost instantly, it seemed, the blackness turned to a dark gray that slowly melted into a lighter and lighter shade gray. The sensation was a little like watching fog being burned away by sunlight. That was enjoyable, but instead of pleasant senses of smell and sound and taste, I regained consciousness smelling fresh paint and hearing Willie Nelson singing and tasting chicken noodle soup.

I slowly became aware of being in a sitting position. A black woman who looked a lot like Pearl Bailey was spooning something into my mouth, and I suddenly realized where the chicken noodle soup taste was coming from. I hate the stuff, so I pushed her hand away and started asking questions. She smiled and walked from the room without saying a word, and that's when I noticed the pink walls. That's right, pink walls! The walls looked new and clean, and that's why I'd been smelling fresh paint. As for the music, your guess is as good as mine, which is that someone up there wanted to make sure the new arrivals didn't panic when they realized they were dead. Maybe they did it because I'm a Texan and wanted to make me feel at home. It likewise makes sense that hardly anyone waking up to Willie Nelson music is likely to jump to the conclusion that they'd died and gone to Heaven . . . unless, of course, you're from Texas.

The walls were pink, I learned later, because the color supposedly has a soothing effect on people undergoing stressful situations. If pink alleviates stress, they wasted it on me. When I woke up wearing a loose fitting, beige jumpsuit - an outfit I wouldn't be caught dead in, unless, of course, I was dead - I suspected what had happened. I checked my chest for bullet holes and didn't find any, and that confirmed my suspicions beyond a doubt. Discovering that you're newly dead, particularly when you just got snuffed out while taking a dump by some slant-eyed commie causes stress no pink walls can cure. Nevertheless, I found myself sitting there surrounded by them, wondering what to do next.

Before long this strange man walked into the room. He looked rather innocuous, but he had a voice like W.C. Fields, and that made me feel uneasy. The goosy feeling passed quickly, though, when he welcomed me to Heaven. I hate to admit it, but I wasn't real sure about my destination. For all I knew, the next person I met could've had horns like a bully calf, been wearing a red suit, and toting a pitchfork. But this fellow - he introduced himself as Pete something-or-other - said that I was at the Training Center for Custodial Services, that I'd be going to school for a while, and that everything was going to be just fine. I'd been assigned to Custodial Services, he said, because my records showed an aptitude for that kind of work. I wasn't at all sure everything was going to be fine when he told me what Custodial Services involved, and he told me only after I demanded a specific job description. He mealy-mouthed his way through it, but I understood enough to register the quick complaint that I didn't apply for or want that kind of job. My complaints didn't seem to faze him, and he answered very few of the questions I asked, saying I'd find out later. He smiled a lot, but it's hard to care about smiles when you've just been killed and then given a crappy assignment.

I spent the next couple of months going to school and learning the ropes for a new occupation. My experiences in the military helped some, but all sorts of things I had no background in at all had to be learned. About a hundred of us "new recruits" went through training, and I tried to approach it the same way I'd approached basic training in the military. We went to classes early and finished late, and I never left the building during my entire stay there. What I saw of Heaven, mostly just glimpses through windows, looked nice, and I'd like to go back one of these days, if for no other reason, just for some R&R. What I saw surprised me because it looked like Dallas. No joke, it really did! I expected to see puffy white clouds, streets of gold, pearly gates, and Angels with wings, but what I saw looked like downtown Dallas. That buffaloed me at first, but once I'd had some time to think it over, Dallas is exactly what it should look like.

Heaven is bound to be full of Texan, and that means lots of Southern Baptists, and if you're at all familiar with Baptists, you know how they are about building things. Someone in Heaven must've noticed their architectural leanings, observed their love of buildings and their ability to raise money to build them, and placed them in charge of stuff like that. I'd like to go back just to see if some of my suspicions about who's running the place are true. I wouldn't be a bit surprised to find Jews in charge of things like banking, clothing, and entertainment. I've always suspected that they may have some pull with the Central Office. J.C.'s one of them, you know, and he's bound to be in tight with the Big Boss. Then again, most of them never recognized him as the Savior, so they may be cleaning sewers and stuff like that. Methodists, Episcopalians, and Presbyterians probably fill nearly all the administrative positions, and Catholics should have a good piece of the food action. Mormons are probably in charge of purchasing, but I hate to ponder what Church of Christ and Assembly of God members are doing. Maybe they're taking care of public relations.

Some celebrities are probably hanging around up there, and I would've liked to meet a few of them. Some of my relatives are there. If my Grandpa and Grandma Anderson didn't make it, nobody did. Grandma Winston, on my mama's side, made it for sure, but it's anybody's guess about Grandpa Winston. I sure thought a lot of my grandparents, and it would be good to see them again. Some of my buddies from Viet Nam probably made it, and maybe even Mary Ellen Wilson, my old college sweetheart. If my memory serves me correctly, she got killed in a car crash about a year before I got it in Nam. I sure hope she made it because that was the best piece of ass in the entire of Texas, and boy, would I like to . . . Damn! If I don't change my thinking, I may never get back there. Forget that last remark.

So that's how I came to be a custodian, and custodial work is all I've done here in the afterlife. I've never cared much for the title because it makes me sound like a janitor. Sometimes I think being a janitor would be a promotion, but that's my title, custodian, so I'll give it to you straight. My training course on Custodial Services taught me quite a bit, but it wasn't nearly enough preparation for the job I was given. Almost all I know about custodial work has come through on-the-job experience.

In human terms, and by human I mean you folks who're still alive, I'm usually called a Guardian Angel. I need to explain that title a little more fully, mostly because there's a lot of confusion about it. Myths or just outright misconceptions concerning what custodians actually do are abundant. Guardian Angels, for instance, shouldn't be confused with Angels of Mercy. One hears a lot of talk about Angels of Mercy, but believe me, it's mostly just talk. It's the Guardian Angels, the custodians like me, who do almost all the work. We're usually assigned on full-time duty at guarding a single individual, but Angels of Mercy are used only in emergency situations and normally work with a group of people. They're like trouble shooters, to be more exact, but custodians are on permanent, continuous assignment.

The confusion about Angels is caused by bad press. Information about Angels invariably comes from the living - a poor source. Doesn't it make you wonder how a living person, someone with no personal experience in the hereafter, could know a thing about Angels? Well, I'm dead, and that's a definite qualification when it comes to knowing about them. Even though I'm not a full-fledged angelologist, I've done quite a bit of research on the subject. Believe me, your average run-of-the-mill custodian is not as well informed on the subject as I am.

An example of the erroneous crapola that goes around concerning Angels relates to Cherubs. They're depicted in literature as beautiful, innocent, fat, rosy-cheeked children with tiny wings on their backs and harps in their arms. The Cherubs you've seen, I'm sure, were hanging around graveyards, perhaps in the presence of a lamb. Some people think the most popular Cherub of all is Cupid - a little fellow who shoots magical arrows into people's hearts, thereby causing a temporary condition of insanity called love. It's bullshit! Cupid was a Greek God, not an Angel at all, and particularly not a Cherub. According to the biblical version, Cherubs are anything but innocent and childlike in appearance. They look fierce and foreboding - like a good guardian should look. To guard means to protect. Would you care to speculate about how protective a fat baby with a harp could be?

Actually, I'm not an Angel, but I am a guardian. As a matter of fact, and just to set the record straight, Angels don't do custodial work because it's beneath their standing. Perhaps I should go a step further and say that full-fledged Angels don't do custodial work, but custodians are like apprentice Angels, much akin to junior aviators who have not yet earned their wings. They didn't teach us anything about rank at the Training School for Custodial Services, so I don't know exactly how or where custodians are placed. It must be real low, I figure, because it's a lousy job. I've never met anyone who held a lower rank, but I think ghosts are lower. I'm not sure about that either because I've never met a ghost and don't know for sure whether or not they even exist. Ghosts are bound to be beneath custodians because they serve no useful purpose, unless you call scaring people a useful purpose.

I'm probably starting to sound like an ingrate, but I'm not. My job has been occasionally enjoyable, often educational, and always challenging. It's just that guarding my mark got to where it spread me too thin to do the job right. You wouldn't believe what all I've been through, and believe me, custodial work can be difficult when you've been assigned to a bad mark. Maybe everyone's first assignment as a custodian is difficult, but I'd be willing to bet that mine was worse than most. Boy, did I get a lousy mark. He nearly drove me crazy at times, and I can't imagine anyone being a bigger pain in the ass than he was.

To make matters worse, they assigned me to western Kansas. A custodian is assigned to a person, not the territory, but my mark just happened to love western Kansas. That alone shows what a goofy bastard he was. Have you ever seen western Kansas? My first impressions were all bad. I kept wondering why the Indians ever fought to keep it, but what really surprised me was the white man wanting to take it from them. When I first arrived, and that was in the middle of August, the thought came to me that maybe they'd changed their minds and sent me to Hell. Damn, it was hot. Two months later I was freezing my ass off in a blizzard.

God, in my opinion, never intended for western Kansas to be inhabited by man. When he made it, he reserved it for buffalo and other wild critters. But man in his eagerness to bring civilization to every square inch of the planet moved in anyway. He killed off all the buffalo and elk and deer and most of the other critters and replaced them with cattle. He ran off the Indians. He plowed up the prairie sod, sank irrigation wells, and planted foreign seeds - wheat and corn and other feed crops. He built big grain elevators and towns and highways and feedlots. All this must've really pissed off the Good Lord, and that's why he makes it so hard on folks who live there. Over the years he's sent plagues of locusts, dust storms, sizzling summer sun, drought, blizzards, hail, howling wind, and tornadoes, but the folks who live there have never taken the hint. I got the message the first time I saw the place, but I'm not a western Kansan.

I'll have to admit that over the years the area grew on me, and I actually got to where I liked western Kansas. My mark grew on me, too, but more like a boil right in the crack of my ass. I've always prided myself in being adaptable, but I could've adapted to being cross-eyed easier than I could've adjusted to Woody. Woodrow Wilson Pickens, my mark for almost fifteen years, was a college professor, a husband, a father, and last but not least, a pain in the ass. Have I said that already? Anyway, I'll give you a bit of background on him, and I'll try to do so with as much objectivity as possible. Keep in mind, though, that it's coming from a custodian who spent nearly fifteen years building up resentment.

For the sake of fairness, I'll start by saying that Woody was basically a decent fellow to start with. He was a psychology professor at Western Kansas University, a small school of scarcely two thousand students. Wouldn't you know it? I got assigned to a psychology professor after making the observation many years ago while still a student at Texas A&M University that nearly all psychologists are nut cases. Woody did very little to change my mind. But let's give credit where credit's due. He was a good teacher, a fine lecturer, and he got along fairly well with the students. Most of his faculty colleagues liked him, but he wasn't overly popular with the administration. They saw him, with some justification, as being somewhat irresponsible.

Nobody, and I mean nobody, knew Woody Pickens as well as I did. I knew him to be reckless, scatterbrained, and occasionally accident prone, among other things, but he never knew I existed and therefore could not have purposefully done a thing to irritate or anger me. I knew that about him but couldn't bring myself to like him. His unpredictability bothered me more than anything else - going from good to bad, bad to good, and with mood swings so rapid that I rarely had a chance to get set for them. Even after fifteen years of watching over him, I wouldn't dare lay claim to having solved the mystery as to what made him tick. Predicting where he might take off to next was nearly impossible, but following him around at least gave me a chance to see a lot of new country.

Even though he was unpredictable, flighty, and reckless, I was able to sometimes forecast what he'd do by watching the behavior patterns of the people around him. He was married to a woman, for instance, who could be a real bitch at times. I know that sounds harsh, but that's the way I saw her. She was a good looking broad - fairly smart, energetic, and a hard worker - but she needed to be in control. The trouble was that she married an uncontrollable man, and that dichotomous mixture created some unfortunate situations. Sometimes she'd try to keep him in line with love and understanding, and that seldom worked, and sometimes she resorted to bitching and nagging, and that never worked. Regardless of what she tried, whenever she went into her control mode, he went wild. They got along well at times, usually when she had her way, but any reasonable compatibility between them never lasted more than a short while. As the years went by, their relationship grew progressively worse, but they stayed together. I guess they were too hard headed to give up. Although it may seem strange, even remote, I think they actually loved each other.

Woody wasn't a chaser, but he wasn't a runner either. Usually shy around women, he showed little interest in them and usually didn't get laid unless confronted by a woman aggressive and pretty enough to capture him. He stayed faithful early on, but then he got to where he'd occasionally wander off and get some strange stuff. His acts of infidelity came more frequently as the years went by. I never knew much about what his wife did because I wasn't assigned to watch her, but from all indications I got, she stayed fairly faithful. She was flirty, but that didn't mean much. The problem was that their personalities clashed, and they had some hellacious fights. When I say fights, I mean verbal and not physical fights. They did a lot of shouting and cursing, but I never saw them exchange punches. I still hated to see them fight because I knew it meant extra work for me.

My assignment to Woody Pickens would've been seen by some people, particularly those who knew me well, as poetic justice. They would say he was well deserved because the way he managed his personal life pretty much paralleled the way I had managed mine- back when I had a life. Woody drank, for one thing, and I don't use the term lightly. I did my share of boozing and fast living, and I've known some hell raisers in my time, but Woody rated right up there with the best of them. Most of his major screw-ups came when he drank, as had mine, but I couldn't hold a candle to the boy. He was a bigger fuck-up than I ever had time to be, and perhaps that's why some people might say I deserved him. I'm not sure about that, but it doesn't matter. The important thing is that he got to be too much of a problem for me to handle.

Woody wasn't such a bad assignment at first because he didn't drink much back then, and he got along well with his wife. He'd been married for just a few years and had recently completed graduate school when I first started guarding him. Then the kids came, a boy and a girl, and his life looked to be working out well. But the situation grew worse year after year, and I was badly overworked before Dewey showed up. I badgered the Central Office, but they're as bad as the army when it comes to bureaucratic dillydallying. It took me forever to get a partner.

Did you ever know a bureaucrat - I mean, like up close and personal? The only thing an administrator cares about is how your performance affects him. Everything is cool as long as you don't make his job any more difficult than it has to be, and almost all bureaucrats are dedicated by-the-bookers. Deviation from the norms, rules, or traditions makes their jobs more difficult, and they're not about to do that unless it suits their needs. Contact with bureaucrats comes, I've noticed, when they want something from you, but it's hard for them to work you into their schedule when you want something from them.

Roosevelt Watson was my only contact with the bureaucracy, and like I said earlier, he was a devout by-the-booker. We'd had quite a few set-tos over the years, but even though he looked bad, I

knew he was a good man. Besides, what did I have to worry about?
What was he going to do, kill me? I kept begging for help every time
he came around. To be completely honest, I asked for a transfer first.
After I saw the futility in that tactic, I started putting on the pressure
for a partner. I have no way of knowing, of course, how many of my
requests made it to the Central Office, but some of them undoubtedly
got through. Otherwise, Dewey wouldn't have come. The thought
has crossed my mind that Dewey became my partner because of
Roosevelt's perverted sense of humor, but I've never mentioned it.

Now that I've given you some background for this story and
perhaps confused you with some of my opinionated ramblings, I'll get
on with the story. That means it's time for you to meet Dewey, and I
hope you like him better than I did when we first met. In all fairness
to him, and since I neglected to say anything other than how terribly
upset I was when he first arrived, I should say he's a fine man. In
time, I came to treasure him as my best friend, and that's not just
because he was my only friend. I cared a great deal about Dewey, but
it took me some time to do it. He's . . . well, he's a . . . little unusual.
I'm pointing this out because I would like for you to withhold
judgment on him until you've been around him for a while.
Sometimes that's not easy. It wasn't for me.

CHAPTER 3
On Your Mark

The day of Dewey's arrival started poorly for me. My mark had been out most of the night trying to inflict further damage to himself. I woke up irritated, but not so much from fatigue and lack of sleep as from having to drive twenty miles over to the Cottonwood bus station to get Dewey. When I said my assignment had put me in an isolated area, I wasn't exaggerating. The town I called home didn't even have a bus station. It was large enough for a bus station, but no main highway ran through it. And can you believe it? The guy is dead already, an Angel endowed with great powers, but he comes on a bus. The man's as hard to see as clean air and can travel completely unnoticed on any conveyance that moves, but I have to drive to a bus station to pick him up. Even worse, he had to arrive at 6:30 in the morning.

The Cottonwood bus station was an old gas station with not even enough parking space in front to accommodate a bus, so I waited across the street near a sign that read, "Bus Stop." The bus arrived ten minutes late and let off three passengers -two old women and Dewey. He stepped off the bus wearing faded jeans, a sweatshirt, and tennis shoes, and toting a book under one arm and a mauve canvas suitcase nearly half his size in his free hand. He was a small man, about 5 feet, 8 inches tall and perhaps 140 pounds. He had short gray hair, was clean shaven, and looked to be about fifty years old. He walked straight toward me.

"You must be Doug. I was told you would be the one wearing a black cowboy hat. Are you one of the bad guys?" he asked, smiling and holding out his hand. It dangled from his forearm like a limp dick, and the way he shuffled his feet and cocked his hip to one side gave me a queasy feeling deep in my stomach.

"Some folks think so. Actually, I just wear a black hat to keep people from thinking I'm a Dodge salesman," I said and grasped his hand. His dead fish handshake caused the queasy feeling in my stomach to get even queasier.

"Cute," he purred.

We walked to the parking lot, got into the car, and headed back toward Forest City. Thinking of the town's name always left me shaking my head. What dumbass would name a town in western Kansas after a forest? There's not one for hundreds of miles, just some cottonwoods and elms where the seasonal rivers flow through, and the town wasn't named after a family or person. I know because I checked.

"I'll show you our mark," I said flatly.

"Right now?"

"Might as well. You need to get used to him."

More silence followed. Dewey didn't seem inclined to talk for the moment, and I sure wasn't in the mood for a conversation. We rode in silence until I decided idle talk was better than absolute quiet.

"I've never cared much for early morning. Just ain't my favorite time of day," I said.

"It *isn't* my favorite either, but I don't mind mornings," Dewey replied. He emphasized the *isn't* to let me know I'd used bad English. I know you ain't supposed to say ain't, but it's part of my Texas upbringing. I say ain't sometimes for the same reason I say "fixing to" instead of "about," or "going to" - like in, "I'm fixing to slap the crap out of you," which was the way I was starting to feel about Dewey. His voice alone made my ass want to eat my underwear. Maybe I felt that way because he'd just corrected my English, but that voice reminded me of my college speech professor. That professor had been a woman, if that tells you anything.

The thing irritating me the most, however, was a bright morning sun that was directly in my eyes. I lowered the sun visor, then reached across and fumbled in the dash compartment for my sunshades. I found them, took a brief look through the smudged lenses, and handed them to my grammar critic. "Want to clean these for me?"

"Sure."

"So your name is Dewey, right?" I asked.

"Yes, Dewey Davvison. That's D-a-v-v-i-s-o-n, with only one "d".

"That's an unusual spelling, isn't it?"

"I'm an unusual person," Dewey said with a sweet, innocent smile that made me even more uncomfortable.

"I'll bet that's true," I mumbled under my breath.

"Beg your pardon?" he asked politely.

"I said what do you do? I mean, what did you do?"

"I was a cosmetologist . . . you know, a hairdresser."

"Figures," I mumbled again.

"Beg your pardon?"

"Nothing, just talking to myself. This sun's really bugging me this morning. It's always in your eyes, that is if you're dumb enough to be up at this time of day. Sunrise is one of the reasons I hate mornings." I tried to adjust the visor, then my sunshades, but nothing helped.

"I love sunrises. Maybe this is what Blake was talking about."

"Who's Blake?"

"William Blake, the poet. He said, 'He who binds to himself a joy does the winged life destroy; But he who kisses the joy as it flies lives in eternity's sunrise.' Well, I guess this is eternity's sunrise," Dewey said, smiling and staring straight into the bright sun.

"This Blake guy had never seen one of eternity's sunrises, and I've seen too many of them. To me, a sunrise is a sunrise, and I don't like any of them," I said.

"What about late afternoons? Do you hate them, too?" Dewey asked, mischief twinkling in his eyes.

"No, I love evenings. Why?"

"It seems to me that you should have the same problem with evenings. The sun must go down, and then it's in your eyes again, isn't it?" Dewey was smiling that sweet smile again, but this time it didn't look as innocent. I got the distinct impression that he was screwing with me, and I could feel my cheeks start to burn. I scowled at him, thinking he might back off.

"It's different," I said firmly.

"How? I mean, sun is sun, regardless of whether it's morning or late afternoon sun, don't you think?" He was still smiling, but by this time, it was an impish smile.

"It's not as bright in the evenings," I said.

"Sure it is," Dewey said, laughing.

"NO IT AIN'T." I made the grammatical error again on purpose.

"Oh, come on, Dougie. It's just as bright, and I think you should. . ."

The sun hurt in my eyes, the early hour made me grumpy, and I was tired and almost in shock from meeting Dewey for the first time, but being called *Dougie* was the last straw. I tried to clench my teeth, but before I knew it, the words were flying out of my mouth.

"Look, you little pansy. I don't give a rat's ass what you think, and don't you ever call me Dougie again. My mother called me that, and I hated it. SO DON'T CALL ME DOUGIE!"

I suddenly realized that the car had slowed to a crawl, which turned out to be a good thing since I'd stopped watching the road. Echoes from my shouting fit still ricocheted around the car's interior, and my eyes were fastened to Dewey like rust to an east Texas windmill. It was one of my bad looks, my best don't-fuck-with-me look - the same one I'd often used to melt down a company of battle-hardened soldiers in Nam. It didn't faze Dewey. He looked surprised, but not at all frightened. What I got from him was a round-eyed stare and a smirk like I used to get from my wife. I never scared her much, either.

"Well, excuse me for breathing," he said calmly and in mock apology. He held his open hand, palm down, against his chest. His remark and feminine gesture only made me angrier.

"Damn! It's bad enough that I've been assigned to the asshole of the world, that I've got a pain in the ass for a mark, and that I've been worked like a pack mule for the past fourteen years, but this is too much. Of all the rotten luck, this tops the list. There's no way I'm going to be strapped with an argumentative fairy," I said and slammed my fist against the steering wheel in frustration.

"Bite your tongue, you . . . you . . . nasty-mouthed, temperamental . . . grouch. I'm not exactly thrilled about this assignment either, you know. I'm not overjoyed to be working with some . . . some . . . redneck."

"Redneck? Who're you calling a redneck, you little faggot?"I shouted, almost loud enough to make my voice break.

I ought to point out that calling a devout Texan a *redneck* isn't a smart thing to do. To me - I do consider myself a good Texan - the word redneck conjures up images of some ole boy who lives way out in the sticks, drives a beat up old pickup, has tobacco stained teeth, drinks corn whiskey from a fruit jar, rolls up his jean's legs, and tries to hump his sister. I'm country, and I have taken a few sips of corn whiskey from a fruit jar, but that's about as close as I've ever come to being a redneck. I'll have to admit to having sex with my first cousin once, but that doesn't count. I was only sixteen at the time, and it was her idea all the way. All I did was cooperate. I have tried screwing a few redneck gals, and unless they're in the mood for it, they're not easy to take down. I guess that comes from all the practice they've had fighting off their brothers.

Dewey continued. "And just who do you think you are, calling me names like pansy and fairy and fruit? You're taking a lot on yourself, aren't you, buster?" His temper was starting to show, but that worried me very little. I felt like I'd just been confronted by a pissed off Chihuahau.

"Maybe, but I think I can handle it. It sure as hell doesn't take a genius to figure out that you're as queer as a three dollar bill," I said through clenched teeth, smirking a bit.

"I've encountered your kind of suppositious arrogance before, and you'll get neither confirmation nor apology from me," Dewey replied, his eyes ablaze with indignation.

"I don't recall asking you for a damn thing," I said, or rather sneered.

"Then we'll let it go at that," Dewey said, after a few moments pause and in a much calmer voice.

Dewey went stone silent after that, and I let him. He looked away, out the window to his right, and I went back to staring into the bright morning sun. All of a sudden I felt despondent - lower than whale shit, actually. I felt stupid, too, and a bit guilty for picking the fight.

"Look, I had a bad night, and I'm a little on edge," I said. "I had no right to come at you like that. Let's forget it, huh?"

Dewey didn't respond. As a matter of fact, it was quite some time before he spoke to me again. I made several half-hearted attempts to break the silence, but he wouldn't buy it. Strained, uncomfortable days passed, and although he stayed at my heels like a hungry cat, not a word passed between us that wasn't absolutely necessary. Even then, I did the talking. Dewey just nodded or shook his head.

Now I was in a real dilemma. In addition to having a problem case for a mark, I'd saddled myself with a muted fruit for a partner. I should've known better. Sensitive people sometimes get offended easily, and I'd been around enough to know that. Still, I needed to find a way to get out of it. Perhaps I felt guilty because I still didn't want Dewey to stay. No matter how lonely I'd been before or how badly overworked I'd been, I didn't want Dewey for a partner. He made me that uncomfortable, but I was going to be stuck with him for a while and would have to make the best of the situation.

I stopped worrying about it after a few days because I knew that Woody was due to break loose on another tear before long. I even looked forward to it. Tailing Woody was better than watching Dewey pout, and I didn't have to wait long. The afternoon of Dewey's fourth day in town, Woody came home from school and stretched out on the couch to take a nap. His two kids, a twelve year old boy named Sean and a ten year old girl named Maggie, came home from school, made themselves a snack, and then headed for a town park a few blocks away. Just before they left, Woody roused up long enough to tell them to be in early. Then he flopped back down to finish his nap. Since he'd turned down an invitation from several of his buddies to go for drinks, I had just about reconciled myself to another boring evening when his wife came home from work.

Wanda, Woody's wife, worked in Cottonwood as a legal secretary and usually got home tired and grumpy. Catching Woody napping on the couch always irritated her, but she usually didn't fuss much about it. She resented his leisure time, I think, but on this particular afternoon her resentment was more apparent. She stood in the doorway to the den for a few moments, her lips screwed up like she'd been sucking green persimmons, watching her husband sleep. Then she wheeled and charged into the bedroom.

"Damn!"

"What does that mean?" Dewey asked. I gave him a weak but savvy smile. You know, one of those look-who's-talking smiles.

"Well?" he asked impatiently.

"It means she's going to screw things up."

"What makes you think that?"

"Because she's a bitch," I said confidently.

"You are surely the most opinionated person I have ever met in my entire life," Dewey said, shaking his head.

"Don't start that again. Just watch and see what happens."

Wanda stripped down to her panties and bra, went to the bathroom and took a whiz, and then came back to the den. She glared at her husband yet again, left the room and finished changing clothes, and before long came back to the doorway. She must have been trying to decide whether Woody was really asleep or just faking it. When Woody didn't stir, she sat down on the edge of the couch and rudely shook him until he was awake. Then she started bitching about the messy house, about how hard she worked to make ends meet, and about how the least he could do was clean up before he took his nap.

"I knew it. I knew the bitch couldn't leave him alone," I said.

"Well, as far as I'm concerned, she has a point. It wouldn't have hurt him to at least pick up some things." Dewey shrugged when our eyes met. He gave me one of those I-can't-help-it-but-that's-how-I-feel looks. "But she could've been more diplomatic," he quickly added. It still pissed me off.

"Why don't you just shut up and watch. After you see what happens because of her bitching, maybe you won't be as sympathetic toward her," I said.

Wanda kept on bitching, and Woody made excuses until he reached his limit. Then he blew his top, called her a bitch, and headed for the door. Wanda stayed hot on his heels, telling him what a worthless sonofabitch he was. "Damn, I knew she'd piss him off. Get your ass ready to travel, partner. We're going for a ride." I motioned for Dewey to follow and headed for the car.

On the way out I made sure to turn off the TV. Sometimes I'd do things like that just to be ornery. I'm sure Woody and Wanda hardly ever noticed because they were too busy fighting, but sometimes I got their attention. Occasionally I'd turn on all the lights before they got home. I've been known to turn off the heat in their waterbed, hide a favorite toothbrush or coffee cup, put some really tough knots in their shoelaces, or simply move something that neither of them had touched for months - just my way of getting even when they'd been giving me a hard time.

Woody pulled out of the drive just as we reached the front porch, and Wanda, standing in the driveway bawling like a fresh-bred heifer, chunked a rock at his car as he drove away. She stormed back into the house, slamming the door with a loud thud. "Where's he going?" Dewey asked.

"Where else? To the bar."

"Does he always go to the same bar?"

"Yeah, but sometimes he moves around to keep Wanda from finding him. It depends on how mad he is and how much he wants to avoid her. She's good at finding him, if she decides to, but he doesn't have many choices. The entire county only has a half dozen bars. He'll go to Frank's first because it's a quiet bar and a good place to drink alone. After his spirits lift, if they do, he'll move to where there's more excitement. Sometimes, he'll just stay at Frank's and get completely waxed."

"Is that all? I mean, that doesn't sound like a big deal to me. Forest City doesn't seem like a place where a person can get in trouble," Dewey asked. His voice was heavy with city-slicker smugness, but he sounded sincere. Boy, did this guy have a lot to learn.

"You don't know Woody. Sometimes he can stir up trouble in a nunnery. He's usually not that hard to keep up with, but every now and then he gets a wild hair up his ass. This man can screw up a one car funeral procession when he's on a tear. I could tell you lots of wild tales about some of the things he's done, but you'll find out soon enough. If we're lucky, he'll never leave Frank's," I said.

Woody went straight to Frank's Bar and Grill on the outskirts of town and took a seat at the end of the bar. He sat there looking lonely and depressed, drinking bourbon and Seven Up. Dewey watched him closely, obviously moved. It had been a long time since I'd felt much sympathy for Woody, but I understood how Dewey felt. I wanted to say something but didn't. Dealing with Woody took some toughening up. An almost empty bar, which this one happened to be at the time, was exactly what Woody wanted. He always sought out quiet places when he was pissed or in the dumps. But he didn't stay at Frank's long. He had four or five strong drinks and then headed across town.

"Where are we going now?" Dewey asked.

"Dusty's Saloon, probably. It's a cowboy hangout. We've got cowboys of all kinds around here - working ranch cowboys, rodeo cowboys, feedlot cowboys, and even pseudo cowboys. Woody likes to hang out with the cowboy crowd, and as strange as it may seem, they like him."

"I guess you've lost me," Dewey said, looking thoroughly confused.

"About what? Cowboys liking Woody?"

"No, about the different kinds of cowboys. I've never met a cowboy and don't know anything about them, but isn't a cowboy a cowboy?"

"Oh, no, not hardly. I've known a lot of cowboys, and there are all kinds. Feedlot and ranch cowboys are the working stiffs of the cowboy world, wage earners who try to make a living tending cattle. Rodeo cowboys, who may or may not be working cowboys, follow the rodeo circuit as bull riders, bronc riders, ropers, doggers, or whatever. Then there's drugstore or pseudo cowboys who're mostly just guys who just look the part by wearing western clothes - you know, like some truck driver trying to look like a cowboy," I said.

"That's interesting, but why does Woody hang around with them? Why do they like him? I mean, he's a college professor, and a relationship like that just doesn't fit. I don't know much more about college professors than I do cowboys, but I can't see Woody wanting to run with them. They don't seem to have much in common," Dewey said and motioned with his head toward where Woody was standing in the parking lot talking with a couple of cowboys. I looked, and it did look strange. Woody, dressed in gray slacks, loafers, white shirt, and necktie, looked out of place in the company of men wearing jeans, boots, and wide-brimmed hats. Explaining this part of Woody wasn't easy, but I took a stab at it.

"One of the first things you need to learn about our mark is that he's not your average college professor. He's not an average anything. He's a complex man capable of showing you several different sides, maybe even opposite personalities. There's a lot of contradictions in this dude, and believe me, it's hard to get set for him sometimes. He can go from a good guy to a jerk, from a compassionate human to an insensitive clod, from an energetic worker to a slacker, and from a scholar to a dumbass in a matter of minutes. The man's a dispositional chameleon - can adjust his personality to the crowd he's with at the time. Maybe he's in the mood for cowboys today. You can never tell about him."

Dewey must've been satisfied with my answer because he stopped talking for a while. I parked beside Woody's car and jumped out to look inside it. He had just walked into the bar with the two cowboys he'd been talking with in the parking lot. "Damn!" I said as I got back into the car with Dewey. "He took the keys with him."

"What difference does that make?"

"Sometimes it doesn't make any difference at all, but I usually hide the keys from him when he gets too drunk to drive. That forces him to leave his car and find another ride home."

"You hide his keys?"

"I sure do, and for several selfish reasons. If he gets in a wreck and hurts somebody or himself, my job gets harder. If he gets totally waxed, which is fairly rare, I have to drive him home. My car gets left behind, and I have to come back after it later," I said.

"Well, it looks like I'm needed after all. Now you have someone who can drive your car home if you are forced to drive for Woody. By the way, how do you handle the driving? Do you get behind the wheel and drive, or do you let him drive and just assist him?" Dewey asked.

"It depends on the circumstances. If he's not too drunk, I just try to stay close to him and correct his driving mistakes. I make sure he doesn't stray over the center line, run off the road, or hit anyone, but I let him do the driving. On a few occasions, I've had to work the gas and break peddles for him. Sometimes I have to work hard at keeping him awake enough to do his own driving."

"Keep him awake?"

"Yeah. Sometimes he gets drunk and sleepy and has a hard time getting home. I slap him, pinch him, or do something to get his attention. Pinching usually works, but sometimes I have to slap him." I couldn't keep from smiling when I said it.

"You enjoy hurting him, don't you?" Dewey asked, his expression alone an accusation.

"Well, we've all got our little quirks. I don't mind getting tough with him, particularly when he's been giving me a hard time," I said. Dewey didn't pursue it, just shrugged it off.

"I think we should check on Woody," He said after a few minutes. I agreed, and we went inside where we found Woody playing eight ball. His mood had perked up, and we settled into a dark corner near the pool table.

"I've got a question," Dewey whispered.

"What?" I whispered back.

"Why are we hiding in a dark corner? We're invisible."

I looked at him but couldn't think of a good answer. It was a good question. Old habits are hard to break, I reckon. Dewey kept talking. "And why are we whispering? They can't hear us, either."

I kept staring at him, feeling embarrassed now.

"Why don't we sit at a table under the lights? I mean, I don't understand why we need to hide in a corner and whisper. Why can't we. . ."

"SHUT THE FUCK UP, DEWEY!" This time I didn't whisper.

"You don't need to shout. I was just trying to . . ."

"I know what you're trying to do, and I don't want to get into another set-to like the one we had about the sun. You can sit or stand any place you like, but I'm comfortable right here. It fits my sneaky nature. I know we can't be seen or heard, but I like it here." I pointed at the floor under my feet.

"That's fine with me," Dewey said, waving his hands in surrender. He mumbled something about me not having to bite his head off just because he asked a simple question.

Dewey's endless supply of questions reminded me of a child, and I suddenly realized that I was treating him like one. I took a silent vow to do better by him, even if it meant being patient with his questions. I didn't want him going mute again. Ten minutes later, after silently watching a dull pool game, Dewey eased my mind by breaking the lull. "I can't believe he's drinking beer after all the whiskey he's put down. That's not good, is it? Haven't I heard a saying that beer after whiskey is mighty risky?"

"Yeah, I think the saying goes: whiskey on beer, have on fear; beer on whiskey, mighty risky. But don't worry about Woody. He's got a cast iron stomach and can drink almost anything in almost any order. Usually, he sticks with his favorite drink, Jack Daniels black with a dash of Seven-Up. He doesn't like fancy drinks or exotic booze, but he likes beer, especially in the afternoon. After dark he moves on to the hard stuff, and what he drinks depends on the crowd he's with and what's available. You'll seldom see him drink scotch, gin, vodka, tequila, or wine."

"Surely he doesn't do this often," Dewey said. It wasn't a question, but I knew he wanted an answer.

"No, he doesn't, but he drinks nearly every day. His daily intake ranges from a few beers to a quart of whiskey. You can count on him getting moderately drunk about twice a week, maybe three times. But once in a while he gets bombed, and it's the really bad drunks you have to watch out for. About once a month he gets completely blotto, throws a real dandy of a drunk. They don't last long, but he sure keeps you busy for as long as they last."

"Does he ever get sick?" Dewey asked but didn't wait for an answer. "A lot of people throw up when they get drunk, and I can't stand vomiting." He shivered and wrinkled his nose.

"You're in luck. This drunk's not a puker. Like I said earlier, the man has a cast iron stomach. He gets hangovers, though, and that gives us a chance to rest up. It takes a while for him to get over a bad drunk, and how long we get to rest depends on how bad he feels. He must be getting tougher in his old age because his hangovers don't last as long as they used to. You can only count on three or four days now, but until several years ago, he might've stayed off the booze for a week. He drinks more now and gets drunk more often. That's why I needed you. He was about to wear me out," I said. I could see some skepticism on Dewey's face, but I just smiled at it. I knew what was coming.

Woody sat at a corner table with some of his drinking buddies. I walked over but didn't hang around long. Listening to a bunch of palaver about the cattle market always bored hell out of me. Woody was still sipping on beer, and I knew he wouldn't get drunk any time soon doing that. Dewey's presence beside me suddenly reminded me that I now had some relief help, and that I didn't have to spend every waking minute with Woody.

"Look Dewey, I'm really bushed. Would you mind if I slipped out to the car and got some horizontal?" I asked.

"Me?" Dewey asked, looking at me like I'd just handed him the reins to an unbroken mustang.

"Is your name Dewey?"

"Yes."

"Then I must be talking to you."

"But . . . I just got here. I've never . . . What if he . . ."

"He'll be all right for a while. All he's going to do for the next couple of hours is drink beer and bullshit with his buddies. You'll do just fine, and if you need me, I'll be right outside in the car," I said, giving him a light whack on the shoulder.

Dewey smiled and nodded.

CHAPTER 4
The Most Dreadful Witness

One of the first things I noticed about being dead was that I still dreamed when I slept. That came as a pleasant surprise at first, but then I started having this recurring dream about how I got killed. The dream wasn't a full-blown nightmare or anything like that, but it was disconcerting in that it distorted almost everything about what really happened except the part about everything suddenly going black. The scene of my death was all different in the dream. I got shot, for sure, but I found myself in a room with bright lights. I was on an operating table or something, and the lights were so bright that I couldn't see anything. I could hear voices, though, and they were calm and reassuring. I was thinking that I must be all right, and that I'd just been wounded and the doctors were fixing me up, and then everything suddenly went black.

I'd been having that dream, and like always when it got to the part where blackness suddenly comes, I woke up. I rolled over and opened my eyes to pitch blackness. I closed them for a few moments and tried again. Same deal, nothing but black, so I blinked and strained hard to see something, anything at all. When I opened my eyes to nothing but blackness again, I panicked. I tried to move but couldn't. I knew the feeling of being frozen by fear, so I waited it out. This is it, I thought; this is what being dead is all about. Then a crazy thought ran through my head. Can a guy die twice? Wait a minute. I have awareness, or otherwise I wouldn't be scared stiff. I can't be dead. My body suddenly came alive, and I jumped up.

"SHIT!" I screamed as my head plowed into the roof of the car. The pain brought me back to reality, and my eyes began to focus. Everything wasn't black after all. Darkness had fallen while I'd been napping, and I started to laugh nervously as I realized that I'd been sleeping on my side with my face toward the back seat. I'd been staring at black seat covers when I first opened my eyes. The top of my head ached, but I felt too relieved to worry about it. I suddenly remembered Woody and jumped out of the car. His car was parked a few feet away, and that told me he was still inside the bar. Regaining my senses also brought back the realization of who was watching him.

Woody was playing pool again when I walked in, but I couldn't see Dewey. I made two laps around the room before I found him in a dark corner, standing on his head with his feet leaning against the wall. "What the hell are you doing?" I asked.

"Contemplating," he replied.

"Contemplating?"

"Yes."

"Contemplating what?"

"The order of things, I suppose," he replied wearily. He opened his eyes, and they looked glazed and out of focus.

"The order of things?" I asked, realizing how redundant I sounded.

"Yes," he replied patiently.

"Standing on your head in a corner seems out of order to me. Why don't you contemplate getting your ass up from there?"

"Because I like standing on my head." It was a childish reply, but his eyes were returning to normal, and he moved his head so he could look around. "Besides, everything is quiet, and no one can see me."

"I can see you, and it bothers me. Get up from there," I said.

"Go away. You're breaking my rhythm," he said, or rather moaned.

"If you don't get up from there, you might end up with more broken than just your rhythm."

Dewey just smiled, the asked, "Are you threatening me?"

"Forget it," I said and took a seat at a nearby table.

"I might as well join you. You ruined my concentration," he said, sitting next to me.

"What time is it?" I asked, not really caring about his concentration. Dewey pointed toward the clock behind the bar. Eight o'clock, not as late as I'd thought. I took a close look at Woody and saw that he was still in fairly good shape. He had a new partner at the pool table.

"Who's the woman playing pool with him?" Dewey asked and then added, "She's very attractive."

"C.W.," I mumbled.

"Beg your pardon?"

"C.W. Her name's C.W.," I snapped.

"Boy, you're sure in a crabby mood. Do you always wake up from a nap like this?"

"Sorry," I said, realizing I'd been short.

"What about her? Does Woody have something going with her? She seems to like him."

"Yeah, she likes him, but Woody's a dumbass when it comes to women."

"What do you mean by that?"

"C.W.'s gone after him several times before, but Woody doesn't respond well to subtle advances. He's slow to figure out when some gal's after his meat. He's too busy getting drunk to notice, I reckon," I said.

"How could he not notice? Have you seen the way she looks at him? He can't be that stupid." Dewey said.

Dewey's comment was an obvious invitation for me to enlighten him, but I really wasn't in the mood for it. Still, I felt obliged to say something. "I've noticed, but I don't think he has. He'll get the message sooner or later, but she'll need to do more than flirt. Woody's a shy man, not at all confident around women. This game could go on for a while, and C.W. will have to play him right to get him. A frontal assault might scare him off, but she's got to be bold enough to capture him. If she's determined and careful enough, though, she'll get him."

The words had scarcely left my mouth when Woody and C.W. laid their pool sticks on the table and headed for a dark corner table. They ordered drinks, whiskey this time, and I knew that was a bad sign. C.W. scooted her chair in close to his, close enough to where she could whisper in his ear. In doing so, she made sure a breast rested on his arm.

"She's making a move. Can he resist her?" I heard Dewey's question but was too busy watching to answer. C.W. appeared to be telling a joke because Woody laughed. He was warming to her advances, and I knew it wouldn't be long before the whiskey warmed him even more. C.W. wanted to get laid, and Woody was starting to realize that he was the layee. I walked over to their table, partly to hear their conversation and partly to help Woody admire C.W.'s lovely tits, when I realized Dewey was trying to get my attention by tugging on my sleeve. "Can he resist her?" he asked again.

"Nope. He's had it. She's too pretty, and he's too far gone to turn her down. She's sure got a dandy set of knockers, doesn't she? The rest of her isn't bad, either. Have you noticed the way her ass wiggles around in those tight jeans? Sometimes it's hard to tell about asses, particularly when the gal's wearing tight jeans. Could be just another fat ass packed in there. I've seen some women's asses pop out of jeans like canned biscuits when you finally get them unzipped, but C.W.'s ass sure looks good in those jeans, huh?" I gave Dewey a man-to-man push with my elbow before I remembered who I was elbowing.

"Yes, I suppose it does," he agreed and tried to smile. I realized the discussion about tits and asses was making him uncomfortable and decided to warn him about Woody.

"Look Dewey, if sex bothers you, then you've got an adjustment to make. Woody's not a chaser, but when he gets juiced up like he is right now, he's as horny as a twelve peckered billygoat. He's not prone to flop down with just any old skank, but he's sometimes available to a gal like C.W. When he finally commits to it, he tries to make a hand, if you get my drift. C.W.'s in store for a good humping if Woody holds true to form."

"Whether or not that kind of sex makes me uncomfortable is not at issue here. I don't need to be a witness to it because we should stop it."

"Huh?" I asked.

"I think we should stop him."

"Stop him?"

"Yes. He's making a big mistake by giving in to this woman, and I don't think we should allow it."

I stared at Dewey for a few moments, fully aware of how dumbfounded I looked while trying to find the words to express what was going on in my head. I decided there was no easy way to tell him. "No, we're not going to stop him."

"Why not?"

"Because that's not our job. You ought to know that from Instructional School. Our job is to protect him from physical harm, and that's all. We can't interfere."

"That's not the way I understand the rules. What about emotional harm? What about psychological damage?" Dewey asked.

I tried hard not to laugh because he looked concerned, but I had a quick comeback for that one. "Dewey, this may come as a shock to you, but screwing a gal like C.W. is seldom psychologically damaging."

"What's so special about her? He's going to feel terrible about doing this. He's being unfaithful, and guilt is damaging. And what if he gets caught? Can you imagine how much suffering will come of it if Wanda catches him? Other people are involved, and they could get hurt."

Dewey had a point, and I knew it. But I wasn't about to give in. "OK, I'll admit it could be harmful, but not under these circumstances. Our boy has some insecurities when it comes to women. Getting laid by C.W. will be good for his self image."

"But he has a wife. Why not improve his self image with her? She's as pretty as C.W., and sex with her won't involve guilt, worry, and self debasement. If anything, sleeping with this other woman will make him even more insecure."

Score one for Dewey. Since I seemed to be getting nowhere, I decided to throw in a little humor by teasing him. "Are you sure you weren't a lawyer?" I asked.

"No, I did hair, but I'm not stupid. You don't want to stop it because you want to watch," he said.

Stupid? Was that what he'd just called me? Now I had to hit him with the heavy stuff. "You're right, I do want to watch. But that's not the only reason. Woody's caught up in an F & F relationship with his wife. By that I mean a fight and fuck situation. They pick at each other, peck around, and throw barbs back and forth. He's constantly throwing out comments, for example, that are an affront to her intelligence. She retaliates by attacking his masculinity. He'll say, 'Any idiot should know that,' and she'll come back with, 'A real man wouldn't act the way you do.' This tit for tat goes on until they get into a big fight and clear the air. Sometimes they fight like cats and dogs. They end up hurting each other's feelings, and then they'll pout until they finally work out their problems in the sack. They'll screw like minks for a few days, and everything will be all right until the next round starts. It's clearly a fight and fuck relationship."

"What you've said may be true, but I still can't see how having sex with C.W. is going to improve the situation," Dewey said, slowly shaking his head.

My chances of winning him over still weren't good, but they'd improved some. I decided to take one last stab at it. "Woody's relationship with his wife is part of the problem. It's a form of sexual masochism. She always keeps him reminded one way or another that he's lacking as a man. He sulks, withdraws, doubts his manhood, and finally fights back by insulting her in some way. After they fight, they fuck. It's their way of making up. It's how they say they're sorry. Wanda is reassured that Woody needs her, and Woody proves to her that he's really a man. But I doubt if he proves it to himself. C.W. doesn't care about all that crap. She just wants to get laid, and she wants Woody. Getting laid by someone who isn't interested in manipulating him, someone who won't rob him of his dignity in the process, will be good for him. Can you at least understand that much?"

"I understand it, but I don't like it," Dewey said, sniffing indignantly. He did that a lot.

"Gotcha," I said, grinning like the proverbial Cheshire cat.

"What's that mean?"

"I beat you. I won the argument."

"You did not."

"Did too. You admitted understanding what I said, and that means I win," I said, giving him the old thumbs up gesture.

"What I admitted to was understanding, but I didn't admit to agreeing with you," Dewey said, looking defiant again.

"Maybe so, but I still beat you in the argument itself, and that's what counts in an argument."

"No it isn't. To win, you must convince me."

"Well, hell, Dewey. If that's the case, nobody ever wins an argument. Is that the kind of relationship we're going to have? Are you always going to be so stubborn about everything? Remember, I'm supposed to be the teacher, and you're supposed to be the student," I said.

"Says who?"

"Says me, that's who."

"On what grounds?"

"Training, experience, and seniority -that's the way it works in the military, and that's the way it works here," I said.

"Poppycock! I refuse to accept those rules," Dewey said, folding his arms and lifting his nose.

"You have to accept them. I'm the manager, and you're the trainee, or put another way, I'm the pundit and you're the pupil. Accept it, Dewey. You're a neophyte."

"Yes, I'm a neophyte, but no, I'm not your pupil."

"Are too."

"Am not," he said, stubbornly.

"All right, Dewey, you win. I lost the argument and you're not a student or trainee, OK? Is it all right if we go and watch Woody and C.W. screw now?" I asked, pointing toward the bar. Dewey had been so intent on the conversation that he hadn't been watching what I'd been watching out of the corner of my eye. He turned to look when I pointed, just in time to see C.W. heading for the front door. Woody was at the bar ordering another drink. Since the bartender was mixing the drink in a large plastic cup, I knew something was up.

"They're not going to do it. She left without him," Dewey said gleefully.

"Don't count on it," I said.

"But she's gone."

"Come on, Dewey, use your head. They just didn't want to be seen leaving together."

I was right because Woody didn't wait five minutes before leaving the bar. He stood on the front steps for a few moments and looked around, then headed across the parking lot. C.W. had parked her car at the far end of the lot, in a dark area away from the other cars. Woody walked straight to her car, looked around again, then quickly opened the door and got in. I motioned for Dewey to get in our car so we'd be ready to follow, but the lights on C.W.'s car never came on.

"Oh no, they're going to do it in C.W.'s car," I groaned.

"Maybe they're just talking," Dewey said. I gave him one of those you've-got-to-be-kidding looks.

"They could've talked in the bar, Dewey," I said and opened the car door to get out.

"Where are you going?"

"I'm going to walk over and see what's happening. Want to go?"

"You go ahead. I'll wait here," he said.

"Suit yourself," I said. I turned and started hustling across the parking lot.

"Pervert," Dewey called after me.

I was lucky. Nothing interesting had happened by the time I got to C.W.'s car and assumed a good viewing position on the hood. They were still talking and laughing as they finished Woody's drink. The talk and jocularity gave way to muzzling and kissing, mostly because C.W. had lost interest. Her mind was on more serious matters. She moved closer and pressed her breasts firmly against Woody's chest. They kissed again - a hard, passionate kiss this time. Woody got quiet, finally, and his hands went to work. He massaged her breasts and then went for the bottoms on her shirt. Next he unsnapped her bra and pushed it up under her chin. I nearly fell off the hood trying to move to a better position.

"Boy, what a nice set of knockers," I said out loud. This was one of those times when I found it beneficial to be able to talk and not be heard.

Woody buried his face between C.W.'s breasts. Her hand was busy rubbing his crotch while he fumbled with the zipper to her jeans. She moved his hand and gracefully slipped out of them. Woody pushed his slacks down to his knees and then went after C.W. like a starving kitten to a bowl of milk.

"Dewey, you'd better come see this. They're getting to the good part," I shouted across the parking lot.

"Peeper!" he shouted back.

I turned back to the action just in time to see C.W. pull off her panties. "Pay dirt!" I shouted. There was no reply from Dewey.

C.W. pushed Woody away just long enough for them to sit up, and that gave me a good look at her. C.W. had the kind of body that made my libido start doing somersaults. For some men's tastes, she might've had too much - large grapefruit sized boobs and fully developed hips. Her small waist made them look even more spectacular, and getting a good look delighted hell out of me. Woody did some close examination himself, and C.W. made sure to momentarily position herself to where he could get a good look. He sat opposite the driver's side, and she swung her left leg over him to a position where she sat facing him. She grabbed his head and pulled his face into her breasts. Her back arched sharply as Woody squirmed around to make entry. Then she sat down heavily, releasing a low moan as she did.

I missed the next few seconds because I jumped off the hood to get a better look through the side window. It was completely fogged up, though, and I had to jump back on the hood. By that time, she was really giving it to Woody - rocking back and forth, moaning and groaning, smashing her boobs into his face, and holding tightly to his hair with her hands. For a few minutes, I had the sensation of riding a motorboat in rough water. Then it all ended in a rush of frenzied jerks, gasps, oooohs, and aaaaahs.

"Disgusting," Dewey said from directly behind me. I jumped like a startled rabbit.

"Don't do that! Don't sneak up on me that way," I said.

"You're sick," Dewey said, self righteously.

"What's sick about watching a natural sex act between a man and woman?"

"I'm not talking about what they were doing. I'm referring to what you were doing - watching. I'm talking about you - you pervert, you peeper." Dewey looked angry, and he was almost shouting now.

"Now you listen to me, you holier-than-thou little shit. I've been stuck in this wasteland for fourteen years. That's a long time to be alone, and I mean completely alone. The only sexual enjoyment I've had during all that time is watching Woody get an occasional piece of tail, so I take my little pleasures where and when I find them. SO, GET OFF MY ASS!"

"That doesn't make it right. You shouldn't watch. People deserve some privacy," Dewey replied calmly.

"**It's my job to watch**." I waved my arms and pointed toward the car.

"Could you please stop shouting? It's not going to help, you know."

He had a point, so I lowered my voice. "Who are you to condemn me for watching, you hypocrite. You were looking over my shoulder, weren't you?" I wiggled my index finger at him.

"I did it to humor you."

"Sure you did. You wanted to peek as bad as I did, maybe for different reasons, but you wanted to see it."

"You're making accusations again, but I'll not dignify them with a response other than to say that I care nothing for viewing someone's . . . someone's . . . organs." Dewey sniffed and lifted his nose in the air again. I was about to renew the debate when the car started rocking again. I stopped to listen and heard C.W. moan.

"Damn, they're at it again," I said and jumped back onto the hood of the car. Sure enough, the action was back. Woody had a good whiskey hard going, and C.W. wasn't about to let it go unemployed.

"Oh, no. You're sicker than I thought," Dewey said, jamming his hands on his hips. Doing that made him look like an irate old maid who'd just been felt up in a crowded elevator. He stood that way for a couple of seconds and then whirled to leave. He took a few steps but suddenly stopped dead in his tracks and said, "Oh, my goodness."

I hated to tear my eyes away from the scene before me, but I took the time to glance back at Dewey. He was holding an open hand to his chest again, palm down like a woman, with his other hand flopping in a limp-wristed wave toward the bar. I looked and caught a glimpse of Wanda as she walked through the front door.

"Was that who I thought it was?" I asked.

Dewey nodded. I looked back into the car just as Woody rolled C.W. onto her back. She wrapped her legs tightly around his buttocks and pulled him into her as hard as she could. Woody responded by giving it his all, but I knew from their motions that they were a long way from finished. My mind started to race, and I looked back at Dewey for a suggestion or hint of what to do. I jumped off the hood and ran to where he was standing, one hand over his mouth and the other on top of his head.

"Got any ideas?" I asked. He snapped his head around and looked at me like I'd just asked him if he wanted to dive off a water tower.

"Me? You're asking me?" he asked, whacking himself on the chest.

"Who else around here can hear me, Dewey?"

"But . . . but . . . you're supposed to be the expert, remember?"

"Don't panic," I said. "Just thought I'd ask. I'll come up with something." I started pacing back and forth, looking intently at the ground.

"What are you doing?" Dewey asked.

"Looking for a stick?"

"For what? Have you forgotten that we have a serious problem here?" Dewey was excited, almost frantic.

"No, I haven't. Help me find a stick."

"What good will that do?"

"I need it to poke Woody in the ass," I said.

"Do what?"

"Poke him in the ass. I'm going to take a stick and poke him in the ass with it," I said, emphatically making poking gestures with my hand.

"You can't do that," Dewey said, slinging his head from side to side so hard that it made his jaws flap in the wind.

"Sure I can. All I need is a stick. Poking him ought to get his attention, and maybe he'll sit up and see Wanda coming."

"Can't you get his attention some other way?" Dewey asked.

"Yeah, there's another way," I said after a short pause. "You got a match or cigarette lighter on you?"

"Of course not. Why?"

"I'll set his pants on fire. That'll get him up for sure."

"Absolutely not!" Dewey fired back. "I'll not stand still for it."

"Then help me find a stick."

The ploy worked because Dewey got busy looking for a stick. Finding sticks where trees are scarce isn't easy, but our search turned more intense when Wanda came walking out the front door of Dusty's. I ran back to the car and looked in. Woody's stroke had quickened and C.W.'s moaning was louder, but they still weren't finished. I ran to the cottonwood and broke off a low hanging limb, then ran back to Dewey, stripping away leaves to make a short but sturdy stick. By then, Wanda was looking inside Woody's car.

"Dewey, I want you to stop her if she starts this way."

"What?" he asked feebly, his eyes going round.

"Stop her. Don't let her get to C.W.'s car until I can get Woody out of there," I said.

"How? What can I do?"

"I don't know. Use your imagination. Maybe you could trip her or something like that," I said.

"No, I just couldn't."

"I don't care what you do, just do it," I said, motioning him toward Wanda.

I raced back to C.W.'s car and looked in. C.W.'s round-eyed stare, clenched teeth, and claw-hook hold on Woody's back, plus the jackhammer action of his ass, told me that they were both in the short rows. I sure hated to poke Woody in the ass right in the middle of the best part. I turned and looked back at Dewey, but he was still standing where I'd left him.

"Get going, Dewey," I shouted and waved toward Wanda again.

"That's interference, isn't it? It would be against the rules to stop her, wouldn't it?" Dewey asked but started taking hesitant steps in Wanda's direction.

"We'll take a chance this time. Get moving."

It was all over except the heavy breathing when I looked back into the car. The side window had been half rolled down, so I reached in and poked Woody's ass with my cottonwood stick. He giggled and smiled down at C.W., obviously thinking she did it. I poked him again but hard this time, and he came up looking wild-eyed and anxious. He was still fairly drunk, but not too drunk to keep him from realizing that C.W. wasn't the culprit. Maybe he thought one of his prankish friends was up to something, but he slowly opened the door and stepped out with his pants still down around his knees. That's when he spotted Wanda. He jumped back into the car and started thrashing around like a wrung-necked chicken in trying to get his clothes back on.

Wanda heard the car door slam and looked across the parking lot directly at C.W.'s car. She just stood there for a moment and then started walking toward us. Dewey was near her by then, but he made no effort to stop her advance.

"Dewey, you chickenshit, you'd better do something. He's not ready yet," I shouted. Dewey froze in his tracks.

"DEWEY!" I shouted again, but he remained motionless.

I was about to call out again when he suddenly went into action. Wanda had just hit full stride when Dewey threw a body

block into her that would've made Bob Lilly jealous. I never saw a
better hit on any football field because he cut her feet right out from
under her. She hit the ground with a thud and lay motionless.
Dewey stood over her, holding his hands to his mouth. A brief glance
back into the car showed that Woody was about ready to make his
escape, so I headed toward where Dewey stood over Wanda. I looked
back and saw Woody ease out of the car and crawl toward the back of
the building. He didn't even look in our direction.

"I said trip her, Dewey, not kill her," I said, trying to choke
back a laugh. Dewey looked pathetic.

"Oh, my goodness! Oh, my goodness," he kept saying.

"Put a muzzle on it, will you? She's all right, just got the wind
knocked out of her, that's all."

I bent down and started looking her over. She seemed to be
in good shape, but I decided to check her out anyway. The parking
lot was deserted, except for Dewey and me, and someone had to help
her. I looked up briefly and saw C.W. drive out the far end of the
parking lot, right across the grass and shrubs in someone's yard. My
inspection of Wanda started at the top and progressed downward
from there. I'd just reached the good parts when Dewey started
poking me in the back. "What are you doing?" he asked, rather
irritably.

"I'm checking her over to see if she broke anything."

"I've never heard of anyone breaking a breast," Dewey said
sarcastically, then added, "Do you have to do that?"

"Sorry, guess I got carried away," I said. My head said move,
but my hands said stay, and I got in another squeeze or two. I hadn't
squeezed a boob in many a moon and wasn't about to let Dewey's
bitching beat me out of an opportunity. Wanda had some pretty nice
knockers herself, better in my opinion than C.W.'s, especially since I
had my hands on them at the moment.

"Stop it!" Dewey demanded.

"OK! OK!" I moved my hands down across her ribs, stomach,
thighs, legs, and right on down to her feet. She groaned when I
squeezed her left ankle.

"Looks like she might have sprained her ankle, but that's all,"
I said.

"Thank God," Dewey sighed.

I put my hand behind Wanda's neck and helped her sit up. She was still groggy, so I balanced her until she could sit up under her own power. She rubbed at her ankle, grimaced and started to whimper. I was thinking how nice it would be if someone would come along to help her because she was too alert by then for me to touch her. Of all people, Woody showed up first.

The fight didn't start immediately. Wanda was too pleased to see anyone willing to help, and Woody felt too guilty not to do a good job of comforting her. What took place when they got home couldn't be called a fight, a quarrel, or even a shouting match. What it was, by good old Texas definition, was a good ass-chewing. Woody ended up being the chewee because he didn't say a word in his defense except that he'd been in the bathroom when she came into Dusty's looking for him. They must've just missed each other, he said. But Wanda wasn't buying it and accused him of hiding from her, saying he'd rather lay out all night with his worthless friends than to be at home with his family. Not a word was said about him being with another woman.

She bitched and moaned about what an inconsiderate bastard he was to go off and get drunk, leaving her to sit at home and worry herself to death until the wee hours of the morning. What made it even worse, she said, was that she had to get up early and go to work to pay bills that ought to be the responsibility of her sorry-assed husband. She bawled and said it sure would've looked bad if she'd been killed when that drunk driver knocked her down in the parking lot, particularly since she never would've been there in the first place if it hadn't been for his sorry ass.

Even after they went to bed, she kept crying and talking about how she'd always loved and looked after him and how he gave her nothing but heartaches. Woody lay beside her, holding her and listening but never saying a word. His face looked dead and ashen, and his eyes turned dull and listless as he stared into the darkness. Wanda finally slept, but fitfully. She twitched and mumbled and made soft sucking noises like a child who couldn't quite stop crying. Woody finally rolled over and stared aimlessly at the ceiling, moving only to wipe the tears off his cheeks and out of his ears.

Dewey and I watched in total silence. After a long while, I turned to him and said, "Well, he got by with another one, but it looks like he's paying a price for it."

Dewey took a deep breath and then said, "There is no witness so dreadful, no accuser so terrible as the conscience that dwells in the heart of every man."

"Another quote?"

"Yes, Polybius."

"Never heard of him, but he's right. I've been through this with Woody before, and he always gets down after he's got some strange nookie. If it bothers him so much, it looks like he'd straighten up. What do you think, pard?"

Dewey didn't answer, but I saw him make a quick swipe at his eyes and immediately knew why. I didn't expect an answer. I'd seen this same scene between Woody and Wanda before - so many times that I'd toughened up to it. But I could still remember how seeing it the first time affected me, and I knew how Dewey felt and what he was thinking. I'd been on the job for a long time, but he'd only had a few days to get set for this. As days with Woody Pickens went, this had been a bad one, and Dewey had held up like a vintage Packard. It was then, standing in the darkness of that gloomy bedroom, that I decided my new partner might not be so bad after all.

CHAPTER 5
The Bone Orchard

"Are we going to sit here all night?"

"Huh?" I mumbled.

"Are we going to stay here? I mean, it seems like a waste of time because they've been asleep for an hour, and we're still just sitting here," Dewey said.

"I'm sleeping, dammit."

"I know that, but don't you think we should go somewhere else to sleep. I'm uncomfortable here," Dewey said.

"Why?" I asked. It wasn't that I really cared, but I felt obliged to ask.

"For one thing, I can't sleep sitting up."

"Then lie down on the floor."

"The floor is hard."

"Anyone who meditates standing on their head ought to be able to sleep anywhere and in any position," I said.

"Well, I can't. I also think we're violating these people's privacy. Bedrooms are like bathrooms, as far as I'm concerned. They're off limits to everyone except the occupant," Dewey said.

"If our being here keeps it from being private, then it hasn't been private for a long time. You may have forgotten, but we're dead. They can't see us and don't know we're here. As far as they're concerned, their privacy has not been violated. Does that make you feel better?"

"No."

"I didn't think it would. Where do you want to go?," I asked, now resigned to moving. Dewey wasn't about to let me go back to sleep.

"I don't know. This is my first week here, so I don't know where we're supposed to go. We have an invisible car to drive that we've been sleeping in up until now, I might add, so I thought perhaps we have an invisible apartment or house somewhere."

"Well, we don't," I said, stood up, and stretched.

"We don't have a place to live?"

"We're not alive. How can you live in a place when you're not alive?" I asked.

"Don't be silly. Terminology has nothing to do with it. Even dead people need a place to stay."

"We don't have one."

"Why not?"

"Because they've never given me one," I said.

"Who is they?"

"The Central Office provides stuff like that, but Roosevelt is the only person I ever see, and I don't see him often, and I've never asked for a place to stay anyhow. Why should I? I can stay anywhere I want."

"Who's Roosevelt?"

Dewey's talking spree would continue until I did something to please him, I decided, but I still didn't feel like getting involved in a lengthy discussion on angeling, and that was exactly where this conversation was headed. "All right, Dewey, you win. Let's go," I said and motioned for him to follow.

"Where?"

"Just follow me." I walked through the bedroom wall into the hallway. Dewey followed, not immediately, but within a few seconds he popped into the hallway with a big grin on his face.

"Hey, that's neat," he said, then walked back through. Then he stuck his head back through the wall and said, "This is fun. Why haven't we done this before?"

"Quit screwing around and let's go. You can walk through anything now," I said and walked through the living room wall right to the front lawn. Dewey followed, giggling this time. I walked down the sidewalk at a brisk pace with Dewey in hot pursuit.

"Who's Roosevelt?" He asked again as he caught up.

"He's our boss, our section chief," I replied. "His name is Roosevelt Watson, and he's a big nigger."

"You shouldn't call him that," Dewey said.

"I don't, to his face."

"You shouldn't call him that at all."

"OK! He's a big spook, if that suits you better. Actually, I suppose he's a spook spook," I said.

"You're not funny."

"Well, he's our immediate supervisor, like I said earlier, and our only contact with the Central Office. In all the years I've been here, Roosevelt has been around maybe two dozen times."

"Where are we going?" Dewey asked, looking around. By then, we'd cleared the house and were standing on the sidewalk in front of Woody's house.

"Get in the car," I said, opening the driver's door to the car.

"But where are we going?"

"You wanted to go somewhere to sleep, and that's exactly where we're going. Get in."

Dewey looked at me and smiled playfully, then tried to walk into the car without opening the door. He bounced off the car and fell backward on the sidewalk, and I broke into laughter. He scrambled to his feet, looking a little bumfuzzled. "You can't do that, you knucklehead," I said.

"Why not? I walked through a wall," he said, struggling to his feet.

"Yeah, but the car operates in the same mode we do. You can't walk through things in your own mode," I said.

"Mode?"

"Yeah, mode. You walked through the wall because it's in another dimension from us, but the car is in our dimension. You're dead, remember?"

"Are you trying to tell me that our car is dead too?"

"Well, in a manner of speaking, yes," I said, chuckling.

"I don't understand."

"Get in. I'll explain it to you later."

"I want to know now. I've been here for several days now, and we just started walking through walls. Until now, we've gone through doors like everyone else, and now this mode thing comes up, and I'm confused."

"Didn't they teach you about all this stuff at the training center?" I asked.

"If they did, I don't remember it."

"You didn't flunk the course, did you?"

"No, I made an A in most of my classes," he said, looking irked. That shut me up on that subject. I'd made B's in most of mine.

"Well, maybe they've changed the way they teach up there."

"I missed a few days due to illness. Maybe that's when they discussed the modes."

"Explaining all that takes a long time, and I don't want to get that started right now. I'll tell you all about it later, but right now, I'm tired and sleepy," I said.

Dewey got into the car, the right way this time, and I cranked up and drove toward the outskirts of town. Just outside of town, I turned onto a county road and proceeded down it for about a mile to a cemetery. As I reached the graveyard and turned in through some ornate, wrought iron gates, Dewey jerked himself upright and looked around. "Why, this is a cemetery," he said.

"Yep, a sure enough bone orchard," I said.

"But, what are we doing here? I don't want to sleep in a graveyard."

"You said you wanted to leave Woody's bedroom. You said you wanted somewhere to sleep, and you even made a point of saying that even dead people should have a place to sleep. Well, pard, this is it."

"I'm not sleeping in a graveyard," he said.

"Then sleep in the car," I said, stopping the car beside a series of graves that were constructed as concrete cashes instead of just mounds of dirt with headstones. I got out, opened the trunk, pulled out a sleeping bag, and headed for the closest cache. Once there, I spread my sleeping bag directly on top of it and proceeded to crawl in.

"You're desecrating a grave," Dewey called from the car.

"Believe me, Dewey, the guy buried here won't care one way or another," I said.

"How would you like it if somebody slept on your grave?"

"I don't have a grave," I said.

"You were cremated?"

"To the best of my knowledge, yes. I have no way of knowing what they did with my body. I left word with some folks that if I didn't make it back from Nam, I'd like to be cremated, but I can't say for sure what actually happened."

"I've never given it much thought, but I don't know what happened to my body either. I suppose they buried me, though," Dewey said, getting out of the car. He looked around uneasily for a few moments before cautiously making his way to the cache where I'd stretched out. The way he moved reminded me of a cat walking through a room full of dogs.

"Why are you walking that way?" I asked.

"Graveyards make me nervous."

"Why? Nobody here can bother you."

"I know, but graveyards are eerie. I've always had the feeling that places like this are haunted," he said, wrapping his arms around himself like he'd just caught a chill.

"If places like this were haunted, the two of us wouldn't be here. Dead folks don't actually stay in the graveyard, you know."

"I know, but they still bother me."

"Well, they don't bother me."

"You still shouldn't sleep on that grave. Don't you have any respect at all for the dead?" he asked.

I sat up and looked at the inscription on the grave, then lay back down. "Depends on the dead, I reckon. I knew this guy, or knew about him, and believe me, he wouldn't mind me sleeping on his grave."

"You knew him?" Dewey asked, looking surprised.

"Well, we never actually shook hands, if that's what you mean. I knew him through looking after Woody. They used to run around together some."

"So this was one of Woody's friends. Figures. You knew exactly where you were coming when you came here, didn't you?"

"I knew he was buried around here somewhere, but I didn't pick his grave on purpose. It doesn't matter, Dewey. None of these folks are any more aware of what's going on here than you are about what's going on at your grave. For all you know, a big St. Bernard is pissing on your headstone right now," I said, grinning smugly.

"Are you aware that you're only about half civilized?" Dewey asked, looking somewhat disheartened.

"Yeah, but that's what makes me such an engaging individual."

"Enraging might be a better description. You seem to have no respect for anything, unless, of course, it's your own ego. It's like you go out of your way to be . . . to be . . ."

"Irritating?" I asked, finishing his sentence.

"Yes, irritating."

"Why do you think folks call me Salty? Hell, I've always been irritating to some folks, but the way I see it, that's their problem. And I'll straighten you out about one thing. I have respect for a lot of things, especially the dead. I liked this guy," I said, slapping the cache under me.

"Is that why you came here?"

"I came here to sleep, but I do come here every now and then to pay my respects. I knew several people buried out here. I've been in this town for fourteen years, and that's long enough to where you can get attached to some folks. This particular man - his name was Don Leland - was a helluva fine hombre. He owned a shirt-tail outfit just outside of town where he ran some cows and did a little farming. All the guy ever did was work his ass off, and all it got him was dead at an early age."

"How'd he die?"

"He died in a ranch accident. He was trying to fix an old tractor, and a chain holding a motor he was trying to remove slipped, and the motor fell and crushed his chest. He died instantly," I said, unemotionally

"How did that affect Woody?"

"Woody loved the guy, and it nearly killed him. Don Leland wasn't a boozer like Woody, but they got to be friends anyway. Don, in his country way, had been doing some quiet missionary work on Woody for some time. If he'd lived, Woody might not be as bad a drunk as he is nowadays. Woody used to go out to Don's place and spend the whole weekend. Him and Don would ride horses and work cattle, and Woody loved it. He hardly ever drank when he was around Don, but that was a long time ago. Don died about eight years ago, and Woody hasn't been on a horse since then. And his drinking got worse, a lot worse."

"Then his death was a tragedy in more than one way," Dewey said.

"Well, I don't know how much of a tragedy it was to Don, but it damn sure hurt Woody. Don left a wife and two kids behind, but they've moved away from here. I've never heard Woody mention Don's death - not once."

"Oh, my. Perhaps Proust was wrong."

"Who?"

"Marcel Proust. He said that happiness is beneficial for the body but grief is what develops the powers of the brain. Undoubtedly Woody's grief has not served him well," Dewey said.

"Sure doesn't look like it, but everybody has their ups and downs. Right now, I'm having one of my downs, and if you don't mind, I'd like to go to sleep," I said.

"I mind. I want to go back to town," Dewey said, sounding like a child again.

"All right, Dewey. I'm moving one more time, but this is it," I said, rolling out of my bag.

I folded the bag, put it back in the trunk of the car, loaded Dewey back into the car, and headed back to town. Just inside the city limits, I turned down Main Street. "Where are we going now?" Dewey asked.

"We're going down the street to a hotel, the old Forest Hotel. It's just a few blocks away. Hardly anyone stays there anymore, so it's easy to find a vacant room. I usually pick a single, but I'm sure we can find a comfortable double room."

"Oh, that would be wonderful," Dewey said, putting his hands together under his chin like he was praying. His mannerisms irritated me less now, and that in itself would've been irritating if I hadn't been preoccupied. What I wanted most was to get to sleep again. Back in Woody's bedroom, I'd been dreaming about Mary Ellen Wilson, a bottle of brandy, and a water bed, and I wanted to see if I could pick up where Dewey had interrupted. We found a room on the second floor, and I went straight to a bed and plopped down in anticipation of getting back to my dream. I was just about there when Dewey started talking again.

"Are we the only custodians in Forest City?"

I didn't answer, thinking that if he thought I was sound asleep, maybe he'd shut up. It didn't work.

"Are we?" he asked again.

I don't give in easy, so I stayed quiet.

"I know you're not asleep because you're not snoring. You might as well answer me."

I snored.

"That's a fake snore if I've ever heard one."

"Go to hell," I mumbled.

"I'm not sleepy anymore, so you might as well talk to me. Sometimes I get sleepy if I talk for a while."

"Talk to yourself," I said.

"I don't know the right answers," he said.

"Hell, you don't even know the right questions. How should I know if we're the only custodians in town? I've never seen one, if that tells you anything. That figures, though, because they probably work in a separate dimension from us. If all us custodians worked in the same dimension, there'd be lots of confusion, and that would make for an unworkable situation."

"Why?"

"Well, because if we could see and talk to each other, we'd sooner or later be at odds over something. And if we got at odds, then we'd be fighting back and forth, and the Central Office would be awful unhappy about that," I said.

"But what makes you think we'd argue, be at odds? It might be nice to have someone around who could help out from time to time," Dewey said.

"If that were the case, you wouldn't be here. I would've asked another custodian to help out when I got worn down instead of asking for a full time partner. People are people, Dewey, even here in the hereafter. We've been given an assignment to one mark, just one, and that means we do what's best for that mark. Sometimes that means we don't do what's best for some other custodian's mark, and that's where the problem comes in. The Central Office couldn't deal with a situation where custodians were at odds with other custodians."

Dewey fell silent for a while. I thought maybe I had satisfied his curiosity, but as it turned out, he was only trying to think of another question. "Why is this hotel practically deserted?"

"It's haunted, according to the rumor around town."

"Haunted?"

"Yeah, you know, like ghosts live here."

"There's no such things as ghosts," Dewey said confidently.

"What do you think you are?" I chuckled.

"I'm not a ghost, and neither are you. How did the rumor get started?"

I didn't answer, but Dewey was already ahead of me. "I don't suppose you had anything to do with spreading a rumor like that. That sounds like something right down your alley," he said.

"Look Dewey, business here was lousy anyway. The only people who ever stay here are a few camel jock foreign students, a few old winos, a few wetbacks, and an occasional traveler who can't afford the motel across town. Besides, I haven't been going around scaring people out of their socks just for the hell of it. There have always been plenty of rooms here, and I just took what was available."

"And you never did anything to encourage the rumor?"

"Not really."

"What does that mean?"

"It means I never did anything intentionally," I said. "Maybe I did a few things like forget and leave a light on, a door open, a bed unmade, or something like that. I caused the biggest commotion by watching television. I had a rare night off and was watching TV down in the lobby when a couple of winos came in. I was right in the middle of a good movie when this wino walked over and changed the channel. I got up and changed it back to the movie."

"You changed the channel with a couple of people sitting there watching the TV?" Dewey sounded amazed.

"You bet I did! I was there first, and it was just a couple of old winos. I've about had my fill of drunks, if you haven't noticed, so it didn't bother me in the least to change the channel. Anyway, only one of them was watching. The other one had nodded off in a chair, so I changed the channel."

"What happened?"

"The wino watching just sat there and blinked a few times. He looked around real good, then got up and changed it back."

"And I guess you changed it back to the movie again."

"You bet."

"Then what happened?"

"The wino got up to change it again, so I kicked his ass."

"You actually kicked him?" Dewey asked.

"Right in the seat of his britches."

"Did you scare him half to death?"

"Hell no. You can't scare a wino. He just stood there for a while and looked around the room. Then he went over to the other wino, the one who'd nodded off in the chair, and socked him a good one. Boy, did that ever start a helluva fight. They woke up everybody in the hotel, and it took three camel jocks and the night clerk to get them separated."

"You should be ashamed," Dewey said, but I could tell he was fighting off a smile.

"Are you sleepy now that you've had your bedtime story? Woody has a light schedule tomorrow and will be out of class by noon. We'd better get some rest because God only knows what he'll do after what happened tonight."

"Do you really think God knows what Woody will do tomorrow, or for that matter, any other time?" Dewey asked.

"Dewey, I'm very tired, and that's too big a question for me to handle right now. Let it rest for a while," I said.

Dewey paused and answered his own question. "I think he knows."

"Well, if he knows the future, he knows I'm about to stuff this pillow in your mouth if you don't shut up and let me sleep," I said and flipped over on my stomach.

"Nighty-nite," Dewey said, sweetly.

"Nite," I mumbled, thinking that was the last of Dewey questions.

"Doug?"

"What."

"You took me out to that graveyard tonight so you could tell me the story about Woody's friend, and I appreciate your caring enough to do that. You're not always as salty as you'd like for people to think you are, and I'm starting to see that in you."

I didn't answer, just breathed hard like I was already asleep. The truth was that I hadn't taken him to the graveyard to tell the story. It just worked out that way, but I was tired, and Dewey was entitled to think that if he wanted to. That was the first time he'd called me by name since I chewed his ass out for calling me Dougie. Doing that and saying what he said pleased me, and I went straight to sleep. Instead of finishing my dream about Mary Ellen Wilson and the waterbed, I dreamed about snakes and spiders.

CHAPTER 6
The Fine Art of Custodianship

Morning came in a hurry, and when I finally started coming back to life, or whatever one could call what I do now when I wake up. Maybe I ought to say that I'd just come back to afterlife, but whatever, Dewey was gone when I did. I sat up and listened. Someone walked down the hall but went into the room next door. I was about to flop back down for a few more winks when Dewey suddenly popped into the room - through the wall, of course. There's nothing worse than a kid with a new toy.

"Good morning!" he said cheerfully.

"Morning," I mumbled. "Where've you been."

"Checking on Woody. He's up and around, teaching a class in developmental psychology. I was amazed at what a good job he was doing lecturing, particularly after the night he had. The man is a true professional."

"He's a good teacher," I agreed. The sound of squeaking bedsprings and bumping from the room next door suddenly caught my attention. I stuck my head through the wall to see what was going on.

"What is it?" Dewey asked as I retracted my head and stood to adjust my clothes.

"International relations," I said.

"Beg your pardon?"

"Some camel jock, I think his name is Faud, is screwing a cowgirl the local kids call 'thunderthighs.' I've seen them together before. You might say what's happening is a meeting of East and West - Middle East and Wild West."

"Well, I'm surprised you're not satisfying your voyeuristic bent by watching," Dewey said.

"Hey, I don't watch just any couple do the dirty deed. I'm picky about what I watch. Thunderthighs in there is about six feet tall and weighs nearly two hundred pounds. She's got a face full of pimples and has stringy blonde hair. Faud is a skinny-legged Arab with an eagle beak for a nose whose only claim to fame is that he's hung like a donkey. I guess thunderthighs got tired of screwing these pencil-dicked cowboys around here and went for the big meat." I turned to look at Dewey and saw that the upper half of his body was in the next room. His face was pale when he pulled his head back into the room.

"Disgusting," he said.

"This time, old buddy, I'll have to agree with you. Are you ready to get out of here?" I asked.

He nodded and we started walking toward where I'd parked the car. As soon as we exited the hotel, Dewey stopped and lifted his head. He looked like someone had just waved a chunk of limburger cheese under his nose, the way his face puckered and all, and I couldn't help but laugh out loud. "What is that awful smell?" he asked.

"That, my friend, is the smell of money," I said proudly, blowing my chest out and breathing deeply.

"Money?"

"Well, that's what the locals always say when some stranger comes through town and asks the same question you just ask. What you're smelling is a feedlot."

"Feedlot?"

"You bet, a feedlot. That's where they put cattle to fatten them up before they go to slaughter. This town has two feedlots - one east of town and one on the north side. The wind here usually comes out of the southwest, so we usually don't get the smell as bad as it is this morning, but when the winds shifts and comes in from the north or east, it gets kind of stinky. Want to go see one?"

"Sounds pretty sickening, but yes, I'd like to see it," Dewey said.

I drove Dewey to the feedlot north of town some five miles, and showed him the feedlot - a big outfit that covered hundreds of acres. The place was called Heartland Custom Feeders, Inc., and it was owned and operated by the richest rancher in all of Sandstone County. Lawson Crowley, a millionaire many times over, had built the feedlot back in the sixties, but it had grown by leaps and bounds since then. I told Dewey all about Crowley and his cattle empire, but he was too spellbound by what he was seeing to be overly interested in the history of the feedlot. Anyone who sees more than 20,000 head of cattle standing bunched up in relatively small pens has got to be impressed, but where another cattleman might see lofty profits, Dewey was seeing anything but that. I explained how the cattle were fed and tried to explain what I knew of how the business end of the enterprise worked, but Dewey listened in total silence. Finally, just as we were leaving, he turned to me and asked, "Do you approve of this sort of thing?"

"No, I don't," I said.

"Good. I think it's absolutely awful. Those poor animals just stand there all day long, waiting to be slaughtered."

"Well, at least they're being well fed."

"That doesn't make up for the way they're being treated. These places are nothing but . . . nothing but . . . but . . . cow concentration camps," he said, finally finding the words.

"You're about right," I said, chuckling.

"Well, you don't seem terribly concerned about it."

"I'm concerned, but there's nothing I can do about it. If I had my druthers, cows would still be running loose on the prairie somewhere, but feedlots are the order of the day around here," I said.

"That's no excuse," Dewey snapped.

"The beef producers are trying to turn out the kind of meat the public wants. You average consumer wants meat heavy with fat because that's what puts the taste in beef. Most folks don't want grass fed beef nowadays, and besides, there's not enough prairie grasslands left to graze out cattle the way it used to be done. Farmers plowed up most of the good grasslands and planted it in wheat and corn. Feedlots buy the grains from the farmers and then feed the cattle in pens like those you just saw. Almost all of the cattle in this country are imported from big cow/calf operations down in Texas or somewhere else. It's a nasty business, in my opinion, but the times, they're a-changing, Dewey," I said.

"Well, I don't care how they try to justify them, those feedlots are wrong."

"Yeah, and wrong in more than just what they do to the animals. Forest City used to be a nice little western town, but now it's too commercial. Lots of undesirable people come in with businesses associated with feedlots, but it gets worse. If you want to see something bad, I'll take you to a packing house," I said.

"No thanks. I've seen enough."

"Don't let it get your drawers in a wad, pard. We're not here to do anything about the Feedlots. Maybe you're next assignment will be looking after a feedlot cowboy or somebody like that," I said, trying to lift his spirits. It didn't work, and when I saw that he might start sulking, I decided to introduce him to some other people. I drove back to Main Street and parked the car. "Come on," I said, motioning for him to follow.

We crossed the street and headed for Clarence's Grocery and Hardware. Clarence Ludwig, the owner-operator of the store, was out front sweeping the sidewalk and greeting the by-passers. He did that a lot, I'd noticed. Amy Ludwig, his wife, was the real store manager. She was known as Miss Amy to almost everyone. Loved and respected by the local people, particularly by the college students, Miss Amy had a kind and generous heart. Clarence, however, was another story. He was a cranky old man, and almost everyone knew he was too lazy to hit a lick at a snake. He wasn't too lazy, on the other hand, to sneak down the street once a week for a little hanky-panky with Marge, a widow woman who owned a laundry and dry cleaners.

I knew that to be true because I'd stumbled upon them screwing on a pile of dirty clothes in a laundry room at the back of the building. I took a short cut through the alley once and saw them getting it on through a crack in the back door. Clarence usually went out to sweep the sidewalk before meandering down the street to Marge's place, and it appeared as if that's exactly what he had in mind. If Dewey thought seeing a feedlot was disgusting, he needed to see Clarence and Marge rolling around in a pile of dirty underwear, sheets, and towels. I quickly dismissed the idea of coaxing Dewey into following Clarence down to Marge's because I didn't want to see that dirty deed again. It's that strong of heart but weak of stomach thing, you know.

"Something is troubling me," Dewey said as we reached the other side of the street.

"Something is **always** bothering you, Dewey."

"Maybe I should say I'm concerned. I'm tired today, almost exhausted, and I've only been up for a few hours."

"What have you been doing this morning?" I asked.

"Nothing much, just followed Woody around."

"Did you walk through any walls?"

"Why yes, I sure have. I've been practicing, you might say. I like it," he said with a silly giggle.

"That's why you're so tired. It takes more energy to walk through walls that it does to walk through an open doorway like everyone else does. You'll have to learn to pace yourself," I said.

"Yes, I know, but I still don't know much about modes. You promised you tell me later, and now it's later," Dewey said.

"Yeah, I did promise, so let's start with the transformation process. Did you get any of that at the training center?"

"Yes, we discussed that. I know that I'm going through a process of being transformed from being a physical being into a spiritual being. They said it was a continuing process that would take some time."

"The modes, as I see it, are part of that process. We have the modes so we can do our jobs, but it goes past that, I think. Sooner or later we'll reach a level of spirituality that's acceptable to the Central Office, and then we'll be ready to take our place in Heaven. I guess you might say we're earning our wings," I said.

"Are we going to have wings when we finish our reconstruction, or transformation, process? I mean, will we have real wings that fit on our backs and enable us to fly around?" Dewey asked, wide-eyed and pale as a sheet. He had stopped walking and was holding his left hand palm to his chest again, while he frantically pointed toward his back with the other hand.

"What's the matter with you? That's what angeling is all about, Dewey. I just told you; it's like being a pilot. You have to earn your wings before you can fly."

"Oh, my goodness!" Dewey said, looking faint.

"What's the matter?"

"Oh, my goodness!" he said again.

"Talk to me, you little shit. What the hell's wrong with you."

"Oh, Doug. I can't stand flying," he said, looking as frightened as a first grader at school for the first time. He was starting to babble now. "I get deathly ill when I fly. That's why I rode the bus here. Planes scare the poop out of me. I may spend the rest of eternity upchucking in a barf bag. Oooooooooooh!" he groaned. His legs gave way, and he collapsed to the sidewalk. Actually, he sat down just off the sidewalk.

"Get up from there and stop being a wimp. You're sitting on Mrs. Johnson's prickly pear cactus."

"I don't care. I can't feel it, and it won't hurt the cactus. I'm invisible, remember?"

"You may be invisible, and you may not feel it, but you're smashing Mrs. Johnson's cactus," I said proudly and pointed to where he was sitting.

Dewey looked down and saw the flattened cactus, then levitated to his feet like a startled deer. "How did I do that?" he asked, bug-eyed with excitement.

"You changed modes," I said.

"I did what?"

"You changed modes," I said again. "You went from I/I to I/T. That can happen when you forget to concentrate. I guess you got upset and lost your I/I mode."

"Oh, my goodness! Now I'm really scared because I don't know what you're talking about."

"Didn't they tell you at the Training Center?" I asked.

"No. I was sick for a couple of days, and they must have covered that while I was absent."

"Come over here and sit down. I'll try to explain it," I said and led him into a small city park and seated him on a park bench.

"First, don't worry about the wing business," I said. "I was just kidding about the wings. Did you see anyone in Heaven with wings?"

"No."

"Well, I think that's because the wings are symbolic. We don't really get wings."

"Thank God," Dewey said, heaving a sigh. "That relieves me more than anything you can imagine. Now I won't have to cut holes in all my shirts and jackets. There's just nothing in my wardrobe that will go with wings."

"We've got two modes: invisible/intangible and invisible/tangible," I said, picking up where I'd left off.

"You're confusing me again."

"If you'll shut up and listen, I'll uncomfuse you," I said impatiently. "Invisible/intangible, called I/I for short, means your mode is not only invisible but is also devoid of any material, or tangible, components. It means you have no substance, weight, volume, or control over anything material. You are like air, if you want to think of it that way. Invisible/tangible, called the I/T mode, allows you to stay invisible but gives you material components and the ability to move and manipulate material things."

"I'm still not sure I understand."

"When you are in the I/I mode, you are like air. When you are in the I/T mode, you are like the wind. Air doesn't move anything, but wind does. Does that help any?"

"No, and I think you're wrong about air because I know that it has some weight and substance. And wind is nothing but moving air, isn't it?" he asked.

"Dammit, Dewey. Quit nit-picking and try to concentrate. OK, air is a bad example. Forget the air and let's go back to basics. Do you remember when I asked you to stop Wanda when she was about to catch Woody screwing C.W. in the parking lot? Do you remember knocking her down?"

"How could I ever forget," Dewey said and rolled his eyes.

"Do you know why you could knock her down?" I asked.

"I didn't think about it; I just did it."

"You did it because you went into an invisible/tangible mode. She still couldn't see you, but you went I/T and took on weight and substance. You took on material components, and that's how you were able to knock her down. You could feel her, and she could feel you because you went tangible. That's what the I/T mode is all about."

"I get it," Dewey said, nodding. "And in order to walk through a wall, I have to become intangible. I have to give up the material components."

"Exactly," I said.

"But how do I know what mode I'm in? I mean, I just smashed that cactus without knowing I'd changed modes," Dewey said, looking buffaloed again.

"Well, that's just due to inexperience. You change modes when you want or need to change. In other words, you think about it.

If you want to walk through a wall, you think intangible and walk through it. Changing modes depends on intent, planning, and desire. You were able to change modes without actually being aware of it, like when you knocked Wanda down in the parking lot, because you really wanted to do it. Otherwise, you couldn't have done it."

"But I didn't. I didn't want to knock her down. I surely didn't want to hurt her," Dewey quickly added.

"I know that, but you wanted to stop her. Somewhere in the span of a few seconds you made a decision, or judgment, that stopping her was better than letting her to catch Woody with his pants down. You just overreacted, that's all. To use mode changes correctly and professionally, it's important to control your emotions. Mastering the art of mode changing takes time, but you'll learn to do it automatically. You'll just do it instinctively. Sometimes I run across a situation where I have to stop and concentrate before I change modes, but that doesn't happen often."

"But I was able to walk through a wall the first time I tried. Why didn't I bump my nose or get knocked down?" Dewey asked.

"There are several reasons why you could do it, "I said. "First of all, you **wanted** to do it. You saw me do it and simply followed suit. You planned it without realizing what you'd done. Second, I think you're smarter than the average run-of-the-mill apprentice, so you pick up on things quickly."

Dewey stared at me, a look of amazement on his face. "I can't believe it," he said. "You actually paid me a compliment."

"Don't let it go to your head," I cautioned. "I only said you were smart, not that you were worth a tinker's dam for anything." I smiled to make sure he knew I was joking.

"There's something else that puzzles me. If I change to the I/I mode, which makes me intangible, then why don't I just drop through the floor beneath me? Why don't I go through anything I try to touch or manipulate?"

"Good question, but I've already explained it. First of all, when you go I/I, you don't have any weight and you're not likely to drop anywhere. You're not going to just float away either. Remember, changing modes is dependent on planning and intent, not just thinking. You didn't fall through the floor or float away because that wasn't part of your intent. If you could just accidentally fall through anything, you could fall right through the earth itself. It's not part of our dimension either, you know. Being able to stand on the earth or a floor isn't something you have to concentrate on, unless of course, you plan on it," I said.

"Oh, my goodness! I just thought of something awful," Dewey said, holding a palm to his chest.

"Like what?"

"Well, when I was still alive, I occasionally had moments when I wanted the earth to open up and swallow me. You know, like when you're really embarrassed or something. What if I do that now? If I really want it to happen, will the earth actually swallow me?"

I broke down in laughter. The thought of the earth opening and swallowing up poor Dewey really tickled me, and I got this mental picture of him just disappearing right through the earth and coming out on the other side and spinning out into space. He didn't see the humor in it. "Well, can that happen?" he asked.

"No, Dewey. That can't happen. I can't really explain why it can't, but it can't, so don't worry about it. Let's give the folks upstairs a little credit for having planned things out a little better than that. They know we're working under a handicap down here, and that's why we've got these different modes," I said.

"Are you sure?"

"Yeah, I'm sure. You might think you've wanted the earth to swallow you up, but in reality, you haven't. My guess is that the situation we're in here is more real than any situation we've ever been involved in before."

"It makes sense to me now. I was tired because walking through walls was using up my energy. I understand now what you meant about pacing myself," Dewey said.

"Yeah, you can't walk through walls as easily as you can tackle people."

"Are there any other modes? Am I going to change into anything else?" Dewey asked.

"There's another mode, but I don't know much about it. It's called the personification mode, and it's when you take on physical characteristics and can be seen."

"Could you look like anybody or anything, or would you look like yourself?"

"I don't know. Like I said before, I don't know much about it. You need special permission from the Central Office to use it. It takes a special energy package, another component capability, or something like that to do it. I used to get lonesome or bored and try to do it, but all I ever did was use up all my energy. I felt like a dead battery and never did get close to pulling it off. Roosevelt finally told me to give it up, that I'd need special permission from the Central Office to use it. He can do it, though, and he says you need to be in really good shape for it. That may be just a bunch of jock talk. Anyway, I quit trying a long time ago. It really doesn't matter because I've never run into a situation where the personification mode would have helped. If we do our job the way we're supposed to, the two modes we have are plenty."

"That's fine with me because I'm having enough trouble trying to use the first two. But it does sound like fun," Dewey said. He noticed the broad grin on my face at about the same time he turned to walk away. "What's funny?"

"Maybe there was a time when having the personification mode would've helped. Several years ago, maybe five or six, Woody went over to Dodge City for a meeting of some kind. He seldom leaves town alone, but he did that time. He stayed around after his meeting was over and did some bar hopping. It was still early, maybe nine o'clock, when he decided to start home. He could hardly walk by the time he walked out of that last bar, and I had to steady him on the way to his car. I'd planned for it, though, and rode with him so I'd be ready to drive him home if need be. I was hoping he'd at least make it outside the city limits before he conked out, but he didn't make it three blocks before he passed out."

"You mean he just went to sleep."

"No, he passed out. He stopped at a traffic light, nodded a couple of times, and fell over in the seat. I slapped and pinched him, but he was out like a light. I couldn't just leave him sitting there under a traffic light, so I scooted him over and drove. I took every back street I could find trying to avoid traffic and make it to the open highway without being seen. Once on the open road, I planned on taking a chance on driving him home. I didn't make it out of Dodge City, though, because a cop whistled me down. I'm sure a driverless car would get any cop's attention, and the one who stopped me had a hard time figuring out what was going on."

"What happened?"

"Woody had started gagging, and I didn't want him puking in the car, so I dumped him over in the back seat and hung his head out the window. I thought the cold night air might bring him around. That part of my plan worked, but then the cop stopped us. He came running up to the car and looked in, but when he saw Woody hanging out the back window, he backed away and stood there with a stupid look on his face. He looked again but still couldn't see anyone but Woody. He scratched his head, walked around the car several times, and looked again. Then he got down on his all fours and looked under the car. Failing to find anyone there, he walked up and down the street, looking in dumpsters and scratching around in scrubs. He finally gave up and arrested Woody."

"He arrested him?" Dewey asked, looking mildly dismayed.

"You bet he did! What else could he do? Poor Woody didn't know what had happened when he woke up in jail the next morning. The cops didn't want to let him go until he told them who was driving the car, but Woody couldn't tell them. They finally got him on a public drunk charge and let him go. The cops decided a drunk driving charge would be hard to prove in court, particularly if some lawyer brought up the question of how Woody could've driven and puked out the back window at the same time," I said.

"If you'll pardon me for saying, you didn't handle that situation very well. You probably cost Woody some money and unnecessary embarrassment by trying to drive him home. You should have pulled the car into a parking lot or over to the curb and let him sleep it off. Perhaps that would have been a good time to hide his keys, or maybe you should have kept him from getting behind the wheel in the first place."

"Yeah, well, you win some, and you lose some. I'll admit I could've done a better job with that one, but I was tired of screwing around with him. You'll learn that sometimes you have to make snap decisions, and sometimes your judgment is a little off. We learn from our mistakes, I guess. I try to keep in mind, in any situation like that, that almost any decision I make is better than the one he's able to make."

"I guess you're right. I spoke out of turn. To be perfectly honest with you, I'm more than a little confused about what we're supposed to do. I remember almost everything they taught us at the Training Center, but there seems to be such a fine line between being a guardian or a nursemaid and between being a custodian or a conscience. I know the rules, I think, but a lot of situations come up that I don't understand. Knowing what to do is a big problem, and I've already learned that this field work is a lot tougher than the classroom was." Dewey looked dejected. I decided it was time for me to make a confession of my own.

"I know what you mean because that bothered me for a long time, particularly when I was a rookie. Occasionally it still does, but I try to remember that my job is to keep this guy alive, not to control him. We're not supposed to direct his actions or steer him away from trouble, but we're supposed to keep him as healthy as possible through what all he gets involved in. It's not our job to reform him, to change his thinking, or to chart a course for him. That's the book on it," I said.

"I know what the manual says, but I just don't see how it's possible to do our job well without occasionally doing some steering. It's difficult to drive a car unless you turn the wheel sometimes, if you know what I mean. Wouldn't it be better to keep him out of trouble instead of trying to straighten out the mess once he's involved? Surely an occasion arises when a little preventative action is useful."

I looked carefully at Dewey for a few moments. This guy, strange as he was, definitely had a good head on his shoulders. I was considering telling him my exact definition of custodial work, but I still has some doubts as the whether he'd been on the job long enough to understand. I decided to tell him, not everything, but enough to ease his mind about what we were doing.

"Sometimes, not often but sometimes, fudging works. Hiding the keys from Woody when he gets too drunk to drive is fudging, a slight violation of the rules. But it's often a better choice than letting him drive home. We need to be careful about the creative ways we use the rules, though, because the Central Office doesn't like it," I said, leaning close so no one except him could hear. I felt foolish. Who's to hear, I thought. "They'd really be pissed if we got too creative. The job of directing his activities is assigned to another division, and we're not supposed to get in their way."

"What other division?"

"I don't know what it's called. Nobody ever tells me anything, and what I know, or think I know, is just speculation. But it looks to me like some people are marked for reconstructive action, that at some point in their life they'll undergo a major change. It only stands to reason that any person who has been assigned a custodian is surely being kept safe and alive for some other purpose. We work for the Division of Custodial Services, so I figure there must be a division in charge of lifestyle changes, reconstruction, or something like that."

"What happens to us when our mark no longer needs guarding?" Dewey looked troubled again, and I knew what he was thinking.

"I don't know, but I reckon they'll give us another mark."

"Yes, I suppose they would. We'd just go from one problem case to another. If Woody gets his life in order, he won't need us anymore. We'd have to start all over with a brand new mark, and he might even be worse than Woody is, and . . ."

"Knock it off, Dewey. You're breaking my heart. I've been assigned to this goofy sonofabitch for over fourteen years, and you just got here. After you've been around for a while, you might be glad to get rid of him. One thing's for sure. If we screw up this assignment to where something bad happens to Woody, we'll get another assignment, all right, but the next one's likely to be looking after a yak herdsman in Outer Mongolia or somewhere like that. We could do worse."

"Yes, being here is decidedly better. You know what else bothers me?" Dewey asked.

"What?"

"We've been given the task of looking after Woody while he's suffering through a bad period in his life. We're supposed to see him through this miserable time and then turn him over to someone else for restoration or whatever. I'd like to see Woody when he's happy, when his life is in order and things are going well for him. Aren't you at all interested in the way he turns out? Won't you miss him?"

"Yeah, I'll miss him for sure, but sort of like I'd miss a bad case of hemorrhoids," I said, looking smug. Dewey didn't laugh, didn't frown, and didn't even lecture me about my remark. His mind was still stuck on the custodial business.

"Do you think everyone has a Guardian Angel? I mean, is everyone on earth who has problems like Woody being looked after by one of us?" he asked.

"I don't think so. Like I said before, only some people are marked for rehab or change of some kind, and I'm sure some people are left to struggle through their problems alone. Too many bad things happen to people for them to be protected. Either that, or there's a bunch of lousy custodians out there. You can go out to the bone orchard every now and then and see where they've buried somebody who got killed in a senseless accident. Any custodian worth a tinker's dam could have prevented it, so I'm sure they weren't protected. Don Leland, Woody's friend who got killed when the motor fell on him, is another story, though. It would've taken a good custodian to stop that from happening."

"If you had been around, could you have stopped it?"

"Maybe, and that's where you really have to be careful not to give in to the temptation to interfere. If I'd been there to stop it from happening, I could've saved Woody a lot of grief and myself a lot of work. I could've thought ahead and made my job easier, but that's something you never do, regardless of how tempting it is at the time. Our business is our mark and no one else."

"Yes, I know. They stressed that to the max at the training center," Dewey said.

"I've been tempted but never came close to protecting anyone except Woody. I think the penalty for going out of bounds on a mark is really tough, maybe even tougher than letting your own mark get killed," I said.

"What would they do to us? Do you think they'd send us to Hell?"

"No, but that's when you might get the job in Mongolia, or even worse. They might even send you back through another life cycle. I've thought about it a lot, and I'm convinced that some people go through several life cycles before they're allowed to stay in the afterlife. I'm talking about reincarnation, of course. It's just a theory, but it's possible that some people go around several times - until they reach a required level of development."

"Do you think there's any way of knowing how many lives you've lived? I have no idea about myself," Dewey said.

"I don't know, but I'm sure of one thing. I don't want to go back again. Maybe it would be all right if I got to choose exactly what or who I was going to be, but otherwise, I don't want any part of it."

"Why not? Where's your sense of adventure?"

"Because I believe that those who go back are being sent to learn more lessons, and I've had about all the education I can stand. My attitude toward women has always been poor, for example, and I wasn't famous for treating them well while on earth. I never did like women much. Don't get me wrong or jump to any conclusions. I'm not one of you guys," I said.

"Thank God for small favors," Dewey said and smiled testily.

I regretted the comment as soon as it left my lips, but I was already knee deep in making a point and kept at it. "It stands to reason that I'd get recycled as a woman. I'd probably be sent back as an ugly gal at that, and I can't think of a worse fate. There's no way an ugly woman could have much fun."

"Oh, I don't know about that. You did all right as a man, didn't you?" Dewey asked, an impish smile on his face. I wiggled a finger at him, stood up, and motioned for him to follow.

"You'd better be nice to me or I'll take you down to the laundry and make you watch Clarence and Marge screw on a pile of dirty laundry."

"It couldn't be any worse than watching that Faud fellow and Thunderthighs do it," Dewey said.

"Want to bet?"

"No, I don't gamble. Besides, I've learned to take your word for some things. Peeping is your specialty, so I believe you."

"Well, at least I got something across to you," I said.

"Don't be so coy. You've been a big help, and you know it. What I've learned today about modes was very helpful."

"Metaphorically speaking, are you willing to admit now that I'm the pundit and you're the pupil?"

"No."

"But you have learned a lot, right?"

"Yes, I've learned some things, but I prefer thinking of it as a junior member learning from a senior member of a duo," he said.

"No, Dewey, it's more like a freshman learning from a senior. You've got a couple of more years to go before you're a junior," I said, flashing a trim smile.

"Gotcha!"

"What's that mean? You didn't win the argument."

"I got you to back off the pundit and the pupil thing, so I win."

"You know something, Dewey?" I asked as we headed toward Woody's house.

"What?"

"You've got a bad stubborn streak in you."

CHAPTER 7
The Accouterments of Angeling

One good thing about Woody Pickens was that you could set your watch by him when it came to quitting time because he went home promptly at three every afternoon. I'd been stretched out on Woody's front lawn, catching a few rays from an unusually warm October sun and waiting for my shift to start. Dewey had taken the day watch alone, and I'd sure enjoyed my leisure time. I watched Woody walk up the sidewalk and go inside, then moved to the shade of a big elm and waited on Dewey. He was trailing along some fifty yards behind, looking sort of droopy.

"You know something, Dewey?" I asked as he sat down next to me. "When you stop to think about it, we're not doing too bad."

"What does 'not too bad' mean?" he asked, perking up somewhat.

"You know, being a custodian. This job's a pain in the ass sometimes, and we're definitely the low rung on the ladder as far as Angels are concerned. Rank-wise, we're lower than a frog's ass, but I'll have to admit that the job does have its advantages. In some ways, we've got it made, pard."

"What are you getting at?"

"Well, for instance, there's the car we drive. I always wanted a '57 Chevy, and now I have one. Just look at that machine," I said and nodded toward the red Chevy convertible parked at the curb. "She's a Bel Aire - 225 horses, dual exhausts, four barrel carb - the works. Plus, she never runs out of gas."

"It's a nice car, but there's more to life than a car," Dewey said.

"I hate to keep reminding you, but this ain't life."

"I know it isn't, but it requires some of the same accouterments."

"Naw, the fixings are even better here - like a car that can't run out of gas. Did you ever hear of a car that wouldn't run out of gas?" I asked.

"Fixings?" Dewey wrinkled his nose.

"Yeah. My grandpa Anderson called equipment 'fixings.' I guess it's fair to use the word here."

"Whatever."

"There's a cooler in the trunk that never needs ice, and every few days it refills itself with drinks. The victuals box - I called it the magic box - always has warm food in it. Most of the time I eat sandwiches from the cooler like bologna and cheese, ham, bacon and tomato, or just a plain peanut butter and jelly," I said.

"Yuck."

"You don't like peanut butter?"

"I can't stand any of that stuff," Dewey said, waving his hand in disgust.

"Don't worry because sometimes we get stuff from the magic box like burgers, hot dogs, fried chicken, chicken fried steak, and . . ."

"Chicken fried steak?" Dewey asked.

"Yeah."

"Boy, you really are a redneck, aren't you?"

"There's that word again. What's redneck about a chicken fried steak?" I asked.

"No truly civilized person would roll a decent cut of meat in flour and fry it. It's . . . It's . . . immoral."

"And eating snails isn't?"

Dewey raised his eyebrows, smiled timidly, and said, "Well, everything can be taken too far. I happen to like escargot, but I can see your point. Perhaps we could compromise and add some things to the menu like pasta, and broccoli, and baked fish, and skinless chicken, a low-fat yogurt, and bran, and particularly fresh fruits. Do we ever have fresh fruits?"

"No," I said flatly. "Monkeys eat fruit."

"What? No fruit?" Dewey asked, looking indignant. I started to make a crack about him already being fruity enough, but better judgment overruled the impulse.

"Nope, nothing like that. Besides, all that stuff you named is healthy. You don't have to eat healthy foods now. Let your hair down and live dangerously," I said.

"Well, occasionally I like spinach quiche, and it's rather fattening. Too many eggs, you know."

"What the hell is spinach quiche?" I asked, wrinkling my nose.

"Quiche is a pie, an egg pie that can be prepared with many different ingredients, spinach being one. It's very palatable," Dewey said, licking his lips.

"The only way you'll ever get spinach in me is to hold me down and poke it up my ass. I'll sure never swallow it." I clicked my teeth to show my determination.

"You should use some imagination in choosing your food. Experiment a little and try some new things. You might even like some of it," Dewey said, looking snooty.

"Never. I'm stubborn about what I eat."

"Suit yourself. What you eat will not trouble me in the least. I would, however, like to help make out the menu from now on."

"There's no menu. We just eat what they send. Didn't they ask you to make a list of what you wanted to eat?"

"Yes, but it was just a check list. It was an ordinary list, and I didn't pay much attention to it," Dewey said, shrugging.

"You should've because that's what you're going to get from now on."

"But I only checked off light foods. I was overweight at the time and wanted to drop a few pounds so I chose salads, fish, and things like that. On occasions I'll want more substantial food. I'm starting to feel tired lately, and I'll need more high energy food. I can't live on what you eat, that for sure."

"No one expects you to live, Dewey. You're dead, so you're going to get real hungry before you starve." I said and sniggered.

"Roosevelt will come around before long, and I'll ask him to change the menu. I'm sure he'll do me that little favor."

"Maybe, but here's something for you to think about. It only took me fourteen years to talk him into giving me a partner."

"That's comforting," Dewey said, wearily.

"Don't get depressed. Think of all the good things." I said.

"Such as?"

"We can wear anything. No one can see us, so no one can complain about how we dress."

"That's even more depressing."

"And we don't have to worry about getting wet, at least while we're in the I/I mode. Hell, our matches can't even get wet."

"Whoopie. We don't have any matches."

"You know what I mean. Since we're invisible, we can sleep, walk, or sit any place we like. We don't have to take baths, or brush our teeth, or go to the bathroom. As long as we stay in the I/I mode, we can even fart and nobody will hear or smell it," I said proudly.

"I can hear and smell it," Dewey said.

"You don't count. I'm talking about real people."

"If we're not real, why do we get headaches?"

"I don't know for sure. We can still feel pain, but you can't get sick, not real sick, anyway."

"That's confusing. I'm having some trouble figuring out why we can do some things, but we can't do others. We still need to eat, for instance, but we never need to go to the bathroom or brush our teeth. We still need to sleep, and we get tired if we don't rest, but we don't get real sick, and we can't die. We still seem to have the same set of emotions we always had, even the same personalities. You are still preoccupied with sex, and that's even more confusing. Why should you be left with an interest in sex? Since you're caught in this invisible mode, you can't actually have sex, can you?" Dewey asked.

"Not unless you do it with someone who's operating in the same mode you are, and you can forget that," I said, almost automatically. Damn me and my big mouth. I'd done it again.

"I wasn't suggesting . . ."

"I know," I said, waving off another confrontation. My comment still irritated Dewey.

"We're obviously left with some prejudices. You're still opinionated and egocentric, and I hate to deflate you, but I am in no way physically attracted to you. Regardless of what you have assumed about my sexual preferences and practices, the matter is moot now. I seem to have lost interest in sex altogether."

"What a bummer," I replied softly.

"It's a blessing. You're the one who has a problem," Dewey said.

"I don't see it that way."

"But you can't do anything. Why have the interest and desire if there's no chance of fulfillment?"

"My condition might change. Maybe I'll get another assignment one of these days. Maybe I'll run into a cute angel with a bad case of hot pants. Maybe I'll learn to use the personification mode and start humping college girls."

"Well, I think it's sad."

"It is sad, but it could be worse. You could be as horny as I am, and then we'd have two guardians preoccupied with sex."

"I was never as . . . as . . . horny as you are," Dewey said, sticking his nose in the air.

Dewey didn't say a word for a full ten minutes. He crossed his legs and stared into the distance. The silence was starting to get uncomfortable when he suddenly turned to me, a strange look in his eyes. The irritation was gone, replaced by a curious, almost troubled look.

"You didn't answer my question," he said.

"What question?"

"Why are we left with certain needs and emotions and not others? Why do we still do some things just like we did when we were living and are spared or denied other things?

"Maybe it's to keep us in touch with humanity. We're left with our human emotions, and that tells me there's a plan of some kind working here. If we lost all our human attributes, then we'd stop feeling human, and if we stopped feeling human, we couldn't do our job. We've been sent here to protect Woody, to look after and care for him, and we couldn't do that well if we weren't able to feel what he feels. Does that make any sense?"

"Yes."

"Good. I'm not as confused as I thought I was," I said and leaned back against the tree behind me. I watched Dewey closely to see if my answer satisfied him, but the look on his face said it had not.

"It makes perfect sense in one way, but in another way it makes no sense at all. Having human emotions is not always an advantage. Sometimes emotions get in the way of doing a good job, don't they?" he asked. He was groping for support, but I couldn't give it to him.

"Now you're in a gray area," I said, shaking my head.

"Well, try to make it light gray or dark gray for me."

"I'll try," I said, then paused momentarily to collect my thoughts. "Woody was marked by someone upstairs because they have plans for him. For reasons unknown to us, he's being tested. He's learning lessons along the way, and in his case, it has been a rough and rocky road. I guess that's why we're here - to keep him alive while he goes through this period of testing and learning. And you may be right about emotions sometimes getting in the way of guarding him. I get pissed at him, really pissed, sometimes enough to be tempted to let something bad happen to him. But I've always been able to overcome my anger and take good care of him. I get tired emotionally and physically, and that's not easy to take either. The only explanation I have for us being left with some human conditions is that we're also being tested."

I thought Dewey would be surprised, perhaps even shocked, at what I had just said, but he wasn't. "I thought you were going to say that," he said.

"Then why'd you make me say it?" I asked.

"I just needed to hear you say it." He shrugged and batted his eyelids. I felt like batting his ears.

"You're worrisome, that's what you are. Are you happy now?"

"I feel better, but I need more answers."

"I was afraid of that," I said and grimaced playfully.

"What exactly are we being tested for?"

"Oh hell, Dewey, I don't want to get into that," I said.

"Is it that hard a question?"

"It is if you don't know the answer."

"Then just say you don't know," he said.

"I don't know."

"No idea at all?"

"None."

"Not the slightest, itsy-bitsy, teeny-weeny, thought about it?" he asked with a childish giggle.

"I'm going to choke the crap out of you, Dewey," I said, trying to sound threatening.

"You can't. We don't do that anymore, remember? You'll have to choke something else out of me." His giggle turned into a silly laugh.

"Maybe I'll choke all the questions out of you, and then I won't have to answer so many."

"Answer my last question, and I'll leave you alone."

"Promise?"

"Absolutely. Just give me your ideas about why we're being tested."

"Well, I figure we're not destined to be custodians forever. It's like I told you earlier, we're just earning our wings. This is a transition stage, and we're working our way toward a higher plateau, or our place in Heaven, or whatever. This is a period of adjustment for us as well as for Woody. We are being given a chance to prove ourselves, but for what purpose, I don't know."

"But . . ."

"You promised," I said, cutting him short. Dewey nodded reluctantly.

"I'll give you this much more. Most of the human attributes we've kept are assets instead of liabilities. We've got a few bad ones left, but most of the leftovers are good. It makes sense to me because maybe that's what Heaven is all about. Maybe it's a continuation of the good things, the things we really enjoyed during our lifetimes. You enjoy eating, don't you?"

"Yes, I do," Dewey said, rolling his eyes.

"But you deprived yourself of certain foods because you thought they were bad for you. You watched your weight. You were afraid you'd eat the wrong thing and make yourself sick, right?"

"Why, yes."

"Well, that's all behind you. Now you can eat anything and as much as you can hold, and you'll never have to worry about getting fat or sick."

"No, I can't," Dewey said, shaking his head.

"Yes, you can. I just said you could."

"I can't if it's not on the menu," Dewey said and puckered up like he was about to cry.

"You not in Heaven yet either. You may have to wait until you're there to get your fancy foods, but we'll keep the pressure on Roosevelt until he gets the menu changed. Since it's just a menu, maybe it won't take fourteen years to get the kind of foods you want to eat - maybe even quiche. They'll probably have foods in Heaven you've never even dreamed of before."

"What a strange pair we make. I'm looking forward to food, and you're looking forward to sex. I suppose you've decided they have fantastic sex in Heaven, too."

"Why not? What's wrong with sex in Heaven? It's the perfect place for perfect sex. Sex could've been the best part of our lives, but most of us mishandled it. We got it all mixed up with guilt, deceit, and all kinds of other bad things. Sex in Heaven won't have all the bad stuff with it. It'll be perfect sex."

"Perfect?"

"Damn right. There were times down on earth when it came close to being perfect. What's wrong with two lovers being reunited in the Happy Hunting Ground? I knew the first time I made love to Mary Ellen Wilson on the back seat of my old Buick, way back when I was a sophomore at Texas A&M, that sex could be almost perfect. Right then I said to myself, Doug, old boy, this is Heaven."

"Somehow I can't imagine you saying anything else," Dewey said.

"Don't sell me short. I'm not totally without principles when it comes to sex. Maybe that's why we were allowed some really enjoyable human functions. Maybe it was God's way of giving us a taste of perfection, a reminder that life in Heaven was even better. Maybe that's why we also got an occasional taste of Hell - like eating spinach, going to the dentist, losing your best marble, losing a lover, or holding your best friend while he chokes on his own blood from a Viet Cong bullet. We had a taste of both hereafters, but I'm sure I'm here because I stayed with the one that meant the most to me. Yeah, I expect to get laid in Heaven, but I don't expect to see any bombs or bullets there."

The conversation suddenly ended when Woody came walking out the front door, headed for his car. A couple of students approached him, and he stopped to visit for a few minutes. When I turned to look at Dewey, he was staring at me with that curious look in his eyes again. My remarks must have moved him in some way, but I had neither the time nor inclination to follow up on it. At first I thought Woody was leaving. He opened the car door, but instead of crawling in, he picked something up off the front seat and walked back toward the house. He was toting a pint of whiskey.

"Let's see what he's up to, then let's go to the car and grab a bite to eat," I said and motioned for Dewey to follow. I fell in behind Woody. Dewey traced my footsteps like a kid following his dad, mumbling something about how he hoped the food would be fit to eat.

Woody stashed the pint in a kitchen cupboard and then opened the refrigerator. He pulled out some leftovers, threw together a ham sandwich, grabbed a beer, and headed for the den. After flicking on the TV, he flopped on the couch and ate his sandwich. His beer was only half finished by then, but his heavy eyelids told me that he'd be asleep in ten minutes. Dewey and I left him to his nap and headed for our car. Watching Woody eat had made me hungrier than ever, and I was digging around in the magic box for food when I heard Dewey say something from the front seat.

"There's a red light on in here," he said.

"What?" I tried to straighten up to hear what he'd said, and in doing so whacked my head on the trunk lid. "Piece of shit!" I howled and kicked the bumper. That was an intelligent move. Now my foot hurt.

"What's this red light?" he asked.

"I probably left the radio on," I said, impatiently while rubbing the lump growing between my cowlicks.

The radio, by the way, was another nice piece of angeling equipment. It picked up any station you wanted it to pick up, and it had sound better than any stereo you've ever listened to. Since we operated in a different dimension from the rest of the world, picking up a local radio station was impossible. But radio in spirit land is really great. Figuring out how it work took me a while, but the radio worked off your mood. If you were in the mood for a little Merle Haggard, you fiddled with it, and that's what it played. If you wanted Pavoratti, on the other hand, you got that. It had knobs and a dial like all radios, but nothing you did with them seemed to make any difference to the music that came on.

Dewey had been having a hard time with the radio. His tastes ran more toward Pavarotti, for instance, than mine did. He'd fiddle with the radio, and it would find opera or classical music of some kind, and he'd sit back to enjoy it, and I'd suddenly get in the mood for Merle Haggard, and the radio would change. My moods must've been overpowering his moods, but whatever, it sure pissed him off. I'd been meaning to tell him about the radio, but I figured he'd figure it out sooner or later. Besides, I'd been having too much fun watching him fiddle-fart around with it.

"It's not the radio; it's this other thing," he said, reminding me of the light again.

I walked to the door and looked. "Roosevelt wants to talk," I said and sat down behind the wheel. "That's our hotline to Heaven. Trouble is, it only works when they want to get in touch with us. The red light means the phone's been activated. Roosevelt's on the other end, and he's our only contact with the Central Office."

I picked up the receiver and punched in the code number. Big deal! It's the only code number I have. Roosevelt answered right away.

"What's happening, bro," I asked in my best black accent.

"Knock off the phony jive talk, Doug." His voice was strong and clear, but he always sounded tired and somber.

"Sorry, just trying to be friendly. What's up?"

"I'm coming to see you before long, maybe in a week or two. Reports are due, and we need to talk. Did your help arrive?"

"Yeah, he's here," I said, unemotionally.

"How's he doing?"

"Great! He's a fast learner, and we're getting along just fine. I really appreciate his help."

A long silence followed. Roosevelt must've been stumped. I got a little uneasy when he didn't answer right away, but I wasn't about to let him off the hook and waited out the pause. "Well, I'll be there in a week or so," he said finally.

"What's going on, Roosevelt? You usually don't come all the way out here just because reports are due."

"I need to check on your new partner. It's policy. Since I'm his supervisor, I'm required to make the visit and see to it he gets off to a good start."

"He's off to a good start. What's the rest of it?"

"I've got something for you. Now that you've got a partner, the Central Office has decided to issue you a motor home."

"Motor home?"

"Yeah, it's used but still in good shape. It will be just the thing for you and Dewey. It's self-contained, and you'll have everything you need and more."

"I didn't ask for a motor home," I said.

"You're getting one anyway."

"Do I keep the Chevy?"

"No, I'm afraid not. It goes back with me, to district motor pool."

"I don't want the motor home," I said bluntly. "I'll just keep the Chevy."

"I knew you'd be upset, but the orders came from upstairs," Roosevelt said with a sigh. He sounded very tired now.

"That's hogwash! Those clones in the Central Office don't do anything without being pushed. Why do you want my Chevy?" I asked.

"Don't make this difficult. It's not my fault. I had nothing to do with it."

"Come on, man, don't take my car. You guys have got cars out the ass. Why do you need mine? You know how I feel about my Chevy."

"Some kid just out of training wants a '57 Chevy. You've got one, we've got this motor home to place somewhere, so you're a natural for a trade. You know how it goes with the boys upstairs," Roosevelt said. He was sounding more apologetic now, but that didn't stop my growing anger.

"Yeah, it sounds like a bunch of bureaucratic crapola to me. I've got fourteen years invested in that Chevy, and I'm not giving it up to some pimple-faced teenager just out of training. Piss on that idea." My voice was getting shrill and loud.

"I'm sorry, Doug. You'll have to give it up."

"What about my seniority?" I shouted.

"This isn't the army, Doug. Seniority doesn't apply to vehicles around here. The Chevy goes back."

"You can't have it."

"Don't cause a fuss. It's orders, man," Roosevelt said wearily.

"Well, change them," I said.

"I can't change them because I don't make them. Can't you get that through your thick skull?"

"Well, do something, dammit! I like my car, and I deserve to have it. A motor home is too cumbersome. My mark moves fast, and I need something that will move around fast enough to keep up with him. The motor home will just be in my way. I need my Chevy. Do you hear what I'm telling you?"

There was another long silence. "Well, what am I going to do with this motor home?" he asked. I resisted a strong temptation to express what was going through my mind, but I held my tongue. Diplomacy was my best bet with a fellow like Roosevelt.

"Look, Roosevelt, you're a smart dude, and a man in your position ought to be able to pull some strings. You've got some pull with the boys in the Central Office, so why don't you see if you can trade the motor home for a trailer. Any kind of trailer would do. A small camper trailer would be perfect for us, and there's bound to be somebody out there who needs a big motor home. It would be a feather in your cap to make a smart trade like that."

"I don't know, Doug," he said.

"Don't you ever get tired of being run over by the Central Office? Don't you ever feel like fighting back?" I asked.

"No one is running over me. I'm just following policy." Roosevelt said, trying to sound confident and convincing. His voice betrayed him, though, and I knew he was weakening.

"If anybody can do something about it, you can. An old crusader like you knows how to get through to the power brokers, knows how to stand up for the little man. The only reason they're trying to pull this on me is because I'm not in a position to fight with them. That's the way it is with bureaucrats. They always pick on the guy on the bottom. It doesn't matter that I've done good work here, and I've never asked for much . . ."

"Never asked for much? Never . . . asked . . . for much?" Roosevelt asked, breaking into a hearty laugh that stopped the conversation for a full minute. As his laughter came under control, he said, "You may be the only custodian in the history of the program who tried to requisition a guard dog."

"That was a long time ago," I said, a little defensively.

"You may have been the first to put beer on your menu, when everyone knows there's not a drop of booze in Heaven."

"I didn't know," I said. I glanced at Dewey, and he was frowning at me. I felt a little stupid.

"You asked for an airplane once, and what about that request for a horse and saddle? You asked for a female partner and even specified her measurements."

"OK, OK. So I've asked for few things, but asking to keep my Chevy is just fair and reasonable."

"I'll agree to that, but your record at the Central Office could be better. You could be more popular with the higher brass."

"Yeah, I know, and that's why I need your help. They trust your judgment. All I'm asking you to do is try. My Chevy is important to me. I do good work in that car, and if I lose it. . ."

"All right, I'll see about it. Would a twenty foot trailer work for you?"

"Fine, just fine," I said eagerly.

"Go for a thirty footer," Dewey said. I'd been too busy with Roosevelt to notice that Dewey had his ear next to mine and was listening to the conversation. I moved the phone to my other ear and shook my head at him.

"What'd he say?" Roosevelt asked.

"Oh, he just said a covered wagon would be fine with him. He really likes the Chevy too."

"Uh huh. I'll see what I can do," Roosevelt mumbled, then hung up abruptly.

"Why did you hang up? I wanted to ask about the menu," Dewey said.

"I didn't hang up. He did."

"But you said. . ."

"Don't worry about the menu, Dewey. Roosevelt will be here next week, maybe the week after, and you can ask him then."

"Is he going to take our car away?" Dewey asked.

"Not if I can help it. He wanted to give us a motor home, and he was going to give the Chevy to some kid just out of training. Can you believe that? I've been busting my balls on this job for fourteen years, and they're wanting to give my Chevy to a rookie. Roosevelt said the orders came down from the Central Office, but it sounds to me like something he'd do."

"Did you really ask for an airplane?" Dewey asked meekly.

"I was a rookie then." I said. It was a poor excuse, and I knew it.

"Did you actually ask for a watchdog?"

"Hey, the dog wasn't a bad idea."

"But a dog must be fed and cared for."

"So must you," I pointed out.

"It's not the same."

"You're right; it's different. A dog would be much easier to take care of than you are."

"No one needs to take care of me," Dewey said, sounding indignant again.

"Well, I don't exactly feed you, but it takes more food for you than it would for a dog. And I sure as hell have been taking care of you."

"You certainly have not! I am perfectly capable of taking care of myself," Dewey snapped.

"Oh yeah? What do you call what I've been doing since you got here, huh? You didn't even know how to scratch your own ass when you stepped off that bus. Who's been showing you the ropes?" I asked.

"You have, of course, but you make me sound completely helpless. I am not helpless and . . ."

"Would you put a plug in it? I'm not saying you're feeble or anything like that. I was just trying to make a point about the dog."

"Well, it didn't come out that way, and besides, I don't like being compared to a dog," he said and stepped out of the car. That's when I noticed that the trunk lid was still open, and I remembered my hunger. I jumped out and went back to the magic box. Dewey looked over my shoulder as I opened it.

"Well, what's in there?" he asked. I threw him a nasty look, but he responded with a well-I-get-hungry-too look.

"Manna," I replied.

"Manna? Sounds worse than chicken fried steak. What is it?" he asked, wrinkling his nose again. He caught me smiling, then cocked his head to one side and lifted an eyebrow. "What are you up to?"

"Nothing."

"What's this manna business then?"

"Didn't you ever read the bible, Dewey?" I answered with a question of my own.

"Some. More than you did, I dare say," he said confidently.

"Then you should know about manna. It was the miracle food from Heaven that fed the Jews wandering in the wilderness. It fell from the sky, remember?"

"Oh, that manna. I remember, it was bread, right? Are you trying to tell me that bread is all we've got for lunch?"

"Nope, and manna probably wasn't bread either. It has been called 'bread from Heaven', but I think that was in a spiritual sense. Manna helped stop the discontent and murmurings against Moses when he tried to lead the Hebrews out of the wilderness to the Promised Land. Actually, manna was a sweet substance that wasn't found on the ground but in low shrubs that grew in the Sinai desert region. I think they're called Tamarisk shrubs. Manna was a growth of some kind, probably a solidified excrement from the shrub caused by insects. Some people believe it may have been plant lice excrement that had solidified in the desert air. But, whatever it was, it wasn't bread that dropped out of the sky."

"That's an interesting concept, but I don't believe it," Dewey said.

"Why not? It makes sense. According to the bible, a double portion of manna appeared on Saturday because no manna appeared on Sunday. Maybe it wasn't seen on Sunday because the Hebrews didn't look for it because it was the Sabbath. Some people think it was there in the morning because it was still cool, but the hot desert days melted it away. Ants, other insects, or animals may have eaten it, just as it would've been eaten on any other day had it not been harvested early," I said.

"But didn't God also send the wandering Hebrews birds to eat?"

"Yes, but there's also a natural explanation for that. The migration of quail from southern Europe to the coasts of Egypt and southern Palestine is also a natural phenomenon. The quail were easy prey for the Hebrews because they were worn out from their long flight. It was an easy source of food for the wandering Jews, and since the quail had historically migrated, they knew exactly where to find them. Anyway, the quail were probably no more of a miracle than the manna was."

"Do you know that for sure?"

"No, but my information came from a good source. A chaplain in Viet Nam told me. We were good friends and spent a lot of time talking. He was a Methodist minister, I think, and he knew a bunch on biblical history," I said.

"I still don't want to believe it," Dewey said.

"Why not?"

"Because I don't want to believe that everything must have a scientific explanation, that's why. Why can't it be a miracle?" he asked.

"Does it really matter?"

"It matters to people who like to believe that God occasionally does things for people to show them that he cares, that he really exists," Dewey said.

"But the Hebrews didn't starve, Dewey. They may have suffered in finding their way to the Promised Land, but they made it."

"But you make it sound like an accident that they did. The gifts that enabled them to survive, the quail and manna, for instance, were just natural events according to your interpretation."

"But it was there, wasn't it?" I asked.

"Yes, but . . ."

I didn't let him finish. "There's your miracle. Some people argue that God set the stage for miracles when he created the universe, when he designed quail to migrate from southern Europe to the Mediterranean coasts of Egypt and Palestine, or when he made the excrement from plants or insects edible. Maybe all the little miracles men like to believe in are just a part of one great miracle - the miracle of the universe and of mankind."

"How profound," Dewey said and smiled. He still had that curious look in his eyes, like he was starting to see something in me he'd not seen before. I handed him a sandwich and soft drink.

"Eat your manna," I said.

CHAPTER 8
Sunsets, Sunflowers, and Sonsabitches

"I don't think I've ever seen a sunset quite this beautiful," Dewey said. I knew he'd been preoccupied with something because I hadn't heard a peep out of him in nearly thirty minutes – almost a record in his case. Woody had a night class, and Dewey and I were enjoying a calm October evening from a park bench just outside Howard Hall. Calm days don't come often in western Kansas, but the wind usually dies down in the evenings.

Dewey was as right as rain about the view. High Plains sunsets are among the most beautiful I've ever seen, and the radiant orange one holding him spellbound was especially spectacular. Watching it hurt my eyes, but its brightness didn't seem to discourage Dewey. Maybe Dewey was starting to feel aesthetically deprived, and sunsets were among the few really beautiful sights around Forest City. He already knew how I felt about the place - that the only reason it ever got settled was because some pioneer's horse died and he ended up getting stranded there. Maybe the wagon broke, or something happened. Nobody in their right mind would see the country for the first time and go, "This here looks like the promised land, so git them kids outta the wagon, maw, and we'll build us a cabin."

Living in western Kansas often made me feel aesthetically deprived. I figured that most folks who lived there suffered from aesthetic blindness, and the fear of that happening to me was bothersome at times. Western Kansas is mostly level country. Nothing in the entire area could be called a hill, and the flatness is only occasionally broken where the rivers flow through. Several rivers, dry most of the year, run through the country, leaving gaping arroyos, or draws. Some of them are almost large enough to be called a canyon, and ancient river floods left wide valleys in other places. The rough country near the river is called "breaks" by the locals, and it is along these breaks that some real beauty can be found. Cottonwoods and willows grow there, and these broken lands with their seasonal rivers and trees and occasional sand dunes help make the country around Forest City more tolerable to people like me.

I once saw a local rancher turn to a visitor and ask, "Ain't this the purtiest grazing country you ever seen?" To me that's sort of like pointing at a shapely woman's navel and asking, "Ain't that the purtiest belly button you ever seen?" My response would have to be, "No, but the area around it ain't bad." Only an appreciator of belly buttons could ask a question like that, and it must take an appreciator of prairielands to think western Kansas is beautiful. I don't like flat country - never have and never will. It looks bleak and lonely to me, and living in country like that can make a person feel the same. It's no Garden of Eden, that's for sure.

Western Kansas University is on the west side of Forest City, on a level expanse of land that tapers off into a ragged break in the earth that's made by the Kiowa River. The cottonwoods growing there turn a golden yellow in the fall of the year, and anyone, even someone who shies away from prairielands, can appreciate them. Dewey had been watching the sun creep below the far side of a giant arroyo, creating a perfect backdrop for the golden leafed cottonwoods. I glanced at the view every now and then, but mostly I was checking out the college gals who kept walking past headed for the library. Sunsets are no match for good looking gals.

"Don't you think the sunset is beautiful?" Dewey asked, noticing my loss of interest.

"Yeah, that's one of the good things about this part of the world. We do have beautiful sunsets," I said. Dewey snapped his head around and gave me an open-mouthed look of surprise.

"We? Did I hear you say we? That's the first time you've called yourself a Kansan."

"A slip of the tongue, pard. Living in an area for as long as I've been here brings on familiarities, I reckon, but I'm damn sure no Kansan. Texas is still home for this old boy."

"I'm still surprised. I never thought you'd ever tie yourself to Kansas in any way. All I've heard for the past few weeks has been derogatory remarks about Kansas. Now you say 'we' like you're one of the locals. It's amazing!"

"You know what I meant. Besides, we're talking sunsets, not states."

"I should've remembered that you love sunsets. It's the sunrises you hate, remember?" Dewey asked. I remembered, but my upbeat mood kept me pursuing it. Instead, I stayed after the state issue.

"I had an uncle who called Kansas the land of three suns. He was a cattleman who'd had a lot of dealings with Kansans and had spent a lot of time up here. It think it left a bad taste in his mouth."

"He called it what?"

"The land of three suns. He said that stood for sunsets, sunflowers, and sonsabitches. He said those three things were what made Kansas famous."

"And I suppose you agree with him," Dewey said, the tone of his voice indicating he'd already decided I did.

"Not necessarily."

"I've heard of Kansas sunflowers, and I've witnessed their breathtaking sunsets, so I know the state is famous for those two things. But I think calling someone a . . . a . . . sonofabitch is shallow, inconsiderate, and blatantly judgmental."

"Why, Dewey, I do believe you said a nasty word," I said, wrinkling my eyebrows at him.

"I only used the word in reference to what you said."

"That puts a new light on it then," I said, then nodded toward Howard Hall and changed the subject. "Want to go in and look around?"

"Sure."

Dewey and I followed a group of jocks into the building. We watched them walk, or swagger, down the hall toward a classroom where they were enrolled in an evening class in manners and social customs. They stopped in the hallway just outside the room and leered at the young women who walked past them. The professor, a plump woman in her early fifties, arrived and entered the room. The jocks followed her, but paused long enough to scratch their balls.

"How crude," Dewey said, puckering up his face.

"You don't scratch your balls?" I asked.

"Scratching is impolite, especially when it involves one's . . . private parts. That's disgusting."

"What do you do when your balls itch?"

"Well, I certainly don't scratch them in public, and I surely don't do it in such a crude, exaggerated fashion. Those boys made a big show of it and right in front of the entire class. They just grabbed themselves by the . . . they just . . . you know what I mean," Dewey said, stammering.

"Yeah, but that's a jock for you. Most of those guys are football players, and they've never been famous for good manners. They're probably lucky to find their balls, much less remember not to scratch them in public. Besides, that's what balls are for. Hell, it's one of man's greatest pleasures. It's hard to beat a good ball scratching."

"But in public?"

"Balls don't have a conscience when it comes to itching. They'll itch any time and any place, and it's usually when you are least able to scratch. Besides, some itches won't wait. When you've got to scratch, you've got to scratch," I said.

"Mine have never itched so bad I couldn't wait until I was alone. But perhaps most men's testicles aren't as disciplined as nine."

"Disciplined balls don't exist. They're born troublemakers, and itching is not nearly the worst thing they do. They're instigators, a couple of real bad eggs. They send messages to other parts of the body. Sometimes they've got control over your hands, sometimes other parts."

Dewey was staring directly at me now, and the look on his face was a mixture of puzzlement and skepticism. "Hands?" he asked cautiously.

"Yeah, balls say, 'scratch me.' But the hands say, 'I can't scratch you now because people are watching.' Then the balls come back with, 'you'd better scratch me or I'm going to make your dick get hard in front of your mother . . . at church . . . sitting right on the front row . . . just before you have to get up and pass the collection plate.'" I was struggling not to laugh, and the look on Dewey's face made it more difficult.

"This conversation is getting ridiculous," he said, then turned and walked away. I followed, still making my point.

"No, it's true. Balls say, 'you'd better scratch me or I'll keep your dick from getting hard the next time you get a chance at a really great piece of tail. Or I'll make you prematurely ejaculate and ruin it for you.' The only thing you can do is give in and scratch. They have you by the balls, so to speak."

"You're a sick man," Dewey said, but the look on his face caused me to break out laughing. He watched me laugh for a few moments, then made a gagging noise and turned his back. He couldn't hold it and broke out into peals of laughter. That was the first time he'd laughed at one of my jokes.

Class had taken up and the hallway became quiet, so I tapped Dewey on the shoulder and motioned for him to follow. We walked up a flight of stairs to the second floor and stepped into Woody's classroom. He was teaching a general psychology class, and Dewey soon became enthralled in the lecture. I'd heard it before, so I eased through the wall and walked back to the car. I popped open the trunk and scrounged around in the ice chest until I found a ginger ale, then headed back toward Woody's classroom.

On the way I stopped off at the men's bathroom to check out the graffiti. Reading bathroom graffiti is a good way to pass the time when nothing important is happening, and this seemed to be one of those times. College students are inventive graffiti writers, much better than soldiers or cowboys. Anyway, I was checking out some typical college graffiti, a poem scribbled on the wall near a urinal, when Dewey suddenly popped into the room.

"There you are. I've been looking all over for you. This is the last place I expected to find you. I checked all the women's restrooms first."

"See anything interesting?"

"They're all empty, but so is this place, so why are you in here?" he asked.

"Reading graffiti," I replied.

"What a wonderful experience for you. Trying to sharpen your sense of crudeness?"

"Just killing time. Sometimes I find one I haven't seen before. Take a look at this one." I pointed at the poem I'd been reading.

"I'll pass," Dewey said.

"Quit acting like a bluenose nun and come take a look at this," I said, or rather ordered.

"I'd rather not."

"Then I'll read it to you. It says:
Oh darling, oh darling, with eyes like a dove,
Come lie down beside me and we'll make sweet love.

Country version:
Oh darling, oh darling, with eyes like a hog,
Break down like a shotgun, we'll fuck like a dog."

"Disgusting," Dewey said.

"It's an American art form, like it or not, Dewey."

"That's ridiculous."

"Centuries from now archeologists may study these writing in order to learn more about our society," I said.

"If they do, then they'll find this one," Dewey said, pointing at an inscription on the wall.

"What's it say?"

"I think you should read it yourself."

I walked over to where Dewey was holding his finger to a poem that read, "Here I sit, my buns a-flexin', tryin' to create, another Texan."

"What's the matter? You're not laughing," Dewey said.

"I've seen it before."

"Here's one I don't understand," Dewey said, moving his finger to another message about foot away. "Jawad is a Jew," it read.

"You'll see a lot of them around campus. Jawad something-or-other is an Arab economics professor who hates Jews. Most of the kids don't like him because he's a tough instructor. Every time he gives a tough test, more of those writings appear on the walls."

Dewey followed me out of the bathroom, then up the stairs to the third floor. It was dark except for the bright red exit signs that hung at the end of the hall over the stairwells. "What are we doing up here? There's no class up here," Dewey said.

"I know, but I want to check on something."

"But . . ." Dewey started to say, but I shushed him with my hand and listened. I'd heard a noise, a something heavy being scooted across a tile floor kind of noise, coming from the room we had stopped directly in front of.

"They're in there," I whispered before remembering no one could hear me. I cleared my voice and repeated it more forcefully. "They're in there."

"Who's in there?"

"A classic Kansas sonofabitch, for one," I said. Dewey followed as I stepped through the wall, holding tightly to the back of my jacket.

"What are we doing now?" he asked as he looked around. We were standing in a receptionist's small office.

"I'm going to show you something," I said.

We moved into the room with Dewey still clinging to me like a timid kid. I stopped to look and listen but couldn't see or hear a thing. The room was almost completely dark except for outside lights coming through the windows, and I was starting to think no one was there when I heard the sound again. I followed the direction of the scrubbing sound around a line of filing cabinets, and that's when I spotted them. I saw them because I knew what to look for, but the bad lighting and his poor vantage point kept Dewey very much in the dark. "What is it? What is it?" he kept asking. So, I moved us closed to the action.

"Now there's a sight that should make every mother proud," I said, making sure it sounded facetious.

"What? What?" Dewey asked, craning his neck to peek around me. What he saw first, plainly visible in the light coming through a nearby window, was a young woman bending over a desk with her hands clasped tightly to the sides. Her dress was over her back, which was sharply arched to keep her bare ass in an accessible position. The other party in this naughty and somewhat bizarre scene was difficult to see at first. A stocky built man with his pants around his ankles was draped over her, breathing heavily as he pumped away in a steady and forceful enough motion to make the desk scoot forward. Apparently reaching the short rows, the man's rhythm was quickening, and he moaned lowly.

"Oh, my goodness!" Dewey said in disgust. He had finally snapped to what was happening and started to back away. I knew what was about to happen and tried to grab him, but he was too quick for me, and I missed him. He stumbled over a trash can and knocked it across the floor, then tried to run through the wall but bounced off like a rubber ball. He fell flat of his back across a desk, and the sound of scattering papers, breaking glass, and splattering liquid filled the room. Then, it suddenly went very, very quiet.

I couldn't find Dewey and didn't have time to grope around in the dark for him, so I flicked on the lights. At first I couldn't find Dewey, but I finally spotted his arms and legs flailing around from beneath an oak desk that had flipped over on him. He looked like a turtle that had been turned over on his back. The man and woman were standing completely erect now, wide eyed with fright and splattered with red printer's ink, and with looks of absolute panic on their faces.

I threw the desk off Dewey, grabbed him, and headed for the hallway. He was trembling and babbling, "Oh, my goodness! Oh, my goodness!" I carried him until we reached the second floor hallway. Once I stood him on his feet, I asked, "Are you OK?"

"Yes," he feebly replied.

"Let's get out of here," I said, then took his arm and led him down the stairs. Once outside, I started to laugh, but Dewey wasn't amused.

"How can you laugh?" he said.

"Oh, come on, Dewey. Don't take it so hard. There's no real damage done," I said, once my laughter was under control.

"You did that on purpose, you . . . you . . . REDNECK!"

"I didn't. I promise, I didn't."

"INCONSIDERATE REDNECK!"

"But . . ."

"PEEPER! PERVERT!"

"Dewey, I . . ."

"You're right about one thing. Sonsabitches do live in Kansas, and the number went up when you got here," Dewey said, lowering his voice and shaking a fist at me.

Dewey's tirade caught me a little off guard, and I stopped laughing. He had actually assumed a fighting stance with his fists clenched, and he was bouncing up and down. "Settle down," I said.

"Because of you, I made a fool of myself and scared those poor people half to death. Someone could have been hurt, and you're to blame."

"Don't get your drawers in a wad, pard. Nobody got hurt, so don't worry about it. Besides, those two had it coming," I said.

Dewey glared at me and said, "Nobody deserves that kind of treatment. And we broke rules. We interfered with someone other than our mark. We had no business being there, and it's all your fault." He waved his fists in the air and bounced up and down again. His antics really tickled me, and I laughed again.

"Stop being a pussy," I said and reached out to grab his arm. He was starting to get under my skin, but I just intended to calm him down. What happened, though, really took me by surprise. As I reached for him, he disappeared from in front of me, and I was abruptly snatched into the air. I turned a complete flip and landed on my back with Dewey sitting squarely in the middle of my chest. His finger was pointed directly at my nose.

"Don't you ever, ever do that to me again," he said in a calm but deadly earnest voice. My first thoughts were to throw him off and give him a good ass kicking, but a tiny voice from deep within told me what a stupid move that would be.

"Are we talking about me making you watch people screw, or are we talking about me grabbing you?" I asked calmly.

"Both."

"Ok, Dewey, I promise. I won't ever do that to you again," I said. He relaxed his grip on me and stood up. I didn't realize how firm his hold had been until he turned loose. He moved away but kept his rigid posture for a few more minutes. The expression on his face changed from anger to concern, and he looked more like the Dewey of old. Even so, I was seeing a side of Dewey I'd never seen before. He didn't look so much like a pansy anymore. I pointed at a concrete bench, and we walked over and sat down.

"Who were those people?" he asked after he'd regained his composure.

"The girl is Tonya something-or-other. She's a senior here at WKSU - one of the local beauty queens. She's won about every contest she's entered here, and that's partly due to what you just saw. The man we just caught her screwing is her boss, the Director of Public Relations, and she's worked in his office for the past three years. From what I've seen, she's ambitious enough to do what it takes to get to the top. Another thing I've noticed is that she's a fad fucker."

"A what?" Dewey asked.

"She fucks fads, whatever is popular at the time. If a particular student becomes popular, you can count on Tonya rubbing a little wool on him. Some jock becomes the campus hero for catching the winning touchdown pass in the Homecoming game, for instance, and the next week Tonya shows up on the back seat of his car. She got on a religion kick last year and screwed a Lutheran Minister."

"A minister?"

"Preacher's peckers get hard too. She enjoys the chase, but she's smart enough to pick on the weak ones. That young preacher, the Director of the Lutheran Student Center, was easy game for her. She's a good looking bitch who can really turn on the charm when she wants to."

"What about Woody? Has she ever gone after him?"

"Nope. He's not been in fashion since she's been around."

"What about the man she was with tonight?"

"She's been screwing him since her sophomore year, the year she won the Miss WKSU beauty contest and went to the Miss Kansas competition down state. His name is Brady Fuller, and he's in charge of public relations and recruitment. Almost everyone knows he's a jerk, but he's politically powerful and does his job well enough to stay out of trouble with the administration. He's a classic phony - goes to church regularly, does civic work, and is a glad-hander. But he's a snake in the grass and a back-stabber. People who work closely with him find that out before long."

"Do you think we should go up and check on them?" Dewey asked, looking toward the third story window where the incident had taken place.

"No, they're all right," I said and chuckled again. The spectacle in the Public Relations Office was too recent in my memory for me to hold back, and the chuckle grew into a deep belly laugh. When I could talk again, I said, "The looks on their faces were priceless. They just stood there with their drawers around their ankles, they're eyes big as saucers, and with red ink all over them."

"Red ink?"

"Yeah. You knocked a big bottle off the desk, and it splattered all over them. They're probably still trying to figure out what happened - how that trash can got knocked over, how the desk turned over, and how the lights got turned on." I had to stop talking and wipe the laugh tears out of my eyes. My sides ached.

"I really blew it," Dewey said, sadly shaking his head.

"Don't worry about it, Dewey. You just forgot to go into your I/I mode. I should've known you'd revert to I/T, but I wasn't thinking. When you stumbled over the trash can, it spooked you, and there was no way you were going to I/I after that. I had to turn the lights on and open the door to get you out of there."

"I'm ashamed," he said.

"Don't be. You probably did them a favor. At least Brady won't be screwing her in his office again, the sneaky bastard. And she's won't be too eager to get close to him again. You did more good than harm."

"But what about the rules? We broke rules."

"It was an accident - just a simple mistake. Nobody will hold that against us," I said confidently. To be real truthful, I wasn't so confident and was hoping Brady or Tanya didn't have a guardian. Word would get back to Roosevelt, and I'd get another ass chewing. Being in the army had taught me to tolerate ass chewings, but I was running out of shorts that didn't have the butt gone out of them. Besides, I was still worried about him taking away my Chevy.

Dewey sat quietly for a long time, obviously still troubled. "It makes me sad," he said, finally.

"How's that?"

"I've been here for a short time, but everyone I've seen thus far seem to sustain your uncle's theory about sonsabitches."

"Thanks a lot," I said.

"I'm not talking about you, even though you've qualified on several occasions. I'm distressed about the other people. Woody is unfaithful to his wife, the old store owner downtown sneaks down the street to fool around with a neighbor, Faud and Thunderthighs fornicated in a room beside us in the Hotel, Roosevelt wants to take our car away, and now we catch Brady and Tonya in that disgusting scene upstairs. It's more than sad - it's depressing. When are we going to meet some normal people?"

"Those are normal people, Dewey."

"No, I mean some nice people, some people who are not underhanded or mean or sneaky."

"It gets worse before it gets better. Keep your chin up. You'll meet some good people. What my uncle said about Kansas was wrong. Oh sure, you can find sonsabitches in any part of the country, and Kansas is no exception to the rule. The sonsabitches are just easier to see, while good folks are hard to notice sometimes. And who's to say there's not a little sonofabitch in everybody? It's hard to find the good in people when we're introduced to their sonofabitch side first. That's the tough part of custodial work, but you'll get used to it."

"Yes, and that frightens me. I'm afraid I'll get hard like you. Excuse me for saying it, but you've become calloused. You're bitter and disillusioned, and I don't want that to happen to me."

"Maybe I am," I said after a few moments of thinking over what Dewey had said, then added, "But don't take what I say so literally. I haven't given up on the human race. Maybe I deal with this job by running off at the mouth, by expressing my negative feelings like my anger and bitterness, instead of holding it. I'm critical of people, sure. Maybe I'm too critical sometimes, but don't take it too much to heart. Most of the people who live around here are just like the folks I grew up around in central Texas. They work hard, treat the neighbors well, go to church, and act like respectable people most of the time. They're boring, but they're good people."

"You see, there you go again," Dewey said and pointed his finger at me.

"That's not being negative or bitter. They are boring, but that's just an honest opinion on my part. At least by my standards, they're boring. That doesn't mean they're not good people. I don't hold being boring against them. They hardly ever do anything more exciting than going to a football game or a rodeo. They don't visit or socialize with one another much. They're sure not your typical party animal. Spuds McKenzie would go nuts around here."

"I understand, but you make them sound like a bunch of old maids," Dewey said.

"The old maids are the most exciting people around here."

"You're impossible."

"I've been here for fourteen years, Dewey. After a custodian stays in this business for a while, he gets to be like a doctor. Doctors start out wanting to help people, but they deal with too much suffering. Almost all of them get to where they look and act hardened and calloused after a while. Maybe that's why they have such a poor bedside manner. It's a defense mechanism and not what the man is really like. He still has purpose and feelings that are hidden beneath that uncaring exterior, so if you think I don't care, you've got it wrong. Don't mistake me for some hard-ass who doesn't care about people."

"I already knew that. I saw through you some time ago."

"Then why didn't you say so? I wouldn't have had to make such a long speech."

"Maybe you needed to hear yourself say it."

"Speaking of seeing though someone, you sure had me fooled. I've always known you were a sensitive, intelligent person, but I never expected you to be so physical. How'd you flip and pin me that way?"

"I've had some training. I'm a black belt in Karate, have been for over twenty years. Living in Chicago and being small and less physical than other men prompted me to take up Karate. I don't like to be pushed around anymore than the next guy. It's been years since I practiced very much, though."

"Well, if you ask me, you're not needing the practice," I said and rubbed my back. Then I stood up and stretched. "Let's go put Woody to bed."

CHAPTER 9
Houston Parker's Last Erection

Dewey yawned, put his hands behind his head, and leaned back in the seat. His eyelids drooped and then closed altogether. It had been a slow morning, but the night before had been anything but slow. Woody had gone to a card party and ended up getting smashed. He had teamed up with several of his friends after the poker game broke up, and they'd all gone to Dusty's. Dewey and I were up until nearly three in the morning, but I'd catch a nap earlier in the day. I finished the last bite of my Butterfinger, then crumpled the wrapper and tossed it out the window.

"Litterbug," Dewey mumbled.

"Nobody can see us. Shut up and go back to sleep."

"I'm too bored to sleep, and nobody being able to see us is no excuse for littering. Just because we operate in another dimension, you shouldn't assume we're here alone, and you could be making a mess for someone to pick up."

"Have you seen anyone else like us around here, Dewey?" I asked.

"No."

"Have you seen any evidence of anyone else being here?"

"No, but that doesn't mean. . ."

"All right, all right! I'll pick up the damn wrapper," I said and opened the car door.

"Thank you," Dewey said.

"You're unwelcome. Your mark is Woody, not me. I don't need a custodian." I crawled in the back seat and stretched out.

"I'm not so sure about that."

"It's too late for me, pard. I'm already dead."

Dewey turned around and stared at me. "No kidding! Now it all makes sense. That's the reason you're always lying on you back."

"Yeah, I'd have made a helluva good whore, wouldn't I? Lying on my back is my favorite position."

"What you would've made is a good rock. Are you going to sleep again?"

"Nope."

"Then why are your eyes closed?"

"I'm checking my eyelids for leaks," I said.

"You sleep too much," Dewey said, flatly. His comment suddenly reminded me of something he'd said earlier.

"What did you mean about being too bored to sleep? That's the silliest thing I've ever heard of. That's the best time to sleep."

"No, you're wrong about that. It's much more difficult to sleep when you're bored."

"Bullshit."

"It's true. Boredom makes you lazy, not sleepy. Some people don't know the difference, but lazy people don't sleep too well. I don't sleep well when I'm lazy."

"You're nuts," I said.

"Let's not discuss it. You have a closed mind about it, so we might as well do something else."

"Like what? I like what I'm doing right now."

"You could show me around. I haven't even seen all of the campus. You can give me the grand tour."

"Now?"

"Why not? Let's do it right now," Dewey said cheerfully, holding his hands under his chin.

"Who's going to watch Woody?"

"He's tied up in class, and I'm tired of just sitting here in this parking lot," Dewey said. I had to agree. We'd been parked in the same spot all morning, and Woody wasn't likely to do any damage to himself in class. I jumped up and crawled over the back of the seat. I'd just pulled away from the curb when I saw Brady Fuller walking down the sidewalk beside Howard Hall. He looked like an overcooked lobster.

"Look who's here," I said, gesturing with my head toward Brady.

"That's the man from the upstairs office, isn't it?" Dewey asked.

"Yeah, that's him."

"He looks terrible. What's wrong with his face?"

"It's probably raw from spending the last few days scrubbing off all that red printer's ink. I wonder what he told his wife when he got home that night. Explaining away red ink is one thing, but explaining how it got all over his legs and underwear is something else. It would have really been funny if he'd got ink on his dick, but that couldn't have happened because he had it buried to the hilt in Tonya."

"You're sadistic," Dewey said.

"Well, you know what they say, don't you? When you play, you pay."

"You shouldn't gloat."

"You're right, I shouldn't. I've seen people worm their way out of worse situations than Brady's. Besides, a good bullshitter can talk his way out of nearly anything. I knew this old boy down in Texas who was the best bullshit artist alive. He could talk his way into or out of anything. One time he got drunk and picked up this gal in a bar over in Dallas. She was one of these kinky broads, and she actually talked him into letting her shave all the hair off his body."

"She shaved him? All over?" Dewey asked.

"All over. She convinced him that sex was better if you shaved off all your hair and lathered up with baby oil. Trouble was, he got too drunk to remember how good it was, but he did wake up the next morning as bald as an egg. Even worse, he had to go home to his wife looking like that."

"What'd he tell her?"

"Well, he came walking in the front door, looked his wife straight in the face, and said, 'Hun, I'd have been home sooner, but I've been to a doctor up in Dallas. They done some x-rays and found cancer. I had to take them radiation treatments all weekend and it caused every hair on my whole body to come out. But, thank God, I'm gonna be OK.' She believed every word of it."

"I don't believe it."

"It happened," I said.

"No one would believe a story like that."

"Dewey, one of the first rules about lying is this: never tell a lie to someone who doesn't care. If you're going to lie, tell it to someone with a vested interest. His wife believed the story because she wanted to believe it. None of his friends believed it because we didn't care if he got laid by some kinky barfly with a fetish for slick men. Folks with a vested interest are sometimes more likely to believe a lie than the truth."

"You may be right. Let's go before I get depressed again."

We drove around campus for a while. I pointed out buildings, gave their names, and told Dewey what I knew about them. Dewey didn't say much, just put in his two cents a time or two. The tour, though, lifted his spirits a little. "This is a nice campus," he said as we finished the tour and parked near the administration building. "I'm surprised at how modern the campus is, and this building is by far the most impressive. What is it?"

"That's Parker Administration Building. Some of the faculty call it ' 'Houston Parker's Last Erection'."

"Calls it what?"

"Houston Parker's last erection. Houston Parker was President of WKSU for over twenty years, and even though academics weren't his strong suit, he was a builder. Buildings are his contribution to this school, perhaps his only contribution. Parker Administration Building is his last construction project. He dropped dead in his private crapper about two years ago, and that building is his last erection. Gaudy, don't you think? Looks out of place on this campus. The field house is the only other building that's even close to being as fancy as this one."

"It seems such a waste to build such fine facilities but then neglect academic matters. Surely Parker had concerns about education other than just beautiful buildings and athletics."

"If he did, they were hard to spot. He was widely disliked by faculty members because he was such a dumbass when it comes to academics. He treated them like children most of the time. Of course, a select group of ass-kissers managed to stay on his good side - almost all of them borderline incompetents. They got along because Parker felt more comfortable with them. Salaries for faculty members at WKSU were among the lowest in the state, but administrator's salaries were near the top. Parker was eager and willing to spend money on sports, buildings, paved parking lots, shrubs, and green grass, but was stingy as hell with faculty development funds, student field trips, academic scholarships, and stuff like that."

"I don't think I would've liked him," Dewey said.

"On the contrary, he was very likeable. He was friendly and outgoing and a master politician when it came to getting funds for this isolated university. He was generous with his friends, and he got along well with the locals. Most folks off campus thought he was a fine fellow."

"He sounds like a typical exteriopsyche personality," Dewey said casually.

"A what?"

"He seems to have developed a parent psyche. Are you familiar with Eric Berne?"

"Never met the man."

"He developed the concept of transactional analysis. He wrote <u>Games People Play.</u>"

"I'm impressed," I said.

"You should be because a lot of people think highly of his ideas, particularly those concerned with leadership. Want a lesson on Berne?"

"Why not? A fellow like me, dead already and caught in a custodial dimension with just one other man, sure needs a lesson in leadership. Maybe I can learn how to lead you," I said, smiling devilishly. Dewey wasn't distracted.

"According to Berne's transactional analysis, we operate in three psyches: parent, adult, and child. The parent psyche is paternalistic because it's protective and even overbearing. The adult psyche is clear minded, composed, and logical. The child psyche is temperamental, whining, and insecure. To be a good leader, it is important to keep the adult psyche from getting contaminated by the other two psyches. The adult psyche needs to stay dominant."

"I'll buy that," I said, nodding.

"Houston Parker wasn't much different from other people in leadership positions. They manage matters through their parent psyche, perhaps because they see themselves as father figures. Parker simply acted accordingly, and that's unfortunate because it hinders good leadership. The entire organization suffers because morale usually sags under a paternalistic leader."

"Where'd you learn that crap?"

"It's not crap; it's good reasoning. And I learned it doing something you should try yourself. It's called reading," Dewey said, sniffing self-righteously.

"Hey, I read."

"What was the last book you read?"

"I don't remember the title, but I read it."

"How can you read a book and forget to read the title? Did you not look at the cover at all?"

"Yeah, it had a naked woman on it."

"I should've known. I suppose you got it in some sleazy bookstore," Dewey said, covering his eyes with the back of his hand.

"Nope, I found it in Woody's office. I remember the cover mentioning something about sex and the American woman. So I sat down a started reading it. I used to sit in his office and read while he was in class, but I had to quit doing that."

"Why?"

"Woody seldom closes the door to his office while he's at school, not even when he goes to class. A book on his desk caught my eye, and I sat down and started reading. It was a quiet afternoon and no one was around. I got interested in the book and forgot about the door being open. A noise at the door disturbed me, and I looked up and found this janitor standing in the doorway, his eyes and mouth wide open. He was staring at the book I'd been reading. He must've been trying to figure out how the pages were flipping themselves. He looked around, then came into the room and waved his hand over the book several times, like he was checking for a breeze. He picked up the book and turned it over in his hands a couple of times, then put it down, shrugged, and walked out of the room."

"You were careless."

"Yeah, but I didn't worry about it. I think the guy was too stupid to get scared and too lazy to run. He's typical of the maintenance people around here."

"That surprises me. I would have thought a person like Parker would've insisted on good maintenance," Dewey said.

"He did, but only in some areas. Five full-time janitors used to work in Parker Administration Building, but only one took care of Howard Hall. The grass could dry out and die around student housing, but not on the football field. The grounds crew spent more time working in the yard at the President's house than they did any other place on this campus. Any part of the campus that's highly visible to the public was a high priority item and well taken care of. But there was a lot of superficial maintenance around here. The library, for example, was poorly equipped and cared for. The field house, on the other hand, had modern equipment and the people needed to care for it," I said.

"What's that got to do with superficial maintenance?"

"Hold your horses, I'm getting there. The equipment budget for the faculty was low, but administrator's offices were very well equipped. They had the money to install a mural in the rotunda of the administration building that cost fifty thousand dollars, but the air conditioning in Howard Hall stayed on the blink half the time."

"A mural of what?"

"A horny toad." I grinned and blinked piously.

"You're kidding."

"Go see for yourself. It's an enormous inlaid tile mural of the school mascot - a horny toad."

"How could they justify an extravagance like that?" Dewey asked.

"Because it's seen, that's why. It's impressive to alumni, parents, board members, and other visitors. That's why it's good politics to maintain the facilities that are the most visible. But maintenance for less visible facilities was usually band aid maintenance. Never replace what you can fix, and never fix what you can do without."

"I'm surprised the faculty would stand still for that."

"They don't have enough power to do anything but bitch, and they do a good job of that. They're the biggest bunch of bitchers I've ever run across in my life, but they seldom did their complaining where it does any good. They learned over the years that their complaints fell on deaf ears when they took them to the administration building, so they went to the faculty lounge and complained to each other. Of course, a complaint aired in the faculty lounge usually found its way to the President's office via one of the ass-kissing snoops. That was always the quickest pipeline to the President's office, but it never changed anything. Of course, all that was then, and now is now."

"It's different now?"

"Oh, yes. WKSU has had two presidents since then. The man who replaced Parker was a firebrand - a real go getter. He came in here and shook this place like a cracker box. Most of the younger faculty members around here, about twenty, came in under his administration. He ran lots of folks off - few good folks, but mostly slackers. He cut athletic budgets to the bone and beefed up academic allotments. He refurbished and upgraded the library and classroom buildings and improved maintenance. He moved almost everything around here in one way or another," I said.

"He sounds like a good administrator. Why'd he leave?"

"Folks hated him."

"What folks?" Dewey asked, frowning.

"Almost everybody. Area residents didn't like him, faculty didn't like him, and even most of the administrators and staff members didn't like him."

"Why?"

"I don't want to get into all that right now, but I'll say this much. Twenty years of Houston Parker left the faculty lazy and spoiled. Parker hadn't done much for them, but he didn't do much against them either. He didn't mind mediocre performance. Perkins, Dr. Owen L. Perkins, to be exact, hated it. He wanted excellence from his staff - administration and faculty alike. Trouble was, he had trouble dealing with people. New ideas and techniques won't cut it in country like this, not unless they're developed slowly and carefully. Perkins was a good man, from what I could tell, but he was blunt, often abrasive, in dealing with folks. That got him in trouble around here, and he didn't last long."

"How'd they get rid of him?"

"It's a long story, and you need to hear it sometime, if for no other reason because it affected Woody," I said.

"How?"

"How'd they get rid of Perkins, or how did it affect Woody?

"Both."

"They got rid of him by banding together against him. Perkins ended up with barely a dozen supporters on campus. They campaigned against him in almost every way they could, and he finally got enough and left. His leaving, particularly the way he left, affected Woody because he was one of his few supporters."

"But . . ."

"Give me a break, Dewey. I don't want to talk about this now. It's not that important, so let's save it for another time," I said.

"All right," Dewey said, "but who's president now?"

"Dr. Ellen Stegnor," I said, grinning broadly.

"A woman?"

"Have you ever met a man Ellen? Hell yes, she's a woman."

"I'm surprised, that's all," Dewey said, shrugging.

"So is everyone else around here."

"What kind of president is she?"

"Too early to tell. This is her first year, but from what I've seen, she's doing fairly well. Looks like she's somewhere between Parker and Perkins."

"How does the faculty feel about her?"

"Professors always seem to be divided into three groups, no matter who the president is: those who support the president, those who hate his guts, and those who don't care one way or another."

"Which group is Woody in now?"

"I don't know for sure, maybe none of them. He doesn't seem too fond of Stegnor, but he's not one of the chronic bitchers. He tries to fit in the don't-give-a-shit group, but he doesn't belong there either. I think maybe he's thoroughly disgusted with campus politics."

"I think he cares," Dewey said confidently. "He's a good instructor, and it stands to reason he's concerned about the university."

"He cares, but he's also slick. Woody's happy just to teach his classes and keep his nose out of the administration's business, as long as they don't hassle him too much. That plan works well because there's a wide rift between faculty and administration. Supervision isn't strict, and as long as a teacher keeps his nose clean, he's left alone. An instructor like Woody gets along with a situation like that, but I'm not sure it's good for him. He may not need more supervision, but he needs more motivation and encouragement. Neglect, I've noticed, usually comes with loose supervision. Woody needs a challenge, and teaching a bunch of Kansas farm kids may not be enough for him. It's hard to excel as a psychologist at WKSU because the students here don't care about stuff like that. Woody may need to be around people who are more academically oriented."

"He should be able to find academic companionship here," Dewey said.

"Look around you, Dewey. We're in western Kansas, a far cry from the cultural capital of the universe. Almost all of these faculty members are Kansans. Many of them graduated from college right here at WKSU, so inbreeding is a problem. Like I said earlier, they're boring people - some of the dullest I've ever been around. What's worse, they're die hard traditionalists who fight change. The last original thought anyone around here died of sheer loneliness. These people are innovative thinkers in the same sense of the word that Woody Woodpecker is a carpenter."

"There you go again, sniping at the locals. No one is that boring."

"Would I lie to you?" I asked.

"You've been known to disguise the truth," Dewey said.

"So I exaggerated a little. Besides, I'm not sure anything I said about Woody is true. He might just be an intellectual snob. If I understood the goofy bastard, I wouldn't need you."

"I am therefore a product of your confusion, right?"

"That's an interesting thought, but I'm too hungry right now to think about it. Let's eat."

CHAPTER 10
All The Angry Children

Dewey took a blanket from the trunk of the car, walked across to a secluded area near the library, and spread it on the ground. I sat on a bench close by and watched him prepare the food. He made a big deal out of placing everything just right on the blanket. I'd spent the last fourteen years eating on the run, and the formalities didn't mean much to me. He was more disciplined than me when it came to eating, and I'd already given up on trying to rush him.

"You'll be pleased. I've got your favorite," he said, holding up a sandwich. I walked over and took it, and Dewey kept chattering. "Thank goodness, they've finally started sending some things I can eat. I've had about all the bologna sandwiches I can stand, and if I eat another chicken wing, I'll fly away."

"If you eat this, you'll die again," I said, staring down at the sandwich in my hand. Out of curiosity I'd pulled the two pieces of bread apart and was staring at the contents - a greenish-brown goop of some kind.

"Oh, that's mine. I handed you the wrong one," Dewey said, looking at it.

"Well, whatever it was, it's ruined now." I was about to trash it when Dewey snatched it out of my hand.

"Don't you dare throw that away. It's perfectly good."

"It can't be fit to eat. What is it?"

"An avocado sandwich, one of my favorites. I quit eating them years ago because they're fattening, but now that I'm dead I decided to occasionally indulge myself."

"It looks like baby shit on bread," I said, then took the first bite of my peanut butter and jelly sandwich.

"Looks can be deceiving," Dewey said, gently taking my sandwich. He opened it and held it up to my face.

"You've got a point," I said as I retrieved the sandwich. "What's that you're drinking?"

"Apricot nectar. Want some?"

"No thanks, I'm trying to quit. Have you ever heard the expression: you are what you eat?" I asked.

"Yes, and I probably believed it until I met you."

"How's that?"

"If it were true, you'd be a dumpster." He giggled and took another bite of his sandwich.

"Food is no fun unless it's loaded with calories, preservatives, cholesterol, and fat. Besides, it won't kill me now."

"That's good because we're going to have a fattening dinner - lasagna." Dewey smiled and wiggled his eyebrows.

"This is dinner."

"This is lunch. Dinner is the evening meal."

"Where I come from, this is dinner. The evening meal is supper."

"You're not in Texas anymore. This is Kansas, and I'll bet they call it dinner," Dewey said.

"OK, Dewey, we'll call supper dinner."

My sandwich was history by then and talking about food bored me, so I excused myself and started walking toward the front door of Parker Administration building. Woody suddenly walked around the corner of the building with none other than President Stegnor, so I stopped and watched. Stegnor had her hand on Woody's shoulder and was smiling amiably. Brady Fuller, his usual smartass grin in full bloom, joined them. They stood on the sidewalk just outside the administration building for a few minutes. Stegnor did most of the talking. Woody listened and smiled politely, but Brady really hammed it up. Dewey suddenly appeared beside me, dabbing at his mouth with a napkin.

"Brady is going to break his neck if Stegnor ever makes a sharp turn," I said, then added, "It almost makes me sick to watch him."

"What's Woody doing with that crowd?"

"Just got caught in traffic, I reckon. He usually walks through the administration building on his way home for lunch." I winked to make sure Dewey picked up on my choice of terms for the noon meal.

"Well, at least Woody has the good sense to be friendly to his boss," Dewey noted.

"Woody's a drunk, not an idiot. Besides, I don't think there's a personality clash or anything like that between him and Stegnor. Besides, for a gal in her late forties, she's a nice looking woman. Woody always notices that. If I don't miss my guess about her, she's an observant woman, and that means she knows Woody's a good teacher."

"Is she perceptive enough to know that Woody has a drinking problem?"

"She's only been here a few months, so I doubt it. If we're lucky, she won't notice. Woody's sure not the only problem case on this faculty, and unless he really screws up, she may be too busy to notice. That's where we come in, Dewey. We need to make sure he stays clean enough to stay out of her road, savvy?"

"But we can do only so much," Dewey said, shrugging.

"That's true, but I've managed to keep him off the hook for fourteen years now. With two of us watching him, our chances of keeping him out of trouble ought to be even better."

The meeting broke up, and Woody walked slowly toward home. Dewey and I fell in like baby ducks. "What do you know about Abraham Maslow?" Dewey asked, stepping in front of me and walking backwards.

"Are you kidding? My mama didn't raise a complete dumbass. He's the man who led the Jews out of the wilderness to the Promised Land," I said.

"That was Moses."

"Yeah? Then he's the one who freed the slaves in the Civil War."

"Get serious," Dewey said.

"I've got it! He picked up a jawbone and whipped the Philistine's ass. No, he picked up the jawbone of an ass and whipped the Philistines. He did something with a jawbone and a Philistine, but I don't remember what."

"Not hardly."

"Discovered America?"

"No, he developed. . ."

"Don't tell me. I've got it," I broke in. "Radial tires; he invented radial tires." Dewey shook his head but didn't answer.

"Birth control pills? Jazz? The microchip? Performed the first successful hemorrhoid transplant?"

"SHUT THE FUCK UP!" Dewey shouted. He stopped abruptly and covered his mouth with his palm. His face turned red with embarrassment when he saw my surprise and spreading grin.

"The things you say," I said and gave him a limp-wristed wave.

"Oh, my goodness," he said. "Your filthy mouth must be contagious."

"Moi?" I asked and tapped myself on the chest in another effeminate gesture.

"Stop mimicking me!" he snapped. I laughed and walked away. When he caught up with me, I turned and grabbed him by the shoulders. Not rudely, mind you. I didn't want to end up on my back again.

"Hey, Dewey, I've got it for sure. Maslow developed the hierarchy of needs." I felt his shoulders sag.

"I can't believe we had to go through that to get to this," he said wearily.

"Well, to be honest with you, I can remember what he did, but I don't remember exactly what it was. I've heard Woody talk about him in psychology class, but you'll have to refresh my memory."

"How uncharacteristic, but I'll do my best to enlighten you. It has been on my mind since we started talking this morning. I meant to mention it earlier, but we got sidetracked and I forgot."

"Lay it on me," I said.

"Maslow placed needs such as food, clothing, and shelter at the very bottom of his hierarchy. Once these needs begin to be fulfilled, several other needs become dominant. The second level is the need for safety, or security. Security needs vary from being a subconscious thing with some people to being a surface thing with others. Some people prefer a clearly defined job that isn't challenging or imaginative because there's less chance of being penalized for failure. Others like challenge and risk. Once this need is fairly well satisfied, the third level becomes dominant. Concurrence seeking is an example of this third level of social needs. People need to have their ideas shared, agreed upon, or accepted by others, and getting this done requires conforming. Informal power groups within organizations are formed as a result of this need. Esteem needs, the fourth level, are things like recognition and prestige - the need to feel important. Most workers, for example, look to their supervisors for support and don't perform well without it. When a person reaches a level at which he feels deserving and one which he can satisfactorily maintain, the final need, that of self-actualization, surfaces. Self-actualizing people are devoted to a job, and they love what they are doing because they have a strong desire to achieve. They set difficult but attainable goals for themselves and are forever trying to figure out a better way of doing things.

"Wow! I'm amazed," I said.

"Why? Because I remembered a little about Maslow?"

"Yeah, that's too deep for me, don't remember things like that. Dirty jokes are mostly what stick in my mind."

"Thanks, but you remember more than you let on," Dewey replied modestly, then continued. "Anyway, President Parker either didn't know much about our Mr. Maslow or chose to reject his principles. Well paid employees are better able to satisfy the basic physiological needs and can move on to the other needs more easily and quickly than those who are not well paid. That's not the problem here at WKSU because faculty members are paid well enough to fairly well satisfy those needs."

"Maybe," I said.

"Nevertheless, they seem well enough satisfied. Their second level of needs, safety and security, are met because they are usually tenured, they have health benefits, and they have a good retirement system."

"Barely adequate."

"And Parker probably made sure faculty responsibilities were clearly defined. He didn't encourage innovation, imagination, or experimentation, but he didn't penalize failure. He probably chose to ignore failure unless it was blatant. I doubt if he did much to recognize or deal with the informal groups that developed among his faculty members. He could've helped prevent that by encouraging individuality, but instead he stressed teamwork. Informal groups can be made beneficial if the leadership shows concerns for their needs, as well as for the needs of the entire organization."

"Parker had a hard time dealing with formal organizations, much less informal. He probably didn't know the difference," I said.

"A lot of organization problems develop when the administrator doesn't find ways to satisfy the fourth need, that of prestige. Rewarding people for their good performances through promotions, merit raises, bonuses, and honorary awards is a necessity. Parker rewarded employees based on who did the best job of brown-nosing. That hurt morale. And he could have encouraged the fifth step, self-actualization, by setting some reasonably difficult, but reachable, goals for his faculty members. To do that, of course, he would've had to tolerate some individuality and innovation. He should've acknowledged their achievements, but unfortunately, he was lax about that too."

"May the bastard rot in hell."

"Well, I don't think his crimes were quite that serious. Are you taking any of this seriously?" Dewey asked, frowning.

"As seriously as a heart attack. If Parker hadn't been such a jerk, my job might be easier."

"But Woody, of all people, should understand all this. He probably grasps the situation much better than the other faculty members, and awareness should be the first step toward dealing with the problem. Perhaps he understands and accepts it."

"I don't think so. Something is troubling our boy, and I think the job is part of the problem. Like I said before, Woody is a lonely, frustrated man. After hearing all this need hierarchy stuff, I'm sure his needs aren't being met."

"That's for sure, but there's a lot more to the man than just his job."

"Yeah, I know."

"He's an angry man," Dewey said flatly.

"Angry? He's temperamental, but I don't know about the anger. He's a laid back kind of guy most of the time," I said.

"I don't mean anger like you're thinking of. Woody feels helpless and that causes anger. Let's go back to transactional analysis for a moment. Woody, like everyone else, would like to deal with his frustrations, resentments, and other problems like an adult. That would allow him to handle his problems rationally, but like many others, he resorts to using his child ego state. He gets angry and throws a tantrum. He may look laid back, but he's probably churning and burning on the inside. Woody's most highly developed emotion is anger because his other emotions are retarded, or underdeveloped. This may be because the large amounts of alcohol he consumes numbs his system and keeps his other emotions at bay."

"I'm not sure I buy it. He gets mad, sometimes real mad, but he calms down in a little while," I said, shaking my head.

"No, you're still not understanding me. Mad and angry aren't the same, at least not in the sense I'm using the terms. Getting mad, or losing one's temper, just lasts a little while, but getting angry is more than just losing one's temper. I've heard anger defined as resentment gone wrong. A person fails to deal with his resentments, stores them, and they end up building into anger. Somewhere in the Bible it says something like, 'Fathers, provoke not your children to anger, lest they be discouraged.' I think that Woody's anger may have discouraged him."

"What are you, a Xerox machine? Do you just sit around and look up quotes?"

"No, but I do remember some of them."

"Well, you missed the mark with that one. I know a little about Thessalonians, and I don't think Paul the Apostle was talking about the kind of anger you're talking about," I said.

"You've actually read Thessalonians?" Dewey asked, looking pleasantly surprised.

"Well, not exactly. My grandma Anderson used to read the bible to me all the time, and besides, that's a commonly quoted biblical phrase."

"I'm still surprised that you know, but that's neither here nor there. Perhaps Paul didn't mean it the way I used it, but it could fit. Houston Parker was a paternalist. He, like a lot of others at the top, liked to think of themselves as father figures, and in treating his employees like children, he encouraged their anger. They resented him, and unused resentment results in anger. Woody, like a lot of others around here, suffered the consequences of Parker's fatherly leadership," Dewey said, ending his spiel with an emphatic nod.

"I understand what you're saying, Dewey, but I'm just not ready to accept the notion that Woody's screwed up because Parker made him angry. Parker's dealings might've contributed to his drinking, but it's not a major cause."

"Again, you're not quite getting the point. Woody's not much different from the rest of us in regard to how he reacts to pressure from above. All of us have some problems with it because the world's full of people who want to be fathers. Whether or not they realize it or would admit to it, they see us as the children, and children are sometimes angry children because they see themselves and small like children. We're surrounded by things that are so much larger than us, and we resent it. We don't like big government or big business or even big bosses. All that bigness makes us feel smaller than we need to feel, and we get discouraged - sometimes to the point where we feel helpless, and helplessness leads to anger."

"Boy, you're smart. How'd you learn all that?" I asked, reaching out and tweaking Dewey's cheeks. He had good tweaking cheeks.

"I could be smug and say I'm gifted, dedicated, and well educated, but it's mostly because I read a lot," Dewey replied, rubbing at his recently tweaked cheek. "And stop that. You'll cause wrinkles."

"You couldn't pack stuff like that in your head just from reading. You must've been a psych major in college."

"I've never been to college," Dewey said, dropping his head like it embarrassed him to admit it.

"You're kidding, right?"

"No, I'm simply being honest about it. My formal education is very limited."

"You sure as hell fooled me. I figured you for at least a master's degree."

"I lived alone most of my life, and that gave me a lot of time to read. Books about what motivates people, what makes them tick, have always interested me. In my profession, or my previous profession, you get to meet a lot of people, and how you deal with them affects your business. You also have a chance to study different personalities. My business prospered, in part, because I took the time to understand my clients."

"You owned your own beauty shop then," I said.

"I owned a salon called 'Impressions by D. Davisson'. It was on Lake View Drive in a ritzy section of Chicago. I had twenty-five employees working in a full-service salon that attracted a rather elite clientele."

"Damn, Dewey, you must've been rich."

"I did all right, but money doesn't mean much to a person who wants to be the best. It is, however, helpful in measuring success in our society. Winning awards, knowing I was highly respected by my peers, and enjoying the gratitude of my clients were worth more to me than the money."

"I can buy that. It was important to me to have the respect of my men. I wanted their confidence as well as the praise of my commanding officers."

The conversation petered out after that, leaving me to sit and think over what we'd just discussed. After listening to Dewey remarks, I needed some time to mull them over. My mulling over periods never last long, and before long I stood up and stretched. We'd been sitting on the lawn in front of Woody's house for quite a while, too busy talking and thinking to note the dropping temperature until I stood up. I scanned the horizon to the southwest and saw that a mean looking front was creeping higher in the sky. I'd seen fronts like that before.

"We're about to run out of good weather," I said. "We'll have snow by tomorrow."

"I don't mind snow," Dewey said.

"Me either, but it's no good for Woody. For some reason, he likes to drink when it snows. Speaking of Woody, it looks like he's not going back to school this afternoon. Why don't you check on him while I walk back to the campus and get the car."

I wheeled around and headed for Parker Administration Building. When I rounded the corner at the end of the block, I looked back and saw Dewey ease through the side of the house into the den. Woody was probably sacked out on the couch, and that meant the only trouble Dewey might run into would come when Wanda came home and caught his napping. But Dewey would probably sit there and watch him anyway because he went at being a guardian with the same enthusiasm and dedication that had made him a successful businessman. For the first time I felt absolutely at ease leaving him alone with Woody, and it wasn't just because Woody was napping.

Dewey had come a long way in a short time. Learning came easy for Dewey, and that was starting to ease the strain of breaking him in. I had joked with him before about me being the pundit and him the pupil, but that's the way I'd seen it all through his first weeks and months with me. He'd never liked being tagged a pupil, but having to show him the ropes had been an extra burden on me, and I was tired. But at the same time, I was starting to understand that I wasn't worn out just from teaching Dewey. The guy was bright, really bright, and just keeping up with him was enough to tax a man a lot smarter than me. I'd never answered so many questions in my life, and I sure as hell hadn't had much practice at it in the afterlife. Answering a question for Dewey, I'd discovered, was like striking a match to alcohol. You can't see it burn, but you can sure feel the heat, and for every question I answered, I got something back. He wasn't the only one who'd been getting an education.

Part 2

Chinese Elms

CHAPTER 11
If Life Gives You Lemons

Late October found the prairie around Forest City looking more bleak than it usually did. My assessment is strictly a judgment call since lots of folks would argue that western Kansas looks bleak all the time, not just when it's dry and parched. Wind had blown all the fall leaves off the trees in town, leaving them naked and ugly. Like any small town, Forest City had a lot of imported trees like ash and mulberry and maple, and even a few evergreens like firs and pines. A tree's beauty is mostly in its foliage, and devoid of leaves, most of them are unattractive. Some, like the Chinese elms, hadn't been pretty to start with and were even uglier naked. The saving feature of the Chinese elm is that it's hardy. Maybe I just coined a cliché. I can almost hear my Uncle Walt saying, "Damn, boy! You're uglier'n a Chinese elm in wintertime."

Hardly any tree is native to the high plains, and Chinese elms are no exception. A lot of people think they're native because they've been there for so long, but the settlers must've imported them, and they grow there like weeds around a hog lot. Not everyone, of course, is in agreement with me about these elms being unattractive. They provide shade, lend a little to the looks of a homestead or town, and they provide a home for lots of birds. But they're still not a handsome tree, and naked of leaves look even worse. Bare elms are signs that winter is not far away, and from the way this particular fall had been shaping up, winter had decided to set in early.

Autumns in western Kansas tend to be fairly nice as a general rule, and bad winter weather usually didn't arrive until December. That doesn't mean late fall and early winter couldn't be colder than a frog's ass on a frozen pond, and I can remember several really bad October snows. Nights were already getting down to the twenty degree range, and the weatherman had forecasted some light snow for later in the week. The land could sure use some moisture, but I wasn't quite ready for a big snow.

Just about everyone has a favorite season of the year, but I don't. Cold weather agrees with me in one regard. I can sleep like a fat dog when it cools down in the fall, and that's just what I was doing on this particular Sunday morning. Dewey and I had sacked out in Woody's garage for the night. Since the night before had been Saturday, he'd been out until past midnight. Woody got drunk, of course, but that just meant he'd sleep longer the next morning, and that in turn gave me a chance to sleep late. Woody's garage was used mostly for storage, and I'd thrown my sleeping bag out on an old mattress.

Dewey, you might suspect, did have a favorite season of the year – winter. Yes, winter, and that struck me as strange because he just didn't look like a winter person. He didn't dislike any particular season, but he loved winter because it gave him a chance to wear nice clothes. In addition, he came from a place that was famous for its winters, so his fondness for them was only logical. Dewey, I was starting to discover, worked hard at liking what he needed to like. He bought into the old saying that if life gives you lemons, make lemonade. Chicago gave him long, cold winters, and Dewey made them likable. In following that line of thinking, he thought that if you loved roses enough, you'd learn to accept the thorns that came with them. The Central Office had given him an assignment in western Kansas, and Dewey was working hard at liking it. The assignment came along with western Kansas, and . . . well, you can figure it out.

"Oh, look! Ice skates," Dewey said, holding them up. He'd been scratching around in Woody's junk for a half hour now, and I'd been thinking about stuffing him into an old sock and hanging him on a nail.

"Shut up, Dewey. Can't you see I'm trying to sleep?"

"It's past nine o'clock. Nine hours of sleep is enough for anyone."

"Not for a bear, it isn't. Now quit making noise."

"I want to go skating," he said.

"Can't. We don't have any ice skates," I said, then rolled over and pulled my head back into the sleeping bag like a turtle.

"I'll wear these. They're just my size."

I popped out of my bag and sat up to look at him. He was sitting down, lacing up the skates. "Now that would be real smart. How do you think that's going to look?" I asked.

"I skate very well, thank you. We had ice rinks all over the city, and I skated all the time. I've been skating since I was very small, and I've always loved it," he said.

"Did you ever water ski?" I asked.

"No. Why?"

"Just wondered," I said, satisfied that my lemon theory was holding up.

"Are there any lakes around here? It's very cold outside, and surely there must be a frozen lake around somewhere."

"Dewey, you can't go ice skating."

"Why not?" he asked, looking puzzled.

"Because nobody can see you, that's why. If you go down to the lake and go skating, all anybody sees will be Woody's ice skates going around and around," I said.

"Oh, my! You're right. I didn't stop to think about that," he said, suddenly looking dejected. I don't know why, but I felt sorry for him.

"If you really want to go skating that bad, I've got a solution for you."

"You do?"

"Yeah, I do. You can go at night, and no one will see you, and no harm will be done. You'll have to skate in the dark, though."

"I don't mind the dark, but do you think it would be all right?"

"Yeah, I've done stuff like that before. I used to love to swim, and I missed it. One day I just jerked my clothes off and dove in the lake. It felt pretty much it always did, and I enjoyed it. I had to do it at night, though. If somebody had come up on me swimming in the daytime, they would've crapped their pants or something," I said, then chuckled.

"When can we go?" Dewey asked, holding his hands to his chest like a child.

"I'm not going. It's too cold outside to swim," I said, scowling at him.

"I know that, silly. I'm talking about ice skating, and it is cold enough out for that. Look! It's snowing out," he said, pointing to a small window just over my head. I looked, and sure enough, it was snowing.

"Just because it's snowing doesn't mean the lake's frozen over. It hasn't been getting cold enough, and you'll have to wait another month for that."

"Oh, poo!"

"Can I go back to sleep now?"

"No. I want to go out in the snow, and I want you to go with me."

"Aw, Dewey, I've been out in the snow before, and it's an overrated experience. Besides, we've got a job, remember?"

"Well, all you're doing is . . . is . . . lollygagging around," he said.

"What I'm doing is recharging my battery."

"Why, did your lights go out?" Dewey sniggered, and I still hated the way he did that. He sounded like a small steam engine trying to crank.

"All right, Dewey. I'll go just as soon as I get some coffee," I said.

After wiggling out of my bag, I headed out to the Chevy to check the magic box with Dewey tagging along at my heels like a loyal dog. I grabbed the thermos and poured a big cup of coffee. I took a swallow and knew immediately that something was wrong.

"What the hell is that?" I asked, staring down at the cup.

"Gourmet coffee," Dewey said, pursing his lips, fluttering his eyelids, and looking pious. He did that often, and when he did, it made him look like a parrot with a new pair of contact lenses.

"What?"

"It's cinnamon and ginger gourmet coffee."

"It tastes like camel piss. Where's the good coffee?" I asked, scratching around in the box for another thermos.

"That's the only thermos. I asked for gourmet coffee when I filled out the food form back at the training school, and they're just now getting it on our menu."

"Our menu? What about my menu? I can't drink this stuff. This is sissy coffee, and I'm used to drinking real coffee," I said, pointing a finger at him and giving him my best don't-be-fucking-with-my-food look.

"Sorry. Maybe it's just a mix-up or something. I'm sure you're regular coffee will be showing up again at least part of the time, and it won't hurt you to drink my coffee for a change."

"And what are these things? Where are my glazed donuts?" I asked, holding up a crumbly, half-mooned thing that looked like a squashed roll.

"Croissants, and I don't know about your donuts."

"Croissants? Who the hell eats croissants?" I asked.

Dewey chuckled. "You're right on the cutting edge when it comes to food, aren't you, Doug?"

"Well, I know what I like, and I don't like this. I need some real food."

"If that's not real enough for you, you'll have to wait until lunch," Dewey said, rolling his eyes skyward. The thought crossed my mind that he must've gone to the same school of sky watching that Roosevelt had, but I didn't mention it.

"Oh, well! I don't guess I'll starve before dinner."

"Can we go walking now?"

"Yeah, let's go," I said, already walking down the street toward the campus.

I should point out that a custodian operating in the I/T mode needs to be careful when he walks around where real people are about. If snow is on the ground, for instance, he'll leave footprints as he walks, and a sight like that would scare your average mortal completely shitless. I'd been doing this angel thing long enough to know that, but Dewey hadn't quite built up enough stamina to handle the I/I mode for too long at one time. We walked a block before I noticed that he was leaving tracks. Even worse, snow was starting to pile up on his shoulders. I pointed it out to him, and he jumped like a shot had been fired at him.

"Don't get goosy. Calm down and switch to I/I," I said.

"How long is it going to take me to get the hang of this," he said, sounding irked.

"You'll get it before long. Are you feeling tired this morning?"

"No, I feel rather rested."

"Maybe that's it. Maybe you're used to being tired, and feeling fresh threw you off balance," I said.

"Could be," he said, taking a few hesitant steps. No tracks.

"I think you've got it, sport," I said, using my best British accent.

As we walked, I explained to Dewey that what I'd said about recharging my battery wasn't just a joke. It took more energy to use the I/I mode, and we'd had a long evening the night before that had required us to stay in the mode the entire time. I'd toughened up to it, but Dewey undoubtedly had not, and regardless of how fresh he felt, his battery was low. He nodded as if he understood, but he was still taking cautious steps. The campus at WKSU had the largest grove of Chinese elms of any place in that entire area. There must've been three hundred of them scattered around, but we headed for a cluster near the mall area around the student union. By the time we got there, Dewey asked to stop and rest.

"What are these trees?" he asked, looking almost straight up.

"Chinese elms," I said.

"They're almost ghostly looking without their leaves."

"Yeah, they're sort of like an ugly woman. She's not so bad with all her clothes on, but naked, she's a scary sight," I said, clicking my teeth.

"Most people aren't attractive without clothes."

"You've been looking at the wrong people, Dewey. Some folks look good naked."

"Some, but not many," he said, granting that much.

"More than you think, maybe. Like C.W., the gal Woody porked down at the bar that night. She looks real good naked," I said, winking at him.

"She's . . . she's . . . chunky," Dewey said, groping for the right word. He should've groped longer because he missed it badly.

"Chunky? Hell, she's just right."

"She has large breasts and hips, and her thighs are thick."

"Haven't you ever heard the saying that the bigger the toys the better the joys? Her toys looked all right to me."

"Maybe she wasn't chunky, but she was too . . . too . . ."

"Endowed?" I asked, finishing his statement.

"Yes, that's a good word. But you've got to admit that a lot of people are not attractive when they're undressed," Dewey said.

"Yeah, I'll sure agree with that. Marge Fink, the old gal that

Clarence is carrying on with - she's uglier than a sack of mad assholes," I said, shaking my head and frowning.

"As ugly as what?"

"Aw, just something my old uncle used to say. It's not worth repeating."

We sat in silence for a while, watching the snow fall and listening to the sounds of a relatively quiet Sunday morning. From somewhere in the distance, the sound of music floated by, and there was the occasional sound of a car passing or a student calling out to another student. Finally, Dewey turned to me and said, "Maybe these elm trees are like people in some ways. They're sure ugly naked, but they're good trees nonetheless."

"Are you about to get philosophical on me again?" I asked, trying to look leery.

"Oh, a little, perhaps," Dewey said, smiling sagely. Since he was sitting on a water fountain encased in concrete, he looked like a Buddhist monk or something.

"Then do your thing. I've got nothing else to do."

"Well, don't you agree?"

"That people are like trees?"

"Yes."

"I some ways they are, I reckon. I'm just wondering how you're going to draw some parallels between Marge Fink and these trees, other than that they're both butt ugly when their naked," I said.

"I wasn't exactly thinking along those lines, but my mind doesn't usually travel the low road like yours does," he said, smugly.

"Are you saying they're not ugly?"

"The trees are ugly naked, yes. Some people are ugly naked, yes. Are all naked, ugly things useless? No."

"What's that supposed to mean? Marge Fink is as useless as tits on a tractor," I said.

"In your eyes she is, but in Clarence's eyes she isn't," Dewey said, lifting a single finger in the air to make his point.

"Just because somebody is useful to just one other person on this earth doesn't mean they're worth anything to everyone else."

"No, it doesn't, but we have no way of knowing how many people think of her as useful. Like everyone, she has relatives and friends, and I'm sure some of them find her useful. But, that's not the point I'm trying to make. What I'm saying is that just because something is ugly to most of us doesn't mean it is useless. These elm trees are ugly right now because they're naked, but when the spring comes, they'll turn pretty again."

"I hate to disappoint you, Dewey, but they're ugly all the time."

"To you perhaps, but to me, they may be pretty. Other people must agree with me, or they wouldn't be planted here," he said.

"They're planted here because they're hardy. They don't need lots of water, and they hold up well against disease and bugs. Maybe they're so ugly that even bugs won't eat them, but whatever, they're sure are hard to kill. The head grounds man here at the college hates trees and tries to kill as many of them as he can. If it weren't for the faculty staying after his ass to leave the trees alone, he'd cut them all back to stumps. As it is, he sometimes trims them back too much. But, they're too hardy for even him to kill."

"You see, that just proves my point. They might not be as pretty as some trees, but they serve a good purpose. They make nice shade in the summer, and they serve as a break against the wind and elements, and they last a long time. What else could you ask for in a tree?"

"Yeah, it all makes sense to me now, Dewey. That's why Clarence Ludwig likes Marge Fink. She's ugly, but she makes good shade. I can believe that. Hell, you could park a greyhound bus in the shade of that woman's ass," I said.

"You're impossible," Dewey said, throwing up his hands in disgust.

"What I am is hungry. Let's go to the house and get some vittles," I said. I walked away giving my best impression of an old cowboy headed for the chuckwagon.

Dewey jumped off his perch and took a few halting steps to see if he was making tracks, and seeing he wasn't, he walked quickly until he caught up. I slowed down a bit, and when he approached said, "There's another angle on the tree thing."

"Let's hear it."

"Well, like I said before, Chinese elms are a good choice of tree for this part of the world. They're hardy, and that's their best quality. Most attractive trees don't last long around here, and the ones that do require a lot of maintenance. I woke up thinking about a saying I saw somewhere that said something about if life gives you lemons, make lemonade. Actually, I was thinking about you when I thought of that saying - about how you're pretty good about making do with what's available and will work. But I think it fits these people around here better than it does you. Life gave them this desolate country, and they made it fit to live in by planting Chinese elms."

"Thank you! I'll take that as a compliment," Dewey said, beaming like new light bulb. I couldn't stand his glee and decided to take him down a peg or two.

"Woody is a little like these folks around here, but he'd take it a step further. Live gives him lemons, and he makes lemonade, all right, but he puts Jack Daniels in it to boot. That's where the two of us are like Woody, but we're also different from each other. Neither of us would be willing to settle for just lemonade. Life gave me lemons, and I made lemon pie. Life gave you lemons, and you made lemon chiffon cake or lemon eclairs. Life gave me eggs, and I made an omelet. Life gave you eggs, and you made quiche. Life gave me a pecker, and I got laid. Life gave you a pecker, and you . . ."

"That's enough," Dewey said, his eyes suddenly slits.

"I was just trying to make the point that neither of us goes for the basics," I said, trying to look defensive.

"The pundit givith, and he takith away."

"What's the matter? Don't like the comparison?"

"The comparison is fine; it's the inference you make that peeves me."

"What, that you're . . . you're . . . refined?" I asked.

"No, sissy. You're insinuating I'm sissy," he said, turning the corners of his mouth down.

"Well, if cinnamon and ginger coffee isn't sissy, what is it?

"Refined."

"Isn't that what I said?"

"Well, yes, I suppose it is," Dewey said, ducking his head.

During the walk back to Woody's house, I elaborated more on the tree theory. Yes, the elms did fit the people who lived in western Kansas. Boring trees fit boring people, I said. Western Kansans didn't get out much, and their biggest social events were things like church revivals, rodeos, barn dances, county fairs, tractor pulls, and the like. But like the ugly Chinese elms, being boring had not kept them from being useful. They were good people - hard working, decent, honest country folk, for the most part. And like the elms, they were tough. They'd stuck it out in a part of the world most people wouldn't have taken a second look at, and they'd even prospered.

What I didn't say to Dewey at the time was that Woody Pickens had been living in Forest City for just over fifteen years and still wasn't a Chinese elm like the people around him. He'd been there ever since he finished graduate school, but no matter how badly he wanted to be like those around him, he just wasn't hardy enough. Maybe that's why he'd stayed in western Kansas, because he wanted to be as strong as the elms. I probably would've told Dewey, but he went into the house to watch Woody for a while. I spent the next hour entertaining myself by trying to figure out what kind of tree Woody was. I was about to decide that he was a nut tree of some kind when I suddenly remembered being hungry. I went looking for Dewey, but not because I wanted to talk trees. Breakfast had been a bust, and I was getting hungry enough to fart fresh air.

We had spinach quiche for dinner.

CHAPTER 12
Dagobits

The last week of October went by without any major problems. Woody got drunk twice - once on Tuesday and again on Thursday. The Thursday drunk was a small one for him, but that's probably because he wasn't fully recovered from the one he threw on Tuesday. That one was a dandy. He started drinking at three that afternoon and didn't quit until three the next morning. Nothing touched it off - no fights with Wanda or at school or anything like that. He just did it. After struggling through two classes on Wednesday morning, he went directly home and to bed, and that's where he stayed until early Thursday morning. He slept for nearly eighteen hours, a new record for him.

Halloween fell on Friday of that week, and it started snowing that afternoon. Unlike the light snow of the previous week, this snow came straight down in fluffy flakes the size of quarters. Most western Kansas snows come in sideways and in tiny, windblown granules that sting your face, but this was a nice snow. It melted almost as soon as it hit the ground at first, but the temperature fell, and before long it covered the ground. Snowfall in desolate country is like spreading a white tablecloth over a dingy table, and it was a refreshing sight. After watching it for a half hour, I gave it up to watch television. I'm may be a lover of snowfalls, but I've always been a sucker for Star Trek reruns.

Wanda came home from work early and was greeted by an unfamiliar sight - Woody and the kids lying belly down on the living room floor looking through a catalog of Christmas gifts that had come in the afternoon mail. Finding Woody spending time with the children put Wanda in a good mood, and before long she busied herself making cookies. Once they were in the oven, she flopped down on the living room floor with the others.

The Star Trek rerun ended and I quickly got bored with the show that came on afterward. I thought about changing channels - "Bonanza" reruns were on channel thirteen - but gave up on the idea. Instead, I got up and meandered into the living room. Dewey was sitting in a corner, watching the family scene through misty eyes. His smile was such that I couldn't help thinking that he was starting to look like an angel. He was literally beaming with delight. "This is the way it should be," he said as I sat down beside him.

I had to agree. The sight was heartwarming, particularly since I'd seldom seen anything like it from him. Woody's daughter, the younger of the two children, was perched on her dad's back, reading the gift book over his shoulder. She pointed out gifts as Woody flipped the pages. The boy was beside his father, helping turn the pages when his hands weren't busy pushing away his sister's eager fingers. Wanda, now lying on the other side of Woody, acted as a mediator in trying to keep the children's hands away. That, of course, only put a fourth set of hands in the picture. It struck me as funny, and I chuckled. I don't know why because I knew how it would end. Wanda got up just long enough to check the cookies, then came back and reminded Woody about it being Halloween. They'd go trick-or-treating after dark, she said, and he was expected to go along. Woody managed an unenthusiastic nod, but it seemed to be enough to please her.

"Where've you been?" Dewey asked.

"Watching TV."

"This is better." He nodded his head toward Woody and the kids.

"Yeah, maybe Woody will behave himself tonight. Snow doesn't bring out the best in him, but this evening is getting off to a good start. Snow is relaxing to some folks, but it makes others restless. There'll be a lot of activity on campus and around town tonight. The students usually get rowdy when it snows like this. Since it's a nice, fluffy snow, they can horse around in it. They'll be up half the night building snowmen, snowballing each other, sledding, and doing other things like that. Most of the stuff they get into is just good, clean fun, but some of it isn't. There'll be some vandalism, especially since tonight is Halloween. Some of the kids are probably plotting mischief already and are just waiting for dark. There's at least one snow time activity, though, you can count on. There will be some panty-packing," I said.

"What?"

"Panty-packing. It's a traditional prank around here. When it snows, and when conditions are right, bands of college boys prowl the campus looking for girls. They hide in the bushes or behind some building until some supposedly unsuspecting girl comes along, and then they jump her and stuff her panties full of snow. The attackers will cover their faces with hoods or bandanas so they can't be identified. This little game, you might've guessed, gives them a chance to get a handful of something other than snow."

"The girls, of course, try to make themselves available," Dewey said.

"You've got it. They'll wear as much clothes as they can get on, and they'll put up a fuss when they're jumped. They'll giggle and squeal, thrash around, and try to pull their assailant's masks off, but in the end, they'll get their drawers stuffed full of snow."

"That sounds to me like something that could get out of hand, if you'll pardon the pun. Don't the school authorities frown on it?"

"Yeah, but they can't do much about it. It doesn't happen very often, usually during the first good snowfall of the year. There's just two cops on campus, and there's no way they can stop the panty-packing," I said, smiling as I remembered an incident that had taken place the year before.

"What's funny?" Dewey asked.

"They may work harder to stop the panty-packing this year because of something that happened last year. A group of jocks got carried away and packed the wrong panties," I said.

"I don't understand."

"They attacked the Hindenburg."

"I still don't understand."

"Her real name is Constance Dougherty, a math professor who checks in at about 250 pounds. She's in her mid-thirties, is noted for her cranky disposition, and is prissy for a fat woman. She's single and is apparently doomed to stay that way. She's so prim-and-proper that she insists on being called Constance, not Connie. All the kids in her classes call her Sourdough Dougherty, but not to her face. Since she's so fat, the students have nicknamed her 'the Hindenburg.'"

"How cruel," he said.

"Hey, man, she deserves it. The gal's a real blimp and an ugly blimp at that. Her disposition is uglier than her body."

"He jests at scars who never felt a wound," Dewey said.

"Shakespeare didn't know this fat-ass," I said.

"My efforts aren't totally wasted. At least you knew the quote's source," Dewey said. "Get on with your story. Did the jocks stuff her panties?"

"Sure did - got her walking home from a night class. Took half a dozen of them, but they got the job done. She nearly tore the door off the Dean of Student's office the next morning. She did some major bitching and demanded the culprits be caught and punished. The dean did his best, but no one was ever caught. Her complaining, put pressure on the school to control the panty-packing, so the next time it snowed, a dozen cops were on campus. Privately, however, almost everyone laughed about it."

Dewey's attention suddenly drifted from panty-packers back to the scene in the living room. The kids were quarreling now, and Woody had gone to the refrigerator to grab a beer. Wanda watched anxiously as he took the first swallow, then made some remark about how she wished he wouldn't drink until after the kids had finished making their trick-or-treat rounds. Woody gave her an expressionless stare before walking through the living room to the front porch. He didn't say a word to the arguing children.

"What's the fuss about?" I asked.

"Their Halloween costumes. They want to wear the same outfit," Dewey said.

"That's no big deal. They're the same size."

"It's a big deal because the two costumes are different. It appears the girl wants the costume the boy picked out. They're not twins, are they?"

"Nope. Sean's the oldest by about two years. He's nearly twelve, just small for his age. Maggie's ten, I think."

"They're good looking kids. What kind of kids are they?" Dewey asked. I gave Dewey a how-the-hell-should-I-know look. "One's a cocker spaniel and the other's a poodle."

"Don't be silly. You know exactly what I mean. Are they well-adjusted? Intelligent? Happy? What?"

"They're pretty good kids. Maggie is a bubbly, enthusiastic kid, and she has the same energy her mother has. Maybe she's a bit flighty, but she's bright, friendly, and talkative. Sean is more like his dad. He's a sharp kid, but he's moody. They both do well in school, and as far as I can tell, they're wholesome, healthy, normal kids. How's that?"

"Good," Dewey said and then quickly added, "I've figured out what the fuss is really about. Sean is reluctant to go trick-or-treating because he thinks he's too old for it. Maybe he doesn't want his parents and sister tagging along with him. Whatever the reason, he's trying to put a kink in the family plan to go out together."

"Don't worry about it. Wanda will fix it. She's decided they're going together, and she'll snatch a knot in young Sean's ass if she has to."

"I'm not sure the boy won't get his way. He's employing a good tactic. He'll fret and fuss until his mother gives in, or until his dad gets enough of it and blows his top. Wanda badly wants the family to go trick-or-treating together, and the boy knows that. His dad is in a rare mood, and Wanda has things going her way right now. She's not about to risk losing the entire evening just because the boy is balking. She'll compromise or give in altogether. If he can't get what he wants, he may go for making his father angry. That way the entire evening will be scrapped."

"I'm on the kid's side," I said.

Dewey stared at me for a moment. "You don't want to have to walk around town with them, right?"

"Right."

"You're a shit, just like Sean. The only difference is that he's a little shit, and you're a big shit."

"You're talking nasty again," I said, wiggling my finger.

"It's excusable, considering the circumstances. I would call you something else, but shit is the only word that comes to mind right now."

"How about asshole?" I suggested, and seeing the dismay in his eyes continued with, "or sonofabitch, or pisshead, or motherfucker. Why, hell, you could even call me a . . ."

"**Stop it!** I wouldn't let words like those cross my lips, and I'm not about to get involved in any game that will let you display your extensive vocabulary of filth."

"Sorry. Got carried away, I reckon. Besides, the kids have quit arguing," I said, nodding toward the children.

Woody suddenly strolled into the living room wearing an outfit he planned on wearing to a costume party later that evening. Wanda had spent days working on their costumes and would have been irked with him for putting it on if it hadn't been for the reaction he got from the kids. They laughed hysterically when they saw their father dressed as an elf. His big ears, pointed nose, cap with a pointed crown, black tights, pointed-toed shoes, and short jacket with big buttons were enough to make anyone laugh. Dewey laughed harder than the kids did.

"He's an elf," Dewey said gleefully, pulling his clenched hands to his chest like a small boy seeing his first puppy.

"No, he's a Dagobit," I said.

"Beg your pardon?"

"Dagobit," I said again.

"He looks like an elf to me."

"The word does come from a tree, I think, but it's a mythical tree. These tiny elves originally lived in dagobin trees, so the story goes. It's a tree that grew over in China or somewhere like that. Anyway, the dagobits we're talking about are sort of like elves, but these particular elves are part of Woody's family tradition. His father's a real storyteller, and many of his stories are about these little elves he invented and passed down to his children and grandchildren. Dagobits caught the blame for a lot of the mischief that went on around the Pickens household, and whenever the kids did something wrong and then denied it, Woody's old man would say, 'Well, it must've been the dagobits."

"My mother blamed it on a mouse," Dewey said.

"I always blamed it on my sister," I said.

"Of course, you would."

"Well, anyway, these dagobits became more than just good-natured elves. Woody's father made them part of a much bigger fantasy world."

"Like a chimera?"

I stared at him a few minutes while trying to decide whether or not I should admit it, then said, "I don't know what a chimera is."

"It's a highly fantastic illusion."

"I don't know about that, but Woody's dagobits were pretty fantastic. Did you ever lie in bed and watch the shadows on the wall or ceiling made by light coming through a window on a rainy night? You know, I'm talking about those squiggly shadows caused by the rain on the windowpanes that danced on your ceiling. I don't know about you, but they used to make my imagination run wild with thoughts of all sorts of monsters and such."

"Yes, and that's what a chimera is. I too envisioned them as monsters or something awful, and they frightened me," Dewey said, fanning his face and rolling his eyes like he remembered them well.

"They scared all small children, and so did the squiggly things and eerie shadows and blacks spots that hid in the corners of Woody's bedroom. Woody's dad always told his kids that those squiggly things were good dagobits who'd come to watch over sleeping children. Sometimes they made those squiggly, dancing shadows on the walls and ceilings just to let you know they were there, he said. When asked why they couldn't be seen with the lights on, Woody's dad said they were much too clever to be seen as anything more than a shadow. Dagobits were always harmless but maybe a tad mischievous. They never hurt people, especially kids."

"Mischievous? What kind of mischief?"

"Dagobits, according to old man Pickens, are responsible for those irritating tangles in your hair in the morning. They also cause the bad taste you have in your mouth, the knots in your shoelaces, the rings around bathtubs, the disappearance of a favorite sock, and the bothersome lump in your pillow."

"How interesting," Dewey said.

"The old man was a weird duck, and his stories about the dagobits may be indicative of more than the old man's far out imagination. Woody grew up listening to his father's stories of fantasy, like the dagobits, but they weren't just bedtime stories. Maybe they show how the old man's mind worked. He must've been a brilliant man, but he had a hard time finding his niche in life."

"Don't we all?" Dewey asked.

"Not like this man. He was a high school teacher, but teaching never satisfied him. Poor health forced him to retire at an early age, and he became a recluse. About all he did after that was read, study, and write, and he turned into a walking encyclopedia of weird or trivial stuff. He wrote a small library of articles, poems, and short stories, but hardly any of them ever got published. Some of his friends and family members read his stuff and listened to his stories, but most folks saw him as an eccentric know-it-all."

"Since you're using the past tense, I take it he's dead," he said.

"No, he's still alive," I said.

"Then why did you use the past tense?"

"Because I'm trying to make a point about the way Woody remembers him. Quit being so tooky."

"What's tooky?"

"It means picky, finicky, hard to please, a pain in the ass. My mother used the word a lot."

"Finish your story."

"Do I have to shift tenses?" I asked.

"Now you're being tooky. Just finish. I'll make allowances for your use of tense," Dewey said, then yawned.

"Am I putting you to sleep? If you're losing interest, say so. I already know the story."

"Oh, no," Dewey said, perking up some. "Please continue."

"There's really not much more to tell. Woody's dad is a funny old man who dreams up fantastic tales. His grandkids, Woody's kids included, love the old man because he's so entertaining. He even calls his grandkids dagobits. Some of his stories are so farfetched that even the kids don't believe them, but many of them are deeply philosophical. In that regard, he's a lot like you. But he tells so many stories that it's hard to know whether they're true or not. I'm not sure if he knows the difference anymore. Anyway, dagobits came from him."

"Woody is actually showing respect for his father's imagination by going to the costume party as a dagobit. Do you think he will explain to people what his costume represents?" Dewey asked.

"I doubt it. The costume was a compromise. Wanda wanted them to go as Anthony and Cleopatra, but Woody axed that idea. Then she suggested Mickey and Minnie Mouse, but he nixed that too. Finally, they decided to go as a couple of elves. To them and the kids, they're dagobits."

"I think it's a neat idea. I just love a costume party. If I were going, know what I'd be?" Dewey asked. I couldn't leave it alone.

"Tinkerbell?" I asked. I knew immediately that it was a bad

joke because the childish smile on Dewey's face suddenly turned into a devilish grin. A fire grew in his eyes.

"Well, at least I'd need a costume. You could go as you are and be a prick. Trouble is, everybody would recognize you instantly," he said.

"Tacky, tacky. You said a naughty word again," I said, wiggling my finger sideways at him.

"You started it."

"Actually, I would wear a costume," I said.

"Attila the Hun, or would it be Judas?"

"No, I'd wear roller skates, leave my dick out and go as a pull toy."

"You are absolutely disgracefully. Did your mother even love you?" Dewey asked and then sighed heavily.

"Adored me, absolutely adored me," I said.

"Did she have other children, or were you her only choice?"

"There were others, but I stuck out like an oasis in the desert, like a rose among the thorns, like a . . ."

"Put a lid on it and finish your story."

"I finished. That's it."

"You were saying that some of the old man's stories might've been true, but there was no way of knowing the difference," Dewey said.

"The way I see it, the old man was real smart, but he had a tough time making it in the real world because he was a knower and not a goer. Maybe he didn't like the real world for one reason or another and retreated into his fantasy world. The guy lived with his nose in a book, and maybe they were his way out. Somehow he just never bridged the gap between mystical and material, between what ought to be and what is. Are you with me?"

"Close enough. Continue."

"He's always been a man of high ideals, but his high ideals never got him anywhere. He was too much of a dreamer to make his dreams come true, but Woody fell heir to them. Being a college professor was his old man's idea. Woody was pushed in that direction from the time he was just a button, and the pressure is still there. Old man Pickens is always quizzing him about his job. Are you studying? Are you writing? Are you reading the right books?

Are you thinking of moving to a bigger University? He wants the best for Woody - wants him to develop both spiritually and materially. Thing is, though, he set some bad examples for Woody."

"Like what?"

"Like his periodic withdrawal into Loony Tunes time. Woody is almost as big a dreamer as his old man."

"There's nothing wrong with dreams. There's nothing wrong with a fantasy world either," Dewey said.

"I know that, but maybe the old man encouraged it too much. Woody dreams but does very little else. He's not oriented toward the fantastic or mystical like his old man, but he's definitely a romanticist. The old man taught him to dream, but couldn't teach him how to get there."

"But Woody is an achiever. You can't say he's not a doer because he's accomplished a lot."

"Like what?" I asked.

"Well, he's a college professor. That's an accomplishment in itself, and being a **good** college professor is even more of an achievement."

"Is it?" I asked, slyly.

"Yes, I think so."

"What's your definition of accomplishment? What's a doer? What's an achiever?"

"It's someone who lives up to expectations, meets goals," Dewey said, then shrugged.

"And whose expectations would that be?

"I see where you're headed. You're saying that Woody has lived up to everyone's expectations except his own, right?"

"Not exactly. Woody knows a lot about lofty ideals because they're a part of his family tradition. It may not be enough for him to reach some goals or perhaps just partly meet expectations. Maybe he wants to please his old man more than anyone suspects. Maybe the problem is that he's set his own goals too high," I said.

"Maybe, but he has an additional problem. He's sick."

"Sick? He's a goofy bastard, but I don't know about being sick."

"He's sick because he's an alcoholic," Dewey said.

"So what else is new, Dr. Davvison? Anyone with one eye and half a brain can see that," I said.

"No, they can't."

"How do you figure that? He goes after booze like a hog to slop. He drinks like a fish and gets drunker than a waltzing piss ant. Anyone who's seen him drink knows the guy has got a drinking problem."

"Most people can see that he drinks too much, but what they don't understand is that he's suffering from a disease. They know he has a problem, but they're not willing to accept alcoholism as his illness. People nearest the sufferer may be the last to recognize his sickness. Family members and friends are sometimes the last to see how sick he really is. They just don't face up to it."

"Hell, Woody even knows it," I said.

"Maybe, but that's another problem in itself. Recognition of a problem and doing something about it are two different things. Woody may know he's addicted, but he may not be willing to do anything about it. On the other hand, he may not be willing to accept his alcoholism because he thinks he's too strong and too smart to get hooked. He may be willing to admit that he's got a problem with alcohol, but he's can't bring himself to admit to addiction."

"You'd think a guy in his position would be able to deal with it. Hell, he's a psychologist and knows all about alcoholism. He ought to know better than to let himself get in the condition he's in."

"Yes, but his intellectual abilities compound the problem. He thinks because he's superior intellectually, he's still in control. Some smart people are control people, but none of us, not even the brightest, is able to live in total reality all of the time. We all need some rest from the real world, so we escape from time to time into a fantasy or dream world. Unreality may be just as important as reality, and we all need an escape mechanism. Some of us find an escape that is not healthy. Woody's father found his in dagobits and a make believe world where he was the master and where he didn't have to deal with failure because he made the rules. For a while, he became the dragon slayer. In Woody's case, he escapes by drinking. I think he tries hard to face reality and to battle his dragons realistically, but dragons are a tough foe. Perhaps seeing his father fail to conquer the dragons of the real world left him with an uncommon drive to succeed where his dad failed, but he can't seem to find the right weapon. Instead, he chose the bottle. Booze has become his dagobits, his escape from reality. Alcohol takes him to a fantasy world where, like his father, he can kill enough dragons to save his sanity," Dewey said.

"Thank you, Sigmund Freud," I said.

"The mind ought sometimes to be amused, that it may the better return to thought, and to itself. That's Phaedrus," Dewey said proudly.

"That's what?"

"Phaedrus said that."

"Was he an alcoholic?"

"I don't know. What difference does it make?" Dewey asked.

"I just wondered why he said it because it sounds like a drunk," I said.

"My words are wasted on unenlightened ears," Dewey said, drawing his mouth into a tight line and exhaling heavily.

"Who said that?"

"I did."

"Well, you'll have to enlighten me later. Besides, I got the message. As bad as I hate it, we've got to go trudging through the snow with our trick-or-treaters," I said and stood up. Woody, Wanda, and the kids were already half way across the street by then.

"I'll play guard dog for a while. You can stay here and catch a nap, and I'll wake you when we get back."

"Bless you, my son," I said and waved my hand over Dewey's head. "I'll be right here when you return." I pointed at the couch.

"You have given a new meaning to the concept of an eternal rest," Dewey said, smiling as he walked toward the front door. If his comment was aimed at making me feel guilty, it missed. I fell asleep quickly and dreamed of tiny men with big eyes and noses, pointed ears, and skinny legs with knobby knees. They danced around the couch where I slept, tying knots in my shoelaces, weaving kinks into my hair, and sprinkling bad taste powder on my lips. But I slept anyway, comfortable in the thought that old man Pickens dagobits were harmless, and that I was much safer with the creatures of his dream world than Woody was with the inventions of the fantasyland he lived in.

CHAPTER 13
Holly-Rollers and Hellfire

Dewey always delighted in waking me up. I don't know exactly what it was about him, but he had something against sleep. He even quoted Shakespeare about sleep being little slices of death, and I kept telling him that we were dead and that made everything just one big slice, and he shouldn't concern himself with how much anyone slept, especially me. I also reminded him that that's why I wanted him in the first place - so I could get more sleep. Still, he seemed to delight in interrupting my slumber.

"Want to go to church with me?" Dewey asked, shaking me.

"Huh? What?" I asked, rising up on one elbow.

"Church. Do you want to go to church?"

"Hell no!"

"Come on, Doug. Go with me," he said, sounding like a kid asking for a cookie.

"Go away," I said, then flopped back down.

"It wouldn't hurt you to go to church, so get up."

"What kind of church are you going to?" I asked. I knew right off that I might as well cut the best deal I could. Dewey wasn't about to let me sleep.

"Episcopal, if I can find one."

"We don't have one of those."

"Sure you do. It's listed here in the paper," Dewey said, holding up an old newspaper. He had me there. Forest City did have an Episcopal church.

"Episcopalians are boring. All they do is mumble and recite and smile at one another."

"Then where do you want to go? I'm open to suggestion."

"I like holly-roller churches," I said, grinning and wiggling my eyebrows.

"Why?"

"Because they look like they're having a good time. They play loud music and clap their hands and holler amen and even roll on the floor. I know just the place," I said, standing up.

"Can't we find a service that's more sedate?"

"Yeah, but if I'm going, you'll have to go where I want to go."

"Fine, you win," he said, looking exasperated.

We got in the car and drove out to an evangelical church on the outskirts of town, called the Apostolic something-or-other. I'd never been there, but I figured it should serve my purposes. More than anything, I wanted to get Dewey's goat. He was far too prim and proper to be able to handle all that holly-roller stuff, and from the sound of the music coming from inside the church, I'd picked the right place. We stepped inside and positioned ourselves on the very back pew, directly beside an old man who seemed to be totally out of it. The preacher, a big fellow with long arms, looked to be just hitting his stride in a sermon that must've been about the choices between the forces of good and evil. He was telling the congregation that they only had those two choices. They could either choose God and good, or they could choose bad and the devil. Many of the people in the congregation were holding their hands in the air and rocking back and forth, and some were chiming in with comments of their own.

I should note here that I'd always had a thing about holly-roller churches, but my feelings about them were very much unlike what I'd told Dewey. I'd never really been to a holly-roller church meeting, but since childhood, I'd had a fear of them. Maybe it went back to a story my uncle Walt had told me about them. He said that all holly-roller churches had pew worms in them, and that you really had to watch out for those pew worms. It was the pew worms that made all those holly-rollers do the things they did, like jumping up and shouting and clapping their hands and such. They did that, he said, because a pew worm had crawled up their ass. Now, I'd long since known that pew worms were just a figment of my uncle Walt's imagination, but I still got ill at ease with holly-rollers. I couldn't even watch those evangelical preachers on television, much less go to one of their churches in person. Being ill at ease sometimes made me do goofy things because I always overcompensated for it.

The old man sitting beside me seemed to be in a trance. His eyes were closed, and he rocked back and forth in rhythm with the preaching, and occasionally he'd say things like, "Thank you, Jesus, thank you," or, "praise the Lord," with no rhyme or reason to what was being said. Dewey looked concerned at all these goings on, but I found it all amusing. The preacher had started into a spiel about all the bad things people had to watch out for, and he began to name them. The old man stopped rocking and mumbling then, and he even opened his eyes to listen as the preacher called them off.

There were lots of evil things out there, he told them. There were liars and killers and thieves and drunkards, and even illicit sex and fornication. He repeated the word fornication again, even shouted it out. When he said it, murmurs of agreement swept through the congregation. The old man sitting beside me went back to rocking, but his only comment was, "Thank you, Jesus, thank you." That's when I jumped up from my pew and hollered, "Amen!"

Dewey nearly lost it. "Stop that!" he said, elbowing me as hard as he could.

"Why? They can't hear me," I said.

"You're being sacrilegious."

"Aw, I don't know about that. I thought I was just getting in the spirit of things."

"Sit down, and don't you do that again." Dewey looked partly pissed, but he looked embarrassed more than anything else.

The preacher finished his sermon by telling his congregation that they'd better shun all the evil things in favor of good things, or else they'd face eternal damnation. He then proceeded to tell them in graphic detail the horrors of hell - you know, the old fiery furnace bit. I looked at the congregation, especially the youngsters, and they squirmed in their seats as he talked about it. Then he ended with a long prayer, and they passed the collection plate. Before passing the plate, though, he said there'd be some testimonials given before closing.

I turned to look at Dewey and found him looking as pious as ever, and that was more than my ornery nature could stand. I jumped to my feet again and said, "Reverend, I've come to testify. I want to say that before I got saved, I used to be the whiskey drinkingest, cigarette smokingest, lyingest, cussingest, whore-hoppingest reprobate in the whole wide county, but since I've come to know the Lord, I've just about quit." When I turned to look down at Dewey, he looked like he was about to piss his pants. His mouth was hanging open, and his eyes had gone as round as tennis balls.

"I am absolutely astounded at your irreverence," he said, after he'd recovered his wits.

"What's the matter, Dewey? Can't you take a joke?" I asked, sitting back down.

"Yes, I can, but what you're doing is a travesty against everything . . . everything holy," he said, still wide-eyed.

"You sound like you believe what this old boy's been saying," I said, nodding toward the preacher.

"Well . . . well . . . well, what if I do?"

"Because . . . Because . . . Because it's a bunch of bullshit," I said, trying to look just as self-righteous as Dewey had been looking. Mimicking him usually irritated him, but since he was already pissed off, he ignored it.

"It is not bullshit," he said, defiantly.

"Oops! Now you've done it. Went and said another nasty word, and in church, no less."

"You said it first."

"If one of your friends went and jumped off a bridge, would you jump in after them? I'm really disappointed in you."

Dewey didn't say a word, and seeing that deviling him was getting nowhere, I folded my arms and turned back toward the preacher. The collection had been taken by then, and the testifying was about to begin. When the first person to give witness stood up, I cackled out loud. Dewey, who'd dropped his head in an attempt to compose himself, suddenly looked up, and when he did, his mouth and eyes flew open again. For a second there, I thought maybe a pew worm had crawled up his ass or something. He grabbed my arm and asked, "Is that who I think it is?"

"Yep, that's her."

"That's the girl we saw having the . . . involved in the . . . doing . . . being naughty with that public relations director," he said, finally able to get it out.

"Tonya, and the guy she was being nasty with was Brady Fuller."

"Well, what's she doing here?"

"Just guessing, I'd say she's about to give witness for the Lord," I said vainly.

"I can't believe it. I just can't believe it," Dewey said, wobbling his head from side to side.

Tonya started her testimony by talking about how she had been selfish and manipulative for most of her life. She talked about how much she'd sacrificed to win all those beauty contests, but left out the part about humping Brady, of course. Vanity, she concluded, was a sin, and she never would've been able to see that unless the Good Lord had revealed it to her. It had come to her all at once, like the Lord had flicked a switch and turned the light on for her, she said. That's when I jumped up again.

"Now, wait just a minute, young lady. Let's not be giving him credit for too much. It was me who turned the light on that night," I said, rather loudly.

I knew before I looked that Dewey was gone. I felt a swoosh of air as he departed and knew that he'd lost enough compose to have switched to the I/T mode. I turned to look around at about the same time the front door flew open. It closed with a vengeance, like suction had drawn it shut, and I knew then that Dewey was in a sure enough huff.

The congregation turned and stared at the door, of course, and I decided to go after Dewey. On the way out, I passed the light switch and almost couldn't withstand the temptation to flick off the lights. That would've really put an exclamation point to what Tonya had been telling them, but I managed to snuff out the impulse. Dewey's opening and slamming the door had caused enough commotion. Once outside, I couldn't immediately find him, so I started walking through the cars in the parking lot. I'd just about made it to the Chevy when a rock whizzed past my left ear. Instinctively, I went I/I and looked around. Dewey was standing twenty feet away, glaring at me and winding up to chuck another rock.

"What the hell do you think you're doing?" I hollered.

"I'm stoning you, you pagan perditionist," he said and then let fly with the rock. He threw pretty well for a sissy, and the rock zipped right through me.

"Tacky, tacky," I said, rubbing one index finger across the other.

"Oh, I wish I had a rock that would work in this dimension," he said, looking skyward, then added, "I'd knock that sanctimonious sacrilege right out of you. I'd stone all that mean-spirited bile of the devil right out of you."

"Dewey, you're starting to sound like those folks inside. Were you a holly-roller down on earth?" I asked.

"No, I was one of those boring Episcopalians, but I have some respect for the way people choose to worship God. I might not agree with what went on in there, but I refuse to be like you. I refuse to belittle them for the way they worship our Heavenly Father."

Poor Dewey. He'd gotten so upset that his arms had gone rigid at his side. His fists were clenched, and his face looked as if he were trying to pass a watermelon or something. I suddenly felt sorry for him, and maybe even a little guilty, but I wasn't about to let him break me down on this particular point. I despised what I'd just seen. "Don't take it so hard, Dewey. I'm just pranking around with you, and you can't take any of that seriously," I said, pointing back toward the church.

"Then what should I take seriously? You? Am I supposed to believe you?" he asked, looking even more distraught now.

"Better me than them. Tonya was laying a big line of crap on those people, and you know that. Do you think she's changed that much since we caught her humping her boss? Five will get you ten that she's fucking the preacher in less than a month," I said, starting to get a little irritated myself.

"Can't you see anything good in people? Do you always have to find the worst in them? You said it yourself that night we walked in on them in that dark office. You said that maybe what I'd done when I caused the commotion may have done some good, and that they might think twice before they did it again. Well, perhaps it did. Perhaps Tonya did realize that what she was doing was wrong, and who's to say that it didn't bring her to some understanding with God. I can't say for sure, but I know one thing for certain. It is not for you to say," he said, emphatically pointing a finger directly at me.

I knew he'd won that round. I had no defense against that, other than to say that I just didn't have that much confidence in Tonya. I started to say that, but I knew what he'd come back with. He'd say that my problem was that I didn't have enough confidence in God's redemptive powers, or something like that, and I didn't want to listen to any more of it. "OK, Dewey, you're right about that. I should have more faith in the good side of folks, and maybe Tonya was really serious about what she said in there. But, I'm not buying that other hogwash about there being just two ways to go in life. All that crap about a fiery furnace where souls burn for eternity is nonsense. It's just not true," I said.

"And you know that for sure?" Dewey asked, moving toward me now. The anger on his face had given way to a look of concern.

"I'm standing right here in front of you. Doesn't that tell you something?" I asked.

"Yes, it does. It tells me that you must not be as insensitive to all this as you act," he said, moving his arms in a circular motion.

"I'll be honest with you, Dewey. I don't know why I'm here. I wasn't a bad person, at least not on the inside. I did a lot of bad things down there, though, and I don't know what saved me."

"Saved you from what?"

"Hell."

"I thought you didn't believe in hell?" Dewey asked, smiling now.

"I didn't say that. I said that I didn't believe in the fiery furnace concept of hell, that's all."

"Then what do you think hell is?"

"I have no earthly idea," I said, shaking my head.

"I wasn't asking you for an earthly idea. You should be past that by now, so give me a spiritual definition of it."

"I can't," I said, softly.

"Then what can you say?"

"Well, I can say that I don't believe in eternal damnation. I don't believe in lost souls, at least souls that are lost forever. People down here use hell as an excuse for religion, and I don't like that. They preach the notion that if you're not with them, then you're against them, and there is no in between. They clump up in their churches and teach intolerance for anyone who doesn't agree with them. You accuse me of being sacrilegious, and you're right, I am. But there's a difference between sacrilege against God and against the people who claim to know and understand God. These folks are phonies, Dewey. That preacher, no matter how well-meaning he is, stood in there and raked those folks over the coals of hell, and that's not right. No one should come to God because he fears the devil. Maybe what people need to understand is that what counts is a life well lived. It's how you treat and serve mankind that brings the greatest rewards, and just joining some church won't save you," I said.

"I agree with you, at least in part. Yes, their approach is wrong, but it may lead some to the exact understanding you speak of."

"It might. I'll grant you that, but I never was a church person, and I'm here."

"I like you," Dewey said, his eyes growing moist.

"Do what?" I asked, completely dumfounded.

"I said I like you. You've got the exterior of a rhino, but you're a lamb on the inside. Yes, that's it – you're a Lamb of God just like the rest of us. That's why you're here. Haven't you figured that out yet?"

"No, I reckon I haven't."

"Want me to tell you?"

"Why not? You will anyway, whether or not I want it."

"Perhaps I won't, at least not this time. I'll tell you this much. Intent is most likely the key. If a person's intent is bad, then his religion will not serve him well, and he, in turn, will not be of much service to his fellow man; but if a person's intent is good, then . . . well, you figure it out," Dewey said.

That was the last of the conversation about holly-rollers and hellfire. We drove back to town in silence and arrived at Woody's house just in time to catch him leaving with Wanda and the kids. Dewey, seeing that and surmising an afternoon of some tranquility, offered to take care of the watchdog duties. I welcomed the opportunity to catch up on some sleep, and that's exactly what I did. I figured I'd dream that same old dream about getting killed all over again, except this time I'd wake up in hell. But, I didn't. Instead, I dreamed of rolling hills and valleys and crystal clear streams . . . and lambs frolicking in belly deep clover.

CHAPTER 14
A Confederacy of Dunces

"Times have really changed," Dewey said, his voice heavy with nostalgia.

"Huh?"

"Times have changed," he said again.

"What times?" I asked without taking my eyes off the beautiful hips swaying down the hallway of Howard Hall. They belonged to a thirtyish, foxy gal I'd seen in one of Woody's psychology class. Though it might seem strange, I'd never noticed what a good looking ass she had, and I couldn't bring myself to tear my eyes away.

"School times. The kids have really changed since the last time I was on a college campus."

"I thought you said you'd never been to college," I said.

"I've been to a college, but I've never actually taken college classes. I read a lot, so that took me to some campuses looking for books. I'm not totally unfamiliar with them," Dewey said.

"Well, I agree with you about the changes," I said, craning my neck to get a last glimpse of that good looking ass before it disappeared into the crowd far down the hallway.

"You're hopeless."

"What I am is helpless," I replied, then added, "It's a good thing I can't use the personification mode. If I could, I'd be trying to jump that gal's bones."

"Would you really?" Dewey asked. He looked genuinely curious.

"Probably not," I admitted after a moment of more sober thought. Not having a good looking butt to gaze upon does have a tendency to bring one back to sober thought, you know.

"I didn't think so."

"Don't mistake my honesty for ethical improvement. I'm just too big a coward. That's about the only thing that would stand in my way. I can't see myself shoveling coal, and I hear it gets hot down there." I pointed down.

"They wouldn't send you to hell for that," Dewey said and sniggered into the back of his hand.

"Says who?"

"You, for one. You told me that weeks ago."

"I was just guessing," I said.

"And you later said that you didn't believe in a fiery furnace concept of hell."

"I did at that, and I don't, but that doesn't mean I'm not guessing at it."

"Talleyrand once said, 'What I have been taught I have forgotten; what I know I have guessed.' Maybe you know more than you think you do," Dewey said, then winked.

"What are you, a walking encyclopedia of quotes?"

"No, but I think Talleyrand is right."

"Not me. A guess is a guess, and Talleyrand didn't know a bit more about hell than I do. He might by now, but he sure as hell didn't when he said that. For all I know the biblical version of hell might be right. Maybe it really is true that Lucifer was an angel once, but he pissed of the Big Boss and got his ass kicked out. Maybe hell really is a fiery furnace," I said.

"Yes, but Lucifer made the mistake of challenging God's authority, and that's more than simply breaking the rules. You've broken many rules, and they haven't sent you to hell yet."

"I don't really break rules, but I fudge. I only do it when there's a good reason, and I sure don't try to rub it in their face. There's very little way I'd ever use my special powers to get some nookie."

"I'm pleased to hear it, and perhaps there's still some hope for you."

"Maybe, and since I can't screw, it's all right for me to check out asses, huh?"

"Humor yourself. I won't complain," he said, looking pious again.

"I've made some interesting observations about women's asses over the years. I even have rating system for them," I said proudly.

"Would it do any good for me not to encourage this conversation?"

"Nope. I hate to see effort wasted, and since I came up with the system, you've got to hear it."

"I've listened to worse, I suppose," Dewey said with a weak smile.

"Here goes. First, you have boney butts. They're the kind that go straight down - no shape at all. Second, there are bubble butts. They pooch out in the back but don't have much shape on the sides. Third, we have the walrus ass. They're the worst kind and don't come in any particular shape. All walrus asses are big, real big. Bottle butts are the fourth kind, and they're the ones that swing out abruptly at the waistline and go straight down - like a bottle. The fifth type is the pear ass. They're the droopy kind because they sag at the bottom. Most women with pear asses have big thighs. Finally, there's the apple ass - the best kind. Apple asses have smooth lines that run down into two well rounded halves at the bottom. Apple-assed women usually have small waists and firm thighs."

"How educational."

"See, I'll show you," I said eagerly, not at all put off by Dewey's apparent lack of interest. "Here comes a gal with an apple ass. See how it has good shape from all angles? Can you see that?"

"I suppose so. She has a very nice shape," he said as the young woman walked by.

"Here comes a bottle butt."

"Can we go into the classroom now?" Dewey asked. He punched me as Woody shuffled past us and into his classroom.

"We might as well. Everyone else is going in. I'd still rather talk about asses than listen to Woody lecture."

We stood in the back of the room for a short time and then sat in a couple of vacant chairs near the front of the class. Woody started his lecture on chemical imbalances and emotional stability, speaking slowly and distinctly as he read from a journal. The material he read was highly technical stuff from a recent research project at the UCLA Medical Center, but he paused occasionally to throw in an observation of his own. I looked at the class of about a dozen students to see if they were getting any of the material. Woody wasn't having one of his better days, and it showed on their faces. They looked more disinterested than he did, and some looked lost and out of place. A few looked completely stupid.

"I don't see how he does it," I said.

"Does what?"

"Stands there and lectures to a bunch of . . . a bunch of . . . dunces. Look at them. Have you ever seen anything like it? They look too stupid to learn their ABC's, much less what Woody's talking about."

"They don't look too energetic," Dewey said.

"Granted, Woody's not having a good day himself, but that's no excuse for the class being such a bunch of deadheads. Not a single question has been asked, almost a third of them are sitting there slack-jawed and dull-eyed, and a couple of them are asleep. That guy in the green shirt, the one on the third row, has his eyes glued to the gal's ass sitting in front of him. At least there's some motivation behind his daydreaming. Woody usually tries to entertain them, tries to keep them alert and listening, but he's having an off day. The material is boring, so the class just sits there like a bunch of retardates. Woody can't be getting much from trying to teach this bunch of lethargic jerk-offs," I said.

"Like I said earlier, times have changed. It seems that these kids aren't as excited about college as we were some years ago. Back then, they seemed to have felt fortunate to have been accepted to college and were trying to make the best of the opportunity."

"Yeah, I remember. I started college at Texas A&M in 1958 and was glad to be there. It wasn't that easy to get in back then, and you had to study to stay in college. Making good grades took even more study. But colleges take almost anything now, particularly small schools like WKSU. I think they must use the warm body theory, which means: if it's alive and breathes, let it in. No wonder academic standards are down. This is what you get now," I said, passing my hand over the class.

"Are they that much worse than they used to be? These kids have had more advantages than former generations. They've had high tech equipment to work with and greater access to information than any generation in the history of the world. They grew up in the computer age."

"Yeah, but standards have changed over the years. We had to pass an English proficiency test to graduate, and the B.A. degree required six hours of English Lit. Not now, though. These kids are lucky to get through six hours of basic English. We had to take twelve hours of foreign language, but that's long gone too."

"Really?"

"Yep, and it gets worse. We sweated it out in zoology, botany, and college algebra. Now they take general biology and general education math. They've got remedial classes in English and math, and there's no minimum standard on the entrance exams. National scores on the ACT exam are down, and they take kids who made less than ten on the ACT here at WKSU. A monkey with a felt tipped pen could make ten on the ACT."

"You're depressing me," Dewey said.

"There's less respect for teachers in this day and age. Discipline is more of a problem now, and that's partly due to the loss of respect. I blame that on the system. We got into trouble now and then when I was at A&M, but we respected authority. The professor was king in the classroom, and students respected traditions. You don't see much of that anymore, and I'm not sure that WKSU is much different from other schools across the country."

"What caused the loss of standards? What happened to higher education?"

"A lot of things caused it, but one big reason is that society puts more pressure on kids to get an education, so more of them try for a college degree. As our society changes from a goods oriented society to a service oriented society, from an industrial economy to a high tech economy, there's less chance for kids to earn a living without a degree now. And, the educational system itself has changed. The liberalism of the sixties brought about changes in attitudes, directions, and curriculums. All those civil rights reforms broke down barriers that kept minority groups out of college, and the college kids of today are a different breed from those of twenty-five years ago."

"What does Woody think about this?"

"It concerns him enough to have caused some changes in him. He's not as gung ho as he was ten years ago. Losing some of his zip could've been caused by his heavy drinking, but teaching poorer students might have something to do with it. He really hasn't mellowed that much, though. Look at the size of this class; scarcely a dozen kids. The economics class down the hall has fifty kids in it because the old fart who teaches it is too simple minded to make it difficult. A lot of students are looking for a pud class, a crip course, where grades are easy. Woody's classes take some study."

"At least Woody is adjusting, and that's important in any business," Dewey said.

"Yeah, he's adjusted some, but it hasn't been easy for him. He may have lightened up on the academic level, but he's still a strict disciplinarian. Notice how quiet this class is," I said, motioning with my head toward the class.

"Yes, and some of them are restless. It's not easy to keep restless people quiet."

"They're afraid of him. Woody, put plainly, doesn't put up with much. He demands respect in the classroom, and the students don't often challenge him. One will try him every now and then, particularly if it's early in the semester, but they learn right quick that Woody's the master of his classroom."

"Perhaps he's too strict."

"Maybe, but at least he keeps them quiet while he's lecturing, and I think most of the students enjoy his lectures. Woody makes it tough on himself because he lives a double life. He enjoys the reputation around campus of being a hard-ass, but he's also well known for his off campus activities. The kids see him off campus quite a bit, and you know what that means. Some of these college kids haunt the same bars that Woody hangs out in. He even drinks and socializes with the kids on occasion, and that may give some of them the wrong idea. Sometimes he sits down at a table with them, buys a round of drinks, talks for a while, and plays the part of a good old boy. His barroom personality is a lot different from his professor personality. Woody probably thinks he needs to keep up the strict classroom discipline to keep the kids from taking advantage of him."

"I understand that, but it's sad that many of his students never see him anywhere but in the classroom. They never see the friendly side of him, just the strict, rigid Woody."

"I reckon that's the price he pays," I said and shrugged.

"The students are paying a big price for never seeing Woody's soft side. He's like a favorite candy I used to eat as a kid. I can't recall the name, but it was hard on the outside but gooey in the middle.

The best part was the gooey part, but you had to spend a lot of time gnawing away at the hard shell to get to it."

"Let's not forget what we're talking about here. This is Woody Pickens, and the gooey part of him doesn't show up until he's had quite a bit to drink. His students don't need to see him that way."

"That's also sad because it doesn't have to be that way," Dewey said.

"I know that, but I don't think he does. He hardly ever lets anyone see what he's really like, particularly his students. He's a very private man, in many ways, and not many people get close to him."

"Withdrawal is a classic symptom of alcoholism," Dewey said.

"Come on, Dewey. It's got to be more than that. He's not always withdrawn, and he's probably been a private person all of his life," I said.

"Perhaps the tendency to be a private person was already there, but alcohol is the culprit. It allows him to deal with his moods to some degree, and even though it may not have been the blame for his problems, it made some worse and even created some."

"What you're saying is that drinking turned Woody into an asshole. Maybe he was just born an asshole," I suggested.

"No one is born an . . . an . . . asshole," Dewey said, barely choking out the word. "Woody uses alcohol to get to where he wants to go."

"I don't follow you."

"Woody is a sensitive guy, wouldn't you agree?"

"Yeah, I reckon he is."

"And he's far above average in intelligence and ability. He's a gifted guy, in other words."

"Yep."

"Do you think he's the only one who knows that?" Dewey asked.

"I'm not so sure he knows."

"Oh, he knows. Believe me, he knows," Dewey said, nodding and squinting wisely.

"So he knows. So what?"

"Do you think other people recognize Woody's superior intellect and ability?"

"Yeah, I think so."

"How do they react? How do they feel about Woody?"

"Some folks see him as an oddball egghead. They probably think he's too smart for his own good. Just for the record, I think he's too smart for his own good," I said.

"Somehow, I thought you would. You also believe, most probably, that there's hardly a hair's breadth between genius and insanity."

"I've heard the saying but never thought much about it. I don't think there's much truth to it."

"That's good because it's a propagation of absurdity invented by those who are less gifted than people with superior intelligence. Perhaps they are green with envy or fearful and are more than willing to sit in judgment from their seats of mediocrity. It's a myth of the common man, created to perpetuate mediocrity. Most psychological studies indicate that people of above average intelligence suffer less from frustration than do their less fortunate counterparts. This indicates to me that advanced intelligence carries with it the ability to deal with living problems. There's no evidence at all to support the premise that high intelligence and insanity are bedfellows."

"I knew that," I said.

"Then you must also know that society brings enormous pressure to bear on people who do not conform to standards and norms, many of them reflective of mediocrity. Those who exhibit a particular genius, or a specific aptitude to perform at a level higher than the average, will run headlong into a wall of societal resistance. Since gifted people are a very small minority of the population, they are often ridiculed and mistreated. Visualize, if you would, the popularity of classical music. How many people in our society are really attracted to Mozart, Bach, Stravinsky and the like?" Dewey asked.

"Not too many, I reckon."

"Since you like quotes so well, here's another for you. 'When a true genius appears in the world you may know him by this sign, that the dunces are all in confederacy against him.' Swift said that."

"Yeah, but he was pissed because nobody wanted to buy his canned beef," I said.

"We're talking about different Swifts." Dewey looked a bit irritated, but he knew I was joking and went ahead making his point.

"There are plenty of good old boys and gals around who ridicule classical music, for instance. They have allowed their lack of education and sophistication to get the best of them, so they laud Hank Williams and poke fun at Beethoven or Stravinsky. What they can't understand or appreciate, they choose to ridicule, alienate, or perhaps even kill. It isn't common enough for them." Dewey almost sneered as he talked, and that wasn't like him. I'd never heard him be so critical of anyone, other than me, of course.

"Does that mean I'm going to have to quit listening to Merle Haggard to be intellectual?" I asked.

"Not at all. Perhaps a person who enjoys only classical music is as bad off as the Willie Nelson purist."

"Thank God! I'm sure common enough to really love Merle. I like Willie too," I admitted.

"I hate country music," Dewey said and rolled his eyes.

"Snob."

"I know," Dewey said, almost inaudibly.

"Maybe you need more education on the subject, and as luck would have it, I'm just the man to free you from your shackles of ignorance," I said and grinned annoyingly.

Dewey frowned and then pressed the back of his hand to his forehead. "Me and my big mouth."

"Quit complaining. It'll be fun. In no time at all you'll be an expert. I'll even show you how the radio works," I said, knowing full well that I dangled the right bait in front of him.

"I would like to learn how to use the radio, but let's not get in a big hurry," Dewey said. "Besides, we have more important business to attend to. My country music education can wait."

"But what about Hank Williams, Ernest Tubb, Loretta Lynn, and Little Jimmy Dickens? What about Charlie Pride, Tanya Tucker, and Larry Gatlin? What about Blue Grass, Texas Swing, and . . . ?

"Larry Gatlin?" Dewey asked.

"Yeah, he's country. So is Glen Campbell, Ed Bruce, Michael Martin Murphy, Dan Seals, Gary Morris, and . . . ?

"Gary Morris? Didn't he sing 'Wind beneath my Wings'?"

"Yep."

"I like that. I also like some of Larry Gatlin's music," Dewey said.

"Well, maybe you're not as big a snob as you thought. I like some classical music, but not all of it, and I refuse to think of myself as unsophisticated just because someone wrote a bad piece of classical music. Sometimes, it's simply a matter of personal taste, you know," I said.

"That's true, but when someone dismisses all classical music as bunk, that shows a lack of proper education. Your point about the country music, therefore, is well made, and I must admit, well taken."

"How about Johnny Cash?" I asked.

"It's not that well taken."

"But he's produced some classics in the field of country music," I said.

"Give me a break. I've had all the country tutoring I can stand for one day. Get back to the original subject, please."

"I forgot what it was."

"We were talking about how most people are intolerant of above average people."

"I was listening; you were talking," I said. "You were making a point about classical music and how all of us rednecks don't like it because we're ignorant."

"You have such a talent at phraseology. Perhaps you should talk," Dewey said, wrinkling his brow.

"Naw, I like listening to you better. Go ahead."

"Well, leaving classical music aside, any number of examples can be useful when it comes to commonness. Television programming is rampant with shows that are tasteless and shallow. The food most people eat, the art they like, if you could call it art, the entertainment they choose, and even their religious preferences are as common as dirt. The average TV watcher will go out of their way to see a soap opera but can't be coerced into watching a real opera on educational television. They might eat shrimp but will scoff at anyone who eats snails. They will drive hundreds of miles to go to football games, boxing and wrestling matches, and auto races, but they won't walk across the street to see a fine art exhibition. They even seek out a church on Sundays that fits their crude, fundamentalist lifestyles. The very same person who screams for blood at a fight or football game on Saturday night might be in church on Sunday morning railing against and perhaps even being willing to persecute those who disagree with him. Their common pursuits, their mediocrities, are even rooted in their religion, and I find that depressing and dangerous," Dewey said, then slumped forward as if he were exhausted.

Dewey's remarks had been delivered in sadness and resignation, but not in anger and bitterness. I waited until he perked up before pursuing the matter further. "So, a guy like Woody Pickens is caught in a struggle between the forces of the commonplace and a drive to rise above the average. He doesn't know whether to lag behind or try to live up to some of his abilities."

"Exactly."

"Who wins?" I asked.

"Too early to tell," Dewey said, smiling slightly. "The contest isn't over."

"I hate to say it, but it looks like the good old boy side of Woody is ahead right now. Sometimes he's so average I can't even stand him myself. To be real truthful, I don't know which side of him I like the best - the scholar or the good old boy."

"That's because the real Woody never comes through either side. When he's scholarly and acting like an intellectual, he's too arrogant, too elitist. When he's common, he takes it too far."

"Yeah, he can't even screw up in an average fashion."

"Woody seems determined to cover up his sensitive, intellectual nature. He probably sees it as a weakness and would like to keep it hidden, or under control. He wants people to recognize his intellect, see that he's above average, but he doesn't want to be ridiculed for it. So he covers it up most of the time, and he usually does it with his good old boy act."

"Why is that? Why not just be Woody and let everybody else go take a flying fuck at a rolling donut?"

"Why do you do it?" Dewey asked.

"Huh?"

"Why do you put on the good old boy act?"

"I give up. Maybe I'm a victim of my Texas upbringing," I said.

"Poppycock."

"Maybe I'm just a filthy-mouthed, hard-peckered old angel with tarnished wings."

"More poppycock, but it's possible."

"A reincarnated pimp from Juarez?"

"Stop it, and answer the question."

"I reckon I'm influenced by some of the same things that have affected Woody," I said after a few moments of thought. "Maybe, just maybe, I'm afraid of getting to be too good. Maybe I feel guilty about being more fortunate than others. Maybe I'm afraid of reaching my potential because I might not like it once I got there, or maybe I'm just afraid I can't make it. Maybe I just need to be accepted."

"Maybe," Dewey replied, lifting his eyebrows haughtily as if he'd just won the debate. Maybe he had. I wanted to keep talking, but Dewey suddenly lost interest in the conversation. His eyes were fixed on a young woman sitting on the second row, directly in front of Woody. She seemed more alert now that Woody had moved around his lectern and was standing directly in front of her. He did that a lot, especially in his smaller classes. The woman was smiling now, taking in every word.

"She's a psychology major. I've seen her in several of Woody's classes before. She's easy to remember because she's a classic apple ass. She must like Woody's classes."

"Is that all she likes?" Dewey sounded a little suspicious.

"Yeah, I think so."

"I hate to ask, but has Woody ever fooled around with one of his students?"

"Never. Not since I've been around, at least. The gals who are prone to go after professors usually leave Woody alone because he doesn't give them any encouragement."

"But this woman looks to be in her late twenties, maybe early thirties. Woody might be more interested in her. She's very pretty," Dewey said. He didn't need to point that out to me. I seldom ever missed a pretty face, particularly one that was attached to a body like that gal had.

"I wouldn't worry much about it. Woody's not about to crap in his own nest. He may be a drunk, but he's too slick to mess around with a student," I said.

"That's comforting," Dewey said.

"Yeah, Woody likes college students, but he has a hard time relating to them. Like most of the other folks around here, they bore him. That makes sense, I reckon, because these kids are mostly from this part of the country. They were raised by boring people, and maybe it's true that boring people begat boring people. If he happens to run across them in a bar somewhere, he'll drink with them, but he usually keeps his distance. He probably sees them as being rank amateurs when it comes to drinking. Woody has a hard time jumping the generation gap. He's not interested in what holds a college kid's attention, and although he tries to talk to them, they seem to run out of things to talk about before long."

"Woody might fare better at a larger university. Perhaps he should be working with students who are more enthusiastic and mature."

"Who said students are larger universities were any better? From what I hear and read, they're not much different than they are right here," I said.

"But large universities have graduate schools. Woody might make an excellent graduate professor," Dewey said.

"Maybe, but I think he likes a low pressure job like this better than he would the higher pressure of a large university. Woody's a teacher, not a researcher and writer. There's no pressure here, no publish-or-perish mandate, and even though he might do better with kids at the larger school, he'd rather be left alone to teach. The kids out here in western Kansas may not be demanding or inspiring, but they're good kids. Most of them are easy to get along with. Discipline isn't much of a problem here."

Woody dismissed class before Dewey could respond, and I was relieved because the good looking, apple-assed gal from the second row had stood up, totally destroying my concentration. We followed her into the hallway, with me giving Dewey a few more tips on the fine are of butt gazing. We were half way down the hall when Constance Dougherty, the Hindenburg herself, charged around a corner and came storming down the hall. She was so fat it took a width of six feet for her to walk. Her face was puckered up like she'd been sucking a green persimmon, and the students in the hallway quickly cleared a path for her. Their moving out of the way like that reminded me of the parting of the Red Sea. Of course, I've never seen the Red Sea or any other sea part, but the way the students scattered as she plowed through them gave me a vision of what it must've looked like.

"Here comes the Hindenburg. Looks like she's on another tear. The pantie-packers must've got her again last night."

"She was at the costume party, wasn't she?" Dewey asked.

"Yeah, she was, come to think of it. They must've got her walking home from the party. She lives in faculty housing, in an apartment near the girl's dorm."

"If she was worried about being attacked, why did she walk home? Why didn't she drive?"

"You tell me. Maybe she likes it," I said with a grin.

"Then why does she protest so much?"

"You know what they say, don't you? A bit dog hollers. Perhaps she protestith too much?" I slapped Dewey on the back and winked to show that I knew a few quotes too, even if I did have trouble remembering the exact quote or who said it. Dewey smiled anyway.

"Dewey?" I asked as I guided him toward the parking lot.

"What?"

"Who's Stravinsky?"

CHAPTER 15
Higher Ed's

I could tell from the way they discussed it at coffee the next morning that Woody was headed for another drunk. Ten o'clock coffee at WKSU was held at the faculty lounge in the student union building. The union, officially marked as the WKSU Student Union by the large sign out front, was unofficially called "Toad Hall" by almost everyone, after the school horny toad school mascot, of course. Gathered at coffee this particular morning were Woody, Duncan Hightower, Reese McDonald, Bob Tubbs, Don Ricks, Ray Wallace, and Nightmare Hawkins. Woody you know, of course. Duncan Hightower, you may remember, was Woody's good buddy from the History Department. Reese McDonald was the Financial Aids Director and Bob Tubbs was the Sports Information Director, and they were thick as thieves with each other. Both, by the way, were assholes. Don Ricks taught geography, Ray Wallace taught in the business department, and Ben "Nightmare" Hawkins was a physical education instructor.

The plans being made were to take off early that afternoon and head over to Cottonwood, a town just down the road from Forest City. The attraction in cottonwood was a bar called Higher Ed's. The place got its name from its owner - Edward Bailey, a retired basketball coach. The bar, mostly a sports bar drinking and eating establishment, was a favorite hangout for jock types, farmers, ranchers, and about anyone else, except students. Ed Bailey was a tall man, so tall that folks had started calling him Higher Ed. His being a college man helped with the nickname, of course. He'd been a highly successful basketball coach, and he was well liked throughout the communities of Forest City and Cottonwood.

I didn't necessarily like the company Woody was keeping. Like I said before, McDonald and Tubbs were jerks, and I didn't like them on general principles. I did like Duncan Highsmith, but you'd have to work at not liking him. He was just an all-around nice guy - soft spoken and generous and just a delight to be around, even when he was drunk. Don Ricks and Ray Wallace, the geographer and the business guy, were all right, but they had a tendency to be argumentative. Ricks, for instance, always had to start a discussion on politics - a subject he knew very little about. Wallace had opinions on everything, and they usually ended up getting testy over some piddling point that didn't amount to a hill of beans. Nightmare Hawkins was too stupid to argue about anything, but he drank like a fish. He was also a big time mooch. He liked Woody because he'd spring for drinks, and that irritated me.

I did, however, like Cottonwood, a nice town of about two thousand people. At first glance, one might wonder why Ed Bailey had chosen Cottonwood as home to his sports bar, but there were reasons. He grew up there, for one thing, and Cottonwood was the kind of place where a nice establishment could thrive. Woody, like lots of other people, liked Ed Bailey and trekked over to Cottonwood several times a month on average to drink and visit with him. He didn't usually get really soused there because Ed frowned on that sort of thing. Drinkers like Woody, though, don't need a place to settle down for a big drunk; they just need a good place to get started on one.

If you appreciate small towns, cottonwood had a lot of charm. The people there were country friendly and eager to please, and the place was just downright attractive. Since it didn't have feedlots and other commercial interests sucking the blood out of it, Cottonwood looked clean and protected and hospitable. It had a main street where all the businesses were located, and some of the nicer businesses, like offices for doctors and lawyers and accountants, were located there instead of in Forest City. I thought it strange that Cottonwood was where most of the doctors in the area lived, but the biggest hospital was in Forest City. Once you saw what a nice town Cottonwood was, though, you understood why doctors chose to live there. The town was quaint in an old fashioned way with all sorts of little shops of one kind or another.

Higher Ed's was a great place to study the sociological breakdown of the western Kansas. The place was almost always busy, and all sorts of people came there. Since we'd been talking about Chinese elms and lemon theory and just people in general, I wanted Dewey to see it. As soon as plans by the coffee crowd to go there had

been made, I went looking for him to lay out the afternoon's agenda.
I found him in the museum.

"Ah, there you are. Culturing yourself?" I asked.

"This is fantastic. Look at all these artifacts," he said, pointing
at a glass encased display of Indian arrowheads.

"Yeah, I used to come here quite a bit. Museums have always
interested me."

"Really?"

"Yeah, really. I like cowboy museums."

"Figures."

"Hey, Dewey! If you're going to understand these people and
how they affect our mark, then you're going to have to get used to
cowboys," I said.

"I know Woody hangs around with them occasionally, but I
don't see how . . ."

I cut him off because I could see that he was headed in the
wrong direction. Our boy needed straightening out, and right then
was as good a time as any. "Just hold your horses, Dewey. I'm fixing
to enlighten you."

"Fixing to? What kind of talk is that?" Dewey asked, screwing
his face into a puckered, pious look.

"Cowboy talk, and you'd better get used to it. Whether or not
it fits your lofty druthers about culture, it is a culture nonetheless,
and it dominates this part of the world. Not all of the people who live
here are cowboys, but the cowboy culture dominates. What I'm
talking about here goes way beyond loving horses and cows. I'm
talking about a way of life."

"I know what you're talking about, but I'm not sure I'm ready
to accept it as a dominant culture."

"You can call it anything you want to, but it's a cowboy
culture. Call it the culture of the prairie, or the high plains culture, or
western culture, but it all amounts to the same thing."

"Just because cowboys settled this country doesn't mean their
culture is dominant, does it?" he asked, looking like he was ready for
more information.

"They didn't settle this country. Squatters and railroad men
and merchants and people like that were the real settlers. Cowboys
moved around too much to settle anything, and they just weren't

settlers by nature. They might've been among the first people in here, but they didn't lay claim to anything."

"Then how did their culture come to dominate?"

"Well, it's a thought process as much as anything, I reckon. Cow men were attracted to this country because of the grazing prospects, and they stayed here for quite a while, at least long enough to set the tone of things to come as far as culture is concerned. Farmers came, as did the railroads and others interested in speculation, and over the years, most of the genuine cowboys got pushed out. Still, a style of living had been established, and it revolved around cows and cowboys. What is here now is a remnant of that, and even though it's different from the way they lived back then, some things remain," I said.

"Like what?"

"Well, like the way the folks around here cling to customs and traditions. That's all a part of the cowboy way of life. These folks are very conservative in an individualist sort of way. Cowboys had to depend upon themselves and their rather tight knit communities, and so do these people. What irritates me is how they seem to mistake individualism for conservatism, and they aren't necessarily the same things. Like I said before, they're good folks, but they're stubborn individualists."

"You get the good with the bad," Dewey said, rubbing his chin like he was mulling over what I'd just said. I took some comfort in at least putting his muse to work.

"Yeah, you sure do."

"I'd like to know more."

"Well, what you see with your own eyes may be the best teacher, so we'll go on a little sociological excursion this afternoon," I said, wiggling my eyebrows.

"Oh, good! Where?"

"To a bar over in Cottonwood."

"A bar? I've already been to a bar," Dewey said, looking disappointed.

"Not like this one you haven't. This one has everything you need to see to understand the cowboy culture."

"Really?"

"Yes, really."

"When do we go?"

"As soon as Woody and his friends get moving around sometime early this afternoon. I heard them making plans at coffee not long ago. I suppose they'll go early this afternoon. Woody usually goes to Higher Ed's several times a month, but it's been quite a while since his last visit," I said.

"Higher Ed's?"

"That's the name of the joint. I'll explain it to you later," I said, motioning for him to follow.

We cracked open the magic box and started digging around for some grub. To my dismay, Dewey's vittles were on the menu that day - asparagus casserole and baked chicken. We seemed to be getting on an every other day rotation of foods, and I dreaded the Dewey days. I ate it, though, and without complaint. We'd just finished when I looked up and saw Roosevelt coming down the street in his big Lincoln. He was pulling a small travel trailer.

Custodians working in a separate dimension from the earthly dimension see things differently from the way mortals see them. We can see everything the mortal sees, of course, but we see other things. I could see Dewey and he could see me, and the two of us saw everything else of an earthly nature the same as anyone else would. But when something unseen by a mortal comes along, a custodian sees it as an object with a slight enhancement in color. It looks vaguely illuminated, like it has a fine outline around it. When I looked at Dewey, for instance, he looked slightly brighter, and he saw me the same way. When Roosevelt drove up, he knew immediately that someone in our own dimension had arrived. He'd never before met Roosevelt, but he knew something was up. He did a double take and then looked at me.

"What and who is that?"

"Just guessing, I'd say that's our new trailer, and the guy driving the Lincoln is our boss, Roosevelt Watson," I said, grinning like a politician at an election rally. Seeing the trailer told me that I'd be keeping my Chevy.

"That's our trailer?"

"Our very own."

"It's . . . it's . . . a cracker box," he stammered.

"Aw, hell, Dewey! What do we need a big trailer for?"

"I hate small places."

"Why, you're small," I said, walking to the curb to await Roosevelt's arrival.

Roosevelt stepped from his car looking like he'd been on a camping trip. I'd known the man for ten years, and he'd always been wearing the same thing whenever we'd had occasion to meet. His usual attire was black suit and shined black shoes with a white shirt and a red tie and no hat. This time, though, he was wearing walking shorts, a flowered Hawaiian shirt, tennis shoes, sunshades, and a baseball cap, which made him look like King Kong on vacation at the beach. I didn't laugh or poke fun at him, though. I was too tickled to see the trailer to mess things up.

"Boy, are you a sight for sore eyes," I said, instantly wishing I could suck back the words. Nobody in their right mind calls a fellow like Roosevelt a boy. Luckily for me, he either missed it or decided to let it pass.

"I have your trailer," he said, smiling.

"So I see. Thanks a bunch. It looks like just the trick."

"Is this Dewey?" he asked, offering his hand. Dewey, as usual, was right on my heels.

"Excuse my lack of manners, and yes this is Dewey Davisson. Dewey, this is Roosevelt Watson," I said, stepping aside.

They shook hands, and I saw Dewey wince as they did. Anybody shaking hands with Roosevelt for the first time had a surprise coming. The man had the grip of a dragline. Dewey managed a smile and then true to character registered his first complaint. "I was hoping for a bigger trailer."

Roosevelt stared harshly at him for a moment, then smiled and said, "Well, this is what we had available. A custodian up in Wyoming had it, but he got transferred to Alaska. It came free, and I latched onto it at the transportation office."

"It'll be just fine for us," I said quickly.

"Does it have two full beds?" Dewey asked. I felt like kicking him.

"It makes into two beds," Roosevelt said.

"Say, what happened to the guy in Wyoming? Why'd he get transferred?" I asked, trying to change the subject.

"He went out of bounds on his mark. I don't know the entire story because he's not in my jurisdiction, but it must've been pretty bad. He got an Eskimo this time," he said, trying hard not to smile.

"That's too bad," I said.

"Yes, it is, and maybe you should keep that in mind."

I knew Roosevelt had just thrown out a mild threat, but I didn't follow up on it. He must've hoped I would because he waited for a few moments before asking his next question. "So, how is your new partner doing?"

"Oh, he's doing very well."

"No problems at all?"

"Well, he's had a little trouble holding his I/I mode, but he'll toughen up to it before long," I said, trying to shrug it off.

"Yes, I heard about that," Roosevelt said. Uh oh, I thought. Here it comes.

"But it only happened a few times. How could you know about it?" Dewey asked. Now I really felt like kicking his ass.

"I heard about the incident at Howard Hall with Tonya Heinz," Roosevelt said, looking back and forth at us.

"Is that her last name - Heinz?" Dewey asked. I couldn't help it and reached out and whacked him with the back of my hand. He gave me a critical glance and then looked back at Roosevelt.

"Yes, that's her name, and that was a sorry spectacle you caused," Roosevelt said, giving Dewey his make-Hercules-piss-his-pants look. From the look on Dewey's face, I thought he might really piss his pants, even though we didn't do that anymore. I decided to defend him.

"It wasn't his fault."

"I already surmised as much," Roosevelt said, shifting his attention to me, then added, "And what about the incident at the church? Did you cause that too?"

"You mean the door opening and slamming? Well, yeah, I reckon I caused that too," I said.

"I can't let him take the blame for this. I lost my composure," Dewey said, looking wan.

"You need to get these things straightened out. We can't have this sort of shoddy work," Roosevelt said, pointing his banana sized finger back and forth at us.

"Just how the hell did you know about all this?" I asked.

"The Heinz girl is under protection. Her custodian reported it," Roosevelt said, sighing wearily.

"The dirty sonofabitch," I said. That brought another bad scowl from Roosevelt, but I didn't care.

"He was just doing his job."

"I've been on this job for over fourteen years, and I've never gone soft on another custodian. I'd rather eat buzzard shit," I said, really pissed now.

"Watch your mouth," Roosevelt said, but it was too late. With me, there's a direct correlation between my level of temperament and what comes out of my mouth, and that's often not to my benefit.

"And what the hell's wrong with the Central Office? Is everybody down here being guarded a loser? That Tonya gal is a conniving little bitch who'd screw a troll if she thought it would get what she wanted. And she's being guarded?" I asked.

"This trailer could go back the same way it came, and so could that '57 Chevy of yours," Roosevelt said, and regardless of how pissed off I was, that shut me up.

After a few minutes of uneasy silence, Roosevelt became more conciliatory. "Look, I know there's been some tenseness with breaking in a new partner, and all I'm saying is that you fellows need to watch you P's and Q's and little better. The Central Office is not overly concerned about what's happened, but I was asked to counsel you about it. I've done that, so let's forget about it."

"I think that's a grand idea," Dewey said enthusiastically.

"Yeah, me too," I said.

Roosevelt stayed around for another hour, and the visit improved considerably after that. Dewey crawled around in the trailer for a while, checking out every nook and cranny of it. Dewey, you might've noticed, was a whole shebang kind of guy. He didn't miss many details in anything, and when he examined something, he examined the entire kit and caboodle. With Roosevelt's visit and all, time crept up on us in a hurry, and before I realized the time had come, I saw Woody drive by with Duncan Highsmith and a couple of other guys headed for Cottonwood. Roosevelt saw them too, and we were excused at that point. Roosevelt left saying he'd park the trailer near Woody's house.

Dewey and I jumped into the Chevy and headed for Cottonwood. Since we could drive as fast as we wanted, I caught up with Woody and his comrades well before they arrived at Higher Ed's. Just as we arrived, Dewey looked at me and asked, "Can other custodians really see what we're doing?"

"No, but they can see what happens around their own mark. They couldn't see us because they're not in our dimension, but our marks work in the same earthly dimension, and they can see that. About the only thing that meddling custodian saw at Howard Hall were chairs and desks moving, and paint flying around, and lights coming on, but that was enough for him to know that something was going on. If I'm guessing, Tonya Heinz has a female custodian on her tail," I said, winking at him.

"I think you may be right," Dewey said, then sniggered.

"Why, Dewey! You usually take offense at statements like that."

"Well, a statement is only offensive when it has no basis in fact, but what you said could be true, and there could be some truth to what you said. Besides, I'm too proud of you right now to be testy with you. Until now, I've always thought your growl was worse than your bite, but you really stood up to Roosevelt. You're very brave."

"Yeah, I'm brave to the point of being stupid sometimes. I almost screwed up the trailer deal, and while we're in the congratulatory mood, I'd like to say that I appreciate your trying to take the blame for the screw ups we've had."

"Think nothing of it. Now can we go inside and observe culture at its finest?" he asked.

"You bet! There's nothing like watching a bunch of farmers and cowboys drink imported beer. Follow me, pilgrim," I said, then screwed my hat down on my head and stalked into the bar using my best John Wayne imitation. Dewey giggled and followed.

I spent the next two hours pointing out patrons and describing as best I could what they were and how they affected the culture of the high plains. Higher Ed's, as usual, was a buffet of people ranging from bankers and doctors down to feedlot cowboys and cattle truck drivers, and like always, they clumped into groups around tables where they could be easily identified and discussed. I started with a section where a group of local merchants had gathered and explained how they affected and were affected by the country they lived in. Later on, a group of cowboys came in and settled into a group around the pool tables. Dewey watched them all intently, studying their manners and conversations and movements. He asked very few question, either during the time in the bar or afterward. I took that to say his concerns about my premise of a cowboy culture were put to rest, at least to some degree.

Driving home later that evening, I thought about telling Dewey that my concept of a cowboy culture could be different from another observer's outlook on it. Cowboys and their culture mean different things to different people, and I felt like telling him that. I decided, though, that he probably already understood that and let it lie. No use in beating a dead horse, you know, and in some regards, I'd already beat that particular carcass enough. I was sure that Dewey also understood that more than just the local culture affected our mark. What we knew for sure was that Woody Pickens was an alcoholic, a drunk, and figuring out what had brought him down to that was not the real problem at hand. Even then, both of us knew that identification of a problem is the first step in doing something about it, and we already knew what the problem was. I'd been dogging Woody for a long time, and one persistent question still came to mind. Did Woody know?

CHAPTER 16
Goofy Golf

Dewey's tendency to lose his cool had been coming less often now that he'd been on the job for a while, but all of a sudden he really had his balls in an uproar. The only bad fit he'd had was when I took him to the holly-roller church, but he'd been relatively calm since then. Like everybody, he needed to blow off steam every now and then, and that's exactly what he was doing when I found him standing beside our car, hands on cocked hips with his palms outward, and with the toe of his right foot tapping at about a hundred taps per minute. Put plainly, Dewey looked pissed. The last time I'd seen a look like that was when my mom caught me trying to peek up a little girl's dress in church.

"This is totally inexcusable," he fumed, almost spewing out the words.

"What's got you so bent out of shape?" I asked as I walked to the rear of the car and opened the trunk. I stared at him a few moments and then started scratching around in the trunk for my driver and some balls. "Lighten up a little, Dewey. We'll eat a sandwich, hit a few balls, catch a few rays, and maybe even get in some Z's. These guys will be tied up playing golf all day, and what can they get into on a golf course? We'll just lay back and take it easy for a while. We'll let them play the front nine without us, then fall in and follow them around the back nine."

"They're going to cheat him, those . . . those . . . four-flushers," Dewey said. Apparently, Dewey was too pissed to listen. He pointed and wagged his finger toward the group of men gathered at the tee box on the first hole. Woody and three of his friends from the college were about to tee up.

"They're going to cheat who?" I asked.

"Those men," he said, gesturing with his hand again. "Those men with Woody are going to cheat the blind guy out of some money. I peeked around the trunk lid and looked at Dewey, then at the foursome waiting to tee off - Woody, Duncan Highsmith, Bob Tubbs, and Reese McDonald. Highsmith was the blind man Dewey had been talking about.

"He's not blind, and who's going to cheat him?" I asked.

"He's almost blind, and those men are going to cheat him. They're betting a dollar a hole," Dewey said.

"Holy shit!" I half-shouted. "They could cheat him out of damn near eighteen dollars. It could mean financial ruin for him."

"The money is of no consequence. It's the principle of the thing. Any amount of money is too much when it comes to cheating a blind man in a game of golf. Woody's friend, that Highsmith man, can't see the nose in front of his face, much less a golf ball."

Dewey was right. Duncan Highsmith couldn't see his own feet. The thick glasses he wore barely improved his eyesight enough to get around, and he was painfully slow and clumsy at most things - including golf. I'd seen him play before and considering his handicap - excuse the pun - was amazed at how well he played, which wasn't very well at all compared to other golfers. He never saw where the ball went after he hit it, probably never even saw his putts fall in, but he loved golf and played at every opportunity.

"Listen, Dewey. Duncan might be almost blind, but he's a long way from almost stupid. No one is cheating him out of anything. Besides, Woody wouldn't do that to him, and he wouldn't let anyone else do it. If anything, Woody is overly protective of Duncan. They've been buddies for a dozen years."

"His not being stupid, which agreeably he isn't, is not at issue here. Duncan will allow them to take his money in order to be just one of the boys. He doesn't want to be seen as handicapped, or even different. It's disgraceful for his friends to take his money under those pretenses," Dewey said, still angry enough to bite off his words.

"You've got it wrong, Dewey. They're taking his money because they like him. They know it's important to Duncan to play and pay his losses. What's so wrong with letting him be a regular guy?" I asked.

"Oh, taking his money is big of them, all right, but are they ever big enough to let him win?"

"Duncan doesn't expect to win. He'd be insulted if they let him win. He expects to play, lose, and pay his losses, and that's what makes him happy. They're not cheating him out of anything," I said.

"Perhaps not, but they're most definitely taking advantage of him, and I think it stinks."

"Well, what do you want me to do about it?" I asked.

"I want you to stop defending them."

"I'm not defending them. I've been through this before, and I'm just trying to explain the situation."

"You're just in a good mood because Roosevelt let you keep your Chevy," Dewey said, sniffing indignantly. Dewey was right again. Roosevelt's change of heart concerning my car had put me in a good mood, partly because I got to keep my classic Chevy, but mostly because I just love it when a peon like me wins one against the bureaucratic monster machine.

"Maybe so, but you're in a crabby mood because you don't like your new bedroom," I said.

"Bedroom?" Dewey asked and then sniffed again. "It's a closet, not a bedroom. I'm mildly claustrophobic to begin with, and that so-called bedroom may drive me stark, raving mad."

"The only reason I made you take the front bedroom is because you fit it better than I do," I said. It was a lame excuse, and I knew it.

"Yes, I might fit, if I sawed my legs off." He had a point. His new bedroom was actually the trailer's living room area, which already doubled as the dining space. His bed was one of those pull down types - the kind that pulled down over the couch and table and was jammed in between the cabinets. It looked like a berth on a train.

"I've already told you how to take care of that. Just open the cabinet doors at the foot of your bed. At least you'll be able to straighten your legs."

"I refuse to sleep while my feet keep company with canned beans," Dewey said, almost shouting.

"It was just a suggestion."

"Besides, I know something you don't," Dewey said after a short pause.

"About the bed?"

"No, about the golf game. I heard them talking," he said, his eyes narrowing down to mean slits.

"Heard who talking?"

"Those men," he said, wiggling his finger toward the golfers who had now teed off and were walking down the fairway toward the first hole.

"Who? McDonald and Tubbs?"

"Yes."

"What about?"

"I heard them talking earlier, when they were alone, discussing how they were going to fleece Woody and Duncan out of some money," Dewey said through pursed lips.

"When did you hear this?"

"When they were all in the lounge having a pre-game drink. Woody and Duncan had gone to the bathroom when they talked about their plan to cheat."

"I don't remember that," I said.

"You weren't there. It happened just after you followed the woman wearing tight pants into the locker room. Remember her?" Dewey asked, looking judgmental. He knew I'd remember because she had one of those fine apple asses I admire so much. I couldn't resist the temptation to sneak a better look at, and I had not been disappointed. It took her nearly ten minutes to shower, and I enjoyed every second of it.

"Yeah, I was gone for a few minutes," I said.

"Since when is twenty a few?"

"It was only ten. So, what was said? What makes you think they have a plan?"

"They made plans to set Woody and Duncan up for the kill. They knew Duncan would be willing to play for money, and they likewise knew that Woody would try to protect him by partnering with him. Therefore, they plan to play poorly for the first nine holes and let Woody and Duncan win. Then they plan to increase the bet to a respectable sum and start winning on the back nine. They're counting on Duncan playing his usual miserable game and on Woody getting too drunk to play well after the first nine holes. In short, they plan to take Woody and Duncan to the cleaners to the tune of about a hundred dollars," Dewey said, still squinting.

"The dirty sonsabitches," I said. This time I wasn't joking.

"My sentiments exactly."

I watched the foursome as they approached the first green. Woody had just hit a chip shot, his third on a par four hole, to within a foot of the cup. Duncan was wandering around in the rough to the left of the green, still looking for his third shot. He usually didn't find his ball, and I knew Woody would have to putt out and then help Duncan look for his lost ball. McDonald and Tubbs stayed in their golf cart, drinking beer and whispering back and forth whenever Woody turned his back. Just thinking about a couple of five handicap golfers cheating a drunk and an almost blind man made my blood pressure rise, but seeing it in progress gave me the red ass so bad my ears started burning.

"Have you ever played golf?" I asked, looking directly at Dewey.

"Yes, but I'm not very good," he said.

"You don't have to be good, not the way we're going to play," I said and flashed him a sneaky grin.

"Are you thinking what I think your thinking?"

"Uh huh. We're going to play some creative golf."

"When you get that narrow-eyed, ornery look on your face, I know we're in for some real mischief. What sort of mischief are you up to?"

"Nothing complicated. We're going to fudge a little, that's all. You might say we're going to give our mark some custodial assistance. He's been needing an ego boost lately, and this looks like a good chance to work a some magic."

"Boosting egos and creative golf aren't specified custodial services, are they?" Dewey asked. He looked a bit worried, but I saw some approval in his eyes.

"No, but we're going . . ."

"I know. We're going to fudge," Dewey said, then burped a giggle. He grabbed his mouth as if the giggle had escaped. Then another giggle jumped through his fingers, and he gave up and laughed out loud.

We watched the foursome disappear down the second fairway without following. Since McDonald and Tubbs planned to lose the first nine holes, our assistance wouldn't be needed for quite some time. I can't lie about it; I looked forward to the back nine. McDonald and Tubbs had been on my shit list for a long. I'd never liked either of them. Tubbs was a squatty, middle-aged, know-it-all who served as the sports information director at the university. He played a mean game of golf, but he also had a reputation for padding his score card. He always tried to record at least one shot less than he made on a hole - one of those guys who always forgot to count his last putt. And he was a terrible loser. McDonald, the financial aids director at WKSU and one of Woody's frequent drinking buddies, was a braggart and chickenshit if I've ever seen one. He delighted in putting other guys up to things he didn't have the balls for, unless it came to sneaking around after some split tail. He considered himself a ladies' man - God's special gift to women. I never could figure why Woody liked to occasionally hang out with him.

The day was perfect for golf - one of those rare warm November Saturdays with almost no wind. Our foursome was playing Western Dunes Country Club, a nice course, especially for western Kansas. Eight Forest City golfers, most of them from the university, had driven the seventy-five miles down to Western Dunes early that morning. In dividing into foursomes, Woody and Duncan had been paired with McDonald and Tubbs. It really didn't matter because almost anyone they'd been paired with could have beaten them easily. Woody usually played in the nineties, but Duncan never broke a hundred. Most of the time he scored about a hundred and twenty and lost a dozen balls in the process.

Dewey and I caught up with our foursome on the eighth hole. Woody and Duncan had won six of the first seven holes, and the betting had already gone up to two bucks a hole. Woody had played pretty good, but it had still been a struggle for McDonald and Tubbs to lose six holes. Duncan's normally miserable game had so far completely gone tits up. I checked his score card, and he'd not scored better than a seven on any hole. Woody was already loaning him golf balls - bad news for our side.

"How well does Woody play golf?" Dewey asked as we walked to the eighth green.

"He drives like a fat woman and putts like a lumberjack. He can hit the ball a long way, but God only knows where it's going. He sprays the ball around a lot, but he usually slices. His play around the greens is poor, and his putting is only fair. Woody doesn't play often enough to be very good," I said.

"What about Duncan?"

"Don't ask."

"He can't be that much worse than Woody," Dewey said.

"Are you kidding? He's already shot a round of golf, and they're just on the eighth hole. The last time I saw him play, and that was last summer, he shot a hundred and thirty, lost two dozen balls, hit another golfer in the fairway, and broke two clubs hitting rocks. He's so blind he'll swing at almost anything that looks remotely like a ball. The goofy bastard even swatted a frog once."

"He hit a frog?"

"Yep, a toad frog. The poor frog was just sitting on a mound of dirt when Duncan waddles up with a three wood, winds up, and smacks him. Splattered frog guts and blood all over him. Damndest thing I ever saw in a golf match." I said.

"Yuk," Dewey said, pruning up his face.

"Yep, he swings at more mushrooms and toadstools than golf balls during a round. I think he's on his third set of clubs in three years. Hardly anything in his bag matches, but he can't tell the difference. He even hit a drive down the wrong fairway once. Sometimes he hits it a long way, but mostly he rolls the ball. Considering he sees like a mole, we can't expect much out of him."

"What are we going to do to help them?" Dewey asked, looking concerned.

"There are lots of things we can do."

"Be specific."

"Golf's a crazy game, so we'll just have to play it by ear. We can change the direction of a putt, improve the distance of a drive, or even make sure a putt doesn't fall. We'll just have to wait and see what needs to be done."

"You're really enjoying this, I can tell," Dewey said with a smirk. I smirked back and walked away, wanting to get a closer look at the game.

Woody and Duncan won the eighth hole when Tubbs missed a three foot putt. He went into a swearing act, just to make it look good. He didn't have to do any acting on the ninth hole because Woody played well, making a par. McDonald could've made a putt to tie the hole, but I diverted it with my foot. He frowned at first, then grinned and suggested raising the ante to five bucks a hole. Duncan hesitated but agreed after getting some encouragement from Woody. He and Duncan had gone through a half case of beer by then, and Woody was starting to feel his oats.

On the tenth hole, a 535 yard par five with a dogleg to the right, Woody went first and drove about two hundred yards, just short of a ditch and to the far left of the fairway. Tubbs and McDonald, long hitters, drove over the ditch and to the right of the fairway, in perfect shape to reach the green in two. Duncan hit a real worm burner that hardly got off the ground and went about a 150 yards.

"We can't have that," I said, walking over and giving Duncan's ball a kick just before it stopped rolling. It spurted down the fairway for another twenty-five yards before I caught up with it and kicked it again, sending it to within about twenty feet of Tubb's ball. Tubbs, McDonald, and Woody were still talking about Duncan's drive when they caught up with the golf balls to take their second shot. Duncan wasn't saying much because he had no idea what the ball had done. The other three men agreed, however, that they'd never seen top spin like that before.

Second shots put Tubbs and McDonald near the green, and no one made the putting surface. Duncan topped his ball, but he swung so hard it bounced high and rolled to where I could kick it all the way to the frog hair just off the green. Woody sliced badly and didn't get on until his fourth shot. On in three, Tubbs and McDonald missed long putts for birdies. Duncan had hit a bladed pitching wedge screamer on his third shot, but I flagged it down with my hand and stopped it about twenty-five feet from the cup.

"Come here," I called to Dewey. He walked over and stood beside me. I reached out and poked him in the chest with my index finger.

"Why did you do that?" Dewey asked.

"Just making sure you're in your I/T mode," I said.

"Why?"

"Because I want you standing over the hole when Duncan putts, with your heels together and your toes turned out. Don't move. I'll make sure the ball gets to your feet. When it does, pull your toes together and knock the ball in the hole. Got it?"

"Yes, we're using my feet to fence in the hole so he can't miss, but isn't it going to look obvious?"

"Who cares? Just make sure the ball gets in the cup."

"Whatever you say," Dewey said, shrugged, and went to stand behind the hole, mumbling to himself something about how I didn't have to be such a grouch.

It was in theory a great plan, but it didn't work as well in practice. Duncan walked up to his ball, stood over it less than five seconds, and then gave it a whack that would've made Babe Ruth turn green with envy. It would've gone completely off the green and to the next tee box if I hadn't stuck a foot in its path and headed it toward Dewey's feet. But the ball was still going pretty fast when it got to him - fast enough to hit his left foot and bounce some three feet in the air. Dewey, acting out of impulse, caught the ball in his hand. I couldn't believe it! He just reached out and caught it. He stared down at the ball for an instant with this really dumb look on his face, then threw it down like a hot potato. The ball bounced about four feet out in front of him. Realizing he'd really screwed up now, Dewey dove for the ball and then crawled back to the hole, herding the ball into the cup with his hands. Then he looked up at me, flashed a silly grin, and shrugged.

"It's in the hole," he said, timidly.

"Dammit, Dewey! Why didn't you just pick it up and drop it in. There's no way it could've looked worse," I shouted.

"But you said it didn't matter how obvious it looked, just as long as it went in. Well, it's in the hole," Dewey said, pointing down at the cup.

"But, Dewey, you should . . ."

"I did the best I could," he said indignantly and stomped off. I turned to look at the players, and all eyes were riveted to the cup. Then they stared at each other, speechless and with their mouths open. McDonald had a sickly smile on his face, but Tubbs completely lost it and threw a stomping, cursing tantrum. He was so pissed, in fact, he missed another putt.

From that point on it got easier for us to manipulate the game. I had to apologize to Dewey for barking at him, even though I still thought he'd deserved it, and he did a better job after that. We decided to start alternating working the greens, starting with me on

the eleventh. On my way up the fairway to the green, way up the
fairway I stopped by Tubb's golf cart to check his scorecard. I knew
he'd try to record the wrong score somewhere along the line, but even
Tubbs wasn't stupid enough to try to make up two strokes with a
pencil, especially after he'd made such a big deal about missing his
putt.

The eleventh hole went smoothly for us, since all I had to do
was stop a couple of Tubbs' putts. They appeared to lip out, but that's
was because I had my hand in the cup. Tubbs blew his top again and
broke his putter against a ball washer on the twelfth tee box. Woody
won the hole with a bogie four. Duncan lost two balls in a small pond
and took a ten.

Tubbs' worsening case of chapped ass was hurting his golf
game now, and I helped it along by kicking his ball into a water
hazard on the twelfth fairway. On the way to the green I found
McDonald's ball in the rough and rolled it under a fence and out of
bounds. Dewey knocked down one of Duncan's bladed pitching
wedge screamers. Then he routed his putt into the hole for a bogie to
win another hole. Tubbs tried to record the wrong score for himself
to tie the hole, but I corrected it when he got out to hit a fairway shot
on the thirteenth. He threw a fit when he saw that his score had been
changed to the six he'd really made. He blamed it on McDonald, who
in turn got mad and refused to ride in the cart with him the rest of the
match.

Tubbs and McDonald, now down by about thirty bucks,
proposed increasing the betting to ten dollars a hole. Only six holes
were left in the round, so Woody and Duncan went along with the
increase. Tubbs hit another water hazard on the thirteenth - without
any help from me - then bent his five iron around an elm tree. I
caught him trying to cheat again on his scorecard as they left the
green. I corrected it and lowered McDonald's score from a seven to a
six, touching off a shouting match between him and McDonald. They
would've lost the hole anyway, but I couldn't pass up a chance like
that. Woody won the hole with another bogie.

Woody and Duncan, both fairly drunk now, seemed
determined to lose the fourteenth hole, and we had to work hard to
keep that from happening. Woody's play turned sloppy, but
Duncan's game went completely to hell. It turned out to be a fun hole

for me because Tubbs had to take a stroke penalty when his ball got lost. He held up the game for fifteen minutes looking for it, and when nobody was looking the sneaky bastard dropped another ball and proudly proclaimed that he'd found his lost ball. That irked me, so when he went to his cart to get a club, the second ball disappeared. He dropped another as soon as no one was looking, but it disappeared too. He finally accepted the stroke penalty and dropped a ball in the fairway. Dewey knocked two of McDonald's putts out of the cup, saving the hole for Woody.

The fifteenth hole went smoothly, mostly because Tubbs and McDonald hit out of bounds trying to take a short cut across a ravine on the doglegged fairway. McDonald lost a ball this time when I found another handy chipmunk hole. Woody won the hole with no help from us. I got worried about Woody and Duncan getting too drunk to play, so I let the air out of their cart's tires. The beer was about gone anyway, but I figured the walking would sober them up some. To keep everything on an even keel, I let the air out of tires on both golf carts.

Nobody won the sixteenth, and we let Tubbs and McDonald win the seventeenth handily. Tubbs, encouraged by winning the seventeenth, suggested a big bet for the final hole. He and McDonald were still down about fifty bucks and wanted their money back. Woody and Duncan reluctantly agreed to the bet, partly out of drunkenness and fatigue, and partly because they couldn't do any worse than breaking even.

Tubbs and McDonald hit good drives on the eighteenth, a rather easy 450 yard par five. It had bunkers on three sides of the green but lots of green to shoot at. A decent golfer could play the hole well, but Woody and Duncan weren't good golfers. They started the hole with terrible drives. Duncan's was the worst, traveling only about seventy-five yards. Woody duffed his second shot and barely got it out of the rough half way up the fairway. Duncan hit a tree with his second shot.

"What are we going to do now?" Dewey asked. "We can't hit the ball for them, and at the rate they're going they may never get to the green."

"We'll just have to make sure the other guys don't get the ball in the hole first. Go down to the green and guard the hole," I said.

"Guard the hole? No one is even close to the green."

"Yeah, but I don't want to take a chance on one of them getting lucky and holing out. Put your foot over the hole. That ought to work."

Dewey stared at me for a moment, then nodded and started off for the green. I went to see if I could do anything to improve my team's game. Duncan was back and preparing to hit, so I stopped to watch him. Much to my surprise, he hit a good shot that went close to 250 yards and dead in the middle of the fairway. Woody duffed his third shot, so I decided to concentrate on Duncan and make him the hole winner. Besides, it seemed to be a fitting way to end the game.

I hustled up the fairway just in time to see Tubbs hit a beautiful second shot. I watched as the ball sailed directly toward the flag, so intent on wishing the ball would catch a sand trap that I forgot all about Dewey. At first I thought the shot would come up short, but I suddenly realized it was headed straight for Dewey. Alone on the green, he was standing beside the flag with his foot over the hole, shading his eyes against the sun. I knew he didn't see the ball.

"DEWEY!" I screamed, but too late. He never saw it. He didn't even flinch before it hit him full in the forehead, propelling him backward like he'd been pole axed, still holding the flagpole in his hand. When he hit the ground, rigid and straight as an arrow, he released the fiberglass flagpole. It catapulted skyward, turned several flips, and landed in a bunker just off the green. The ball, having bounced off Dewey's hard head about thirty feet in the air, landed near the flagpole in the soft sand of the bunker. I made a mad dash for Dewey.

He was as still as a statue when I got to his side. A big blue lump had started growing in the middle of his forehead, and he was out cold. I turned and looked down the fairway and saw Tubbs breaking his three wood by furiously pounding the ground. McDonald stood beside him, calmly watching until the head flew off the shaft. Then he casually addressed his ball and stroked it toward the green. All I saw was the swing.

"Damn!" I said, then grabbed Dewey by the arm and pulled him off the green. I turned and started back across the green just in time to see a ball scurrying toward me. McDonald had hit a really good shot. It would've gone past the hole by some twenty feet, but to make sure he didn't have a makeable putt, I kicked the ball into the nearest bunker. Then I walked over, took my finger, and poked it down into the soft sand.

Dewey was starting to stir around by the time I got back to him. The blue lump had really come of age since I'd last seen him and was now a full inch tall and twice as wide. He struggled to sit up but couldn't get his balance well enough to do anything but flounder. I propped him up and supported his back against my knee.

"Wh. . .wha. . .what happened?" he managed to ask.

"Wow, Dewey! You're starting to look like a unicorn," I said. He failed to see the humor in it.

"Oooooh!" he moaned as he rubbed at the lump. "What hit me? What happened?"

"You got conked on the head by a golf ball," I said, then turned around to check out the green. Tubbs and McDonald must've found their sand-trapped balls because I could hear cursing before I turned around. McDonald seemed particularly unhappy about his lie.

I dropped Dewey and ran back to guard the hole because the action was picking up on the green. Woody had just hit his shot to the green, a nine iron from about a hundred yards out. Duncan's shot came just a split second after Woody hit his ball, and it was another of those bladed pitching wedge screamers that came in like a rocket. It would have gone fifty yards over the green, had it not hit a bunker. But it was going so fast the bunker couldn't even hold it and it bounced twice and rolled up on the green, no more than fifty feet from the cup. He was on in four.

It took McDonald two shots to get on the green. Tubbs also got on in four, using the same technique: one shot to dig the ball out of the hole, and one shot to pitch the ball on the green. Woody was the only player not on the green in four. I hadn't counted, but he was at least two strokes behind everyone else. He was away, so he putted up close and then putted out. He said he made a seven and no one contested it. Why should they? Everyone was on in four.

Tubbs hit a good putt that stopped about three feet short of the cup. He spotted. McDonald putted next, about four feet past the hole. I started turning to watch Duncan's putt, but barely in time to see the ball roll past my right foot. He'd hit early again, the blind bastard, and all I could do was watch the ball roll away from me.

"You elephant-eyed sonofabitch!" I shouted at him. I knew it didn't do any good to shout at someone who couldn't hear me, but I felt better. Out of the corner of my eye I saw Tubbs and McDonald look at each other and wink. I was really pissed now. Duncan waddled over to his ball and lined up another putt. Woody coached him, telling him to hit it easy. He did. It rolled about ten feet and died.

"Leave him alone, you Coors powered hophead," I shouted. "I can't do a thing unless he gets the ball to me." Dewey was looking at me like I'd gone crazy, and I felt a bit foolish. I was too pissed to feel a lot foolish.

Duncan tried again. This time he rolled it right between my feet, and I directed it into the cup with my toe. He'd scored a seven, the same as Woody. Tubbs and McDonald had cause to feel cocky because they were both laying five. If either of them sank one of their next two puts, it was all over. I didn't have a choice. Moving in close, I stuck my hand in the cup and then knocked out four straight putts, two from each man. Tubbs nearly took his partners head off when he threw his putter after missing his final short putt. McDonald called him a no play sack of shit and walked off. Tubbs broke two more clubs on his way back to the clubhouse. Woody and Duncan stood on the green and watched them for a few moments, then turned and smiled at each other. They'd won a hundred dollars, fifty bucks each.

CHAPTER 17
The Fox and the Possum

"How's your head?" I asked Dewey as we drove away from the Western Dunes Country Club, following a van full of golfers headed back toward Forest City.

"Throbbing, thanks to you," he replied.

"Hey, I didn't hit you," I said.

"You told me to stand there. You knew I was vulnerable because I was in my I/T mode. You told me to put my foot over the hole." Dewey sounded like an abused child.

"You'll live."

"That's easy for you to say. It's not your head," Dewey said, then moaned as he readjusted the ice pack I'd rigged for him.

"I'll make it up to you. I'll even trade beds with you, if it'll make you feel better," I said.

"Would you?" he asked.

"Sure. My feet will sleep with beans anytime. They're not proud."

Dewey seemed pleased, so pleased that he did something I'd rarely seen him do. He went to sleep in the middle of the afternoon. It worried me, so I woke him up.

"Dewey?"

"What?" he mumbled

"Wake up."

"Why?"

"Because you're not supposed to sleep when you've had a head injury. You could have a concussion, and going to sleep could be fatal," I said. Dewey looked at me like I'd taken complete leave of my senses.

"Fatal to what?"

"You could go into a coma."

"Good! That's exactly what I want right now - a good coma," he said and closed his eyes again. That wasn't hard to do because they were almost swollen shut anyway.

"Come on, stop that! It's dangerous for you to sleep," I said, shaking his shoulder.

"It's not near as dangerous as what you're doing," he said and opened one eye to give me a menacing look.

"You'll have to wake up to hit me," I said.

"You're a real pal, you know that?" Dewey said and then abruptly changed the subject. "Speaking of pals, how'd Woody and Duncan end up being such close friends?"

"They came to WKSU the same year and just grew to be friends. Duncan teaches history and does a good job of it, from what I've seen and heard. They were casual friends for a while, then became drinking buddies. Sometimes they'll get a couple of bottles of whiskey and spend the entire night drinking and talking. I've listened to some of the wildest, most complicated, conversations in the history of modern civilization. Listening to a couple of normal drunks babble is bad enough, but hearing two eggheads discuss world politics, Freudian theories, the Prussian Empire, and things like that is enough to drive you nuts. Anyway, they're close friends who spend a lot of time together. They're seen together so much, in fact, that many people think they're brothers. The students call them 'the fox and the possum.'"

"Woody is the fox, I suppose," Dewey said, smiling.

"Yeah, that sandy red hair of his earned him that nickname."

"And I suppose they call Duncan 'the possum because of his white hair."

"Woody's the one who tagged him with the name. Duncan has a slew of kids, five I think. When his children were smaller, they crawled all over him and stuck to him like a bunch of sucking pups. Duncan can't drive, so he walks everywhere. Seeing him walking down the sidewalk with three or four kids clinging to him reminded Woody of a mama possum with a litter of young on her back. Anyway, Woody called him 'the possum' so much it stuck, even became popular with the faculty and students," I said.

"What happened to the kids? I've never seen Duncan with children."

"They're only here during holidays now. Duncan and his wife split several years ago, and she took the kids. It nearly killed him, but he got used to it. Part of the adjustment, I think, is that he drinks more now. Taking care of kids kept him busy back then, but now he has more time for drinking."

"That's sad," Dewey said.

"Yeah, it is, but the good thing is that his wife left with them. Woody's wife is a queen, a real sweetheart, compared to what Duncan had for a wife. The man's a lot better off now, despite losing his kids. Besides, Woody takes up the slack where he can."

"It's a poor trade," Dewey said flatly. "Woody doesn't treat Duncan very well."

"How do you figure that?" I asked.

"Well, for one thing he talks rudely to him. Haven't you noticed that? Duncan is such a gentle person, such a sweet man, and Woody is terrible to him. Haven't they ever had a falling out over it?"

"No, not over that. They had a falling out several years back, but it was over campus politics. Woody sided with the president, a guy named Perkins, and Duncan sided with the witch-hunters. It was a messy situation. Woody usually stays out of campus politics, but he became a Perkins man from the start. The locals and some of the faculty hated his guts, and it split the town and the university. Perkins ended up leaving, and within a year Woody and Duncan were back on good terms. Woody has always playfully picked on Duncan, but it's just in jest. He's not being mean to him."

"Yes, he is."

"You've got the wrong idea, Dewey. Woody loves Duncan like a brother. They're drinking chums, comrades, fellow intellectuals, and general buddies. Duncan is like family around Woody's house, and there's nothing under the sun that Woody wouldn't do for him."

"Then why does he talk to him the way he does? He calls him a possum, for instance. I've heard him refer to Duncan as the Pillsbury Doughboy, Casper the Ghost, and even a Smoo. And the other day, when Duncan was standing in the hall holding his coffee cup in his hand, Woody walked up and dropped a quarter in it like he was a blind beggar. I don't know what you call it, but I call it being mean," Dewey said.

"That's just sort of a game, or ritual, that goes on between them. The teasing, joking, and name calling is Woody's way of showing his affection for Duncan. Duncan understands and accepts it as such. Duncan would be offended if woody catered to him," I said.

"Are you sure?"

"Yeah, I'm sure. I'll admit that Woody overdoes it sometimes, but he doesn't mean any harm."

"Well, I'll take your word for it because you should know if anyone does," Dewey said with a sly grin.

"Understand what? The way Woody treats Duncan?"

"No, overdoing it."

"Moi? Are you saying I'm an excessive person?"

"There's not a moderate bone in your body," Dewey said confidently.

"I won't argue that point."

"Maybe that's why Woody and Duncan are such good friends. Like you, they're passionate men," Dewey said.

I looked hard at him for a few moments while trying to figure out how to ask him the next question. I couldn't find a better way, so I just blurted it out. "Are you saying that Woody and Duncan are queer for each other? Better yet, and you saying I've got a queer streak?"

"Oh, my, no!"

"Then, what are you saying?"

"I'm just saying they seem to have the ability to feel things more strongly than some people, that's all. They have strong opinions about things, just like you."

"That's what passionate means, huh?"

"Yes, at least in part," he said.

"I've got another theory," I said.

"Of course you do."

"Yeah, I think they hang together because neither of them is a Chinese elm. Remember when we talked about how people are like trees?"

"Yes, I remember. What about it?"

"Well, I figure that Woody stays here because he wants to be a Chinese elm, or at least he'd like to be as hardy as they are. He may find these western Kansans boring and hard to understand from time to time, but I think he admires their staying power. They're too conservative and fundamentalist in their beliefs for him to be comfortable around them, but he works hard at understanding them. Duncan is pretty much the same, except he stays for a slightly different reason. He's a historian, and they have a hard time finding jobs anywhere nowadays. Still, he likes it here, and he likes the people around here. Both men, though, don't quite fit in, and almost everybody craves companionship."

"Perhaps you're right. They are aspiring Chinese elms, and they haven't quite made it yet," Dewey said.

"What kind of tree do you want to be, Dewey?"

"I have no aspirations of being a tree of any kind."

"Yeah, but perhaps we're more like trees than we think we are. What do we call a tree that's dead?"

"A dead tree?"

"No, dumbass! Once dead, we call it wood, or lumber, or firewood, or something like that."

"What's your point?" Dewey asked, raising himself up on an elbow.

"A tree dead is sometimes worth as much or maybe more than a tree alive. Alive it adds beauty to the earth, provides shade, and things like that, but once dead, it provides all sorts of things that are useful. Buildings like houses are made of wood, and what about furniture and things like that?" I asked.

"I see your point, but a live redwood standing in a forest somewhere is much more useful than it is in someone's deck or fence," Dewey said.

"That's true, but it's still very useful dead, right?"

"Right."

"And what about mahogany and beech and maple and walnut? They make excellent wood that is highly sought after, and there are lots of trees like ebony that are even more highly prized. The scarcer the tree and the more beautiful the wood, the greater the prize," I said.

"What kind of wood does a Chinese elm make?"

"Not too good, I'm afraid."

"Then it's more useful alive than dead, right?"

"Probably."

"Then it puzzles me why anyone would want to be a Chinese elm. Everything dies, and I'd rather be more valuable dead than alive," Dewey said.

"Then what kind of tree do you think you were?"

"Teak, perhaps. I always loved the look of teak, and it lasts for a long time. What kind of tree do you want to be?"

"A pussy willow," I said with a smirk.

"Figures."

"Well, I'm glad we got that settled."

"Good! So, let me alone while I finish my nap."

"Do you promise to wake up without brain damage? I don't want a brain damaged partner," I said.

"I promise. Besides, two brain damaged custodians working together would be a disaster," Dewey said, then closed his eyes.

CHAPTER 18
The Bobble

After living on the High Plains the high side of fourteen years I should've learned to expect anything from the weather, but it always seemed to catch me off guard. Just a few days after our golf game, the weather suddenly turned bad. A snowstorm blew in, bringing a swirling downpour of sleet and snow. The weather was bad, but even worse Roosevelt had called saying he'd be in that day. He needed to see us, he'd said, and that worried me because Roosevelt never got around that fast unless something was wrong.

Dewey and I were sitting in the car just outside Parker Administration Building waiting on Woody to get out of a faculty meeting. That didn't help my day either because Woody usually got drunk after faculty meetings. I usually went with him but decided to sit this one out. My mood just wasn't up to any boring faculty talk, and I didn't expect any trouble to develop. Faculty meetings reminded me a lot of military briefings. High ranking officers came in and talked to lower ranking officers and enlisted men who listened with a jaundiced ear. At faculty meetings, administrators came in and talked to professors who listened the same way - with suspicion and trepidation.

Dewey was resting on the back seat, which means not sleeping, which means talking as usual. Mostly, he was either asking questions or complaining about his sore head. My only enjoyment on this otherwise miserable day had been watching Dewey, and I giggled every time I looked at him. The lump on his forehead had gone down, but the two badly swollen black eyes made him look like a raccoon with acute hay fever. The sunglasses he wore to hide his injuries really tickled my funny bone. I tried to point out to him that nobody could see him but me, something he obviously knew already, but he insisted on the shades. Roosevelt was coming, but he would be polite enough not to laugh at Dewey's looks. I wasn't.

"Sit up and let me look at you. I'm starting to feel depressed again, and I need another good laugh," I said.

"Go suck an egg," Dewey said.

"You're nearly as boring as the faculty meeting. I might as well be in there with Woody."

"You're not nailed down, are you?"

"I don't want to get out in the cold. Look at that," I said, pointing at the near blizzard conditions.

"I think it's nice. It's invigorating."

"Well, I can't see where it's done much to invigorate you. Get your ass up from there and quit feeling sorry for yourself. You'll feel better," I said.

"I feel fine right here. Besides, there's nothing else to do."

"Yeah, but don't count on the rest of the day being so easy. Woody may come out of the faculty meeting pissed off and go throw a big drunk. That happens sometimes."

"Why should attending a faculty meeting cause him to do that?" Dewey asked.

"Because he's a drunk, and sometimes it doesn't take much to set him off."

"Just going to a faculty meeting?"

"Maybe you ought to go in and see for yourself. Sitting through a couple of hours of that makes anybody want to throw down a couple of strong belts. It's almost sickening, depressing at least."

"It can't be that bad. What are they doing?"

"Being developed. According to the agenda I saw on Woody's desk, they're involved in faculty development, and that means they're going to tangle assholes."

"Tangle . . . assholes?"

"Yeah, they'll get into an argument," I said.

Dewey let the subject drop, and I dozed off for a while. My nap would've lasted longer, but Dewey started shaking me. "Wake up. We have company."

"Huh?"

"Roosevelt is here," Dewey said again. I straightened up and looked over at Dewey. He was smiling.

"Where?" I asked.

"Right there," Dewey said and pointed over my shoulder. I turned around and found Roosevelt's big, black face staring through the window at me. It caught me by surprise, and I jerked back before I realized he wasn't the abominable snowman. He was wearing a parka with a fur lined hood pulled up over his head, and his nose had been pressed against the window.

"Damn, boss man, you nearly scared me out of my socks," I said, rolling down the window and offering my hand. Roosevelt smiled and took my hand. When I say he took my hand, I'm not exaggerating. It would take four hands like mine to fill one of his, and he had a firm grip. You never knew if you were going to get your hand back when you offered it to him.

"We need to talk," he said abruptly. Roosevelt had a way of cutting right through the crap and getting straight to the point. "Can Dewey handle your mark while we have a conference?"

"Sure thing," I said and then looked at Dewey. He raised his eyebrows and frowned slightly. I got out and followed Roosevelt, who was already walking off toward the library. We went inside and made our way to a quiet area in the reference section.

"What's the beef?" I asked as we shed our coats and sat down at a table covered with musty smelling books.

"I have a confirmed report that you've been involved in a flagrant violation of the rules," Roosevelt said. "The Central Office is concerned, shall we say, about the way you and Dewey handled the incident at the golf course several days ago."

"Confirmed? Who squealed?" I asked.

"One of golfers is under protection. His custodian notified the Central Office, saying some strange things happened. Since you're operating in a different dimension, he couldn't see you, but he was aware of some monkey business going on that could've been pulled off only by someone with supernatural powers. That means you and Dewey were messing around," Roosevelt said and scowled at me.

"Yeah, we messed around some, but those two peckerheads playing Woody and Duncan were trying to cheat their asses off," I said.

"That's not what I'm talking about, and you know it. You know you're not supposed to tamper with things like that, and you were blatantly obvious about it. Golf balls bouncing out of the cup, balls buried in sand traps, shots that bounced off at ninety degree angles, and even a flagpole flying up into the air are not good methods of guardianship. What were you guys trying to pull?"

"It was justified, believe me. Those guys were going to . . ."

"It was not justified," Roosevelt cut in. "The manual specifically states that under no circumstances are you to . . ."

"Screw the manual. You needed to be there to understand the situation. They had it coming. Besides, it was harmless," I said, taking my turn to break in.

"Harmless? You interfered with another custodian doing his job. Your antics so upset his mark that it made his job almost impossible for days. What you did caused a great deal of trouble because the custodian in question had to call in reinforcements for a few days. The Central Office gets concerned when it has to send in a troubleshooter."

"No balls, huh? Well, I can tell you one thing for sure. He's a puss, and that's for sure. Neither McDonald nor Tubbs is anywhere close to being the trouble Woody is, and I've busted my ass for a long time looking after him, and never once have I called for a troubleshooter. Then, out of the wild blue, they up and send in a troubleshooter when some limp-dick custodian can't handle a small crisis. Who is the coward, anyway? Who's he guarding?" I asked.

"That's confidential information, and it's none of your concern. What is your concern is that you do your job properly. I've known for some time that you occasionally stretch the rules, but I let it pass because you were overworked and alone. But you have some help now, and you seem to be getting braver about breaking rules." Roosevelt's voice jumped an octave, and he started in with that finger shaking business again.

"What do you want me to do about it - go sit in the corner?" I asked, folding my arms defensively.

"You're taking this too lightly, and that would be a grave mistake on your part. This is a serious matter, and it could be dealt with harshly. You're playing it much too close to the edge, my friend, and if you push too hard, I may not be able to help you. I'd like for you to know and understand that I'm on your side, that I regard you highly as a custodian, but you need to give me some help with this," Roosevelt said, reaching out and touching my shoulder to make sure I got the point.

"What do you want me to do?" I asked, trying to sound sincere.

"I want you to cool it for a while. Play it by the book, and play it close to the vest for a couple of months. Things seem to be going pretty well for you now, so don't spoil it. There's been some discussion about a transfer for you, and regardless about how you feel concerning Woody, I don't think you'd like what's been suggested," he said.

"What suggestion?"

"I'm not at liberty to say."

"Good grief, Roosevelt, the least you can do if you're going to threaten me is to be more specific. Where are they wanting to send me now?"

"I'll only say that you should learn to tolerate cold weather and speak Russian if you are determined to continue breaking the rules. It could even be worse than that." Roosevelt's eyes narrowed down and he nodded wisely as he spoke. He sure got my attention.

"Now just hold on a minute, Roosevelt. That's out of the question. I can't guard some vodka sucking Russian. I don't parley vous the lingo, and I don't like the commie bastards. You might think you've got me by the short hairs, but you can send my ass to hell first," I said defiantly. Roosevelt couldn't hold back a chuckle.

"You'll not be sent to hell, but you should keep in mind that you could have a worse assignment," he said.

"I just put it on file. I'll be a good boy for a while," I said and waved my hand in surrender.

"Good! How's Dewey doing?" Roosevelt asked.

"He's working out fine. I never would've thought it to begin with, but he's learning quickly, and he's dedicated," I said in all honestly.

"I'm glad to hear that too because I had already decided that he needed the opportunity and challenge of doing some work on his own. But just for a couple of weeks, mind you," Roosevelt said, grinning broadly.

"What about me? What am I going to be doing?" I asked, not just because I was curious but because I was concerned.

"You're going to Las Vegas," he said flatly.

"Huh?"

"You're on your way to Vegas."

"Me? Going to Vegas? How . . . how . . . come?" I stammered.

"You're going on special assignment," he said.

"Special assignment? But . . ."

"That's all I can tell you right now, but I thought you should know about it so you could make some plans. You'll need to prepare Dewey for his first time alone with Woody. I will say this, however. I think you'll welcome this temporary assignment. This is a great opportunity for you because the Central Office is considering you for a promotion. I think they want to see how you perform under fire, and I'm confident that you'll do a good job. Otherwise, I wouldn't have recommended you." He smiled again, but I couldn't think of anything to say.

Roosevelt took me back to the car, shook my hand and disappeared into the blowing snow. I jumped into the car, ready to tell Dewey about my new assignment, but he was gone. I got back out, ran into Parker Administration Building, and found Dewey peering through the door of the conference room. When I say peering through the door, that's exactly what I mean. His ass and legs were outside the door, but the rest of his body was inside the conference room. I snuck up and goosed him in the ass.

I should've given it more thought, but I was feeling really good, and goosing him in the ass seemed like the right thing to do at the time. It scared him so bad that he jumped completely through the door and crashed headlong to the floor. Then he jumped up, still rattled, and tried to run back through the door. Unfortunately, he'd lost concentration and reverted to the I/T mode, and that of course made it impossible for him to exit. He smashed into the door with a loud thud, bad enough in itself, but then he fell back into the crowd of faculty members.

This all happened at a very inopportune time. The Dean was just in the process of trying to restore order after a lengthy and heated debate between various faculty members concerning greater emphasis on liberal arts courses in the general curriculum. Several members of the chemistry department had taken exception to remarks made by a few historians and political scientists. Tempers had flared just before Dewey, dazed and confused after running into the door, plummeted to the floor right beside a chemistry prof. One of his arms flew up and whacked the prof across the back of the head.

It was a good lick because it made a loud "splat" and snapped the man's head forward a full foot.

It gets worse. Sitting right behind the chemistry prof was a huffy historian who'd started the argument in the first place. The chemistry professor automatically assumed that he was under attack from the rear and retaliated. He jumped to his feet and smacked the history prof a good one right in the nose, knocking him out of his seat and to the floor. The situation really deteriorated after that. A political scientist took up the fight in behalf of his downed comrade and threw a nice roundhouse right that put the chemistry prof flat of his back. By the time the fracas was over, it involved twenty-five faculty members and a dozen departments. I really didn't get to see how it turned out because Dewey regained his composure and came charging out into the hall after me. Boy, was he pissed - so much so that his eyes matched the color of his ass, which apparently was cherry red at the time. I took off down the hall like a scalded-assed dog. It is to my credit and good fortune that I was faster afoot than Dewey, but he chased me all the way back to the car. I had to lock myself inside until he cooled down in the blowing snow. When I was sure he no longer wanted to kill me, I let him get in. By then, he could talk a little.

"You are absolutely, unequivocally, and audaciously the most disgracefully callous and uncaring person I have even met. What you did, or caused, back there was unforgivable," he fumed.

"I agree, and I'm sorry," I said. My apology caught Dewey by surprise.

"You do? You are?"

"Yeah, and I mean it. I wasn't using my head, but I have an excuse."

"I knew it," Dewey said.

"Saying I'm sorry doesn't mean I can't give an excuse, does it? Don't you at least want to hear it?"

"I'll listen, but it had better be good."

"I was excited because I'm going to Las Vegas," I said. Dewey didn't say a word, just stared at me. I couldn't read the expression on his face.

"Did you hear what I said?" He nodded, but said nothing.

"Since when did you get to where you couldn't talk? What the hell's wrong with you?" I asked. Dewey shrugged.

"I've been given a special assignment." Still no response.

"I may get a promotion." More silence.

"TALK TO ME, YOU LITTLE SHIT!" I shouted. Dewey flinched and batted his eyes, but didn't respond.

"Aren't you going to say anything? How about congratulations? Good luck, maybe? Hope you have a good time? Take a hike? Kiss my ass? Go fuck yourself? Take a flying. . . ?"

"OK! OK! Congratulations. When are you going?" Dewey asked, still looking pickle-pussed and sounding disappointed.

"I don't know. Roosevelt didn't say. As a matter of fact, all he told me was that I was going, that it was a great opportunity for me, and that I'd probably be gone for a couple of weeks," I said.

"It's not a permanent assignment?" Dewey asked, sounding uplifted.

"No, it's just temporary," I said. The expression on Dewey's face was plainly one of relief. That made me feel good, I'll admit.

"Then, why didn't you say so to begin with," he said irritably.

"You didn't ask. You didn't say nothing."

"Anything. The word is anything," Dewey said, sniffing.

"OK, anything, but if you'd bothered to ask, you would've known. You're not worried about me being gone, are you?"

"Not at all. I'll enjoy the peacefulness left in the wake of your absence," he replied and lifted his nose in one of those la-te-da poses.

"That means, then, that you don't want any advice about how to handle Woody or what to do if he cuts loose on as big drunk while I'm gone, right?"

"I didn't say that. Feel free to make any suggestions you feel are in order," Dewey said.

"I don't have any. You're a big boy, and I'm confident you'll do as good as I could," I said.

"Really?" he asked with a surprised smile.

"Really. Just don't break any rules. They're on to us about the creative golf we played at Western Dunes, so you might be watched. Roosevelt says the Central Office is pissed about it. They found out because either Tubbs or McDonald is being protected. Anyway one of those dingleberry custodians filed a complaint with the Central Office because his mark went nuts on him for a few days after he lost the match. They even had to send in a troubleshooter to help him out, Roosevelt says. Can you believe that?"

"One of those . . . cheats is being protected?" Dewey asked in near disbelief. "Well, of all the . . ."

"Don't worry about it. I think most of the heat's on me. Roosevelt says he knows I've been fudging for a long time but didn't take it too seriously until this jerk custodian squealed on us. I guess the Central Office came down on Roosevelt, and he had to come talk to me about it. He told me to cool it for awhile, that there'd been some talk at the Central Office about transferring me. He said I wouldn't like being transferred."

"That doesn't sound too good," Dewey said, frowning up again.

"Aw, you can't take them too seriously. They just wanted to threaten me. That's just like an administrator. They sent Roosevelt out here to chew my ass out about a minor infraction of the rules over a stupid golf game, then turn around and want me to take a special assignment in Las Vegas. Roosevelt sounded like it was an important operation, but said he couldn't tell me anymore about it. I wonder what they want me to do in Vegas?" I asked.

"It's beyond my comprehension," Dewey said, shaking his head.

CHAPTER 19
Dreamers, Schemers, and IBMer's

The fracas at the faculty meeting took away any anger or hostility Woody might've taken with him. He went straight home and flopped down on the couch for a late afternoon siesta. Dewey was still down in the dumps about that had happened at the faculty meeting that afternoon, and maybe he was a little worried about me going to Las Vegas. Something had him in a blue funk because he was slumped down in a corner of Woody's living room looking like a sore-dicked hound in a pen full of bitches in heat. After watching him pout for two hours, I decided to try to make him feel better.

"Look, Dewey, you're not the blame for what happened there this afternoon," I said.

"Oh? You think faculty members just fight that way every time they get together? Just wait until word about this gets back to Roosevelt. He really will be mad then."

"Oh, come on, Dewey. You've been on campus long enough now to know how it works. All it takes is the right mixture and the fight's on. Today they were viewing a video tape discussing computers in higher education. Some distinguished scientist from back east was on the tape, supposedly talking about using modern technology, namely the computer, in collection and dissemination of information in higher education research and education. That's a touchy subject, especially with some segments of the faculty. Liberal arts and humanities folks aren't as keen on that sort of stuff as are those in the natural sciences and technical fields. It was a readymade battlefield for the schemers, the dreamers, and the IBMers."

"I don't follow you, not exactly," he said, sitting up straight. I must've aroused his curiosity because he leaned over the back of the seat. "Who are the schemers, dreamers, and IBMers?"

"That's my own personal grouping of college personnel. Over my years of hanging around this place I've been able to place certain faculty members into certain categories. The dreamers, first of all, are people mostly from the humanities and liberal arts. They're history, art, literature, political science, sociology, philosophy professors, and the like. Since they're more idealistic and traditional than some, they tend to be somewhat naive about the world they live in and teach about. The IBMers are almost the opposite, since they're concerned with facts and figures about things. These folks are mostly from the natural sciences, business, accounting, etc. Their approach is more down to earth. More pragmatic than the dreamers, they seem to lack vision. Maybe they can't see much beyond their machines and labs and such. The schemers, the worst of the three, are the people who actually run the university. They're the administration and staff and some faculty who seem to be willing to adopt any approach that will get the job done. They probably lean toward being more like the IBMers because they can't grasp the intellectualism of the dreamers. Does any of that make sense to you?" I asked.

"Yes, it makes perfect sense," Dewey said.

"Good! Then, I won't have to waste a lot of time explaining it, and that's good because I'm not sure how well I understand it myself," I said.

"Where does Woody fit in?" Dewey asked while he was crawling over the back of the seat.

"Oh, he's definitely a dreamer. He's into computers and doesn't shy away from new technology, but he's still an idealist. Maybe that's part of his problem."

"For once we're in complete agreement, and being such an idealist may be more than just a part of his problem; it may be the very root of it."

"How do you figure that? His idealism sure as hell doesn't get in his way of being a jerk sometimes. I always thought idealism went hand and hand with some ethics and morals."

"If you think about it carefully, you'll see how it all fits. His moral character lags because his own personal principles are too high for him to reach. Woody has placed himself in the position of having to choose between working toward his high ideals or not trying at all. Perhaps he tried and found himself lacking, and having come up short chose to stop subjecting himself to failure. He opted for nothing instead of only a part of something. He behaves badly to prove to himself that he either has no principles at all or that his goals are unrealistic and out of reach." Dewey shrugged when he finished speaking, and I took it as a hint that he wanted some elaboration on his theory.

"You're right down the middle on that one, Dewey. He's rebelling against his own ethics, but why? If they're too lofty for him, then why doesn't he lower them?" I asked.

"That's easier said than done, and if anybody should know, you should. You're the guru of lowered standards," Dewey said, smirking.

"You're right, I do know about lowered standards. I humped a married fat gal once, and that meant I had to lower two standards. I don't believe in messing with another man's wife, and the other standard's obvious," I said, grinning.

Dewey sighed, shook his head and then asked, "Did you feel guilty about it?"

"Not much. She was a good lay, and I never liked her husband much."

"I should've known better than to try using you as an example. You're practically devoid of principles, but some people find dealing with guilt very difficult. Still others, like you, have a hard time recognizing guilt."

"What does guilt feel like?"

"It means feeling culpable, or shameful."

"In that case, I know about feeling guilty," I said, grinning to make sure he knew I'd been jacking around with him.

"There's a difference between being guilty and feeling guilty. Some people, those without conscience, don't feel guilt. Others handle guilt feelings like Woody does, by getting angry. Their anger leads them into things that violate the very same set of principles that made the feel guilty in the first place," Dewey said.

"Almost anybody knows the difference in how they feel, don't they? I mean, they ought to know the difference between being angry or feeling guilty about something," I said.

"Oh, but they don't. Accepting guilt as such may mean accepting their failure to meet ethical goals, so they suppress the guilt, and suppressed guilt turns into anger."

"So, what you're saying is that Woody's screwed up because he set ideals too high, and he can't turn loose of them, so he violates them out of protest. Have I got that part right?"

"In a nutshell, yes."

"What puzzles me is where those high-brow ideals come from. Why does he refuse to lower them?" I asked.

"He can't lower them because they're too deeply ingrained. They're a product of the society we live in - come from our families, churches, government, and all sorts of institutionalized things. Most of our institutionalized ethics, even our prejudices, are too much a part of us to lower."

"Damn, that wore me out. Wake me up when Wanda gets home, would you?" I leaned back in the seat and pulled my hat down over my eyes.

"But you didn't finish explaining about the dreamers, schemers, and IBMers."

"Later."

It seemed like I'd barely closed my eyes when Dewey started shaking me. I looked up and saw Wanda strolling across the floor, headed for the den where Woody was sleeping. I had misgivings about what her reaction would be when she came home to a cluttered house and a napping husband, but she surprised me. She even let him sleep while she cleaned up and fixed an early dinner. Her good mood, it turned out, was due to the annual faculty Christmas party being held that evening. The party might've improved her mood, but it didn't do a thing for mine. Wonderful, I thought. What perfect timing for the party to come on the heels of the disaster at the faculty development meeting. I wasn't worried so much about Woody because he usually didn't screw up at a faculty affair. I just dreaded the party on general principles.

Dewey, of course, was delighted. My little talk perked him up some, but when he found out about the party, he turned all smiles. With the kind of disposition he had about parties, he should've been the madam of a whorehouse. We barely seated ourselves in a corner of the ballroom that evening when he said, "Now that we have most of the faculty and administration assembled, you can finish your discussion about schemers, dreamers, and IBMers."

I acted like I didn't hear him and kept looking over the crowd. The annual affair was being held at the local country club, and we showed up late because Dewey had to dress up. I bitched about it, but he put me off by saying he enjoyed wearing nice clothes but seldom had a chance to do it, and he would not allow my complaints to spoil it for him. I went to the shindig in my jeans and sweatshirt, but Dewey wore his mint green tailored suit with reddish specks all over it. In addition, he had on white shoes, a white shirt, and a reddish ascot to match the suit. Being invisible is a blessing sometimes.

"Well, are you going to tell me or not," he asked again, looking peeved.

"Dewey, you look like a lime with the mange," I said, turning to scowl at him.

"I look just fine, and you know it."

"You look silly."

"What I wear is none of your business. Now tell me about the faculty," he said curtly.

"Didn't I already do that? Besides, most of these people are too boring to talk about," I said.

"To you, perhaps, but I don't know most of them. I need to know about them because you may get transferred or promoted, and I'd be left here with no way of finding out about these people."

"First off, I'm not going to get promoted or transferred, and second, you can learn like I did."

"And how was that?" he asked.

"By keeping my mouth shut and watching."

"You are not going to intimidate me with you mean mouth. I want information, and you have it. The more I learn about these people, the more prepared I'll be for whatever happens."

I was tired and not feeling particularly informative, but the way he put it left me in a position where I couldn't refuse. "Where do you want me to start? There are over a hundred people here," I said.

"The dreamers," Dewey said quickly. "Start with the dreamers."

"You would pick the hardest bunch first. They're scattered all over the place, but that fits their style. They're too scatterbrained to be organized into a tight group. Liberal arts and humanities people aren't nearly as tightly knit as the technologists and natural scientists. Maybe that's because there's such a big difference between them. My theory about dreamers, schemers, and IBMers doesn't hold true in every case, at least not when it comes to rigid departmental lines. It doesn't always hold up from individual to individual, but it fits most of them. We might as well start with the historians, since they're bunched up tonight."

"Where are they?"

"The group over by the fireplace, under the elk antlers - that raggedy-ass bunch with the unhappy looking wives." I indicated with my hand.

"You're right. They're sloppy looking, and their wives don't look happy. Why is that?" Dewey asked, craning his neck to get a better look.

"They can't get their husbands separated and quiet long enough to dance with them," I said and started moving toward them.

"Some of them look too old to dance."

"You're right about that. There are about half dozen historians here, and four of them actually named animals on the arc," I said.

"Why are they so old?"

"Because they've been here for years, that's why. Historians are plentiful, and when they find jobs, they stick. The two younger history guys, Duncan being one of them, hang out with the political science staff," I said, pointing toward a larger and more active group huddled near the bar not far away. Woody was in that bunch, standing near Duncan. Both looked sober. "More dreamers," I said, passing my hand over them as we walked by.

"Oh my! Who, or what, group is this?" Dewey asked, pulling at my arm and pointing to a group that had put together a long row of tables. The group stuck out like a warthog in a litter of duroc piglets - easily the loudest and best entertained group in the room. Someone in the group had just told a joke and was strutting around and scratching his balls while the others laughed. "Who is that?" Dewey pointed directly at the man.

"Gordie Mazurski," I said and chuckled. "He's the head football coach here at WKSU. All those people are coaches and physical education instructors. Mazurski's not a bad guy, as far as I can tell. He's a Polack from back east somewhere, but he's been around for quite a while now, maybe five or six seasons. That's a long time for a coach at this school. If they win, they move up to a better school before long. Parker always pumped enough money into athletics to make sure they were respectable, but the last couple of presidents put a quietus to that. Mazurski probably won't be around much longer."

"What group do they fit into?"

"None. They're too stupid to dream and too lazy to scheme. I did hear, though, that the athletic department has a new computer system. I don't know about you, but that troubles me some," I said.

"That's a large group. Are all of them coaches and physical education people?"

"No, but most of them are. Some are just faculty members with a jock intellect, but some are from administration."

"That reminds me. Where are the administrators?" he asked.

"At the first table near the door. They'll be the first to leave because there's no chance they're going to cut loose and have a good time in front of the faculty. In the old days they went to Parker's house and partied, but Stegnor isn't much for that sort of thing. They'll probably gather at one or the other of their houses, maybe some dean's place. Some professors will go with them, but most will hang around here after they leave. That's when the activity around here will pick up some."

"What about this group?" Dewey said as he pulled my sleeve and guided me toward another section of the room.

"That's looks mostly like business department people from accounting, finance, management, and even economics - a bunch of IBMers for sure. Some are from the computer science and math departments. They're definitely the most boring folks on the faculty and will be the first to leave as soon as Stegnor goes home."

"And this group?" Dewey said, indicating with his head toward a group so tightly packed you could hardly see space between them.

"That's the natural science people, mostly chemists, biologists, earth sciences, physics, and the like."

"They're the worse looking group I've seen so far," Dewey said, wrinkling his nose.

"That's because they've sniffed too many lab fumes, I reckon. Actually, most of them are good folks," I said.

"Can you identify any other specific groups in the room?" Dewey asked, stretching his neck and looking around eagerly.

"No, not really. There's a few others, but nothing out of the ordinary. There's a group of industrial arts people over there, and there's some home economics people there, and there's library science there," I said and pointed out three small groups across the room.

"And the large group on the other side of the room?"

I had to look twice because they were in a poorly lighted area, but as we got closer, I recognized them. "That's education," I said.

"Dreamers, schemers, what?"

"I've never been able to figure out what they are. Education is a weird field of study, and there are so many different kinds of education people. They're the biggest department on campus, though, because this is an old teacher's college. I'd say they're schemers, mostly because they've managed to scheme themselves into jobs. Education is weak academics wise, and almost anyone can get out of college with an education degree. I've never been able to figure out why they even teach it, other than the state requires it of teachers. That's how they schemed their way into college academics - by creating a need for what they do."

"Couldn't the same be said of other fields of study?"

"No," I said flatly, and Dewey didn't pursue it.

We walked around the floor again, and then Dewey suddenly stopped dead in his tracks and gawked. "What about this group?" he asked, turning me toward another small group. I'd seen them earlier, but had decided not to point them out. "That's a strange looking group of people."

I had to stifle a smile before I explained who they were. "Most of those people are from the English, drama, speech, and library science, and various other departments like music and humanities and foreign language."

"If they come from so many different departments, why are they lumped up like that?" Dewey asked.

"Have you ever been on a college campus before?"

"No, not really. I've visited them but didn't pay close attention."

"Well, if you had, you recognize them right off. Let's move closer and maybe you'll probably recognize them."

We moved a bit closer. He looked down at his suit, then back at them, and then back at me. "Well, they're . . . they're . . . a little strange, but that doesn't mean there's anything wrong with them."

"I didn't say there was."

"Artists and actors and writers are many times strange, a little different."

"I'm sure they are, Dewey," I said, still smiling.

"That doesn't necessarily mean they're . . . they're . . . queer," he said, a bit defensively.

"I didn't say . . ."

"Oh, shut up! I hate it when you're patronizing," he said, then turned slowly and walked away like a shoplifter the store dick had just yelled at. I hustled after him and caught up just before he made the door. Then I gently took his arm and led him to the table nearest the bar.

"I know exactly how you feel," I said, putting my hand behind his neck and guiding him toward a table not far away. The entire group consisted of uniformed military science people and a few western dressed animal science professors. "Do you know who they are?" I asked. Dewey gawked for a moment, then smiled and nodded, and I continued. "Even if these army types were out of uniform, the haircut would be a dead giveaway, but everybody who wears a cowboy hat is surely not a cowboy. A soldier is just what he looks like, but the uniform doesn't automatically make him one. A cowboy hat doesn't make a cowboy either, and I'm fully aware that weird clothing doesn't make someone queer. It just might make them look that way," I said.

Dewey looked at me for a few seconds, then smiled understanding and walked away, this time like a kid that had just been awarded a blue ribbon at the county fair. Come to think of it, he walked away more like a beauty contestant who'd just won Miss Congeniality. I watched him as he poked around the room, carefully examining the various groups assembled there. After a short while, he settled into a corner near a group of liberal arts people.

The annual Christmas party officially ended at about midnight, but Woody and Wanda went from there to Duncan's house where another party lasted until past three in the morning. Woody got drunk, of course, but nothing out of the ordinary took place other than he got loud and obnoxious. Dewey and I followed him and Wanda home, and after making sure they were safely asleep, went to our trailer and sacked out. The day had been long and exhausting, and I was dog tired. But I couldn't get my mind off what Roosevelt had said about the Las Vegas deal. Mostly, I kept wondering what Roosevelt wanted me to do out there, but I also worried some about Dewey.

As for Dewey's performance to date, he'd done well. But Roosevelt had more confidence in him than I did. Dewey had every attribute to be a good custodian, but the jury was still out when it came to whether or not he had the stamina for it. In my way of thinking, he still hadn't toughened up enough to handle the job alone for a lengthy period of time. The I/T mode was still giving him trouble, and he still lost his cool every now and then. I kept thinking that maybe I should've told Roosevelt that. As far as Las Vegas was concerned, I didn't know what to think. I even tried to make some wild guesses but couldn't come up with anything that made sense at all. Finally, I slept.

Part Three

The Lower Road

CHAPTER 20
The Personification Mode

My assignment in Las Vegas lasted only a few short weeks, but I made the best of them. After fourteen years of being holed up in Forest City, Kansas, Vegas was just the glitzy kind of town I needed for a short escape. The town itself was a blast, but I had more fun with the assignment than anything else. That's because I got to do some things I've always wanted to do, and one of them involved winning lots of money. I hated for it to end, but at the same time, I looked forward to my regular job. Admitting this isn't easy, but I missed Kansas - even Dewey and Woody.

I'd had done some worrying, too. The time between the Christmas party and my departure from Kansas, about six weeks, had gone too smoothly. Christmas had come and gone without incident, partly because Woody and Wanda had lots of company. Woody's parents spent the week of Christmas with them, then one of Wanda's sisters and her family came the week after. Woody behaved well through it all, and only drank enough to get drunk a couple of times. I figured him for a big drunk as soon as all the relatives cleared out, but two weeks went by and nothing happened. Then Roosevelt called and sent me to Las Vegas, and during my time there, Kansas and Dewey and Woody kept creeping into my thoughts.

"How're they hanging?" I asked, loud enough to wake the dead. Actually, that's exactly what I did. Dewey jumped three feet in the air when I spoke out. He was sitting on a bench in the hall, just outside of Woody's classroom, half asleep when I walked up beside him. He landed on his knees after the start I gave him, but he jumped up quickly and rushed to me.

"Thank heavens, you're back."

"You can thank Roosevelt. He's the one who brought me back," I said.

"Then thanks to Roosevelt," Dewey said, hugging me. I've never cared for hugs from men, but I indulged him. The look on his face had told me that Dewey was more than just relieved and happy to see me. He looked exhausted.

"Has Woody been a problem since I've been gone?"

"That would be the understatement of the year. He's been a real jerk," he said, his voice suddenly turning surly.

"That must mean he's been on another bender, huh?"

"That too would be an understatement," he said, plopping down heavily on the bench. I sat down beside him.

"You look like a nap would do you some good. Why don't you go home and stretch out. I'll look after Woody for a while."

Dewey jumped at the chance. "Would you?"

"Sure thing. I've had a nice vacation, so take off. You can tell me all about our bad boy later."

"Thanks," Dewey said, then shuffled away, shoulders slumping and feet scuffing the floor. I'd never seen him too tired to stand up straight, and that worried me some. Either he just wasn't ready to handle Woody alone, or Woody had really pulled a bad one this time. Maybe it was some of both, I decided.

I peeked in the window of Woody's classroom to check him out. He looked pretty much the same as always, except he looked more rumpled than usual. His hair was longer, and he looked pale. I checked the clock in the hall and noticed that class wouldn't be out for another thirty minutes, so I thought about checking out the girl's bathroom. The idea quickly passed, and I couldn't figure out why I'd lost interest in peeping on college girls. Then it hit me like a bolt from the blue. I'd been overexposed. The smorgasbord of tits and asses I'd been subjected to in Vegas for the past three weeks had dulled my appetite for peeping.

I sat down to mull over the dilemma, but my mood refused to make room for reflection. I paced the halls until Woody turned class out and headed home. Although I'd prepared myself for action, nothing happened - at least, not at first. Woody ate a sandwich, drank two fast beers, and then flopped down on the couch. Within minutes he was fast asleep. I checked the trailer and found Dewey asleep, and that was all the excuse I needed to stretch out on my bed and do the same. The next thing I remember, he was shaking me.

"What are you doing?" he asked, his eyes filled with anxiety. He looked like a diarrhea sufferer ten miles from the closest bathroom.

"It's called sleeping. You close your eyes, lie real still, and fall into a somnambulistic state," I said, rubbing my eyes.

"Where's Woody? Where'd he go?" Dewey asked, half shouting.

"Relax, Dewey. He's in the den sleeping."

"No, he isn't. I just checked, and the house is empty. Get up. Get up right now. We've got to find him," he said, tugging at my arm.

"Take it easy, Dewey. He's around somewhere. There's no way he could've gone far. What time is it, by the way?"

"Nearly seven o'clock."

"Damn," I said, peeking out the window. It was already dark, but I could see that Woody's car was gone.

"We've got to find him," he said, pacing nervously back and forth across my tiny bedroom. It was only about a two step pacing job, so he was flicking back and forth in front of me like people through a turnstile in a busy terminal.

"Quit it!" I said sternly.

Dewey looked at me but kept pacing. "Hurry. Get dressed."

I obliged him, mainly because I had to go anyway. Woody had probably gone no farther than Dusty's Saloon, but telling Dewey that wouldn't help. He was wound up like a cheap watch, and so I moved as fast as I could. We pulled into the parking lot at Dusty's bar five minutes later, but Woody's car wasn't there. We drove to Frank's Bar and Grill, but still no Woody.

"Turn left and go that way," Dewey said, pointing toward Front Street. I hooked a quick left and then looked at Dewey for more instructions. He just stared straight ahead, his face drawn into a concerned expression I'd seldom seen him wear.

"Shall we drive through the park, sir?" I asked. Dewey didn't smile, just waved me on with a deliberate motion of his hand.

I drove until he motioned for me to turn left again. I turned down Jefferson Drive, and slowly motored along, all the while watching Dewey out of the corner of my eye for an indication of what to do next. We turned right two blocks down Jefferson onto a narrow street. The street narrowed even more and then dead ended near a group of dumpsters. Parked under an elm beside a row of hedges and almost hidden by the dumpsters was Woody's car.

"What's he doing down here?" I asked.

"Woody has a new friend."

"That means he's humping somebody down here, right?" I asked.

"She's a student, that pretty lady with the derriere you admire so much," he said. He should've known better than trying to narrow it down that way. I admire lots of derrieres.

"That doesn't tell me diddly-squat, Dewey," I said, chuckling.

"She's the one from his developmental psych class last semester - the one you said had an apple ass," he said irritably.

"Oh, that one," I said, actually surprised. I couldn't believe Woody had got up enough courage to make a move on her. Besides, she didn't seem like the kind who'd be receptive to a move.

"Yes, that one. She lives in that apartment building, first floor, apartment three. It's a nice two bedroom, but the furnishings are too rustic for me."

"Chippendale is too rustic for you," I said. Dewey usually took up a challenge like that, but he let it slide. I waited, but he just sat there staring toward the dumpsters. "So why are we sitting here? Let's go in and see what's going on."

"You go. I've seen enough," he said, sighing heavily again.

"How long has Woody been at this?" I asked.

"For about two weeks - ever since Wanda left."

"Wanda's gone?"

"She's gone to her parent's home. Her father had a heart attack, and she went to help her mother," Dewey said, almost matter-of-factly.

"What about the kids?"

"She took the children with her. Woody was drinking heavily, and she didn't trust him with the children. They had a big fight before she left."

"Is the old man in bad shape?"

"It sounds serious."

"How did all this get started?" I asked, nodding toward the building.

"She recently went through a divorce, and Woody had been giving her some informal counseling. It was all innocent enough at first. Then she came to his office one afternoon, just after Wanda had left, and before I knew what was going on they . . . standing up, they . . . they . . . "

"Fucked," I said.

"If you must put it crudely, yes," Dewey said.

"Woody got to her in his office, huh?"

"It's disgusting."

"Screwing a classic apple ass like that gal is never disgusting. Sure you don't want to come along?"

"I'll stay."

Apartment three was on the far end of the complex next to the stairwell, but I didn't learn that until I'd been through half a dozen apartments. I could've saved myself the trouble by walking around to the front and reading the numbers over the doors, but I was too lazy for that. Instead, I started in the middle and walked toward the west end of the building. I got in a few good peeks at a big boobed gal in apartment six and then caught three coeds in apartment four sitting buck naked in the middle of the living room floor smoking dope. I nearly missed Woody in apartment three because all the lights were out. I couldn't see a thing in that pitch black bedroom, but I could hear well enough to know what was happening. I stepped back into the living room, flicked on the TV, and waited, making sure to keep the sound low.

Ten minutes later and in the middle of the ten o'clock news, the bedroom door opened and the woman came out and headed for the bathroom in the hall. But the glare from the TV screen caught her eye, and she walked into the living room wearing nothing but a confused look and her toenails. Excuse me, but I gawked. Hot damn, what a good looking woman! I watched her closely as she moved over to the TV, turned it off, and quickly walked back to the bathroom. Missing the rest of the news would've really irritated me if it hadn't been for that beautiful ass. I checked the bedroom to make sure Woody was there and then went back to the car in the alley.

"Back so soon?"

"I couldn't take it anymore. That's too much woman for me," I said.

"I didn't think you'd even admit that."

"Well, I'm caught up on watching naked gals. I've been in Vegas for three weeks, remember?"

"I remember, and I've been meaning to ask about your trip. How did it go?" Dewey asked. He didn't sound sincere, just polite.

"We'll talk about it later. It's a long story, and you're tired, and . . ."

"Tell me about it. You have a way with a story, and perhaps it will pick me up," he said, smiling feebly. But the smile quickly faded, and he turned almost tearful. "I've missed you, Doug."

"I missed you, too," I said. That made Dewey break into a genuine smile.

"So tell me all about your trip."

"Sure you want to hear it? It's a long story."

"I'm sure," he said.

"I got to use the personification mode," I said proudly.

"Did you?"

"Yep, and for three weeks. Can't do it now, though. My assignment was temporary, and so were the powers, but that's all right because I had a helluva time for a while," I said, giving Dewey a playful nudge with my elbow.

"You didn't . . . take advantage . . . did you?" Dewey asked, looking concerned.

"If you call indulging every fantasy I've had for the past fourteen years taking advantage, the answer is yes," I said.

"But you didn't do what you always threatened to do, did you? You didn't . . . didn't . . ."

"Nope, but I did everything else."

"That's a relief, a least. I was afraid you'd get in big trouble out there and get shipped off to Russia."

"Actually, I was preoccupied with other things. The first thing I did was rent a car and drive all over Las Vegas. I got a ragtop and just cruised. And, I ate. Boy, did I ever eat," I said.

"Anything else?"

"I talked to people, to real people."

"So what am I, chopped liver?" Dewey asked.

"You're dead, Dewey. I've been talking to dead people for fourteen years. These people were alive, really alive," I said.

"So what's the difference?"

"Well, it's . . . it's . . . different."

"So is drinking water through your nose, but I don't think I care to do it. Besides, you've talked with the living before," he said.

"Yeah, but it's been a long time since I actually touched people. People bumped and nudged and rubbed skin with me. I felt warm bodies against mine again. Even though I wasn't one of them, I was among the living again, and that was exciting," I said.

"Yes, I suppose it would be."

"I'll have to admit that I got carried away once and tried to get laid."

"I should've known. What happened?" Dewey asked, squinting at me.

"I picked up some woman, a tourist from Iowa, and took her up to my room. After fooling around a bit, we hit the bed. She was a good looker, a gal with a nice shape and lovely face, and I was really looking forward to getting some nookie. But it never happened. We rolled around on the bed until we got steamed up pretty good. She reached down and grabed my dong about then and suddenly went stiff as a carp. Her eyes flew open wide, and then she jumped up and started putting her clothes on. After getting about half dressed and with her clothes barely hanging on her, she made a dash for the door. I jumped up thinking maybe I could talk her into staying, and that's when I saw myself in the mirror and almost fainted. My pecker was a foot long and almost as big around as my wrist, and that's when I knew why she ran," I said.

"You mean . . . your . . . thing . . . was . . ." Dewey said, then broke down and laughed like a fat man. I should say he laughed like a tired fat man.

"Yep, it sure was. The only dick I've ever seen that big was on something wearing hair, and I couldn't figure out where it came from. It sure wasn't mine."

"That's hilarious," he said, wiping at his eyes.

"Do you want to hear the rest of the story?" I asked. Dewey's sense of humor was starting to get on my nerves.

"Yes, please continue," he said.

"Well, the shock of seeing my dick caused it to go down, and it shrank back to normal size. I was relieved, but seeing it swivel up that way scared me. I ran to the door to call after the gal, but nearly bumped into Roosevelt. He was standing in the hall, leaning against the wall just outside my door. He looked like the proverbial cat that had just eaten the canary. That's when I knew where the big dick came from. The Central Office had fixed me so I couldn't get in trouble."

"Roosevelt told you that?"

"Yeah, he told me not to worry, that nothing about me had changed, and that I was still the same person I'd always been. I told him not quite, that at least one thing had changed a lot. That's when he told me that my new mode came with some slight modifications. Since it was my first time out, the Central Office had made some adjustments. They didn't want me to fall victim to worldly temptations, which is exactly what I was about to do. Roosevelt said I could think of my new pecker as a governor, sort of like a restriction on a carburetor to keep a car from going too fast," I said.

Dewey laughed again, but he managed to gather himself in a few minutes. "I suppose you had something to say about that," he said. He knew me well enough to know that I didn't take things like that lying down.

"I sure did. I called the folks in the Central Office a bad name, several bad names, actually. Roosevelt told me to bite my lip, that those folks were just looking after my best interests. He said the adjustment was temporary and would go away when I learned to control myself. That didn't calm me down much, though, and I told him it was a dirty trick. I was so pissed that my mouth got the best of me. I threatened to go out and find some black gal, said they were used to dicks like that."

"You said that to Roosevelt?"

"Yeah, and it pissed him off. He told me to watch myself, or otherwise my dick could get even bigger, might even end up dragging the ground. That's when I shut up. Having a donkey dick is one thing, but an elephant dick is out of the question," I said.

"So, what happened then?"

"I didn't get laid, that's for sure."

"What about your assignment in Las Vegas? What have you been doing for the past three weeks?

"Gambling."

"Gambling? Was that really your assignment? You've been gambling in Las Vegas for three weeks while I've been slaving and worrying myself sick over Woody? You've just been gambling?"

Dewey asked. His voice went up half an octave and his face started getting red.

"What can I say, Dewey? So I got an easy job, and you had to work your ass off. I'm sorry you had a bad time of it, but I refuse to apologize for having a ball in Vegas," I said.

"There's no justice, not even in the hereafter," Dewey said, sadly shaking his head.

"I don't want to hear about it, Dewey. I was here for fourteen long years all by myself with Woody, so don't cry on my shoulder. If anybody's earned a vacation, it's me."

"You're right, and I beg your pardon for downgrading your job in Las Vegas. It's just that Woody has been . . . such a . . . such a . . ."

"Shit?"

"Yes, a shit," Dewey said, nodding emphatically.

"Want to tell me about it?" I asked.

"No, I want to hear the Las Vegas story first. Why were you gambling?"

"That was my job, or at least it was most of my job. What made it such a fun deal was that I couldn't lose - no matter what game I played, how I played, or where I played. I won more money than I thought existed in the whole world."

"Was that part of the plan?"

"That's what we were sent there to do. My only job was to go to these casinos and break the bank. It was a dream come true, especially for somebody with my luck. I couldn't win a dime when I was here as a mortal, and that's why I hardly ever gambled. But I won millions, literally millions, of dollars over the past three weeks."

"I'm assuming you didn't do this alone," Dewey said, stifling a yawn.

"No, I had some help. As soon as I got to Vegas, Roosevelt took me to Caesar's Palace and introduced me to my new partner. You should've seen her. What a babe! I nearly got a hard on just looking at her," I said.

"Given your state of confinement, or adjustment, that would've been some situation," he said through a brittle smile. The idea that I had a different partner miffed him some, not the boner.

"Yeah, I might've busted a zipper, but I didn't. Anyway, she was a real doll. Her name was Phoebe Foster, and she's a former hooker. She used to live in Vegas, worked there, and that's why they sent her on the assignment."

"There had to be a valid reason. Otherwise, teaming you with a prostitute ranks right up there with the appointment of James Watt as Secretary of Interior," Dewey said.

"Who's James Watt?"

"I'd explain, but it's not worth it. Go on with your story."

"Phoebe helped me work the casinos. She knew Vegas like the back of her hand, but the thing that made her so valuable was that she knew lots of people. Having her around made my job easier, and a lot more enjoyable," I said, grinning.

"I suppose you tried to . . ."

"I never laid a hand on her. Our association was strictly professional, but I sure enjoyed her company. Her sense of humor and mine seemed to jive, and that made working together easy."

"That doesn't speak very well for her, I'm afraid. You have the sense of humor of a gutter snipe," he said, matter-of-factly.

"She was a bright woman with a realistic outlook on life. A drug overdose killed her, but she's changed a lot since then. Her transformation brought out the best in her," I said defensively.

"That's good. Did she have any observations about how your transformation was going?"

"We didn't discuss it."

"Was she using the personification mode too?"

"Of course, but she didn't look like she used to. She still had too many old acquaintances living in town to use her old image. Anyway, she was my partner, and we met when we got briefed upon arrival. This fellow named Hubie Sinclair served as our contact there. He'd been sent in by the Office of Special Operations, and all I can say about him is that somebody in the Central Office is doing a helluva job of typecasting. Hubie used to be a Detroit cop, and he headed up our sting operation."

"Ah, yes, the operation. The plot thickens," Dewey said. His manners were starting to rankle me, but I went on.

"It's like I said before, we gambled. Our job was to hit these casinos and break the bank. Some mobster named Lieberman ran a half dozen casinos in town, and it was our job to clean them out. At the briefing Hubie told us that Lieberman's casinos were funded by dirty money, mostly from cocaine and other drugs, but partly from funds from prostitution, pornography, toxic waste disposal, and loan sharking. The Office of Supernatural Effects rigged the gambling devices, and that's why we couldn't lose," I said.

"And you and Phoebe did this alone?"

"Nope. A guy named Clayton worked with us - an accountant in charge of keeping up with winnings. He didn't gamble, though. Phoebe and I took care of the gambling chores."

"Was that all there was to it? Did you just go in, clean the casinos out of money, then leave?" Dewey asked.

"That's pretty much it, but it's not quite as easy as it sounds. Casinos don't just let a fellow walk in and win all their money. They usually run you off if you start winning too much, and they refuse to take any bet they don't feel comfortable with. We had to set it up where they had to take the bets I made. This sting operation went far beyond what I was doing in Vegas. They had other teams working all over the country, even out of the country. While we worked on the casinos in Vegas, teams were hitting their network branches in other places - where their loan sharking outfits were, where their drug distribution branches were, or where their toxic waste disposal units were, and things like that. I haven't heard about the others, but the operation in Vegas was a success. We took twelve million bucks out of that town," I said, whacking myself on the chest.

"What happened to the money?"

"Gave it all to charity - higher education research, to be exact. It went to some university doing research on infant illnesses. I saw a blip on TV about this research center and asked that the money be sent to them," I said.

"Bless your lecherous, but obviously sometimes charitable, heart," Dewey said, patting my knee. "Now tell me how you won the money?"

"I just strolled in and started gambling. Phoebe took me to this casino called High Rollers, a second class casino on the new strip. Some rich Texan had just dropped a quarter of a million in there the night before, and they were ripe for the picking. I walked in looking like I owned Dallas, Stetson and fancy boots and all the trimmings, and started playing blackjack. I turned a hundred dollar bill into five thousand in less than an hour, then moved to the crap table. Ten thousand later, I went back to the blackjack table and waxed them for about fifty thousand. They changed dealers on me, but I still couldn't lose. I tried to put down a fifty thousand dollar bet at the blackjack table, but they wouldn't take it. I went back to the crap table and got to them for about fifty grand before leaving. On my way out, I dropped a quarter in one of those jackpot one-armed bandits. It paid me twenty-five thousand, so I got out of the place with better than two hundred thousand."

"Two hundred thousand isn't enough to break a casino, not even a small one," he said.

"No, but it'll cause some concern, particularly when more than one person walks out with a bundle. Phoebe got to them for more than I did, about three hundred grand. They had to send out for the money to pay her, probably to one of their other casinos. The next night we split up and carted off nearly a cool million, about five hundred grand each. We changed images the next night and collected another million," I said.

"You changed images?" he asked, looking a bit shocked.

"Sure did. They made me into a short, fat, baldheaded guy with a Yankee accent. I raised hell with Roosevelt about it. He said I'd get to change again in a few days, and that being an ugly Yankee would be good for me. I didn't argue the point, but I couldn't see how being that ugly was good for anybody. I should've kept my mouth shut because two days later he turned me into a Japanese businessman."

"How fitting."

"Some twerp from Supernatural Effects actually did it. Every two days the mode mechanic - that's the twerp - came around and changed me into somebody else, and he never let me be what I asked for."

"Need I ask what you wanted to be?"

"We won't go into that, but I sure as hell didn't ask for what I usually got. After being the Japanese guy, I was a doctor from Nebraska, a peanut farmer from Oklahoma, a bank examiner from Philadelphia, and used car salesman from Phoenix - most of them ugly, I might add."

"I love it," Dewey said, chuckling.

"I didn't care for it very much, but by the end of the first week we had a suitcase with nearly five million bucks in it. The losing plague had spread to all six Lieberman casinos by then, and his money suppliers were starting to get goosy. This, of course, was part of the plan. He called in some out of town money, drug or prostitution or loan sharking cash. We went out the next day and took another two million off him, then gathered another million and a half the next day. Within days, his out-of-town sources dried up, and he turned to banks. They wanted assurances, and he spent thousands having his machines checked for bugs. He changed dealers, pit bosses, and floor managers, but we just kept taking his money. We didn't completely break him, but we hurt him. Another team is working him now. There's a lot of dirty money involved, and it may take a while. We were never told what the overall plan is, but undoubtedly the Central Office wants to cause the big crime bosses to start fighting among themselves. Maybe they're just trying to raise money for some worthwhile charities, but whatever their goal, they're doing some good."

"Is that the entire story then?"

"Well, almost. We had a little harmless fun on the side," I said.

"Tell me about it," Dewey said, sitting up straight for the first time since we'd pulled into the alley.

"There was this hooker Phoebe knew from way back. She's a greedy bitch, and when I say greedy I'm not just talking small stuff. She's a high dollar hooker who works out of a fancy casino penthouse, and she's supposedly in tight with Lieberman. Phoebe said she'd do nearly anything for enough money. She's a vain woman, too, who takes care of her business, and you know, of course, what her business is. Phoebe said she used to brag about her unusual muscle control, and about how her business was the best in Vegas."

"So?"

"So it just happened that I was personified as some peanut farmer from Oklahoma that week - a big drink of water well over six feet tall and not too hard to look at. He looked ripe for the picking if anybody did, and that gave us the idea about setting up the greedy hooker. I called this gal up and asked for an appointment. She sent some big meathead down to the lobby to get me, then gave me a good going over when I got up to her penthouse. I told her I just wanted a good lay, and she said it would cost me a thousand. I whipped out a thousand and laid it on the table, and we went back to her bedroom. We got naked and jumped into bed, and she reached for my dick. I got even more of a reaction from her than I did from the tourist gal from Iowa. She jumped straight up in bed and stared down at me with her mouth hanging open. Then she told me to get my clothes on and get out. That's when I went to my pants, pulled out my wallet, and laid ten crisp thousand dollar bills on the dresser. She stared at the money for a minute and then shook her head. I laid out another ten thousand, but she still shook her head. That's when I pulled out all the money - a smooth fifty thousand dollars. She offered me all sorts of kinky stuff, but I said a good lay was all I wanted. All she had to do for the fifty grand was take what I had."

"Did she?"

"Nope, but she tried. She greased up her business and tried sitting down on it, but it wouldn't go in. After that she tried every position known to hookers, but nothing worked. The more she tried, the more frustrated and pissed off she got because the more she tried, the bigger and harder my pecker got. She'd try and try, and then she'd get up and run around the bed. Finally, she fell down in the floor and threw a screaming, cursing fit. Then she threw me out," I said.

"You're a louse," Dewey said, unemotionally.

"Yeah, I know."

"Did Roosevelt catch you?"

"Yeah, he found out, and it pissed him off. I spent the next two days being a skinny bank examiner from Philadelphia with crossed eyes and a big wart on my nose."

"Serves you right. He should've done worse than turn you into a man with crossed eyes and a wart on his nose. He couldn't have made you have sex with a woman who looked like that."

"Roosevelt's stern, but he's not mean," I said.

"And Phoebe, what happened to her? Is she still in Las Vegas?"

"She went back to her mark, somewhere in Minnesota. She's breaking in a new partner, too. They're watching over a teenage doper. She said the kid's a mess."

"So is that kid in there," Dewey said.

"That bad, huh?"

"I've never seen him in this condition. He functions, but Woody seems different somehow. His teaching has been only mediocre lately, but maybe that's because of the drinking. He's been drinking heavily, particularly when he's alone. And his mood has been gloomy, real gloomy. He comes out of it while he's with the woman, but it comes over him again as soon as he's alone. That's why he works so hard at filling his hours with wild outings, I suppose. I dread the weekends. He goes crazy from Friday until Monday, and that's been driving me crazy."

"He's on the run again. He does that when he gets crowded too much, when he can't handle things. The fight with Wanda and this new thing with the woman in there have him on the run. I've been through it with him before, but I learned to deal with it."

"I don't want to talk about it," Dewey said, looking out the window at the dark.

I allowed the conversation to die at that point. Dewey was right, and there was no use worrying about it until the time came. With Woody on the run again, my job was to keep him safe, or as safe as I could manage. Surely the Central Office would let us know when the job was over. Vegas had been fun, but it sure felt good to be just me again. The personification mode had been a new and exciting experience, but being home and back in a mode structure I understood was a better feeling.

CHAPTER 21
The Worm That Will Not Sleep

The growl of Woody's car engine brought me awake with a start, not my favorite way of greeting a new day, but I was relieved as I straightened up and looked around. I'd been dreaming of Las Vegas and Phoebe, and it was a dream fraught with both pleasure and pain. The pleasure part had to do with a warm waterbed and Phoebe's hot body writhing under me. The pain part came from guilt caused by trying to abuse the personification mode and thereby break my trust as a custodian. It also came from having that donkey dick the Central Office had endowed me with, thereby ruining my fun with Phoebe. Waking out of the dream brought the reality that none of it was true, and I leaned back with a big smile on my face. I woke up holding my crotch. I was back to normal, all right, because all I had was a comfortable handful. Dewey was staring at me, a deep frown furrowed into his forehead.

"Are we playing with ourselves?" he asked.

"Just checking. I was having a bad dream."

"Was a monster after your penis?"

"The monster **was** my penis," I said, causing Dewey to snigger into his palm.

"Woody's leaving," Dewey said, motioning toward the taillights disappearing down the narrow lane to my left. I cranked up and fell in behind him.

"It's still dark. Does he usually go home this early?" I asked.

"This is late for him. He's usually home by one or two, and it's nearly five now. He'll go home now and wait on Wanda's call. She always calls about six to make sure he's up in time to make his class at eight. Old habits are hard to break, I suppose. She's been his alarm clock for too long."

"Well, at least she's still calling."

"They even fight over the phone," he said, sighing heavily. He'd been doing that a lot lately.

The call came just as Dewey predicted, and Woody ended up slamming the phone down on the receiver within minutes after he picked it up. Then he sat and stared at a blank wall, looking lost and confused. At fifteen before eight he checked his watch, then washed his face and slipped on his sports coat. He headed for the front door but nearly tripped over a stuffed animal that one of the children had left on the hall floor. He stooped to pick it up and then stared at with a look of deep remorse on his face. I thought for a moment that he'd break into tears, but he didn't. His face and eyes went blank, and he dropped the stuffed animal and quickly exited the room.

Dewey caught my concerned expression. "It gets worse. Sometimes he sits and stares for hours. Sometimes he cries."

"He's done that before."

"Has he held a gun to his head before?" Dewey asked. I turned to look and caught him staring at the floor. He never did that when saying something important.

"No, he hasn't. When did he do that?" I asked.

"A week ago, give or take a day. The gun wasn't loaded, but he held it to his head. He didn't pull the trigger. I'd seen him remove the bullets, but I was horrified and changed to the I/T mode and moved closer him, just in case he tried to load the gun. I almost didn't hold my mode. That's how scared I was. He got up and walked around the bed, still holding the gun, and when he turned his back, I grabbed the bullets and dropped them into the dresser drawer with his underwear. He paced back and forth for a few minutes and then came back for the bullets. He got confused when he couldn't find them. Finally, he put the gun back on the shelf."

"You done plumb good," I said.

"I done plumb good? What kind of talk is that?"

"That's redneck for 'you did exceedingly well'", I said, winking at him.

"All I did was hide his bullets. What if the gun had really been loaded? What then?"

"We'd have another assignment, and maybe they'd send me back to Vegas with Phoebe. Where's the gun. I'll load it for him," I said, trying to inject some humor. Dewey didn't go for it.

"You're awful," he said.

"Yeah, but you love me anyway," I said, playfully whacking Dewey on the shoulder.

He looked too tired and despondent to respond to my joking around, so I told him the truth. "I was just kidding. Actually, I'm worried. Woody's never done that before. He's been wild and reckless, and he's given me more than my share of headaches, but he's never actually threatened to take his own life. What worries me is this: if he's gone as far as holding a gun to his head, he's bound to be thinking about using it. That means our boy is having a real crisis. We're going to have to watch him awful close."

"Yes, I know," Dewey said, solemnly.

"Dewey, I think I ought to say something. You're worn out, and I'm beginning to see why. You're worried sick over this mess, and there's something you need to know. We can't keep Woody alive if he really wants to die. If and when he makes up his mind to pull the plug, we might not be able to stop it. We can't monitor everything that goes into mouth, or hide every bullet and gun, or drive a car for him, or walk for him. We can't watch him that close."

"What can we do?" he asked, looking more despondent than ever.

"Our best, that's all. If he pulls the trigger, or whatever, we'll have to accept it. He's in a black mood, that's for sure, but it might be more than that this time. Woody might be losing it, going crazy."

"And oh! that pang where more than madness lies, The worm that will not sleep, and never dies," Dewey said.

"Huh?"

"It's just a couple of lines. From Byron, I think."

"I should've known it was a quote. Here I am, trying to talk frankly, and you're talking about worms."

"I'm talking about Woody and his present dilemma, you literary twit. The quote, although apparently of little use to you, was symbolic. Woody is lonely and guilt-ridden, and he can't put it to rest," Dewey said, looking genuinely irked.

"If he'd straighten his ass up he wouldn't feel that way," I said.

"You mean stop drinking?"

"That'd be a start in the right direction."

"He's too far gone to just quit. Woody needs help, some professional help," Dewey said.

"Like a psychiatrist? A psychologist, maybe? Damn, Dewey, he's one of them. How can a shrink do somebody like Woody any good?"

"Woody's a teacher, not a practicing psychologist. He may know the language, the jargon, and the ideology, but he's a long way from being a psychiatrist. Psychiatrists are more skilled, better trained, and . . ."

"I know what they are," I said.

"Then you should know better than to say what you did, even though it's forgivable. Woody feels the way you do. A psychiatrist is the last person in the world he wants to talk to, but that's not what I had in mind. I was thinking of a treatment center."

"He won't go to a treatment center," I said flatly.

"Did you want to go to Viet Nam?"

"Hell no! My reserve unit got called up."

"Woody may end up in treatment the same way you ended up in Viet Nam," Dewey said.

"Nobody's going to send Woody off for treatment. Nobody cares about his drinking problem, except maybe Wanda, and sometimes I wonder about her. His friends might think he drinks too much, but they don't think he's an alcoholic. His bosses don't know how much he drinks, and probably wouldn't care if they did, just as long as he doesn't cause them any trouble," I said.

"You're right, but that's because a real crisis hasn't developed. His drinking is getting bad enough to draw attention now, and he could create that crisis at any time."

"I've been thinking that for years, but even though he gets his ass in a sling from time to time, he always slips out of it," I said.

"This affair he's having might be the straw that breaks the camel's back," Dewey said, rubbing his chin and squinting. Doing that made him look perceptive because when he was thinking and focused on a problem, his eyes took on the hue and brightness of a computer's high resolution color monitor.

"Don't count on it. He'll probably straighten up some when Wanda comes home. He'll get rid of apple ass and fly right for a while, and then he'll pull the same thing again. The guy's good at worming out of things," I said.

"Perhaps not this time. He's changing. I can't explain how, but something is different. He may decide to continue his affair with this woman, and Wanda will catch him, and that will touch off a crisis. Someone at school may find out and confront him. It's not easy to keep something like this hidden in a small town like Forest City," Dewey said.

"Who is this gal, anyway? Where's she from, and what's she doing humping a drunk psychology professor? All I know about her is . . ."

"That she's got a nice bottom," Dewey said, finishing my sentence.

"Right."

"She's 31 years old and recently divorced from a blue color type man who drank a lot. Woody, however, is not surly and mean like her husband was. They moved here from Denver, and she started attending college to get her mind off a bad home situation. She's fascinated by Woody's intellectual prowess, but it's more than that."

"Well, Woody's no Robert Redford, but he's not bad to look at. Maybe she's just horny," I said.

"Woody is tailor-made for her. He's good to her, for one thing, and he's understandable and predictable. Woody, to some degree, is even controllable. The sex, in my opinion, is secondary."

"I'll buy that."

"You will? I never thought you'd admit that sex is second to anything."

"I wasn't easy, but I know Woody too well. He might be tailor-made for her, but she isn't for him. Woody's addicted to fight and fuck situations, remember? Unless she's hooked on the same thing, apple ass won't hold him long, and he'll run back to Wanda. She's what really turns him on because she knows when and how to treat him like dirt. If this new gal wants a real romance, she'll be very disappointed in Woody."

"That's very perceptive of you, but how long will it take this woman to find that out?" Dewey asked.

"Until Wanda gets back," I said.

"Will Wanda catch him this time?"

"Nope."

"What if she does?"

"Then our job will get even tougher," I said.

"Not if her catching him creates a crisis severe enough to get him into a treatment center," he said.

"I just had a thought. We could set Woody up and cause the crisis. We could fix it to where . . ."

"How dare you suggest such a thing," Dewey said angrily.

"It was just a suggestion," I said, but too late. Dewey was already walking away.

Woody plowed through three psychology classes - two general psych classes and a senior class in abnormal behavior, and then he headed for home. He left a note on his door saying he'd be reading in the library. That was a lie, and by two o'clock he was at Frank's drinking beer with a couple of cowboy cronies. Three beers each and an hour later, the cowboys drifted away, and Woody headed for Dusty's. A light snow had started falling, and that put me ill at ease. Snow had once been pleasing to me, but Woody's tendency to act up on snowy days had ruined that for me. I started thinking of other things he'd spoiled for me, and I suddenly found myself feeling gloomy and resentful.

Apple ass showed up at Dusty's just before four with several other women about her age. The other gals were commuters who drove in from surrounding towns rather than live in a dorm or local apartment. The commuter set liked Dusty's, and the crowd picked up about four every afternoon. Woody usually avoided the commuter crowd, preferring instead to hang out at Frank's until well into the evening. Somehow, I got the feeling that apple ass's showing up and Woody's early arrival at Dusty's was no accident.

Dewey and I sat in the corner and watched Woody play a corner pinball machine, something he seldom did. Then I noticed something else unusual - a vodka and tonic drink on table beside him. A devout sour mash bourbon drinker, Woody hardly ever screwed around with vodka. "Has he done that before?" I asked.

"Playing pinball?"

"No, the vodka tonic."

"Just since he started having some stomach problems. He must be trying to ease up, but it's not working because he drinks more now."

"That's not like him," I said.

Woody played a second game of pinball without ever looking over his shoulder. Apple ass kept sneaking looks in his direction, but he didn't let on that she was anywhere around. I was starting to think he hadn't seen her and was wondering how he'd handle it when he did. "What's this gal's name?" I asked.

"Faith Appleton," Dewey said, grinning boldly.

"You're kidding. Appleton?" I asked.

"Yes."

"Well, I'll be. Apple ass Appleton, what a moniker."

"I like Faith better. It's a beautiful name," Dewey said.

"You're right; it's a nice name. The gal wearing it ain't too shabby herself."

"Ain't?"

"Naw, she sure ain't," I said, watching her closely as she swished past on her way to the ladies room.

"You're English is getting worse."

"Yeah, but my eyes aren't. That's a fine looking woman, and there's more to her than just ass. I might have to take back what I said about Woody dumping her when Wanda gets home. Woody might not be able to break away from this gal too easy, and there may be your crisis. Getting caught usually happens when you get so proud of what you're humping that you get brave. You want everybody but your wife to know you're getting it, and that leads to trouble. They may have set up this meeting, and if so, he's playing it awful loose this time, and that's not like him."

"They've met here before, but they never leave together," Dewey said.

"It's coming. Woody will get braver and braver, and that's going to put him at risk."

Dewey looked as if he'd been prepared to say something sharp, but my remark apparently disarmed him. "Is that a compliment?"

"Sort of. Now let's get out of here. Let's go outside and watch it snow."

"What about Woody?"

"He's not going anywhere right now," I said, pointing to show that he had just moved nearer the table where Faith was sitting with her friends.

"You're right. I accept your invitation."

Dewey and I sat on the Chevy's hood and ate sandwiches while we watched it snow. The falling snow, particularly since it was another of those nice snows that floated straight down in big fluffy flakes, lifted my spirits, but so did the roast beef sandwich in my hand. Dewey nibbled at his asparagus sandwich and sipped at his apricot nectar, never saying a word but occasionally taking deep breaths and expelling them in vapor puffs. His antics so amused me that I didn't notice right off what was happening. When I saw snow on his head and shoulder, it dawned on me.

"What are you doing in the I/T mode?" I asked. Dewey looked at me, blinked, and then grinned feebly.

"I don't know. I didn't realize I was, I guess. I was just making frosty breaths and . . ."

"You're so tired you can't even hold your I/I mode," I said, cutting in.

"No, I was just . . ."

"Don't lie to me! You're pooped, Dewey."

"I must be," he finally said, realizing he didn't have an argument. He'd screwed up, and he knew it. His concentration level was low, dangerously low.

"What if some drunk came out of the bar and saw a layer of snow hanging in the air making vapor breaths? He'd crap his corduroys. Knock it off and change modes."

"O.K.," Dewey said, shrugging.

He closed his eyes and tried to concentrate, but nothing happened. He was just too tired to get out of the I/T mode, and that meant he was too tired to work. I loaded him in the car and drove him back to the trailer. I would've given him the car, but he looked too tired to drive, and I didn't want to ride home with Woody. A good night's sleep might bring him back to normal. Still, his inability to change modes worried me. I'd been tired before, but never so tired I couldn't change modes, and I decided right then and there that if he wasn't better by morning, I'd call Roosevelt.

On the way back to Dusty's, I started thinking about what Dewey had told me about Woody's episode with the gun. Just thinking of it nearly spooked me, and Dewey's comment about how Woody had been changing sure hit the nail on the head. I'd been back from Vegas for just a short time, but I'd seen it. It wasn't something you could put your finger on, but more like something you had a gut feeling about. The feeling sucked. Whatever had taken place in Woody wasn't good, and he'd need more supervision for a while.

Keeping a closer eye on him started immediately, and for a while it was downright fun. He followed Faith home from Dusty's just after midnight, fairly well drunk but then. They didn't even bother going to the bedroom this time and did it right on the living room floor. I watched for about ten minutes, then went back to the car and waited. Leaving a scene like that was rare for me. Faith was sitting astraddle Woody making motions like a belly dancer, but I tore myself away from it. Maybe it was too much for me to take, or maybe it was a premonition on my part. Whatever, I went back to the car and waited. That's when I saw him - a man sitting in a car close by staring toward Faith's lighted window. I didn't know him, but I knew he was trouble when I first laid eyes on him.

"What's this guy up to?" I asked out loud, so used to having Dewey with me that I forgot he wasn't there. I suddenly found myself wishing he was when the man stepped from his car and slipped something into his coat pocket. I didn't see it good, but it looked like a pistol. That's when I got out and made a dash for Faith's apartment. I stepped through the apartment wall and found them still on the floor, looking satisfied and still naked as a new egg.

"Get up, you stupid jerk," I shouted, very much aware he couldn't hear me. Sometimes I yelled out loud just to let off some steam, but this time I was really shook. I stepped back through the front wall to check on the man and saw him moving closer as he gingerly walked across the darkened courtyard. Watching him walk across the icy ground gave me an idea, and I changed to the I/T mode and waited just outside Faith's door. When the man got close, I braced for him.

He stopped just in front of the door and looked at the lighted window. Then he leaned forward and tried to peek around the drapes. He couldn't see anything, of course, and when he started moving back toward the door, I tripped him. I just stuck my foot out, and he hit the deck like cowshit on a flat rock - even went "splat" when he hit. I couldn't help sniggering at first, particularly at the way it all came about. When I tripped him, his feet started peddling and then his arms started wind milling around, and then he went down. After he landed, I started feeling bad about it because he hit hard.

All the commotion drew attention, and the front door to Faith's apartment flew open within seconds, and Faith, wearing a heavy terrycloth rope, peeked out. Then Woody came to the door and peeked out. The fallen man's wind started coming back and he began moaning. Faith came out first, then Woody, still buttoning his shirt. They bent down over him and assisted him until he was up and walking again. When they helped him to another apartment just down the walk, I started getting a heavy feeling deep in the pit of my stomach. Obviously, the man wasn't who I'd thought he was - Faith's jealous ex-husband. I felt sicker by the second.

I waited outside Faith's apartment, pacing back and forth. In my anxiety, I forgot about still being in the I/T mode until Faith and Woody returned. I was pacing with my head down when I suddenly noticed the deep trough I'd cut into the snow. Then I saw my vapor breaths and looked up. Faith and Woody were standing not ten feet from me, clutching each other and staring at me. Their eyes were wide, nearly as wide as their mouths. I lost my composure and ran - a stupid move because I turned and ran straight into a snow covered hedge row. Snow flew everywhere as I plowed through the hedges and then ran toward my car. I couldn't concentrate hard enough to change modes, so I cranked up and drove off, leaving a stream of vapor breath behind. I glanced over my shoulder and saw Faith and Woody still staring in my direction.

After three laps around the block, I parked on a corner and waited for Woody to start home. I didn't have to wait long, and by then I'd calmed down and was back in my I/I mode. Woody drove straight home, and I followed him into the house and watched as he waddled to bathroom. When I heard the shower running, I sat in a corner of the bedroom and waited. My day had been demanding, but my wanting it to be over with didn't hurry Woody. He stayed in the shower for half an hour, and by then I'd dozed off. Movement nearby aroused me, and I looked up and found Woody sitting on the edge of the bed staring at the clock. Four in the morning, it said, but he kept staring at it. After a short while, his eyes shifted to the phone, and he started at it a long time. Wanda's call wouldn't come for hours, but he just sat there and stared at the phone. I felt like whacking him in the head, but then he did something I hadn't seen in a long time. He lowered his head and cried.

I hate seeing men cry, but I hate hearing it even more. With the house empty and with no reason to hold back, he let it all out, and the hollow sounds of his sobbing got to me. I tried to stay in the room with him, but he kept crying, and I got up and went to the living room. After a while, the house got quiet, and I went back to the bedroom and found him looking into the top drawer of his dresser. I moved closer and saw that he was staring at his pistol. I almost dirtied **my** drawers! My heart started to race, but I couldn't move. He kept staring for a few more minutes, then sniffed a couple of times and reached into the drawer. That's when I switched to the I/T mode again and moved in like a cat going after a mouse. Just as I was about to grab him, he picked up a T-shirt and started putting it on. I breathed a sigh of relief and slumped to my knees, and at that moment, I knew for sure why Dewey was so worn out.

Woody went back to his bed and stared at the phone again. After a few minutes, he fell over and went to sleep with the lights on. I craved sleep about as bad as anyone can, but that old saw about there being no rest for the weary holds up sometimes. I'd had a bad day. Roosevelt would probably get wind of the incident at Faith's apartment, but that's not what had me so bumfuzzled and agitated. My mark was in a tailspin, and I had no idea what to do about it.

CHAPTER 22
Crossroads

Dewey slept until nearly ten o'clock the next morning, but that didn't matter. He needed the rest, and Woody had given us a break by missing all his morning classes. He'd gone to sleep without setting his alarm, and he slept almost as long as Dewey did. I welcomed the break - not because I wanted to catch up on some sleep but because I needed some time to think things out. Maybe I was too tired to think, but whatever, nothing came of my feeble attempts at it. Woody got out of bed long enough to call in sick at about nine o'clock, then went back to bed. The morning was cool but clear, and I deposited my weary ass under a tree out front and waited. Shortly after ten, Dewey popped out of the trailer and headed my direction. He had a thermos of coffee in his hand.

"Regular or sissy?" I asked as he walked up.

"Sissy, but you look like you need it," he said.

"You got that right. I had a rough night. Almost killed some guy."

"You what?"

"I pulled a stupid trick at apple ass's apartment last night. Some guy showed up, and I thought it was her ex-husband, and I tripped him, and he lost his balance in the snow and busted his ass. Then I couldn't get back in my I/I mode and pulled one of your stunts. I stomped down some snow, ran through some bushes, and right in front of Woody and Faith. I really fucked up," I said, taking the coffee Dewey had just poured for me.

"Oh, my! It does sound like you had a rough one. Who was the guy?"

"I have no idea, other than he was a neighbor, and he was trying to peek through Faith's window."

"Well, that's something you should have some sympathy for."

"Tacky, tacky," I said, wiggling a finger at him.

"Speaking of tacky, were you ever unfaithful to your wife?"

"I've learned some hard lessons that aren't easy to forget, but what's that got to do with anything?"

"Oh, you mentioned something about Woody's unfaithfulness, and I got the feeling that you were speaking from experience. Want to enlighten me?"

"Nope, just take my word for it."

"No? How unlike you. You're usually willing to share almost any point of view. Share is too mild a word, since you are seldom reluctant to lay your wisdom on anyone polite enough to stand and listen, particularly me, since my patient and understanding nature is a good depository for your . . ."

"All right, I'll tell you," I said.

"You got caught being unfaithful, didn't you. Is that what killed your marriage?"

"No. It ended because we got to where we couldn't stand each other."

"You weren't unfaithful?"

"I didn't say that."

"Then you were unfaithful."

"I screwed around some," I said.

"And you got caught?"

"You might say that."

"Either you did or you didn't. Why is a direct answer so difficult for you?"

"Because I did, and I didn't. I didn't get caught with my pants down, but I'd left a trail any fool could've followed. Still, I followed my father's advice about confessions. He once told me that a man should never confess to any sexual indiscretion. Lying was bad, he said, but better than owning up to the truth. 'Always deny it. Even if your wife catches you doing the neighbor lady on the living room floor, don't confess. Tell her you thought it was a pile of clothes on the floor and you were just looking for a soft place to lie down,' he said to me."

"There must be some logic in advice like that, but I can't seem to find it," Dewey said, scowling.

"The logic is simple. A confession might be good for the confessor, but it's hell on the confessee. The confessee gets dumped on, and not much good comes of it. And according to my wise old father, the woman never forgets. She might forgive, or try to forgive, but she never forgets."

"I'm not sure I agree."

"I didn't think you would."

"Confessions, properly given and properly taken, clear the air. A marriage can survive an act of infidelity, but it seldom survives deceit."

"What if the person being deceived, maybe for their own good, never finds out? What then?" I asked.

"One of them knows, and therein lies the danger," Dewey said.

"You've got a point," I said, but only after thinking it over for a few moments. "What you're saying is that Woody knows, and regardless of whether or not Wanda ever gets wise to him, he has to live with it from now on."

"Precisely."

"I'm still not sure my old man's advice isn't better. Ignorance is bliss."

"Ignorance is seldom blissful."

"That's crap! I don't know squat about nuclear physics, astronomy, Greek classics, poetry, and opera, or even about polo, hockey, and tennis. As far as I can tell, I haven't missed a thing. There's lots of things I do know, and that's enough for me. Maybe Will Rogers said it best when he said that we're all ignorant, just on different topics."

"I agree to some extent, but you have missed some things. You would be better off knowing something about those things you mentioned, even hockey. I love hockey," Dewey said, smiling sweetly. I still didn't like that smile.

"You love hockey?"

"Sure. I used to go watch the Black Hawks quite often."

"But hockey is a violent sport. You hate violence. You've always scoffed at rodeo, and now you're telling me you love hockey," I said, squinting at him.

"I don't like violence in most forms, but I like hockey. Hockey is much like ballet in that it requires skill and grace."

"So does rodeo, Dewey," I said.

"What's graceful about jabbing sharp spurs into an innocent animal, or trying to jerk their heads off with a rope?"

"Hockey players try to smash in each other's faces. Besides, who said the animals were innocent?"

"It's a given, and it seems so unfair and unjustified."

"It's unfair for a one hundred and thirty pound rider to jab his spurs into the side of a fifteen hundred pound bull that would dearly love to kill him?"

"The bull is a dumb animal, therefore he's innocent. He acts on instincts, not hatred or any other emotion."

"Are we trying to draw a parallel here?" I asked.

"Not really, but there seems to be one, particularly if we view it from this angle: Why would a small man want to try to ride a big bull? This is a classic mismatch, is it not?"

"I don't see it that way. Some bull riders, blessed with skill and experience, ride even the toughest of bulls. It seems to me that it comes out fairly even."

"Want to know why?"

"No."

"Well, listen anyway. I've been reading up on this sort of thing, and I want to see how much of it I remember. The bull rider's motivation comes from his need of finding a way to relate to the world around him. Like all men, the bull rider needs to overcome his fear of being a tiny grain of sand on the beach of life. Not all men choose the same forms of making themselves feel more at home on this planet. The need is the same, but the method of dealing with it varies according to social conditions."

"What do you mean by social conditions?"

"The way of relating oneself to the world is found in his passions: love, hate, or even individualism and independence. Our passions are tied together in what we generally call character, which is something we don't have in common. We share common drives, but not passions, and the differences in character are due to the differences in social conditions."

"I'm not sure that makes sense to me."

"A cowboy's passion may lie in his independence, his individualism. He expresses that by challenging the bull, a fitting reflection of his social conditioning. It's part of his western traditions and customs; it's something he understands. Win or lose, he proves to himself that he somehow fits into his natural environment."

"Cowboys fit into their natural environment better than anyone walking around on this planet, Dewey. He doesn't have to make himself fit; he already fits because he helped create that environment. Now, a guy like Woody has more of a problem, and Duncan, his half-blind buddy, really has a problem," I said.

"Well, he can't see well, but I'm not sure he'd be a good example of what we're talking about."

"Sure he would. I remember a time when Duncan insisted on going to Cottonwood to eat at a nice restaurant. Woody took him, and once in town, they located a restaurant and went in. People were waiting to be seated, and the waitress told them there would be a thirty minute wait. Duncan, a lover of newspapers and magazines, spotted a convenience store across the street and trudged off in that direction. Within minutes he started back toward the restaurant with a half dozen newspapers and several magazines, but poor eyesight and too much to drink got him disoriented, and he stopped on the street corner to get his bearings. So there he stood wearing dark glasses, a crumpled hat, an old raincoat, and with his arms full of magazines and newspapers. Woody decided to go rescue him, but he didn't quite get there before a Stetson clad man boldly approached him, grabbed a couple of newspapers out of Duncan's arms, shoved a quarter in his hand, and walked off. This left Duncan standing there, babbling something about not wanting to sell his newspapers. Woody almost doubled over in laughter, and so did I.

"That's shameful and irrelevant," Dewey said, sniffing.

"Shameful, my ass. That's funny; you've got to admit that Duncan looks like some blind guy selling newspapers. Those guys just assumed . . ."

"It's still shameful, and what is even more shameful is your laughing about it. Duncan couldn't help the way he looked."

"What he looked like, Dewey, was some derelict wino, or a flasher. He always looked that way. He even got thrown out of a shoe store one time."

"Thrown out? For just looking blind?"

"For looking like a derelict. Sometimes he really looks rumpled and ragged, and he was looking that way when he went to a mall up in Denver with Woody. Woody was in this shoe store trying on shoes, and Duncan wandered in and sat down in a chair. In a few minutes, some security guards came in and asked him to leave. The shoe store manager had called them and asked that Duncan be asked to leave. Duncan took it well, but Woody got pissed and stomped out of the store."

"Good for Woody."

"Like I said before, Woody's protective of Duncan. He pokes fun at him, but he doesn't like other people doing it. He does it because he cares about Duncan, and that's his way of showing him. Other people may not know that, but he does, and doing that may help Duncan find his niche, don't you think."

"I see where you're headed with this. You're saying that Duncan, despite his appearance, is looking for a way to fit in."

"Yeah, but he doesn't go about it like the cowboy does. He's different and he knows it, and maybe he overcompensates for that. I'm just guessing at a lot of this, but it makes sense to me," I said.

"You analogy might be poor, but you're on the right track. If man didn't work toward fitting in, toward altering his environment, he would feel lowly and useless and small and alone. Like everyone else, he comes into this world the most biologically helpless and frail of all animals, but unlike other animals, he is born with few basic instincts to rely on and be guided by. What he has is intelligence, the ability to reason. Man's intellect, however, is often an inadequate substitute for his weakened instincts. His ability to reason makes living difficult because he is aware of his frailty. Man knows he is apart from the rest of nature, knows how vulnerable he is, and even knows how it all will end, in death. His existence is a problem because he's the only animal that does not feel at home in his environment. He can't live the way an animal lives, by repeating the patterns of his species, but he must live, and in doing so must solve his problems."

"Man has instincts, Dewey."

"No, he doesn't, not really. What we often misjudge as instinct is really character."

"Now I know what to blame it on. I always thought my instincts were at work when my dick got hard and I started looking to get laid. Are you telling me that sex is not instinctive?" I asked.

"No, it isn't. What man has mostly are biological drives and some basic elementary reactions, not instincts."

"What about survival? There's no instinct for survival?"

"Not really. You learn how to survive. A bull rider learns how to ride bulls and that aids his survival because he has found his roadmap through life. There's no instinct in riding bulls."

"And the roadmap, I'm guessing, is his character, right?"

"Right.

"You beat all I've ever seen, coming up with notions about man and his environment and his passions and character. Where'd you come up with all that crap?" I asked.

"I've been reading Fromm," Dewey said piously.

"From what?"

"No, not from, but Fromm, like in Erich Fromm," Dewey said, giggling.

"Who's he?"

"THE ANATOMY OF HUMAN DESTRUCTIVENESS. He wrote that. He's a famous psychiatrist and a well known writer."

"Not in central Texas. I've never heard of him," I said.

"Why doesn't that surprise me?"

"Because you're a man of considerable perceptiveness."

"But without instincts," Dewey said.

"I'm still not convinced that man doesn't have instincts," I said.

"Perhaps it will help if I say it again, but with more emphasis this time on specifics. Man may not have lost his instincts, but they are badly weakened. What he has is biological drives and some rudimentary reactions, but no real instincts. Those are Fromm's words. Fromm also says that unlike an animal, man doesn't have a built in program that tells him what to do. What he has is self-awareness, the ability to reason and decide. His awareness, however, makes him aware of how stupid, powerless, and frail he is. He's is even aware of his own death. His biggest problem is his own existence. Erich Fromm calls this problem 'existential disequilibrium,' and he says that man is only able to overcome it by finding stability within his culture. But this cultural stability is fragile and the dichotomy between his lack of instincts and his self-awareness never goes away. He must deal with it always."

"But man reacts to things, and some of those reactions are instinctive, aren't they?" I asked.

"No. He reacts through character, not instinct. He deals with this existential disequilibrium that Fromm spoke of by developing what he called 'character-rooted passions.' People have different characters because of different social conditions and some genetic dispositions, and these character-rooted passions are their substitute for missing animal instincts. These passions are critical in understanding our fellow man. We've been through all of this before," Dewey said, wearily shaking his head.

"Is that why we're so different, you and I?"

"Try thinking of it this way. If life is a journey, then living is the road we travel. Like any traveler, man needs a map to guide him. He'd get lost without one. Along this highway of life, man is going to encounter a lot of crossroads, and which road he takes will determine where he arrives. Are you with me so far?"

"Yeah, so far."

"To most animals, the roadmap is instinct. Since his instincts are badly weakened, man's map is made up of his family, religion, class status, and other things. Even if the map is wrong, it works for him because he'll end up somewhere," he said.

"Yeah, but what good's a map if you don't know where you want to go?" I asked.

"Well, it isn't much good if that's all he has. Man also needs an object of ultimate concern - an object of ultimate devotion that can be used as a basis for his values and for continuing his travels. Man needs to find a harmony with nature, a unity with the world around him."

"So, Woody's screwed up because his map and his object of devotion are screwed up."

"Yes, but there's more. Let's say that the traveler comes to a fork in the road. One road goes downhill, and the other goes uphill. The downhill road is smooth and wide and inviting, but in reality it is the road to disaster. It has no other destination. The uphill road is rocky and winding and uninviting, but it has a rewarding destination because it leads to higher ground. As long as one follows the lower road, he'll never be able to pick his way through life because he can't see much from down there. But if he manages to make it to higher ground, he has the great advantage of being able to see where the low road leads."

"And Woody has taken the lower road."

"Yes. Men like Woody turn to things like alcohol and sex in an attempt to gain this unity with the world and some harmony with nature. But whatever unity or harmony he finds, it's always temporary. Even worse, it cripples him, impairs his judgment, and makes him dependent on his passion for drink and sex."

"Why does he do that?"

"Because he's bored. Woody, like all people, needs to overcome boredom. To overcome boredom, he needs to be excited, and to be excited he needs to be stimulated. What stimulates a person to be active depends on the person, and Woody has chosen the wrong stimuli. What he has chosen is momentary excitation through drink and sex. That, of course, simply anesthetizes his boredom, but does not cure it. He remains bored, even though he doesn't realize it. Some people try to work their way out of boredom, but that seldom works either," he said.

"If sex and drinking won't work, what will?"

"By using what Fromm called 'activating stimuli'. This sort of stimuli is ever changing and therefore produces good results, but only when a person is capable and willing to use it. A person who can respond productively to activating stimuli doesn't get bored. Other people rely upon simple stimuli, the kind that produces drives. These simple stimuli produce only immediate and passive responses and don't alleviate boredom. The people who rely upon simple stimuli, like sex or drinking or greed, must keep increasing the stimuli for it to work because the novelty of it wears off. They may have to constantly change sex partners for it to be effective, if sex is what they use to alleviate boredom. If they drink, they have to increase the amount."

"That sounds like our boy, all right."

"Yes, it's a tragic situation."

I would've pumped Dewey for more information, but I heard the phone ringing inside the house and went to see who was calling. I reached the bedroom toward the end of the conversation, but I heard enough to know that Wanda's father had died. Woody would be leaving for Ohio that day, and that was bad news. Dewey couldn't make the trip, not in his condition, so I'd be going it alone for awhile. I was already dreading it.

CHAPTER 23
The Board of Regrets

Dewey was sad when I told him about Wanda's dad, but I knew he would be. Dewey got sad about people dying, even if he didn't know them. His I/I mode was working again, but he still looked tired, and I insisted on him taking a break. He argued about it, but Roosevelt finally stepped in and convinced him to take some R and R time. He packed a bag and left with Roosevelt, but he had a wistful look on his face as they drove away.

Woody got up and around by ten, and we were on the road to Denver by noon. He called Faith to tell her about Wanda's dad, and we drove out of town without him seeing her. Surprisingly, Woody looked and acted fresh that morning. I felt like forty miles of torn up road. Woody didn't take any booze along, and the road was long and straight, so I curled up on the back seat and went to sleep. Half way to Denver, I woke up and looked around at the miles of prairie surrounding us. Colorful Colorado, my ass, I thought as we drove along. The country was as flat and drab as any I'd ever seen - even worse, in my opinion, than western Kansas. Something else crossed my mind. It's the pits when you live in country so isolated that Denver, Colorado is closer than the nearest major airport in your home state.

We were in the air for just a few short hours, and it was good to see Ohio again. Ohio has real trees, and that always impressed me. For the past fourteen years about the only kind of trees I'd seen were cottonwoods and Chinese elms, and I had always looked forward to Woody's short trips back to Ohio. The trees at this time of year were just trunks and leaf barren limbs, but I enjoyed them anyway. I also enjoyed seeing the open countryside between the Columbus airport and the town of Clarkston. Wanda sat close to Woody, her head on his shoulder, telling him about her dad and plans for the funeral. Walter, her brother and a local farmer himself, drove the car. He didn't talk much.

Once at Wanda's parent's place, Woody moved through his in-laws with considerable grace and understanding. He hugged and kissed Wanda's grief-stricken mom, he hugged her two semi-ugly sisters and a few aunts, then shook hands with the men folk. With that out of the way, he spent some time with his children. They walked around town, not a long walk because Clarkston wasn't much of a town, and stopped at a school playground to ride the teeter-totter and swings.

Later when he went to the upstairs bathroom to shower, Wanda followed him in and locked the door behind her. She stepped out of her panties, and pulled Woody to her. He looked surprised and confused, but he met her half way. He was already undressed, but Wanda was too eager to undress. She simply hiked up her dress, and guided Woody into her, supporting herself by half sitting on a corner vanity table. She finished quickly, and Woody made it a point to do the same. I didn't intend to watch, but it happened so fast I couldn't escape. I stayed, partly because I was amazed at Woody's behavior. How could he do that, I asked myself as I watched. Less than a day ago he was stroking Faith on her living room floor, but now he was going after Wanda like a frenzied teenager. Was it an act? Couldn't be, I decided. Woody wasn't that good at acting. He was really excited by her, at having her again. He was so excited, in fact, that he could get off in less than a minute.

Wanda slipped out of her dress, and showered with her husband. They took their time, and even though I didn't watch, I knew they were getting it on again because of the heavy breathing and bumping around in the shower stall. Finally, Wanda emerged, toweled off, dressed, and left the bathroom. Woody stayed in the shower for another ten minutes, so long that I peeked in to check on him. I wished I hadn't because I caught him crying again. He was standing with his head under the water and with a bath rag up to his mouth. That bugged me because Woody wasn't drunk this time - hadn't had a drink since the night before, but he was crying. That confused me bad enough to want to cry myself, and I started missing Dewey. Maybe he could explain what was going on with Woody because I sure as hell didn't know. My only notion was that he had a guilty conscience, but it had to be more than that.

The funeral went well, as far as funerals go. I'm glad I didn't have to go to my own funeral because I hate them, and knowing whether or not a funeral went well isn't my strong point. Being dead for a decade and a half hasn't helped me face up to funerals very well, but I've been to a few, and Wanda's dad got a nice enough send off. She held up well, and Woody was really good with her. That surprised me. I thought he might try to be a good husband for a change, but I likewise thought he was too much of a weak ass to pull it off. I'm not complaining because it made my job easier. He even made it through a second day without a drink.

He didn't make it through the third day, though. He started drinking at the airport before they took off for Kansas, and the three drinks he had on the plane finished the job. Wanda didn't get cross with him for getting drunk, partly because the drinking improved his mood, and that in turn made her feel better. She drove from Denver back to Forest City with Woody talking the entire way about a book he was thinking of writing. The kids slept.

I figured the good rapport between them would end when Wanda walked into the messy house Woody had left behind, but she didn't say a word. I rushed off to the trailer to see if Dewey was back from his R and R, but he wasn't. By the time I got back to the house, the kids had been put to bed and Woody and Wanda were screwing again. I'd been gone for less than ten minutes, and they were already at it. Since I'd seen more than my share of that lately, I went back to the trailer and crashed.

Woody beat me to school the next morning, and by the time I got there, he was in the faculty lounge talking about Ellen Stegnor with several colleagues. The Board of Regents had come to campus for a special meeting, and rumor had it that the new president was in trouble. The lounge crowd was almost gleeful, but Woody looked stunned. How could she already be in trouble, Woody had asked. She'd only been on the job a short while, not a full year even. She'd been indifferent and ineffective, some replied - not at all what the university needed. But she'd not had time to do anything, Woody then replied. Her not doing anything, some replied, was the problem. Woody went silent after that, and it seemed to me that he'd just realized something. He'd been too preoccupied over recent months to notice what was going on around him. An organized effort was obviously underway to unseat the new president.

"What's going on?" Dewey said from directly behind me. I jumped into the next room and then poked my head back through the wall and looked at him.

"Dammit Dewey! How many times have I told you about sneaking up on me?"

"Several."

"Then why do you keep doing it?"

"I don't do it on purpose. I was simply announcing my presence," Dewey said, piously.

"Do it from farther away next time. I could've run into. . ." I started to say and then suddenly remembered that I'd jumped into the girl's bathroom and had caught a glimpse of something that should've been of interest to me. I pulled my head back into the bathroom and looked at it. There it was as big as life - a rubber machine.

"Come in here and look at this," I said, poking my head and shoulders back into the hall and motioning for Dewey to come.

"And cater to your voyeuristic leanings? Not on your life," Dewey said.

"I don't have a life. Neither do you, so come here. I'm not peeping at naked girls."

Dewey hesitated and then grudgingly followed me into the bathroom. I pointed at the machine. "So?" he said.

"So don't you see anything strange about that? It's a rubber machine, Dewey."

"Actually, the machine is metal. It contains condoms, or to some, prophylactics. There's nothing rubber about it," Dewey said, sniffing lightly.

"But it's in the girl's room."

"Why not? They get social diseases, too."

"Yeah, but this is WKSU, the Mecca of High Plains conservatism. Folks around here just don't go for this sort of thing," I said.

"Even conservatives are realist. College kids are among the most sexually active people on the face of the earth, therefore they need more protection. I read recently where the college crowd seems to be the most convinced that they will not get infected with the aids virus, and colleges are trying to protect them."

"But this is WKSU, Dewey. This would be the last school in America to put rubber machines in the girl's john," I said.

"Maybe they are the last. Have you been on any other campuses lately?"

"No."

"Then pipe down and show me to the car. I'm hungry."

"Follow me, sir," I said, shuffling off toward the Chevy like a waiter.

I've never been much of a breakfast person, but the donuts and coffee we found in the magic box hit the spot. Dewey had a cup of tomato juice and an English muffin. His appetite didn't come close to mine because I gulped down a half dozen donuts and had three cups of coffee. Dewey watched me eat, daintily munching his muffin, with a mixed look of astonishment and displeasure on his face.

"I'm hungry," I said, defensively.

"I've seen garbage disposals devour food more slowly than that," he said.

"So I eat fast - so what?"

"It's bad for your digestion."

"You really knock me out, Dewey. I'm dead, and you're worried about my health."

"I'm not worried about your health, just your digestion. Eating like that gives you gas, and I'm the one who must put up with your farts," Dewey said.

"Fart? Did you say fart?"

"Yes, fart. When some people make gaseous emissions, it should be called breaking wind, or passing gas, or something polite. In your case, they're just farts." Dewey tried but couldn't hide a smile.

"Speaking of farts, have you heard the news? The Board of Regrets is coming to town."

"Beg your pardon? Board of what?"

"Actually they're called the Board of Regents, but I call them the Board of Regrets. In Kansas, the Board of Regents is the top dog in higher education. It has eight members, I think, appointed by the Governor. They meet about once a month to oversee the functioning of the various colleges and universities."

"The board runs everything?"

"No, not everything. University presidents are powerful, but the board is stronger, partly because they hire presidents. They also dole out the money and keep a close watch on the financial aspect of higher education," I said.

"Why are they coming?"

"Talk has it the new president's in trouble. Don't ask me over what, though, because I don't know."

"Who's on the board?" Dewey asked.

"A bunch of political hacks, mostly. I haven't kept up in recent years, so I don't know exactly who's on it. We can find out right quick. Their pictures are hanging on the wall of the conference room in Parker Administration Building."

"Let's go look," Dewey said.

The conference room was vacant, and we slid through a wall and started checking out pictures. I should've remembered that a new Governor had been elected, and a change of administration usually means a change in the composition of agencies, boards, commissions. Kansas had just gone from a Republican Party to a Democratic Party governor, and the nine member board had four new members, two of them women. They looked much younger than the other board members. I pointed the new members out to Dewey.

"What does that mean?" Dewey asked, looking at the younger faces on the wall.

"It might mean things will be different around her for a while."

"Four new faces on the board could change things that much?"

"It could indeed. See that guy there?" I said, pointing to the picture of an elderly, square faced man. Dewey nodded.

"That's Winford Bliss, the chairman of the board. He's a sharp cookie, and this is his first tour as chairman. He's a progressive, a free thinker, and he'll push for changing some things. Other board members have sometimes accused him of being an unrealistic liberal, but he may get more support from these younger members. The picture next to his is that of H. M. Richardson, and he thinks a lot like Bliss. H. M., by the way, stands for Horace Mann, and he tries to live up to his billing. Those three, the ones on the end, are all political hacks. The woman, the black gal, is a civil rights activist who got on the board for political reasons. All she cares about is making sure her race gets their share. Good academic standards and civil rights don't always run in the same direction, you might've noticed. The other two are conservative ranchers, both strong Republicans, and not too savvy about academics either."

"What about that man?" Dewey said, pointing to the picture of a balding man wearing thick glasses.

"That's Lewis Franks. He's a wimp who'll go with the crowd."

"How do you know so much about the board? None of them are from around here," Dewey said, having noticed that the home towns of each member were written just beneath their names.

"There's not a board member from within a hundred miles of this school, but they meet on this campus once a year, usually in the spring. I used to sit in on their meetings when I had some spare time, mostly because what they do affects my mark. Watching them work is what gave me the idea of calling them the board of regrets. So much of what they've done is regrettable, believe me."

"Like what?"

"Like choosing Houston Parker as president."

"But that was a different group of people. The current board didn't choose him."

"You're right, they didn't, but they kept him propped up. They seldom ever gave him any guff and just went along with what he wanted. That's the way it is with politics, Dewey," I said, winking.

"Did this same group of people hire the current president?"

"Yeah, but they were under pressure at the time. They'd just hired some high school superintendent from Wichita or Topeka as president of another college down state, but he spent one day on campus and ran into so much hostility that he resigned. The board, this new board, had named him without asking for input from the faculty or students or anyone, for that matter. Having their new man run off in just one day was an embarrassment, and they tried to do it right after that. When Houston Parker died, we had several committees going around here - a search committee and a selection committee. They narrowed a list of fifty applicants down to three, and Perkins was chosen by the board from that number."

"Perkins is the president the locals ran off, right?"

"Well, they didn't actually run him off. They just hassled him until he wanted to leave. I don't know whether or not they would've fired him, but most politically appointed boards do what is politically feasible. Most of them liked and supported Perkins, but they'd been bombarded with hundreds of letters and phone calls about Perkins. A well organized campaign was taking place to get rid of Perkins, and even though the board didn't give in to it, they were probably relieved when he resigned," I said.

"You told me about Perkins earlier, but I've forgotten the story," Dewey said.

"I'll refresh your memory, but I'll keep it short. Perkins took over about three months after Houston Parker died. Personally, I didn't care who headed the university, just as long as he didn't make my job any harder. Woody was already causing enough trouble to worry the calluses off a baboon's ass, and I worried what would happen if Perkins decided to take an interest in his faculty's personal problems. I had a feeling he was fixing to stir up a hornet's nest around here, and I didn't want Woody being one of the hornets."

"Undoubtedly he did stir up a hornet's nest." Dewey said.

"Yeah, he stirred them up, all right. I should've known how he would react to the new leadership, particularly when I saw what kind of man Perkins was - a dedicated academician with a list of publications as long as your arm. The man had a wide array of management skills, and his straight forward approach to problems made him popular with Woody right off. But a change of leadership always causes some problems, and I could tell right off that Houston Parker's old crony pals would suffer the most."

"Did they?"

"I'm getting there. Anyway, out goes paternalistic, political, Houston Parker and in comes energetic but abrasive Dr. Owen Perkins. He was an aggressive and savvy money raiser and manager, but he didn't know much about finessing people. Woody stayed in the shadows and watched Perkins start the process of derailing the old Parker gravy train. Some of his friends were affected, but that didn't seem to upset Woody. The gravy trainers initially tried to win Perkins over by getting him involved in the same circle they moved in, but he wasn't buying it. All the Parker ass-kissers took a run at him, then fell back. By September, as the anti-Perkins forces started to rally around those who were on the new president's ever growing shit list, Woody had decided for sure where he stood. He was a Perkins man, though he hardly knew the man, mostly because he admired his vigor, his aggressive style of tackling problems, and his professional approach to management. It looked like some real changes might take place at WKSU. The Perkins haters put some pressure on him, but Woody wouldn't go with them."

"Perkins and Woody became friends, I suppose."

"They were friendly but not buddies. I don't know how much Perkins knew about Woody's personal problems, but he looked the other way. He must've known something because Woody kept getting worse about his drinking and escapades, and I worried that Perkins might feel forced to do something about it. He never did, though, and I don't know whether it's because he liked Woody or just didn't know how bad he was screwed up," I said.

"Perhaps it's some of both, but perhaps Perkins saw in Woody something that was useful to him. 'A hen is only an egg's way of making another egg,' said Samuel Butler, and Woody might've just been Perkin's way of reaching other faculty members. Tolerating Woody's escapades might've been his way of showing others that he did indeed care about his faculty."

"Maybe, but when Woody sided with Perkins, his friend and colleagues shut him out for a while. His marriage started going bad about then. He might've become more involved, but he was too withdrawn by then. No one in administration had paid any attention to him in years, and that had caused a big build up of resentment toward the system. He wasn't about to rush to the new president's aid, and that was probably a blessing because he was too screwed up to be of much help to anyone."

"You still haven't explained what Perkins did to upset so many people."

"Perkins didn't fool around once he took over. He canned some of the old Parker gravy train administrators, a half dozen faculty members also resigned between terms, not all of them caused by Perkin's coming. Several teachers took early retirement, and a couple moved up the ladder to better jobs elsewhere. Still, rumors started flying. In a special faculty meeting called midway through the first semester, Perkins fingered a half dozen problem areas he intended to upgrade. Academics would be emphasized and athletics would go on the back burner. He pointed out that an intensive search for more academic scholarship funds was underway, and that the

WKSU Foundation, which provided most scholarships, would be targeted as a high priority item for upgrading. The library would be remodeled, and a bigger part of the budget would go into building up library holdings. The old admissions system under the Parker regime would be scrapped and replaced by minimum standards requirements. Campus discipline would be strengthened, particularly in the dorms where strict visiting hours would be set and strictly supervised. The campus would be policed more carefully. The cafeteria would be remodeled, as would several dorms. The campus grounds would be beautified, and maintenance would be improved. He said a new student activities center was on the drawing board," I said.

"And that made people mad?" Dewey asked, looking a bit baffled.

"It made some people mad, but what really got them was his talk about upgrading the faculty. A greater emphasis would be placed on terminal degrees, which meant that anyone hired from then on would have to have a doctorate. He saw inbreeding as a problem and talked of bringing in "new blood." He would press hard for higher salaries for faculty but said he expected a merit system for pay increases to be in place within a year. He said he planned to reorganize administration under three vice-presidents - one for academic affairs, one for student affairs, and one for business affairs. A half dozen new administrative offices would be created. A definite chain of command would be established, and a new budgeting system would be put in place."

"Did he do all of those things?"

"He did a lot of them, and in doing so alienated a lot of people. By the end of his first year here, he was thoroughly disliked."

"Then the faculty resented him because he made their jobs more difficult, and they were accustomed to being left alone under Parker," Dewey said, nodding as if the story was starting to come together for him.

"Yeah, that's mostly it. Some didn't like him because he kept pressure on them, and some didn't like him because he was blunt, even abrasive with them. Almost everything he did was a move in the right direction, but his method of getting there is what cost him. The newer faculty members leaned in his direction, particularly at first, but many of them knuckled under to pressure from the older heads. Students didn't like him, either."

"But he was working toward helping them."

"Most students didn't care about upgrading academic standards, Dewey. They just wanted a diploma. Just look around this place. Have you seen any of these kids clamoring for better instruction or anything like that? They may have appreciated some of the things he did, but they resented most of them - particularly his moves toward more discipline."

"Perhaps, but the students might have been afraid to take his side, particularly with all their teachers going the other way," Dewey said.

"Yeah, but some of them got actively involved in the plots and moves to get rid of him. After Perkin's first year here, a witch-hunt committee was formed - composed of disgruntled alumni, townspeople, and even some faculty and students. They called in witnesses and took testimony and ended up presenting to the Board of Regents a report based mostly on rumors and half truths and some outright lies. The board, having appointed Perkins, was not willing to dismiss him, but it nevertheless put the man in a bad position. Not long after the report came out, he resigned."

"Woody was unhappy, I suppose."

"He was pissed, so much so he finally came out of his shell and attended one of the witch hunt committee's meetings. He stood up and told them what he thought - that they were trying to do a hatchet job on a man who was just trying to do his job, and if that they should disband and stay the hell out of it. Most of them just sat there and stared at him, but a few got mad and flared up. Some openly ridiculed him."

"Poor Woody, he tried to do what he thought was right and got persecuted for it."

"They didn't really persecute him, but some were cold toward him for a while. It hurt him some, and he tried to drink it away." I said.

"The same people who opposed Perkins are opposed to Stegnor, I suppose."

"Some are the same, but not all. My guess is that Stegnor has been moving too slow in taking apart the things Perkins did, which was their reason for getting rid of him in the first place. I've heard that some of the old Parkerites who were run off during Perkin's stay have been trying to get their old jobs back. Actually, she's changed very little of what Perkins did."

"What is the Board of Regents meeting about today? Are the Parkerites behind it?"

"I don't know the answer to either question, but the meeting's at two this afternoon, and I thought I'd drop in. What time is it now?"

"Not quite ten."

"Good. We can stop talking about this boring crap and talk about your vacation,"

"It was wonderful," Dewey said, rolling his eyes.

"Tell me outside," I said, throwing my arm over Dewey's shoulder and pulling him toward the door.

We strolled across campus and sat under a tree on the library lawn. It was a pleasant day, particularly for late February, a month that can be the pits in western Kansas. Some of the worst blizzards I've ever seen came in late February or early March, but we'd had a relatively mild month, and that was fine with me. We'd already had the snowiest winter I could remember in recent years, and I was happy to see the snow from the sudden storm of several days past melt away. Hardly a breeze stirred, and the warm sun felt good. So we sat, enjoyed the nice weather, and talked. I was happy to see Dewey back in good spirits and looking spry and energetic.

He told me all about his short vacation. Roosevelt had taken him to San Francisco for three days. He'd been to the opera, the ballet, and to a recital of a world renowned string quartet. He'd eaten lavishly, he said, and named off a dozen dishes I'd never heard of. What made the trip so nice, he said, was the company of a beautiful young woman named Phoebe. When he got to that part, I broke in.

"Phoebe?

"Yes," Dewey said, smiling impishly.

"Phoebe Foster, my Phoebe Foster?" I asked.

"The very same," Dewey said.

"But . . . she's . . ."

"A delightful person," Dewey said, finishing my sentence. He didn't do a good job of reading my mind because I was going to say she was an ex-hooker who now worked in Minnesota.

"But . . ."

"Roosevelt said she needed some R and R, as you call it, so he killed two birds with one stone and put us together. Her mark, the kid she was watching, got hurt in an accident and was temporarily hospitalized, and she needed a break. The trip to Vegas had exhausted her, so we took our brief vacation together."

"Well, I'll be damned."

"I seldom trust your judgment in women, but you were right about Phoebe. She was wonderful, just wonderful."

"Yeah, she's a real piece of artwork," I said.

"She loves opera and fine food and museums and . . ."

"Knock it off, Dewey."

"Are you jealous?"

"You're right, I'm jealous. She's my idea of the perfect woman. What a face! What legs! What an ass! What a set of . . ."

"You just can't get past the tangibles, can you?" Dewey asked, making it sound more like a statement than a question.

"Get past them? Hell, I didn't even get to touch them," I said.

"There's much more to the woman than looks. Besides, you don't know what she really looks like, do you?" Dewey asked.

"Yeah, I know. She used the personification mode most of the time we were in Vegas as someone else, but I got to see her as herself at briefings. I don't like thinking about how good she looks. It makes me lonesome, not to mention what it does to my nuts. Go ahead with your story."

Dewey took up where he'd left off, but my mind was only half on what he said. Phoebe Foster was back in my mind now, and I started wondering if I'd ever see her again. The sad thought that we'd probably never meet again almost overcame me. By the time Dewey finished his story, full of references about Phoebe, I was depressed.

Woody's office door was open when we returned to his building, and Faith Appleton was standing in the doorway. The conversation between them had just ended, and she looked torn and confused when she turned to walk away. Woody closed the door after her and then sat staring into space through expressionless eyes. The staring always got under my skin, and I was glad when several students showed up at his door to draw him out of his trance.

Nothing much came of the Board of Regents meeting. The rumors that President Stegnor was in trouble with them turned out to be nothing more than that, rumors. Several representatives of the defunct Perkins witch-hunt committee came before the board with a list of grievances against Stegnor, most of them relating to her reluctance to roll back Perkin's policies. Then they presented the board with a petition signed by nearly a thousand people asking for the removal of the rubber machines from the bathrooms at WKSU. The petition, of course, didn't refer to them as rubber machines.

The board rejected the list of grievances against their new president hands down. Not one complaint was taken seriously - except for the rubber machine controversy. Four of the nine members wanted the machines out, but five members wanted to make sure condoms were made available to students. A compromise allowing the distribution of condoms through the university health department, but disallowing the machines, was proposed. Stegnor objected, saying most students wouldn't use such a service. She wanted condoms made available to students under more private circumstances than having to ask a school nurse for them. The board agreed and by a 6-3 vote allowed the continuance of machines in bathrooms. They did, however, ask that only bathrooms in dormitories have the machines. Bathrooms in other buildings, they said, were too public - a nice way of saying they were too visible to the public.

"Do you think that will be the end of it?" Dewey asked when I told him about the meeting. He'd watched Woody while I attended the meeting.

"No."

"But, they didn't get a thing out of the board," Dewey said.

"That's true, but this deal with the board is just a pattern of harassment. They may not expect to get anything from the board, at least not this early in the game. Like I said before, politically appointed boards usually do what's politically expedient. The campaign against Stegnor may just hope to wear her down, like they did Perkins. By the time that takes place the board will be sick of having to deal with it and will accept her resignation.

"How long will that take?"

"Beats hell out of me. It took them two years to get rid of Perkins."

Dewey surprised me and stopped asking questions, maybe because I'd said about all there was to say about it. Then maybe talk about boards and petty policies and campus politics bored him as much as it did me. All this didn't seem to be affecting our mark, at least not immediately. Woody let it all pass with but one comment. He bumped into Stegnor on campus shortly after the board meeting and told her how pleased he was with the work she'd been doing. She took the support warmly. Stegnor liked Woody, and as I watched them exchange pleasantries and then walk in separate directions down the sidewalk, I got a warm feeling about her in thinking that the time might come when I'd get some help from this lady in dealing with him.

CHAPTER 24
Baseball, Hotdogs, Apple Pie, and Chevrolet

The controversy involving campus politics wasn't the only thing heating up around Forest City. Winter finally gave way to warmer weather, and Dewey started acting like a just hatched ducking. I didn't complain about it because he'd been tired and down in the dumps, but he started getting on my nerves to where I wanted to hold his head under water. For one thing, he started getting up at the crack of dawn every morning. He'd drink a glass of juice, then go walking or jogging for the next hour. After that he'd come back to the trailer and do weird exercises, and sometimes he'd even meditate.

He'd been doing the meditation bit on and off ever since he'd arrived, that same standing on his head in a corner thing. The weird exercises and the jogging were new, and I finally ask him what was going on. He said that he was trying to get in better shape and that the exercises and walking and running were all part of his new regimen. I reminded him that he was dead and in about the best shape he could hope to be, but he just scoffed at that, so I shut up about it. But he also took up other things, like feeding birds and messing with flowers. Doing those things, you might've guessed, isn't all that easy for a custodian.

Our Angel equipment worked only in our dimension and therefore only on things pertinent to us. The Chevy, for instance, moved us around from place to place, but we couldn't have moved anyone or anything on mortal earth with it. We couldn't use an angel's spade, for instance, to dig a hole in the ground. If we had wanted a hole dug, we would've had to change to the I/T mode and use an earthly spade. We didn't have an angel's spade because there was no need for one. We didn't have any spirit world dirt to dig in. But Dewey wanted to mess with flowers all of a sudden, and I had on occasion caught him changing to the I/T mode to pull up a weed that didn't belong in a flower bed he'd taken the time to look over. And he loved touching the flowers. I decided to wait until he started flinging dirt around to say anything, but it was plain that Dewey had spring fever. I, on the other hand, had a cold.

"Quit that," I said.

"I'm not hurting anything, and besides, no one is looking," Dewey said. I'd just caught him scratching around in a flower bed with his hands.

"What about Mrs. Johnson, the old lady who lives here? What's she going to think when she comes out and finds her flower beds weeded?"

"She will just think some kind soul helped her out, and that's exactly what's happening. I'm just helping."

"Yeah, but . . ."

"Mind your own business. You're just grouchy because you have a cold, so go fuss at someone else," Dewey said.

"You're the only one around, and you deserve it. You're probably the one who gave me this cold."

"I haven't had a cold."

"You're right. I've been getting colds since I got here, and that's hard to figure. How can that happen? I can't catch colds from these people."

"Sure you can. You breathe the same air," Dewey said, grinning.

He had me there - almost. "But I'm dead."

"You keep saying that, but maybe you're not. Wouldn't you consider a cold proof that you're alive?"

"Not like them, I'm not."

"We both know that, but maybe a cold bug doesn't."

Now he had me for sure. "You're right about that, I reckon, but you're not right about the flowers. Playing with them is fine, but you shouldn't be digging around in them."

"Digging in flower beds is a civic minded thing to do, and I've been feeling good lately. This town could use some spiffing up, and I might as well lend a hand when the opportunity presents itself. Winter's over, spring has sprung, we're not very busy right now, and tending flowers is one of those real things people need to do occasionally," he said.

He was right about one thing. We hadn't been busy at all, and the lull had lasted almost a month. Woody had been such a good boy that I almost forgot who I was guarding and fooled myself into thinking he might be starting to get his act together. He drank less, even tapered off to getting tight just a couple of times a week. He stayed home more, now that he'd dumped Faith. Yeah, he's the one who called it quits, and that mildly surprised me. Faith wasn't like the other women Woody had messed around with. She's more of a lady, not some barfly or round heel. Besides that, and I can't say it too often, she was a knockout when it came to looks. But Woody broke it off, and Faith did her best to go along with it.

Not long after that, I started seeing Faith around campus with another man. I'd even see her walking to and from church with him on Sundays. Boy, what a switch, I thought, but that didn't fool me in the least. She was heart sore over Woody and wanted to get him out of her system. Maybe she wanted to make him jealous, but whatever, Woody didn't seem to mind . . . at least not at first.

Wanda looked happier than I'd seen her in years. She'd recently changed jobs and was now working as a legal secretary for a new attorney who'd just set up a practice in Forest City. Wanda had worked as a legal secretary for the past ten years, but her old boss started getting senile and inactive. She obviously liked her new job, which meant she threw herself into her work. A hard worker, Wanda sometimes went too far. Some folks who worked around her had problems dealing with her because she made them look bad, but her new boss, a man in his mid-thirties, admired her energy and efficiency. Unfortunately, he admired more than that. The few times I'd seen them together, he'd been sneaking looks at her physical attributes. I didn't like the guy's looks or manners - too much of a pretty boy who carried himself like he was vain to the core. Then again, I never did think much of any lawyer, so I tried to take that into account.

My job didn't involve watching Wanda, and I can honestly say that I'd never spied on her. I hardly ever saw her unless Woody was around, but when the new boss came into the picture, I broke a long standing precedent and spied. I don't know why I did it. Maybe it had something to do with the way she'd been acting, like she was getting ripe for wandering. She'd always been a flirt, but I'd never seriously suspected her of screwing around. I wouldn't have blamed her for it, but I just didn't suspect her.

I didn't start watching her right off, but I happened to see something by accident. I had followed Woody downtown, and he happened to stop off at the office of Frederick Lomax, III, Forest City's newest lawyer and his wife's new employer. Freddy was always cordial to Woody, and that's what tipped me off. He was too cordial. Woody stood around and talked for a few minutes, then wandered off toward the campus. I stayed behind for a few moments - Dewey walked Woody back to school - and they were barely out of sight when Freddy moved in on Wanda. It wasn't a heavy move, but it was a move, nonetheless. He didn't touch her - just looked at her in a suggestive and subtle way. She knew it, even encouraged it. Freddy had a boner for her, and she was enjoying it. From then on, I watched her.

Woody and Wanda started reverting to their old ways not long after that. Woody stayed home more, but that might not have been a blessing because he became restless and grouchy. Wanda was working harder, so she often came home from work in a bitchy mood. They got started back into that same old tit-for-tat thing, got pissed, then sulked. At first they didn't fight, just sulked. Woody started drinking more, and after a few weeks of light bickering and sulking, they finally got into a big fight. Woody stomped off, went to the bar, and got blasted. They didn't speak to each other for three or four days after that, and the same old F and F routine was back in full bloom. They fought again and made up by screwing like minks, and I could see trouble on the horizon.

Next came a real humdinger of a fight. Wanda came home from work in a bitchy mood a few days later and started it with her bitching. They fought, and Woody slept on the couch that night, but not before going out and getting drunk. The next afternoon, while Woody was home sleeping off a bad hangover, Freddy moved in on Wanda. This time he did more than throw suggestive glances in her direction. He'd been admiring Wanda's body for too long, and he couldn't stand it any longer.

Wanda brushed aside his advance, but it was a half-hearted brush off. Freddy was an opportunist, and he knew what was going on between her and Woody. He knew it was just a matter of time before he got to her, and so did I. Faith Appleton was about the only thing Woody noticed those days. I'd been watching the way he looked at her, and I knew watching that beautiful butt swish up and down the halls at school had been working on him. The look in his eyes said it all. I didn't bother Dewey with all this for a while, but a rainstorm came through the next morning. He couldn't walk or jog or weed flower beds, so I hit him with it.

"Woody's about to screw up," I said.

"You've noticed too, huh?" Dewey said.

"Yeah, he's getting horny for Faith again. Things aren't going well at home, and that means trouble. It's just a matter of time before he's humping Faith again, and to make matters worse, Wanda's getting ready to screw up too. It's a contest now as to who does it first. Her new boss has the hots for her. He even rubbed his hard on her the other day at the office, so I think it's getting serious."

"Really?"

"Is a hard dick serious, Dewey?"

"Yes, I suppose it is," Dewey said, shaking his head.

"That means we've got troubles coming, and all we can do is get ready for it. I figure one more fight will do the trick. One of them will get hurt bad enough to jump the fence, and I figure it'll be Woody. He usually starts it, whatever *it* is."

My telling Dewey turned out to be a good thing because I was wrong about Woody being the first to wander. Wanda broke down first, and only a few days after my talk with Dewey. I didn't even get to see it, but he did. I sent him down to Freddy's office to watch her. He objected but did it anyway, and as luck would have it ended up being the one who brought me the news. Dewey's not the kind to watch, but they caught him by surprise. I don't think he thought it would really happen, especially not then. Wanda had stayed late to help put together some court briefs, and it happened, and Dewey got caught flat-footed.

"Well, they did it," he said, walking up and sitting down beside me. I was sitting on Woody's front porch watching a nice Kansas sunset when he came trudging down the sidewalk. He looked almost forlorn.

"They did?"

"Yes. They were just standing there, and all of a sudden they were doing it. He just reached over and grabbed her, and they did it right in his office, right by his desk. He just pulled up her dress and they . . . did it."

"Lordy, Lordy, that woman does love to screw standing up. Beats all I've ever seen," I said.

"Is that all you've got to say about it?" Dewey asked, looking irked.

"I'm not surprised enough to say anything else."

"No, I suppose you're not. You predicted it."

"Yeah, I'm a real wizard."

"What now? What about Woody? Do you think he'll find out?"

"Who knows, but even if he does, it might take a while. Once he starts up with apple ass again, he might not care," I said.

"That's doubtful. He'll care, no matter what."

"You're probably right."

"Where is Woody, anyway?" Dewey asked.

"He took the kids to a baseball game at the college," I said.

"You let him go alone?"

"He took the kids, Dewey. He's not going to get into anything with the kids along," I said.

"He could get hurt."

"Yeah, a baseball might conk him on the noggin or something. How's he going to get hurt watching a baseball game?"

"One of us should be there."

"OK Dewey, I'll go," I said, standing up.

"I'll go with you. I love baseball. It's a game of skill, similar in many respects to ballet."

"You said that about hockey."

"That's true, I did, but I like baseball because it's a real thing - an American traditional like hotdogs and apple pie and Chevrolet. Remember the television commercial?"

"Yeah, I remember. Maybe that's why Woody went to the game,"

"He probably went to take the kids, or maybe he loves baseball."

"He likes it OK, but I just had the thought that maybe he's trying to do something that's ordinary and wholesome. I've never seen him eat a hotdog or apple pie, and he drives a Ford. He hasn't been to a baseball game in years, and maybe he's trying to do something that most people do," I said.

"You may be right. Drinking has made his life so unorthodox that he's trying to establish some ties to normalcy. Perhaps this is his way of dealing with his insecurities."

The conversation about baseball was as boring as the game we were watching, so I didn't encourage it. Dewey didn't seem to mind, and the game wasn't boring him. He appeared to be one of the few people in the stands having a good time. He sat right behind the backstop and watched the balls come to the catcher, and he clapped with almost every good pitch the pitchers made. After a bit he came and sat beside me, giving a pitch by pitch analogy of the game. To my surprise, he knew the game of baseball very well. He even spoke the jargon.

I watched Woody as Dewey talked. He looked tired, almost exhausted. His kids were running with other children behind the grandstands, totally oblivious to the game being played a few yards away. Woody stared at the playing field and players, but his eyes were dead, and it was plain to me that he was seeing nothing, hearing nothing. He looked numb, but I knew that he really wasn't and suddenly felt sorry for him. If I've ever seen a man who needed a hotdog or piece of apple pie or a drive in the country in an old Chevy, it was him.

I really didn't feel bad that his wife was downtown humping her new boss. He had that coming. I felt sorry for him because he was lost again, and I knew about that feeling. For a short while he'd had a purpose in life. Wanda had needed him, due to her father's death, and he had responded to her need. He'd been placed on a very important committee at work, and he'd tried to get his act together by ending his affair with Faith. But it hadn't worked for him, and he was lost again, maybe more lost now than he'd ever been before. Now his wife was having an affair of her own, and that started me wondering what it would all lead to. Maybe I felt sorry for him out of respect for my own feelings. If Woody fell apart, my job was going to be much tougher.

"Get up and buy yourself a hot dog, you dumbass," I said.

"I beg your pardon?" Dewey asked, looking shocked.

"Sorry, Dewey. I was talking to Woody. He looks like he needs a hotdog," I said.

"You right. I think he does."

Wanda, looking and acting cheerful, was home cooking supper when we got there, and her blitheness both surprised and irritated me. Maybe she deserved an affair of her own, but the least she could do was show some signs of guilt. Woody always did, but she seemed lighthearted. Her mood, though, didn't rub off on Woody. He stayed gloomy, even through dinner. After eating, Wanda stretched out on the living room floor with the children and read to them while Woody crashed on the couch in the den and watched TV until he fell asleep. Later, he got up and groggily stumbled to the bedroom, undressed, and fell into bed. Wanda came to the bedroom door, turned on the light, and stared blankly at him for a few moments. Then she switched off the light and put the children to bed. After a hot bath, which took half an hour, she came to bed and snuggled close to Woody. She muzzled the back of his neck, but he brushed away her kisses. She kept at it for awhile, but when her kisses failed to bring him around, she reached over him and grabbed his pecker. Woody knocked her hand away, groaned, and flipped over on his stomach.

"Would you look at that? The woman screwed her boss this very afternoon, and now she's trying to put the make on Woody. What the hell's going on, Dewey?"

"My only observation is that she's feeling very insecure right now and needs some reassurance," Dewey said.

"I figured you say something like that, but I'm ready for you this time. Just how in hell is getting laid twice in less than four hours by two different men going to make her more secure?"

"For the same reason Woody went to the baseball game, perhaps, and for the same reason I like taking care of flowers. A marriage between two people doesn't necessarily constitute homemaking. People do things like mowing lawns, washing cars, furnishing and cleaning houses, and even digging in flower beds because it's a part of housekeeping that goes along with homemaking. What she's trying to do is the normal thing. Husbands and wives are supposed to have sex together. That's the way a normal marriage works, and that's what she's trying to recover - that and her loss of purpose. She's Woody Pickens' wife, not Freddy Lomax's wife, and sex with Freddy might be exciting for the moment, but it's not the same as sex with her own husband. She's trying to reconnect with normalcy," he said.

"All this mess is getting too complicated," I said, rubbing my temples.

"I know what you mean."

"There may be good explanations for what's going on here, but it's shitty business," I said.

Wanda didn't turn out the lamp beside her bed for quite some time. She stared at her sleeping husband's back and looked lost and lonely, and that was more than I could take. We left them that way, him sleeping and her staring, and went to the trailer. I tried thinking about Phoebe, but that only made me horny. Dewey went straight to sleep, and I didn't mind at all because I wasn't in a talking mood. Talking without knowing what you're talking about is sort of like trying to drive a car on an almost empty gas tank. You might get started, but you know you're not going far with it. Maybe the same thing can be said about thinking, but I did a lot of that for the next few hours. We'd had some of Dewey's food for supper, stir fried veggies over noodles, and I dozed off hoping the coming day's dinner would be hotdogs and apple pie. I already had the Chevy.

CHAPTER 25
Pickens' Charge

Woody stayed depressed for the rest of the school term. He taught class each day, and then went home and slept the remainder of the afternoon. He went to Frank's regularly, but hardly ever to Dusty's. There were no major screw ups - just a procession of relatively quiet drunks. He spent some time with Duncan Highsmith, but not a lot, and he had no involvement with any woman other than Wanda, and he had very little with her. I didn't watch them closely during that stretch, but I hadn't seen them have sex at all. He started looking gaunt from not eating right, and I don't mean just thin. Woody, put plainly, looked sad and defeated.

Graduation came and went in a routine manner for him, with the exception that Faith Appleton graduated summa cum laude with a psychology degree. She'd taken a job as a high school counselor in Denver, but she made it a point to come by Woody's office and tell him that she wouldn't be leaving until August. They'd been stepping around each other until then, but I'd seen in her eyes what I'd been seeing in his, and I knew it would pull them back together before long.

Wanda allowed Freddy to have his way with her at intervals, usually in his office and usually standing up. Like I said before, I wasn't assigned to watch Wanda and can't say for sure what all went on between her and Freddy, but it seemed to me that she controlled the relationship. Whenever it happened between them, she usually determined when and under what conditions, and I don't think it happened all that often. Freddy kept his nose to her butt like a hound after a bitch in heat. He'd try and try, and finally she'd give in. With her sex life pretty much shut down at home, I think she went as long as she could stand it before giving in. Their screwing sessions seemed to be quick but frantic, and only once did I see Wanda really lay a good one on him.

Things had got so boring around Woody that'd I walked down to main street to see what was happening. Wanda had stopped by the house about the middle of the afternoon and found Woody where he usually was, on the couch sound asleep. Seeing him that way was nothing new to her, of course, but for some reason it really ticked her off. She stomped out of the house and straight back to Freddy's office, and as soon as the last client of the day had exited the door, she took him down. She pushed him over on top of his desk, then hiked her dress up and crawled on top. He looked taken back at first, but he rose to the occasion.

I've read about retaliation sex before, but Wanda put the meanest screwing on him I've ever seen. She wooled him around until he just couldn't function anymore, and when she finally crawled off him, she had one of those spiteful take-that-you-sonofabitch looks on her face. A couple of days later she broke off the affair, and that really buffaloed Freddy. He griped, of course, but she gave him a choice. Either they stopped the mischief, or she quit the job. He opted for stopping the mischief because finding another legal secretary as good as Wanda in a small town like Forest City would be impossible. Maybe he went along with it because he knew she couldn't hold him off forever. She had too many problems at home for that.

Woody's depression stayed about the same until just before the start of the summer term in early June, and that's when he went on a real bender. It started at Franks Bar and Grill, as usual, and ended up at Dusty's. I figured he'd end up at Faith's apartment before the night was over, but C.W. Laney captured him before he got there. C.W. was the gal Woody had humped in the parking lot at Dusty's the previous fall and almost got caught by Wanda while doing it. Dewey remembered her.

"Oh, no, he wouldn't," Dewey said when he saw C.W. rubbing up against Woody at Dusty's. The last call for alcohol had been sounded, and Woody was too drunk to drive. C.W. had showed up about an hour earlier with a girlfriend, but the friend hooked up with some cowboy and took off.

"Oh, yes, he would. He's drunk - blitzed, bombed."

"Yes, he's drunk, but I sure hope he doesn't get taken in by that woman again."

"She's a good looking filly, and he's ridden that pony before. Sometimes a feller likes to walk back through plowed ground," I said, winking.

"Perhaps, but Woody's been spoiled. He's accustomed to . . . finer things now. He's been with Faith . . . and this C.W. woman has . . . has a big behind. She's this wide," Dewey said, holding up his hands to indicate.

"Yeah, she's got a big ass, but it's a nice ass. She's a big gal, and big gals have big asses sometimes. I kind of like her ass," I said, turning my head to size it up.

"I thought you were an apple ass man?"

"I am, but that doesn't mean I can't appreciate some of the others."

"From the looks of things, Woody must like it too. He's going for it," Dewey said, motioning toward the door. I turned just in time to see Woody and C.W. leaving.

"Good. I haven't had a good show in months."

"And just when I thought you were getting better," Dewey said.

"I'm getting better, but I'm not cured. Let's go."

"Do I have to go?"

"No. You can go watch Wanda if you want to. She's probably off somewhere with Freddy."

"That's over. She broke it off."

"Yeah, for how long? She's probably pissed off because Woody's not at home. She might be with Freddy right now," I said, knowing better. Wanda might be out looking for Woody, but she wasn't with Freddy. I knew that to be a fact because I'd heard Wanda mention that he was handling a case in Dodge City that week.

"I'll go with you. You might need me, but I'm telling you right now that I'm not tackling anyone. If Wanda finds him this time, he's just going to get caught. I won't stop her," he said, wagging a finger at me.

"That's fine with me," I said.

Woody followed C.W. in his car, and that meant I had to ride with him. He was far too drunk to be driving, but he didn't want to risk leaving his car at Dusty's. C.W. took the lead in a pick-up with a fancy topper camper. Dewey followed in the Chevy. She took a country road that ended in a grove of cottonwoods along the river, some ten miles south of Forest City. It was a very remote area where no one would bother them. Once there, she parked near the river, and they sat on a stump and drank straight from a bottle she'd pulled out of the camper. Then she rolled a joint, took a puff, and handed it to Woody. He shook his head, and even though she kept pushing it at him, he kept refusing. Smoking grass made sex more fun, she told him, but Woody still refused. Finally, she gave up and started necking on him.

I'd been hanging around Woody for a long time, and I'd never seen him stopped by impotency. There's a first time for everything, though, and his state of drunkenness almost thwarted her efforts at getting him primed for action. She'd stripped down to nothing but a horny smile, and that's when I moved closer to enjoy the show. Dewey, of course, stayed in the car.

Woody got undressed and went after her. They stood in the moonlight clutching and clawing at each other like a couple of clumsy teenagers. Woody seemed unenthused at first, but he finally got worked up to the action stage. C.W. was whipped into a near frenzy by then, and they fell to the ground and rolled around in the sand like a couple of playful bear cubs. He'd be on top for a while, then her, until finally she ended up on bottom - squealing like a trapped pig and kicking sand in all directions. It ended when they both collapsed in a sweaty, sand-covered, puffing head. After laying there panting for a few minutes, they got up and headed for the river. I shuffled back to the car feeling disappointed and relieved that it was over, a strange feeling for me.

"Back so soon?"

"I must be getting sick or something. I didn't even enjoy it."

"They may be hope for you yet," Dewey said, smiling wisely.

"I hope not. Maybe it's just that I'm too used to seeing him go at it with Faith, but it looked . . . looked . . ."

"Disgusting," Dewey said, finishing my sentence.

"Yeah, I reckon you're right. I don't know that I'd say it was disgusting, but it was unrewarding. C.W.'s a good looking gal, but you were right when you said she wasn't a Faith Appleton. As flowers go, Faith's a rose, and C.W.'s a daisy. Maybe I just thought she was a rose, and it turns out she's a faded rose."

"The fairest things have fleetest end, Their scent survives their close; But the rose's scent is bitterness, To him that loved the rose."

"Who said that?"

"Francis Thompson the poet. It comes from a poem called 'Daisy'," Dewey said.

"What does that mean?" I asked.

"It means that a rose's scent linger long after the rose is faded, but the scent that lingers is a bitter reminder to the one who loved the rose itself. Put another way, you found the experience less rewarding because the rose itself is gone, and the lingering fragrance is pale in comparison."

"Yeah, that's what I was afraid it meant. That means our boy Woody misses the rose too, huh?"

"Yes."

"And that's what keeps him sniffing around. He still knows the scent, and he's trying to find the rose again."

"Something like that."

"I could ask if you think he'll ever find the rose again, but there's no answer. I'm starting to understand what I don't understand, if that makes any sense to you. I'll have to admit that it's not a good feeling. I liked it back when I thought I knew what was what and didn't concern myself with all the whys and hows of things. I'm changing, and it's your fault, you know. If all this talking we've been doing is leading me to losing an interest in peeping, I'm going to be really pissed at you."

"You could lose worse," he said, smiling.

"Considering my lack of recreation, I can't see what. Maybe I just wasn't in the right frame of mind. Maybe I didn't get a good look or something. I think I'll go back and try again," I said, then headed for the river.

The river hardly ever had much water in it, but there was just enough for Woody and C.W. to wash off. They could've saved themselves the trouble because they'd no more than finished when it started raining. At first it came down slowly, but by the time they'd reached the camper, it was coming down in sheets. After coming down hard for about fifteen minutes, the rain settled to being light but steady. Woody and C.W. sat in the doorway of the camper and watched it rain. They were still buck naked except for a blanket they'd pulled over their shoulders.

I sat in the car with Dewey until the rain eased up and then went back to the camper. C.W. was busy trying to get Woody hard again, but she wasn't having much luck. She kissed on him and pulled at him, but he was as limber as a worm in warm mud. She kept at it until he became half hard, and seeing that she'd do no better, she settled for it. After pushing him down on his back, she crawled on top and went to work. I moved closer to make sure I got a good look - so close in fact, I could've touched them. Woody didn't respond much, but he let her flop, bounce, and squirm around on him until she got off again. You could almost see the relief on Woody's face. If I could've seen myself, I could've seen the relief in my face, too.

C.W. rolled off him in a few minutes and suggested he get in the cab of the pickup and turn on the heater while she got dressed. The rain had put a sharp chill in the air, something she was not aware of until her sweat soaked body started cooling down. Woody got up, slipped on his clothes, and jumped into the cab of the truck. He cranked the engine and revved it a few times, but the engine promptly died when he lifted his foot from the accelerator. He cranked it again, this time keeping his foot down on the accelerator. His left foot, covered with mud now, was on the clutch.

I had no idea what was about to happen because I had started walking back to my car. C.W. was standing up in the camper, right in the back door, pulling up her jeans. They'd barely made it to her knees, though, when Woody's foot slipped off the clutch. The truck lurched forward, and that shot C.W., her pants still down below her knees, straight out the door onto the ground. She hit with a thud, and I ran to see about her.

She started screaming in pain just as soon as she got enough breath. Woody jumped out of the truck to see what had happened, but I got there before him. I could see right off, as anyone could've, that her right leg was broken. C.W. choked off her screaming some, mostly so she could heap obscenities on Woody. He didn't know what to do and was starting to look like a hunter who just killed somebody's cow. When he bent down and tried to touch her, she cursed at him even more. When he stood up, she cursed him, telling him to do something. Finally, he scooped her up in his arms and laid her in the camper. She really raised a ruckus then, screaming and cursing at the same time. He tried to pull her pants up, but that brought the worst round of screaming and cursing yet, so he left them down around her ankles. Then he got in and started driving toward town.

"What's he doing?" Dewey asked.

"Taking her to the hospital, I hope," I said.

"In that condition?"

"Most people with broken legs go to the hospital, Dewey," I said.

"But, her ... her pants ... and she's all covered with sand and mud and ... her pants are down," Dewey stammered.

"I know that, Dewey, but what can he do? She won't let him touch her."

"I suppose he must take her the way she is," Dewey said, looking timid.

"Boy, this is going to be rich," I said, laughing. I knew it wasn't funny to them, but I was wondering how Woody planned on getting C.W. to the emergency room.

"He's going to get caught this time, isn't he?" Dewey asked, his voice a bit strained.

"It doesn't look good. The people at the hospital will know him, and hauling in a woman with a broken leg and with her jeans down around her ankles might look suspicious, wouldn't you say?"

"Oh, my goodness, yes," Dewey said, holding his palm to his chest.

Woody drove fast to Forest City, but he drove right past the turn to the hospital. He headed right down main and then hooked a left on Lawrence.

"Where's he going? The hospital's back there," Dewey said.

"He's going to Duncan Highsmith's house."

"How's that going to help? Duncan's no doctor, and he can't see to drive."

"I know, but Woody's got something in mind," I said.

I was right because Woody went straight to Duncan's house. He went to the back door and started pounding on it. It took him a while, but Duncan answered, and by then I was near enough to hear the conversation. Woody wanted Duncan to ride with him to the hospital. Once there, he'd get out and walk away, back to Duncan's house. Duncan was to go into the emergency room and get help for C.W. Then he'd walk home. Woody would spend the rest of the night there and then Duncan would walk over to Woody's house early the next morning and tell Wanda that Woody had passed out on his couch the night before. Wanda would believe that because it had happened several times before. Duncan was quick to point out that Wanda had already been to his house, hours earlier. Woody said he'd tell her that he came later, that he'd make up some other excuse about why he was late getting to Duncan's house. Right now, he needed help getting C.W. to the hospital. Duncan quickly dressed and followed Woody to the truck, where they opened the back door of the camper and told C.W. the plan. At that point, she didn't care, just as long as somebody got her to the hospital.

"I can't believe he pulled it off," Dewey said later, after C.W. had been delivered to the hospital and after Woody and Duncan had met back at the house. Woody put his clothes in the washer, then the dryer, just to make sure all the sand and mud was gone by the time he wore them home the next morning. It was nearly five a.m. by the time Woody flopped down on the couch. Dewey and I sat in a corner and dozed until daylight. Duncan didn't have to walk to Woody's the next morning because Wanda came knocking at the door by seven o'clock. Woody got up and told her the story he'd made up. Duncan dutifully corroborated it, and Wanda seemed convinced. Being convinced didn't keep her from crying and telling Woody what an inconsiderate sonofabitch he was. I had to agree.

A slight hitch developed in the plan, though, when Wanda noticed that Woody's car was nowhere around. Woody said he'd loaned it to someone at the bar, and they hadn't brought it back. Later that day, while Wanda was at work, Woody got a cowboy friend to take him back to the river to recover his car. It took hours because the area was still muddy, and the car was mired up to its axles. A neighboring farmer had to bring his tractor across from a nearby field to pull him out of the wet sand. And while Woody unstuck his car, Wanda was back in the Freddy's office working off her frustration. This time they did it laying down on the bathroom floor, a first for Wanda. She finally got laid with her feet pointed in the right direction, at the ceiling of Frederick the third's bathroom.

CHAPTER 26
Just Another Chapter

Roosevelt was pissed.

"You could've killed the man. What were you thinking about?" he asked, glaring at me over folded arms.

Just perfect, I thought. Since so much time had gone by since the incident, I'd been hoping he'd missed hearing about it. I didn't need this ass chewing coming on the heels of a night like the night before, and I opted for the coy approach. "I got caught up in the moment, I reckon. I thought it was her ex-husband. It was late, and he had a gun and . . ."

"He's a night watchman. They carry guns, Doug."

So much for the coy approach. Maybe the stupid approach would work. "How was I supposed to know that? My mark's inside getting laid, this guy parks in the alley, puts a gun in his pocket and starts that way, so what am I supposed to think? Huh?"

"The man's in his fifties, much too old to be Faith Appleton's husband, and don't call her apple ass. Records say she's a fine person," Roosevelt said, almost snorting the words out.

He wasn't going for it. A try at taking the shock effect dodge might not hurt anything. Maybe I could get him sidetracked and talking about something else. "Yeah, she's fine all right. She's so fine she's trying to fuck my mark down to a nubbing," I said.

"Knock off the vulgarities. Everyone has biological needs, and Faith is no different from the rest. She's made an unfortunate choice in choosing your mark to . . . to . . ."

"Fill her needs?"

"Exactly."

"She's still fucking him," I said.

"That doesn't excuse your actions. You could've needlessly hurt the man. And what about your mark? You couldn't change modes and nearly scared Woody and Faith to death."

So much for coy, stupid, and shock effect diversions. Time for my last resort - the truth. "Yeah, I know, but I was up tight. I lost my composure and screwed up on that one, but so what?" I asked.

"That's not like you Doug. You're impulsive sometimes, but this isn't like you," Roosevelt said, moving forward to look more closely at me.

"Woody's been thinking suicide, and that's got me a little on edge," I said.

"Suicide?"

"Dewey says Woody's been playing with a pistol. He says he even held it to his head once."

"That's serious," Roosevelt said, rubbing his chin.

Now's the time for a bit humor, I thought. I struck a pose like his, rubbed my chin, and said, "No shit, Sherlock."

I should've let well enough along. "Sending you to Las Vegas might've been a mistake. It might've given you a bigger head than you already had. Maybe it took the edge off."

"The only big head I got in Vegas was on that donkey dick you stuck me with, but it's gone now, and what edge are you talking about?"

"Your guardsmanship edge. Maybe you've grown complacent and inattentive."

"I'm in good shape compared to him," I said, nodding toward the trailer where Dewey was sleeping. I'd slept a couple of hours, until nearly nine o'clock, and had just rolled out when Roosevelt showed up. Dewey had roused up briefly when Roosevelt knocked on the door, but he rolled over and went back to sleep. Roosevelt and I were talking in his car - a new, four door Lincoln.

"What's wrong with him?"

"He can't hold his I/I mode," I said.

"Not at all?"

"Not last night, he couldn't. He's not up to snuff."

"Mode malady," Roosevelt mumbled.

"Mode what?"

"It's called mode malady," Roosevelt said, louder. "At least that's what guardians call it. It's not uncommon, but it's nothing to be taken lightly. How long has he been this way?"

"I just noticed it last night. I think he'll be all right after he gets some rest," I said.

"Hummmm," Roosevelt said.

"What's the hummmm about?"

"This entire situation has me concerned. Woody may be coming to a crisis stage. That means you and Dewey need to be sharp, and neither of you are looking too sharp to me. You might need some help."

"Another guardian? Oh, no, we can handle it," I said.

"I'm not so sure. Dewey's down, and that thing with you last night worries me. Maybe I'd better . . ."

"Just leave it alone, Roosevelt. A third person would really screw things up. I can stand a partnership, but a committee is something else again. Don't send anybody."

"Are you sure?"

"Positive. I can handle it."

"What about him?" Roosevelt asked, pointing to the trailer.

"He'll be fine, just needs to rest a little."

Roosevelt had been sizing me up carefully while we talked, and I could see his expression soften. "I get the picture, and I'm going to trust you on this one and take you at your word."

"Thanks," I said, then opened the door of the Lincoln. "Nice wheels. When did you get this?"

"Last week. The Central Office liked the job we did in Las Vegas. That reminds me. I've been authorized to commend you on your efforts there. So I'm doing that now by saying thanks for a job well done."

"Do I get a medal or something? How about a new car for me? I want something like a Porsche, or a . . ."

"Get out of the car, Doug," Roosevelt said, smiling.

Dewey sat on a park bench nearby and watched the last of the conversation take place in Roosevelt's new Lincoln. He'd been watching Woody lecture at nearby Howard Hall, but Woody had gone to dinner, and that gave him a break. Since it was lunch time, we ate on the library lawn and then relaxed a while. I'd been looking for a chance to talk with Dewey about what was going on between Woody and Wanda. Nearly three weeks had passed since Woody's encounter with C.W. at the river, and it had been a quiet time. Nothing much had happened because Woody had been sick for a good week after the big drunk and river party.

Just saying he was sick won't cover it. Besides a bad hangover and upset stomach - poor Woody just about crapped himself to death

- he was wounded. He'd learned a hard lesson about screwing in the sand because his pecker looked like a sapling pine that had been run through a debarking machine at a tree processing plant. It was so sore, in fact, that he could barely wear his pants, and keeping it hid from Wanda had been a tricky situation. His being sick had been a blessing in one respect since it kept her from wanting sex with him. Not even the most avid fight and fuck fan wants to get laid by a cotton-mouthed, diarrhea ridden hangover victim. But Wanda wanted to nurse her husband, even bath him, and when Woody rebuffed her efforts at caring for him, she started sulking again.

Those three weeks had passed quietly as Woody slowly recovered from his stomach problems and sore pecker. He was barely healed enough to get around, though, when he jumped back in the sack with Faith Appleton. Seeing her hanging around another man bothered him some, I'm sure, but there was more to it than just jealousy. Woody missed her, and things hadn't worked out well at home. He called her into his office one morning as asked if he could see her again, and even though she groused some by saying it was wrong and they shouldn't be doing it, she agreed. She must've had it bad for Woody, and her new boyfriend, a young bachelor professor in the business department, had apparently been a poor replacement. I'd been hoping she could hold out against Woody, but I reckon it's hard to think straight when your hormones are doing all the thinking. Anyway, Woody snuck over to Faith's apartment as soon as his pecker got back into using condition, which was nearly two weeks after the river incident.

C.W., in the meantime, had been discharged from the hospital. Her husband, a gentleman rancher twenty years her senior, believed the story she told, whatever it was, and took her home. Maybe he didn't really believe it, but he took her home anyway. Woody managed to sneak by the hospital once to see her, and she forgave him. She even laughed about it. Anyway, she went home to nurse her broken leg, Woody went back to Faith, and Wanda went back to keeping her boss happy. It looked like she'd finally given up on keeping Freddy panting after her, at least for the time being.

Woody and Wanda stepped around each other for a while, speaking only when they couldn't avoid it. Then something happened that really surprised and confused me. Wanda went to work and got drilled twice, once that morning and again that afternoon, and while she was getting it on with Freddy, Woody was holed up in a motel in Cottonwood with Faith. That very night, Woody and Wanda went to bed and screwed like minks. That had been just two nights before, and I hadn't had a chance to ask Dewey what he thought about it.

"What going on, Dewey?" I asked, stretching out on my back to stare up at the sky. He stared at me a few moments and then flopped down on the grass a few feet away.

"You'll have to be more specific than that. All I see is blue sky," he said, folding his arms behind his head.

"I'm talking about Woody and Wanda. What's going on with them? Is something really new happening, or is this just another chapter in the continuing saga of Woody and Wanda?"

"It's not just another chapter," Dewey said.

"Then what's going on."

"I don't know, but it's not the same old routine."

"Brilliant observation, Dr. Freud. Hell, even I know the routine has changed. Wanda's getting punched by her boss, for one thing, and Woody's drinking has changed to sporadic bouts and benders. Worse yet, they're both acting real strange," I said.

"A lot of what they do is strange, so what exactly are we talking about?"

"Their bed habits, that's what. Don't you think all this is weird? The first time Freddy got to Wanda, she went straight home and tried to screw Woody. That didn't made sense to me, and when I asked you about it, you said she was feeling insecure."

"She is."

"But what about the other night? Wanda had screwed Freddy twice that day, and Woody had gone over to Cottonwood to hump Faith, and then Woody and Wanda go home and screw like a couple of newlyweds. What's going on? Are they both nuts?"

Dewey frowned for a minute as he thought about it. He'd been tailing Woody that day, so he didn't know about Wanda's double-dip with Freddy until I just mentioned it.

"I still think it's the insecurity thing," he said.

"They've been insecure for a long time, so why is all this happening now? How come both of them have lovers, and they're still acting like newlyweds? It doesn't make sense to me. It's almost like they're getting primed up on other people just to enjoy a good roll in the hay at home. How can they both get laid by other people, twice in one day even, and then go home a screw for an hour? You can't tell me that's just insecurity."

"Yes, I can. You might not believe it, but I can because it's at least part true."

"What's the other part? Try something on me I'll believe," I said.

"What I mean is this: Woody, like all men, needs a sense of identity. He needs a frame of reference, a sense of orientation. Without it, he's lost. Woody's place in life relates to his family, regardless of what condition it's in. Wanda is not only part of Woody's world; she's perhaps paramount to it. Woody has little else with which to relate, and he has chosen Wanda as a particular point of devotion. To some this devotion is religion or country or values and ideals, but to Woody, it's family, and Wanda and the children are about the only family he has. The same is true of Wanda, particularly since she recently lost her father. Woody is her world, her frame of orientation. She's just as lost without him as he is without her. Their actions don't seem to support such a notion, but it's probably true."

"That won't explain why they act like a couple of teenagers who've just discovered sex," I said.

"Oh, but it does. Their behavior with others has frightened them because their respective frames of reference have been put in jeopardy. They are fearful of losing their places, their identity. Being frightened isn't easy to live with, and they're willing to do almost anything to avoid it. They took lovers to help cope with their anxieties, perhaps. In addition, Woody gets drunk to deal with his. What they're doing is making substitutions for proper aggression."

"By screwing somebody else? By going at each other like a couple of sex-starved kids?"

"That's one way of getting rid of fear and anxiety," Dewey said. He gave me a curious look and then continued. "It's like the parable of the man who ran from the mouse. As he ran, the mouse got larger, and the faster he ran away, the larger the mouse grew. Finally, the mouse had turned into a charging elephant, but the frightened man had run as far as he could. Too tired to run anymore, he stopped and waited to be trampled, but he was not. When he looked, he saw that the elephant had stopped and had come no closer. He took a couple of steps toward the elephant, and it grew smaller. Then he chased it, and it grew ever smaller. In the end, the elephant had shrunk to a mouse and was chased into a hole. The man, in short, had conquered his fear through aggression."

"That makes sense. Neither Woody or Wanda know how to handle the situation they're caught in, so instead of taking proper aggressive action, they use sex as a cover up,"

"That's about it in a nutshell," Dewey said.

"What would be the right kind of aggression?" I asked.

"Confronting the problem. They need to face the charging elephant. Neither of them is self-confident enough for that, however. They're too insecure."

"But, if sex is just a cover up, why are they acting the way they are? Why don't they just rely on their new partners instead of keeping up the affairs and still acting like newlyweds at home?"

"They're not acting like newlyweds," Dewey said, sniggering. "The answer's simple, really. They're not happy with what is happening. They're not happy, period. The answer is not in their new sex partners, either, and they sense that. You explained it cleverly when you called Woody and Wanda as being caught up in a F and F relationship. They fight, hurt each other and then end up working out their difficulties in bed. It proves to him that he's still her husband and lover and the father of her children. He's still the man of the house that way. She proves to herself that she's still his wife and lover and the mother of his children, and still in her proper place."

"Yeah, that **was** clever of me, wasn't it," I said.

"You could be even more clever and add a new dimension to your concept. The problem is worse now because they're dealing themselves more misery. They're having affairs, and even though they haven't been caught at it, they are hurting themselves. That makes having sex together even more important to them. Both of them need the reassurance they get from that unfortunate relationship even more now."

"You're right, of course," I said, slowly nodding my head. "The old fight and fuck relationship is getting even worse, isn't it."

"Yes, it is."

"There's one more thing I don't get. If these two need each other so much, then why don't they act like it? Why are they both headed in a direction that, in the end, is bound to kill the very thing they seem to need the most?"

"It's part of being frightened, I suppose. Perhaps they're trying to prove to themselves that they don't need each other. Part of it is simply boredom," Dewey said, shrugging and lifting his eyebrows.

"They're acting like a couple of horse's asses because they're bored?"

"Do you remember the discussion we had about the bull rider and why he rode bulls?"

"Yeah, he does it to find his niche in this world," I said, nodding.

"Right, but there's more to it than that. We've already talked about Woody and Wanda's devotion to each other. It might be a faulty devotion, but it is one nevertheless. All of us, since we're very much aware of our separateness, need to find strings and workable ties to the world we live in. We come into this world ill-equipped because we must get along without animal instincts. At the same time, we must deal with self-awareness."

"Some people lack the endurance, stamina, patience, or understanding to use activating stimuli. Woody and Wanda's F and F relationship is a kind of masochism, and masochistic people have trouble initiating excitation. They can't react well to normal stimuli, so they react to what overpowers them. A marriage like Woody and Wanda have gives them a chance to experience things like hate, fighting, sadism, and even submission. It may be why they stay together - not in spirit of their difficulties, but because of them. Nothing they do, however, stops their boredom."

"What's going to happen to a couple of people who are as screwed up as Woody and Wanda? Will they ever turn into healthy, productive, happy people?"

"I don't know what will happen, but there's always a chance of them recovering. Their situation looks hopeless, but something could happen to alter their course. We may be on the verge of a crisis, a confrontation, and that could start them in the right direction."

"What's the right direction? Staying together? Going opposite directions?"

"The right direction is that they get well, whatever direction that takes. As for the marriage, its chances aren't good."

"You don't think either of them can forgive the other, do you? You think their screwing around is going to kill the marriage."

"On the contrary, I think just the opposite. Their sexual promiscuity won't kill the marriage. Like I said before, the marriage gives them a chance to feel hate and frustration and mental anguish. They stay together partly because of that, not in spite of it. Catching each other in affairs might only strengthen that support," Dewey said.

"It could go the other way too. It might destroy them," I said.

"Yes, it might, but we must try to be optimistic. We must do our job with the conviction that things will work out for the better. You need to keep in mind that these people don't know what's wrong with them. Woody is a very sick man. Alcoholism isn't his only problem, but it complicates things. Since he has chosen to deal with his boredom through character-rooted passions that are not productive, since he seeks to anesthetize rather than cure the problem, he is a very confused man. Wanda is no better off, since she has chosen approximately the same course. Something needs to happen that will shock them into seeing what is happening, and that may take quite a shock. It may take a lot of help from someone else, someone outside this situation."

"Who would that be?"

"I don't know."

"You don't? I thought you knew everything," I said.

"I don't know a lot of things. I'm not even sure what I just told you is completely true," Dewey said.

"Then why'd you tell me?"

"It helps alleviate my boredom," Dewey said, flashing that ornery smile of his.

"What about my boredom?"

"You can always go peeping, since that seems to be your thing. With all the sexual activity that's been going on around here, you've really been stimulated lately, which I might point out is not very productive."

"You read your books, and I'll keep peeking. And speaking of peeking, there goes Woody," I said, sitting up. "Maybe he's headed over to Faith's to get a little nookie. I think I'll tag along. Want to come?"

"No," Dewey said, rolling his eyes. "I might walk down town and check in on Wanda."

"That won't keep you from seeing anything. She'll probably be humping Freddy. What do you think she sees in Freddy?"

"He's nice to her, and he desires her."

"What he is, Dewey, is an asshole," I said.

"Yes, but he's novelty, at least for the moment."

"Are you saying there's going to be more?"

"Perhaps," Dewey said, turning to walk toward town.

"Don't you want to ride?" I called after him. He shook his head and walked on.

Woody didn't go to Faith Appleton's apartment. He went home, changed into jeans, sneakers, and an old sweatshirt and went straight to Duncan Highsmith's. I hated to see that because Woody and Duncan sometimes got into day long drinking sessions. Besides, their drunks were usually boring. They always ended up sitting down at Duncan's living room table and talking and drinking and that's about it. Their conversations bored hell out of me, and this session would probably be no different. They'd talk about everything from ancient philosophy to sports, but all they'd do is talk. The only good thing about these sessions was that Wanda usually came over and broke them up about dark. Woody, of course, knew that, and whether or not he hung around until then depended on how he felt.

The television was going in the den, so I sat down to watch while Woody and Duncan drank and talked in the next room. An old rerun of Wild Kingdom was half over - Marlon had just jumped into a swamp and was wrestling with a giant anaconda - when I heard Woody mention something about fishing. I got up and moved to the door and listened. Out of the corner of my eye, I saw Dewey sneaking up behind me. He, of course, would deny that he was sneaking, but he was. He'd say he was just being quiet, but why should an invisible guardian bother with being quiet? He just wanted to see how high he could make me jump.

"What's going on?" he asked, rather loud.

"Nothing here. What's going on at Freddy's?" I asked.

"Nothing. Freddy's out of town and Wanda's busy typing."

"Woody's talking about going fishing," I said, nodding toward the table. Duncan was pointing out all the bad things about fishing, but that rang true to form. Duncan hated almost everything involving the great outdoors.

"That would be a novelty," Dewey mused.

"Not really. Woody used to fish quite a lot."

"I've never seen him fish."

"You haven't even been here a year, so what do you know about Woody's recreational interests?"

"I didn't think he had any interests in recreation."

"Screwing is recreation," I said. "You've seen him do that."

"I don't consider it recreation," Dewey said.

"What is it then?"

"It's . . . it's . . . it's . . ."

"Recreation," I said, flashing one of those I-got-you-that-time smiles.

"Call it what you like," Dewey said, sniffing.

"Woody hasn't been fishing in several years, probably three or four."

"Why'd he quit?"

"I don't know. Maybe it was getting in the way of his drinking," I said.

"Then why is he talking about going again?"

"Maybe he just needs a break. Maybe he wants to get back to nature for a while. Maybe he's up to something," I said.

"Like what?"

"I don't know. Let's listen," I said, nodding toward the table again.

We listened, and the scheme that unfolded over the next hour was simple enough. It would, for the most part, be just a fishing trip. Woody and Duncan would pack up and go to Pawnee Lake, a small but scenic lake in a state park some one hundred miles to the east. It was only a two hour drive from Forest City, and it was one of Woody's favorite fishing holes. The nice thing about Pawnee Lake, as far as Duncan Highsmith was concerned, was its closeness to home. He could've cared less about fishing, he hated camping, and he didn't like riding in a car. Duncan's poor eyesight kept him from driving and made him dependent on other people to get him around. He avoided automobiles as much as possible, but he enjoyed a good time out with the guys. They'd invite others, of course, and spent half an hour making a list of people who'd be good candidates.

Before long, I lost interest in the conversation and let my mind drift back in time to days when Woody was glad to be alive. I hadn't lied to Dewey about the fishing because Woody had once been a dedicated fisherman. Actually, he'd been a very active man who enjoyed all sorts of outside sports. He and Wanda and the kids had traveled a lot. But that had been a long time ago, and it had been several years since I'd been on the road with Woody. I didn't care who they took fishing with them. It would be nice to get away again, and I was already looking forward to the trip.

CHAPTER 27
Angling Angels

I laughed until my sides ached. Watching Duncan Highsmith try to fish would've made anyone laugh - anyone except Dewey, that is. He sat beside me, under the shade of a large cottonwood, as poker-faced as a funeral director. That didn't stop me, though, because Duncan had just hung his plug in Reese McDonald's shirt sleeve. He'd been trying to cast for five minutes, but all he'd managed to get done was hang limbs and ball up the line. This time he'd caught Reese's shirt, and from all the noise Reese was making, he must've caught some skin to boot.

"You should be ashamed," Dewey said, sounding like a mom who'd just caught her four year old trying to run the kitty through the spin cycle on the washing machine.

"For what?" I asked.

"Laughing at that man. He's doing the best he can."

"He's a disaster zone. I've never seen a bigger klutz in my life," I said.

"But he can't see."

"That's true, but it's still funny," I said, then laughed again.

"You don't look like such an expert yourself," Dewey said, grinning for the first time and nodding toward my line. I'd been trying to fish but without much success, but fishing equipment wasn't included in my angeling accouterments, and I'd fashioned a fishing rig from a skinned limb and a discarded fishing line and rusty hook I'd found on the bank. It wasn't much of a rig, but at least I could fish. Just to be fair, I'd rigged a pole for Dewey, and both poles were sticking in a soft bank in front of us. We hadn't had a bite, and my line had drifted into some snags and was tangled.

"I'll never catch anything if I don't get my line untangled," I said, then stood up and looked around. I'd been careful not to touch either pole because I didn't want some innocent passer-by to get spooked by a fishing rig dangling around in the air. I couldn't see anyone except Duncan and Reese, and they were across a small inlet of water from us, maybe fifty yards away. Besides, they were too busy fussing about Duncan's casting to notice me, so I picked up the pole and untangled my line from the snags.

"You're taking chances," Dewey said.

"Nobody's looking," I said, gently poking the pole back into its hole in the bank. I checked my worm first to make sure the hook was still baited.

"You're still taking chances. Someone you can't see might be watching."

"Want me to check your bait?" I asked, ignoring his warning.

"No. I don't want you hurting another worm."

"Worms can't feel pain, Dewey. It's a scientific fact," I said.

"Says who?"

"I read it in a fishing magazine."

"You call that scientific?" he asked.

"It's scientific enough for me," I said.

"How would anyone know whether or not it hurts the worm? Did they ask?"

"Yeah, that's exactly how they found out. Some scientific fisherman picked up a worm, stuck him on a hook, and then asked, 'Did that hurt?' The worm didn't say a thing, so that must mean it didn't hurt."

"Then why do they wiggle around so much when you're putting them on the hook?"

"You'd wiggle too if somebody was trying to stick a hook up your ass?"

"Yes, because it would hurt," Dewey said, giving me an I've-got-you-this-time smile.

"OK, Dewey, so it hurts. Who cares besides you. It's just a worm, and fish like worms, so that's just the worm's tough luck."

"It wouldn't be if people didn't feed them to fish. Won't fish eat anything else?"

"Yeah, as a matter of fact they do. I read somewhere that they'd eat dead hairdressers from Chicago. Want to find out?" I asked, making a motion like I was going to grab Dewey. Since he made no motion to escape, I went ahead and grabbed him.

I should point out that Dewey Davisson was about as ticklish as a person can get. I'd goosed him or tickled him a few times before, but you had to be careful about it. I knew that if you caught him off guard and scared him, you could end up on your back gazing up at the stars flying around your head. If he saw you coming, though, he'd easily slip your grabs. I rarely got to tickle him because he was so slippery, but this time I got him by an ankle and held on. He kicked sand everywhere, but I got in a few good tickles to his ribs before he wrestled free. I went after him on my hands and knees, but he jumped over me, still giggling. About then I looked up and saw Duncan and Reese staring in our direction. They were probably trying to figure out what was making all the commotion just across the lake from them. Since Dewey and I were both in I/T modes, we were kicking up sand and moving the tall grass and bushes around quite a bit. It didn't worry me much about it because Duncan couldn't see anything that far away, and Reese was already about half drunk. Still, I quit chasing Dewey and went back to fishing.

Watching a couple of lines dangle in water got boring before long, and we went I/I and wandered over to where the guys were camped. All told, the fish and frolic group from WKSU amounted to eight people. Besides Duncan, Reese, and Woody, there was Bob Tubbs, Gordie Mazurski, and Lane Allen. Tubbs, you probably remember, was the sports information man. He was Reese McDonald's best friend, and they went almost everywhere together. Lane Allen was the young business professor that Faith Appleton had screwed around with for a while. The other two members of the party were Sean Pickens and Danny McDonald, a couple of 12 year olds.

Woody's kid Sean and Danny, Reese's boy, came because Wanda wanted it that way. The kids were school chums, and sending them along was a good way of keeping Woody out of trouble. She tried to send a kid along with him as often as she could, but Woody usually wormed out of it. He hadn't even argued about it this time. Sean tried to argue some, but Wanda nearly pinched his ear off, and he buttoned his lip. So the two boys joined the fishing party, and the plan seemed to be working. Woody had done more sleeping than drinking, and sleeping was exactly what he was doing when Dewey and I reached the encampment. On the way to the campsite, we passed the two boys on their way to where Reese and Duncan were fishing.

"Boy, this is a lively bunch," I said, looking around the campsite. Woody was stretched out on a recliner, cutting Z's like an old dog. Mazurski was lying on his sleeping bag, reading a book. That struck me as peculiar until I noticed the title, something about defensive strategy against the option offense. Bob Tubbs was napping too, just feet away from Woody, and Lane Allen sat staring into the fire and poking at it aimlessly with a stick. He looked out of sorts, but that might've been due to his recent break up with Faith Appleton. He'd undoubtedly taken their brief fling more seriously than she had. I sympathized with him. I'd seen the gal in action, knew what that free from all clothing fanny of hers looked like, and I could see how that would be easy to miss.

"They don't look too active, do they?" Dewey asked.

"Look at poor Lane. Kind of reminds me of a young bull in a pasture full of heifers and old bulls. In case you missed that analogy, a young bull isn't likely to get any under those conditions," I said.

"He looks bored."

"Yeah, but not getting any nookie will make you look that way. Faith probably rubbed some wool on him, and now he's down in the dumps because she's cut him off. What do you think? Think he got to her?"

"Who knows? Who cares?" Dewey looked irritated, but I didn't let up on him.

"Aren't you at all interested?"

"No. It's none of my business. It's none of yours either."

"I think she must've been so heartsick over Woody that she broke down and let Lane have a little. That's why he brooding," I said.

"Do you think she's that easy?" Dewey asked.

"No, but I think she might've been willing to do something like that."

"So what if she did?"

"Nothing. I just wondered, that's all. Like you said, it's none of my business," I said.

"Are they just going to lie around like this all weekend?" Dewey asked, after a few minutes of watching nothing happen.

"Probably not. They'll get into the beer after they've eaten lunch, and that'll get them started. They'll do some card playing, and some jabbering about this and that, and some fishing, and then more beer drinking."

"What about the boys? What'll they do?"

"They'll just be boys, probably. They'll explore every square inch of this place, and they'll sit around and listen to the men talk," I said.

"That's not good."

"Maybe not. I've often wondered if Wanda's plan of sending the boy along to keep Woody out of trouble really works. Either one of two things will happen. Either Woody will stay straight, or the boy will end up being the orneriest little shit in western Kansas. He could get a real education, you know."

"That bothers me," Dewey said.

"Don't fret much because Woody's not about to do anything really bad in front of the kid. He may run his mouth some, but he won't do anything."

"Running his mouth might give Sean the wrong impression."

"I'd say it'll give him the right impression, which might not be good. But all boys grow up listening to their dad's yarns and tales. Woody's got lots of tales to tell, but I doubt that he'll say anything bad around the kid. The kid probably needs to spend some time with his dad," I said.

"Were you close to your dad?" Dewey suddenly asked, staring straight at me.

"Yeah, I think so. Why?"

"Just wondered. You've never told me much about yourself. You talk a lot, but you don't say much about your family. Are your parents still living?"

"Yeah, as far as I know. They'd be in their seventies."

"What about brothers and sisters?"

"One of each - a brother that's older and a baby sister. What is this anyway, the life and times of Salty Anderson?"

"Salty. That's such a good name for you," Dewey said.

"I got the name from my rodeo buddies," I said.

"Were you good at rodeo? Were you a star or anything?"

"I was good enough, but I wasn't a star. I never won a world championship, but I might've if I hadn't gone to Viet Nam and got shot."

"What are your brother and sister like?

"They're just folks, Dewey, just folks," I said.

"That doesn't tell me much."

"My sister married a preacher and teaches school in Texas. They still live in my home town, as far as I know. She's a good gal, has a couple of kids, loves her husband, and all that good stuff. My brother, the last I heard, was working in Dallas at an aircraft factory. He never went to college, but he's done all right. Like me, he had a hard time getting his act together for a while, but he's probably doing fair by now."

"What about your ex-wife. Whatever happened to her?"

"Beats me. We married about the time I got out of college, but it only lasted about six years. She married an architect the second time, I think, but I haven't heard anything about her in years. She wrote me once in Nam. Out of the blue, I got this letter from her. She said she just wanted to wish me well."

"That was nice," Dewey said.

"Yeah, she was a good woman, and I wasn't much of a husband - gone too much, I reckon. She always felt like I was wasting myself on rodeo, being as I had a college education and all, but rodeo was all I ever really wanted to do. I made a living at it most of the time, but she didn't like being left alone. She didn't like going with me either, so it was a bad deal. Finally, we just kind of drifted away from each other. She finally ran into some guy she liked, and I came home from a long road trip, and she was gone. I found out later that she'd moved in with the guy."

"Any children?"

"No. She didn't want the stretch marks," I said, then chuckled as I remembered how vain she was about her looks. I also remembered how good she looked, and that made me want to change the subject.

"What about you? I'm not the only one who doesn't talk much about their past. All I know is that you're from Chicago, and you were a hairdresser."

"There's not much more to tell. I went to work right out of high school, and that's about all I ever did - work. My dad died young, and my mother's health got bad. She lived with me until she died. I had some aunts and uncles but never had any contact with them. No brothers or sisters. Compared to your life, mine seems boring, but it wasn't. I enjoyed life. I took care of mother, worked, and spent my spare time reading. I did other things when time permitted."

The conversation petered out after that. Talking about our former lives had started us thinking about things and people long gone to us. In my case, it left me thinking about my parents and wondering how they were getting along. What I didn't tell Dewey, probably because I hate owning up to being a sentimental type, is that my folks meant a lot to me. I could've turned out a lot worse, but they gave me some solid support and did their best to get me started in the right direction. I wandered some, got off track from time to time, but at least I knew where I was supposed to be going. Maybe it's arrogance on my part, but if I'd lived I would've made it there, whatever or wherever **there** is. From what he'd told me, Dewey's life had indeed been boring compared to mine. He'd worked hard and nursed a sick mother in the process, and he'd still managed to make a good life of it, and I admired him all the more for it.

"Want to go check our lines?" I asked, not wanting to think about the past anymore.

"Sure. Fishing isn't as boring as these guys," he said, jumping up.

When we got back to our spot on the bank, we found the two boys, Sean and Danny, fishing with our lines. They'd been exploring, and although we'd tried to hide the poles in some weeds, they found them. To my surprise, they were catching fish. "Would you look at that?" I asked.

"He just caught a fish," Dewey said, giggling like a kid.

"The little shits! I sat there for hours and never got a nibble, and now they're catching fish - with our poles," I said.

"They're nice fish," Dewey said, still giggling and looking at the fish that were flopping around on the bank.

"It's just a perch, Dewey. Besides, aren't you pissed about the kids throwing them out on the bank?"

"Not really. They eat worms, and I'm not much of a fish person. You're just jealous because they're catching them."

"Yeah, I am," I said, then dropped down to a squatting position. Dewey did the same, and we spent the next fifteen minutes watching the boys catch fish. They caught several more small perch, but the size didn't matter because they were loving every minute of it.

"Do you wish you'd had children?" Dewey asked after a bit, staring inquisitively at me.

"It wasn't up to me, Dewey. Women have the babies, you know. My woman didn't want any."

"But did you want one?"

"There was a time when I did, but considering how it all turned out, it's a good thing I didn't."

"I wanted children," Dewey said.

"You're kidding." His statement surprised me - a bunch.

"No, I wanted a child. I even thought about marrying just so I could have children."

"But. . . "

"But what?" Dewey asked, cutting me off. I was glad he did.

"Nothing, I just never pictured you as the fatherly type."

"What do you have me pictured as?" Dewey asked. He seemed more curious than irritated, so I decided to be semi-honest with him.

"Well, it's not that I can't see you making a good father because I think you would, but it's just that I can't see you making the kid. You've got to do that first, you know."

"No, I suppose you couldn't," Dewey said.

I let that subject drop real fast. Dewey had made his point in a subtle way, and I was willing to let it go at that. What he'd said, though, started me thinking over Dewey's recent remarks about his life. He obviously wasn't manly in a manly sense, but regardless of that, he'd had very little chance to develop a lasting relationship with anyone. Maybe he just never wanted to. Thinking about all that gave me the thought that a man's background is sure important, but I really didn't want to bog my mind down with anything heavy at that time. Still, my thoughts kept coming back to it, and I started thinking about Woody and wondering how and why he got to be so screwed up. I was thinking about asking Dewey that very question when Woody sauntered up with a rod and reel in his hand. Sean and Danny showed him their fish, so Woody dropped his line in beside theirs. That's when the fish quit biting because nobody caught a fish after that. Woody's bad luck even extended to fishing.

Woody and the boys drifted off toward camp after a while, leaving the two fishing poles on the bank. I waited for them to get out of sight, then picked up my pole and baited the hook. The kids had left my can of worms behind, much to Dewey's chagrin. He grimaced as he watched me snake the worm onto the hook. "You like that, don't you," he said, squinting at me.

"Yeah," I said, flashing an evil grin. Then I held the hook and worm up to my ear. "If you listen real close you can even hear them scream when you jab the hook in."

"You know what? I hope you get recycled as a worm next time, and I hope someone just like you digs you up and goes fishing with you."

"It'll never happen. Next time I'm coming back as a millionaire playboy," I said.

"You were too much of a playboy in the last life. You probably won't get another chance at that game."

"I was just practicing so I'll know what to do next time."

"What are you doing now?" Dewey asked as he watched me unwind line from the end of my pole. Like all good pole fishermen, I'd wound up quite a bit of line around the tip of the pole, just in case I needed it later.

"I need to get out into the water farther, just about to where that stump is sticking up," I said, pitching out my line. The hook plopped into the water right beside the stump, just where I wanted it. I was about to say something else to Woody when a fish struck.

"Crap!" I said, yanking the pole up. At first I thought it was hung because there was no give. Then I felt the fish jerking and started trying to pull him in.

"Is it a fish?" Dewey asked excitedly.

"Damn right, it's a fish, and a big one," I said, bracing myself for the fight. This fish wasn't giving an inch, and I was afraid to put too much pressure on the old line I was using. Instead, I started walking down the bank, following the direction the fish had taken. He was running deep and still pulling hard.

"Real big?"

"Get the gaff. Get the scales. Call the newspapers. This one's a state record for sure," I shouted.

That's about when the fish took a run to the surface and broke into the air. That's when I knew what a big fish I'd hooked. It must've weighed nearly ten pounds. "Holy shit!" I hollered.

"Holy shit!" Dewey hollered. That's when I took a quick look at Dewey and found him standing bug-eyed behind me. His mouth was so wide open a sparrow could've flown right in without touching a thing. Even though I was busy at the time, I had to look because Dewey had never said that before.

The fish flopped a couple more times, but I still had him on the line. I wasn't gaining much ground, though, and the thought crossed my mind that I might lose him. I moved closer to the water's edge and followed as the fish made another run down the bank. He was really pulling hard now, and I gave him all the slack I could. Then he came to the surface again, and for the first time, I pulled in some line. He landed close to the bank but made another run for deeper water. I gave him some slack again, then braced for another tussle. Back and forth we went, from shallow to deep water, from the surface to another run down the bank. After about ten minutes, the fish started tiring, but so was I.

"Pull him in! Pull him in!" Dewey said.

"I can't. He's still too strong," I said, then got a real brainstorm. "Hey, Dewey. Why don't you wade out into the shallow water there and catch him with your hands. I'll try to pull him in close, and when I get him to the shallow water, you grab him."

"Me?"

"Yeah, you," I said.

"But the only fish I've ever touched was a dead one at the fish market," he said.

"Then you shouldn't mind touching this one. Now get your ass out there and catch that fish."

"No."

"What do you mean, no?"

"Just no, that's all. I'm not touching him. He might bite me."

"Fish don't bite, you ninny. They don't have teeth. Now get the hell out there," I said, taking the time to give him a mean look.

"No," he said firmly, folding his arms and assuming the stance of a Boston banker.

"Dewey, this fish can't bit you. My line's old and could break at any time, so please go catch him," I said.

"You go."

"I'm holding the pole, so quit being a sissy and grab the fish."

"They have sharp fins, don't they?" Dewey asked.

"They have fins, but they won't fin you if you pick them up right. Just stick your hand in his mouth and pick him up by the lower jaw. He can't fin you that way."

"Are you sure he doesn't have teeth?"

"Positive. That's a bass, and bass don't have teeth."

"I'm going to hate myself for doing this, but all right," Dewey said, slowly walking to the water's edge. He looked down into the water, now muddy from all the fish's flopping around, then gingerly stepped off the bank. The fish was really getting tired now and wasn't fighting nearly as hard, but I was still afraid to put much more pressure on the line. I watched Dewey wade out into thigh deep water and then started directing the fish toward him.

"He's about had it, Dewey. When he gets up to you, reach in his mouth and grab his lower jaw, like I said before. Then just walk straight back toward the bank."

"All right," Dewey said.

Catching a fish, even a big one, didn't seem like much of a chore to me, but I'd failed to recognize two things. First, Dewey wasn't your average fish catcher. He was scared of the fish, and besides that, he was a rank amateur at fish catching. Second, the fish turned out to be a walleye instead of a bass. I didn't notice that, though, until Dewey had already stuck his hand into the fish's mouth and grabbed his lower jaw. I couldn't see it well because Dewey was between me and it. He must've zeroed in on the fish, then closed his eyes and grabbed, and maybe that's why he never saw the teeth. Walleye pike, you may already know, do have teeth, and even though it may have been worn out by then, it still had the strength to chomp down on Dewey's fingers when he grabbed his lower jaw.

Dewey grabbed the fish, wheeled around, and took a step toward the bank. Then he stopped dead in his tracks. His eyes bugged out and his mouth flew open and he screamed, "Aaaarrrrrrrggghh!" He threw the big walleye into the air about twenty feet, and it went flying over his head and into the deep water. I would've been upset about losing the fish, but Dewey, now free of the fish, came straight at me. I threw the pole down and headed for high country, with Dewey hot on my heels, howling at the top of his lungs. "LIAR! LIAR! LIAR!" he screamed as he chased me through a knee deep slew infested with cattails and tall grass and slime just off the lake's edge. Running through a slew while laughing your ass off isn't easy, but I made a hand at it. Dewey was pissed, and I knew it.

We tore through the slew, leaving behind more bubbles than an underwater hippo fart. I glanced back to see how I was doing, and the path we were making looked like a herd of Moose had charged through it. Then we broke across an open field and headed for a rock outcropping some two hundred yards away. Dewey was still behind me, screaming his head off. I reached the rocks, clamored over them, and headed up the ragged side of the mesa. I figured if I got to the top of the mesa, I'd have it made. About half way up, though, I looked back and saw that Dewey was making up ground on me. I gave it my best effort after that and managed to get to the top of the mesa still in the lead. He might've caught me if he hadn't tripped over a rock near the top of the escarpment. I heard a thud and turned to see Dewey keel over backwards and tumbled off the mesa.

The fall didn't hurt him, but he dislodged lots of rocks in falling. It did knock the breath out of him, and that took most of the fight out of him. I scurried off the mesa and gathered him up. His mouth was popping open and shut like an oxygen starved goldfish in a fish bowl, but he soon got his breath back. His hand was bleeding from where the walleye had chomped down on it, and he was too exhausted from the chase to hurt me. His eyes, though, still had a murderous look about them, and he'd developed a twitch - you know, one of those bad tic douloureux things.

"I'm really sorry, Dewey. I never would've told you to grab the fish if I'd known it was a walleye," I said. I'm sure my words sounded like they lacked sincerity, probably because I couldn't keep from grinning after I said them. The lethal look in Dewey's eyes deepened despite my apology, but the tic started going away. I finally snuffed my smile and helped him up. I cleaned has hand with my bandana and found some good sized teeth prints. By the time I finished doctoring him, he'd started to cool down a bit. Ten minutes went by before he said a word, and by then I'd been able to convince him that it had all been a mistake.

Seeing Dewey tie up with the walleye was funny, but what we saw back at the campsite a few minutes later was downright hilarious. Bob Tubbs and Reese McDonald, both fairly drunk by then, were trying to explain to the rest of the group what they'd stumbled up on down at the lake. They were telling about a fishing pole and taunt line dancing around in thin air, and about a shark-like fish that jumped twenty feet out of the water. They waved their arms and tried to show what had happened, even the splashing of water in the slew and of reeds and weeds that parted and fell flat to the ground. They told about sand swirling around in the air like a dust devil had come through, and of limbs breaking and loud footsteps and heavy breathing. Nobody, of course, believed a word of it. They even took the others back to the bank and showed them the proof - the trampled reeds and weeds, the disturbed sand, the abandoned pole and line, and the muddied, twisting path through the slough. Still, nobody believed a word of their story. The only reaction they got was being accused of getting drunk. Even the two boys laughed at them.

"We could've really messed up today. Roosevelt will hear about this," Dewey said as we watched the crew from Kansas roast weenies around the campfire.

"Yeah, Tubbs is being guarded by some tattletale custodian, so he probably will."

"Will he do anything about it?"

"I'll get another ass chewing, but this ass has been chewed before," I said, pointing at my butt.

"What if Roosevelt decides to do something this time? What if he decides to give one of us another assignment?"

"He won't do that. He needs us here."

Our tired bunch of campers from Kansas finally made it home just after midnight. Woody dropped Duncan off at his house and then went straight home. I was really grateful for that because my ass was really dragging by the time we got back. Dewey looked worse for wear and went straight to bed. I followed Woody inside to make sure he got to bed. Wanda was already sacked out, so Woody crept into the bedroom and slipped under the covers without disturbing her. She mumbled something to him, then flipped over and snuggled up against him. Woody, I'd noticed over the years, didn't care much for snuggling, so he moved away from her and stared into the darkness until sleep overtook him.

Dewey had a hard time getting to sleep that night, and that kept me awake until past two. Maybe his sore hand was bothering him, but he thrashed around in his bed for the longest time. Finally, I got up and opened the cabinet door so he could straighten his legs out. That didn't seem to help much because he still kept tumbling and tossing. The last thing I remember of that night was hearing a can of beans rolling around in the cabinet as Dewey tried to get comfortable.

CHAPTER 28
Dog Days

Western Kansas can get hot during the summertime, but I'd never seen it get as hot as it did during Dewey's first summer there. Occasional rains usually kept it tolerable, but our last rain had fallen in late June. Not a drop of moisture fell during July, and by the middle of August, the prairie started to wither under a bad spell of heat. Daily afternoon temperatures usually rose to at least 100 degrees, sometimes to as much as 110. Being a native Texas, I was accustomed to the heat, but Dewey started looking like a hunted fox. Heat, like the wind, can wear hard on a man.

"I'm hot!" Dewey said, fanning his face with his hand.

"Everybody's hot. It's probably over 110 today," I said.

"Why doesn't Woody turn up the air conditioning? It must be ninety degrees in here."

"Air conditioning doesn't do much good in a house with a couple of kids that don't know anything about closing doors. Besides, Wanda is part lizard. She reminds me of those sand streaks I used to find laying out under a blistering sun down in Texas. Right now, she's happier than a possum in a persimmon tree," I said, nodding toward where Wanda was stretched out on a blanket in the back yard. Dewey and I were in the den with Woody, but watching him sure wasn't as much fun as watching Wanda.

"Well, at least the children are cool," Dewey said, calling my attention to Sean and Maggie playing under a water hose.

"Nothing's going on here, so you might as well go to the library," I said, grinning impishly.

"You know about the library, huh?" He said, ducking his head.

"Yeah, I've known you sneak over there every chance you get for some time. I started wondering how you kept coming up will all that stuff about Maslow and Berne and Fromm, so I followed you one day."

"You spied on me?"

"I followed you, and that's different from spying. Besides, nobody cares if you go to the library, especially me. If that's what turns your crank, then do it. It just tickles me that you thought you had to sneak around to do it," I said.

"I wasn't sneaking. I just didn't think it was any of your business," he said, hoisting his nose in the air.

"Well, whatever, so go on to the library. I'll hang around here. The kids will get tired of the water hose before long and head off down the street somewhere. Maybe Wanda will flip over on her back to get some sun on her boobs, and I don't want to miss that. If she doesn't I'll mosey over to the girl's dorm. They're starting to move into the dorms for the fall term, and I might go over and check out the new crop," I said, grinning and wiggling my eyebrows.

"I thought you were quitting that."

"I didn't say anything about quitting. I just said it wasn't as much fun as it used to be."

"You're a sick man."

"Maybe so, but it's been a boring summer. Worst run of dog days I've seen in years. You'd think with all this hot weather, these town gals would be wanting to run around naked, but the only naked gals I've seen lately are Wanda and Faith Appleton."

"I thought you liked peeping on Faith, since she's got such a nice behind."

"Variety is the spice of life. Even a fine apple ass like Faith's gets boring after a while."

"Maybe that's an omen," Dewey said, grinning at me.

"I don't believe in omens. I do believe in boredom, though, and I'm about ready for something to happen."

"I'll agree that Woody is getting restless. Even though he won't recognize it as such, he's getting bored with Faith. He's just hung up in the dealing with dog days in more than just the dog days of summer," Dewey said.

"What do you mean by that?"

"Woody is going through dog days in that he's listless and inactive, and that means he's seriously bored. We've talked about boredom before - all about Fromm notions about taking care of boredom through flat stimuli. Maybe that's your problem. If you'd go to the library and read, you're boredom would be dealt with through activating stimuli. Instead, you go to the girl's dorm and apply flat stimuli to it, and in doing so, you only temporarily relieve your boredom. That's why Woody's relationship with Faith is not working for him, and it's why Wanda's affair with Freddy will not work for her. It works for a while, and then it starts to become stagnant. Drinking and rowdy behavior works the same - sooner or later the dog days return. You might also remember that the danger in flat stimuli is that it needs to be increased or changed in order for it to work."

"If the pattern holds true, he'll have to find another sex partner to make the flat stimuli keep working for him."

"That seems to be the pattern."

"What about Wanda? Will she start screwing someone else besides Freddy?"

"That's a very real possibility, too."

"Where and how is this mess going to end?" I asked, after thinking it over for a few moments.

"I don't have an answer for that," Dewey said, shaking his head.

"Speaking of dog days, where did the name come from in the first place?"

"It's a term for the hottest part of summer, from July to late September. It gets its name from Sirius, the Dog Star - the brightest star in the sky."

"Good. There for a minute I was worried that they'd named it after real dogs, and I like dogs," I said.

"Do you? I like dogs, too," Dewey said, beaming like a child.

Finding out that Dewey liked dogs gave me a great idea, or at least I thought it was a great idea. "Want to have some fun?"

"Sure. What do you have in mind?"

"Let's go pet a dog," I said, waving him toward the door.

"We can't do that," he said, frowning up.

"Sure we can. I've done it before. You just shift to I/T mode, find a dog, and give him a few pats."

"But what about the poor dog? Being touched by something it can't see must terrify the animal."

"Naw, it doesn't bother them much. It spooks them sometimes, but sometimes they act like they like it."

"I don't believe it. I think the poor confused animal will run off."

"There's only one way to find out," I said, motioning toward the door.

"No."

"Why not?"

"It's cruel, that's why not. Certain senses, like seeing and hearing and smelling, are important to animals. They can't see, hear, or smell us," Dewey said.

"But they can feel us, and that's a sense that's just as important. Besides, I've done it before. The worst that can happen is that the dog runs off."

"But they can't see you," Dewey said, loudly this time.

"Well, maybe we can find a blind dog and pet him," I said, just as loud.

"You're absolutely impossible."

"Are you coming?" I asked, heading for the door.

"I guess so," Dewey mumbled.

We stepped outside and started down the sidewalk toward the campus. Dogs seem to like campuses, and I was certain we'd find one there. Dewey followed, still complaining. Several dogs trotted by, but none of them looked like good petting prospects. Then, lying in the shade of a shrub near the library, I found a good one - a slick haired mongrel hound of some kind. I watched him for a few moments and then looked around to see if anyone was around. I could see a few people, but they were a considerable distance away.

"What do you think of that one?" I asked.

"He looks mean," Dewey said.

"Dammit, Dewey! If that poor old hound looks mean to you, then you're probably scared of Chihuahuas."

"But he's got big teeth."

"Lucky for him, huh? He's a big dog, and big dogs usually have big teeth. He'd look sort of funny with itty bitty teeth, don't you think?"

"Dogs with big teeth can bite harder than dogs with little teeth."

"Then don't pet him where his teeth are. Pet him on the back."

"I'm not going to pet him at all. This is your idea, so you pet him."

"O.K., I will," I said, moving toward the dog.

I wasn't lying when I told Dewey I'd petted dogs before. When I first got killed and came to the hereafter, I got really lonesome for dogs. Finally, I tried petting one. He ran away, of course, but not before I got in a few pats. I didn't do it often, but every now and then, I'd pet one. I finally decided that a dog would have to be sound asleep or dead to be petted, and I've always abided by the old saying of letting sleeping dogs lie. This particular dog, though, wasn't sleeping. I moved in behind him, reached out, and stroked his back. Sneaking up on a dog from the rear isn't easy, even if you're invisible. The movement of grass under my feet alerted him, and he looked around just as I touched him. Since he saw nothing, he came out from under the shrub like I'd stuck a hatpin in him.

"You see!" Dewey said, pointing toward the dog, which was now loping away and looking back over his shoulder.

"Aw, he's probably half wild anyway," I said and then added, "but he didn't try to bite me."

"But you scared him."

"He'll get over it. Come on, let's go find another one."

The next dog I tried was a cocker spaniel I found drinking water out of a fountain. Spaniels are usually dumb and friendly, but this one ran off faster than the mongrel hound. Then I tried petting an Australian shepherd with the same results. I was about to give up on the idea as a lost cause - Dewey wouldn't touch one at all - when I spotted another mutt. This dog looked like a mop with the handle sawed off, and I've always loved shaggy dogs. He was jet black, about a foot tall, and with short legs you couldn't even see because of his shaggy coat. The hot weather had him panting and trying to cool off under a sprinkler system. I walked right up to him and started rubbing his head. He looked around and then started wagging his tail.

"You see, he likes it," I said.

"That's because he can't see much to start with," Dewey said, giggling. He was right because the dog's eyes were completely covered with hair.

"Want to pet him? He's sort of soggy from standing under this sprinkler, but petting a soggy dog never hurt anybody."

"Well, maybe just a few pats," Dewey said, moving toward me. He bent over and touched the dog with his index finger, then pulled it back and grinned like a child who'd just touched his first dog. Then he reached out and stroked the dogs back a few times. The shaggy mutt, probably a stray, just stood there wagging his tail. We were so involved with petting the dog, I almost didn't see them coming, but out of the corner of my eye I spotted a couple a grounds maintenance men sneaking up on us.

"Uh oh," I said.

"What!" Dewey said, jerking back his hand.

"Here comes a couple of dognappers," I said.

"They're just maintenance men," Dewey said, looking around at them. The men had stopped and were talking lowly back and forth, probably trying to decide how to capture the dog.

"Yeah, but they're after this dog. From the looks of him, he's a stray, and the college doesn't like strays hanging around. They've always had trouble with dogs around here. College kids who live off campus, and that's about half of them, bring dogs with them. When school turns out in the spring, lots of dogs get left behind and turn into strays. They hang around the campus because it's easier for them to find scraps of food around here, and that causes a problem for the grounds people. They hate dogs and kill them when they get a chance. This mutt doesn't have a collar, so he's probably a stray," I said.

"Kill them? They kill them?"

"Yeah, they haul them out to the landfill and shoot them."

"But, don't they have a dog pound or animal shelter," Dewey asked, starting to look frantic.

"They've got a pen outside of town where they hold dogs for a few days to give owners a chance to claim them, but hardly anybody ever claims them. Most of the time, the city and the college street and grounds workers don't even go through the formality. They catch them, haul them off to the dump, and shoot them," I said.

"Well, they're not shooting this puppy," Dewey said, snatching up the dog. The dog struggled at first, but Dewey clamped down on him and took off at a high lope across the campus toward Woody's house.

"What the hell do you think you're doing?" I shouted after him. Dewey didn't answer, just ran faster.

I started chasing him and then remembered the two grounds workers. When I turned to look at them, they were staring in Dewey's direction, mouths agape, and with looks of absolute shock on their faces. I guess seeing a dog fly off like a startled duck would surprise almost anybody, and it sure had these two men's attention. After a few moments of gawking, they looked at each other, then turned and hustled off toward the maintenance building.

I walked up and down the block Woody's house was located on looking for Dewey but couldn't find hide nor hair of him. I checked all the sheds and garages and was about to decide he'd gone elsewhere when I thought about Woody's basement. Mostly just a storage area for junk, the basement was the one place around Woody's house where Dewey could hide a dog. I found him there, hiding in a corner behind some large cardboard boxes, counting the holes in his hands and arms.

"Where's the dog?" I asked. Dewey kept counting without looking up, but took time to point at a large cardboard box a few feet away. I looked down into the box, and sure enough, the dog was there.

"What now?" I asked. "We can't hide this dog forever."

"I've already figured it out," Dewey said, lowly.

"Figured what out? That dogs don't like to fly?"

"I found that out, too," Dewey said, holding up his hands. His forearms looked like a flesh eating woodpecker had got a hold of him.

"What'd you expect," I said, then thought of the grounds workers.

"I expected to keep this puppy from being killed, that's what."

"You should've seen the looks on those maintenance men's faces when you took off with the dog."

"Serves them right. They shouldn't kill little dogs."

"You want them to just kill the big ones?"

"I don't want them to kill any of them," he said.

"Listen, Dewey. We can't start getting involved in things like this. You know the rules about custodianship, and they don't involve us getting mixed up with the normal flow of life around us," I said.

"Killing helpless animals is not within the normal flow of life," Dewey snapped.

"Yes, it is. Like it or not, right or wrong, that's the way it is. Man is a predator, the most cunning and dangerous of all God's creatures."

"Are you saying God created us as predators? If so, I reject that. God did not make us predators; we took that upon ourselves. The idea that God put animals on this earth for us to kill and use as we see fit is strictly an invention of man. It's called anthropocentrism."

"I don't care what it's called or who started it, the fact remains that man is a predator," I said.

"It doesn't have to be that way," Dewey said, so softly I could barely hear him.

"But it is that way, and the two of us can't do a thing about it."

"Well, perhaps we can't change the entire system, but we can change this one situation. There's no reason this dog should be killed, and I'm going to make sure it doesn't happen. Besides, I've caused too much of a fuss to stop now."

"It's that kind of thinking that kept us in Viet Nam. We'd caused too much of a fuss to get out, and we ended up not changing a thing for the better. What can you do to save that dog? Sooner or later the grounds people will catch and kill him."

"Not if Woody's family adopts him," Dewey said, smiling up at me.

"Adopts him? Woody hates dogs and dogs hate him. I've never seen him touch a dog."

"But Wanda and the kids love dogs. I've watched the kids around dogs, particularly Maggie, and they'd love to have one of their own. I've even heard Wanda ask Woody about getting a dog," Dewey said.

"And Woody said no, didn't he?"

"Yes, but that doesn't mean much around here sometimes. I'll see to it that the kids find the dog first, and they'll love him, and that will be that."

"What if the dog bites the kids like he did you?"

"He won't. He just bit me because I scared him."

"O.K., Dewey. Do your bit for dog kind. I'm not going to kick about it," I said, then headed back upstairs.

I went directly to the couch in the den looking for Woody, but he was gone. Water was running in the shower, so I peeked in and found Wanda taking a shower. I checked the driveway and saw that Woody's car was gone, which meant he'd probably either gone to Duncan's house or to Frank's Bar. The kids had wandered off down the street, looking for other kids to play with.

Dog days hadn't affected Frank's Bar and Grill much, but a nuclear attack wouldn't have hurt his business during daylight hours. The only two patrons in the place were Woody and Duncan, about the only dependable afternoon customers Frank ever had. Frank seemed to be in his usual cheerful mood. He sat gawking with a dumb-faced stare at a soap opera on television while Woody and Duncan drank at a table across the room. I didn't want to hear their conversation, so I eased through the wall and sat in the shade of an elm tree near the sidewalk.

My mind kept going back over the conversation I'd had with Dewey about man's predatory nature, and I kept thinking of things I should've said and wondering why I didn't. My relationship with Dewey, although vastly improved since it first started, still had some kinks in it. My reluctance to tell him how I really felt about man's treatment of animals, I decided after thinking on it a while, came from the role I'd assumed. I'd spent too much time playing the tough guy, the rodeo cowboy, and that put me in a negative stance with Dewey. He wore his sensitivity on his sleeve, but I'd been reared around men who never did that. His positive approach to situations, sometimes too high brow and refined for my tastes, usually took the lead in our discussions, and I in turn ended up trying to put a damper on them. Looking back on it, I'd been the loser in most of those discussions.

But our most recent talk caught me at an even more pronounced disadvantage because I was in sympathy with his ideas about how mankind treated animals. I had introduced Dewey to feedlots early on, but I hadn't told him how badly I detested them. I loathed seeing thousands of cattle standing hock deep in their own dung, packed by the dozens into small pens, being fed growth enhancing grain products and feed, and waiting for the slaughter houses and packing plants. I hated the packing plants themselves, and my visits to them had left me distressed and wondering what kind of people it took to work in them.

I hated seeing the prairie plowed and planted into endless fields of corn and milo and wheat needed to supply the feedlots. I often found myself longing for the days when cattle roamed the vast prairielands in herds that were moved about by real cowboys, not some cow shit booted feedlot cowboy who punched cows from pen to pen. I hated all that, knowing all the while that feedlots weren't the worst of what had happened to the cattle business.

I should have told Dewey how I felt about overgrazing, the tampering with special high yield beef breeds, and all the other things that went with the exploitation of cattle. I should have said how I felt about using horses for racing, polo, and fox hunting. Now, there's a really honorable sport - fox hunting. Dozens of mounted hunters sic dozens of hounds on one fox and then chase it through briars and fences and hedgerows until the dogs catch it and tear it apart. I should've admitted that I'd always felt a bit guilty about my own treatment of animals - how I'd spurred bucking horses sometimes so hard I'd drawn blood, how I hunted and killed hundreds of game animals, and how I passively stood by and watched men do much worse to animals without a word of criticism. I should've told him all of that and more, but maybe I didn't because I already knew what he'd say. He'd say that maybe us humans had hit the dog days of our existence; that our lives had become so stagnant that we looked more and more to our predatory nature as some sort of flat stimulus that justified or added meaning to our existence.

My thoughts took me back to Viet Nam, and I remembered how I felt in battle. I thought about the bullets and bombs and death, and I remembered how it felt to know you'd ended the life of another human being. I even thought about my own death and wondered how the Viet Cong sniper who ended my life must've felt. I learned at least one thing before he pulled the trigger that sent a bullet that struck me dead. Man's predatory nature carries a high price tag, particularly when it involves killing. Regardless of what a man thinks at the instant he releases the arrow, pulls the trigger, swings the blade, flings the stone, or even drops the axe toward an animal's head, he eventually pays a dear price. The predator, no matter how cunning or convinced of his rightness, is himself the prey in the end because a man can't survive without a conscience. In time, the predator himself becomes the hunted . . . and the haunted.

The next day, while Dewey watched Sean and Maggie play in the back yard with their new dog, I sat down beside him and told him how I really felt. But I didn't tell him just to change anything between us or to get myself off the hook as a spokesman for tough guys, or even to show him that I really had a heart after all. I wanted him to know that we agreed on something, and that my being a cowboy didn't always put me in a position of being a hard case. As a matter of fact, my being a cowboy is what made me sensitive to the issue of animal exploitation. Hardly any breed of men uses animals more, and although we sometimes use them wrongly, we care about them. Maybe I told Dewey how I felt because I wanted him to know that cowboys, even though they're very much a part of the predatory process, are reluctant participants.

CHAPTER 29
A Lover, A Fighter, and a Cowgirl Rider

Dewey's first rodeo almost caused him to throw up. I even felt sorry for him, but not too awful sorry. That's because I was having too big a time to worry much about Dewey. Being at a rodeo again had put me in a good mood. I kept trying to give Dewey some pointers on rodeo, but he wasn't very interested. He took it kind of like he had my pointers on butt gazing, and I view my tutoring as a damned-if-you-do, damned-if-you-don't situation. I stayed after him with the rodeo pointers, but he was too upset about the treatment of the animals to listen.

"Oh, my goodness!" he said, just as the calf roper reined his horse to a stop and snatched the calf off his feet. The calf scrambled up and knocked the cowboy sprawling as he tried to run down the rope and throw him, but Dewey didn't pay any attention to that. "That's absolutely criminal."

"Yeah, I know," I said, then added, "He ought to stomp the daylights out of that goofy calf."

"Bit your tongue, you . . . you . . . sadist," Dewey said, sharply.

"The calf's not hurt, Dewey."

"He's not any better off, either," Dewey said.

"You're going to have a hard time with the team roping. That's when two cowboys rope a steer, one the head and one the back legs, then stretch him out on the ground," I said.

"They try to pull him apart?"

"Naw, they don't try to pull him apart, just stretch him out so they can get a time. They'll do it in about ten seconds or less, too."

"I don't care how quick they do it. It's still cruel."

It should've been plain to me from the start that Dewey wouldn't take well to seeing a college rodeo, and I was starting to think that bringing him along had been a mistake. He had a closed mind on the subject of rodeo, and what he was seeing obviously wasn't doing much to change it. So the calf gets jerked around. Anyone who can compare hockey to ballet ought to be able to appreciate rodeo, but my efforts at getting Dewey involved in the sport as an appreciative spectator weren't working. What we were watching was the annual Western Kansas State University College Rodeo. WKSU usually sponsored a pretty fair college rodeo team, and from what I'd seen so far, they were better than fair this particular season.

We'd come to the first performance of the rodeo partly because Woody, Wanda, and the kids had come. Mostly, though, we came because I wanted to. This particular rodeo was something I always looked forward to, and I hadn't missed a single performance in fourteen years. Luckily for me, Woody was a big rodeo fan and hardly ever missed a performance either.

College rodeo kids are pretty fair hands, and since I'm a former college rodeoer, I'd kept up a keen interest in the sport. Having Dewey along gave me a chance to pay closer attention to what was going on in the arena instead of watching my mark. That wouldn't have been much of a problem anyway, particularly since Wanda and the kids had come, but it was nice to have Dewey with me. At least it was nice until he started his bellyaching about the cruelty to the animals.

"Maybe you ought to go on back to the trailer. You're not enjoying this, and I'm getting tired of listening to you gripe about it," I said.

"I'll stick it out," he said firmly.

"Well, don't force yourself. Either you like it or you don't, and there's no use in you being miserable. Why don't you just get your ass up and go on home."

"You might need me."

"For what? Woody's sober, Wanda and the kids are with him, and there's not a thing you can do around here that can help me," I said.

"No."

"But you won't like any of it."

"Maybe they will do something I like. I see here on the program that they have barrel racing. That should be better."

"Yeah, it's pretty good. I always liked watching those college cowgirls turn the barrels and race against the clock. What I really like is seeing those cute asses bounce up and down on that saddle," I said.

"You would," Dewey said, sniffing.

"Well, you might not like it as well as you think, especially when you see those gals spurring and whipping their horses to make them run faster," I said, then stood up.

"Where are you going?"

"Down to the bucking chutes. They're about to ride saddle broncs, and I want to be up close. Want to go?"

"No, I'll stay here for a while. I have a feeling it looks worse up close."

I took my time getting around to the bucking chutes. Although September still had a few days to go, the nights were starting to cool off. A stiff breeze had come up, so I stopped off at the Chevy to get a jumper out of the trunk. I left Dewey sitting on the concession stand roof, a good place to watch the rodeo from. Dewey was a pansy about a lot of things, but not when it came to braving the elements. He was sitting there in just a cotton shirt, jeans, and tennis shoes - munching on a carrot and watching the rodeo. Actually, he was watching the crowd more than the rodeo.

The bronc riding was a bust. The horses didn't buck well, but that was about par for a college rodeo. After that came the goat tying, the steer wrestling, and the team roping. Some kids did well, but mostly it was boring. I crawled up to the roof of the announcer's stand just over the bucking chutes and watched from there, glancing over at Dewey every now and then to see what he was doing. He perked up considerably during the specialty act, a trick roping act featuring several trained animals. He liked the clown, too, but Dewey would, of course. You might've noticed that Dewey had lots of kid in him.

The wind had really picked up by the time the team ropers and barrel racers had finished their runs, but it didn't keep me from enjoying the bull riding. Several cowboys turned in excellent rides, but one kid got thrown off and hooked pretty bad. I glanced over at Dewey when they were hauling the kid off on a stretcher, and he was holding his hand over his mouth. The poor bull rider wouldn't agree with this, of course, but the hooking he took might've been a good thing. Maybe it gave Dewey a slightly different perspective about rodeo. Seeing a fifteen hundred pound bull viciously attack and hook a downed rider sort of takes the edge off any argument that says the animals are badly abused in rodeo. Cowboys, I can promise you from years of experience, take some abuse themselves.

Even though the rodeo ended on a down note with the injury to the bull rider, I'd enjoyed myself. The kid, it turned out, had a few broke ribs but no really bad injuries. On the way back to the Chevy, we passed a truck with a bumper sticker that read, "I'm a lover, a fighter, and a wild bull rider." I'd seen that same sticker on lots of truck bumpers, but Dewey hadn't and pointed it out to me.

"I used to have one sort of like that," I said as we got in the car.

"You didn't ride bulls, did you?"

"I tried a few but gave it up early. I was a bareback bronc rider," I said.

"Then why did you have a sticker like that?"

"It wasn't exactly like that. Mine said, 'I'm a lover, a fighter, and a cowgirl rider.'"

"That's not hard for me to believe. Now I suppose you're going to brag about all the cowgirls you rode back in your rodeo days," Dewey said.

"I rode a few."

"Did you ever get bucked off?" Dewey asked and then sniggered.

"Not me. I'd hook a spur in their flank if they tried to throw me," I said, flashing an evil grin.

Dewey knew I was kidding, but he still asked anyway. "You were a devil, a real devil, weren't you?"

"I've been known to let my mean streak surface every now and then."

"I can attest to that," Dewey said.

We followed Woody to his house. I figured on hitting the sack early, but that got vetoed when Woody decided on going to the bar. A big crowd usually gathered at the bars in town after a rodeo, and Woody wanted to be there. Wanda didn't, and that's when the trouble started. Don't get me wrong. The trouble didn't start because Wanda was opposed to bars. She enjoyed a good time as much as the next gal, but she objected to going, saying she didn't have anyone to stay with the kids. Even kids as old as Sean and Maggie couldn't be left alone that late at night. Since that kept her from going to the bar too, she wanted Woody to stay at home.

I'd seen situations like this come up before and knew exactly how it would turn out. Woody sat in the den in front of the television and sulked while Wanda put the kids to bed. Wanda tried to sooth his ruffled feathers by bringing him a beer when she came to the den, but that didn't help much. He drank the beer while Wanda kept harping about why she didn't want him to go to the bar. She knew how to work most situations to her advantage, but Woody was no slouch at manipulation himself, and watching these two at work struck me as funny. Wanda figured she'd lose, but she'd decided to inflict some damage on the way down. She'd lay some guilt on him, and guilt is heavy artillery when it comes to dealing with a drunk. Woody, on the other hand, needed to manipulate the situation to where he'd have an excuse for going out, and getting a fight started was the best excuse. It didn't have to be a big fight, just enough for both of them to get pissed off.

That's exactly what happened, of course. Wanda's argument about why he should stay home appealed to his role as a father and husband. Guilt works like a laxative sometimes - not immediately but by the next morning. This particular dose gave Woody an excuse to flare up in his own defense, and she flared back, and that's when the sit hit the fan. Sharp remarks flew back and forth - insults from him aimed at her sincerity and intelligence, and insults from her aimed as his integrity and manhood. It ended like always when he got mad enough to call her a bitch, and that's the magic word. She bawled and called him an inconsiderate asshole, and Woody stomped off toward Dusty's.

This is where the old fight and fuck relationship between them had started taking a new twist. Woody was on the loose for a while, but he couldn't go to Faith Appleton because she'd moved to Denver. His only path of retreat was the bar, so that's where he headed. Wanda usually stayed at home and sulked, figuring her husband would end up back at home hauling a harvest of guilt from the seeds she'd planted before he walked out, but she didn't stay home this time. She went to the phone and called around until she found some college girl willing to watch the kids, and then she called Frederick Lomax, III.

Dewey followed Woody to Dusty's Saloon, but I stayed back until the babysitter came and Wanda went her not so merry way. She still looked genuinely pissed when she jumped into her car and slammed the door, and I couldn't help but think about Freddy. If he thought the anger retaliation humping he took at his office that day taxing, he didn't know the half of it. Wanda had that look in her eyes, and Freddy was more than likely in store for the revenge fucking of his life. Woody was my object of concern, though, and I spent the next hour in a dark corner at Dusty's Saloon telling Dewey what I thought about how Woody and Wanda manipulated each other. The place was crowded and loud, not a good place to talk. Dewey nodded a lot but didn't say much. I figured him for some comment, but when he stayed quiet, I was relieved. I liked listening to his high brow notions and concepts, but I'd had about all the Maslow, Berne, Freud, and Fromm I could take for a while. He didn't even have a quote for me.

Woody mingled back and forth across the bar, but only after he'd downed a couple of stiff drinks. Before long he fell in with a bunch of college rodeo kids and started buying rounds of drinks. That was unlike him because he was pretty much a tightwad drinker. He seldom carried more than twenty dollars in his pocket, but this time he had his checkbook with him. I watched him write a check for fifty bucks, but an hour later the money was gone. He wrote another, and the crowd around him got larger and larger as the night went on.

Dusty's shut down about one, and the crowd quickly disappeared - all but a fairly large group that stood around in the parking lot finishing their last call for alcohol drinks before hitting the road. Woody hung around with that group for a while, then got in his car and headed home. I heard one of the college kids in the crowd tell him about a party at an apartment across town, but Woody turned down the invitation. When he got home, he found the babysitter asleep on the couch in the den. She roused up long enough to tell him that Wanda was out, but instead of taking her home, Woody told her to stay and stomped out. I knew that was bad news.

"Where's he going?" Dewey asked as Woody drove off.

"Probably to that party the kids invited him to. I don't like this," I said.

"Has he done this before?"

"A time or two, but never in the condition he's in tonight. I've seen some of those kids around town and on campus before, and that's a wild bunch for sure. Woody doesn't have any business over there."

"Who are they?

"I don't know their names. Most of them, you probably noticed, are cowboy types. A couple of them are pretty heavy dopers, I think, and a few of the girls are as wild as jackrabbits. If my guess is right, it'll be a rowdy party."

The party turned out to be wilder than I expected. Some dope, mostly grass, got passed around, and the tiny living room apartment got thick with smoke. Woody looked and acted out of place for a while, but before long the booze took care of that. I watched him closely, getting more worried by the minute. I got even more worried when some gal started stripping down. Woody got bug-eyed when he saw those wholesome tits flapping in the breeze, but he tried to ignore her. Then another girl went topless and even offered a feel to anyone interested. The crowd had thinned down to about fifteen people now, but that was still too many for Woody to act up in front of.

The second topless gal finally got around to Woody, but he hesitated when it came his time for a squeeze. With some encouragement from the other, he finally reached out and cupped a boob in his hand. Everybody roared with laughter when he did, and that gave him even more encouragement. Minutes later, he felt up the first topless girl, who didn't resist. Woody was too drunk by then to be easily discouraged, so he followed the first topless girl into a hallway moments later and got himself a good feel. He even got a handful of crotch while he was at it, and the gal seemed to be liking it more all the time. They stood in the hallway exchanging rubs for a minute or two, and then the gal took him by the arm and pulled him into a small bedroom. I stepped through the wall and watched as the gal slipped off her jeans and grinned at Woody.

"What the hell are we going to do now?" I asked Dewey, as soon as I'd stepped back into the hall. "Woody's about to hump some eighteen year old kid in there." Dewey, usually quick with an answer of some kind, didn't say a word. He just stood there and looked distraught.

"Talk to me, dammit," I said.

"I . . . I don't . . . know," he stammered.

"We can't just stand here and let it happen. Screwing is one thing, but screwing a gal that young is another deal altogether."

"Maybe they won't do it. Maybe Woody's too drunk."

I stuck my head back into the bedroom and took a good look. Woody had his pants down by then, and his dick quickly told me he wasn't too drunk. "He's getting ready to hump her, Dewey," I said, once back into the hall. Dewey looked even more distraught, but he didn't say a word.

Seeing that Dewey wasn't going to be any help, I jumped into the bedroom in time to see Woody and the girl go together. In all my years as a custodian, I'd never even thought about keeping Woody from getting laid, but now I was getting almost panicky. The only thing I could think to do was start a disturbance bad enough to distract him, so I went back to the living room, changed to the I/T mode, and pushed the biggest cowboy in the room. Nothing happened because he stumbled backward a few steps and grinned. I went around behind him and gave him a push, but still, nothing happened. Time was short, so I walked around in front of him and punched him in the jaw. I hit him a good lick, and he crashed into a wall. He shook his head, rubbed his jaw, then took a wild swing at some guy who'd come to see about him.

That started a pretty good fracas because within seconds a half dozen guys were throwing punches. I went back to the bedroom, but in spite of all the noise going on outside the room, Woody and the gal were still going at it. She was spread-eagled on the bed with her feet pointed skyward, and Woody was right in there, his ass pumping like a jackhammer. I started to just grab him by the hair of the head and yank him off, but then I thought of something else. I went back through the wall into the living room, then grabbed Dewey and pulled him back into the bedroom. He squawked, of course.

"What are you doing?" he shouted.

"Do you see that?" I asked, taking him behind the neck and forcing him to look at what was happening on the bed.

"Oh, my!" Dewey gasped, slapping a hand over his mouth.

"We can't let this happen, Dewey."

"But . . . but . . . it's already happening."

"They just got started, so it's not too late. Woody's drunk so he'll be slow. We can't take a chance on him getting this teenager knocked up," I said.

"But . . . what can we do, pull him off?

"Nope, we're not going to touch him. He'd probably just think he fell off or something, and he's too drunk to remember it. She might, though, if we jerked her out from under him."

"No," Dewey said, shaking his head vigorously.

"Don't tell me no, Dewey. Now you get over there and help me," I said, pointing at the foot of the bed.

"I can't."

"Yes, you can," I said, jumping up on the foot of the bed and pointing at a spot beside me. Dewey looked confused for a moment, but then he joined me.

"What we're going to do is grab her by her ankles. Get a good hold because she might kick. When I give the word, jerk backward as hard as you can. Got it?" I asked. Dewey still looked like he was about to commit the crime of the century, but he nodded.

The gal's feet were still pointed straight up, so I grabbed her left ankle, and Dewey grabbed the right one. She didn't fight at first, but when she started to kick a little, I shouted, "NOW!" We couldn't have timed it better because we yanked at exactly the same instant and in one rapid motion. Since that was my first experience with trying to jerk a carnal coed out from under a pie-eyed professor during an act of copious copulation, I learned something of interest. It's not that hard, particularly when they're already lathered up. Dewey and I must've really put our backs into it, thus overdoing it just a tad. The girl came out from under Woody like a cake of bathtub soap from under a fat lady.

I didn't see exactly what happened because all three of us - that'd be me, Dewey, and the gal - went flying off the foot of the bed. Dewey and I ended up in a heap on the floor, but the gal slammed ass first into the wall behind us. That knocked the wind out of her, which turned out to be a blessing because she couldn't scream. Woody looked around wild-eyed for a few seconds and then started feeling around all over the bed. When he couldn't find her, he jumped up and started putting his clothes on. The room was dark, and he had a hard time finding everything, including his boots. He almost forgot them, but I took a chance and grabbed them up and stuck them in his hands. Finally, he got dressed and moved out into the hall. The gal had got her wind back by now, but she didn't scream. Instead she jumped up and ran headlong into the wall across the room. Unhurt, she got up and charged again. Same results. Figuring she'd kill herself at that rate, I opened the door, and she charged out into the hall - holding her bare ass and blubbering.

The fight that I had started minutes earlier had cleared most of the people out of the apartment onto the lawn out front, but a few of them were still inside. Woody was bad drunk and reeling around, so I just grabbed him and pushed him toward the back door. Once there, I threw him outside and went back to the bedroom to look for Dewey. Several kids were standing in the hall and staring into the bedroom, and the blubbering, bare-assed coed Woody had been diddling was hysterically trying to explain what had happened. In slipping past them I saw the object of their attention. All the bedcovers were piled in the floor, and they were rippling and billowing as someone thrashed around in them, and I knew exactly who that someone was. I rushed in and untangled Dewey.

"Change to I/I, Dewey," I said, shaking him. He looked angry at first, but he saw the people peering in through the doorway and mellowed a bit.

"I'll try," he said, closing his eyes.

Within seconds he went I/I, and we eased through the apartment building wall and found Woody stumbling around in the back yard. He looked pathetic. Barely dressed and obviously too buffaloed to know what was going on, he couldn't possible get home without major assistance. "Go get his car, Dewey, and meet us around the corner on the next block. Just pull into the alley, and I'll get Woody and meet you there," I said, pointing directions.

"What about the keys?" Dewey asked.

"Yeah, keys," I said, then took off after Woody. It only took seconds to chase him down, and then I tripped him. He went down flat on his face, and I rifled through his pockets until I got the keys. Then I ran back to Dewey and pitched them to him.

"What if somebody sees me? I mean, what if they see a driverless car going around the block."

"Don't worry about it, just do it," I said.

Woody started giving me grief the moment Dewey disappeared around the corner of the apartment building, and to make matters worse, we hit a snag. Someone had called the police, and several cop cars were in the parking lot in front of the apartment building by the time Dewey got there. Woody had parked right up front, and one of the cop cars had Dewey blocked in. Thirty minutes went by before he came around to the alley, and I had to hide Woody in a dumpster until he got there. He'd been too much to handle - thrashing, and twisting, and swinging, and even shouting. That got under my skin, and I couldn't chance him drawing attention, so I stuffed him in the dumpster.

The dumpster, it turned out, was half filled with rotting garbage, and poor Woody smelled like a sewer by the time I finally got him out. Keeping him in hadn't been too easy because I had to close the lid on him and then sit on it. I hated to take him home in that shape, so we drug him over to a nearby hydrant and sprayed him with a garden hose. Even the hosing down with cold water didn't bring Woody around, and he finally passed out on the way home. We carried him to the porch, then leaned him against the door and rang the doorbell. Wanda's car was home, and I knew she'd take care of him from there.

"That was a close one," I said to Dewey as we walked to our trailer.

"Yes, perhaps too close. We'll probably hear from Roosevelt on this one for sure."

"Yeah, that's a safe bet. It could've been worse, though. Folks at the party were pretty screwed up, and they might not remember exactly what happened. Hell, I'm not sure I can remember what happened. I'm not even sure anybody saw Woody go into the bedroom with that girl. I remember someone saying they thought he'd gone home. The girl's going to remember, but she might not say much about it."

"I hope not, but I'm worried about it," Dewey said, heaving a sigh.

"Damn Woody, that stupid sonofabitch. Of all the dumbass things to do, I sure as hell didn't expect him to get mixed up with a college gal," I said.

"He getting worse, isn't he?" Dewey asked solemnly.

"I'm afraid so."

"Perhaps it would be best if something did come of this incident tonight. That might be the crisis Woody needs to start him toward recovery," Dewey said.

"By losing his job? By ending up the laughing stock of the university? I don't think so, Dewey."

"No crisis intense enough to shock Woody into getting some help is going to be easy for him."

"I know that, but I hope this isn't the one."

"Woody's morals are deteriorating. That often happens to alcoholics, you know."

"It's either that or he's taking his interest in rodeo more seriously now by starting to get a liking for young cowgirls. Maybe he's taken to heart what my old bumper sticker said about being a lover, a fighter, and a cowgirl rider," I said, hoping to lighten the moment.

"C.W. is a cowgirl, so that's nothing new," Dewey pointed out.

"Yeah, but tonight's cowgirl was a kid, a teenager. The only thing we can be thankful for is that we got it stopped in time. Knocking up a college gal is a lot worse than just humping her."

"Are you certain he didn't . . . didn't . . . ?"

"No, I'm not positive, but I think we got him stopped in time," I said.

"We're back to the old deal about improper stimuli, aren't we?"

"Don't start that, Dewey. I'm just not in the mood for a psychology lesson right now."

"I'm not going to start, but that's it, isn't it?" Dewey asked.

"Yeah, I guess that's part of it. Woody's been really bored lately, particularly since Faith moved to Denver last month. Maybe that's why he's been playing it so close to the edge. Maybe it's because he's just increasing his dosage of whatever it takes to kill his boredom and make him feel alive for a change."

"You summed it up well."

"Can we go to sleep now?" I asked, flopping down on my bed.

"Will he push it to the edge until he falls over?"

"How should I know?"

"I think he will because he wants to get caught," Dewey said.

"Huh?" I asked, sitting up.

"He wants to get caught, subconsciously, at least."

"I don't think so," I said.

"Getting caught would ease his guilt feelings. I read somewhere, I can't remember exactly where, that people drive things like this to a conclusion because they need to justify their guilt. That's what makes it so frustrating in trying to deal with a person like Woody. Wanda, for instance, seldom does what might work best on him. Woody goes out and misbehaves, and she either reacts by bitching and screaming at him or by forgiving him. Both responses help alleviate Woody's guilt and just make it easier for him to do the same thing again, which is go out and get drunk and misbehave."

"What the hell else can she do?"

"She could act unconcerned. They teach that in Alanon, I think. They call it 'tough love', or something like that. What Wanda should do is to detach herself from Woody's drinking. She should go on being a housewife and mother and stop trying to control Woody. Her indifference to his problem might be the best way to handle him because it would stop enabling him to act the way he does. It would shut him off from his reinforcement, from the temporary alleviation of his guilt."

"I've never thought of it exactly that way, but you may be right," I said. "What she's doing now sure as hell isn't working."

"Do you think Wanda went to Freddy tonight?" Dewey asked.

"Where else would she have been?"

"Do you think that's her reinforcement, her way of getting back at Woody, or is she just trying to build some guilt of her own?"

"I don't want to analyze Wanda. I'm having enough trouble figuring Woody out. Let's let it lie, huh Dewey?"

"You're right. It's been a long, hard day, and tomorrow will come soon enough," Dewey said, slipping under the covers.

"I hope Woody wakes up so sick that he doesn't get out of bed for a week, and guess what? I don't feel a bit guilty about feeling that way."

I didn't, either.

CHAPTER 30
Witch-Hunters

When it came to throwing a drunk like the one that ended at the cowboy party, Woody's timing couldn't have been worse, and my hankering for it to pass without incident didn't pan out. Maybe it would've, but other goings on in the community suddenly took a keen interest in Woody's problems. Dewey and I had been so involved with watching our mark that we hadn't noticed, but the witch-hunters were out again.

Ellen Stegnor's second year as president of WKSU was now underway, and the disgruntled group that had caused the ruckus over the rubber machines earlier in the year had regrouped. This time they'd organized as the Concerned Citizens Study Committee, but the real issues were still the same. They wanted to be rid of Stegnor because she'd done little to put things back the way they were when Huston Parker was president. But even though that was the thorn in their side, they couldn't attack her directly on those grounds. The Board of Regents loved Stegnor and thought she was doing a terrific job. The board, now dominated by more liberal thinking members, obviously wanted change, and President Stegnor was their chosen representative on campus. The new president didn't have to make change because Perkins had done that before her. Her job, at least for the present, was to make sure those changes stayed in place.

Change, particularly the progressive variety, comes hard to isolated areas like western Kansas. The witch-hunters, therefore, got lots of aid and comfort from the locals. Stegnor was an outsider, and even though she had a pleasing manner about her and did her best to get along with the folks in the community, she wasn't one of them. And, she had a stubborn streak in her. Almost all attempts on the part of former Parker gravy trainers to get Perkin's changes changed met with failure. From what I could tell, she didn't like the gravy trainers.

A dozen new faculty members had just been hired during the summer - all Ph.D.'s and all young. Not one former Parkerite who'd been dumped by Perkins had been re-hired, and at least a half dozen of them had applied. Reese McDonald had managed to hold his position under Perkins, but Stegnor had recently demoted him by splitting his former job into two jobs. Reese took it in stride as best he could, but his wife had not, partly because she also got pushed down. June McDonald, a bright and witty woman who did a good job of teaching, had only a master's degree in history, yet Parker had hired her some ten years before because the McDonalds were good friends. June had managed to hang on during Perkin's two years, but Stegnor had made sure she ended up teaching nothing but freshman and sophomore courses.

There's more, much more. Stegnor had just hired a new Vice-President for Academic Affairs, a Dr. Don Early. Early was a right now kind of man, and most of the faculty at WKSU were next month kind of people. In just three months Early had pissed off nearly half the faculty. Both the Vice-President for Student Affairs and the Vice-President for Business Affairs had come within the past year, and neither of them was well liked. Athletics suffered under Perkins, and Stegnor seemed unwilling to do anything to beef up sports. Rumors about dropping football altogether were circulating. Gordie Mazurski, the popular football coach, had resigned during the summer after three straight losing seasons, and the current football squad had not won a single game. About the only winning team at WKSU was the rodeo team, and that was because most of their money came from private sources.

The Board of Regents supported all these moves, and the witch-hunt committee needed an issue that could hurt the new president. Woody's behavior showed promise as being an issue, and he had been more closely observed in recent months than before. Woody had angered some folks over his siding with Perkins, and even though that had been some time before, some associates had neither forgotten nor forgiven. Stegnor had been friendly toward Woody - too friendly, some thought. Folks around town had talked about Woody for a long time, but almost everybody saw him a being harmless. He got drunk and acted up, but so what? Woody wasn't the only professor at WKSU who got drunk and acted up. In the past his indiscretions had been overlooked, but that was in the past. The witch-hunters obviously had plans for Woody.

Someone from the rodeo party blabbed, but the worst of what happened that night never came to light. Woody had been seen at the party, drunk and putting his hands on college girls in ways a college professor should never touch a student. There'd been a free-for-all and some injuries, and that got talked up some, but there was never any talk of Woody's escapade in the bedroom with the coed. The girl involved had clammed up, partly because what happened scared her. She undoubtedly knew who Woody was, but she kept her mouth shut. But talk of one incident led to talk of other incidents. Woody had been seen drunk on other occasions, and he'd been seen with women other than his wife.

I know all of this because I snooped around. After the rodeo party incident, I kept my eyes and ears working overtime. Kids at school talked about it, but that talk just passed around as sniggers-and-whispers gossip. Then I got wind of the witch-hunt committee and started worrying more about it. For the next three or four days, I pushed guardian duties off on Dewey while I did some investigating. Dewey didn't mind because Woody had hit a momentary lull, mostly because he felt bad.

Just as I expected, The Concerned Citizens Study Committee turned out to be a bunch of malcontents. It had about a dozen members, most of them from the local towns of Forest City and Cottonwood. Clarence Ludwig, the grouchy old grocery store owner, was a member, as was Duke Fitzgerald, a merchant from Cottonwood. Both were still angry because Stegnor wouldn't let them back on the gravy train. Under Perkins, the university had gone to a mandatory state bidding system. A lot of local businesses got hurt when bigger outside suppliers undercut their bids. The state had always required the university to accept the lowest bid, but Parker always manipulated the system in order to reward local businessmen. Perkins refused to do that, and Stegnor held to his policy.

Chuck Stone, another member, was a former football jock turned local politician. Stone's wife had recently lost her cushy job at the university when Stegnor abolished it. Les Woodrum, a staunch Church of Christ member, had volunteered to be on the committee because Stegnor did away with most of the religion courses. Florence Akers, a senile retired school teacher, joined the committee because her granddaughter had been expelled for being in the men's athletic dorm after hours by the new Vice-President for Student Affairs. Wimp Winters, a former jock and yet another member, was hopping mad about the rumors of dropping football. There were other members, of course, but their stories were much the same as the others. It was plain from the outset that the committee had been formed to harass the new president, and I worried that Woody would be caught right in the middle of it.

"Woody's neck is out a mile on this one," I told Dewey as we watched kids file into Woody's classroom. I'd spent several hours the day before filling Dewey in on what I knew of the witch-hunters. The room was filling up fast, but Woody wouldn't get there until about five after.

"Yes, but this thing with the witch-hunt committee might be a blessing in disguise. Perhaps it will get his mind off his other problems," Dewey said.

"Groups like that are never a blessing, and what's happening here is just another problem for Woody to deal with. Half the faculty is suspicious of him, and the other half is pissed off at him. Up until now Stegnor has been friendly toward him, but that may come to a screeching halt," I said.

"You're right, I suppose, but perhaps it won't turn out to be a big problem. Stegnor probably won't allow the witch-hunters to make Woody a sacrificial lamb, and his friends will stick with him."

"Don't count on it. The opposition to her has done a good job of intimidating them, and they're not going to speak up. Other than Duncan Highsmith, Woody doesn't have any friends on this faculty. The rest are just acquaintances, and they'll knuckle under to peer pressure. That's the way it goes, you know. Negative voices always seem to be heard first and last. Folks around here are slow to move on anything positive until it's too late. By the time they finally get around to closing the door, the horse is out of the barn. The good folks will sit back and watch the worst happen before they finally realize a wrong has been done. Then they'll raise hell about it."

"That's because they aren't mobilized," Dewey said.

"Yeah, and they usually don't start getting organized until it's too late," I said.

"Are you saying that Dr. Stegnor will lose the fight?"

"She'll lose, all right - if you're talking about the battle over upgrading academics and bringing progress to WKSU," I said.

"I'm not sure I agree. She looks like a determined woman to me."

"She's determined, but she's not a fool. She strikes me as a positive thinker, and most positive folks know when to quit and move on. They can usually find an out," I said.

"You think she'll just quit?"

"No, she won't just walk off, and she sure won't let them run her off. She'll find an escape route, and when she's figured an angle that will let her get out with her pride still intact, she'll be gone. Why stay here and take a beating when there's better jobs other places?"

"That makes sense," Dewey said.

"Yeah, and that's what really chaps my ass. Stegnor will be the only winner in this deal. She'll get something out of it, then move on in good shape. The folks left behind are the ones who'll suffer. Even the folks who'll think they got rid of her will be hurt."

"How so?"

"She's in demand, so she'll find a better job. Woody, for instance, is just another psychology professor, and they aren't in demand. Neither are the rest of these numb-nuts around here. They'll have to sit here and stew in their own juices after Stegnor leaves."

"Do you think Woody realizes that?"

"Probably," I said, shrugging.

"I don't think he does."

"Then why'd you ask me what I thought?"

"I was just curious, that's all," Dewey said, lifting his eyebrows. He stared at me a few moments and then asked, "When and where is the witch-hunt committee meeting?"

"Tonight, I think, but I don't know where. They'll probably have it in one of their homes, and I'll have to do some snooping around."

"Are you going?"

"I need to be there, and for more than one reason. Our job is to look after Woody, and that's getting harder by the day. Woody's on a run right now, and when that happens, anything can happen. It wouldn't take much for him to go over the edge, and we need to make sure that doesn't happen. These Witch-hunters might help give him the push he needs," I said, nodding slowly.

"Yes, but we can't do much about that," Dewey said, looking concerned and suspicious at the same time.

"No, we can't do much, but that leaves room for a little," I said, wiggling my eyebrows.

"Should we do anything at all?"

"I saw something in Vegas, though, that worried me some. I'm not real sure what I saw, but it worried me anyway. I didn't say anything to you about it when I came home because you were worried sick and worn out from watching Woody, but I saw something that started me thinking. Remember that rich Texan I mentioned, the one that dropped a quarter of million in one of Lieberman's casinos?"

"That's been some time ago, but I vaguely remember."

"Well, he was on a run like Woody is right now. I've seen it too many times before not to recognize it. The thing is, this Texan was running and causing a lot of trouble at the same time. We were trying to hurt that Lieberman guy, the casino owner, and the Texan was out there losing a bundle every night in some casino. They said he had lots to lose, but after the second night of big gambling, he stopped losing."

"What stopped him?"

"Death, that's what. He keeled over and died on the sidewalk. His limo pulled up in front of the casino, and he stepped out on the sidewalk and fell dead. I saw the crowd gathering and went over to see what was happening. There he was, staring up at the stars, taking his last few gasps. A man in a chauffeur's uniform was bending over him, gently rubbing his face. I didn't think much of it, but later on I saw the man talking to Hubie, the operation chief. I went to a briefing - we had them about every four days - and saw the man. He wasn't a chauffeur then, but it was the same guy. I asked Roosevelt about him, but he told me not to concern myself. I figured it out on my own, though. That chauffeur fellow was a hit man, a death angel," I said, staring straight at Dewey.

"Death angel?" he asked, looking frog-eyed.

"I can't be sure, but that's what I think. That Texan finally ran out of running room, the way I figure it. He was in the way, and his time was up, and they took him out," I said.

"Maybe the chauffeur was just his guardian angel. Maybe that's why you saw him talking with Roosevelt, and you know how Roosevelt is. He seldom volunteers information about anything. I think you've misread the situation."

"Maybe, but it worried me. I thought about some of Woody's runs and wondered if the same thing might happen to him some day."

"I just have a hard time entertaining the thought of Death Angels," Dewey said, wagging his head.

"Maybe I did misread the situation, and I hope you're right," I said.

Dewey fell as quiet as a room full of snails after that, and I knew he was thinking about what I'd just told him. Figuring everything had been said that needed saying about it, I didn't pursue it. When Woody dismissed class, we followed him back to his office and watched him try to grade papers. Within ten minutes, though, he wrote out a note, tacked it to his door, and started to leave his office. The phone rang however, and from the gist of the conversation, it was plain that he'd been called to the dean's office. He stood over the phone for several minutes after hanging it up. He didn't look well at all. His color had turned ashen, and he was sweating.

"That must've been some chewing," Dewey said.

"I don't think that's the problem. Something's wrong with him, so keep your eyes skinned. He's headed for the dean's office, and then he'll probably go home. I'll meet you there in an hour," I said to Dewey, then headed for Parker Administration Building.

I snooped around Stegnor's office for a few minutes, but since nothing was happening there, I headed downtown to Clarence Ludwig's place. Nothing much was happening there, either, but I overheard Amy Ludwig saying something about a meeting at one of the witch-hunt committee member's home. Since it was close by, I hustled over.

A group of about ten people had gathered in the living room, and it didn't take long for me to see what they were up to. Within minutes they started talking about how they planned to bring Woody into the picture. They'd talk about his drunkenness and his supposed affairs and finally about the incident at the rodeo party. They'd make sure to put Stegnor in a position of having to defend him. They got off that topic after about ten minutes and moved to more important matters, but by then I was really pissed. I felt compelled to do something ornery.

I got lucky when I found a couple of inflated balloons left over from a recent kid's party. I grabbed one, changed to I/T mode, and then stepped into the dining room. The living room and dining room had no wall between them, just a drawn curtain. I stepped in behind the curtain, held the inflated balloon under my arm, and untied the knot around the stem. With my index finger and thumb on my right hand holding the stem closed, and with the balloon between my arm and side, I started putting pressure on it. It's a trick I played all the time as a kid, that of making a sound like a fart. Five of the committee members were sitting in chairs with their backs to me, just a few feet away and with only the curtains between us.

I squeezed the balloon and let air ease between my fingers and made my first synthetic fart. I did it right behind Harley French, and it almost broke up the meeting. Everybody looked at him with surprised expressions on their faces, but Harley just cleared his voice and started talking louder. Recognizing that he didn't have enough class to handle the situation, I squeezed off another one - a high-pitched, squeaky fart sound that made the other people around him wrinkle their foreheads. Harley scooted his chair around and simpered like an idiot.

I squeezed another big one right behind Wimp Winters, a loud flutterblast fart, and everyone started looking as goosy as a trapped rabbit. They kept talking witch-hunt talk, though, so I moved over behind Florence Akers and squeezed off the best one yet. She jerked herself erect and looked around with a silly grin on her face. Harley French screwed up big when he grinned, and for a few seconds I thought Florence was going to slap him. Bob Tubbs, the sleazy bastard, was sitting by the wall two people down, and I got him next. It sounded like tearing canvas, and that one did the trick. Two women on the other side of the room jumped up and stomped from the room. I probably got off ten good phony farts before running out of air, and I didn't even have to go with my back-up balloon.

Dewey tried to look disappointed when I told him about what I'd done to break up the witch-hunt meeting, but he couldn't pull it off. He even giggled, but then turned somber when he started telling me about what had gone on in the dean's office. Dr. Early, the academic dean, had given him a moderate ass chewing over the incident at the rodeo party - moderate because he talked calmly and politely, but he got his point across. Such an incident was not to happen again, he'd said sternly. Woody took the reprimand silently, offered an apology, and walked out looking dull-eyed and dazed.

I went into the den where he was reclining on the couch and looked at him. His face was still white but the sweating had increased. The dressing down he'd taken from Early hadn't helped, but Woody was obviously sick. As it turned out, he was sicker than I thought. Wanda came home from work and got busy cooking supper, and Woody had just got up to walk to the kitchen when he fell. Wanda saw him fall and rushed to him, but she couldn't get him up. Dewey was there before me, looking distraught and holding his hand to his mouth. I headed toward them at about the same time Wanda rushed toward the phone to call for an ambulance, and as I did, I saw a dark shadow move quickly from the corner of the room into the hall. I took a quick look at Woody and then bolted for the hallway. No one was there.

"Did you see that?" I asked, walking back to where Dewey was bending over Woody.

"See what?" he asked.

"That shadow. What the hell was that shadow?"

"I didn't see . . . I saw no . . . shadow," he stammered.

At the time, I was too concerned about Woody to worry much about what I'd seen, or thought I'd seen. Woody was motionless and out cold. Wanda came back and hovered and fussed over him, but nothing she did brought him around. The gal had her hands full, that's for sure, and to make matters worse, the kids came in about that time. Sean stood against the wall and stared at his fallen father, but Maggie went into hysterics. The ambulance came and hauled Woody away, but Wanda stayed behind to make sure the kids were taken care of. Dewey and I jumped into the car and followed the ambulance to the hospital.

CHAPTER 31
Chickenshititis

Dewey looked green. Twice already I'd asked him if he was sick, but both times he'd said no. Still, he looked green, and I couldn't figure out what his trouble was. I watched him fidget around in his chair, crossing his legs and folding his arms and moving his body into more sitting positions than I'd ever seen. His antics got on my nerves, so I asked him one more time.

"What the hell is wrong with you?"

"Nothing."

"Then why are you acting like a worm on a griddle?"

"I'm just nervous, that's all. Aren't I allowed to be nervous? Is that against the rules?" he asked irritably.

"You're driving me nuts," I said. "If you can't sit still, why don't you get up and walk? Better yet, why don't you just go on back to the trailer. I can watch Woody by myself for a while. He sure ain't going nowhere."

"Ain't going nowhere?" Dewey asked, pruning up his face in response to my bad English. I did it to get even with him for his squirming.

"Not in the condition he's in."

"No, I suppose you're right. Maybe I'll go outside and walk around a bit."

"Uh oh, Dewey. I think you're getting it. Come here and let me look at your eyes," I said, motioning for Dewey to move closer.

"Do what?" Dewey asked.

"Come here and let me look at your eyes. You might be catching the bug that's been going around these parts."

"What bug." Dewey moved closer, and I took my thumbs and index fingers and widened his eyes. I moved close and stared intently at his eyeballs.

"Hummmm."

"Well?"

"You might have a slight case, but I don't think you've got it. Have you had an overwhelming urge to enforce some sort of petty rule lately?" I asked.

"This is silly."

"Does your asshole pucker up with jealousy when someone outdoes you? Do your palms sweat when someone suggests an idea better than the one you had? Do you get giddy at the thought of starting a groundless rumor about someone? Do you feel euphoric when you've been mean to someone just to get even with them even though you know they were right? Do you suddenly feel lethargic when everyone is in a hurry to get you to do something you're not eager to do? Do you . . ."

"STOP IT!"

"How else do you expect me to diagnose your illness if you won't cooperate?" I asked.

"There is absolutely nothing wrong with me that needs diagnosing, especially by you," Dewey snapped.

"Oops! You just exhibited a classic symptom, so you might have it after all."

"Classic symptom of what?"

"Optirectitis."

"What is that?"

"It's a rare disorder involving the malfunctioning of the optic nerves. Somehow they get crossed up with rectal nerves, and it causes you to have a shitty outlook on life. An outlook like that can make you do all sorts of chickenshit things, so some folks call it 'chickenshititis.' I've seen lots of it lately, especially among the faculty and members of the witch-hunt committee. Woody's got it, but not as bad as some of the others."

"Well, I certainly don't have it," Dewey said, sniffing.

"Oops! That's another symptom – self-righteousness," I said, shaking my finger at him.

"You're the one who has it. You have all the symptoms."

"There's another one - false accusations."

"You know it's true," Dewey said, sniggering.

"You're right, partly. But nobody's immune from being an occasional chickenshit. The problem with some people is that they're like that all the time," I said.

"No one is that way all the time."

"Most people aren't but Freddy is, and Bob Tubbs is, and so are those jerks on the witch-hunt committee," I said.

"You're not qualified to make a judgment like that because you're not around them all the time. Other people seem to like those people."

"Yeah, but that's because they're chickenshits too."

"I'll admit that you're making a good point, but I'm still not ready to accept the idea that some people are that way all the time."

"Optirectitis is a dangerous disease that spreads like wildfire. I've seen it spread through an entire company of men in the military, and it can start with just one chickenshit. Before long, everybody's got a shitty attitude. Just take a close look at this faculty at WKSU. One chickenshit can infect an entire department, and just a few of them can screw up the whole kit and caboodle."

"Well, maybe you're overstating the problem, but I'll agree that . . ."

"Yeah, and it works that way because the people who've got it don't like suffering alone. They want to infect other people," I said, interrupting.

"Why is that?" Dewey asked, sincerely. I think he already had his mind made up as to why it worked that way; he just wanted to hear the cowboy explanation.

"If somebody came along with a turd in his hand and offered it to you, would you take it?" I asked.

"Of course not."

"Do you think most people would?"

"No."

"If somebody walked up to you with a turd smeared on his face and told you that some bully had smeared it on him, would you help him clean it out of his eyes?" I asked.

"In that case, I probably would," Dewey said, puckering up his face in disgust.

"Well, if you did, you'd have a handful of shit, wouldn't you?"

"Yes, I suppose I would."

"Well, Dewey, a handful of shit is a handful of shit, any way you look at it," I said, grinning wisely.

"That's true, but I surely wouldn't try to give it away to someone else," Dewey said.

"What if the bully who rubbed the shit in the first guy's face came by? Would you feel an urge to rub it back in his face?"

"The thought might cross my mind, but I surely wouldn't do that to some innocent person," Dewey said.

"Maybe not directly, but nobody likes toting around a handful of shit, and most people look for someone to share it with. If they can't find the original bully, they'll simply pass it along to someone who is willing to take it. That person in turn will do the same, and so on, and so on."

"If that's the case, the disorder should be easily cured. All it takes is for someone to stop the cycle by refusing to pass it on."

"You're right, but lots of folks aren't strong enough to reject it. It takes a pretty good immune system to fight off chickenshititis."

"Where did you come up with a concept like this?" Dewey asked, smiling inquisitively.

"The Army, of course. We applied the term 'chickenshit' to petty rules that were applied harshly, and the person enforcing the rule got called a 'chickenshit captain', or 'chickenshit colonel, or whatever. The term octorectitis came from an old warrant officer I knew. He said it came from having your head up your ass too much of the time. I just sort of put them together," I said, shrugging.

"It makes sense, sort of, but I'm weary of the subject. Could we talk about something else?"

"Yeah, we can talk about what's wrong with you. I just figured it out. You're scared of hospitals, aren't you?" I asked.

"That's silly," Dewey snorted.

"You're scared of doctors and nurses, too."

"That's even sillier."

"Quit being a chickenshit and admit it. It's true though, isn't it?"

"I don't like hospitals, but I'm not afraid. They just make me nervous, that's all," Dewey said.

"What they do is scare you," I said, grinning my best I've-got-you-now grin.

"I'm not afraid, just . . . just . . . irritated. Hospitals smell bad. I hate that antiseptic smell."

"Feedlots smell bad too, but a lot of good tasting steaks come out of them," I said, chuckling.

"I'm not really keen on doctors, either," Dewey said.

"Nobody likes doctors. What's your beef?"

"One of them caused me to be here," Dewey said, lifting his nose.

"A doctor killed you? Is that how you died?" I asked, suddenly feeling foolish. After all the time we'd spent together, I'd never asked how he died.

"He didn't exactly kill me. He just did a bad job of treating me."

"What caused you to die?"

"A ruptured appendix," Dewey said.

"Aaaah," I said, slowly nodding. It all made sense now. We were in a hospital keeping watch over a mark that just had an emergency appendectomy. No wonder Dewey looked so green around the gills. The entire affair had brought back some bad memories.

"I'm going for a walk. Want to come?" Dewey said, jumping up.

"Might as well. I don't like the way hospitals smell, either."

Once outside, I almost wished I'd stayed in the hospital. The temperature was in the high nineties, and that's a little unusual for autumn in western Kansas. I'd about had it with hot weather because we'd had one of the warmest summers in the record books. July and August had been scorchers with most days soaring into the low one hundreds. September stayed hot, and it hadn't rained since back in June. The prairie had browned to the point of looking bleak and barren. I looked at the sky as we walked out the front door, hoping to see some sign of rain, but just saw a sea of pale blue. Dewey proceeded to a bench near an old elm and sat down. Thoughts of going to the trailer were running through my mind when I spotted Roosevelt's big Lincoln cruise around a corner and head straight for us.

"Oh shit!" I said.

"My sentiments exactly," Dewey said.

Roosevelt pulled to the curb and slowly crawled out of his car. Most folks don't have to crawl out of a Lincoln, but Roosevelt did. He was just about too big to even fit comfortably into a big car like that. It was my turn to fidget now. Seeing Roosevelt brought to mind what had happened at the apartment party a few nights before. I was also reminded of the fishing incident at Pawnee Lake. Roosevelt plodded toward us, still wearing that Deputy Dog face.

"How're they hanging?" I asked.

"You tell me," Roosevelt said, starting to look peeved.

"Tell you what?"

"Well, you can start by telling me what's going on with your mark."

"He just had his appendix out, that's all. He's feeling pretty bad right now, but he'll be all right in a few days," I said.

"Is that all that's wrong with him?"

"He's still a drunk, if that's what you're after."

"You're being evasive, so I'll get right to the point. What's the damage from the incident of last Friday night? Any repercussions?" he asked.

"Not that I know of," I said.

"Will there be any?"

I shrugged and then looked at the ground. Looking at the ground didn't help much because I could still feel Roosevelt's eyes burning a hole in me. I tried to wait him out, but the silence got too much for me. "Look, Roosevelt, we did the best we could. If you've got something to say about it, get on with it."

"You are bound and determined to play by your own rules, aren't you? You're interfered again. You . . ."

"So maybe we went out of bounds, but Woody was getting ready to screw up bad. He was down on the bed with an eighteen year old girl with fifteen other people in the next room. What am I supposed to do, stand there and watch him fuck her brains out?" I asked.

"You've certainly done that before, haven't you? Why the sudden change of heart?" Roosevelt asked, looking dead at me.

"Because this gal was a kid, that's why,"

"You started a fight by striking someone. You caused a big commotion in the bedroom, the details of which are unknown to me, and you operated an unauthorized vehicle. Police were involved."

"Yeah, I sure did all those things. At lot was happening all at once, and I didn't have much time to think about it. What else could we do?"

"People were injured. Granted, no one was hurt badly, but people got hurt bad enough to need hospital treatment, and had you stayed out of it, the incident would not have happened," Roosevelt said.

"Maybe I missed the point here, but what about the girl? What about Woody? What if he'd kept humping her and ended up knocking her up?"

"He was already in the act when you stopped him. You may not have prevented a thing," Roosevelt said, wagging that big finger at me again.

"Maybe I didn't, but I just couldn't stand there and do nothing," I said.

"There's another matter to discuss. What about that incident at the fishing lake? What about that?"

"I figured that was coming. Tubbs's snoop custodian spilled his guts, huh?"

"The incident was reported," Roosevelt said.

"We were just horsing around, and it got a little out of hand."

"It got more than a little out of hand, wouldn't you say?"

"The incident didn't really involve anyone but me and Dewey. I asked him to help me catch a fish which happened to have teeth, and he got bit and . . . Aw, hell, what am I making excuses for. It was all innocent fun, and nobody got hurt," I said.

"You've always got an excuse, don't you, Doug?" Roosevelt asked, nodding slowly.

I didn't say anything, and to keep from having to look at Roosevelt, I glanced at Dewey. I expected to see him looking meek and intimidated, but instead, he looked mad as hell. I'd seen the look several times, that snooty you-about-to-get-yours-buddy look, but I surely didn't think he'd really say anything. I was just about to say something else to Roosevelt when he stood up and moved to within a foot of Roosevelt. Standing that close made him look like a toadstool under a Redwood, but once he started talking, he grew about an inch per word.

"Now you listen here, you big bag of wind. Just where do you get off coming around here making accusation like that. You drive around in your big Lincoln acting important while we're out here trying to take care of business. Whenever you show up, which I might add is seldom, all you ever do is bitch, bitch, bitch. So we fudged. So what? If you think this job is so easy, then you need to try it yourself. And if you're so dedicated to rules, then here it is right straight from the codes, and I quote: 'Should said custodian(s) meet a situation that requires drastic action, meaning said situation is critical to the extent the guarded mortal's physical and/or mental well being is jeopardized, then said custodian(s) may use physical force to remedy said situation,' end quote, from Section 3, Clause 4 of The Custodians Field Guide For Protective Services. The situation you're complaining about fit those circumstances, and furthermore, sometimes certain conditions dictate bending the rules, and if you haven't learned that by now, you're not much of a supervisor. If you want to do something constructive for a change, you can try being supportive of a couple of hard working custodians, and it might also help if you stopped being a . . . a . . . chickenshit."

Dewey's voice was high and shrill by the time he finished unloading on Roosevelt, but he hardly took a breath during the entire tirade. Once he got it all out, he wheeled around and stomped off toward the hospital, leaving Roosevelt standing there with his mouth hanging open. We both watched him go, too shocked to say a word for the next few minutes. Finally, Roosevelt cleared his throat.

"You know, I like that guy," he said, then chuckled. I wanted to laugh like hell, but I just chuckled, too.

"Dewey's good help," I said.

"And he's right, of course - at least about the criticism. My job is to make sure the job is done right, and sometimes I forget how hard you guys work. That doesn't mean I approve of the way you work sometimes, but overall, I'm pleased with your performances. Now, on to other business," Roosevelt said, moving closer.

"What other business?"

"I've got another temporary assignment for you."

"Vegas?" I asked hopefully.

"No, not this time. You're going to Cleveland."

"Cleveland, Ohio? That's the worst town in the country."

"I know, but you'll only be there for a few days. We need you there because you've got a knack for the kind of job that needs to be done. You'll be troubleshooting for an undercover police detective," Roosevelt said matter-of-factly.

"I don't know squat about police work, but it sounds exciting. It also sounds dangerous. What'll I be doing?"

"I couldn't say. They'll brief you in Cleveland. I'm just supposed to send you on your way."

"What about Dewey? He got sick the last time I went off and left him by himself," I said.

"It won't be as hard on him this time because Woody's laid up for a while. Besides, I brought him some help. We're breaking in a new kid, and Dewey's got enough experience now to show him the ropes," Roosevelt said, turning toward his Lincoln and motioning for someone to come. The deeply tinted windows of Roosevelt's Lincoln had kept me from noticing the passenger until he stepped out and timidly moved toward us. I looked him over good as he approached, and out of the corner of my eye I could see Roosevelt watching me. The man was thirtyish, clean cut in a jock sort of way, and a light skinned black.

"Winston Frye, meet Doug Anderson," Roosevelt said, stepping back and motioning us together with his arms. I reached out and shook hands with him.

"Howdy," I said. Winston just smiled and nodded.

Roosevelt stayed for another five minutes, then crawled back into his Lincoln and drove off. Winston and I stood there for a few moments, smiling and shuffling our feet, then sat down. We visited long enough for me to find out that he was from Alabama, same as Roosevelt. He indeed had been a jock, he got killed in a boating accident, and he was just out of training. He looked a little scared. I figured he'd be even more scared when he met Dewey, so I tried to cushion the blow by telling him about Dewey. It didn't help a lot because Winston almost turned white when he first shook hands with Dewey. He looked like a homophobic who'd just stepped into a john full of queers.

Dewey had calmed down by the time I introduced him to our rookie, and he even seemed excited about being asked to show him the ropes. I hung around until past noon and then caught a bus up to

Garden City. From there I jumped on a small plane to Wichita, waited around there for an hour, and then grabbed a big jet on to Cleveland. Dewey stayed on my mind the entire trip, mostly because of his outburst against Roosevelt. I felt a little bad about leaving without bragging on him, but at least I wasn't worried about him this time. Woody's stay in the hospital would last at least a week, and Dewey would have his new partner to talk to. Winston was the one who'd have a tough adjustment period.

Part Four

Tracks To Higher Ground

CHAPTER 32
Cleveland Cowboys

I'd been to Cleveland once before and left nothing there, not even the bad memory of the visit. Going back again had me feeling apprehensive and cranky, especially after my contact didn't show at the airport. I missed a plane in Kansas City that would've had me there on time, but I still wasn't more than an hour late. My contact either didn't show at all or just didn't wait around, but regardless, my mood got worse. I followed the backup plan, which was to check in at a north side precinct with a detective Reynolds. I caught a ride downtown in a limo hauling a couple of out-of-town business execs. A little later, I hopped in a truck headed toward the north side of town not far from the lakefront.

My previous trip to Cleveland had lasted only a few days, and that had been close to thirty years before. I remembered very little from that one brief visit - just enough to convince me that Cleveland was the asshole of the universe. The city had changed some since then. I rode through areas with modern buildings and wide boulevards and neatly landscaped parks - not the decaying old city I'd seen thirty years before. Even the Cuyahoga River, back then little more than a rust colored sewage canal draining into Lake Erie, looked almost like a real river now. But the view changed as I entered the neighborhood of the police precinct where I was to meet Reynolds. This was the Cleveland I remembered - dirty and run down and mostly populated with blacks. I walked the last half dozen blocks, and even being invisible didn't keep me from feeling ill at ease. I found Reynolds sitting on the steps of a half gutted brick building, smiling as I approached.

"They said you'd be a cowboy, but I sure wasn't expecting Salty Anderson," he said, shaking his head.

"You know me?" I asked, looking him over carefully. He was a fiftyish, husky built man with a face almost as craggy as the elephant hide boots I used to wear. Yeah, I know. Elephants are endangered critters, and I shouldn't have worn the boots. I checked, though, when I bought them and the salesman assured me that that particular elephant hide had come from a road-killed elephant that got run down by a pygmy on a moped.

"Naw, we never met, but I know who you are. Seen you ride lots of time back in the sixties. Used to live in Oklahoma - had a mark down there for about ten years. Went to lots of rodeos. Yeah, I remember you real good. Welcome to Cleveland," he said, then leaned forward and offered his hand.

"Thanks. I'd say I'm proud to be here, but I'm not. When my supervisor said he was sending me here, I felt like telling him that I'd just as soon try poking a bowling ball up a gorilla's ass as to go to Cleveland, but that wouldn't have helped any. By the way, who was your mark down in Oklahoma?" I asked, taking his hand and giving it a few good pumps.

"Boy named Innis Brooks. Remember him?"

"Yeah, a bull hooked him and killed him out in Arizona. I didn't know him that well but always thought he was a pretty good hand."

"I liked that kid, mostly 'cause he liked rodeo. Me, I was born and raised up in Texas. Cowboying, that's all I ever knew anything about. Then on one of my assignments, I got sent down to Oklahoma to watch over this young bull rider. I really liked that job and hated seeing it end. Felt real bad about losing him like that, but there ain't much any of us can do sometimes. He drew this bull that hardly anybody ever rode. Had the reputation of being bad to hook a feller. Innis got throwed off right at the tooter, and that big twister come back and hooked him 'fore I had a chance to do a thing. 'Course, he's doing all right now. Somebody said he's working down in Arkansas, making a good hand at being a custodian."

"I've only had one mark," I said.

"Me, I've had quite a few - Cribbs being the most recent."

"Cribbs?"

"Yeah, that's his name, Lester Leroy Cribbs, the feller you're gonna be looking after. Everybody calls him 'cowboy.' That used to rankle me, them calling him that, but I've come around to thinking that real cowboys like me and you have to cut these city slickers some slack when it comes to shit like that," Reynolds said, winking.

"Yeah, I reckon, but I don't know much about city slickers.

I've been in western Kansas for almost fifteen years, and not many folks live out there."

"Sounds like a good assignment to me. Most of mine have been in cities, and I'd rather have western Kansas any time. After a few weeks here, you'll be liking Kansas a lot better."

"My assignment area is fine, but my mark is a pain in the ass," I said.

"Aw, hell, boy! They're all a pain in the ass. That's how come they're being guarded. If they weren't so bothersome, they wouldn't need no help," Reynolds said, grinning broadly.

"Yeah, I reckon."

Reynolds started talking about Texas then, so I parked myself on the step beside him and listened. His life's story and mine turned out to be much the same. We'd both been cowboys - him as a rancher and working hand, and me as a rodeo cowboy. I liked hearing him talk. His down home sense of humor made the listening enjoyable, and I was disappointed when he finally got around to talking about my new assignment. He described Cribbs as 'a scaly sonofabitch,' meaning he was difficult and unpleasant. I'd have to work in the personification mode to keep up with him, but he said I'd come highly recommended, and that I had a reputation for being able to handle the hard cases. I didn't tell him the only thing I'd ever guarded was a drunk psychology professor, and the thought of working around real bullets again gave me the willies. Other cops had started calling Cribbs 'cowboy' because he was so wild and wooly. He loved danger, Reynolds said, almost to the point of having a death wish.

"Did Cribbs get too much for you to handle? Is that why I'm here?"

"Well, not exactly. I was doing all right with him, but then I up and got killed," Reynolds said, lowering his head and giving me a sideways grin.

"Killed?" I asked, not knowing whether to grin or look sad. Since it was a toss-up, I just looked stupid.

"Yep, got it right here," he said, pointing to a spot just over his left ear. He didn't grin this time, and the look on his face told me that he was - excuse the expression - dead serious.

"But . . . but . . . you can't die," I said.

"How many times have you worked the personification mode?" Reynolds asked, squinting at me.

"Just once."

"And nobody told you that you could go tits up?"

"No, I just assumed . . ."

"Damn, Salty, you cain't assume nothing - gotta ask about shit like that. 'Course, it's just like a supervisor not to tell you. Me, I made sure and ask."

"But . . . you're sitting . . . right here," I stammered.

"Yeah, I sure am, ain't I," he said, feeling his chest with both hands. Then he looked up and smiled broadly.

"Then you're not dead . . . or . . . er . . . dead again."

Reynolds threw his head back and laughed hard this time, slapping his knees with both hands and rocking back and forth. It took him a full minute to get his wind back. "Naw, Salty, I ain't dead again. There's only one dead, but a feller working in the personification mode can sure get killed again. I've been working this assignment as Dub Reynolds, but my real handle's Virgil Jacks. What that means is that Virgil's still going strong, but Dub Reynolds is deader'n a dried carp."

"Damn," I said, lowly.

"Yeah, I know what you're thinking. Getting killed, no matter who you are, is still getting killed. But, it's different - sorta like having a good horse go dead under you. Ever have a horse drop dead while you was riding him? Well, feels sorta the same. You fall, get up, look down at the body, then walk away feeling sorta weird. Seeing your body, a personification you've been using, laying dead makes you feel like your favorite horse died. I felt bad about losing Reynolds, but I knew the real me was still here. Sabe?"

I nodded, then asked, "But what about Reynolds? What about the body?"

"Aw, they're out burying him right now. That's how come this place is sorta deserted. Folks around here liked me pretty good as Reynolds, so they're giving me a good send off."

"How long were you Dub Reynolds?"

"Five years. They sent me in as a transfer from Texas - gave me a whole history and everything. It's been a helluva job, boy, I can damn sure tell you that. Got shot twice, broke an arm once, and been cut three or four times. Put lots of bad guys away, though," Virgil said.

"But what if you're working a case as yourself and get killed? What then?" I asked.

"Don't nobody ever use PM as themselves."

"I've done it," I said, shrugging.

"You personified as yourself?" Virgil asked, leaning forward and looking concerned.

"Sure did. They sent me out to Vegas for a sting operation on some crooked gambling. I was personified as several guys, but I was me for a while."

"That ain't too smart, Salty."

"Nobody told me not to, and that's before I knew about this getting killed business. What would've happened if . . . if somebody had shot me in the head," I asked, pointing at my head.

"I ain't sure," Virgil said, scratching his chin.

"I can see how you might get another personification killed, since it's not really you, but what if it's really you and . . . and you get shot or something?"

"I know what you're asking. I just ain't sure what the answer is. What the hell were you doing using yourself anyway?" Virgil asked, frowning.

"I was trying to get laid," I said lowly.

"Do What?"

"Get laid. You know, get a little tail," I said, louder this time.

"Hell, Salty! You can get laid as anybody. Feels just as good, and there ain't near as many risks involved."

"Yeah, but I wanted it to be me that was getting laid."

"Well, I reckon that makes sense in a weird sorta way. It's still risky, though, and it's kinda stupid. You're always you, regardless of what you're personified as. Get it?"

"Kind of, I reckon."

"We'll get back to that in a minute, but right now what I want to know is this: did you really get laid?"

"Nope," I said, shaking my head.

"Naw, I didn't think so. Did they pull that big dick thing on you?" he asked, cocking his head sideways again.

Hearing that question caused me to snap my head up and stare at him. "Yeah, that's exactly what they did. Said it was a precautionary thing. How'd you know about it?" I said.

"Aw, hell, boy! You think you're the first custodian to ever try and get laid? They've been doing that for years. What you should've done is personify as somebody else, and then you might've got by with it."

"How would that help?"

"Well, for one thing, you'd be less obvious. The Central Office would know who you was, but other folks wouldn't. Other custodians working the I/I and I/T mode wouldn't be ratting you out 'cause they couldn't see you as who you really are. Most supervisors, except, of course, your own, wouldn't know you either. And, here's the good part. Custodians working the personification mode wouldn't know you either."

"I hadn't thought of that."

"You're a corker, you are, and you're gonna make a helluva guardian for Cowboy. You're about as goofy as he is. You're the first custodian I've known of to risk going PM as himself just to get laid," he said.

"Maybe I like pussy better than most folks," I said, starting to get irritated.

"Yeah, but the Central Office put the kibosh on that. How big did they go with you?"

"About like this," I said, holding my hands about a foot apart.

"That big, huh? Well, that's enough to keep most anybody honest. Proves several things, though. First, you ain't gonna get laid till they want you to, and second, somebody up in the Central Office has sure got a sense of humor," he said, then laughed out loud.

The incident was still too fresh in my memory for me to see that much humor in it, but I waited until he got down to giggles before asking my next question. "You never finished telling me about the personification mode. How does all that work?

"All I can do is tell you how I think it works, but I've been around for a while, and I'm a fair hand at observing. There's several kinds of personification modes, I think. One is what I just used in being Reynolds. They created him for me, and just put me in his body. I don't know how they do it, but they do. Another way is that a feller can be born into the personification mode, and he may spend a long time doing it, at least till he dies out of it," he said.

"You're saying some folks are born as angels?"

"Not necessarily as angels, but maybe as custodians."

"How can that be? How would they ever know what they're supposed to do as custodians?" I asked.

"Well, they really don't know, or they don't exactly know. Did you ever hear anybody talk about cowboying as being a calling?" he asked.

"Yeah, they believe they were born to be cowboys."

"Exactly, and maybe they were. Ain't everybody who can look after cows and horses and other critters, and cowboys, if you've bothered to take account, are fair hands at looking after their friends and families. Maybe for the same reasons folks become preachers and teachers and doctors and anybody else down there who's in the business of looking after folks. They don't really know they're custodians, not exactly, but they just might've really been born to it."

"Thinking that lots of those folks I knew down there were custodians is staggering. If what you say is right, the world is full of millions of living custodians, and I find that hard to believe."

"Try thinking of it this way. There's things those personified custodians can't do 'cause they ain't operating in the spirit modes. They can't change from one to the other, and they don't have the powers of observation that we've got. Put plain, they cain't do the job by themselves, and that's why we're needed. If you think about it hard, it makes sense. There's so many dimensions to this spirit stuff that it's sorta mind boggling, but it has to be that way, or otherwise, we'd be stepping all over one another," he said.

"Were you ever a born custodian?" I asked.

"Well, I ain't sure. I only remember living one life down there, and I died out of it in 1912. Made it to being 61 years old. Had me a nice place out in west Texas, but I just got old and died. Worked too hard, I reckon. I don't figure I was a born custodian 'cause I really died - none of that getting up and walking off stuff. Next thing I knew, they had me going to school to be a custodian. I spent the next twenty years with a banker in Dallas, then eighteen years with a cotton farmer in Oklahoma, then damn near forty years with a politician in New Mexico, and then five years here in Cleveland. And I looked after Innes Brooks for a while."

"Forty years with the same mark?"

"Yep, and he was a flannel-mouthed sonofabitch. Listening to him was the worst part. Slow learner, too," Virgil said, shaking his head and smiling.

"There's something else that bothers me. What about death? You mentioned dying out of earthly life before. What did you mean by that?" I asked.

"Well, it's sorta like this, I think. Somebody upstairs in the Central Office has got it figured out that a feller cain't come into the spirit world till he's ready. Maybe it's that some folks down there ain't really born with a spirit or soul or whatever you want to call it. Some, like them that's called to be cowboys or preachers or whatever, are born with souls, but some folks have to develop one. If he don't get a soul developed before he dies out, then he gets recycled as somebody else. This goes 'round till he's ready for the spirit world."

"But what if he is born with a soul?"

"He just dies and comes here. Remember what I said about how it feels to walk away from your body?"

"Yeah."

"That just happens to folks who've got a strong enough spirit to walk away. If they ain't developed it, they go back again," he said.

"The two of us are here, so we must've had a strong enough spirit. But, where do we go from here? What's next? Is this the end of the cycling process, and is this all there is?" I asked.

"I don't know."

"Aw, come on, Virgil. You're not going to run out of answers on me now, are you?"

"Naw, but I don't have an answer to that question. I've thought about it lots, but I don't know where it's going. It's sorta like traveling a long road, I reckon. I don't mind the hills and curves and hard to travel stretches as long as I get a smooth and straight stretch ever now'n then. I just do my job and wait to see what comes along next. Maybe the road will level out one of these days and end up somewhere nice. Ask me something else."

"What personification will I be using here?"

"Agent Albert Brown, just in from Dallas," Virgil said, without hesitating enough to bat an eye. He produced a crumpled sheet of paper and started reading. "Thirty-eight years of age, Viet Nam vet, Afro-American, former footballer, worked DEA a short while, etc. You're PM lasts for two weeks, just till my full-time replacement gets here."

"Albert? Everybody's going to call me Al. I hate the name," I said.

"It only lasts for two weeks."

"Sometimes I wonder what goes through those folk's heads up there in the Central Office."

"I've had trouble with that, myself, but I believe there's a master plan working here. I don't understand it, but something's going on that's past my learning and understanding. Us being cowboys sorta complicates things, I reckon."

"What's that got to do with it?"

"Why do you figure a feller wants to punch cows or go rodeoing? Why don't he just fall in and get a regular job like most everybody else?" Virgil asked, squinting again.

"I don't know about other cowboys, but I liked the freedom of being able to go my own way," I said.

"There you go. Us cowboys value freedom and independence more'n your average feller, and that causes us to think a little different from most folks. Maybe it all goes back to the cowboy's way of doing things."

"I never earned my keep punching cows, but I did my share of it."

"How'd you take to the work?"

"It was hard, damn hard."

"But, did you learn anything?" he asked.

"Yeah, a little," I said.

I ought to point out about here that talking cowboying, and I'm using the word like a verb here, with a real working cowboy always made me nervous. My being a good professional rodeo cowboy always seemed to make me a real cowboy in the eyes of most folks, but it didn't carry much weight with working cowboys. They're almost arrogant about their abilities in handling horses and cattle, and lots of them see rodeo as a waste of time. I've never laid claim to being much of a working cowboy, so I was being careful about how I answered Virgil's questions.

Seeing that I was inexperienced in that area, Virgil proceeded. "Well, if you did, you learned it from the older more experienced hands. You sure didn't learn by asking a bunch of silly questions first. Cowboying sorta goes against the grain when it comes to the regular way of educating people. Seems like folks learn by being told how first, and then by going out and trying it. Cowboying is almost backasswards from that. Older hands want to see a youngster try first, and then they'll step in and do the educating. A feller wanting to be a working cowboy needs to do some careful observation, then jump in there and give it a try. That shows the older hands that he's willing and eager to learn. Then, and only then, will he get the education he's needing."

"I've been through that - even with rodeo. I learned mostly by watching and trying," I said.

"Yeah, if you'd stood around a waited on somebody to come tell you what to do and how to do it, you'd be waiting a while. Most other folks do exactly that, even here in this afterlife, but a few folks like me and you are still expecting to get things done the way we're used to doing them. That don't always sit well with the boys upstairs," Virgil said, pointing toward the heavens.

"Maybe what we need around here is more cowboys."

"I'd go for that, but mostly what we've got is people like this dude." Virgil nodded in the direction my back faced, so I turned around to look. The man walking toward us looked familiar at first glance, but I didn't fully recognize him until he got within a few feet of us. I'd seen him in Las Vegas when I worked the sting operation out there - that twerp from the Office of Supernatural Effects.

Our meeting with the mode mechanic didn't last long, but long enough for him to turn me into a black guy. He fiddled-farted with this gadget that looked like a TV remote control device, and I went from being semi-handsome Salty Anderson to full-ugly black guy in the bat of an eye. Virgil started laughing immediately, but I failed to see the humor in it. Somehow, I had the feeling Roosevelt was behind this, but I didn't say anything. The only good thing about my personification was my new size. I went from a moderate six feet and 180 pounds to a large six foot four inch three hundred pounder.

The mode mechanic twerp said I'd be in the mode for two weeks or until the Central Office asked for a change, then walked away. I'd just seen myself in a window in the building and wasn't about to let him get off that light.

"Hey, what the fuck's this?" I asked, pounding myself on the chest with both hands.

"That's your new mode," he said, giving me a look like Dewey did when he was getting pious. The dude, by the way, was distinctively Jewish.

"I don't like it. Turn me into somebody else."

"What's the matter, Mr. Anderson? You're not a racist, are you?" he asked, looking mean now.

"No, but the least you could do is make me look like Billy D. Williams or somebody like that. Hell, I look like Fat Albert," I said, looking down at myself.

"I think it's a good look for you. Remember, you're in Cleveland now," the twerp said, throwing me an ornery look.

"I might be in Cleveland, but when I finish kicking your ass, you're going to be somewhere in Mississippi," I said, heading straight at him. I didn't get there in time, though, because he fiddled with the sticks on his machine and vanished into thin air.

"Damn, boy, you do look like Fat Albert," Virgil said, smiling broadly.

"Well, at least I'm not me," I said, looking down at my new body. That's when I noticed my hands. What a set of hands! I'd never seen hands that big. "Did you ever see hands like these?"

"Naw, but they match your feet. What size are those tennis shoes, sixteens? Big hands, big feet, and that means you probably got one of them foot long dicks again," he said, then started laughing hard again.

"I wonder how Cowboy's going to like me like this," I said.

"Aw, hell, he'll hate your guts, but don't take it personal. He hates working around anybody."

"A loner?"

"Yeah, worst kind. Took me damn near a year to get him warmed up to me. 'Course, he's gonna be sorta blue about me getting killed and might be hard to work with for a while. Just hang with him, and he'll come around. That's how come I gave you that little talk about cowboys. This feller don't have no idea exactly how cowboy he really is. The dumb sonsabitches that hung the moniker on him done it 'cause he's so reckless and gung ho. Truth is, he sorta lives like a cowboy, even though he don't know come here from sic 'em about a cow. Cribbs is an individualist, but he's loyal to his calling just like a cowboy is to his.

"Are you going to be around for a while?" I asked.

"Naw, just waiting on you to get here. Done got my orders to move on. Wanted to sorta get you started, and that's about done, so I'll be easing on out of here pretty quick."

"That's too bad. I'm not really craving this assignment. I don't know who figures out these things in the Central Office, but they've got me pegged wrong. I'm not really cut out for violent lifestyles. Viet Nam took all that glory boy crap right out of me," I said.

"Yeah, but you wasn't Fat Albert then," Virgil said, then offered me a farewell handshake. For a man I'd met only an hour before, I sure hated to see him go.

Lester 'Cowboy' Cribbs really turned out to be just as reckless and crazy as I'd been led to expect. He wasn't insane crazy, but he was definitely don't-give-a-shit crazy. Within twenty-four hours of meeting him, I was glad that mode mechanic had turned me into Fat Albert because I soon found out that being a cop is a lot different from being a soldier. Lester had a knack for finding trouble, and when he found it, he liked jumping right in the middle of it. During my two week association with Lester Cribbs, he got me shot at twice, kicked in the balls once, punched in the face three times, and bitten in the ass once. I've been shot at before, so I handled that all right. Being punched in the face sure as hell wasn't new to me, and I'd even been kicked in the balls. Nobody, though, had taken a bite out of my ass since I wore knee pants. The ass biting, the least of my injuries while in Cleveland, happened the second day on the job.

We'd just finished up a bust in a raggedy-ass old apartment building near the lakefront when I got bit. The place was hardly lived in, except for a few empty apartments used mostly as crack houses. We - that'd be Lester and me and two other narcs - rousted a pusher from one of the apartments and ran into more flack than we figured on. We got the pusher cornered and cuffed without a shot, then started out with him. That's when about a half dozen gals jumped us. They weren't armed, but they were sure putting up a fuss - kicking, screaming, scratching, and flailing away at us. They didn't like us hauling off their dope, and during the scuffling, one of them bit me on the ass. It hurt like hell and sure pissed me off. I wasn't about to walk out of that building with nothing but teeth marks on my ass, so I got Lester to hold her while I yanked down her pants and bit her ass. I bit the bitch good too. Then I went across the street, bought a bottle of peroxide, and washed my mouth out good.

Cribbs had been sullen and unfriendly toward me until that incident, but he actually grinned at me afterward. I soon found out that Virgil's description of him was right on the money, but he forgot to tell me about the cursing. I've always considered myself somewhat of an expert at cursing, but Lester was the first person I'd met who could use the word motherfucker in a sentence a dozen times. All women were "bitches," and personal references like "my ass" or "your ass" came up frequently. In trying to make a point to me once about how fat some gal named Brenda was, he phrased it this way: *"That mutherfuckin' Brenda's so mutherfuckin' fat that the porkchop eating bitch has to make two mutherfuckin' trips to get her oversized walruss ass across the mutherfuckin' room."* The thought of simply telling me that Brenda was fat would never have crossed his mind. Brenda, by the way, was a lady cop who worked with us. Calling her a "walrus ass" didn't miss it far because Brenda was a big gal. She took a liking to me when we first met, and I spent the remainder of my time in Cleveland trying to avoid her.

Just about the time I started getting used to Cleveland slums, they yanked me off the job. We'd just about wound things up when my replacement showed up and told me to get back to Kansas right away. I asked why the rush, but he said the message just told him that I was supposed to get home pronto. So, that's what I did. The twerp mode mechanic showed up shortly after my replacement arrived and changed me back to Salty Anderson. That alone was a big relief, but it took me a while to get used to looking at my small number ten sized feet again. I had to adjust to looking at other smaller things, too, but that's neither here nor there to this story.

Leaving Cleveland didn't bother me a bit, but I hated saying goodbye to Cribbs. In some ways he reminded me of Woody. He wasn't a drunk, but he liked living on the raw edge of disaster. Instead of booze, his fix was danger, and he reveled in it. After a couple of days around him, it came to me that Cribbs was too lucky to need a guardian, and that's where he wasn't at all like Woody. Cribbs lived a charmed life, and I got the feeling right away that the only person in real danger was me. His lifestyle scared me some, but I liked him anyway. Meeting him started me seriously considering chucking the word nigger from my vocabulary.

CHAPTER 33
Green Studebakers

Getting back to Kansas took an entire day. Time had flown since I'd been in Cleveland, and my time away from Kansas sure as hell didn't seem like two weeks. Being busy with a new set of circumstances had caused me to lose track of time, but a glance at a ticker tape style sign in the Kansas City airport brought me up to date in a hurry. Woody would be up and around by now - unless something had happened. I started worrying about why they'd called me back to Kansas with just a few days before my job was done in Cleveland.

I finally got to Cottonwood on a bus in late afternoon and caught a ride on a delivery truck to Forest City. Once back in town, I went straight to Woody's house. The Chevy and the trailer were back in their usual parking places, but Woody's car was gone. I checked the house, found no one there, and then went to the trailer. Winston was sleeping in my bed, and I woke him up. He still looked like a pre-teen Jewish boy in a room full of Rabbis, but maybe he always looked scared.

"Where's Dewey?" I asked.

"Gone to Missouri. Roosevelt told me to stay around until you got here to give you the news. Dewey had to go to Missouri because Woody's father passed away. They left this morning."

"Old man Pickens is dead, huh?"

"Died just yesterday," Winston said.

I packed a bag, tossed it in the trunk of the Chevy, and hauled ass for Missouri. I'd had it with airports and planes and wanted to drive. It wouldn't take me long. When you can go 100 miles an hour and not have to worry about running into anything, a six hundred mile drive isn't too bad, and in just over six hours, I drove into Laswell, Missouri.

Finding someone in a town the size of Laswell doesn't take long, but I'd been there many times before and knew just where to go. Woody had always tried to go home twice a year, once at Christmas and once in the spring, but in recent years he'd barely averaged one trip a year. It had been over a year since he'd last visited, and now he was home to bury his dad. I dreaded seeing him because I knew what old man Pickens' death would do to him. I didn't hate seeing Dewey, though. I found him sitting on the front porch of the Pickens residence, a small wood frame house at the end of main. Actually, main was the only real street in Laswell.

"Boy, are you a sight for sore eyes," I said.

"I'm the one with sore eyes," Dewey said, standing up to shake my hand. His eyes looked puffy and red.

"Is Woody taking this hard?"

"Yes, very hard," Dewey said, wiping his eyes with the back of his hand.

"Looks like you've been taking it hard too."

"I hate funerals."

"Yeah, me too. What about Wanda? How's she doing?" I asked.

"She's been really good with Woody, I think. She tries too hard to help, but at least she's trying."

"That's good because I don't think she cared much for the old man."

"That's strange because I haven't seen any signs of that. Wanda has been just wonderful with Woody's mom," he said.

"Woody's dad thought his son had married beneath himself. Woody was a graduate student when he met and married Wanda, and she'd only been out of high school a couple of years and was working as a waitress in a restaurant when they met. The old man thought he should've married someone with a college degree."

"Wanda doesn't have a degree?"

"She does now. She graduated at WKSU," I said.

"That should've satisfied Woody's dad," Dewey said.

"It did, I think, but Wanda always felt out of place with the Pickens clan. She's from a blue collar background, and I don't think she ever really left it. As you can see from the way they lived, the Pickens don't have much. What they've always had, though, is a family tradition of being highly educated. Woody's mother has a master's degree, as did the old man. Both of his sisters have master's degrees."

"Woody the oldest child, I take it."

"He's the middle. His older sister married a college professor, and his younger sister married a doctor. Both of them still live in Missouri somewhere, I think."

"Woody's mom seems nice. She's handling this very well."

"You should expect that from a woman like her. She a sweet gal, but she's tough enough to handle crises like this. I've always thought highly of Mrs. Pickens. In lots of ways, she reminds me of my mother. Maybe you've already figured this out, but Woody's a big mama's boy."

"I guessed as much. One of the first things I noticed about him was that he called home every week, mostly to talk to his mom."

"Yeah, I reckon they do," I said, remembering that I had always talked more with my mom.

"How will this affect Woody?" Dewey asked.

"It's hard to say. Since I've been guarding him, he's only lost a couple of people close to him, but no relatives at all. He was difficult to deal with for a while after that cowboy friend of his got killed, so God only knows what this could do to him. Then again, maybe he'll straighten out some."

"I fear the worst."

"Death affects people in different ways, but it seems to me that the folks who handle it the best are the ones who have something to hold on to. Sometimes it's their religious beliefs and sometimes it's family and friends. I guess it all depends on how important the person who dies is to those who're left behind."

"Woody didn't seem particularly close to his dad, but he's sure taking this hard. That surprised me," Dewey said.

"He feels that way because he had debts to pay, and he feels like he came up short with his dad."

"Do you really think so?"

"Yeah, I'm almost sure of it. Old man Pickens did a better job of indoctrinating Woody than he ever suspected. Maybe he didn't mean to, but he left Woody thinking he hadn't lived up to what was expected of him. The old man had lofty ideals and big dreams, and some of them, at least, were wrapped up in his son. Sometimes he pushed Woody pretty hard, too hard maybe. I don't know how it was when Woody still lived at home, but the old man always wanted Woody to do more."

"But Woody hasn't been a failure," Dewey said.

"No, but he could've been a lot more than he is, or at least that's what his dad thought. Woody must've been a bright kid, and maybe old man Pickens couldn't stand seeing talent go to waste. Since he never was an achiever, maybe he didn't want his boy to make the same mistakes he'd made."

"Perhaps, but if he left Woody feeling like a failure, he made a big mistake."

"Parents make mistakes with their kids, Dewey. Maybe the old man pushed too hard, but I don't think that's the problem. His pressure was mostly rhetorical because he was one of those do-as-I-say not do-as-I-do people. He must've felt obligated to encourage his kids, and since he couldn't show the way, they talked a good story instead. Maybe that's the reason for all the lofty ideals and goals."

"What about Woody's mother? Did she push?" Dewey asked.

"Yeah, but in a different way. She didn't preach to Woody, but she's always been a steady person. Didn't talk high ideals, but she set them by example. Woody's parents had a strong sense of direction, but his mother's style might have been more effective than his father's since it was based on leading the way instead of just pointing it out. She's probably not aware of it but her ways are sort of like cowboy ways. I was just talking about that the other day with Virgil, and he . . . "

"Who's Virgil?" Dewey asked."

"A cowboy custodian in Cleveland, and he . . . "

"Is that the person you worked with up there?"

"No, he was my contact, and he . . . "

"Then who did you work with?"

I stopped and stared at Dewey, trying to figure out if he was just bored with the conversation about parenting or what. "What are you, the new conversational speed bump around here? Why do you keep breaking in?"

"Conversation speed bump, huh? I like that," Dewey said, nodding.

"I got that from my mama. She used to say that her main function in life was being a speed bump for my daddy, or otherwise, he'd end up in a wreck from going too fast. That would make a helluva title for a country song, wouldn't it. I can just hear somebody on the radio, singing, 'You're just a speed bump, darlin', on my highway of life.'" I said.

"Oh, Lord, spare us from that, but your point is well taken. Your mother at least had purpose and a strong sense of direction, but parents aren't always successful in getting through to their children. You're a good example. Undoubtedly your parents tried hard to set directions for you, but you turned out semi-rotten," Dewey said, smirking.

"Yeah, they did, but it's hard to raise kids when you're as busy as they were."

"Busy? What did they do for a living?"

"Bank robbers," I said, not cracking a smile.

"Give me a break."

"Actually, they were just good country folks. Daddy farmed and messed with livestock, and mama raised kids. I got a good raising."

"Parents can lead the way or point out the way, but kids often get lost. Woody may have been given proper directions, but he seems to have missed a turn somewhere."

"He's missed a bunch of turns, but that can't be blamed on his folks."

"I wasn't trying to blame them. I was just pointing out that Woody perhaps misinterpreted their intentions for him," Dewey said.

"That's a pretty fair bet, I'd say. Woody's folks, not even the old man, have been disappointed in him. The old man, though, just wanted more. What really counts is that Woody wanted more."

"I think you're absolutely right."

"The trouble with Woody is that he's like a car he used to own - a green Studebaker. Remember the Studebaker?" I asked.

"Yes, of course. I owned several and loved them," Dewey said.

"Yeah, you'd sure had to love one to drive it. They were about the dumbest looking car on the road."

"I thought they were beautiful."

"You would, Dewey, but that's my point. You're the kind of guy who'd buy a stupid looking Studebaker just to make sure it had a home. Not everybody wanted one, and that's why the company went broke," I said.

"The Studebaker wasn't dumb looking; it was just ahead of its time," Dewey said, sniffing.

"Yeah, like about twenty years ahead. Nobody wanted to be seen driving around in one of those bullet nosed bastards."

"They drove well, got good gas mileage, and lasted a long time."

"That's just it, Dewey. Nobody in the fifties cared about gas mileage. They wanted style. Everybody was driving big gas guzzlers with tailfins and fancy chrome grills."

"I suppose you're right, but I still think it was a good car."

"I know I'm right. I owned one too," I said.

"You owned a Studebaker?"

"Yeah, but it sure wasn't my idea. My dad bought it for me when I was still in high school. It was green, like Woody's. That's how I know what he must've felt like driving the thing around all the time. Half the kids at school made fun of mine, and I couldn't even get girls to ride in the thing. Other kids had '55, '56, and '57 Chevys and Fords, but I was driving a 1951 slime green Studebaker."

"You should've considered yourself fortunate to have a car to drive," Dewey said.

"Yeah, I should've. Looking back on it, that old car was a good set of wheels."

"Woody had a Studebaker like yours, huh?"

"That's what old man Pickens drove, as long as they made them. After the early sixties, he drove Nash Ramblers. When Woody got old enough to drive, and since the family didn't have much money, he had to fix up an old Studebaker his dad had junked years before. He drove it around for a year or two, I think. It was either that or drive his old man's Rambler or whatever car he had at the time. I see old man Pickens had moved up to Dodges," I said, nodding toward the old Dodge sitting in the driveway.

"Woody liked the car because sensitive people who've suffered at the hands of insensitive people harbor a special affection for things like green Studebakers. They may never show it publically, may not even admit it to themselves, but they do. Woody's sensitivity toward green Studebakers is the little boy in him trying to reach out again, but that boy has been covered up with too many years of calloused living, and he can't get through."

"I reckon that means that I need to let the little boy out."

"Yes, and so does Woody. He wants to be a sports car, and you want to be a pickup truck, and you're both Studebakers."

"It takes one to know one," I said.

"I'm also a Studebaker, maybe not green, but still a Studebaker."

"What makes us all Studebakers?"

"We're streamlined," Dewey said.

"Huh?"

"The Studebaker was ahead of its time in design. It was more streamlined, more aerodynamically designed, than other cars. The public couldn't really accept it because it was advanced years beyond what they could understand."

"So, folks don't understand us, huh?

"Perhaps that's human nature. What people can't comprehend, they sometimes choose to dismiss as being foolish, or even stupid."

"Right, and from what I can tell from listening to Woody's mother, Woody was always a strange kid. He was a bubbly youngster with lots of energy. I think he had an adventurous nature and was always into things. He spent lots of time out in the woods and fields around here looking at plants and animals. Any of his toys that had parts ended up in pieces before long because he had to know what made them work. Woody wasn't a nurd or anything like that, but he was too nosey for his own good. He had trouble at school sometimes because teachers thought he was a smartass."

"That's true of many children, so I don't see how that makes Woody weird," Dewey said.

"Woody was an Opie clone with big ideas," I said.

"Opie clone?"

"Yeah, you know, like that kid on the Andy Griffin Show on television. He was just a small town kid, like Opie, but he was too smart. What made things bad for him was his inquisitive nature. He wanted to know about things, so he asked lots of questions that most kids wouldn't ask. Other kids thought he was stupid, or weird. What I think happened was that he got made fun of for being a bright, sensitive, open-minded kid, and it turned him off. Being a sensitive kid might've been the worst part of it because that made the teasing hard to take. Woody didn't want to be any different from the other kids, so he learned to shut off the part of him that offended the others."

"Yes, and in doing so he shut off the best part of himself," Dewey said, nodding.

"Woody developed a tough guy image to stop the teasing. Maybe he even learned to like it. Anyway, he still doesn't want anyone thinking he's sensitive. I reckon he'd rather have them think he's an asshole, and lots of them do."

"That's too bad."

"In more than one way. If he wasn't such an asshole, we wouldn't have to work so hard," I said.

"Perhaps, but that's what you like about him. He's a Studebaker, just like you are. If a person judged you just from your exterior, you'd be considered an insensitive bore."

"Not me. I might be a Studebaker, but I'm a Golden Hawk, and there's nothing boring about them. Remember them?"

"No, I can't say that I do. I didn't pay much attention to cars."

"Well, the Golden Hawk Studebaker came out in about 1957 and was a helluva machine. It was low and sleek and had this big Packard engine and would run about 140 mph."

"You're not a Golden Hawk, you're a dump truck," Dewey said, sniggering.

"Me? You're calling me slow?"

"I've seen faster slugs. Woody isn't too fast either, and perhaps that's why the two of you make such a good match."

"Slow ain't always bad. I know some women who really like slow men, particularly when it comes to . . ."

"Stop saying 'ain't', and please spare me another analogous dialogue involving sex, would you?" Dewey asked, rolling his eyes.

"But it's about my old green Studebaker. Don't you want to hear about how I got my first piece of ass on the back seat of that old Studebaker?"

"No!" Dewey said, standing up abruptly.

"Where're you going?"

"To check on Woody."

I followed Dewey to the back of the house, to room filled with little more than books and papers. This room was old man Pickens special room, his place of retreat. Woody, alone now for the first time, was shuffling through a stack of papers on an old oak desk. After finishing that stack, he dug through the drawers until he found a scrapbook stuffed full of yellowed papers. After a brief search, he pulled a small manuscript from the scrapbook and started reading. At first he smiled as he read, but before long his face clouded up and tears started rolling down his cheeks. Dewey and I moved closer to see what he was reading. The lead page, laid face up on an old Underwood typewriter nearby, read: THE DAGOBIT LEGEND AND MYSTIQUE, by Bernard E. Pickens.

Wanda coaxed Woody out of his father's room long enough to feed him a sandwich for supper. Dewey started reading the manuscript as soon as the room had cleared, so I sat down beside him and read along. I had known about old man Pickens' dagobits for almost fifteen years, but in reading over Dewey's shoulder, for the first time I got the real story about them. I only saw the manuscript that one time, but the story has stayed with me. Paraphrased here due to my less than perfect memory, the story was about how dagobits had come to America as stowaways from Asia. Tree people since time first began, they were threatened with extinction because their beloved dagobit trees, the trees they'd taken their name from, had all be destroyed by disease, wars, and greedy merchants.

I remember looking the word up in a dictionary, and found that Woody's dad had probably taken the word for dagoba. A dagoba, I found out, was a dome shaped shrine where Buddhist relics were stored. He would've known about things like that. In checking further, I found nothing about a dagobit tree, and I didn't find anything about dagobits. By then, however, I was interested enough to read the entire manuscript.

Old man Pickens' dagobits made their way to America by following the tracks of a great leader who'd risen among them. This leader, a man who'd overcome great obstacles to become one of the most revered dagobits to ever live, set off on a long journey looking for a land where dagobit trees grew. He walked across the Aleutian Island chain one cold winter when the waters were frozen. He stayed in Alaska for a while, explored some, but didn't find trees there to his liking. After resting up a while, he walked all the way down to Oregon, where he found a beautiful stand of Golden Dagobit trees. It turns out that what the Chinese called dagobit trees were actually just hazelnut trees . . . big hazelnut trees. He sent word back to Asia by way of a silver dolphin who'd befriended him, telling his people that they'd know the way by the tracks and signs he'd left along the way.

Although it took many years for them to accomplish it, every last one of the dagobit people migrated to Oregon to live in the grove of Golden Dagobits there. In time, some of them moved on to places like Missouri, where another variety of dagobit trees grows, and it was there that old man Pickens came to know his first tiny person. They'd been with him ever since, and having a dagobit friend was a stroke of wonderful luck. Although very tiny, these little guys have great powers when it comes to looking after people. No one has actually seen them, he said, but they exist.

Dagobits, Woody's dad contended, are low maintenance friends. They always take care of themselves, they protect their chosen big friends, and they are very loyal, but on one condition - that the person befriended by a dagobit never lose faith in them. If he does, he can't be helped by them. These tiny elves are passed on from generation to generation of dagobit believers, and this is never broken until someone stops believing in them. In bequeathing the friendship of a dagobit to a loved one or friend, a great honor has been bestowed. *There is no greater gift because unlike other fine gifts that eventually wear out, a dagobit never dies. No fine gift ever has a condition attached to it, old man Pickens wrote, but it should be understood that in accepting a dagobit as a gift, the receiver accepts the unwritten condition of not doing anything to repay the giver. His obligation of dagobit possession is that he must someday pass along to someone else what has been given to him.*

Woody stayed away just long enough for us to get the manuscript read, then came back to the room and prowled until the early hours of the morning, disturbed occasionally when Wanda came in to urge him to get some sleep. But he kept putting her off, saying he needed to find something. Finally, she went off to bed alone. Woody found what he was looking for - a sealed envelope with his name scribbled on it. He should've seen it earlier, but the lead page to the dagobit story had covered it up. His father had stuck it in the old typewriter, no doubt to make sure his son wouldn't miss it.

Woody opened the envelope with trembling hands and read the following note:

Dear Son,

I write this note knowing my time is short. You will no doubt be looking for this, expecting perhaps some farewell instructions from me. I've been famous for that, I suppose. You probably think you have had too many instructions, so you will be relieved to know that I have only one for you. Look after my dagobits. They've been with me for a long time, and they are all I have to leave you. They will stay here with your mother as long as she needs them, but when she is gone, they are yours.

You've never really cared much for dagobits, but the time will come when they are important to you. You've had a few with you all along. I sent them with you when you left here many years ago, and they have stuck with you.

When the time comes, my dagobits will want to reunite with yours. Remember the obligation of possessing them? You must pass them along to someone else from time to time. Make sure the grandchildren have a few. Perhaps you have a friend who needs a couple. My final instruction to you, therefore, is that you must learn to use your dagobits. They are more real than anything else in your life.

Your loving father,

I expected more tears from Woody when he read the note, but they didn't come. Instead, he looked confused and agitated, and he spent the next fifteen minutes pacing back and forth across the room. This was a new one on me. I'd been bird-dogging him for a long time, and I'd never seen him vapor lock like this before. He read the letter again, but still, no tears. He read the dagobit story again, but didn't even get moist eyes. I started getting a little confused and agitated myself about then.

"What's wrong with him?" I asked, turning toward Dewey.

"He doesn't understand," he said, sadly shaking his head.

"What's to understand? Any fool could see what the old man's trying to tell him," I said, waving my arms.

"Could they?"

"Well, I got it, and if somebody like me can get it, anybody can."

"Don't sell yourself short. You're a lot more perceptive than most people. I'm not exactly sure how it happened, but you never lost contact with the little boy in you. Oh, you've worked very hard at losing him, but he stayed with you."

"What's that got to do with Woody not being able to understand dagobits?"

"Woody has shut down the little boy within him. It all goes back to what we talked about earlier. The tough guy won't allow the boy to be heard anymore, and that is part of everything that's wrong with him."

"I know all that, but it's such a simple story," I said.

"In some ways it is, but there's a great philosophy of life wrapped up in the Pickens' dagobit story. It's a story of giving, of unconditional giving. Even more important, perhaps, it's a story of conditioned receiving. Some people know how to be a giver, but don't know much about being on the receiving end. Woody could learn a lot from this story because he knows how to love. He just doesn't know how to give it away. Even worse, he doesn't know how to accept love."

"Maybe I don't understand the story after all."

"Woody knows the story as well as anyone, but he doesn't understand some parts of it. He fully understands what he can't feel. He understands that loving and showing love carries certain risks. He's know that since boyhood, and his problems about showing his feelings for other people goes back a long way. People aren't born into the world hating life. But a love of life is acknowledged through a showing of love for the other things God created, especially people. Animals usually respond well to a show of affection, but people sometimes don't. People like Woody, those people with a special affection for other people, learn early that reaching out to other people with a show of affection can be risky. They keep reaching out, however, and they keep getting hurt, and in time, the rejection beats them back," Dewey said.

I knew all I could handle for the time being, so I stopped talking and let Dewey fall asleep. Woody kept pacing until the first light of dawn appeared, and then he finally crashed on the living room couch. I dozed in a corner of the room for a while, but the sound of children's laughter brought me around just before nine. A half dozen kids, including Woody's two youngsters, were swinging on an old tire that had been hung in a tree from a rope in the yard, and watching them play suddenly made me nostalgic. I'd spent many an hour as a kid swinging in an old tire, just like those kids were doing. I'm sure Woody had done the same, since he was from the same kind of small town I came from, and that meant we shared more in common that just swinging in an old tire. Maybe that's why so much about him pissed me off sometimes. Realizing there's things about yourself that you don't like, particularly when you come to that conclusion from judging someone else, isn't easy to take.

The sound of children laughing was a far cry from the sounds inside the Pickens house. Actually, there was hardly any sound at all, just the noises made by people moving around and talking in low tones. Disturbed by people moving around, Woody got up from the sofa and moved to his old bedroom. I followed and found Dewey standing in a corner. Woody sprawled on the bed, face down, and Wanda sat on the bed rubbing his back. The room smelled of mothballs, and it still looked more like a kid's room than a guest room. The walls were covered with pictures from Woody's childhood and teenage years, but one picture stuck out like a sore thumb. I tapped Dewey on the shoulder and pointed it out. He smiled as he looked at a blown up snapshot of a sixteen year old Woody Pickens proudly standing beside his green 1951 Studebaker. Mama Pickens must've snapped the picture when Woody had been working on his car because he looked sure enough grungy . The car looked worse, though, but everybody's proud of their first car. Maybe that's what made Dewey smile. He stared at the picture for a minute and then went back to his corner. I went outside and listened to the children laugh.

CHAPTER 34
Diagnostic Doodling

Whenever Dewey turned up missing, I usually knew just where to find him - the library. Dewey, of course, couldn't read in the library during working hours for fear of being noticed. Folks usually get spooked when they see books moving around or pages being turned without any visible means of movement, and a library can be a spooky place to begin with. Since the library was closed, I knew for sure I'd find Dewey there.

"What are you reading now?" I asked when I found him beside a window in the political science section.

"Drucker," Dewey mumbled, without looking up.

"What?"

"Peter Drucker. He's a management theorist, supposedly one of the best," Dewey said.

"What's all this other stuff?" I asked, pointing at several books and journals scattered on the desk in front of him.

"More management material," Dewey said, still half mumbling.

"So what have you learned?" I asked.

"Not much, and I'm not likely to with you standing there asking questions. Go watch Woody. I'll tell you everything as soon as I find out what is going on," Dewey said, finally looking at me.

"I don't mind watching Woody, but reading that stuff seems like a waste of time to me."

"Perhaps not. I have a feeling the new president's troubles aren't over, and I'm trying to find out whether or not she knows what she's doing," Dewey said.

"A book's going to tell you that?"

"These books may tell me what I want to know about management. That, in turn, may tell me something about Dr. Stegnor."

"Stegnor's not our problem."

"No, but she could be. On the other hand, she may turn out to be a good ally. Now go away," he said, returning to his reading.

I don't know how long Dewey stayed at the library, but he hadn't returned by the time Woody got up from his nap and started drinking. He went to Frank's, and sat in a dark corner, at a dark table, in a dark mood. Frank, the owner and only other person in the place, brought him a drink every fifteen minutes. Then he went back to his stool and television behind the bar.

Woody's dark mood hadn't lifted since his return from his father's funeral in Missouri almost a month before. Other than occasional trips to Frank's, he didn't go out much - just sat around the house and nearly drank himself into a stupor every night. With Faith out of his life now, Woody had nowhere in particular to go. Wanda tried for days to get him to open up and talk about his grief, but Woody had gone stone cold. He didn't cry or complain, but he refused to talk unless someone forced him. Woody was a hard man to force into anything. Wanda's attempts to open him up turned into bitching sessions for a while, but she finally gave up and quit trying. So Woody sat at home and brooded, while Wanda wandered back to Freddy. He was willing to give her plenty of sympathy, but that, of course, wasn't all he wanted to give her.

Woody ended up back at home by eight o'clock, and by then Dewey was at the trailer. Woody went to sleep in front of the television, leaving the kids to take care of themselves. They didn't have any choice because neither of them could get Woody awake. Wanda called twice to make sure they were all right, but she didn't make it home until nearly midnight. Woody was still sleeping on the couch, and that's where she left him. Maybe it was for the best because Wanda had that fresh fucked look. She looked so rumpled, mussed, and wooled around that she almost looked like Freddy had just crawled off of her. I don't guess it would've mattered, even if Woody had been awake to see her, because he was too screwed up to see straight, much less notice anything.

"What'd you find out about management?" I asked as I walked into the trailer.

"I'm not sure. I've studied enough, and perhaps what I should do is sit down and do some diagnostic doodling," Dewey said, scratching his head.

"Do what?"

"Diagnostic doodling - you know, thoughtful scribbling. Doing that sometimes helps me put facts and figures in the proper perspective."

"I thought doodling meant to draw cute things on a scratchpad or something."

"No, it means to scribble," Dewey said, firmly.

I looked around until I spotted a dictionary. After walking over and bringing it back to the table where Dewey was sitting, I dropped it in front of him. "Look it up."

"You're a glutton for punishment," Dewey mumbled, flicking pages rapidly. Finally, he zeroed in and started reading. "Doodle, the verb, means to make a doodle or to dawdle or trifle. Doodle, the noun, means - an aimless scribble, design, or sketch. So, you see, you were wrong again."

"No, I wasn't. Webster didn't say a thing about diagnosis, and besides, it said aimless scribbling. What you're doing isn't aimless, so it's not doodling."

"I added the word diagnostic to make sure that particular emphasis was understood, but you obviously missed it. Diagnostic doodling is a euphemism, better than saying something like scientific informationalization."

"You win, Dewey. Diagnostic doodling it is. Besides, I must be missing the point. How does doodling help you sort things out?"

"Seeing it sketched out helps me think. So, I start with Perkins, the most recent former president. He was undoubtedly an MBO man, and the new president seems to lean in the same direction," Dewey said.

"A what?"

"A management by objectives man. Want to hear how it works?" Dewey asked, reaching behind him to pick up his notebook.

"No," I said, sitting down on the bed beside him. Then I yawned to make sure he knew I was tired and sleepy. It didn't work.

"The least you could do is listen. I've done some reading, have taken all these notes and . . ."

"OK, OK! Lay it on me, but keep it simple."

"I'll try, but this is all hard to understand. The basic principle is easy, but it takes some explaining. I'll start by saying that MBO is a way of implementing organizational goals. A lot of organizations don't function very well because organizational objectives are unclear, unrealistic, improperly communicated, and therefore are shunned by subordinates. MBO tries to cure these problems by, first of all, getting managers and subordinates to agree on objectives that are reachable. They develop a plan that not only allows but encourages workers to try to reach these goals, and they will agree on some criteria to be used to measure and evaluate progress toward reaching them."

"That sounds easy enough."

"Yes, but it's easier said than done. To make it work properly, managers need to know how to delegate authority downward while at the same time holding people under them accountable if they don't do what they should. Subordinates, in other words, need to reach their agreed upon level of performance."

"That's still easy," I said.

"Yes, but some organizations jump into it without really knowing what they're doing. One of the first things they need to realize is that MBO takes time before it becomes effective - about three to five years. Also, it takes a lot of effort to make it work right. Periodic reviews are essential, and both managers and workers who get their jobs done have to be rewarded. To reach objectives, goals should be well defined and priorities must be set up. Once goals are set, an evaluation process should measure results to know if goals are being reached," Dewey said.

"I'm still with you, and it still sounds simple enough to me."

"Here's another catch. Management must be willing to allow what Peter Drucker calls, "informed dissent." They even need to encourage it, he says, because disagreement is a good way to reach goals that are realistic and obtainable in a reasonable time span."

"So what's the hitch?"

"Most managers have a hard time doing that. They just set goals and then expect people under them to see to it that they're met. What I'm saying is that MBO takes a different management style than is found in most organizations. Some organizations have failed at MBO practices because it needs to be integrated with budgeting. Since budgeting is done annually, MBO sometimes has trouble breaking into the budgeting routine."

"It's going to have another problem here," I said.

"What's that?"

"It's new, and folks around here won't like that. They're used to Parker's way of doing things, and I can guarantee you that he didn't know beans about MBO. All he knew was the old kiss-ass system."

"That's typical of the leader/follower organization, where leaders run things by arousing in followers emotional responses such as love, hate, and fear. Charismatic rule replaces common sense. Hitler's Germany is an example. Other leaders have run organizations through legal or traditional authority, like in constitutional governments or monarchies. Houston Parker understood this organizational concept best, although he probably couldn't have named or explained it."

"Where'd you learn that?"

"Max Weber," Dewey said.

"Sounds like the army to me," I said.

"It is like the army, and perhaps that explains why former army officers have made poor presidents. They came to power in a system like this because they led an army to victory, but they are seldom able to duplicate their first successful feat when they try to deal with the next problem because they get overconfident."

"Who said that?"

"Arnold Toynbee, the historian."

"That might be true, but the leader/follower system worked pretty well in the army."

"It probably does work well in the military, but it's not the same in other organizations. Universities are staffed with people who've earned doctorates, and they're not kids. The army recruits young men, eighteen and nineteen years old, because they are pliable. Older men wouldn't bend over when the sergeant you referred to barked a vague order."

"Who said that?"

"Dewey Davisson," Dewey said.

"What's all that got to do with Ellen Stegnor's administration?"

"Dr. Stegnor knows a lot about management, but most of what she knows probably relates to pyramidal organizations, which also has some drawbacks. According to Weber, this hierarchial system of having a leader at the top and subordinates scattered at different levels down the pyramid. This creates a division of labor, a ladder of authority, a span of control, and staff and line divisions. The division of labor divides people into specialized tasks, and that tends make them more concerned with their own specialty than with the organization's goals. Communication between these specialties is often difficult, and that hurts coordination of effort and makes it hard for an institution to find presidents and vice-presidents from within their own ranks. People who've come up through the ranks find it hard to turn loose of their specialty and therefore can't see the entire picture. Cooperation suffers because specialists may not try to get along with people from other disciplines."

"I can see how that's a problem on a college campus. Some of the folks around here are so specialized they're damn near goofy. Remember the fracas at the faculty development meeting? That's a good example of how jealous and narrow-minded some of these professors can get," I said.

"I think that probably happens in all organizations, but that could be better handled if the span of control was improved. Sometimes organizations have too many people reporting to the managers or supervisor, and what makes that particularly bad is when those reporting have to work together. Most departments around here are small, but the people work so closely together that it could cause a big problem."

"I can see another problem coming up. Perkins added administrators like crazy, and that went over like a three inch dick at an orgy. The faculty's still mad about it, and Stegnor hasn't done much to trim administration. Think she needs all those positions?" I asked.

"Perhaps, but that's another problem with organizations. Managers rely heavily upon staff members, so they have a tendency to create too many positions."

"I understand all of that, but I still don't exactly see how it fits in here. This is just WKSU, a country college. You're talking about big organizations."

"Dr. Stegnor may have in mind a master plan of some kind, and that means she has some dreams for the University. She will try to pass those dreams, translated into objectives, down through his staff and line positions to the students. That will cause problems because she must rely on people who were already here. They aren't going to see her dreams as clearly as she does, or they may totally disagree with them. Some of her subordinates have spent years building little power bases within the university, and they will fight to keep them. That will cause a power struggle."

"What she ought to do is fire the sonsabitches," I said.

"I can't see her getting rid of troublesome people, but she may move them around to where they're less of a bother. Doing that may be the only way to get her programs implemented. She will also need to be patient with those who are trying to work with her because they will be clumsy with the new system at first."

"This old pyramid system has got too many bugaboos in it. Why don't they just scrap it and use something else?"

"They could, but the other types of organization available don't lend much to change around here. The pyramidal system is based upon the notion that people are interchangeable parts, and it's hard to dislodge people of the idea. She'll probably have to work with something people understand."

"Well, in the case of western Kansas, she might have to go back a hundred years to find one. This country is way too traditional for much change. Stegnor seems bent on cleaning this place up and making it into a decent college, and regardless of how she goes about it, she'll likely run into a stone wall. Folks around her may not want a good University." I said.

"Oh, I think they do."

"I don't. I think what they really want is students who spend money, and sports to watch, and jobs that pay good money for very little effort in return, and . . ."

"I see your point. What it all comes down to is whether or not they're willing to pay the price for a well managed school," Dewey said.

"If they're interested in quality and efficiency, they're only willing to take as much as they can get without paying much for it. That's why so many of them are fighting change."

"Yes, it's a matter of self interest."

"It's more than that, Dewey; it's a matter of survival, or at least that's the way some of them see it. Stegnor doesn't understand these people like I do. These folk come from tough pioneer stock - rugged individualists who settled these plains. They endured some tough times in sticking it out here, and they've done that by sticking to some rules and traditions. Anything that flies in the face of their way of doing things is going to bring out the stubbornness in them," I said.

"But their survival also depends on change. Sticking to tradition is fine, to a point. Inflexibility is a killer, and these people could die of their own reluctance to meet progress."

"They change, some, but it comes slow in this part of the world. Stegnor is moving too fast, and they can't handle that. She needs to slow down, and I'm not sure even doing that will please them. Change is change, and they might fight it no matter how fast it comes. She's an outsider to these people, and that's part of the problem. When it all gets down to the nitty gritty, they'll fight any change that threatens them, and there's lots of folks in a position to feel threatened. Some of those folks will move away and find greener pastures, but some will stay and fight because they don't have anywhere to go. They don't have the talent or qualifications to find other jobs," I said.

"That's sad," Dewey said.

"Yeah, but that's the way it goes. Efficiency and good management takes some sacrifices, and the people who make them should be the slackers. Some of these faculty members should never have been hired, and some of these students don't belong in college. As academic standards go up, faculty requirements rise and enrollment goes down some, and a trend like that will not be well received around here."

"It's still sad."

"You're just a bleeding heart when it comes to things like this. If you need to feel sorry for somebody, feel sorry for all the folks who suffered under the old system. It was sure unfair to people like Woody," I said.

"I do feel sorry for Woody," he said.

"Good, then we can quit talking about management. I already know too much about bureaucracy, and what I know, I don't like much. I always thought it would be different in the hereafter, but it's the same old bullshit. Do you think there's anywhere in the universe that doesn't have an organizational structure?" I asked.

"I don't know," Dewey said.

"Well, if you figure that part out, I want to know about it. You find us a place that doesn't have bosses or supervisors, and we'll haul ass. At least while I was alive, I had a few options, but now I was just a custodian assigned to a drunk college professor in western Kansas. I can at least sympathize with the plight of some of the anti-Stegnor folks because I don't have anywhere to go either. Maybe that's why I argue with Roosevelt so much. I sure resent being read the rules, but they aren't about to change the system."

"I've got an idea," Dewey suddenly said.

"Uh oh," I said.

"Why don't we both do some doodling. I'll sit here a do mine, and you can go over there and do yours," Dewey said, pointing toward a nearby table.

"But, I don't know how to doodle," I said.

"Everyone can doodle."

"I'm not a diagnostician, either."

"Perhaps not, but you've been on the job a long time, and that means you've made certain observations that I have more than likely missed. We'll write down our observations about how Woody's environment is affecting him, and perhaps we'll come up with something. Doodle down everything that comes to mind," he said gleefully.

I gave in again, mostly just to humor Dewey. Woody was asleep, or passed out, on the couch at home, so I might as well keep him happy. Funny thing, though. I enjoyed doing it, once started, and it took me nearly two hours to get my doodling done. Dewey finished first, but he sat patiently waiting on me to join him.

"Which one shall we go over first?" Dewey asked as I sat down beside him.

"Let's do yours. Mine's sort of messy," I said.

Dewey pushed his doodling, done on a large legal sheet of white paper, in front of me. It looked like this:

⊛ Woody has a job that makes him feel ineffectual and frustrated and alienated, which tends to encourage him to drink.

⊛ Woody is involved in an unhealthy relationship with his wife, and this encourages him to drink.

⊛ Woody has low self-esteem, and this encourages him to drink.

⊛ Because of his extra-marital relationships and other acts of irresponsibility, Woody feels guilty and this encourages him to drink.

♡ Woody doesn't know much about how to give or receive love, and this encourages him to drink

♱ Woody doesn't have much of a spiritual life, and therefore he drinks.

✍ Woody is highly intelligent, but his intelligence leads him to believe he can handle his problems without help.

☎ Woody is withdrawn and does not communicate his feelings well, and this encourages him to drink.

⊛ Woody is sensitive and refuses to accept it, and this tends to encourage him to drink.

❐ Woody is an individualist, and is seen as being different, and this encourages him to drink.

I stared at it a while, then smoothed out my rumpled sheet of paper and placed it beside his. Mine looked like this:

月 Woody gets drunk 'cause he's too damn smart for his own good.

☺ Woody's gets drunk 'cause his wife is a bitch!.

♂ Woody gets drunk 'cause he thinks he's a failure.

ਰੇ Woody gets drunk 'cause he works in a job that looks like a pyramid

● Woody gets drunk 'cause he's a goofy bastard!

✡ Woody gets drunk 'cause he's a chickenshit.

√ Woody gets drunk 'cause he's pissed off.

✔ Woody gets drunk 'cause he's a green Studebaker.

Dewey frowned and squinted as he carefully read over my page of doodles. Then he looked at me, smiled feebly, and said, "They're a lot alike. Yours is crude and rather limited, of course, but we've both diagnosed our mark in practically the same light."

"Surprised?"

"Yes, and I'm not exactly sure what this means, but I think it must mean we're on the right track," Dewey said.

"Yeah, that's kind of what I was thinking, and maybe that's what it's all about, being on the right track. That talk we had back in Missouri about how parents set examples for their children might work here. People aren't like cows or sheep, but there's another cowboy practice that shows how that works. Cowboy call a steer that leads other steers to slaughter a 'Judas steer,' and a 'bell-mare' was a mare used to keep horses or mules from wandering off somewhere. Sometimes even with cattle or horses or sheep, critters that are usually driven from place to place, it's sometimes easier to lead them. Herding people is almost impossible, but a smart leader might get them to follow. Maybe Stegnor needs to be a bell-mare."

Dewey nodded, and we spent the next few seconds staring at each other, both of us still a bit surprised but pleased at our efforts. After a year of discussion and haggling, we seemed to be coming to a junction of ideas about the problem at hand. Maybe we'd done it in separate ways, but we'd done it just the same. Nothing needed saying after that, but I made one final comment. "We're sure some pair to draw to, huh Dewey?"

CHAPTER 35
The Dewey Delicate System

The long drought finally broke in late October with a heavy rain that lasted for three days. It rained like hell the first day, maybe two inches worth, then settled into a slow drizzle the second day. The temperature started dropping on the third day, turning rain to sleet and wet asphalt streets and roads to sheets of black ice. Traveling on snow slick roads can be bad enough, but driving on black ice is almost impossible. Of all things I didn't need at the time, black ice was one of them.

Woody's mood remained the same, but his physical condition had gone downhill. He'd lost down to barely 160, nearly twenty pounds under what he usually weighed. I'd noticed some gray hair along his temples for the first time, and he was starting to look as gotch-eyed as a Bloodhound on downers. He looked gaunt, but his stomach extruded slightly, and sometimes I'd catch him rubbing at it. At first I thought maybe his incision from the appendix operation bothered him, but he'd started gagging and throwing up some. Woody's liver might be giving out, I decided. After his surgery and the witch-hunt attack and his father's death, he'd slowed down his drinking some, but for the past couple of weeks he'd been hard at it again. He'd almost given up beer in favor of the hard stuff, and his boozing started much earlier in the day now. On the afternoons he didn't have a class, he didn't bother going back to the campus, and instead of spending hours drinking at Frank's or Dusty's, he drove around in the country with a bottle between his knees.

I'll have to admit that watching over him had been a lot easier since he'd gone gloomy, mostly because he wasn't out getting into mischief. Faith Appleton's move to Denver had cut off his major source of mischief, but C.W. Laney hadn't gone anywhere. Woody had stopped hanging out in the local bars since his blues set in, and that made it tougher for C.W. to find him. But she finally got horny and bold enough to call him at school, and even though Woody wasn't feeling very sociable, she managed to talk him into getting it on with her at some fleabag motel in Cottonwood one night.

That one dalliance had been about the extent of his fooling around since back in September when he'd humped the college gal. That girl, by the way, had stayed clear of Woody. What happened in the room that night, if indeed she remembered exactly what happened, couldn't have been much fun for her. Woody apparently remembered very little of it, and the girl's reluctance to come around him tickled me. I didn't care what kept them apart, just as long as they stayed away from each other.

Wanda must've given up on working out her insecurities by screwing her husband. They'd not only stopped fighting; they'd stopped fucking. With their F and F relationship on hold, and perhaps over with for good, they merely tolerated each other's presence. Wanda's fling with Freddy was in high gear, and Woody didn't seem to care about anything except his bottle. The marriage had hit bottom, and I was wondering what it would take to cause the final break. Nothing much would've surprised me at that point, and I'd about convinced myself that anything capable of ending it would be nothing less than a mercy killing.

Dewey had predicted long before that an act of infidelity wouldn't kill Woody's marriage, but that had been mostly textbook talk. Infidelity might not be the **real** reason marriages die, but it can sure be a killing blow when a marriage is already in serious trouble. I always figured Woody to be the one who'd get caught first, but sometimes people the closest to a situation get fooled, and I was too close. In a small town like Forest City it's not easy to carry on an affair and not draw some attention, but the conditions were such that Wanda must've stopped caring what kind of attention she drew. Maybe that's why she got caught with her pants down.

I never would've thought it would've happened that way, but Woody stumbled in on her and Freddy. I figured he was too screwed up to suspect them, and maybe he didn't, but he still caught them. There they were, with Wanda sitting on the edge of Freddy's big oak desk, leaning back on her elbows with her legs in the air like plow handles and with her panties dangling from one ankle, and with Freddy giving it to her like a runaway jack hammer. They must've forgotten to lock the door, and Woody walked right in with me a few steps behind.

I'd seen Wanda and Freddy in this position before, but Woody hadn't, and it took him by surprise. Stunned is a better word for what it did to him. He stepped back a few steps looking about as discombobulated as a nun in a nudist colony, but he never said a word. Knowing what was running through his head was anybody's guess, but Wanda's reaction was easy to read. She looked like she'd just been harpooned. Freddie froze, but he didn't stay between Wanda's legs very long, and that's because she put a foot in the middle of his chest and kicked him half way across the room. He hit the wall and then slid down it until his ass hit the floor. Wanda quickly slipped her panties back on, stood up and smoothed out her dress. She looked at Woody, then puckered up and started bawling. Woody's only response was to smirk at her, shake his head, and walk out of the room.

"Woody's in a real shitstorm now," I said as I burst into the trailer. Dewey dropped his book and stood up.

"What . . . storm?"

"He just caught Wanda humping Freddy down at his office. Woody's inside changing clothes now, so we'd better get rolling. I've got a feeling he's about to go on a sure enough bender."

"Oh, my goodness! He actually caught them in the act?"

"Like a couple of hung up dogs."

"That's too bad," Dewey said, sighing.

"Maybe so, but this might be that crisis you talked about. One thing's for sure. Something's going to happen because of it, and we'd better be ready. You going?" I asked.

Dewey nodded, grabbed up his jacket, and away we went. Woody was already pulling out of the drive by the time we came out of the trailer, so we jumped into the Chevy and fell in behind him. He stopped at a local liquor store long enough to buy a couple of bottles, then walked across the street to a phone booth. I followed and listened. He called Faith Appleton and asked if he could come to Denver, but she apparently said no. I couldn't hear what she said but judging from Woody response, she must've told him that it would be better if they didn't see each other again. Woody didn't tell her about Wanda or any of that stuff, and he didn't try to push her. He mumbled something I couldn't quite understand, something about wishing her well, and then hung up. After standing in the phone booth for a couple of minutes staring blankly through the glass, he ambled back to his car and drove off.

We followed him out of town, then down a county road for about five miles to an old bridge that crossed the river. He pulled off the road just beyond the bridge, opened a bottle, and took a sip. We pulled in behind him, and I got out to see what was going on. Woody was just sitting there, staring straight ahead through dull eyes. The sun had come out but was setting, and about all that could be seen was glare off the icy road ahead. Every minute or so, he lifted the bottle to his lips, but he hardly blinked as he drank.

"What's he doing?" Dewey asked when I got back to the Chevy.

"Staring. Drinking. The poor bastard looks like his asshole fell out, and he don't know where to start looking for it. Catching Wanda that way must've really got to him," I said.

"Don't you think he's known for a long time that it was coming to this? He might not have expected her to be unfaithful, but he's been expecting it to end."

"Yeah, but expecting it and going through it are two different things. He probably thought he could handle it, but now that he's up against it, he's hurting. He's about to learn something else."

"About what?"

"He's going to really miss Wanda," I said.

"Aren't you taking something for granted? He might not leave her, or she might not leave him."

"No, Dewey, they'll split. They might get back together, but they'll split for a while. Who knows, they may even split for good."

"They might, but do you think he'll really miss her?"

"Oh, yeah, he'll miss her. He'll miss almost everything about her - even her bitching. What he's going to miss the most, though, is her pussy. It's been his, or mostly his, for a long time, and he's going to get lonesome for it."

"That's right, Doug. Boil it all down to something base and disgusting. Is everything a matter of sex with you, and even so, couldn't you just say it that way?" Dewey asked, frowning.

"I could've, but that's not what I meant. If I say he's going to miss her pussy, that's what I mean. It's sort of like you're favorite pair of old boots. New boots look better, maybe, but they don't feel as comfortable as your old ones." I said.

"Oh, please, spare me," Dewey groaned, then quickly added, "and besides, you're wrong anyway. It doesn't seem to me that he's been missing anything about Wanda lately. They've hardly had sex in months."

"Yeah, but that was before what he knows now. Maybe it's something in the male ego, but men start missing what they've been getting when somebody else starts getting it. Like boots, when you get them shaped to fit, you don't want anybody else wearing them."

"That's true, I suppose," Dewey said.

"Not only is he going to miss it, he's going to feel real guilty about not taking care of it while he had a chance. Put the two together, missing it and feeling guilty over it, and a man will go back and get it again, if he gets the chance."

"Really?"

"Yeah, it's a fact. When my old lady left me, I was off in San Antonio shacked up with a cute Mexican gal. At the time I thought she was the best lay I'd ever had or ever would have. When I got home, I found this Dear John letter and an empty house. It took me a month to find my wife, and when I did, she'd moved in with another guy. I cornered her and tried to talk to her, but she wouldn't listen. I tried to hold her, but she pushed me away. That even made me want her more, but she wouldn't let me touch her. Finally, I went to the apartment where she lived, threw her down on the floor, and screwed hell out of her."

"You raped her?" Dewey asked, his eyes round with surprise.

"Naw, I didn't have to rape her because she didn't put up a fuss at all. I gave her the best screwing she'd ever had from me, and she acted like she really enjoyed it. It didn't change a thing. Once we finished, she got up, put on her clothes, and asked me to leave. I was too confused by then to argue with her, so I just got dressed and stomped out. That was the last time I saw her."

"How strange."

"Dewey, this might come as a real surprise to you, but women are strange about a lot of things. Losing my wife didn't teach me a thing about women, but I learned something about myself, and that's that a man by nature is possessive about his pussy. I didn't want her until somebody else had her, and I needed to go back and prove to myself that I could still get between her legs. What I learned, though, was that getting a piece of ass was all I could get. Woody might go through the same thing."

"You think the marriage is really dead then, huh?"

"Dead as the two of us. They might end up back together for a while, but there's too much damage. The two of them staying together makes about as much sense as an Eskimo scuba diver. They'd be better off if they never saw each other again."

The sun started going down before long, and since it was getting too dark for us to watch Woody from the Chevy, Dewey went to sit in the car with him. Letting him do that turned out to be a big bobble on my part, but it was an even bigger bobble on Dewey's part. Trying to help a drunk drive a car was something Dewey had never tried before, but he sure as hell got his chance. We were just sitting there when all of a sudden Woody cranked up and drove off.

"Oh shit!" I said, taking in after them. I could see Dewey peering through the back glass of Woody's car and looking like a diplomat who'd just been kidnapped by terrorists.

Darkness, I should point out, is different when you work in another dimension. A custodian sees night in terms of light gray, and never pitch blackness. I reckon it's that way so we can do our jobs, and once you get used to it, it doesn't bother you at all. Dewey's driving, though, was something hardly anybody could get used to. He wasn't much of a driver, but he could handle a car well enough to get around. Maybe he would've been better if he got more practice, but I hardly ever let him drive. Since he knew his limitations as a driver, he didn't complain. Woody drove pretty well sober, but he was the pits to ride with when drunk. Riding in a car with Dewey driving would've been better, even on black ice. Nobody drives well on black ice, and Woody hadn't gone a mile before I knew he'd never make it to wherever he was heading. Every few hundred yards the car would fishtail and head for the ditch, but he somehow managed to keep it on the road.

Dewey was working in his I/I mode, which meant he couldn't do a thing to help Woody. What worried me was whether or not Dewey could jump into the I/T mode without getting hurt. Once in the I/T mode, a custodian can manipulate objects, but that's just half of it. Object can also manipulate us, and if Woody's car happened to crash, Dewey was at risk, not to mention what might happen to Woody. It would've been silly for me to worry about Dewey getting killed, but he could get bunged up, and I didn't need a crippled partner on my hands. I didn't need a dead mark either.

Woody made it to the main highway and headed for Cottonwood. Maybe he knew where he was going, but I sure didn't like the idea of him heading in that direction. Dewey must've changed to the I/T mode because he moved close to Woody and hovered over him. For the first ten miles or so Woody drove fairly slow, no more than thirty miles per hour, and that made it easier for Dewey. He had to help with the steering a time or two, but we were on the open highway with no stop signs and very few turns. Drunks, though, are unpredictable when it comes to driving, and Dewey found that out the hard way. Woody might've been getting sleepy, but for whatever reason, he rolled down the window. The car quickly filled with cold air, and Dewey started shivering. He was still in the back seat, and to get away from the flood of cold air, he started crawling over to the front seat.

Dewey's timing couldn't have been worse because he started crawling to the front seat about the time Woody drove up on a cattle truck pulled over to the side the highway. The big truck was backed up to a loading ramp just off the roadway where several cowboys were herding cows into the trailer. Two horses were tied to a fence nearby, and as Woody's car approached the loading scene, they suddenly bolted and broke free of their ties. A horse suddenly ran right in front of Woody's car at about the same time Dewey started crawling to the front seat. When he saw the horse, Woody went for the brakes, but booze and black ice saw to it that he didn't get stopped in time. Brakes on black ice are about as worthless as handles on a hippo, so the car didn't slow down much. It wouldn't have slowed down at all if it hadn't been for a short section of road that was covered with salt. The trucker had probably thrown it out so he could get his rig rolling again, and that might have saved a really bad accident. What happened anyway turned out to be bad enough.

The unfrozen patch of road gave the tires enough traction to slow Woody's car and dip the nose down, but when it hit ice again, it started cutting circles. I didn't have a very good view of what happened, but it went something like this. Woody hit the brakes, Dewey hit the floorboard under the dash, the car hit the horse, the horse hit the windshield, the car hit the ditch and slid into a telephone pole, and the telephone pole hit the cattle truck. My Chevy won't slide on ice, so I pulled over to the side of the road and ran up to Woody's car. The horse, jammed ass end first through the windshield, was still kicking some, but it was a goner. Woody and Dewey were wedged in under the dying horse, and even though I couldn't see them at first, I could hear Dewey. His words were muffled, so I couldn't understand what he said, but I could sure hear him.

I thought maybe the two cowboys would try to help Woody, but cows scattered everywhere, and they were frantically trying to herd them back through the gate that had been left open. When I saw that they weren't going to help, I started trying to free Dewey. I tried the doors on both sides, but they were jammed tight. I managed to reach inside and grab the keys so I could unlock the trunk and grab a tire iron. Then I used it to pry open the door on Woody's side. There he was, smashed down in the seat under the horse's ass, blinking like crazy and spitting out horse hairs. I couldn't help it and started laughing. I was still laughing when I went around and pried open the door on Dewey's side. When I saw him, I really laughed.

Dewey was on his back with his legs pointed toward the top of the car. They pointed that way, but they sure as hell weren't sticking up because the horse had them crumpled up under his chin. Dewey's head was jammed under the heater vents, and he was still letting out muffled screams. He was flailing his left arm around like a Chinese orchestra conductor, so I grabbed it and started pulling. He wouldn't budge, though, so I went back around to Woody's side. By then, he had squirmed out from under the horse's ass and was nearly free. He looked all right, so I went back to Dewey. He hadn't gone anywhere, but he'd picked up the volume on his shouting.

"GET ME OUT OF HERE!" he screamed.

"I can't, Dewey. There's a horse on top of you," I said.

"Oh, my goodness! I'm allergic to horses," he said, puffing heavily.

"You're in big trouble then, Dewey, because there's a dead horse right on top of you."

"Move it."

"I can't move it, Dewey. It's too big."

"Then move me." Move puffing.

"Move yourself. All you have to do is switch back to the I/I mode," I said.

"I can't, you ninny. Can't you see that I'm too upset to concentrate?" he shouted.

"Well, you're going to have to because I can't move you," I said, tugging on his arm again. He still wouldn't budge.

"Horsehockey!" Dewey puffed.

"Yeah, there's some of that too," I said. I wasn't lying about the horseshit because Woody had it all over him. Woody, by the way, was out of the car now and stumbling around in the road. Actually, he was slipping and sliding more than he was stumbling.

The cowboys only managed to get a few of the cows back through the gap. Most of them ran off down the road, and since neither of them had a saddled horse around to give chase, they couldn't do a thing but watch them go. Then they spotted Woody and started in his direction. I could tell from the pissed off looks on their faces that Woody was in for a bad time, so I ran around the car to help him. Woody was pretty drunk, half in shock, and babbling out of his head, but that didn't stop the cowboys from grabbing him. They pushed him around some, and then one of them wound up and punched him right in the face. Down he went.

I never could stand an uneven fight, particularly when the one being teamed up on is almost defenseless. Seeing Woody go down really chapped my ass, so I hauled off and cold-cocked the guy. The punch, a good one if I do say so myself, sent the cowboy reeling backward into the ditch. He struggled to his feet, shook his head, and headed back toward Woody. I socked him again, sending him right back to the ditch. He didn't get up so fast this time, but he came back anyway. I hated to, but I poked him again. He didn't try to get up after his third trip to the ditch.

The other cowboy, I noticed when I turned around, was as bug-eyed as a bullfrog. He stared at his fallen friend while scratching his head under his hat. His mouth hung open so wide a dove could've flown in without tucking his wings. He sort of regained his senses when he saw Woody struggle to his feet. Finally the guy must've decided he'd missed something in the dark, that Woody must've been the one who'd socked his friend, so he took a swing at him. I wasn't close enough to stop it, and Woody went down again. I might've let that punch slide if it hadn't been for what happened next. The cowboy started kicking at Woody, and I couldn't tolerate that. Maybe I should've let it alone because when I punched the guy, he fell right on top of Woody. I was getting warmed up by then, and my punch took all the fight out of the guy. Woody, though, looked like he'd been in a hatchet fight and everybody had one except him. His nose was bleeding and he had a couple of nice sized gashes on his face. The cowboy who'd landed on him knocked all the air out of him, so I rolled the cowboy off him and bounced Woody on his butt until his breath came back. Then I went back to see about Dewey.

"How's it going?"

"Shut up and get me out of here, you . . . redneck!" Puff, puff, puff.

"Take back the redneck part first," I said.

"You're enjoying this, aren't you?"

"Maybe just a bit."

"GET ME OUT OF HERE!"

"Take back redneck."

"OK, I take it back," Dewey said.

I don't know why I made Dewey take it back because there wasn't much I could do. Dewey couldn't hold his concentration long enough to get out of the I/T mode, so he had to wait until a motorist came by. Within thirty minutes a state trooper and wrecker showed up. They hooked a tow line to the horse and pulled him out of Woody's car, and that finally freed Dewey. By then he was not only puffing, he was sneezing his head off.

The traffic cop arrested Woody, and that really made me mad because I had to spend the night in jail with him. He'd been in jail before, but never in the condition he was in on this particular night. The cops should've taken him straight to the hospital, but instead they just locked him up and left him to roll around on his bunk and groan the night away. Every hour or so he got up, stumbled across the cell to a urine encrusted toilet, and threw up. The cops let him out at noon the next day, once Woody had called for help. C.W. Laney came right over and bailed him out, then checked into a motel.

Calling her was probably a good move on Woody's part because C.W. had money, and she was sure glad to see him. I don't know how anybody could've been glad to see Woody because he looked awful, even after he showered away the horseshit. Ghost white and with eyes sunk back in his head, he could barely move without help. C.W. talked him into seeing a doctor who stitched and bandaged him up. Taking care of him wasn't too hard after that because he went directly to sleep, and even though it was only three in the afternoon, he didn't wake up until the next morning.

Dewey wasn't talking much, but his being mad at me didn't have anything to do with it. He wasn't just kidding about being allergic to horses because he looked almost as bad as Woody. The sneezing finally went away, but his nose stopped up like he was having a bad sinus attack, and his eyes were swollen and beet red. Watching Woody sleep soon got boring, so I went to where Dewey was sitting in the grass just outside the motel restaurant. My opening remark didn't do much to get the conversation off to a good start.

"Damn, Dewey, you're eyes are looking like a couple of buzzard's assholes in a power dive," I said.

"Go suck an egg."

"Just trying to cheer you up."

"I really botched it," Dewey said, sadly shaking his head. I'd expected him to take the blame for what had happened, so I was ready for him.

"You didn't screw up, Dewey. You just got caught in the wrong place at the wrong time. It could've happened to anybody."

"Would it have happened to you?" he asked.

"Maybe, and that's because I would've done the same thing you did. The only difference might've been that I would've done it another way. I'm not as delicate as you are. You're real gentle, and I'm not, and sometimes you need to be heavy-handed with a drunk."

"What should I have done?"

"I wasn't there, so I can't say exactly what you should've done. I probably would've been a lot rougher with him, though."

"How rough?"

"I don't know. Probably would've tried to outmuscle him - if there'd been time. I'd have stayed real close to him, and if the need had come up, I'd have pushed him aside and done the driving. In your case, though, there wasn't hardly time for you to do anything, so quit worrying about it."

"I'm delicate, huh?" Dewey asked, smiling slightly.

"I'm not being critical, just observant, and I'm not saying you can't handle a job like that. You're just gentler than me, that's all."

"Yes, I suppose we do handle Woody differently. Perhaps we could name out styles. Let's see, there's the Salty system versus the Dewey delicate system. How does that sound?"

"Uh, like crap."

"I like it anyway. From now on, you handle all the situations that call for the salty system, and I'll handle the delicate situations. We'll create a division of labor, so to speak."

"How are we going to know when to apply what system?"

"That should be obvious, shouldn't it? When the situation dictates a soft touch, I'll do it. If the situation demands a firm approach, you'll do it."

"You've got a deal," I said, sticking out my hand.

Woody didn't leave Cottonwood for three days, which meant he missed his Monday classes. He called in sick and then spent most of Monday humping C.W. He had a hard time cutting the mustard at first, but C.W., being wise in the ways of getting a man primed for action, finally brought him around. Once started, Woody got with the program, and that really amazed me. The man was still stove up from a wreck, he'd been sick from a drinking spree, and there he was going at it like a college kid. I didn't watch much of it, but every time I checked the room, they were at it. Being married to an old man must've really been tough on C.W. because I've never seen a woman who liked sex like she did.

Dewey's delicate system versus my salty system turned out to be as much a prophecy as it did a division of labor. Dewey couldn't have known at the time that he'd play a big role in Woody's crisis stage, but he did. After the car wreck and the rendezvous in Garden City with C.W., Woody went home, but this time to an empty house. Except for a few old pieces of furniture and his personal belongings, the place was empty when Woody walked in. I think he knew it would be, but it was still too much for him to handle.

Woody had stayed sober for nearly three days, but coming home to an empty house sent him straight for a bottle. At first I couldn't understand why he stayed. An empty house filled with nothing but memories was the last place he needed to be. But he stayed, sitting on the floor of his bare bedroom and drinking whiskey straight from a bottle. Then it came to me why he didn't leave. Woody's loneliness went beyond being alone in an empty house. He had nowhere to go, at least from his muddled mind's point of view. Even Duncan Hightower, his closest friend, was out of reach this time. I knew better - knew that help was only a phone call away, but Woody either couldn't or wouldn't see that.

Dewey and I sat silently in the corner and watched, expecting almost anything, but Woody just sat and drank until he could barely sit up any longer. Finally, he struggled to his feet and stumbled to his dresser. I elbowed Dewey and jumped to my feet as Woody opened the top drawer and stared down into it. I knew the I/T mode was on because the hairs on my arm were standing up, and I could feel the blood racing through my veins. I moved closer when Woody reached into the drawer and picked up the pistol. "Don't do this, you stupid sonofabitch," I said, moving even closer.

Woody fumbled with the gun, but he finally got the clip out to make sure it was loaded. It was. He clumsily jammed the clip back into the handle and jacked a shell into the chamber. I moved closer, about to pounce, when a soft touch on my shoulder distracted me. I turned and found Dewey staring at me. "Don't mess with me now, Dewey. I think it's getting down to the bedrock."

"We have a deal, remember? Let me do this," he said softly. I started to argue, but time wouldn't allow it. Besides, the determined look in Dewey's eyes broke me down, and I moved back.

Woody stepped away from the dresser a few feet, then switched off the safety and lifted the gun to his head. His eyes had taken on a glaze, like he wasn't even there anymore, and his hand was steady for the first time in hours. Then a tight smile formed on his lips as he tilted the gun toward his temple. I looked at Dewey, ready to shout at him to do something, when he moved in on Woody.

Dewey moved like a cat, very fast and smooth as silk. He gently pushed the gun away and then gathered Woody in his arms. I heard Woody suck in breath when he felt Dewey embrace him, and he looked startled for a moment. But Dewey held on, gently rocking Woody back and forth in a motion so slight I could barely tell they were moving. Within minutes, Woody's arm fell to his side, and the gun tumbled to the floor. I stared at it for an instant, and when I looked back at them, tears were starting to trickle down Woody's face. His eyes had changed from glazed to gentle, and he looked more like an injured child than anything else.

"Well, I'll be damned," I said, mostly under my breath.

Woody went to sleep on the floor, curled in a fetal position and with the gun that almost ended his life laying no more than ten feet away. I started to pick it up and hide it, but there was no use in moving it. Dewey lay between him and the gun until Woody had gone to sleep. Then he rolled over and stared at the pistol. He got up and left the room for several minutes, and then returned carrying a small screwdriver.

"What the hell are you doing? I asked.

"Fixing this gun," he said, sitting down beside the pistol. He picked it up, and went to work, and within a few short minutes had broken the gun down into at least a dozen pieces. He gathered up the pieces, walked to the drawer, and gently laid them in a corner.

"Well, if that don't beat all. Where'd you learn to do that? It would've taken me ten minutes to do that, and you just zipped it apart."

"I had a gun like that once. I fired it infrequently, but I took it apart often. I despise guns, and tearing it up made me feel good," he said.

"If you hated guns, then why did you have one?"

"Someone thought I needed it and gave it to me."

"You're full of surprises, you know that, Dewey? I never would've believed a situation like that could be handled like you handled it. I reckon the Dewey delicate systems works sometimes," I said.

"Yes, I suppose it does," he said, smiling proudly.

"You know, partner, something tells me that my time here may be about up. Woody can't go on like this much longer. Before long he'll either be dead or on the way toward getting well, and when that happens, I won't be needed anymore. I'm betting he starts uphill before long, and then you'll have this job to yourself. You won't need me. I never would've thought of doing what you just did."

"Perhaps, but it may be some time before he starts uphill. God only knows when that will happen, so don't plan on leaving yet."

"I don't know. I've got this gut feeling that it's all coming to a head. Something, I don't know what but something, is going to happen and pretty soon," I said, tapping Dewey on the shoulder to make my point.

"Got any predictions about what?"

"Nope. I've just got this feeling, that's all. Everything is happening fast now, and there's nothing we can do to slow it down. Old man Pickens is dead, Wanda's gone, Woody's not in good physical shape, and now he's got a DUI charge hanging over him."

"Yes, we've got more trouble coming, but we can handle it," Dewey said, then eased himself down to the floor.

"You get some sleep. I'm going for a walk," I said.

I didn't want to think about what had just taken place that evening, so I walked and tried to think about Phoebe Foster. I tried, but my mind kept going back to the gun, and I spent the next few hours thinking how stupid suicide really is. Woody couldn't possibly know what I'd learned the hard way - that a bullet wouldn't end his pain. I walked until my legs got tired, then went back to Woody's bedroom and sat in a darkened corner. The moments when Woody put the gun to his head had gone by so quickly and anxiously that I almost forgot something. When Dewey touched me on the shoulder to ask to handle the situation, and when I'd turned to take a quick look at him, a dark shadow had moved rapidly from the room. I would've mentioned it to Dewey, but the shadow had been behind him, and he couldn't have seen it. Caught up in that moment of madness, my mind must've refused to allow me to get distracted by anything other than the task at hand.

I was glad to see the sun come up the next morning, and as the first rays of light started to light up the windows of Woody's bedroom, my mind flashed back to the morning Dewey first came to Kansas. We'd argued about sunrises and sunsets, about which was better, and I lost my temper and shouted obscenities at him. But now I welcomed the morning light that chased away all the shadows, real or imaginary, and I suddenly realized that guarding Woody was making a sunrise person out of me.

CHAPTER 36
The Salty System

A for sale sign went up in front of Woody's house within the next week. He moved into a one bedroom furnished apartment across town, and even though his new place was only about a mile from his old home, it might as well have been a million. He looked and acted like a man abandoned in a foreign land. Wanda had moved to an apartment in the same building where Freddy Lomax lived. She didn't look a bit abandoned, but her actions told a different story. Her romance with Freddy had cooled a bit, but that could've been for several reasons. Maybe her split with Woody had taken too much out of her to enjoy getting it on with Freddy, or maybe having to keep tabs on a couple of kids and earn a living at the same time spoiled it for her. I really don't know much about what was going on with Wanda because Woody kept me too busy to notice what she did. Whenever I saw her, which wasn't often, she looked out of sorts.

Hardly anything had been said between Woody and Wanda since he'd caught her with Freddy, other than a brief confrontation when he finally came home from his Cottonwood adventure. She'd been worried to death about him, and even the rumors flying around town about his wreck on the icy highway and subsequent stay in jail hadn't pissed her off enough to keep from worrying. She had called all over the county looking for him, even to the county jail. They'd confirmed his being in jail earlier but had no idea where he'd gone from there - just that he'd been bailed out by C.W. Laney. After that, Wanda stopped trying to track him down, but when he finally showed up for class during the middle of the week, she went to his office. Their short meeting lasted just long enough for them to decide it was time to split the sheet. Woody sat and stared at the wall like a zombie while Wanda tearfully said she'd had enough. Her words were forced and halting, but she finally got it out and left.

Woody kept staring at the wall until a student came to the door and disturbed his stupor. After answering a few questions, he followed the student into the hall, closed his office door, and trudged off toward his apartment. He walked because his car was still in the shop being fixed - that and because the cops had taken his license and the insurance company his auto coverage. Insurance companies get nervous about covering anyone with a DUI charge on their record. Worse yet, he was still staring a court date in the face, but that wouldn't come until after the first of the year.

I expected Woody to go into an even deeper gloom after all his new problems, but knowing what Woody's thought or felt was hard to figure out. He functioned, but poorly, mostly because he stayed stoned. Sometimes he went straight home from work and drank himself into a stupor, but most of the time he drank until moderately crocked. Nobody came to see him, other than Duncan Highsmith, and Woody hardly ever left the apartment. He got some anti-depressants and tried taking them, but the pills just made him antsy and even more anxious. Breakfast had now become a blender mixed concoction of beer, tomato juice, and several eggs, and he'd started eating Tums like candy. Teaching class kept him going while at school, but once back in the apartment, he hit the bottle again.

Although he'd nearly stopped going to the bars, C.W. didn't lose contact. She'd sneak over to his apartment as often as she could, usually a couple of times a week, and her coming around may have kept Woody from starving. She brought food and forced him to eat, and she kept him from drinking while she was around. That's partly because it's hard to screw and drink at the same time, and C.W. had more on her mind than keeping Woody sober and healthy. Woody refused to talk much and therefore wasn't good company, but that didn't discourage C.W. That started me wondering if she didn't have plans for him other than just having someone around to rub her horns off every now and then.

Thanksgiving holidays came and Woody perked up enough to spend a few days with his mother in Missouri. He flew, which meant I had to go with him by myself. Dewey still wouldn't get on a plane. Woody put up a good front while he was there, or at least it was a good act for Woody. Mamas, though, are hardly ever fooled by their sons. Several times she asked about his welfare, and I could see the concern in her eyes. She knew about his split with Wanda, and although she knew almost nothing of what caused it, she questioned him very little. Mostly, she tried to reassure him with some motherly support. Woody tried to be receptive, but he didn't want to talk about Wanda, and he didn't want to listen. Mama Pickens looked more worried than ever as she kissed her son goodbye when he left for Kansas. The brave smile she gave him on the front porch just before he walked away might've fooled him, but it sure didn't fool me.

Once home, Woody bounced back some. At first I felt relieved, but then I got worried. I'd read somewhere that people didn't kill themselves during the depth of their depression. They usually pulled the plug when they were coming out of it and realized how far down they'd been. I'd been concerned about a suicide attempt ever since Dewey had stopped him that night in the bedroom, and we had stayed with him constantly since then. Since moving, he'd packed the gun away some place, but I still worried about it and started watching him closer than ever. I hadn't seen the pistol, but I knew he'd had it put back together by a friend who knew guns . . . and that worried me.

That night Woody got on a mean drunk, and to make matters worse, Wanda decided to come by to talk to him about their divorce. But they never got around to talking divorce - not after Wanda saw what kind of shape Woody was in. Too drunk to talk reasonably, Woody turned especially mean once they'd started talking. Wanda ended up bawling and pleading with him to get some help with his drinking problem, and that prompted Woody to retaliate by calling her names. He ended up calling her a cunt, and that ended the discussion. That word, I've noticed, will kill a conversation with most women in a heartbeat, but when delivered the way Woody spat it out, it went through her like a lance.

"Woody shouldn't have called her that," Dewey said, watching Wanda run down the sidewalk to her car, still bawling.

"No, he shouldn't have," I agreed. "It doesn't help her any, but Woody doesn't know what the hell he's saying right now."

"Why do people have to hurt each other when they're going through a separation?" Dewey asked.

"I don't really know, Dewey. Maybe they're just driving a few final nails in the coffin."

"Will that be the end of it?"

"I doubt it. They're addicted to the pain, remember? They'll have to go at it some more before they finally get enough."

"That's too bad," Dewey said, shaking his head.

Woody's fight with Wanda must've started him thinking about Faith Appleton again, so he called her. But a man answered the phone, and Woody recognized the voice as belonging to Lane Allen, the young business prof from WKSU. He must've gone up to Denver over the weekend to see Faith, which could only mean that she was involved with him again. Woody's whiskey muddled brain still worked well enough for him to realize now why Faith didn't want to see him again. Lane recognized Woody's voice and told him not to call again, and Woody responded by calling him a jerk before slamming the phone down on the receiver.

Next, he tried to call C.W., but the old man answered. Woody hung up without saying a word and then paced around the apartment, sulking and kicking anything that got in his way. Actually, he was too drunk to pace, so I should say he stumbled. After about fifteen minutes of reeling around the apartment, he started looking for his wallet. That was a waste of time because I hid it. I'd noticed earlier that he was running low on booze, and I didn't want him walking the streets in the shape he was in. The cops might've picked him up, or somebody might've seen him, even if he'd just walked to the local liquor store and back. So I slipped his wallet under the toaster. He really got mad when he couldn't find it, but that didn't bother me because I knew what was coming. He'd call Duncan Highsmith and ask him to come over with a jug of something. True to form, he had just picked up the phone to call Duncan when someone knocked on the door.

"Oh shit!" I said.

"Who would that be?" Dewey asked.

"How the hell would I know? Maybe it's the cops. With all the racket he's been making kicking stuff around, somebody probably called them," I said, then stuck my head through the wall to see who it was.

"Oh, double shit!" I said when I saw who it was.

"Who is it?" Dewey asked.

"It's that girl from the apartment party - the one we yanked out from under Woody," I said.

"What's she doing here? I thought she'd been avoiding Woody." Dewey looked worried.

"She has, and I don't know what she's doing here. You'd think she'd learned a lesson or two."

"Each man reads his own peculiar lesson according to his own peculiar mind and mood. Melville," Dewey said.

"Yeah, but this is a girl, not a man," I said.

"The same rule applies."

"Not when it comes to women. You can't figure them."

Woody was standing in the middle of the living room floor, still staring at the door. The gal knocked again and then rang the doorbell, and this time Woody started wobbling toward the door. I had an urge to kick his feet out from under him, but that wouldn't have helped much. He'd already called out to the gal to come in, and by then she was opening the door. She stepped through the open doorway a few feet, then stared at the floor and started talking. She said several of the people who'd attended the party had told her that some people had been asking about Woody's presence there. Some had asked about the ruckus in the bedroom, even asked point blank if Woody had been involved. They'd said they didn't know anything about it, but her name had come up and now she was worried that someone would make the connection between her and Woody. She was afraid she'd be expelled.

Woody stared at her like he didn't have any idea what she was talking about. It was an honest reaction on his part for two reasons: first, he didn't remember much of what had taken place, and second, he was too drunk to think. His reaction angered the girl, and she said his playing dumb wouldn't help matters, and that if she got in trouble over it, she wouldn't be the only one. She reminded him of what they'd done in the bedroom that night, and that's when Woody started to grin. Maybe he remembered bits and pieces, but he obviously was in no mood to care. Then he invited her to sit and followed her to the couch. He stumbled on his way there, but she didn't seem to notice how drunk he was.

Woody collected himself and watched the girl as she talked about how somebody had pulled an awful trick on them that night by throwing her on the floor. She told about the bed covers billowing around mysteriously. Woody's eyes had been switching back and forth from the girl's eyes to her tits, but when she said that it was too bad about the interruption because she'd really enjoyed what they'd been doing, his eyes stayed on the tits. Then he mumbled something about how as long as all the fuss had already been caused, they might as well finish what they'd started. The girl shook her head at first, but Woody moved closer to her and started rubbing the back of her neck. When his hands went for her boobs, she giggled and twisted away, but Woody kept after them.

"Damn you, you stupid sonofabitch," I said.

"That won't help," Dewey said.

"Kicking him might help. Yeah! I think I'll just kick the crap out of him. That'll slow him down for a while," I said, moving toward him. Woody had just grabbed a big handful of boob when I kicked him, just below the knee. That got his attention, but he must've thought the gal did it. He looked at her and frowned, then grabbed at her crotch. I had just pulled my leg back to give him another boot when Dewey grabbed me and threw me down.

"Don't you dare," he said.

"But Dewey, he's about to really screw up bad again," I said.

"Well, if you're going to stop him, you'll have to find another way."

"OK," I agreed, sitting up. "I'll wait and see what happens."

What happened was exactly what I thought would happen. Woody pawed at the gal, she pawed at him, and before long they went to the floor. They rolled around for a few minutes, clutching at each other and snorting like a couple of hippos. She had a leg lock on Woody that would've made Hulk Hogan jealous, but Woody tore away from her and struggled to his feet. He started shucking his clothes by kicking off his shoes and stripping off his pants. He peeled off his shorts at about the same time the gal slipped out of her panties. Woody still had on his shirt, so I grabbed the back of his collar, right at the nap of the neck, and yanked him. He reeled backward, looking startled. The startled look went away, though, when he looked back at the naked gal lying on the floor across the room. I'll have to admit that I took time to look at her myself because she was worth a second look. My mind got back to business when Woody took off for her. That's when I dropped to my knees and grabbed him around a leg and started pulling him away from the girl. She was squirming and writhing around with her legs spread wide apart, and holding Woody back wasn't easy.

"What are you doing?" Dewey shouted.

"I'm going to keep this goofy bastard from screwing that college gal if I have to break his leg," I said.

"Stop that!"

"Forget it, Dewey. The only way that gal's getting laid tonight is by a one legged drunk."

Dewey kept complaining, but I barely heard him. Woody had stopped straining and was looking down at his leg with a perplexed look on his face. Maybe he thought he was having a cramp or a muscle spasm or something because he whacked his leg a couple of times, then started dragging me. I pulled even harder, but Woody was hell bent on getting to the gal. She was now sitting up watching him with a confused look on her face. I reckon watching a guy come at you like Woody was, dragging a leg behind him and with a demented look on his face, could cause one to look confused. I hate to admit it, but the drunk bastard was starting to get the best of me. I couldn't get a good hold on the slick carpet, and he kept scooting me as he moved closer and closer to the gal. Every now and then he'd whack his leg again, still thinking he was having spasms or cramps, but his aim wasn't too good. Mostly, he was whacking my head, and that pissed me off. That's why I bit him on the calf of the leg. I didn't bite him hard enough to draw blood, but it was a good enough bite to make him cry out and jump.

Woody, unfortunately for me, was in no shape to be struggling and jumping, and he lost his balance and started falling. I didn't want him to hit his head on a table or piece of furniture, so I reached up and grabbed him. But one of his arms swung around, and he whacked me right across the nose with the back of his hand. That's when I lost my grip, which threw him off balance even worse, and he fell face down right on top of me. As he landed, his right knee caught me flush in the nuts, and that's when I forgot all about Woody, the gal on the floor, and my smarting nose.

"Huuummpph!" I went, as my breath left my body. I could almost feel my face turning blue, but it's hard to care about a blue face when your nuts feel like a dump truck is parked on them. I grabbed my crotch and rolled over on my stomach. At that point, the last thing in the world on my mind was Woody Pickens, who was now free to crawl over to the gal and go about his business. Nuts, nuts, nuts – that's all I could think about.

"Are you all right?" I barely heard Dewey ask.

"Umph! Umph!" I went. Anyone who's ever had it happen to them knows that talking is a practical impossibility when you've just been kneed in the balls. That's because you tongue swells up to four times its normal size, and your lips feel like they're the size of ping pong paddles.

"Are you all right?" Dewey asked again. I still couldn't talk, so I gave him a few more umphs. I could feel him trying to turn me over, but I resisted that move. All I wanted was to stay still until the pain eased a bit, and it took a while for that to happen.

"You're nose is bleeding badly. Do you think it's broken?" Dewey asked. I had finally rolled to my side but was still clutching my balls.

"Fubct da nobse," I managed to almost say.

"Beg your pardon?"

"Ma nubst ara flabt," I grunted.

"I still can't understand you."

"Shubt da fubct upt, Dewby," I said. He understood that, I think, probably because he'd heard something like it before.

It was about five more minutes before I could talk plain again, and by then I was up on my elbows. I looked over at Woody and the gal on the floor just in time to see him roll away from her. At first I thought it was too late, that they'd finished, but then I noticed that Woody wasn't breathing heavily. The girl looked puzzled, but Woody looked mad, and that's when I knew something new had happened. Woody had gone impotent - couldn't cut the mustard for a change.

"Well, I'll be go to hell," I said.

"He couldn't do it," Dewey said, sniggering.

"That's what it looks like," I said, snorting blood out my nose.

"You're still bleeding."

"I'll live."

"But you turned blue," Dewey said.

"I was born blue," I said, struggling to my feet. "One thing's for sure. Turning blue won't kill me now."

The girl didn't stay long after Woody couldn't get it up. Women sometimes take it personally when a man can't cut the mustard, thinking maybe he isn't attracted to her or that she did something to cause the dysfunction. I knew the real reason for it but was glad to see the girl leave. Woody got up, stumbled to the couch, and quickly fell asleep.

Exams kept him busy all week, and he got through them without a major hitch. One problem arose when Lane Allen came to his office to tell him that he was resigning his teaching position at WKSU to take a teaching job in Denver. He said he knew all about Woody's affair with Faith, but that it didn't matter to him. They had a good thing going between them, and he didn't want Woody fooling around with her anymore. Woody didn't say a word, just stood behind his desk and glared at the man. Finally, and just before he left, Allen said that if Woody tried to see Faith again, he'd take the matter to a higher authority.

On the last day of exams and after Woody's last final, Dr. Don Early, Vice-President for Academic Affairs, came to Woody's office. Woody pushed aside the exams he'd been grading and invited Dr. Early to sit. Early closed the door before sitting down, then got straight to the point. What he said, in a diplomatic way, was that Woody's off campus activities had him in trouble. The administration was aware of his bouts of drinking, his recent arrest for driving under the influence, his impending divorce and the circumstances involved with it, and even his affairs with other women. He said that while it was not the intent of the administration to get involved in the personal lives of employees, it took an interest when a professor's lifestyle started affecting his work. Woody needed to get his life in order, Early said, and he strongly encouraged him to seek counseling before the matter got completely out of hand.

Woody's first reaction was to try to explain it away by saying he'd been under a lot of pressure lately, but Early didn't back off. He again encouraged Woody to get help and said the administration could no longer ignore his behavior. Woody dropped his head after that and said nothing. When Early bluntly asked if Woody would start looking for help, he nodded. Early then said he had great faith in Woody's ability as a teacher, patted him on the shoulder, and walked out of the room.

"Will he do it?" Dewey asked, looking a hopeful.

"Probably not," I said, shrugging.

"But his job's on the line now."

"Woody may be too far gone to care. Early means well, but someone like Woody isn't likely to respond to encouragement that comes in the form of a threat. That's not going to send him looking for help."

"But the man clearly got his point across. Either Woody straightens up or he gets dismissed, and Woody may be confused, but he's not stupid," Dewey argued.

"Are your ears plugged up, or are you just not listening? Early could've threatened him with anything, could've even told him that unless his dries us and quits screwing around that they're going to whack off his nuts. He could've said they'd form a firing squad and shoot his sorry ass, and it still might not faze Woody. I won't argue the fact that Woody's not so screwed up that he doesn't want to keep his job, but just coming into his office and telling him to get help or get out won't get the job done."

"What should he have said, then?"

"I don't know, Dewey. Maybe if Early had told Woody exactly what to do, and exactly what to expect, it might have a chance of working. But Woody's already confused and frustrated, and now he's got one more thing to worry about, and he still doesn't know what to do about it. He's not about to just up and say, 'Hey, I think I'm a drunk and need to go to treatment?'"

"No, but Woody is surely thinking about it, don't you think?"

"Yeah, he's thinking, but that doesn't mean he's going to do anything. What he needs is a strong push toward doing something, and what Early just told him isn't push enough."

"What will it take?"

"Something drastic, I'm afraid. I just hope when it comes that Woody survives it. He's in a tailspin right now, but you know what they say about falls, don't you, Dewey?"

"No, what?"

"It's not the fall that hurts, but it's that sudden stop at the bottom that's the problem," I said, winking.

We stayed at Woody's office for a while longer, but Dr. Early's visit upset him to the point that he couldn't grade papers. After about thirty minutes, he gathered up a stack of exams and headed for his apartment. Once he'd downed three or four strong drinks, he halfheartedly graded the tests and averaged grades until the numbers stopped making sense to him. Duncan Highsmith stopped by to invite him to have dinner at a downtown cafe, but Woody refused the offer. Duncan had one drink and went on his way. Woody watched TV for a while, then fell asleep on the couch.

Dewey curled up in a corner and nodded off. Nothing was on the tube except dull sit-coms and Christmas specials, so I prowled around the apartment building for a while. Most of the occupants were college students who'd already gone home for the holidays, and since I was too bored and restless to sleep, I went downtown and watched people walking up and down Main Street. Some were doing late evening Christmas shopping, some were coming and going from restaurants, some were delivering and fetching, and some paused long enough to greet friends. I listened to the sounds of a small town, and from somewhere down the street heard people laughing.

Observing normal people go about doing normal things made me think of Woody and about how pathetic he'd become. I caught myself wondering why he couldn't be like these people, knowing the answer all the while and hating it more and more. The people on the street had to deal with problems of their own, just like Woody and everyone else, but their problems had not consumed them. Woody was like most of these normal people in almost every respect - except for one thing. He was an alcoholic, a drunk. The burden of that one problem outweighed all others, and still, he couldn't see it. What set Woody apart from these people, the thing that made him pathetic, was that his problem had blinded him and perhaps robbed him of his best chance of defeating it.

CHAPTER 37
The Shadowlopers

Wanda took the next week off from work to go back to Ohio for Christmas, but she came by to see Woody before she left town. She brought Mark and Maggie so they could have a present opening session with their dad before going to grandma's for Christmas. That was decent of her, I thought, especially since Woody would be spending Christmas alone. He stayed sober for his kid's sake, but he looked like warmed over death. The presents he gave them were meager compared to what they usually got, but if they were badly disappointed, they didn't show it. Wanda had probably already told them that Woody couldn't afford much, and considering his financial situation, Woody came up with some decent gifts.

Woody had never been a financial wizard, but he'd never been reckless with his money. Wanda had a tendency to be scatterbrained about money, but she wasn't a big spender either. Since their break-up, she'd not been overly demanding of him, and he'd given her what he could. Her lawyer, which surprisingly was not Freddy, had earlier in the week sent the divorce papers to Woody. Wanda hadn't asked for much - all the furniture and profits from the sale of the house, which had been about $5,000; full-time custody of the children with visitation rights for Woody; $600 a month in child support, approximately one/fourth of his take home pay; and the newer of the two cars, a ninety-two model Ford Thunderbird. She'd stuck him with a few other expenses, like keeping all existing life and health insurance policies on the children in effect, and payment of all legal and court fees. Woody had signed it and sent it back the next day.

His current financial woes were due to nearly a thousand dollars he'd forked out to have his car fixed. His collision insurance on his ten year old Ford sedan had lapsed a few days before the wreck, and he still owed the garage another two thousand. January didn't look much better because he had a court date to meet. The fine for his DUI would probably run at least five hundred bucks. But he'd managed to save back about three hundred dollars for presents, and the kids didn't squawk about them.

The present opening session lasted for only an hour, and then Wanda and the kids headed out for Ohio. Christmas sometimes has a way of stirring emotions, and I expected their parting to be tense and maybe even tearful. Too many Christmas's past, too many remembrances of times when life seemed richer and fuller, sometimes get in the way of Christmas's present. But their parting went quickly - no lingering in doorways and no misty eyes and with only a few clumsy hugs from the kids. Woody paced the floor for thirty minutes after they left, then dropped down in a chair and fell asleep.

I was sitting in front of Woody's apartment building, waiting for him to wake up and wondering how he'd hold up during the holidays when Roosevelt drove up. He stepped out of the car and headed toward me. Winston Frye was right behind him, and that told me something right off. Roosevelt probably wanted to send me on another special assignment, but I quickly decided that whatever he had in mind was out of the question. Woody needed me, and Winston was more of a nuisance than a replacement. Woody could go over the deep end at any time, and Dewey might need a competent partner.

"I'm not going," I said.

"Are you sure? You might like this assignment," Roosevelt said, smiling like a bandit.

"Don't play games with me. I'm not in the mood for it," I said. That wasn't a lie because I'd been sort of down in the mouth lately. I'd been getting too involved with everything that had been going on with Woody, and that had left me in a bad mood.

"It's no game, and it's not really an assignment."

"Then why's Winston here?"

"I came to make you an offer," Roosevelt said.

"What kind of offer?"

"If you could go anywhere, where would you want to go?" Roosevelt was still smiling, but for the first time I knew he wasn't just teasing me.

"Minnesota," I said flatly.

"OK, Minnesota it is. Where in Minnesota?"

"Where's Phoebe Foster?"

"Deluth."

"That's where I want to go then," I said.

"OK, it's Deluth, Minnesota."

"Are you kidding me?"

"Not a bit, Doug. You need some time off, so I brought Winston along to fill in for you while you're gone. You're free to go at any time. I anticipated your response and warned her that you might be on your way up there before long. She'd like to see you," Roosevelt said, smiling slightly.

"But what about Woody?" I asked, suddenly thinking about what a problem he'd been lately.

"Dewey and Winston can handle it. You just go to Minnesota and enjoy yourself."

"How much can I enjoy myself," I asked, flashing a sneaky grin.

"That's up to you. This is an unsupervised visit."

"Something's up. I know you too well to believe that. What's the deal?" I asked. It was a good question, I thought, because I still couldn't see Roosevelt turning me loose with Phoebe without restrictions.

"Listen, Doug, it's like this. Phoebe is very fond of you, and I think you're equally as fond of her. You've grown a lot in the past year, and I'm ready to give you more freedom from now on. Maybe you're ready for some unsupervised time of your own," he said.

"Well, I'll be damned," I said.

"You'll be late if you don't get started before long. I told Phoebe you'd probably be there late tomorrow. Here's the address. By the way, I've got another surprise for you," he said, handing me a slip of paper.

"It couldn't be better than this one," I said, staring at the address.

"Someone you know is waiting in my car."

"Yeah, who's that?"

"Why don't you go see for yourself. Winston and I will be at your trailer visiting with Dewey," he said, then walked off toward where the trailer was parked under a willow tree.

I walked to the big Lincoln and opened the back door, only to find no one there. I stuck my head in and saw a gray haired man in the front seat, but he didn't turn around. "Who are you?" I asked.

"Hey! Hey! Hey!" the man said, then laughed and turned around.

"Virgil Jacks, you old geezer. I figured I'd seen the last of you," I said, whacking him on the shoulder.

"You're looking lots better'n you did last time I saw you, but just about anything would've beat being Fat Albert Brown, huh?"

"I didn't mind, but it's good to be me again. Say, what are you doing hauling with Roosevelt? What's up?" I asked.

"Aw, hell, they've done give me a new job. Been a custodian for sixty years, and all of a sudden they up and promote me. I ain't ever wanted to be a supervisor, but they've been poking the job at me for about forty years," he said.

"So you finally broke down and took it, huh?"

"Naw, they made me a better offer this time. I'm gonna be a supervisor's supervisor. They give me the regional job, which means I've got all of Kansas, Colorado, Wyoming, Nebraska, Montana, and the Dakotas under me. Hell, boy, I'm the big wagon boss now," he said, grinning from ear to ear.

"You mean Roosevelt's working for you now?"

"Yeah, one of a dozen district supervisors I've got to ride herd on."

"Then that means you're my boss too," I said.

"Sure enough, but don't let that bother you much. I ain't hard to please, as long as a feller does his job, and I hear you're a good hand," he said, looking serious now.

"So, why are you riding with Roosevelt?"

"He's showing me around his territory. They said I could office out of any place I wanted to, so I picked Cheyenne, Wyoming. That ain't too far from here, so I thought I'd drop down for a visit."

"Well, it's good to see you. Come on, and I'll introduce you to my partner," I said, motioning for him to follow.

We went to the trailer and called the others out. The trailer was barely big enough for Roosevelt, much less the five of us. Depending on Winston for support in a crisis was like asking a horse to walk a tightrope. Dewey wouldn't like it when he heard I was heading for Minnesota to do nothing more than visit with Phoebe. With that in mind, I broke it to him gently.

"Bad news, Dewey. Motorcycle gangs have taken over some town up in South Dakota and are terrorizing the locals. They need somebody to go in and help get them straightened out, and Roosevelt wants me to go," I said, giving Dewey my best Kingfish look.

"I've already told him about Minnesota," Roosevelt said, then sighed and shook his head.

Dewey smiled, but it was a sideways smile if I ever saw one. I felt like saying something encouraging, but decided to wait a while for that. Then I remembered the shadows I seen on several occasions. Since he'd been in the field for a long time, I directed my first remark at Virgil. "I've been seeing something strange lately, and maybe you can tell me what it is. On several occasions I've seen a shadow moving around. It moves so fast that I can't get a good look at it. Did you ever see anything like that?"

Virgil looked at me first, and then at Roosevelt. The two men's eyes stayed hooked together for a few seconds. Then Roosevelt asked, "When did you see them?"

"I've been catching glimpses for some time, but I just wrote them off as my imagination or from being tired. Twice, though, I've seen it well enough to know that I really saw something, and both times it happened, Woody was in a shitstorm - once when he passed out and had to be hauled off to the hospital, and just the other day when he put a gun to his head," I said.

"Shadowlopers," Virgil said, still looking at Roosevelt. He nodded in agreement, but that didn't help me a bit.

"What in hell are shadowlopers?"

"Well, you might have part of it figured out already. They sure just might be from hell, or headed that way," Virgil said.

"Nobody really knows what they are or where they come from," Roosevelt quickly added.

"Yeah, Roosevelt's right, they're probably not from hell. The Central Office admits they exist, but they don't blab it around much. I ain't ever heard of 'em causing real trouble, and till that happens, the boys upstairs will officially ignore 'em. If you're asking me, though, I think they're ghosts or something like that," Virgil said, squinting wisely.

Dewey had been listening, but his only contribution to the conversation had been the wincing he'd done each time Virgil used bad English. He could've winced himself into spasms listening to Virgil, had it not been for the statement about ghosts. At that point, his eyes went round, and he asked, "Ghosts? There really is such a thing?"

"That's what I call 'em, but I've heard 'em called things like lost spirits, trapped souls, dark spirits, and the like. Amongst custodians they're just called shadowlopers, and that's a pretty good moniker for 'em," Virgil said.

"Well, I've never seen them," Dewey said, looking sort of mind-boggled.

"A lot of custodians have never seen them. I've never seen them," Roosevelt said.

"Well, I don't mean any disrespect to you boys, but it takes some savvy about field work to notice 'em. A keen eye, that's what it takes. Takes a keen mind to boot, and that's how come Salty here just saw 'em in a time of crisis. He must've been all charged up and keen of wit when they caught his eye. That's when I spotted 'em, and even then you never really draw a good bead on 'em. They move fast, and all a feller ever sees is the dark shadow forms," Virgil said.

Roosevelt looked a little peeved, but he didn't say a word in response. I almost grinned when the thought crossed my mind that he had some adjusting to do. For one thing, Virgil called everybody 'boy', and Roosevelt would have to get over his sensitivity about it - either that or just keep his mouth shut about it, which is just what he must've decided to do. Dewey, though, seldom kept his mouth shut, especially when he felt frustrated. "But you still haven't said what they are. They've got to be more than just shadows, so what are they?"

"Maybe they really are lost or trapped souls. The best guess is that they're folks who somehow slipped through the cracks between the mortal world and the spirit world. They died in such a way as to keep 'em from crossing over to our world, and some think they're looking for a way to get in. Others think they don't want in, that all they're about is running wild in their own world of shadows. If that's true, then they really are ghosts, I reckon," Virgil said.

"But you said something about them being from hell," Dewey said.

"Yeah, but don't be taking that too serious. There's some who think that's what hell really is, the world of shadows, but I kinda think the shadowlopers are more like escapees from hell. They might've been folks that lived bad mortal lives, knew they were headed for hell, and just refused to go by refusing to accept their own deaths. They're just so scared of the hereafter, that they keep running to keep from being caught up with," Virgil said.

Roosevelt had stood it about as long as he could and said, "Yes, but the Central Office prefers to think of them as wandering souls that have not come to grips with eternity, and therefore become shadowlopers. Should they ever accept that, they'd be able to come over, and many of them would belong with us, and not in hell."

It was time for my two cents. "I tend to agree with Virgil. Who'd want a chickenshit like that here with us? Maybe hell really is just a world of shadows, or maybe they're really escapees from hell. As long as they're just a mild nuisance, I don't really care. I just wondered what I'd been seeing, and now I know."

"Well, I care what they are," Dewey said, still looking concerned.

I started feeling bad about ever bringing it up about then. Dewey would have enough on his mind without having to worry about shadowlopers, and given his sense of wanting to know something about almost everything, he'd fret about it. But where Dewey appeared to be concerned, Winston Frye, who'd been sitting and listening to the conversation, looked gut shot. Roosevelt must've noticed the look because he put his arm around Winston's shoulder and walked him to a place where he could calm him down.

"That boy's got a long ways to go," Virgil said, watching them walk away.

"Yeah, but Dewey here can show him the ropes. He's a good hand, and I'm not going to be gone but a few days," I said, hoping to perk Dewey up a little. It worked because he smiled and looked pleased.

"Well, I'm needing to get on down the road, boys. Where'd you say you was headed to?" Virgil asked.

"Deluth, Minnesota."

"Tell you what, Salty. I've got this fancy new airplane, and I still ain't learned how to fly the thing too good. I'm needing some practice, so I'll just fly you on up there," he said.

"You've got a deal."

A round of brief good-byes followed, and Roosevelt and Virgil and I departed in the big Lincoln, leaving Winston and Dewey standing on the sidewalk in front of the apartment building. Woody had just walked outside, so their day of guarding was just beginning. My few days of unrestricted R and R were just starting, and boy, did it ever start with a bang. Roosevelt drove us to Garden City, where Virgil's plane was parked, and that's when I started having regrets about accepting the offer to fly. The plane was an old bi-wing, open cockpit, 1920's aircraft that had more dings in it than an eight day chime clock, and when Virgil said he needed some practice, he sure told the truth. He scared me so bad on several occasions that I had trouble holding my I/I mode, and I was sure glad to get my feet back on the ground in Deluth.

"I've been mulling it over while we flew up here, and I've decided there's something you need to know about shadowlopers," Virgil said.

"This isn't going to be one of those bad news things, is it?" I asked.

"Naw, nothing like that, but over my years of doing what you're doing, I figured out something about 'em. The shadowlopers I spotted appeared to have attached themselves to the mark I was guarding at the time. I don't exactly know why, but I figure it was 'cause they're lonesome. It seems to me they're waiting around on somebody they knew from the mortal world to die off so they can have some company in the shadow world. Maybe that's why you only see 'em when you're mark's in real danger."

"You're saying that the shadowloper I've been seeing used to be a friend of Woody's, right?"

"Probably, but he could just be somebody he knew."

"You're also saying that this shadowloper is hanging around so he can steal Woody's soul, aren't you?" I asked.

"Well, I wouldn't exactly say that he's wanting to steal anything, but I think he's probably wanting to recruit a pardner to go shadowloping with him," he said.

"Damn, Virgil, that's some heavy shit," I said, shaking my head.

"Yeah, it's heavy, all right. Shadowlopers are the leeches of the spirit world. I figure they're not powerful enough to actually steal anything, especially a soul, so they ghost the shadows of places where they're likely to find somebody who's as weak spirited as they are. They couldn't have stolen a spirit like mine or yours 'cause we're too damn strong for 'em, but weak spirited people die every day, and they're the ones whose souls are at risk. Your mark is a hard drinking man, and booze weakens the spirit. He could be at risk, and that's why the shadowloper's leeched onto him."

"What can I do about it? Is there any way I can get rid of this shadowloper?"

"There's not much you can do about it, unless . . . unless . . . "

"Unless what?" I asked, breaking in. I was starting to get the willies, and they got the best of me for the moment.

"I was just gonna say unless you can identify the shadowloper, and that's not likely to happen," Virgil said.

"There's no way at all?"

"I cain't say for sure, but I've heard of an instance or two where a custodian actually caught one of them. The world of shadows ain't a dimension in itself, and Shadowlopers have to leech off somebody else's dimension. They cain't operate in the mortal's dimension, so they undoubtedly use yours. That being the case, this custodian said he latched onto a shadowloper by paying attention to certain things that were going on around his mark. He claimed he could smell 'em," he said, grinning.

"Smell them?"

"Yeah, he allowed as how they smell sorta like ammonia."

"You're kidding me."

"Naw, that's what he said - just a faint smell of ammonia."

"How'd he catch it?" I asked.

"Well, he picked up the scent, then laid back and acted like he didn't notice nothing till the thing got bold and got close enough to where he could grab it and take it down. According to him, they're fast but not too hard to hold. Anyway, he caught it, and knew who it was. Then he told it to get the hell away from his mark and never come back," he said.

"Well, did doing that work??

"Don't know 'cause the feller said his mark died shortly after that."

"That beats all I've ever heard of, but the part about the smell is sure interesting. I don't remember smelling anything when I spotted the shadowloper, but then again, I wasn't paying much attention."

"Well, keep your wits about you, and you might be able to identify your ghost. Me, I've got to get on back to Cheyenne," he said, sticking out his hand. We shook, and he flew away still wobbling and weaving like a toy plane on a string.

I watched him fly away, thinking about Woody and who his shadowloper might be. We had talked in terms of it being a him, but the thought struck me that Woody's shady spook could be a gal. I was tempted to start trying to remember all the weak-assed people Woody had known since I'd been guarding him, but doing so would've put my brain in vapor lock. This shadowloper could be most anybody he'd known, and I dismissed trying to figure out who it was because it really didn't make any difference - unless I wanted to try to get rid of it. Up until then, it had been no more that a nuisance to me, but if Virgil was right about them being out to recruit a weak soul from a weak-ass mortal, this shadowloper was more than a nuisance to Woody. I'd already started thinking about ways to catch it when I arrived at Phoebe's place, but when I got a look at her, I didn't think about shadowlopers again for quite a while.

CHAPTER 38
Phoebe

Phoebe Foster, like I said earlier, was a real piece of work. A small gal at about five feet three inches tall and with strawberry blonde hair and fair skin, she had just enough freckles across her nose to make her cuter than a pile of puppies. She had a nice body with all the curves in the right places, but I loved looking into her beautiful green eyes best. Seeing me again seemed to thrill her because she rushed up and hugged me. Her doing that started my nuts to aching right off. Since my wrestling match with Woody at the apartment that night, they had been a bit tender.

As it turned out, Phoebe's mark had just been checked into a rehab center, and her partner had taken over the guardian duties for a while. She'd already been reassigned, but she didn't know where or to what mark and was just waiting around for orders. That tickled me pink because that meant she'd have lots of free time to spend on me. The first thing we did was bundle up and walk the downtown streets of Deluth. The Christmas decorations almost gave me a holiday spirit, and I say almost because I've never been much of a Christmas person. Being with Phoebe would've made me feel festive if I'd been in Juarez at a bull fight, and you can imagine what I think of bull fighting.

Phoebe had a magic box a lot like mine, but hers had more goodies in it, and we ate like royalty for the next couple of days. Her car was a Porsche 911, one of my favorites, and I spent hours driving it up and down the snow covered streets of Deluth. She lived in a Winnebago motor home - much nicer than the trailer Dewey and I lived in. Women custodians must have more pull with the central office, I decided. Maybe they had some women's lib action going on back in Heaven, but I didn't fuss about the accommodations.

A mode mechanic showed up my second day there with his gizmo for personification. This guy was different from the one I'd threatened in Cleveland, so I made sure to tell him that I wanted to be personified as myself. He didn't like doing that and suggested all sorts of personifications, but I refused all of them. Finally, he did what I asked and changed me, and when he turned to Phoebe to change her, she waved him off. Then he wiggled the joystick on his gizmo and disappeared.

"Why'd you send him away. I was hoping we could go out on the town like regular folks tonight," I said.

She smiled, then closed her eyes and took a step forward. In just one step she suddenly turned into a personification of herself - a sure enough flesh and bone Phoebe. She brought along the good parts too, and that caused me to break into a big grin. "How'd you do that?"

"I just moved into the same dimension with you, that's all," she said, smiling and tilting her head to one side.

"I thought we were already in the same dimension," I said.

"When we talk about working in a dimension, we're talking about a scope of activity and the aspects associated with it. Out here in the spirit world, some of the same properties apply that applied on mortal earth. A large chunk of granite has a set of properties to start with, but once the artist finishes making it into a statue, its properties change. The properties, in other words, determine the dimension of something. All I did was change properties," she said, extending her arms and smiling generously.

"But you look the same as you did while you were in the other dimension. If you changed properties, you should look different, shouldn't you?" I asked.

"Not necessarily. A statue can be made of wood or stone or clay or any number of things, but it can still look the same. If it helps you understand, my changing into a personified me was like changing a statue from clay to stone."

"But how'd you do it? You just closed your eyes, stepped forward, and changed."

"I met a nice mode guy who showed me how to do it. That little gizmo he carries around doesn't really change anything about you. All it does is open a door between you and the dimension you're going to be using. You can learn to open the doors yourself with a little practice and proper thought process. I opened the door just now by concentrating on what I really wanted, and then I just stepped through. You can step out of it the same way."

"How long did it take you to learn how?"

"Not long, maybe a week," she said, smiling again.

"When I first heard about the personification mode, I used to try to get it. I tried so much that I'd get exhausted from trying, but I couldn't do it, and then you tell me that you did it in a week," I said, flapping my arms to my sides in disgust.

"Well, like I said, some nice mode mechanic showed me how. The big trick is that you can't do it for some spurious reason. You probably tried doing it because you wanted something for no good reason other than satisfying yourself, and the door doesn't open for greedy purposes."

Oops, I thought. Now I know why I never could do it. I had getting laid in mind, and that's greedy, I suppose. To be real truthful with you, I still had that in mind, and now I was starting to worry whether or not my personification mode would allow that. Based on what Phoebe had just said, I might be in big trouble if I tried anything greedy. Maybe that's why Roosevelt had been so willing to give me an 'unrestricted' vacation. He probably knew that I couldn't get into any mischief unless it was through some guiltless intent, and I'd hardly ever heard of mischief without just a little guilt. My head was starting to ache from the thought that I might never get around to some mischief with Phoebe.

"What's the matter. You don't look well," she said, stepping closer.

"I just had an awful thought, that's all."

"What kind of thought?"

"I've had this fantasy about us . . . and . . . it involves . . . and you see it . . . well, it . . . Aw, hell, it involves me and you getting it on together, and now I'm starting to have second thoughts about it, that's all," I said, finally getting it out.

"You mean, you don't want to now?" she asked.

"No, I still want to, but I'm thinking that I can't do it now."

"Are you getting sick or something?"

"Naw, I feel fine, but . . . "

"Then don't worry about it. What's meant to happen will happen, and there's no use worrying about it," she said, reaching out to pat my face. Then she walked away, motioning for me to follow.

"Yeah, but what's meant to happen may not be what I want to happen," I mumbled, mostly to myself and with my head down as I shambled along behind her.

We taxied around town for the next few days, mostly because Phoebe's accouterments, including the Porsche, wouldn't work for us now. We could've used it in the personification mode, but nobody would've seen it, and a couple of people flying down the road at sixty miles an hour with nothing around them but thin air tends to spook most folks. So we took taxis and buses and did the town up right. On my second night in Deluth, we ate out in the best restaurant in town. While there, I might add, the waiter tried to pour us a glass of wine, but I brushed it aside. I'd been through too much with Woody to ever let booze cross my lips again. Phoebe smiled when I did it, then pushed hers away. We went to a Christmas concert that evening, then checked into a nice room at the best hotel in town. If you're wondering where all the money for this came from, there's a simple explanation. Phoebe paid for it.

We spent the evening talking, mostly about our lives and some of the things that had happened to us. We compared notes on being custodians, and we even talked about sports. Phoebe was a horse lover, so we talked horses, and that gave me a chance to tell her all about my rodeo career. We probably never would've run out of things to talk about; we just ran out of endurance. I'd kept my hands off her about as long as I could, but finally I gave up and pulled her to me and kissed her. Within minutes we were peeling off clothes, not knowing if anything would come of it. Once we were naked, I looked down and checked to see if that donkey dick was back, and seeing it wasn't, I proceeded with what I'd started.

You probably think I'm going to blab and tell you every detail about what happened, but you're wrong. It's not that I don't remember every detail because I do, and it's not that I've got something against writing about sex, because I don't. But it's different when you're writing about yourself, and I'm not a kiss and tell all guy. I'll tell, but I just won't tell much. This is where a good imagination comes in. I will say this much - YIPEEEEE!

We didn't roll out until noon the next day, but instead of waking up refreshed after putting to rest a fifteen year dry spell, I felt a bit blue and somewhat agitated. I kept trying to make myself feel great, but I didn't, and I couldn't pull it off. I'd just enjoyed the best sex of my existence anywhere, life and afterlife, but something wasn't right. A gnawing feeling that I should be back in Kansas kept after me, and I couldn't push it out of my mind. We showered and then went out for a nice lunch. Phoebe had noticed my change of moods and asked what was bothering me. I didn't know exactly how to tell her that I felt torn between being there with her and being with Woody back in Kansas, but I tried.

"I know the feeling," she said after listening for a while.

"Other things are bugging me, I reckon. Maybe it's just my suspicious nature, but I'm having trouble with Roosevelt's generosity in letting me come here. Why would he pull me out of Kansas unless . . . unless he's trying to get rid of me for a while? My mark is having a rough go of it, and he comes in with some rookie to stand in for me, and then sends me up here. I keep asking myself that, and the only answer I can come up with is that he wants me out of the way for a while," I said.

"That seems strange, him wanting you to come at a time like this, but why would he want you out of the way?"

"Remember that rich Texan who dropped dead in Vegas?"

"Yes."

"Remember that custodian chauffeur, that dead-eyed sonofabitch, who was with him?"

"Yes."

"I wanted to know who he was, but when I asked Roosevelt, he just told me not to concern myself about it. But that bastard gave me the willies so bad that I couldn't quit thinking about him, and I finally figured out who, or what, he was. He was a death angel, Phoebe. I know it sounds farfetched, but that's exactly what he was," I said, leaning forward and staring her straight in the eyes.

"You can't be serious," she said, leaning back in her chair and looking away. For just an instant, I saw something in her eyes that I didn't like.

"You're not part of this, are you?"

"Part of what?"

"This little conspiracy to get me out of town so a death angel can take out my mark. You're not a good liar, so look me in the eyes and tell me you didn't have anything to do with it," I said, gritting my teeth.

"I have no idea what you're talking about, and I refuse to believe God employs death angels," she said, looking me dead in the eyes. She looked sincere to me, but that didn't disarm me of my death angel idea.

"No, but some bureaucratic dumbass in the central office might decide to snuff my mark, and Roosevelt, being the dutiful supervisor he is, will go along with anything they tell him to do. They might not even tell him what their plans are, but they might use him to get me out of the way."

"This is all too bizarre to be true," Phoebe said shaking her head.

Since she was having so much trouble with my worries about death angels, I decided to give her a taste of the sure enough bizarre. I spent the next fifteen minutes telling her what I recently learned about shadowlopers, and by the time I finished, she was getting a little more receptive to my death angel talk. Still a long way from being convinced, she asked a question that brought me to a new level of consciousness. "I can buy the idea that someone in the Central Office might think of employing a death angel, but I just can't see how they could pull it off. You're a good custodian - so good, in fact, that you even picked up on the shadowlopers. How could they possibly get a death angel past you?"

"By getting me out of the way," I said.

"But you have a keen sense about things like that, and if you thought a death angel was really lurking about, you wouldn't have come here. You already admitted being suspicious from the beginning, and . . . "

"Jesus Christ!" I said, jumping straight up. What she'd said had suddenly set off a sudden realization that went off like a grenade exploding in my head.

"What is it?" Phoebe asked, looking alarmed.

"You're right. I never would've come, no matter how bad I wanted to see you. But he brought in this wimpy young custodian to help Dewey while I was gone. And, he had the big boss with him - a guy I think a lot of. Hell, he even flew me up here. That's it! The kid's the death angel. They knew I never would suspect him, and that's why they brought Winston to stand in for me. This is all a set-up. We've been had, Phoebe," I said, holding my hands to my head.

"I guess this means you're going home, right?" she asked, looking dismayed.

"I don't have a choice. I've got to get home, and fast."

"Want me to drive you in my Porsche? It goes 160 miles per hour. I can get you there is six, maybe seven, hours."

"Let's do it," I said, taking her by the hand.

When we drove away from Deluth headed for Forest City, I felt like somebody had shoved a knife in my gut. I kept having visions of me bouncing ton sized boulders off Roosevelt's head, and I could see myself choking the crap out of some double-breasted suit wearing, chickenshit bureaucrat from the Central Office. I could see Winston, his eyes sunk back in his head like a zombie, hiding in the shadows waiting to take Woody. Worse yet, I could see Woody stretched out in a coffin, all ashen-faced and dead as a dinosaur bone. Through it all, I could see me standing around looking like the stupid sonofabitch who let it all happen. The only good thing about the deal was finding out that Phoebe wasn't part of the plot to get me out of the way. The trip home was an anxious ride for me, and I prayed that Woody would still be alive when I got back to Kansas.

CHAPTER 39
Stoned Angels

Getting back to Forest City took only six hours, just as Phoebe had promised, but it seemed like an eternity to me. We drove straight to Woody's apartment and found Winston sitting on a bench just outside the apartment building. When he saw Phoebe's bright red Porsche drive up, he walked over with a grin on his face as big as Texas. I'd never seen him smile before, and his demeanor set me back a few pegs. "Nice wheels," he said, gawking at the Porsche.

"Where's Woody? Where's Dewey?" I asked, shooting both questions at him in rapid succession.

"Upstairs," he said, pointing toward Woody's second floor apartment.

I breathed a sigh of relief and then said, "This is Phoebe Foster. This is her car."

"Nice wheels?" Winston said again, still holding that goofy looking smile.

"Hello," Phoebe said.

"Nice wheels," Winston said again, and I suddenly started seeing him as an old phonograph machine whose needle had got caught in a bad record groove. The thought of whacking him a good one to see if I could unstick him ran through my head, but that idea quickly passed.

"Want to take it for a spin?" Phoebe said, smiling at him like a teacher might at a student in the slow learners section.

"Yeah, that would be neat," he said. Good deal, I thought. She'd found a way to get his tongue unstuck, and he'd be out of our hair for a while.

Phoebe stepped out of the Porsche and made room for Winston. He got behind the wheel and drove away. "That's the guy you think is a death angel?" Phoebe asked, and when I nodded, she broke into laughter.

"I know it sounds stupid, but like I said before, nobody would suspect him," I said.

"You're right about that," she said, once she was able to stop laughing. To be real truthful, I started having doubts myself. Being around Winston, even when he wasn't looking scared, would give anyone the idea that he was too stupid to be anything other than just Winston, the wet behind the ears trainee.

We joined hands and went straightway to Woody's apartment, and found Dewey watching some nature show on television. "What's shaking," I asked as I tiptoed up behind him. He jerked, then jumped up. "Oh, for the love of Pete!" Did you have to do that?"

"I was just announcing my presence," I said, smirking.

"You're just getting even, that's all," Dewey said, fanning his face like he couldn't breathe and looking embarrassed.

"You remember Phoebe?"

"Yes, I certainly do," he said, then took a couple of steps forward and hugged her.

We visited for a few minutes before I finally got around to asking, "Where's Woody?" I asked. Dewey motioned with his head toward the bedroom.

I went down the hall and poked my head into the bedroom. Woody was lying on his back, staring at the ceiling while C.W. fondled him. Nothing much was happening, though, because Woody's pecker looked as limp as a day old diaper. C.W. was bare-assed naked, so I stuck around for a few minutes to check her out. I still liked her big ass and nice round boobs, but they didn't do as much for me as they had before my trip to Deluth. I suddenly became aware of Dewey and Phoebe's presence behind me. "How long have they been at it?" I asked.

"Oh, since about midnight, on and off. I haven't watched, so I don't know what they've been doing. They may have been sleeping," Dewey said, sighing.

"Since midnight? No wonder Woody can't get it up," I mumbled.

"Beg your pardon?"

"Oh, nothing, just making an observation."

"Disappointed?" he asked, then suddenly remembered Phoebe was standing right beside him. He looked at her, smiled, and shrugged.

"She's pretty. Who is she?" Phoebe asked.

"C.W. Laney. Woody has been carrying on with her lately," I said.

"He's not a bad looking guy himself," she said.

"He used to be a nice looking guy, as far as guys go, I reckon. Booze has beaten him down to looking like that now," I said.

"That's too bad," she said.

"Dewey thinks C.W.'s too well endowed. He thinks she's chunky," I said.

"She is . . . chunky," Dewey said, sniffing.

"Do you hang around and watch them together like this often?" Phoebe asked, her left eyebrow curving into the shape of a teepee.

"Aw, sometimes," I said.

"Prevaricator," Dewey mumbled.

"What's that?" Phoebe asked, but by then I was already standing on Dewey's foot.

"Just clearing my throat," he said, smiling innocently.

We went back to the living room and sat down on the floor. I needed a chance to talk to Dewey, and since it looked like Phoebe was going to stick around for a while, then was a good a time as any. "How have you and Winston been getting along?"

"Getting along with Winston is like making friends with a cat," Dewey said. "All he does is sleep, eat, follow you around, and eat and sleep some more."

"Yeah, he's docile, but I think the bastard's a death angel," I said.

"A what?" he asked, looking back and forth from me to Phoebe.

"I said he's a death angel. I figured something out while I was in Minnesota. Roosevelt was just trying to get me out of the way when he sent me up there. I think the Central Office has decided to snuff Woody."

"Are you serious?" Dewey asked, looking shocked.

"As serious as lung cancer."

"What makes you think that?"

"It all adds up, that's why. They sent me up there so Phoebe could keep me busy and out of the way. She's not in on it, but Roosevelt knew I'd jump at the chance to be with her. They sent

Winston to do the job because nobody would ever suspect him of being the hit man."

"Are you sure?" Dewey asked.

"Yes."

"And you believe this story?" he asked, looking at Phoebe.

"I did at first, but after meeting Winston, I'm not sure what I believe. He sure doesn't look very dangerous to me," she said, giving me an apologetic look.

"That's the way it has to be, don't you see. If they sent in somebody who really looked like a killer, then we might be able to stop him. Winston is perfect for the job," I said.

"I'm not convinced," Dewey said, wagging his head from side to side.

"Well, I reckon there's nothing I can do to convince you, so I'll have to handle it on my own. I'm going for a walk," I said, then stood up and marched out of the room. Phoebe caught up with me outside the building, and we headed toward the campus. From Woody place to the center of the campus couldn't have been more than a half mile, and it didn't take long for us to get there. Just as we reached the gymnasium, I spotted Phoebe's car parked by the curb out front. Winston was nowhere to be seen.

"I wonder why Winston left your car there?" I asked, pointing it out to Phoebe.

"I have no idea," she said, staring at the red Porsche.

"Maybe he broke it."

"He can't break it," she said, chuckling.

"I don't know about that. Winston's sort of a klutz, and just judging from what little I've seen of him, he could break a railroad spike," I said.

"Oh, he's probably around here somewhere."

It turned out that Winston was around somewhere, and finding him turned out to be just what I needed to prove my theory about him being a death angel. We'd just rounded a corner near the gym when I spotted him talking to a couple of football jocks just outside a side entrance. They were joking and laughing and doing that male bonding thing that jocks are so famous for. I caught Phoebe by the arm and pulled her back and behind the trunk of a large tree, then pointed toward Winston.

"Why, he's working the personification mode," she said, her mouth dropping open in surprise.

"He sure is."

"No rookie trainee can work the personification mode," she said.

"Sure can't," I said, flashing an I-told-you-so smile.

"You may be right about him. At the very least, someone has misled you about who and what he really is."

"Shall we go tell Dewey?" I asked.

"Yes, I think we should," she said, and we backed away staying low to make sure Winston didn't spot us.

Dewey took it hard when we told him. The first words out of his mouth were, "What can we do?"

"I don't know, but I'll figure something out," I said.

"We can't fight them, Doug. They're much too strong," he said.

"Yeah, they're strong, but we can sure as hell make their job hard for them. If they think I'm just going to walk away and let them snuff my mark, they've got another think coming. This old boy's going to do some real fudging this time," I said, gritting my teeth.

"But ..."

"Are you just going to lay down for this?" I asked.

Dewey stared at me for a minute, and as I watched his eyes, I could see the determination build. "No," he said. "No, I'm not. Just tell me what to do, and I'll do it."

"That's my man," I said, taking a line from L.L. Cribbs.

"I hate to miss out on all this, but I've really got to get back to Deluth," Phoebe said.

"You don't hate it near as bad as I do, but can't you hang around for a couple of days? Today is Christmas Eve, and if you went back to Deluth, you'd just have to spend Christmas alone. Come on, stay a couple of days," I said, gathering her in my arms.

"Well, I am unemployed right now," she said.

"Good! We'll go out and do something tonight."

"Can I go?" Dewey asked.

"Who's going to watch Woody and Winston? That kind of like leaving the cat to watch the canary, isn't it?" I asked.

"Aw, poo! I'll stay," he said.

Winston drove up then and went straight to the trailer. Phoebe, partly because she felt sorry for him, tagged along with Dewey when he went to check on Woody. I started pacing. I don't know about you, but I've never been able to do much quality thinking while sitting. Maybe that's why I didn't make A's in college, and I might've been if they had let me take tests standing up. I may be the only man in the history of the world who wrote a book standing straight up. That's right! I typed most of this book standing, and you can blame the bad parts on when I got tired and sat down to type.

Some things need to be done sitting, I reckon, but I always avoid thinking and sitting at the same time. There must be a kill switch in my ass or something because sitting puts me to sleep about as fast as lying down does. I know what you're thinking. I've made numerous references in this book about sitting, but it was easier to do that than to try to explain what I usually do, and that's to hunker down. Hunker is an old time word for squat, so that's what I do most of the time - hunker.

My pacing and thinking got me nowhere, and I gave up and joined Dewey and Phoebe in Woody's living room. Woody was wobbling around the kitchen in his shorts, and C.W. had on a smile, and that's all. I still liked the way her boobs jiggled when she walked, and I gawked at her until Phoebe elbowed me in the ribs. The two naked people made some sandwiches and then retreated to the bedroom. Since nothing much was happening at the moment, we decided to raid the magic box.

Winston was sound asleep when I peeked inside the trailer, and I wasn't about to wake him up to eat with us. I motioned for Dewey and Phoebe to follow, and we went to the car to see what was for supper. We sat on the ground behind the Chevy and ate. The sun had gone down by then, but the evening was surprisingly warm for a Christmas Eve. We talked a while, and then returned to Woody's apartment. Several couples were entering just as we arrived, and once inside, we found several more couples sitting around the living room. Within the next half hour, a dozen more people showed up - most of them strangers to me. They must've been C.W.'s friends.

The party would've turned out to be boring for us custodians if it hadn't been for the dope smokers. After all those years of hanging around Woody, I sure didn't expect what happened. He'd never once smoked grass, and he didn't that evening either. Others at the party did, though, and before long Woody's tiny living room was thick with smoke. Whenever people started smoking, Dewey usually left the room. He hated smoke of any kind, but this time he stayed put. I thought he stayed because Phoebe was there, and he seemed to enjoy her company. I was telling Phoebe something unimportant when Dewey suddenly started giggling like a teenage girl.

"What's wrong with you?" I asked.

"Did you hear the joke that guy just told? It was hilarious," he said.

I didn't think much about it, but in a little while he started laughing again - this time until tears ran down his face. Watching him cut up that way got me tickled, and I started laughing. Something must've set Phoebe off because she got cranked up then, and before long we were rolling around on the floor, laughing at every little thing that came up. This went on for about thirty minutes, and then Dewey struggled to his feet and said, "I'm hungry."

"But we've already eaten. All that's left is Winston's part," I said.

"Then let's go eat it," he said, his head wobbling around on his shoulders. His eyes looked weird, and it suddenly dawned on me what had happened.

"You know what?" I asked, looking at Phoebe.

"No, what?" she said. Her eyes looked like Dewey's.

"We're stoned."

"Yes, I think we are," she said, then laughed like crazy.

"Stoned?" Dewey said and then started laughing too.

I saw then that we'd better get out of there, and that's just what we did. My head cleared some once we got outside, but I knew it would be a while before we got straightened out. After checking to make sure Winston was still sleeping, we raided the magic box and ate his supper. Then we flopped down on our backs in the grass and stared at the stars. Maybe it was the dope smoke mood, or maybe it was seeing Winston sleeping that gave me the idea, but it finally came up with one. The plan I devised was a stroke of genius, and I immediately tried it on Phoebe and Dewey.

"Hey, guys, I've got it," I said, rolling to my side and facing them.

"Got what?" a thick-tongued Dewey asked.

"I've got a plan about what to do with Winston. We're going to kidnap him."

"We'll get in big trouble," Dewey said, then broke into giggles.

"Maybe that's just what we need - some big trouble. I know we can't get away with it, but maybe if we caused a big enough fuss, the Central Office might listen to what I've got to say about their plans to take Woody out. Being in the military taught me how to be a good bullshitter, and even in the army I could always find somebody who'd listen to me. I wouldn't mind taking a crack at those bastards in the Central Office. Somebody needs to speak up in Woody's behalf," I said.

"Here, here," Dewey said, pounding his fist on the ground.

"We'll kidnap Winston, and that will get it started. Roosevelt likes the kid, so he'll come to his rescue, and when he does, we'll demand to talk to the Central Office. It's the only way Roosevelt will set it up for me, and if he doesn't, nothing is lost. At least we will have flushed their plan out into the open, and they may give up on it."

"You won't get to talk to the Central Office, but you're right about drawing attention to their plan. If they know they've been discovered, then they'll probably back off. I like the plan, but how are we going to kidnap Winston?" Phoebe asked, raising herself up on one elbow.

"You won't hurt Winston, will you?" Dewey asked, looking concerned.

"We won't hurt him," I said.

My idea of capturing Winston came from a trick that had been played on me back in college. A bunch of my buddies sewed me up in my sheets while I was passed out on my bed, and that's exactly how I planned on capturing Winston. As soundly as he slept, sewing him up would be no problem. Then we'd take him some place and stow him away until I figured out what to do next. This could be done because a custodian usually sleeps in the I/T mode. He can sleep in the I/I mode, but that requires some energy, and he rests better if he can go I/T. That's no big problem if he uses his head and sleeps out of the way of anything that might come his way. Any sleeping custodian is vulnerable to some degree because he's not aware of what's going on around him, but no custodian can be trapped by anything worldly. He could be confined by our sheets, and that was what Winston was sleeping on. The logical place to put him once we'd captured him was in the trunk of the Chevy. Winston would probably wrestle free of the sheets after a while, but he wouldn't be able to get out of the trunk.

Catching Winston and getting him in the trunk of the car was no problem. Dewey and Phoebe did the sewing, and then we moved him to the trunk of the Chevy. He didn't even wake up. Once that was done, I started thinking of ways to raise a big enough ruckus to get Roosevelt back to Forest City as soon as possible. With several snitch custodians around town, that shouldn't take long. In thinking of ornery things to do, Frederick Lomax III came to mind. I thought of him first because the bastard had it coming on general principles alone. Wanda was out of town for while, and that left Freddy with time on his hands.

"You guys want to have some fun? We're already stoned, and there's no use in wasting a good high," I said.

"Sure," Dewey said.

"Count me in," Phoebe said.

We found Freddy about fifteen minutes later at Dusty's Bar downtown. He usually didn't go in there, but it was Christmas Eve, and someone had invited him down for a drink. Freddy was drifting around the bar and visiting with folks he knew, and it was a while before I could get him where I wanted him. Most of the bar's patrons that evening were cowboy types with their wives or girlfriends. I waited until a gal I'd seen earlier with a big cowboy got close to Freddy. She'd come to the bar and was standing back to back with Freddy, so I moved in, went I/T, and pinched her on the ass. She looked over her shoulder and frowned at Freddy, who was still looking the other way, but she didn't say a word. Seeing that she needed a harder pinch, I repeated the maneuver. She winched and jerked around, only to find Freddy turned the other way and visiting with someone else.

Most gals I've known would've already been on Freddy like white on rice, but this one seemed to have more tolerance for getting her ass pinched that most women. The big cowboy she was with walked up about that time, but she didn't say a word to him about it. She tried keeping a wary eye on Freddy this time, but when she got distracted by something for just a second, I got her again. Figuring the ass pinching wasn't working, I went for the boobs. That worked. She wheeled on her toes and fired a shot that caught Freddy just beneath the right ear, and he stumbled forward a couple of steps. Doing that caused more of a ruckus because he stumbled into several cowboys, causing them to spill drinks and bump up against one another. Freddy wheeled around to see who'd hit him at about the same time the gal turned to her escort and said, "He pinched me."

It was a hell of a fight, but not because Freddy contributed in any way other than getting knocked cold. I know what you're thinking, and you're right. It was a mean thing to do, but Freddy had it coming, and all those people should've been at home instead of out partying on Christmas Eve. No one should have pleasant memories of a Christmas Eve night in a bar, and I just did my little bit to make sure these people didn't go away with fond recollections of that particular evening. I was hoping some of those folks had custodians. A good free-for-all might get back to Roosevelt quicker than anything else, so I went around the room pinching lots of ladies boobs and butts. I knocked hats off cowboy's heads, and did other little irritating things until the fracas was in full bloom. Then I walked outside. Two cop cars were already pulling up in the parking lot.

"What did you do in there?" Dewey said, looking alarmed. I could see that he was getting back to normal, but not all the way back. His eyes still looked a little glazed.

"Started a fight, that's all," I said.

"Sounds like a dandy," Phoebe said.

"Aw, the cops will have it under control in a few minutes. Other than a few bloody noses and such, there won't be much to it. Are you guys ready for some more action?"

"What now?" Dewey said, looking gleeful again.

"Let's play Santa, won't to? There are some kids around town who won't get much in the morning because they're poor. Let's raid some stores, gather up some goodies, and leave them around for kids," I said.

"You mean steal things?" Phoebe asked.

"It's not exactly like stealing. After all the money they've made, these merchants can afford a little charity on Christmas. We won't wipe them out, just take a few things from each place. Let's hit the ones who started all this witch-hunt stuff. They deserve it, and that ought to get back to Roosevelt pretty quick."

"I think that's a fair estimation," Dewey said, then giggled.

The party at Woody's apartment had broken up, and he was out like a light when we went by to check on him. He was alone and sleeping face down on the couch in the living room. C.W. must've gone home, or had wandered off with her friends. Raiding the stores downtown didn't take long. We didn't take much - just a few things for the poorer kids in town. Forest City didn't have a lot of poor people, so delivering the toys didn't take long. I had a few places in mind, and we picked out a few other places that looked like candidates for a little Christmas cheer. Moving the toys was a tricky situation. A large Pooh bear heading down the street on its own would have caused quite a commotion, but the hour was late and no one was around. Once at the house, we had to count the kids to make sure we left enough presents.

By the time we'd finished with the night's business, all three of us were dog tired. I crashed in the apartment with Woody, knowing he'd sleep late and looking forward to doing the same. Phoebe curled up beside me, and Dewey went back to the trailer. I went to sleep thinking about what I could do the next day that would bring Roosevelt to town. I planned on keeping things stirred up until he appeared, and instead of counting sheep to bring on slumber, I thought of things I could do to the people in town who had incurred my ill will.

CHAPTER 40
The Bushwhacker

It's strange how things work out sometimes, because something happened the next morning that made my efforts at causing a ruckus totally unimportant. It's not that what happened caught me totally by surprise, but the way it happened sure as hell did. The day after Christmas started out bad when Phoebe announced that she was leaving for Minnesota. I stood around and watched her get her things together, then walked her to the car. She said something about hating to run out on me but needed to check about her new assignment. I said that she sure didn't hate it as bad as I did and then gathered her in my arms. "When will I see you again?" she asked.

"I don't know, but you'll be seeing me," I said.

"Promise?"

"Yeah, I promise."

She drove away, and I stood there wondering if I'd made a promise I couldn't keep. The mischief we'd caused the night before was bound to bring repercussions from Roosevelt and maybe even the Central Office, and a showdown was coming up about the death angel business. Winston was still trapped in the trunk of the Chevy, and Roosevelt would be one big time pissed of supervisor when he got wind of it. The thought had crossed my mind that by the time this mess with Woody ran its course, I might be in so much trouble that an assignment guarding a salt miner in outer Siberia would've been getting off light. It addition to being some worried and a lot despondent, I was starting to get tired.

I sat on the curb near the trailer and watched traffic go by for a while. Sundays around Forest City were always slow, but a Sunday after Christmas meant that it was real slow. A few cars passed, and some kids were in the yard playing with their new toys. The unseasonable warm spell had held, and the temperature was well into the sixties. I watched a man in his fifties and a boy of perhaps seven play catch with a football, and a wave of nostalgia swept through me like lobo wind. I thought of my grandfathers and how they'd played with me, and I could see myself at fifty playing with one of my grandkids. But I'd never had children, and even if I'd lived to be fifty, would not have had grandbabies to play with. I tried to think about some Mexican kid across town out playing with a gift he hadn't expected, a gift we'd left on Christmas Eve, but that didn't help much.

A week passed, and the New Year came, but Roosevelt still hadn't appeared. I was starting to think that my antics of Christmas hadn't been sufficient to provoke the kind of response I wanted. Dewey and I stuck to Woody like stink to a rotten egg, but nothing out of the ordinary happened. I still hadn't given up on the notion of a death angel being on his tail, but I'll admit to having a few doubts by then. I was still tired and preoccupied with it all, and maybe that's why I didn't see it coming.

Woody walked out his apartment building with Dewey just a few paces behind him. He seemed to be headed for the street out front and was half way there when it happened. I was looking in their direction and saw Dewey's eyes suddenly go round. I started gathering my legs under me to rise, and I saw Dewey suddenly dart in front of Woody. Then I heard the crack of a rifle firing, and both of them went down. Dewey landed first, catapulted backward by the force of the bullet tearing into him. He'd had the presence of mind to go I/T, but the bullet had passed right through him and hit Woody. I'd been in a war, so I'd seen people hit before by rifle fire. They had gone down quickly, but that's not what happened with Woody. Dewey had slowed the bullet, easing the impact some. Woody crumbled to his knees, then clutched his chest and looked down. Blood was squirting from between his fingers and spreading across his white shirt. His head jerked a time or two, and then he pitched forward on his face.

I turned quickly and looked toward the street. A late model Cadillac sedan parked up the street suddenly sped away from the curb, but not before I got a look at the driver. He glanced over his shoulder momentarily, and I got a good enough look to recognize him. I'd never seen him before, but I knew who he was. I'd screwed up big time. The Central Office must've known I'd never expect a shooting, especially from a white haired old man in a Caddy. But I saw his eyes when he looked back - the same dead eyes I'd seen in Vegas.

I rushed to where they'd fallen and checked Woody, then Dewey. Dewey looked the worst for wear, but I knew he wouldn't die. Woody had a hole in his left shoulder, about four inches left of his heart. In looking closer, I saw that the bullet had not passed through him. Several people rushed up about that time, and I turned my attention to Dewey. The bullet had sure gone through him, but he was conscious. I grabbed his arms and dragged him to the shade of the elm tree where the trailer was parked. I knelt beside him and held him up to get a better look at him. He looked back at me and blinked, then asked, "Did I stop it?" I shook my head. He frowned in disappointment and then collapsed in my arms.

I picked him up and took him inside the trailer and laid him on the bed. He was bleeding badly, and I started applying pressure with towels to get it stopped. The bullet had gone through the right side of his chest and came out right between his shoulder blades. A lung shot like that would've killed almost anyone, and I kept thinking about what Virgil Jacks had said about getting killed a second time. Dewey couldn't die again, not really, but everything else about what would actually happen to him was a mystery. I didn't want the person I knew as Dewey Davisson to die, regardless of what happened to his spirit, but I didn't know what to do with him. I needed some help about as bad as I've ever needed it, and that's when I remembered Winston.

He came out of the trunk of the Chevy looking like a bear just coming out of hibernation - all squinty-eyed and groggy. It looked to me like he'd been asleep the entire time, but I knew that wasn't true because he'd done a bunch of yelling the night before when Dewey and I went after the toys. I told him what had happened and said I was sorry about what we'd done to him. He still looked scared, but I told him how much I needed his help. Someone had to take care of Dewey while I looked after Woody. Once that death angel in the Caddy figured out that he'd botched the job, he'd be back, and I needed to be ready for him.

"Can you help me?" I asked, finishing my spiel about how sorry I was about locking him up that way.

"Sure. I was a doctor for a short time, you know," he said proudly.

"You were what?"

"A doctor. I was going into sports medicine. I'd just graduated med school when I died. I can't promise anything, but I know what to do."

It came to me then why Winston came out of training able to use the personification mode. Central Office people must've had plans for using him as a doctor somewhere, and he'd be worthless at that unless he could go personification mode. I never would've figured him for a doctor, not in a million years. I hustled off to the hospital feeling more like a fool than I'd ever felt in my entire like. I'd mistaken a former doctor for a death angel, and I didn't even want to think about the parallels a mind like mine could draw from that one. I might've made more of it if it hadn't been for the crisis at hand. I was in jeopardy of losing my mark and my partner, and that was enough to get my full attention.

I took up guard at the hospital just outside the emergency room. Within minutes, doctors had decided what should be done. Moving him to a larger hospital was too dangerous, and they'd do the surgery there. Fortunately for Woody, one of Forest City's doctors had been an army doctor who'd done two tours in Nam. Another thing in his favor was that the Forest City Hospital was unusually large for a small town. Since the next really large hospital was hours away, the local hospital had grown over the years to be big enough to attract several good doctors to the community.

Woody stayed in surgery for four hours, and I kept sticking my head into the operating room to see how things were going. I heard one doctor say that he thought Woody had a good chance of making it. The bullet had missed his heart and lodged next to a lung. I stayed around until they rolled him down to the recovery room, and then to the intensive care unit a little later on. I stood over him for a while and watched him. The doctors were more optimistic at that point than I was. I've seen pickled eggs with better color.

A nurse finally got Wanda on the phone, and from the sound of the conversation, she'd be coming home immediately. I parked my weary ass at the foot of Woody's bed and waited. A few of Woody's friends were starting to show up in the waiting room area. Most of the faculty was out of town for the holidays, as were the students, but a rigid and distraught Duncan Highsmith showed up. Reese and June McDonald came next, and then others trickled in. Don Early, the academic vice-president, dropped by, and Ellen Stegnor, the university president herself, showed up. Others came, but I didn't pay much attention. A dark mood had hit me - the worst case of melancholy I've ever experienced. I was sad to the core and depressed beyond tears. I had felt it coming, even before my trip to Deluth, but I wasn't ready for it. I'd never felt so helpless and worthless. There I sat, waiting for that dead-eyed death angel to come and finish his job. I didn't have much confidence that I could stop him, but I was hell bent on trying.

The death angel never came, but Roosevelt did. With all that had happened, I'd almost forgotten about my ploy to get Roosevelt to Forest City, and it startled me when he stepped through the wall and stared down at me. "How is he?" he asked, looking tired and somber as usual.

"Oh, he's fine," I said, trying hard to flash a smile to accompany my sarcasm. "Somebody put a bullet in him, and some doctors just got through digging around in his innards to get it back, but he's going to be fine. He may die, of course, but we can always use another poor frustrated sonofabitch in this fucked up afterlife."

"What kind of crack is that?" he asked, scowling.

"Don't lay any of that innocent crap on me," I said, rising to look him square in the eyes.

The tired look in Roosevelt's eyes turned angry. "I have no idea what you're talking about. I'm here because of the reports that have been flooding into the Central Office this morning. From the sound of it, you've gone completely mad. Why are you terrorizing these people?"

"I needed to get you here, that's why, and I knew that would do it. Even though Dewey and I can't get through to you, obviously someone down here can. Why is that, Roosevelt? Why is it that other custodians can get through to you, and I can't?"

"That's not of my doing. The Central Office decides things like that, but that's neither here nor there. What is important is what's going on here. What happened to Woody? How did he get this way?"

"You know damn well what happened to him. One of your boys shot him," I said, biting the words off.

"One of my boys?"

"I don't know who he works for, but you know who I'm talking about."

"That's not true. We don't kill people, Doug. Whoever did this is of this world," Roosevelt said, sadly shaking his head.

"Bullshit! I saw the sonofabtich. I've seen those eyes before, and I know who he is."

"You can identify him?"

"Yeah, he had dead eyes, just like that hollow-eyed death angel I saw in Vegas," I said.

"You have very little faith in your Heavenly Father, don't you? Do you honestly believe that God would send in a death Angel?" Roosevelt asked, a look of deep disappointment on his already sad face.

"I didn't say I blamed it on God, but I can blame it on some piss head bureaucrat up there who handles the roll call, or whatever you want to call it. Somebody up there decides when and how people die, don't they?" I asked.

"No."

"If they don't, then who does?"

"Most of that is decided down here. No one at the Central Office makes those decisions. Sometimes we're aware of the situation, know that someone will die, but we don't order it. It just happens, that's all. Everyone down here isn't under protection, for one reason or another, and bad things happen to people. Death is a natural thing, whether or not you want to believe it."

"Hey, that crock of crap won't work on me. I've been busting my ass for fifteen years trying to keep this goofy sonofabitch alive. If the Central Office didn't make life and death decisions, I wouldn't be here," I said, almost shouting by then.

"I didn't say we didn't make life decisions. That's what custodianship is all about. You're here to keep him alive and as safe as possible. I know of no plans to end your custody of Woody. You're all worked up about something that doesn't exist. You've fabricated this wild scenario in your mind, and that has led you into making some critical mistakes lately. You really messed up, Doug."

"What did I do that was so bad? So I played a few ornery tricks on folks. So what? Every one of them deserved it, one way or the other."

"What about the innocent people you've hurt?"

"What innocent people?"

"What about those people in the bar where you started the fight? What about the people you stole from?" he asked, waving his arms around.

"They had it coming," I said.

"That's not for you to decide. You've stepped way out of bounds this time. Stretching the rules to take care of Woody, even though they were sometimes flagrant violations, were understandable if not excusable. But what you've done this time is totally inexcusable. You hurt people," he said.

"Piss on them. I've had it up to here with all your bureaucratic bullshit, and why the hell were you trying so hard to get me away from here? What about the set-up with Phoebe in Minnesota, huh? That was pretty low, Roosevelt. You use people, and that's a lot worse than what I did."

"I sent you to Minnesota because you were tired and needed some rest, and for no other reason."

"I don't believe you."

"What can I do to convince you?"

"You can't say a thing to me that will change my mind," I said, then sat back down at the foot of Woody's bed.

"I'm very sorry to hear that because it leaves me little choice about what to do with this situation. I'm pulling you off this assignment. It will take me a few days to make ready a replacement for you, and I'm ordering you to stand by to be transported elsewhere," Roosevelt said sadly.

"Do what you have to. I'll do the same," I mumbled.

"What does that mean?"

I didn't answer, and after staring at me for a few seconds, Roosevelt turned and walked out of the room. Within minutes, though, I started wishing he'd stayed around. He was such a by-the-booker that he would've learned something about believing everything the Central Office told him. Had he stayed, he would've seen his first shadowloper. Darkness had fallen outside, and the lights inside the intensive care room had been lowered for the night. A light over Woody's bed kept that part of the room fairly well lit, but the corners had gone dark and shadowy. I was hunkered down in a corner on the far side of the room. The long day had started catching up with me, and I lowered my head to my knees to rest for just a few minutes. Maybe I dozed for a short while, but something caused me to look up at an opportune time.

Death angels had been on my mind so much over the past few days that I'd pushed shadowlopers aside, and when I saw this thing moving in a corner to the left of Woody's bed, I thought the death angel had come to finish his business. I went rigid for a moment as every nerve in my body came alive, and then I suddenly realized that I was not looking at a death angel. This thing was dark and almost formless, not an old man with white hair and dead eyes, and it hovered near Woody's bed like a thick fog. It moved a bit closer, and that's when I went for it. I'd gone to school on the first two shadowlopers I encountered and had noticed that they'd moved from left to right. I knew it would move fast, too fast for me to charge it and have any chance of grabbing it, so I drew a bead toward the right of it and lurched forward.

My luck had been poor for a while, and maybe I was due for a change, but whatever, I got lucky and plowed right into the thing. When I knew for sure that I'd hit something solid, I clamped down and held on for dear life. I had no idea what I'd caught until I pinned it under my knees and started wrestling it around with it. The fog around it must've been an ambience of some kind because my hands went right through it, and in the light of the open room, my shadowloper turned out to be just a man. I rolled him over, and what I saw nearly shook me out of my boots. The shadowloper I'd captured was none other than Don Leland, Woody's cowboy friend who'd died when the tractor motor fell on him some eight years before.

"You cowardly sonofabitch," I shouted, shaking him as hard as I could. "What are you doing slinking around here? Are you trying to steal my mark's soul, you chickenshit bastard?"

He tried to speak but made no sound at all, but I could see his lips making the word, "I'm sorry." He kept mouthing those words to me until I loosened my grip and little. I suddenly felt compassion for him. This had been a good man, not some sleazy bastard that had somehow evaded the clutches of demons from hell. This guy should've been somewhere in the spirit world with me, not ghosting around in a world of shadows. He kept mouthing the words, and I started wondering if he'd been able to hear exactly what I'd said. Maybe the world of shadows cut him off from the sounds of my world. I pulled him up to where his face and mine were close because I wanted him to understand exactly what I said next.

"You can't go on this way, Don. You've got to find the courage to step into the spirit world with the rest of us. This is not a bad place, and you belong on this side with us. If you care anything at all about Woody, you'll go away and leave this to me," I said and then turned him loose. He stared back at me for a few moments, then nodded as if he understood. His face suddenly disappeared back into the fog, and in the bat of an eye, it whisked from the room.

I stayed with Woody for the rest of the day and most of the following night. By that time, Wanda and the kids were back in Forest City. Woody was conscious by the morning after the shooting, but he was in no condition to see anyone other than close family. His mother had been called and was on a plane headed for Kansas. Wanda hovered over him, sniffling and rubbing his face, but Woody didn't seem to care who was around. His children were brought to the hospital that afternoon. They stared at him through a glass petition, but when Wanda turned his head toward them, he closed his eyes.

I made a quick run back to the trailer when Wanda showed up. She looked distraught but in control, so I felt comfortable leaving the hospital for a while. After my confrontation with Roosevelt, I also felt comfortable with the idea that the death angel wouldn't come to the hospital to finish his dirty work. If I'd accomplished nothing else, I thought maybe I'd put a kink in the death angel operation. At the trailer, I found Dewey still in dreamland, but Winston said he'd been moving around and groaning some. Winston said that Roosevelt had predicted about three bad days for Dewey, then a rapid recovery. His color had improved a bit. I felt torn between staying and leaving, but I couldn't stick around long. Apprehension got the best of me, I went straight back to the hospital and took up guard at the foot of Woody's bed. Stegnor came by to see him and then stood in the hall talking with Wanda for a while. I followed them out to hear what was said.

Stegnor told Wanda that she wanted to help Woody, and then she said something that nearly knocked me a double loop. She's said she knew Woody could recover from alcoholism because she had done it herself. She used the term 'recovering alcoholic' when she described her current status. I'd heard the term before, but an alcoholic was a drunk to me, and a sober alcoholic was a recovering drunk. A drunk is still a drunk, any way you turn them. I thought I knew a drunk when I saw one, but I never would've guessed Ellen Stegnor as having been one. She pointed out that other people were concerned about Woody, then pulled a letter from her pocket and handed it to Wanda. She started bawling as she read, so I moved in behind her and took a look. It went like this:

Dear Dr. Stegnor:

I am writing out of concern for Dr. Woodrow Pickens, one of your faculty members. Dr. Pickens is a very ill man, and he needs help desperately. He is suffering from alcoholism, and I fear that his illness has become a life threatening situation. It is my hope that you can intervene, somehow, and help him recover.

Dr. Pickens is a wonderfully gifted and intelligent person who has much to offer his fellow man. Sadly, he cannot live up to his potential due to his difficulties with alcohol. He respects you and is a devoted employee that you can ill afford to lose. It is in your best interests, as well as his, for him to get help for his sickness. Time is of the essence, so please, act quickly. Should much more time pass, I fear that he will be lost. I'm sure you will know what to do.

Sincerely,
A devoted friend.

I knew at first glance that the handwriting belonged to none other than Dewey Davisson. Bless his heart, Dewey had stood it as long as he could, and given his gentle and considerate nature, he had written a letter to the one living person he knew could help. Wanda graciously accepted her support and then went back into Woody's room.

I've never thought of myself as sentimental, but seeing Wanda standing beside her fallen husband, holding his hand and with tears streaking down her face, got to me. I had to knock a few tears off my own cheeks, and it started me thinking about what Roosevelt had said. My anger was beginning to fade, but my blue mood deepened with feelings of loneliness and despair. What's it all coming to, I asked myself. Roosevelt would hold true to his word and ship me off somewhere, and where would I be sent next? Phoebe was gone, and I might never see her again. My partner was lying in the trailer with a hole in his chest, my mark had been shot down like a mad dog, and some killer angel might still be stalking him. Furthermore, I had the feeling that Woody didn't care anymore. I was the only thing left between him and the forces that wanted to do him in, and my confidence level had fallen to where a snail could've crawled over it. Everything had gone to hell in a hand basket. Life on earth was screwed up, and life in the hereafter wasn't looking any better. Don Leland may have lurked in the shadows long enough to have seen that, and given his options between shadowloping and doing what I'd been doing, I wasn't sure he wasn't one up on me.

I've never been the kind of guy to get down, but the deteriorating situation had finally beaten me to my knees. I've always tried to follow my mama's advice, which was to keep my head up. "Don't ever let them catch you looking at your feet," she'd say. Something else she used to say was, "Remember who you are." I never really understood what she meant by that, but I always took it to say, "Hey, boy, you're OK, and you'll come out fine." That simple philosophy of life had always worked pretty good for me before, but this wasn't life. I was dead now, and this afterlife hadn't turned out to be what I'd expected. So the same old question kept coming up. What's the use? What's the fucking use?

CHAPTER 41
The Beaten Path

Two days passed and no one came to transport me to another job. Roosevelt had said that making arrangements might take some time, but I figured he'd stir around and get it done as soon as possible. Virgil Jacks was the big boss in my region, and the thought had crossed my mind several times that I should go to Cheyenne and have it out with him about this transfer business. Virgil could make Roosevelt sit on a block of ice if he wanted to, but I couldn't make up my mind as to whether or not he'd want to. Virgil liked me, but I'd screwed up bad this time. He wasn't likely to overrule Roosevelt's decision to yank me. I'd seen promotions ruin several good men, and maybe the Central Office had already indoctrinated him the way they had Roosevelt.

Woody took a turn for the worse two days after surgery, and the doctors seemed a little baffled by it. He'd been able to speak for a couple of days, but he spent most of his time drifting in and out of consciousness. Wanda stayed by his bedside constantly, and Duncan was there most of the time. Other than them and Woody's mother, who'd now arrived from Missouri, only a few visitors drifted by. I sat in a corner and watched and waited on the death angel to come, feeling lower each passing hour.

I left the hospital briefly to check on Dewey. He could talk a little by then, and he understood everything I told him. He broke into a big smile at the news that Woody was still alive, and I couldn't bring myself to tell him that he was just barely alive. Winston was making a hand at taking care of him, and I didn't spend much time at the trailer. I hurried back to the hospital and took up my watch again. I'd hang tight and try to stay alert. Doctors had been telling Wanda that Woody would make it. I'd been around a lot of death, and I kept telling myself that he wouldn't. If he died, though, I was determined that a death angel wouldn't take him.

A nurse had just come in to check Woody, and that's when I saw someone move into the room in a corner across from me. He had white hair, and I immediately starting thinking death angel. But then he moved into the light, and I saw that the intruder was Virgil

Jacks. I probably would've recognized him earlier if he'd been wearing his normal attire of hats, jeans, and boots. He still had the jeans and boots, but the hat was missing. He looked down at Woody, then at me.

"I was expecting Roosevelt," I said.

"Roosevelt won't be coming, boy. He's been kinda out of sorts lately, and the Central Office moved him. I gave him a little pep talk, then sent him on his way to Alabama," he said.

"They transferred him to Alabama?"

"Yeah, and that's good, I reckon. He's still gonna be a supervisor, but it's a smaller district, and he probably won't have no pain in the ass custodians like you working for him," he said, scowling at me.

"They didn't transfer him on account of me, did they?"

"Naw, but you helped some. They shouldn't have ever had him in Kansas in the first place. He had a hard time getting a handle on the way folks think and act out here. Anyway, you've seen the last of him. A new supervisor will be coming in here before long, and I'm taking up slack till then. That's why I'm here," he said.

"I've been thinking about trying to get in touch with you, but Dewey's shot up bad, and I didn't want to leave Woody. He's not looking good, and I'm still worried about that dead-eyed sonofabitch coming back to finish him off," I said.

"Roosevelt told me all about this stupid notion you've got about some death angel trying to do in your mark. You've made a helluva big mess over it, and for no reason at all. You can forget the death angel business. They don't exist."

"You're starting to sound like Roosevelt. I know they exist because I saw the shooter. He was the same hollow-eyed bastard I saw in Vegas some time back, and I know that's who did it," I said, trying hard to meet Virgil's gaze.

"I believe you saw something, but Roosevelt knew for sure that you hadn't seen no death angel."

"Yeah, but Roosevelt didn't think I'd seen a shadowloper, but I did. I even caught the bastard," I said.

"You really caught him?"

"I sure did. He came sneaking around here and I got lucky and took him down. I know the guy. He used to be one of Woody's friends. His name is Don Leland, and he got killed about eight years ago. He was a good man, and him ending up a shadowloper threw me for a loop. I gave him a good cussing and told him to get gone to wherever he's supposed to go.

"That don't surprise me. Truth be known, the feller used to be a custodian like you."

"You've got to be kidding me," I said.

"Naw, he probably had a bad mark and just couldn't toughen up to it. I probably should've told you that earlier, but I figured there was no need in bothering you with the particulars."

"What particulars?"

"Like I told you before, there's some that think shadowlopers are the souls of sleazy sonsabitches that somehow escaped hell, but that's probably wrong. Do you really think anybody's gonna escape the clutches of hell? That ain't the way it works. These shadowlopers escaped from our side, and they've got no place to go except where they are now. That's the big reason the Central Office don't say much official about them, 'cause it's embarrassing to admit to having somebody who'd want to escape from this side," he said, looking grave.

"How do you know that?"

"Well, I don't know it for an absolute fact, but it just makes sense. A feller dies and comes here, and they assign him to something like custodian duties, and he cain't hack it. He gets a bad case of rabbit blood, and before you know it, he's gone. It don't happen often, but it happens. I've run across a few fellers who've done duty trying to catch 'em. The Central Office don't advertize it, but they've got some trackers out trying to bring 'em in," he said.

"All that may be true, but it still doesn't mean that I'm wrong about the death angel. I saw him, and I know what I saw," I said.

"You need to come with me for a while. You're worn down to where you're not thinking straight, and I can put some things in perspective for you. We won't be gone long," he said, motioning for me to follow.

Since Virgil had flown down to Kansas in his airplane, we had to take my car. I had no idea where we were headed, so I just acted as chauffeur while he directed. We proceeded west of town by some twenty miles and then turned onto a farm to market road. Several miles down the road, he motioned me down a primitive track that dead ended at a ranch house. Cattle grazed pastures nearly, and I remember thinking that whoever owned the ranch must've been pretty well off. When we got to the house and pulled around back, I was shocked to see a Caddy sedan. C.W. Laney's car was parked beside it.

"What the . . . ."

"Let's go inside," Virgil said, nudging me with his elbow.

Once inside, we went into a large den where a white haired man sat staring into the flames of the fireplace. I moved around to get a closer look at his face. "That's him. That's the bastard who shot Woody."

"Yes, I know," Virgil said calmly, just as C.W. walked in holding her coat. She asked the man if he was ready to go, and he nodded. His face was blank, like his eyes, and he moved slowly as he got up and put on his coat.

"What's going on?" I asked.

"He's burdened, this man, with the sin of trying to take another man's life. He knew about Woody and C.W., and that's why he shot him. But now he cain't live with it, so he's going to town to turn himself in."

"But . . . but . . . I thought he was a . . . ."

"Yes, I know - a death Angel. But he's just a man, Salty. He couldn't stand the thought of losing his wife, so he took that hunting rifle and used it," Virgil said, pointing toward a rifle hanging on the wall.

The sudden realization that I'd been totally wrong about the death Angel business hit me like a thunderbolt. I couldn't say a word, but I don't think Virgil expected much of a response from me. He motioned for me to follow, and we walked back to the Chevy and got in. We drove back to town in silence, but I'd recovered enough by then to start wanting some answers. Once at the parking lot back at the hospital, I turned him and asked, "Where do we go from here?"

"The beaten path, that's where," Virgil said without hesitation.

"I don't get it."

"Yeah, I know you don't, and that's been your problem all along. I'm starting to see how you got so involved in your mark's problems. Like him, you think you're one of God's special creations -

that cain't nobody else in the universe compete with you. You think you're so unique that what works for everybody else cain't possibly work for you. Well, I've got news for you, Salty. You might be some different from other folks, but you got made from the same mud all the rest of us come from. You've got it figured where God must've picked up a handful of really good clay to make some special folks, and then a handful of wet sand to make others, or even a handful of shit for some. That ain't the way it works."

"I didn't say it was."

"Naw, you didn't say it, but you act like it. You're not the first person who figured there had to be another path for him, that the beaten path walked by most folks just wouldn't fit his feet one way or another. I ain't got a thing against somebody wanting to venture off the beaten path every now'n then, but all of us need to remember where it is. If you don't, you're sure as hell gonna get your ass lost, and that's just about what's happened to you," he said.

"If you're getting around to reading me the book on how I ought to do my job, you can cut the crap and get straight to it," I said.

"What I'm talking about don't have shit to do with the book. What it has to do with is learning something about getting along, and the rules for doing that don't come from no book. They're rules that have been learned and passed along for centuries by people. They're not written in stone, but if you hold your head up and listen hard, you can almost hear 'em in everything around you. You learn to notice 'em by paying attention to what's going on around you. That beaten path got laid by people who had some notion about where they wanted to go, and because they paid attention and learned something in the process, others followed it."

"Maybe I didn't want to go the same place all of them were going. What's so damn bad about that?"

"Nothing, except a feller ought not break ranks unless he's got some idea of why he's doing it. Anybody who thinks he's got the forthwith to find a better way of getting there, then let him have at it. But a feller that wanders off the path just for the sake of wandering is dangerous to the whole bunch of us. Being an individualist is fine, but you sure need to know your business to do it that way. It might not be a fair judgment on my part, but based on what I know about you so far, you're wandering around out in the boonies somewhere with no idea of where you're heading."

He had me. I was lost and knew it, but I still wasn't humble enough to accept the beaten path. "So, what happens to folks like me who can't walk the beaten path? What happens to people like Woody?"

"Well, hell, boy! That ought to be as plain as the nose on your face. You're mark is shot all to hell, and you ain't getting along so well yourself. The both of you have got to learn to deal with the beaten path. You cain't go on thinking you're so different from the pack that what works for them won't work for you."

"But what if it doesn't work for me?"

"Everybody's always using mountains as examples of obstacles in life, so I'll do the same. Let's say that you need to get over a mountain, and there's only one road that goes over it. Let's also say that you don't know the mountain, and you know even less about road building, but the road looks to you like some idiot built it. Maybe it's crooked and winding and all sorts of things, but it's pretty well traveled 'cause it's the only road to the other side. You decide to take out on your own and cut a new trail that will go straight up one side and straight down the other. You strike out cutting this new trail, and somewhere up the mountain you start realizing that the old boy that built the road ain't quite as stupid as you figured he was. You learn, for instance, that making a road winding and crooked is a smart thing when you're trying to go up a steep mountain 'cause it's just plumb stupid to cut one that's too steep for anybody to climb. Are you still with me?" he asked.

"Yeah, so far."

"There's always been mountains around that had to be passed over, and folks figured out all sorts of ways of doing that. They used whatever they had to do that, like just walking or riding a beast of some kind. The pioneers coming west had to get over the Rocky Mountains in wagons, and a wagon cain't go just any old place. They sought out the best route, and then cut themselves a path. All those famous passes are now named after those folks, and millions of other folks, many of 'em folks who came a century later, are still using the same routes through the mountains. Pretty soon other vehicles came along, like cars and such, and the old beaten paths got made better and changed some. Airplanes can even fly over the mountains now, but that don't mean the old paths completely lost its use 'cause even planes need something to navigate by. Any good explorer looks for the signs of earlier explorers."

"I can understand that, but . . . "

"Just hold on till I'm finished. I'm on a roll here, boy, so let me get finished. Here's the upshot of the whole thing. A feller that heads off on his own needs to have some idea of where he's going. You might not figure that out unless you do like wild critters and sniff the breeze, keep your head up and pay attention . . . and if you do, before long you see that your new path and the old road start crossing one another. That's more'n likely gonna happen, since you're probably going straight up, and the old road's winding around the mountain several times on its way up. Now, you might not want to jump right back on the old road the first time you cross it, but after you've about beat yourself to death trying to make a new path through all them rocks and thick timber and all, you'll start liking that old road lots better.

"That might be true, but just because everybody follows the old road all the time doesn't mean I have to. The old road might be a proven way of getting over the mountain, but if nobody ever tried finding a new way, then we'd be stuck with the old road forever," I said.

"That's right, but anybody cutting a new road needs to remember where the old road is. That's the most important thing, and you cain't get away from that. When a new road cutter finds the going too tough to handle, he ought to take advantage of the old road when the occasion presents itself. All new roads don't have to be completely different from the ones that came before 'em. Let me ask you something. When you cut a road over a mountain, which side is most important, the going up side, or the going down side?" Virgil asked.

"The going down side is."

"That's right, and do you know why?"

"Yeah, because you can see where you're going from there. The view is better, and you can pick out a better route."

"Right again, and do you think the view looks any different to you than it did to the first road cutter who went to the top of that mountain?" he asked, squinting hard at me.

"Not much, I reckon," I said.

"Then, there you go. Sooner or later, you're likely to join up with the beaten path anyway. Folks who went over the mountain before you more'n likely found the best way down a long time ago, and only a fool would start cutting a new path from there. He might get lucky and find one, but the chances of him doing it are real remote. The time comes when all of us need to trust the judgment of folks who came before us. Everybody cain't be an explorer or road builder."

"I see what you're getting at, but I just can't do that. I can't just accept the wisdom of others because they got there before me, and I sure as hell can't go the same road everybody else takes. Woody can't do it either. Beaten paths are for folks who live their lives in moderation, and the two of us aren't built that way. I can't speak for him, but I don't think I could ever learn to accept moderation," I said.

Virgil took a deep breath and then exhaled slowly as he thought of what to say next. "There's enough real mountains in life without going around creating imaginary ones. Maybe the first thing you ought to ask yourself is whether or not what you're facing is a real mountain or just a make believe one. I never was a well educated feller, but I did some reading one time about planets and how they circle around their sun. Planets cut a sorta lopsided orbit around the sun, I reckon. The book called the longest distance in the orbit away from the sun the aphelion stage. The closest distance was called the perihelion stage. The planet cools some at the aphelion stage and heats up at the perihelion stage. People might be like planets in that they're either aphelion types or perihelion types. Some like it up close to the heat, and some like it out where it's cold."

"So, you're saying I'm an aphelion person."

"Naw, you're just the opposite, and that's part of the problem. A aphelion person would be the kind that wouldn't get involved. They'd be observers, but they wouldn't want to be part of the action. The danger with being that way is that a feller could freeze staying that far off the fire, and to survive, he has to move in closer every now and then. A perihelion kinda feller wants to be right up next to the fire. He wants to be involved in the action. The trouble here is that he just might burn his ass up, and since he cain't stand it there for long at one time, he has to run back from the fire every now and then."

"But what about the beaten path thing? Neither one of these folks, either aphelion or perihelion, is moderate enough to go the beaten path," I said.

"You right about that, they're not. Most folks figure out that it's a helluva lot easier to find the warm zone and stay there. Their orbits may vary a tad from time to time, but they stay pretty much to the path. They don't have to look for it either because it's already there waiting for them. It's the pain in the ass special folks that spend all their time running in and out of the fire," he said, smiling for the first time in quite a while.

"Yeah, but we're right back where we started. If I can't live in the warm zone, or stay with the beaten path, then what am I supposed to do?"

"Well, just like a feller needs to learn something when he journeys off the beaten path, he needs to do the same on your trips to and from the fire. I'm not saying that you'll sooner or later learn to live in the warm zone with most other folks, but you'll learn how to get along with 'em. I wouldn't want to make a smooth orbit or beaten path kinda feller out of you, Salty. You'll always be a guy who has to climb the up side of a mountain on your own, regardless of how hard it is. There can be an advantage in doing it that way 'cause lessons learned hard might stick better'n lessons learned easy, but you've got to learn something. Otherwise, you just wasted the effort. I've always been a lonesome climber myself, but I have learned a few things about knowing when to join up with moderate folks on the beaten path."

"All right, boss man. What do I do next?"

"Next, you need to talk to somebody who knows a lot more about what's going on that I do. We need to take a little trip."

"But what about Woody? I can't run out on him now. I've been looking after him for a long time, and the least I can do is stick around until he . . ."

"Till he dies? Is that what you're planning on?"

"I don't want him to die, but he doesn't want to live. To be truthful with you, if I were in his shoes, I don't know whether I'd want to live either," I said.

"So, what do you plan on doing for him, sit in a corner and watch him die? What happens now is up to him. He'll more'n likely still be here when you get back. It ain't an easy trip, but you may get the answers you're looking for."

CHAPTER 42
Tender

I went inside and took a look at Woody, then stood around long enough to hear some medical folks talking about his condition. His vital signs were good, they said, but he seemed to be in a depressed state that was hampering his recovery. The semester break was coming to a close, and a few more friends had trickled in. From there I dropped by to see Dewey, and was surprised to find him sitting up in bed. He still had a big bandage around his chest, but he smiled when I walked into the trailer with Virgil. "Damn, Dewey! You're looking like a bull's eye on a practice target," I said.

"Yes, I suppose I do," he said, looking down at himself.

"Looks like Winston did a good job of fixing you up. It's a good thing I remembered to let him out of the trunk, huh?"

"I'm so embarrassed about that. My only excuse is that I was under the influence of a drug," he said, ducking his head and looking sad.

I turned and saw the perplexed look on Virgil's face and felt he needed some enlightenment. "Our mark and some friends decided to get smoked up on marijuana, and we breathed too much of it. We decided that Winston was a death angel and locked him in the trunk of the Chevy," I said.

"I didn't decide anything. I was too stoned to think," Dewey said.

"That's the wildest story I ever heard," Virgil said, then added, "No wonder Roosevelt transferred out of here."

"Roosevelt transferred?" Dewey asked, looking shocked.

"Yep, gone to Alabama. He'd been asking for a new assignment for a long time, and the Central Office finally came through for him," Virgil said.

"Who will be our supervisor now?" Dewey asked.

"A gal named Sophie Roy. She's a corker, that one. Used to be a helluva stage performer back in the thirties. You'll like her."

"And what about a partner? Since Roosevelt is gone, does that mean Doug gets to stay?" Dewey asked.

"Naw, he's through here. Winston will stay for a while, and then we'll see what happens next."

"Is he leaving now?"

"Not for a while. He's going on a little trip with me, and then he'll be around for a few days. You boys will have plenty of time for goodbyes," Virgil said.

Winston drove us to the airport after a brief visit, and I spent the next few minutes trying to prepare myself for another ragged flight with Virgil. I still had no idea where we were going, but a trip over to Cottonwood with Virgil flying the aircraft would've made me nervous enough to sweat blood. My mood had lightened somewhat, though, and that made the thought of the flight a bit more tolerable. We jumped into his old rig and taxied down the runway. The take-off went smoothly, and he leveled it out at about five thousand feet and cruised for a little while. I was sitting in the cockpit behind him, and I saw him lean forward like he was adjusting something, and then we suddenly took off like a rocket. I'd been keeping an eye on the ground below, but that started going by so fast that it made me dizzy, and I had to close my eyes for a few minutes. When I opened them again, we were headed in a slightly upward direction at such a speed that everything around me blurred into bright streaks of color that seemed to swirl and form into a tunnel directly in front of us, and when we flew into the mouth of the tunnel, there was a sudden explosion of brilliant white. Seconds later, the tunneling streaks of color reappeared, and then clouds, and finally clear blue skies again.

I looked down, and the ground was coming up fast, and the scenery had changed dramatically. Instead of the flat prairielands of western Kansas, we were flying over rolling hill country. Virgil banked the plane to one side and headed toward a valley dotted with small lakes and grassy pastures. I saw no fences, telephone poles, highways, or any other marks of man except for a few small residences. Just at the mouth of the valley, a small village popped into view, and Virgil set the plane down smoothly on a dirt road just outside of town.

I stepped out of the airplane and looked around. The terrain around us looked a lot like central Texas, except more hilly and with less trees. The land was dotted with occasional patches of trees and low-lying brush, and farm houses. "Where are we?" I asked, looking around at the people who'd walked to the edge of the township to gawk at us.

"It's just a town," Virgil said.

"Where? When?"

"None of that matters. You'll see soon enough."

Virgil's airplane definitely stood out in the small village, mostly because it was the only one there. The only other things around with wheels were carts and wagons. The town, as best I could tell, looked pre-twentieth century, but dating it was impossible. In some ways, it reminded me of towns I'd seen in New Mexico, but the countryside was much too green for that. Most of the houses and buildings were made of stone or wood - Spartan but attractive. Children played on the square, and old people sat around small tables playing a game of some kind. Other people were busy doing one chore or another. Everyone smiled, and no one seemed surprised or concerned that an airplane had just landed carrying two crusty looking cowboys.

We walked to the square. Virgil stopped briefly to visit with a few people, and then we went directly to a general mercantile style store just across the way. A pleasant gray haired woman there came forward and asked what we needed. Virgil said he wanted two days provisions for hiking in the hills, and then he smiled and said, "This feller's gonna take a little walk up to Tender's place." The woman smiled graciously, nodded, and then retreated to fetch the provisions.

"Who is Tender?" I asked.

"He's the feller I brought you to see."

"Are we going to see him now?"

"Naw, you're going, but I'm staying here. Like I said before, it ain't an easy trip, and I've made the walk before. You'll be going it alone, but you ought to be used to that. It's uphill all the way," he said, then grinned.

"What are you going to do? You're not going to leave, are you?"

"I'm staying right here in the village. Best food in the whole universe, and the fishing is even better. Besides, these folks are fun to visit with. They'll take good care of me, and I'll be right here when you get back."

"But I don't know where this guy lives. How am I supposed to find him?"

"Keep your head up and sniff the wind now and then. Use your wits, and you'll go right to him. Damn, boy! You're a Texan. You know how to track, don't you?" he asked, cocking his head sideways.

"Yeah, but it's been a while. The last tracking I did was in Nam, and I was looking to kill somebody then. What do I do when I find this man?" I asked.

"Well, you cain't kill him, that's for sure. He is a good listener, though. Maybe you ought to tell him what's on your mind. Maybe you could ask him a few questions fellers like me cain't answer for you."

"I'll do that," I said.

Virgil gave the lady in the mercantile a small bag of something as exchange for the provisions. "What was that?" I asked.

"Seeds," he said, smiling broadly.

"You traded a little bag of seeds for all this?" I asked, looking down at the pile of stuff at my feet. In addition to a new pair of hiking boots, I had a backpack and enough food for two days.

"These folks don't care about money. I gave her some seeds for vegetables, and since they're mostly gardeners, they appreciate it. They've got all kinds of plants here, but not much southwestern stuff."

"What'd you give her?"

"Rattlesnake beans."

"You're shitting me. You gave the gal a pile of rattlesnake beans for all this stuff? You know, Virgil, I'm starting to think there's more devil in you than there is angel," I said.

"She's happy, so why should you be disappointed? I didn't cheat the gal. It's all in the value you put on things. Rattlesnake beans to me and you don't amount to . . . well, to . . . anything more'n a hill of beans. But to her, they're like gold. I don't feel bad about giving 'em to her 'cause I gave 'em with an open heart, and that's the way she took 'em. Cheating somebody's a matter of intent, and my offer was an honest one. You oughta keep that in mind, maybe."

"What's that supposed to mean?"

"I'd tell you, but you'll be learning what it means fast enough. Meeting Tender will teach you that," he said, looking cock sure of himself.

"I get it. You're telling me not to try to peddle Tender a line of shit, right?" I asked.

"Well, kinda. I don't need to tell you that, though. Nobody with good sense lies to the feller. He brings out the best in folks, and that's honesty. Folks like you feel like they've got to give more than they're able to give. I'll bet you were the shits to trade presents with come Christmas time," he said.

"Come to think of it, I probably was."

"Yeah, you had to be Salty Anderson, big time rodeo cowboy. You probably bought big 'cause you felt like just Salty Anderson wasn't enough of a gift. Did you ever have a dog that you loved?"

"Yeah, I had several."

"Were they smart dogs, or special dogs?"

"Not really. They were just dogs."

"There you go. You loved the dog 'cause it gave you the only thing it had to give, and that was the love of a dog. That's the most honest gift that can be given, and if a feller could learn to do the same, just give what he had to give in an open hearted way, he'd be a helluva lot better off. I'm done talking now. Like I said, you'll be meeting up with Tender pretty quick, and I'm just wasting my time with all this palaver."

"What if I can't find him?"

"Aw, hell, you'll find him. I'll tell you this much. He lives on top of a big mesa where the view's the best around. It ain't necessarily the highest spot of ground you'll cross, but it's the most fitting for a feller like him. And, remember to keep your nose in the wind. If you ain't back in a few days, I'll figure the wolves ate you up, and I'll go on back by myself," he said, then turned and walked back toward the square.

"What wolves? Where the hell are you going?"

"Back to the mercantile. I kinda like that gal, and I ain't run out of rattlesnake beans yet," he said, without looking back.

"What wolves?" I asked again. He didn't answer.

I sat down just outside of the village and put on my new hiking boots. I hated the notion of wearing new boots and almost left them behind, but cowboy boots aren't made for long hikes, and I didn't know what to expect. I tossed my old boots into the cockpit of the plane, strapped on my backpack, and headed down the valley toward the distant hills. I've never seen a more beautiful valley. Occasionally I'd walk past a tidy homestead of rock or stucco, and only around these settlements did I find plowed fields. Mostly, I walked through grasslands. I'd worn a jacket on the flight, and that turned out to be a blessing. By the time I'd walked out the valley, the sun had started going down, and the temperature dropped dramatically.

Where the valley narrowed to a wide arroyo, I started following a stream upward. I stopped long enough to watch foot long trout play in the shallows along the shoals, and several large deer like animals came up to the stream and drank. I could see clouds gathering in the hills above me, and I decided to trek on until it got too dark to keep climbing. Just as the first few drops of rain started falling, I came upon an abandoned shack near the stream. It looked like the line camp shacks I'd seen on the mountain ranches of the southwest, but this particular hut must've been a herder's abode. The roof leaked some, but it kept me dry throughout the night. I went to sleep listening to wolves howling out in the hills. Morning came around, cold and damp from the night's rainfall. I built a fire just outside the shack and made coffee long before the sun had risen. After drinking several cups and eating a hard roll, I headed on up the trail toward the high country.

It rained again that morning, and my hiking boots were starting to come in handy. They fit well, and I had no problems with them. The country turned incredibly rocky at one point, and the going got difficult. In a two hour span of time, I probably made it no further than half a mile, and that's when Virgil's words started coming back to me. "Keep your nose in the wind," he had said to me. "Don't forget the beaten path," he'd said. But I'd seen no beaten path since I'd been following the stream upward, and the only thing I smelled in the air was the strong scent of evergreens. If anything, I'd just about run out of a path to follow. I stopped, ate lunch, and thought it all over.

Tender lived on a mesa, Virgil had said, but all I'd seen were hills. Where he lived fit the man, he'd said. *Tender*. What kind of name is that, I asked myself. I tried thinking in terms of legal tender, like in money, but that didn't make any sense at all. *Tender*. Could mean sensitive or considerate or loving, but that didn't make much more sense. *Tender*. Sounds like it might mean to tend to something, or to look after. That's it. This man must be a shepherd. That makes sense because he lives in the hills. He could be some kind of sensitive, like a guru of some kind, but this fellow was probably just a herder of sheep or some other critter. Virgil had sent me trekking into the wilderness looking for a sheep herder. The thought of turning around and going back crossed my mind, but I'd come too far for that. Besides, my curiosity was starting to get the best of me.

I stuck to my course of following the stream until it narrowed down to a mere trickle, and then I started looking for trails. I also stopped occasionally and sniffed the wind, and I paid attention to every sign that looked like it could've been made by a man. I headed for the tallest hill I could find, and I went the direct route - straight toward it. Doing that took me through some rough country with heavy brush and treacherous rock outcroppings, but I kept at it until I got there. Once there, I saw the flat-topped mesa Virgil had spoken of, but I saw no path of any kind. The mesa was shaped like an oval table with one end being covered with a heavy growth of evergreens. I headed toward the end with the trees.

I located a path - narrow but apparently occasionally traveled. I saw no human tracks anywhere along the trail, and the hills I went through on the way to the mesa presented less walking problems than I'd encountered on the way up. I moved quickly through low-lying shrubs of trees that looked like scrub oaks. Willows grew around the several small lakes I passed, and I saw an abundance of animals of all sorts. Beaver built dams along the creeks, and hoofed animals of all sorts darted across the narrow path in front of me. Eagles and hawks and other birds soared above me or darted from tree to tree, and all sorts of small critters like rabbits and ground squirrels scurried around. A large cat, perhaps a puma, slinked away from a rock he'd been sunning on, and I saw wolves occasionally.

By late afternoon, I'd reached a hilltop directly overlooking the mesa. I could now see animals grazing the flatlands of the mesa top, and they appeared to me to be nothing more than domesticated goats. Not only had Virgil sent me all the way here to talk to a shepherd, he'd sent me to talk to a goat herder. I still couldn't see a house of any kind, so I held my head high and sniffed again. I smelled smoke. Someone had a fire going, so I started looking for the smoke itself. Must be in the trees, I decided, and headed toward them. Within an hour, I was walking toward a stand of what looked to be fir trees, and that's when I spotted the small settlement. It consisted of a small house and barn and several sheds, all made of rock with wood shingled roofs. A dog suddenly started barking, and a man turned to look toward me. In the distance, the wolves had started howling again.

I kept at my pace, even when the three border collie dogs ran out to meet me. I was sore and scratched all to hell from climbing through the brush, and dogs weren't about to keep me from my destination. At the last minute, they lowered their hackles and started wagging their tails. The man stood his ground and waited patiently, smiling and carefully sizing me up as I approached. "You've come far. How was your trip?" he asked, offering a calloused hand in greeting.

"Not bad," I said, taking his hand.

"Come to the house. We'll eat and have something to drink. Are you a coffee drinker?" he asked.

"Yeah, I'm a coffee lover. Been drinking it since I was a kid," I said.

"Well, I've only come to appreciate it in more recent years, but I too enjoy it. I developed a taste for it after I left where you come from," he said, smiling graciously.

"You know where I'm from?"

"You're language betrays you," he said.

"Can I help with chores?" I asked, noticing that he'd been chopping wood when I arrived.

"There's not much to do. I need to feed the chickens and livestock out back, but that's about it. But you may help, if you like," he said, gently waving his hand in the direction of the sheds out back.

"This place is beautiful, but how can you raise goats here? I came through some wild country today, and you're surrounded by lions and wolves and all sorts of predators," I said.

"There are no predators here."

"But I saw a puma, and gray wolves."

"Yes, they're about."

"But they don't kill the goats?"

"No. The dogs keep them away," he said, smiling.

"But they didn't keep me away. I came here, and all they did was bark," I said.

Tender turned at that point to stare at me. "Are you a predator?"

"I used to be," I said, then dropped my eyes to keep from meeting his gaze. I was beginning to see what Virgil had meant when he said people didn't lie to Tender. He had the most penetrating gaze I've ever encountered.

"But you aren't now. Otherwise, you wouldn't be here," he said, giving me a reassuring pat on the shoulder.

I walked with him as we scattered feed for chickens, a few hogs, several cows and horses - all animals that ran free on the mesa. There were no fences, no pens with gates. Once inside the house, I saw no doors, not even doors to keep out the chill of the evenings or the wild beasts that roamed the hills around him. My curiosity had peeked by then, and I couldn't hold back any longer. "Who are you? I still don't know why Virgil sent me here. I mean, I know why, I just don't know why he sent me to you."

"Around here they call me Tender. It's just a name, but it fits me. I like to tend," he said.

"But why did Virgil send me to you?"

"Because you have questions, I suppose."

"Yeah, I've got lots of questions, but I can't see how a tender of goats can answer them," I said.

"Who would you rather have answers from? Would you be more likely to believe a prophet, or philosopher, or psychologist, or perhaps a . . . ?"

"No," I said, breaking in.

"Then, let's have something to eat and drink, and then we'll talk about serious matters. But while we're doing that, tell me about where you come from. I would guess the southwestern United States from some time in the middle of the twentieth century. Am I right?" he asked, smiling wisely.

"Texas, to be exact, and I died in a war in southeast Asia in 1969," I said.

"Oh, and were you still young at the time?"

"Yeah, I was 34 years old."

"Then we have something in common. I was there before you, but I departed early too. Tell me more."

He worked at putting together a supper of goat's cheese, cow's milk, hard bread, roasted corn, and green beans, and all during that time and whatever time it took us to finish eating, I talked about Texas and what I remembered of life there. I even told him a little about what I'd been doing since as a custodian. He listened intently without interrupting except to qualify certain things of interest to him, and after brewing some stiff coffee, we settled by the fireplace and got down to business.

"So you have questions that need answering, and I take it that you're unwilling to accept the answers given by your supervisors," he said.

"Well, I like my supervisors fairly well, but they work for the Central Office, and I don't trust that bunch of bureaucrats as far as I can throw them," I said.

Tender threw back his head and actually laughed for the first time, then said, "You know, I don't trust them much either."

"Yeah, but you're way out here, and back there where I work, they've got lots of control, especially over me," I said.

"Well, they don't have control here," Tender said, smiling and pointing at the floor under his feet, then continued. "You came looking for answers, and perhaps I have them. I'm not God, of course, but you can trust me."

He smiled again at that point, and I was starting to notice what an unusual effect it had on his otherwise rugged face. Although bearded and with fairly long hair that swept back over his ears, he looked well kept. His tanned skin wasn't badly wrinkled for a man that looked to be in his early fifties, except for deeply etched crowfeet in the corners of his eyes. His even, white teeth and clean features made him easy to look at, but his eyes reached me first because they were the most impressive eyes I've ever seen. Deep blue and intense, they were soft, compassionate eyes that made me feel enough at ease to want to talk to him.

So, I told him. I told him everything I could remember about being a custodian, from when I first started looking after Woody right up until Virgil brought me to that village. I told him about what all Woody had been involved in, about his drunkenness and his affairs. I couldn't tell the story without throwing in some of my own opinions about what had happened, so I didn't hold back. I told him all about Roosevelt and Dewey, and about Wanda and about the kids, about Woody's few friends and people he worked with at the college, and I even told him about the shadowloper. For well over an hour, I told him everything I could think of, and in the end I told him about the stupid trick I'd pulled in trying to stop a death angel. He looked concerned while I talked about the sad things, he smiled when I talked about the lighthearted things, but he laughed when I spoke of death Angels. Then I told him something that made him look sad. I said, as frankly as I could, that I'd lost faith in almost everything, even the hereafter. I asked him the very question that had been bugging me for months - if nothing ever works out right, what's the use? Is what I've been going through for the past fifteen years all there is for me?

Tender smiled when I finished, then moved closer to me. "What do you see here?" he asked.

"Just a beautiful mesa and a little farm with animals and a small crop. I see a place that shouldn't exist," I said.

"And why not?"

"How can you live here? You have no fences or pens or even doors. You have no protection to keep the wolves from coming in here and tearing you apart," I said.

"But it's like I said before. There are no predators here."

"Where I come from, almost everything is either a predator or the preyed upon, and sometimes they're both. That's the way it's always been down there."

"You're not down there anymore. You're here with me, and what do you see in me?"

"Well, you're not just a simple goat herder, that's for sure," I said. "I don't know who or what you are."

"I am just a simple goat herder. Do you know why?"

"No."

"Because it's what I wanted. It's what I asked to have, and it's what I have. I wanted a place where killing, ever killing for the sake of survival of the species, did not exist. I wanted a place where there were no predators and no preyed upon. This is a place of my creation, and here, nothing is sacrificed so something else can live," he said, looking firm.

"That's hard for me to understand. How do the animals live? How do you live?"

"They just live, that's all. Oh, it's not a perfect system. I'm not quite perfect enough for that. I take some eggs from the chickens, and I harvest some plants that are grown to eat. But I never kill the animals, and they don't kill each other. The wolves prowl these hills and valleys, but they don't kill the lambs of the flock, or the children of the villages. The lions don't kill the deer, nor does the bear eat the trout from the streams and lakes. We do not prey upon each other. You must remember that your experience is from a mortal world, and mine is not mortal. Nothing dies here, not really. Some things change, but nothing is killed."

"It all sounds great, but how did you come by all this?"

"I created it to meet the conditions of my own expectations," he said, smiling fondly.

"Then all of this isn't real. I'm in your make believe world," I said.

"Oh, it's more real than anything you know from a mortal world."

"But you made it up."

"All things are made up, one way or another. People live in a real world while they're mortals, but few of them ever really grasp reality. It's all around them, but they go through life as if they're sleep walking. They don't pay attention, don't really grasp the reality of reality. It's almost as if they're not fully aware that they're alive, if that makes any sense to you."

"No, it doesn't. I felt alive while I was down among the living," I said.

"Did you? Did you really have a sense of being? Were you fully aware of what was going on around you?" Tender asked.

"I thought I was fully aware of everything, but now I'm not sure. I must've missed some things."

"We all missed a lot of things during our mortal lives, and that's due to our lack of awareness. And that in turn kept us from thinking about some things we should've considered. I'm not being overly critical, just pointing out that what we think is real is just the way we experienced it, the way we felt it, or saw it. That's part of the human condition, so it's excusable. But we've moved on from that, and now we should realize our limitations and learn to fully experience reality. My environment now is not a dream world. You can touch it, and it won't crumble under your touch. You can experience it in all manner of ways, and it won't fade away. Did I create it or was it here waiting for me all along? Does it matter as long as it's real?

"No."

"Let me ask you something important now. What do you want?"

"Well, I sure didn't want what I ended up getting. What I got was assigned to a drunk. I didn't even want to be a custodian. They just gave it to me - said that's what I had an aptitude for."

"But what do you want? You must have wanted something somewhere along the line."

"I don't know for sure, but at one time I wanted to be a rodeo cowboy. I ended up being a pretty good one, but I practiced hard and tried hard. Then I got killed, and there doesn't seem to be too much of a demand for dead rodeo cowboys where I'm at now," I said.

"Is that where you want to be?" Tender asked.

"If you mean forever, the answer is a definite no. It's had its ups and downs, but the downs outnumber the ups by a considerable margin."

"Then it all comes back to the question about where you want to be, and in time, you'll need to decide."

"What do I do until then?"

"You keep working, and thinking, and learning."

"But it all seems like such a waste of time. It's the same thing over and over, and nothing ever seems to come out right. People down on mortal earth are . . . are . . . depressing," I said.

"They have their faults," Tender agreed, then smiled again.

"Then I die and come to the afterlife and nothing's changed. It's still the same deal. There's all these people still making the same dumb decisions and manipulating and managing, and it all stinks. I thought it would be better, but it's just more of the same. What's worse, I'm trapped in it. They can send me anywhere they want, make me do what they want, and they've got all these rules to follow, and the people aren't much different than when I was alive."

"What if it had been different? What if you'd suddenly died, left earth, and come to a place like this? Would you have liked that? There's no Central Office here - no supervisors, no rules, no people who need guarding. We don't need any of that because life is simple, just like the people who live here. Rules and managers disappear when people no longer have a use for them. Could you live in a society without rules and management?" Tender asked.

"I don't know," I said.

"I think not, at least not yet," Tender said.

"I know one thing. I've had enough of the way it is down there," I said, pointing down.

"Perhaps you have, and that's why you've been sent to me. You are growing and moving toward a higher plane. Many others have not been as fortunate as you," Tender said, smiling wisely.

"You mean like the ones who went to hell or ended up being shadowlopers?" I asked.

"What is hell, and what about the world of shadows?" Tender asked.

"I don't really know much about them, but I figure they're worse than where I am now."

"To be a little more specific, what do you think hell is?" Tender asked.

"I don't know," I said.

"I don't know either, but this much I'm sure of. Hell is for people who need it, or think they need it."

"Are you saying that folks make their own hell?"

"I think so. I made this place," Tender said, smiling again.

"Yeah, but . . . you wanted it. You just said you were here because this is what you wanted. People don't want to go to hell."

"Don't they?"

"Not if it's anything like some of the stories I've heard," I said.

"People get what they work toward. It's a part of their dreams. I dreamed of this place for many years before I finally arrived. I had a vision of what lay ahead for me, just as you will have. There are others who have no dream, no vision of what exists on the final plateau."

"But I don't know either," I said.

"But you will know because you have vision, the ability to dream. Only dreamers can see the final plateau. I could show others what you are being shown now, but they would see nothing because they cannot dream."

"Everyone has dreams."

"Do they?"

"Yeah, they do. Even bad people, really bad people, have dreams."

"What they have, Doug, are plans and intentions. They don't dream because they can't. One cannot dream without being able to see. People without vision are limited to seeing only what their greed, their conceit, and their self-centeredness allow them to see. In truth, they are able to see very little, and that keeps them from dreaming. Not being able to dream becomes their doom because it takes them no further than temporary gratification. Therein lies their hell because they have created it. Even if the final plateau was theirs to see, they would see nothing in it."

"Is that why you asked me what I saw here?"

"Yes," Tender said, nodding slowly.

"But I don't know what I see," I said, suddenly feeling inadequate.

"You've seen more than you think. You have the eyes of a dreamer, and even though you haven't put it all together yet, your dream is alive and well."

"You're talking about waking dreams, aren't you?"

"They could be waking, or you might envision these things in your sleep."

"The thing I dream most about in my sleep is an operating room situation at some hospital in Viet Nam. I'm on this table and there are bright lights all around, and even though I can't see them, people are hovering around me. I get the feeling from what they're saying, which isn't all that distinct either, that I'm going to make it. Then the lights go out, just like somebody flicked a switch, and I'm dead," I said.

"Is that how it happened?"

"I don't remember it as being that way. All I remember is getting hit, then lying on the ground staring up. Then, just like in the dream, there's nothing. The next thing I know, I'm coming to in a pink room at the Training Center for Custodial Services."

"The dream is what really happened," Tender said.

"Then why don't I remember it that way?"

"Like everyone who has had a mortal experience, you have difficulty in accepting your own death. You still speak of yourself as being dead, but you're sitting here right in front of me. Accepting an end to you mortal experience is important in moving on, and you haven't completely come to grips with that. That dream will end in time, and you consciousness will make room for more productive dreams. Those dreams, both waking and sleeping, will eventually lead you to a place like this."

"When will I be ready for this place?"

"Perhaps never because what I have here may not be what you want," Tender said.

"I just had a scary thought. What if you change your mind and decide you want something else? Since you created this place, will it just go away when you don't want it anymore? What will happen to all these animals and hills and village people?" I asked.

"Oh, I will never change my mind, but if I do, someone will want it. I may have created it, but my dreams aren't so different from a lot of other people's dreams. Eternity is big enough to hold a lot of places."

"What you're saying then, is that there's already a place out there waiting for me, and I can't get there because I haven't figured out where I want to be."

"That's fairly well sums it up. I judge you as being an individualist, so your place might be as seemingly lonely as mine. Once you reach a destination, it's not just some place that's set to stay that way forever. It adapts as you continue to grow, and that will be quite a change for someone at your level of development. You accustomed to adjusting to your surroundings, and that's not the way it is here."

"Will I get exactly what I want?"

"Defining exactness isn't easy, but yes, when the time comes. If it makes more sense to you, think of it this way. You are working your way to the top of a long stairway, and each step of the stairway is just another phase in your life. Up until now, you've thought of yourself as being dead, but you're very much alive. Actually, you're more alive now than ever before. Your staircase of life, however, is not one that you can just run up without some preparation. Sometimes it is physically demanding and difficult. Our human conditioning teaches us to take it in leaps, perhaps jumping some steps, but it can't be navigated that way. You must take each step as it comes because it is important to feel each one of them under your feet. That prepares you for the next step, which in turn prepares you for the next, and so on. As you take steps you learn and understand, then you move to the next and master it. Eventually, you get to the top."

"I reckon I've got a long ways to go," I said.

"Yes, still a long way, but not as far as some. You've come a long way already. The top may not be as far away as you might think," Tender said.

"So what I do is go back to being a custodian until I'm ready for the next step, huh?" I asked.

"Something like that, but you've already taken a step or two. You're role will change some until you've mastered that step, then another comes along."

"That means I've got to go back down there and mess with the Central Office again. That means more bureaucrats, and nit-picking people to take care of, and . . ."

"Yes, but it will be different this time. There will be new challenges and new people."

"But what about Dewey? What about Woody?"

"Don't worry about them. They're taking steps too - growing some and moving on. You did your job, and you did it well. You learned a lot from the experience, and now it's time . . ."

"I know, to move on," I said, breaking in.

"The time will come when you'll move beyond central offices and supervisors and rules. Keep that in mind, always. Someday, perhaps soon, you'll start to get a picture of what awaits you in the end. Seeing the end will help you on your journey because you must keep taking the steps and moving up the stairs. That's why you're here now. We wanted you to see where it all leads," Tender said.

"I didn't come to see this place. It's unique and beautiful, but it wouldn't mean much if you weren't here. I've never met anyone like you."

"Have I been helpful in any way?"

"Yes," I said, nodding.

"Why?"

"I can't say, exactly, but maybe meeting you helps because you've already walked those stairs to the top. You must know about the pain and sacrifice it takes," I said.

"Yes, I know a little about that, but I also know of the joy that comes from understanding what it's all about. The sacrifices are small compared to what awaits you, Doug. You still have many earthly trappings that must be shed before you come to where I am, but you have a good heart. In the end, that's what counts," Tender said.

"Will I ever see you again?"

"That's up to you, but you know the way now. You climbed all the way up here."

"But I don't know how I got to this place, or dimension, or world, or whatever it is. Virgil brought me in his old airplane," I said.

"Then you know someone who knows the way, and in time, you'll learn how to get here on your own."

We talked until the chill of night drove us to the warmth of warm covers. I slept on a pallet near a fireplace and dreamed the Viet Nam dream again. Nothing changed about it, and I woke up with a start when the switch flicked in my head, just like I always did. I drifted back into a light sleep until a splash of sunlight ended it early the next morning. Tender was already up making breakfast. After eating, I said goodbye, shook his hand, and started to walk away. Then I remembered something I'd meant to ask him earlier, and turned around.

"Will I ever see my folks again, Tender? Will I see my mom and dad, and grandmas and grandpas, and folks like that?" I asked.

Tender smiled and said, "When I first came here, that village down the road was very small, but some of the people who lived there were waiting for me. Some came later. Perhaps you saw a woman in the square, bustling about and keeping busy. If you did, you saw my grandmother. My grandfather was probably whittling and talking with other men near the village square. My sister is there, as are my brother and my parents. They, like me and the other people, are here because we shared the same dream. Many people and some relatives I knew from my worldly days are not here, but I don't fret about them. Their dream was different, so they stay elsewhere. Perhaps someday our paths will cross again, either here or somewhere else. You may have noticed in your worldly dealings that life there is not worth much without people who share your dreams. Without them, this place wouldn't be worth much either."

"Then I'll see them again," I said confidently. Tender nodded, and I started my walk back to the village.

I made it back to the tallest hilltop before noon, and when I looked down the far side toward the village, I saw a well beaten path leading to the top where I stood. On my trek to Tender's mesa, I'd made better than half the trip through rough country along a line that ran no more than half a mile for an easy access. I hadn't even had the presence of mind to look back at where I'd come from. Virgil would've died laughing if he'd been with me. I walked home via the beaten path, but I never did admit my mistake to him.

CHAPTER 43
Requiem for a Fallen Angel

I found Virgil sitting with a group of elderly men around the well in the center of the village square. He was so enthralled with the game they'd been teaching him that I had a hard time tearing him away from it. Finally, he gave up the game and followed me back toward the airplane. "Did you get your answers?" he asked.

I nodded, not knowing exactly how to answer him. Instead, I asked a question of my own. "Who is he, Virgil?"

"Tender. That's about all I know."

"I know what they call him here. I want to know who he was down on earth," I said.

"Does it really matter?

"Yeah, it matters. He's too savvy just to be a goat herder. He didn't get that smart looking after a bunch of goats, and he's bound to have been around a long time."

"Yeah, he's been around a while, I reckon, but I don't know who he was. I just know who he is now, and that's Tender."

"But somebody had to bring you to him the first time. How'd you get to know him?" I asked.

"I did what you did and screwed up a couple of assignments. I lost one mark to a suicide. Just turned my back on him for a few minutes, and he jumped off a building. That's the first time I came here. Got down on myself, got that old rabbit blood going in my veins, and needed some advising. And I had a bad run-in with the Central Office once and tried to quit the guarding business, and I came back again that time. The last time was when that Innis Brooks kid got killed by the bull, and I started laying it all on myself. I kept thinking I should've stopped that from happening, and the Central Office kinda felt the same way. I got to feeling sorry for myself, and that's when a wiser feller saw the need to haul me up here. I'm a slow learner, so I had to come back more'n once. Supervisors brought me, but they told me the same thing I'm telling you, and that's that I don't know who he used to be," he said.

"I was hoping you'd know."

"Quit worrying about it. He's special now, and that's what matters. He told you what you needed to hear, didn't he? Thing is, do you believe what he said?"

"Yes. I don't know why, but I did?"

"He has a way with people, and that's why I took you to him. I knew you'd believe him. Everyone who has met him believes him, and that's his special gift."

"Yeah, but that's why I'm asking. If he's got such a good way with folks, then why's he out here herding goats? Why isn't somebody like him running the Central Office?"

"He's way past that lowly stuff, and I don't know why he's up here. If you're asking for my personal opinion, which is, you know, subject to some scrutiny, I think it's 'cause he did his thing on earth a long time ago, and what he did down there was enough to last mankind for a long time," he said, squinting at me.

"What contribution? Who the hell was he?" I asked, starting to get irritated.

"Don't get testy. I'm telling it the best I can. Let's put it this way. Does the word carpenter mean anything to you?"

"Jesus Christ! You're not saying he's . . . "

"I ain't saying nothing for sure, but you asked what I thought, and I'm telling you. 'Course, you can take that with a grain of salt. There's a rumor going around that I'm sometimes full of shit, you know. For all I know the feller could've been Joan of Arc, or Mohammed, or Buddha, or even Gandhi, or Abe Lincoln."

"Abe Lincoln? Are you crazy? I could believe Robert E. Lee, maybe, but not Lincoln," I said.

"Yeah, your right. I got carried away there for a minute. Are you ready to head on back to Forest City?"

"Might as well. I've got to start climbing that staircase sometime," I said.

"What staircase?"

"Didn't Tender tell you about the staircase, about taking steps and all that?"

"In so many word, yes. He talked about beaten paths, building roads, and climbing mountains," Virgil said, grinning impishly.

"I should've known. I can see that working for you is going to be a big change for me," I said.

"Who said you're going to be working for me? They may be fixing to transfer your ass to Alabama."

"They wouldn't do that. They like Roosevelt too much to send me down there. Where will I be going?"

"We'll talk about that later. Right now we need to get back to Kansas and get some things smoothed out."

Virgil cranked the plane and took off. We climbed up to five thousand feet and went through the same routine again. Just like before, watching the colored streaks twist into a funnel in front of us made me dizzy and gave me a headache. I closed my eyes and waited it out, and when I opened them again, we were cruising through Kansas skies again. Darkness had fallen on the prairie, but I recognized familiar landmarks. Virgil flew to the airport and put the plane down rather gently. He must've been getting the hang of flying because even with the colored streamers and tunneling, this trip hadn't been near as bad as the one to Minnesota.

Since there was no car for us at the airport, we had to walk to town. We walked briskly down the dark streets until we rounded a corner a half block from the hospital. I'd been trudging along with my head down, but I stopped dead in my tracks when I lifted my head and looked toward the hospital. The entire hospital grounds and the small city park just across the street were filled with people, literally hundreds of people. They were just standing, holding lighted candles. Some were bunched in groups, talking lowly, while others stood silently looking toward Woody's second floor hospital room window. "What's going on?" I asked.

"Sure beats me. Maybe all these folks are Woody's friends," Virgil asked, scratching his head.

"Woody's got a few friends, but a crowd like this wouldn't gather . . . unless . . . he died or something," I said.

Virgil frowned and shifted his weight as he turned to stare at me. Then he slowly shook his head. "Well, we'd better get up there and find out, I reckon," he said.

"What if he is dead? What then?"

"We'll cross that bridge when we get to it. Right now, we need to know what's happened while we've been gone," he said.

Inside the hospital, the mood seemed even more somber, and that spooked me some. I hustled up to Woody's room as fast as my sore legs would carry me, and to my relief, he was still breathing. I'd say he was still alive, but what he was doing at the moment didn't quite come up to living standards. Wanda was at his bedside, as was Duncan Highsmith. Ellen Stegnor and several other faculty members were keeping the kids company in a nearby waiting room. Woody appeared to be conscious, but showed no emotion whatever. The folks around him had the same looks of concern on their faces that had been there when I left on my trip to see Tender, and I knew instantly that little had changed.

I soon learned that word had spread concerning the shooting and Woody's grave condition among students and faculty returning from the Holidays, and with some support from people like Ellen Stegnor and Don Early, a candlelight vigil had been organized to show support from him. Since it was Sunday evening, local churches had thrown in with the students and faculty members, and that accounted for the size of the crowd. Woody had been told, but if he understood what was happening, he showed no sign of it. The disappointment from his reaction, or lack of one, was plainly written on Wanda's face, and she was starting to look threadbare at the seams.

I paced. All sorts of thoughts were running through my head. My job there was nearly over, and I was torn about what to do to bring my time in Forest City to a close. I walked to the window and stared down at the crowd of candle holders below. I knew some of them, but most were just faces to me. I walked back to Woody's bedside for just long enough to look down at him. His breathing seemed a little more shallow than when I'd seen him last, and his face had lost some color. Virgil moved closer, and even though I knew the answer to the question before I asked it, I still blurted it out.

"What good can come of Woody's dying?"

"I don't know, Salty, but then again, there's lots of things I don't know. I reckon I'm old fashioned enough to believe in certain things being God's will, and that's what I go with in a case like this."

"But before you said that it's up to Woody."

"I know, but I meant in a worldly way. In the long run, everything is up to the Big Feller."

"Then why doesn't he stop this? If there's any such thing as a miracle, one right now wouldn't hurt anything," I said.

"Neither one of us knows that for sure."

I grabbed Virgil by the arm and pulled him to the window, then pointed at the several hundred upturned faces - faces illuminated by the glow of tiny candles. "Look down there, Virgil. Look at those people. They're just folks who have to fight it out every day in this lousy world, and like Woody over there, they sometimes lose faith. How can God ignore that? How can he miss a chance to show these people that he's really out there?" I asked.

"Don't you think those people already know that?" Virgil asked.

"Some of them might, but most of them don't. I spent a while down here with folks like that, and I know how I felt. I wanted to believe in God, but mostly I just hoped there was something out there to believe in. Couldn't he give them more proof that he's really there? There they are, standing there waiting on somebody to come out and say that Woody's going to make it. Then they can all go home secure in the knowledge that God let him live."

"That's wouldn't be enough, Salty. If Woody dies, they'll go home believing it was God's will. God won't come out a loser, no matter what happens. And maybe that's how it's supposed to be. If everybody knew for an absolute fact that God really existed, then there might be even less faith out there. The way I see it, folks who find God have to go looking for him, and they go looking 'cause they've got doubts about it all. Without some doubt, most folks don't bother to look. Maybe a little doubt is a good thing, especially if he helps somebody come to the conclusion that God's really out there."

"But don't you think people need more assurance that God's will sometimes ends in something other than death?" I asked.

"Is that what's been stuck in your craw for all these years?" Virgil asked, his eyes searching my face for some hint of what was going on in my head. I didn't respond immediately, so he asked again. "Is it?"

"I doubted, if that's what you're asking. Maybe I doubted too much."

"I'm slow, but I'm starting to figure you out. You've spent all this time thinking you're dead - thinking you're something other than what you were when you were with them," Virgil said, waving toward the crowd below.

"But that part of me is dead and gone. Salty Anderson bit the dust in Nam, and that was the end of that. That wasn't so bad in my case, but if Woody dies, somebody else will end up raising his kids, and he'll miss something important. Kids in college that could've learned something will miss that, and any way you look at it, Woody Pickens is going to be dead and gone," I said.

"The one thing you didn't learn from dying is that there ain't no dying. That body you walked around in down here is dead, yes, but Salty Anderson is still alive. You're standing right here with me, close enough to touch. We are talking to one another. Get that through your thick skull. YOU AIN'T DEAD! YOU WILL NEVER BE DEAD!"

"All right, so I'm not dead. But if I could talk to Woody right now, knowing what I know now, I'd say, 'Hey, Woody! Hang in there pal. If you're expecting it to get better by just kicking the bucket, you've got another think coming. Get your shit together, and get on with what you've got left of this worldly existence.' That's exactly what I'd tell him," I said.

"Sounds like a sure enough good idea to me," Virgil said, grinning big.

"What?"

"Do it! March your ass right over there to his bed and do it. Well, maybe you oughta wait till everybody's out of the room, but I think it's a great idea."

"You nuttier than a California fruitcake."

"Well, it's up to you, but if it was me, I'd go for it."

"You mean go personification mode and really tell him that?"

"Naw, the shock of actually seeing you might kill the poor bastard for sure, but you can find some way of doing it without going that extreme. There's lots of ways to talk to people. Me, I'm needing a nap, so I'll be waiting on you back at the trailer," he said, then turned and stalked out of the room.

I walked back to the bed and stared at Woody again, and the reality of what might happen to him suddenly hit me. Within a few days I'd be gone from there, and I just might be taking my last look at him. I thought back over the years I'd spent with him and about everything we'd gone through together, and I knew him as well as I'd ever known any man. The thought that he didn't know me didn't bother me much, but I hated to think that he felt like he'd gone through all of that by himself struck me as being awfully sad. Now our association was coming to an end, and I didn't want to leave without doing something to let him know that he wasn't alone in this thing. Maybe he'd never know, but at least I would know that I tried to tell him. Even if I could've told him face to face, he wouldn't have believed it.

I stood there looking down at him, thinking about what I could do that might let him know he wasn't alone. Nothing came to me, and so I decided that I'd do something that would at least cast some doubt on the idea that he was completely alone. So, I did the only thing I could do. I moved closer to him, switched to I/T, and touched him. At first he didn't respond in any way, but I kept rubbing my hand across his forehead until I saw his eyelids twitch. I let the palm of my hand rest on his forehead until he opened his eyes. He rolled them around in an attempt to see who was touching him, and when he saw no one, he did something that gave me the strength to walk away and not look back. He sucked in a deep breath, and then he smiled.

Daylight the next morning came with a bang. "All right, you maggots. Drop your cocks and grab your socks, it's daylight in the swamp," Virgil hollered. Dewey sat up with a start, then grimaced in pain and eased himself back down. Winston, like usual, didn't wake up at all.

"What are you up to?" I asked.

"Well, I just got back from the hospital. Woody's eating breakfast," he said with a broad grin.

"Well, I'll be damned," I said.

"Whatever you did must've worked. He's just nibbling, but at least he's making an effort now. Say, I've been thinking. I need to get on back to Cheyenne for a couple of days. Got more folks to check on, you know. I'll be back in a couple of days and pick you up. Maybe I'll bring your new car when I come."

"Bring Dewey a car. I'm keeping the Chevy," I said.

"I want a larger trailer," Dewey said.

"The Chevy stays here, but we'll see about a trailer. I'm leaving pronto, so I'll see you in a few days," Virgil said, then slammed the door.

"I want my Chevy," I hollered after him, but there was no reply.

"Why did he go away without you? If you're being transferred, why didn't he make you go right now?" Dewey asked, sitting up again.

"He's giving me a couple of days to sew up loose ends."

"And I'm the loose end, I suppose."

A year earlier, I couldn't have let an opportunity to dig Dewey slid by, but I must've been growing a little because I did exactly that. "Yeah, Dewey, you're the loose end."

"Well, I must admit that I'm going to miss you in the worst sort of way. We made good partners, don't you think?"

"We were better than just good. We made some mistakes, and we might've figured some things wrong, but we did a great job of getting Woody through some rough times. I'm proud of our work together, but I've got to go now. You and I will have different paths from now on. Maybe we always did have, but we at least crossed paths and found a way to work things out. I've been learning a lot lately. I met Tender, you know," I said.

"Who is Tender," Dewey said, frowning.

"He's a very wise man who lives on a mesa somewhere far from here. I'd tell you about him, but you'll be meeting him one of these days. Maybe someday I'll take you there myself," I said.

"Well, if we're not going to talk about Tender, what are we going to talk about?" Dewey asked, smiling innocently.

"I don't know. Maybe we can talk about the things we've learned together. Who knows, I might want to write a book about it."

"That'll be the day," Dewey said, then giggled.

"Well, we can talk anyway. Want to do that?" I asked.

"Sure," Dewey said, slapping his palms down on the covers and grinning like a kid. Seeing him do that was almost too much for me, and I had to turn my back on him for a few minutes. I was missing him already.

Epilogue

Sunsets aren't as pretty in Montana as they are in western Kansas. I thought you might like to know that, just in case you haven't had a chance to compare them. The winters are colder up here too, but that's about where I run out of things that Kansas has got over Montana because this place is really nice. Kansas has at least one more thing that Montana doesn't, and that's Dewey Davisson. I see him occasionally, but I still miss having him around all the time. Kansas has Woody Pickens too, but I'm still trying to decide whether or not I miss him. I'd say the irritation is what I probably miss the most, but I'm still getting a healthy dose of that.

I've had a busy year. Not only have I been trying to adjust to new country and write this book, I've had to deal with the rigors of a new job. You know how it goes. When you're really busy and can't afford the extra time, that's when shit happens. Just last week, right in the middle of me trying to get a new custodian started over at Livingston, one of my boys down at Red Lodge decides to screw up royally. The Central Office called and said they'd received reports that a rookie custodian on my watch had flagrantly violated article four, section three, clause four of The Custodians Field Guide For Protective Services, which means he'd used physical force. I scrounged around until I came up with a copy of the field guide, and then I high-tailed it on down to Red Lodge.

"Just what the hell do you think you're doing?" I asked. I'd just walked into a bar in time to catch Lester Cribbs cleaning blood off his knuckles. You remember Cowboy, don't you? Yeah, he's the goofy narc detective from Cleveland who led the charmed life. Well, the charm wore off, I reckon, because he got shot and killed about six months ago. Since then he went through training and was assigned to my district. I was tickled pink to have him at first, but that was before I found out what a pain in the ass he could be. I don't mind saying that I was a bit ticked off.

"We just finished whipping these mutherfucker's asses," Lester said, looking up and grinning like he was proud of what he'd done. He nodded toward four men lying on the floor, all looking worse for wear. His mark, a boozed up bronc rider, was sitting at the bar nearby, getting even more boozed up. I knew this particular fight couldn't have been the one the Central Office had alerted me to. They're not that fast, so what I was looking at was a brand new situation.

"Do you have to use that word?" I asked, giving him my best you'd-better-get-your-ass-in-line look.

"OK, boss man. We just finished whipping those mutherfucker's butts," he said, flashing me one of his cocky grins.

"That's not the word I'm talking about, and you just went out of bounds again. How many times am I going to have to read you the rules?" I asked, waving the field manual in the air.

"Fuck the manual. These mutherfuckers had it coming."

"You can't use that kind of force, and you know it. What you've done here is way out of line. Do you understand what I'm telling you?"

"Yeah, I hear you, man, but this shit's different. I hit the muther . . . the bastard . . . because he was kicking my mark," Lester said, frowning up as he spoke.

"Do what?"

"My man - Lester always calls his mark 'my man' - tangled assholes with these miners, and they ended up fighting and whacking at one another. My man there did good for a while, but they finally got him down. I tired keeping it even by pushing them back so he could get up, but there was too many of them. I finally decided to deck one, and when I did, it started getting hairy."

"That's exactly what I'm talking about. You butted in and made the situation worse," I said.

"Worse, my ass. How much worse can it get than having four guys stomping the shit out of you? I was just trying to clean out some space and give my man a little breathing room. Once he got on his

feet, I didn't have to hit but one other guy. He cowboyed up good and flattened the other two."

"The two of you knocked out all four of them?" I asked, looking at the men on the floor, then at Lester's mark. The boy couldn't have weighed more than 150 pounds.

"Yeah, man, we sure did. Four punches, four KO's," Lester said, grinning proudly.

"What'd you hit the mutherfuckers with?" I asked, trying to keep a straight face. Lester broke out laughing, and that broke me down.

"You're all right, boss man," Lester said, wiping laugh tears out of the corners of his eyes. "I liked your ass the first time we ever met back in Cleveland."

"Yeah, and that's where both of us might end up if you don't watch your step," I said, wagging my finger at him. "The Central Office gets nervous about things like this, so keep it down to a low roar, OK?"

Lester nodded, and I left him sitting there. Several of the miners they'd whipped were starting to groan and move around. I checked them over before I left to make sure they weren't hurt badly, then jumped into my pickup and headed back up here. If you're wondering where here is, I've been staying out west of Billings along the Yellowstone River. Got me a gooseneck travel trailer parked out there in a meadow. Virgil got me a new pickup for transportation, and he did fine by me. It's a big Ford crew cab four-wheeler with all the trimmings, and that's not a bad replacement for my Chevy.

You probably thought this book was going to have a bad ending, but as you can see, it doesn't. Things could've turned out better, I reckon, but what the hell, that's life. Yeah, that's what I said - life. I've been thinking about that a lot lately, particularly since my talk with Tender. Anyone who says, "life goes on," probably has no idea exactly what a profound statement it really is. It's too bad that folks get hung up on the notion of dying because it's not that big of a deal. My life's been better since I stopped thinking of myself as being dead, but it took me a long time to learn that life goes on, and on, and on, and on, and on.

This book can't just keep going on, though, so I have to draw the line somewhere. As for Dewey, he's getting along pretty good. Sophie, his new supervisor, is making a good hand, and Dewey likes her. Winston spent about six months with Dewey and then transferred down to Alabama to work for Roosevelt. To replace him in Kansas, they sent in a guy named Wilton Ricks, a former stock car driver from North Carolina. He stumbled around in a state of shock for the first three months he was with Dewey, but he's coming around. He's a good listener, I hear, and that's good because Dewey needs somebody who'll listen to all his high brow talk on sociology and psychology and things like that. Dewey says he's bright and is learning the ropes fairly well, and that it sure as hell doesn't take them long to get to where they need to go.

Dewey was correct all along about what it would take to get Woody Pickens straightened out. I don't remember most of the quotes he popped off from time to time, but one of them has stuck with me. That's the one that goes, "There is no witness so dreadful, no accuser so terrible as the conscience that dwells in the heart of every man." I thought all along that I was the witness that might turn him around, but just being a witness wasn't my job. I did my job well enough to keep him alive long enough to where he became the witness, the accuser, who made the difference. He finally saw himself for what he was, a drunk, and that's when he started his long climb out of the hole he'd dug for himself.

There's always a new challenge in this business, and Dewey still reads all the time. Lately he's been studying up on alcohol recovery, but that stands to reason. You know how he is about things like that. Woody went to treatment after he got out of the hospital which means that Dewey went along. I figured his job would be easier after Woody got off the sauce, but that's not what happened. Dewey says he's still a pain in the ass but in a different way now. He's making the transition from being a practicing drunk to a recovering alcoholic, and according to Dewey, that's a whole new ball game. *Woody and Wanda are still together, but I've got my doubts about it ever working out. At least they're trying, and that's what counts. The big winners in the deal have been the two kids. There are still some problems, but having a drunk daddy in the house isn't one of them. Dewey says that Woody's starting to see himself in his kids, and for a man like him, that's where his hopes of recovery will settle. That's a good place for anyone's hopes, I reckon.*

Woody has made friends with Ellen Stegnor, and that's helped some. He's trying to adopt a live-and-let-live attitude toward life, but that's a waste of time for a man like Woody. That's just my opinion, of course, but Woody won't ever be able to stay far away from the action. He's not a beaten path kind of guy. Dewey says he's active in Alcoholics Anonymous, and he's right in the middle of campus politics. A first teamer, that's what he's destined to be, and he might as well get ready for it. I figured he'd leave western Kansas, move to a bigger university once he stopped drinking. Word has it that Ellen Stegnor has been offered the president's job at a larger school in Nebraska, but so far she's still in Forest City. As for Woody, he's hanging tight there. That doesn't mean he won't move in the near future. I learned a long time ago that predicting what he might do next is an iffy proposition. He's sober now, but he's still Woody.

The reformers and the traditionalists are still fighting it out over campus policies, but that comes as no surprise. Some of the reforms might be too strong for western Kansas, but most worthless folks hate change of any kind because it threatens their worthlessness. Woody seems to have found a home with the progressive set, and that may give him a feeling of purpose and support. Some will dislike him for it, that's just the way it goes. I doubt if there's a college campus anywhere without some dissention.

The Parkerites and witch-hunters are still around, but they're no longer strong enough to screw things up. Clarence Ludwig died of a heart attack back in the spring. They found him on a pile of dirty towels in the back of Marge Fink's laundry, so you can figure out what happened. I hear he's been recycled as a camel driver in Afghanistan, but that's just a rumor. Miss Amy sold the store and moved to a retirement village in south Texas, and I hear she's doing well. Harley French had a stroke and turned into a vegetable. I haven't heard about any of the others.

Faith Appleton married Lane Allen in Denver last year. C.W. Laney left town shortly after her husband went to jail for shooting Woody. He got a short sentence, but C.W. didn't hang around. Dewey giggled when he told me she'd left town with Freddy Lomax. Sometimes poetic justice is a bitter pill to swallow, but sometimes it's a hoot. Duncan Highsmith still drinks a lot, but Woody's been doing some missionary work on him. Fred's Bar closed for good early last year, but I understand that Dusty's Saloon is still going strong.

Don Leland got captured by a team of shadowloper hunters and was sent back to custodial school for a refresher course. They assigned him to my district, and he's guarding a geologist over around Billings. He's still shaky at times, but he likes his mark and says he's enjoying the work. The geologist is bipolar and queer as a three dollar bill, but he's intelligent. Don is your typical good old boy, and I've encouraged him to apply some common sense to his work. I've been in his shoes. Woody had me outclassed when it came to book smarts, but there's always room for practicality. I had that, he didn't, but it all worked out.

As for me, I'm adjusting. I once envied Roosevelt's job, but not anymore. It's funny how your perspective about management changes when you get to be a manager. I've got about thirty custodians under me, and it's a good thing Virgil gave me a new pickup because I spent ninety percent of my time on the road. Some of my squad members could screw up a one car funeral procession. Half of them don't have a lot of experience, and my district is a tough one. I've got part of southeastern Montana and a small chunk of northeastern Wyoming, and that takes in parts of several Indian Reservations. Looking after a boozed up cowboy is one thing, and a boozy Indian can wear the horns off a billygoat. I still don't get along well with the Central Office, but I probably never will.

One of the really nice things about my new assignment is that a cute redhead has taken over as supervisor of a district over in South

Dakota, and that's not far from here. We get together on a fairly regular basis. She's still trying to teach me to use the personification mode without calling in the mode mechanics. I may be one of the few supervisors in the country that can't just jump into it at the drop of a hat, but I'm learning how. Phoebe says I can't do it well because I've still got too many self-centered thoughts in my head. I may never get it down until I find another teacher. I still can't look at her and not have a few naughty thoughts.

Virgil and I have formed a fine friendship. We visit on a regular basis, but I haven't seen Tender again. I'm still thinking about what he told me, and I'm still working toward taking the steps he talked about. Whenever I have time for serious thinking, I take walks and ponder over what I want in the long run. I dream about it sometimes, but I don't have the Viet Nam dream now. Once I got past the notion of being dead, it went away. In so many words, Tender told me that I couldn't look backward and forward at the same time, and a backward looker can't dream about anything but the past. Looking forward and dreaming about what's ahead isn't easy, but I'm getting better at it. I don't worry a lot about it. Like Tender said, eternity is a big place, and I'm in no hurry.

When I think about it real hard, I get these glimpses of what it might be like when I finally get to the higher plateau. I can't get a real clear picture of what it looks like, but I can see some things as clear as crystal. Sometimes I dream about my parents, my grandparents, and some of my old buddies. I get little glimpses of a small ranch with horses and cattle and maybe a couple of nice fishing ponds. Once in a while, I see myself riding a strawberry roam horse across rolling green prairies, with a good dog trotting along beside me. Up ahead, a gal stands waiting for me in front of a small house with a barn out back. I'm not real sure because I'm still too far away, but she might be sort of a strawberry, too.

That's about it. Maybe now you know what I meant when I started this story by saying it was based on practical thinking. Sagacious practicality, I called it. A horse sense approach to critical thinking, I defined it. What it all comes down to is purpose, and I've *got one last metaphorical story for you. There's an old saying that it's hard to remember that your original purpose was to clear the swamp when you're up to your ass in alligators. Drunkenness is a lot like that, I think. Woody Pickens started with a purpose, but he got caught up in a swirl of alkigators and lost sight of that. If the alligators you're wading through are really bottles of booze, they're alkigators. And they nearly ate him up. But Woody finally got started toward higher ground where they couldn't snap him up. Some scars remain because the alkigators gnawed at him while he was wallowing around in the muck and mire with them. He'll carry those scars for the rest of his life, but he doesn't have to live with the open wounds unless he falls back into the swamp again. The alkigators will always be there waiting for him down by the lower road, and he knows that. He also knows that nobody can fight them alone and hope to win.*

I'd like to take some credit for it, but I didn't save Woody Pickens from the alkigators. I might've been the one who threw him the lifeline, but I wasn't around to pull him in. I didn't stay behind and point out the tracks that led to higher ground, didn't take those first few halting steps with him, didn't prod him along when the going got tough, and wasn't there when he scrambled to firmer footing. People who loved him did that for him. You may have figured out that Woody's journey and mine are the same in lots of respects. I didn't fall into a swamp full of alkigators, but I walked the lower road with him, and it's a treacherous track indeed. I helped him out of the swamp, but Woody's lifeline turned out to be his family and friends. My lifeline turned out to be the same thing.

You've been a good listener, but I knew you would be. Getting this story told has taken quite a while, but you're still here, and you deserve a good ending. Here it is: If you ever find yourself walking that lower road, keep a wary eye on the swamp because if you do, you'll see those yellow-eyed alkigators staring at you from out in the darkness. Take it as a warning. They're waiting on you, so don't mess around on the lower road any longer than you have to. You just might not get out of there as lucky as Woody Pickens did.

www.ingramcontent.com/pod-product-compliance
Lightning Source LLC
Chambersburg PA
CBHW080816020726
47501CB00009B/2318